~Eyes Behind Belligerence~

This novel is a work of fiction. Any references to real people, events, establishments, organizations, or locales are intended only to give the fiction a sense of reality and authenticity. Other names, characters, places, and incidents portrayed herein are either the product of the author's imagination or are used fictionally.

EYES BEHIND BELLIGERENCE. Copyright © 2011, 2012 by K.P. Kollenborn. All rights reserved. No part of this book may be reproduced, stored, or transmitted by any means—whether auditory, graphic, mechanical, or electronic—without written permission of both publisher and author, except in the case of brief excerpts used in critical articles and reviews. Unauthorized reproduction of any part of this work is illegal and is punishable by law.

SECOND EDITION
ISBN 978-1470168162
eBook ISBN 978-1-4524-7114-3

book design by K.P. Kollenborn

~Eyes Behind Belligerence~

A Novel

K.P. Kollenborn

CreateSpace

This book is dedicated to the Bainbridge Island community, including the people I interviewed as well as the Bainbridge Island Historical Museum, whose support was overwhelmingly generous. And I would like to thank the Manzanar Historical Society for providing me free resources about the intimacies of Manzanar's camp life. Without those resources I could not have recreated the social and political attributes, which made Manzanar unique. I also want to thank my Leonard Bishop Writing Group whose insight, talent, and friendships have given me the confidence to write such an intensive novel. Last, but not least, I would like to thank my husband for indulging me with all my collective research and visits to Seattle, Bainbridge Island, and Manzanar. It's not clinical obsession once everything has been set free into the written word.

CHARACTERS & TERMINOLOIGIES

CHARACTERS	PRONONCIATIONS
The Yoshimura Family	Yo-she-moo-ra
Haruko Yoshimura (mother)	ha-roo-koh
Toshiyuki Yoshimura (father)	toe-she-you-kee
Jimmu/ Jim	jeem-moo
Bethany (sister)	
Rose (sister)	
Tom (brother-in-law)	
The Hamaguchi Family	ha-mah-goo-che
Setsumi Hamaguchi (mother)	sate-soo-mee
Fujita Hamaguchi (father)	foo-jee-ta
Russell/ Goro	gore-oh
Sadaye (sister)	sah-dah-yeah
Meito (brother)	mate-oh
Gertrude (sister-in-law)	
Joe & George (cousins)	
Kunio (brother)	koo-nee-oh
Kay (sister-in-law)	
Harry & Clara (cousins)	
Chiyeko (sister)	chee-yeah-koh
Tadao (brother-in-law)	tah-dayo
Masako (sister)	mah-sah-koh
Osamu (brother-in-law)	oh-sah-moo
Ruth (cousin)	
Others	
Mitsuru	meet-sue-roo
Tomiko	toe-me-koh
Katsuji	kaht-sue-jee
Shikami	she-kah-me
Sumida	sue-me-dah
Ikki	ee-key
Mr. & Mrs. Morimoto	more-ee-moe-toe
Toru	toe-ru
Choichi	cho-ee-chee
Saburo	sah-boo-ro

TERMINOLOGIES

Issei (ee-say) "First generation." People who emigrated from Japan to the Americas.

Nisei (nee-say) "Second generation." People born in the Americas.

Kibei (kee-bay) "Returning to America." People born in the Americas, raised in Japan, then return to the Americas.

Hakujins (ha-koo-gins) White people.

Omono (oh-moe-no) Slang for "wise guy."

Inu (ee-noo) Although the direct translation is "dog," it is slang for "spy."

~PART I~

They Will Live in Infamy

CHAPTER ONE

Early Winter, 1938

NO ONE turned off the radio as the sheriff and mortician carried a body down the stairs; their large feet popping the creaky steps. A sheet covered the boy's face, hiding his lips that were frozen in a death grin. He was only seventeen. Jim watched the two strangers haul his older brother on a stretcher as if he wĕre luggage; as if scraps. The broadcaster's voice straggled up the staircase, pursuing a haunting image. Each whitewashed wall, with flowered borders peeling at the tips, reflected streaks of drizzle and snow from the windows. Jim stared out the window. Away from the body. Away from his parents. He felt like vomiting. Only five hours ago he had asked John if he could borrow one of his Count Basie records.

"Take the whole damn collection," his brother retorted. "*Ka-mai-ma-sen*." He then crumbled a Valentine's card he made for his girlfriend, uttering, "Worthless!" and tossed it into the trash.

Jim didn't understand his brother's sarcastic tone. He didn't take any records, fearing his brother would lash out, or that it was some sort of test. Because his brother had been irritable all month, Jim maintained an amicable distance. John's bruises had remained dark after arguing with their father. And that was unusual. Normally their father showed restraint by keeping his fists relaxed; calmed. But John's girlfriend was pregnant and dishonor had blighted the family name.

The mortician's wide shoulder bumped into a family portrait, slanting the frame. Jim recoiled. His brother's rigid mouth suspiciously resembled a smirk.

"Harold!" the sheriff snapped. His leather coat squeaked with his movements. "Watch yerself!"

The mortician scowled. His youthful appearance implied clumsiness like a newborn calf in the field. Glancing up, he uttered, "Sorry!"

They proceeded to step down; their knuckles grazing by the wooden rail on one side; family photos on the other. The mortician trampled to the bottom of the staircase, and balanced the stretcher to his chest. He shifted and crimped the rug. Swinging his head back and forth, grumbling, he tried to avoid bumping into the radio that sat on an end table. The sheriff thumped down the last two steps. A dizzy odor of fried shrimp and seaweed wafted under their broad noses; the stench of an unfinished dinner lagged in the air. The sheriff and mortician never got used to the odd smell of the Japanese. Even after all those years living on the same island.

Jim's father calmly sat on the couch with his hands over his knees. His clean, shaven face became petrified; his small frame transformed into frigidness. He had forgotten to remove his polished shoes and damp coat, not realizing he still had them binding his body. Jim's mother cradled Bethany, Jim's youngest sister, in her lap. Her cotton *yukata*, a delicate housecoat, wrinkled underneath the child's heat. Both parents retained composure in front of the strangers as they sipped down their son's death like a glassful of razor blades. To expose their pain to outsiders was simply not done. They felt once they cried out they would never stop bleeding.

Stroking Bethany's hair, the mother wondered how much of John her daughter would remember. At seven, she was too young to comprehend everything. The mother was only two when her eldest brother was killed during the Russo-Japanese war. She had no memory of him. The familiarity of her brother came from an old, discolored photograph that hung with her other ancestors' portraits. Every week she was forced, by her parents, to pay respects to an unknown dead brother. She would not do the same to her daughter. She accepted the grief and agony she felt for her son, but would not force guilt onto her daughter as if her life bore less value than her brother's death.

Dr. Ellis, a middle-aged man with reddish hair, stood in the living room with the family. He wiped off droplets of sweat from his forehead. "Mr. Yoshimura," he said. "We'll take care of the rest. Don't you worry."

The father shook the doctor's hand and bowed his head. Dr. Ellis couldn't disguise his pity. The circumstances of John's death would torment Mr. Yoshimura for the rest of his life. Having children of his own, Dr. Ellis understood the fear of not only losing a child, but also claiming responsibility for that child's death. He had known his friend since he stepped off the boat to work in the lumber mills. Their friendship lasted through war and Black Tuesday, never wavering under the pressures of politics. He had always perceived Mr. Yoshimura as a good man.

"We'll get you through this," Dr. Ellis continued, "if that's what you want. Anything else I can do, let me know."

Mr. Yoshimura said nothing, and only bowed his appreciation. He was grateful for his friend's immediacy and discrepancy, declaring his son's death as accidental. No other white doctor would have done the same. He was grateful, and yet all he felt were shards of grief and guilt; his tongue shackled by pain. No father could ever prepare himself for the death of his oldest son. Especially in that fashion. Especially when he had pushed his son to that brink. The pride he had possessed now seemed ridiculous. It wasn't worth it. It wasn't worth it.

The sheriff and mortician paused to listen to the radio. Reports of the Japanese Imperial Army ravaging China amplified the details of executions, beatings, and violations against women. The sheriff shuddered with a series of grunts, and glanced at the mortician.

Walking through the front door, Jim overheard one of them disdainfully utter, "These Japs don't even cry for their dead son! Go figure!"

The doctor quickly shut the door, nervously looking at Jim, wondering if he had heard the cruel remark.

Jim bruised his tongue with his teeth until it bled. Hate began to bloat inside. These outsiders knew nothing, not a goddamn thing, about his family. About his grief. About being Japanese in America. Now the war in China began castrating horrible images, and the public winced. What Jim couldn't believe was how these men spat out judgment on the day of his brother's death. What goddamn right did they have?

The car door slammed. He heard their large feet sloshing over the mud. Roughly exhaling as if breathing out boiled water, Jim looked at his father. His father had not protected John, and now John was dead.

"Doc!" the mortician yelled. "Ready when you are!"

Jim turned his attention to the doctor; although avoided eye contact. He knew Dr. Ellis was observing him while he tightly folded his arms across his chest. The doctor's worried expression only aggravated him. He hated pity. Pity meant stupidity.

The doctor gently rested his hand on the father's shoulder, and said, "I'll give you a call tomorrow." He then reached for his hat and long coat that lay on an easy chair. He browsed through the drafty house, examining the painting of Jesus on one wall, and two Japanese scrolls on the other. It was a superbly tidy home. Too tidy, in fact. Organized, dust free, and not cluttered. Unlike his home. His four children, all teenagers, managed to overrun his household. Swing music blaring. Magazines, coats, lipsticks, and jock straps crowded him out of his living room and into his tiny office. But he wouldn't have it any other way. As frustrating as it often was, at least they were content. Glancing at the father, then the son, he opened the door and left.

Jim finally gazed out the window. He relived the image of John's face and body as he lay beside a box of rat poison; stiff like an iron rod; lips curled over his teeth like a decomposed corpse. There Jim found his brother dead on the attic floor.

The men started the hearse. Mist outlined the black vehicle like pebbles in a pond, enforcing the unwanted change. It pulled down the dirt driveway. A soft layer of snow sunk in the dusk's darkness.

Jim suddenly ran upstairs to his bedroom; the very room he had shared with his brother. The walls were covered in stripes, but bare of pictures except one. The portrait of their great-grandfather hung in an oval frame glared down at their beds. Dressed in traditional Japanese garments from the Meiji era, his stern expression locked an implication of customs. His deteriorating portrait seemed primitive in a modern world. Jim spat at the picture. Slamming the door, he fell on his bed, and plunged his face into the pillow, weeping. He felt like his chest had been crushed by an avalanche of rocks. Choking on his saliva, he had difficulty breathing. He wanted to die. To end this piercing pain. To escape. Jim knew once the doctor departed, John's name would never be repeated in the house. It would be as if he had never existed.

Late autumn, 1941

RUSSELL traced his finger tips over her Maria's neck, flicking away her long, dark strands of hair. Her bronzed skin softly framed her small nose and sable eyes. He kissed her. Standing behind a row of short pine trees, he leaned his body into hers. She tasted of peppermint and black licorice. Her wooly sweater tickled the palm of his hand while he rubbed her back. She coiled her fingers through his thick hair. Gray clouds fogged the sun as if fogging windows in the backseat of a car. They heard snickering behind the pine bristles and cones.

Irritated, Russell barked, "Who's there?"

A shadow shifted. "Hamaguchi doin' the hoochi coochi!"

"Leo!" Russell stepped away from Maria, and poked through the limbs. "Is that you, lug head?"

"In the flesh," he replied. His sandy hair stirred between the gaps of the branches as he lurked like a grizzly bear. Chuckling, he persisted, "Of course, not as fleshy as you, maybe! Listen, the guys been lookin' for ya! Wondering if you wanna go to Seattle this weekend."

"Just a minute!"

Russell, who stood barely over five feet, brushed his bangs aside. For the past two weeks they believed they had found a secret spot just off the high school grounds. Away from families. Away from friends. The small community grew smaller each year while their desires flourished. It became harder to be discreet. Looking at Maria, whose cheeks flushed in embarrassment, Russell bit his bottom lip and tugged at his belt. He picked up her school books wrapped in a leather strap, and reached for her hand. Trying to smooth the awkward moment, he squeezed her hand.

"I'm sorry, "he whispered. "How about Sunday? Go see a movie?"

Annoyed, she strayed backwards to adjust some distance between them. Russell glanced at her checkered skirt, wanting to touch the curves of her legs. She rocked on her heels; her white Bobbie socks perfectly trimmed around her ankles; her long skirt swaying. He then looked up and studied her displeased face that splintered the mood. She glared at the tall blond prowling behind the trees. It was obvious Maria did not like his friend.

She finally replied, "I can't. My fadda, he tanks maybe you ah too serious. He not trus' you." She hesitated, and slowly revealed a smile. "Bud maybe . . . maybe nest week we study in library."

Russell curtly sighed. "Oh, sure! I hope he can stand over us to watch too!"

Pivoting in half circles, she coyly said, "Bud de Winta Dance is only a couple weeks." She winked.

He eased forward to kiss her again. She brushed his chin with her knuckles, feeling no growth of a beard yet. Not for a few more years, anyway. It didn't matter that he was Japanese or that she was Filipino, only that they were on the verge of becoming a man and woman. Curling her moist lips, she again moved back, grinning, and walked into the fort of cedar trees. Russell could only watch, aching for more, yet knowing his best behavior protected his family's honor. He felt as if he would shrivel like a prune, die in frustration, and harvest rotten fruit before he got married.

Leo quipped, "Took ya long enough! Jesus, thought I might hafta send in the fire department!"

Sweeping down to pick up his book strap, he wished Leo could be a little less offensive. People tolerated him because of his football legacy as a great linebacker. His temper and strength assumed respect from fellow athletes; fear from others.

Russell asserted, "Like you would know!"

"Rusty," he leered, "I've dated half my class! Believe me, I've done my share!"

"Yeah, Leo. You're a real charity case."

Leo looped his elbow around Russell's neck, and pounded his fist on top of his head like a jackhammer. Laughing, he said, "Hey, man! How do you make Chop Suey?"

Clutching Leo's massive fingers, he strained to peel them apart. His books slipped, stabbing at his side. Russell was a stocky-built jock whose curved muscles advertised his physical capabilities. His popularity revolved around wrestling, triumphing as one of the best in the Seattle-San Juan region. He deserved better respect from Leo.

Gasping, he retorted, "I don't know! I'm not Chinese!"

"You flog a Chink with a noodle! Get it? Noodles and a Chink?"

Leo unfastened his arm. Russell jerked away. Yanking down his varsity coat, he suppressed the urge to whack Leo in his fat belly. The guy could be such an asshole at times! Breathing heavily, Russell stared up at him, frowning. "That joke really isn't funny, Leo."

"Why? It's not like you're Chinese." He pressed his thick hands on his hips. "Or are all you Orientals just super sensitive?"

Carefully watching Leo, wanting to tell him to stuff noodles up his ass, he answered, "The joke's kinda corny. And it's not- polite."

He rolled his eyes and sniggered, "Oh, okay! I'll remember my manners next time! Don't be such a Fuddy-Duddy!"

Swinging his strap of books over his shoulder again, he marched past Leo, trying to calm himself. The columns of thin trees lined the trail and released a sweet, musty scent that comforted the air. At the bottom of the hill, Russell's friends gathered in a circle. A few smoked cigarettes. Each wore a varsity jacket, representing football, basketball, and wrestling. They spoke of girls and upcoming games. Russell was the only Asian among them. Leo demanded a smoke, slapping his hands together and rubbing them as though receiving a gift. He boasted about Russell's embarrassing moment, exaggerating the details. Everyone chuckled or jeered, except Dave Lundberg. He observed Russell narrowing his eyes; cheeks reddening. Dave knew Russell wouldn't say anything, afraid to insult his friends; afraid of rejection.

"Okay, guys!" Dave exclaimed, clapping his hands in an attempt to quiet everyone. He wore a baseball cap to cover his curly, brown hair. "That's enough! We've got more serious business to talk about!"

"Yeah!" Leo hollered. "Like pickin' up girls in Seattle!"

THE door squeaked, bumping into a dangling bell, then closed. Jim glanced up. Another high school sophomore entered his father's shop, Yoshi's Groceries, one of the few Japanese businesses on the island. His father had sliced his last name in half, believing that the rhyming of "Yoshi" and "groceries" would be an effective gimmick for business. And supposedly it was. Jim resettled his attention to his studies; disinterested in his male classmate. Standing behind the register, he leaned over his math book and swayed his pencil. One day he was going to be an engineer, and thus become an important man. More important than his father; the *oyabun*; the deputy of the *Issei* community. One day he planned to leave Winslow, fleeing from this damned rural, industry that kept dripping like a rusty faucet; slowly and with empty endurance. Bainbridge was too small; cluttered with illiterates, farmers, and mill workers. And clogged with his father's impossible traditions.

Minutes later his classmate set down bottles of vinegar, horseradish, and a bag of rice. Jim glanced up once more, noticing Russell's hair was dampened from the mist; unruly from the walk. Russell Hamaguchi used to live ten acres from the Yoshimuras outside of town, and would cove over to his house with his parents for tea. The adults would discuss local politics and business. But after John had killed himself, Jim's family moved to another house.

"How's it going?" Russell asked.

Jim stared at him. All those years they preserved a stranger's distance. As if Russell were so damned superior strolling past him at school with his jock friends; ignoring him. Jim looked at the items in front of him, automatically punching the register, knowing how much each item cost by heart.

"Fine," he finally replied "That'll be forty-eight cents."

Russell peeled off a polite smile, waiting for Jim to say something else. An uncomfortable silence pulled along as though a tractor plowing through rocky ground. He studied Jim with mutual frustration. Jim had height, making him taller than most *Nisei* boys; like his brother, Meito. An unusual trait. Jim's broad face strengthened his sharp cheekbones and lean nose. His rounded glasses balanced on his cheeks, creating an intelligent spectrum. His stiff mouth and righteous eyes seemed to criticize Russell's every movement. These characteristics made him a bit intimidating. Since he could recollect as a child, Jim looked like someone who had regular constipation. Maybe he did. At each public gathering, all Jim did was sulk in a corner somewhere with that constipated look.

"Well," Russell persisted, thumping fifty cents on the counter, attempting to draft a conversation, "My mother's planning on making *sukiyaki* and *sushi* tonight. Normally she gets this stuff, but she's not feeling well, and so," he shrugged, "she volunteered me."

Jim continued to stare, completely uninterested. Russell's babble pricked at his nerves. They weren't friends. Never had been. Never will be. He slid the money to the edge of the counter, and dipped his fingers inside to exchange the pennies.

"Thanks," Russell sighed.

Jim was *too Japanese,* in his opinion. How did Jim expect to fit in when he continued to exclude himself? He remembered Jim's brother behaving in the same manner: quiet and stern. Maybe if the poor sap had a girlfriend he would be less prudish.

Jim reached for a brown paper bag under the counter, and carefully placed the bottles between the soft bags of rice. He still said nothing.

Russell sustained his smile. "See ya Monday."

Jim nodded his reply. *Baka*, he thought. What a complete fool. He watched Russell slip outside the door. Russell's image, blurred by the rain droplets, rippled across the front window. In the sixth grade Russell had changed his name from Goro to a sturdy American name; as if endorsing popularity votes. Jim was proud he didn't pretend to be someone else in order to be accepted by the white community. Mutating one's name to strip off their parents' heritage, as Goro did, signified weakness. How could someone replace his birth name without replacing his dignity?

Mr. Yoshimura coughed twice in the back room where he organized his order forms for the month. Jim cringed. Soon his father's footsteps aggravated the peaceful surroundings; his flawless and crisp strides controlling the silence and announcing his presence in the room. Wearing wire-thin glasses that touched his thick brows, his father consistently dressed in a suit and tie; even at informal events such as birthdays. Each morning his father polished his shoes to purposely shine like glass. Prestige defined his function in society. Jim interpreted his father's virtue as obsessive. Growing up in Hiroshima, and coming from a family of eleven, Japan offered no mobility for his father. The United States whispered prosperous promises, and his father absurdly believed in these golden words.

Mr. Yoshimura walked to Jim. Before he opened his mouth, another customer walked in with his nine-year-old son. The man was the father of John's unfortunate girlfriend. Rarely did his neglected friend walk inside his store. Usually his wife or daughter, Tomiko, would come by. The shame still lashed at their backs; and yet, no one spoke of it.

Breaking a grin, Mr. Yoshimura exclaimed in Japanese, bowing his head, "*Mitsuru-san! Always a pleasure. It has been too long.*"

Mitsuru, short and muscular from years of laboring in the strawberry fields, removed his hat and bowed. "*Yes. The years are easy to forget, my friend. But today I come for advice.*"

Mitsuru gently tugged at his young son's shoulder. The boy scrunched his nose out of impatience, and slid out a folded piece of paper. Mitsuru glanced at Jim, shocked to see how much he appeared like John. He felt sorry for the Yoshimura family. The inexplicable cause of John's death left the town baffled; coming up with inexplicable answers. Although rumors of suicide often came up.

Mitsuru yanked the paper out of the boy's hand. Biting his chapped lip, he walked to the counter, unfolding the thick paper.

"*Before I sign this contract, I would like for you to read it, Toshiyuki-san, and tell me if it is favorable. The last time I leased land, my landlord made me pay double on the deposit and charged interest for late payments. I do not understand any of this. Please help me.*"

Mr. Yoshimura carefully read the English words. He had become the middleman between the two communities. Tax advice. Banking advice. He also sold health and life insurances on the side. And before the Depression, he even acted as a travel agent to Japan.

Jim looked down at the small, wearied boy who seemed he didn't want to be there; swinging his hip and rolling his eyes. Jim didn't want to be there either. He reached over the counter to grab two toothpicks. Smiling, he put one toothpick between two fingers and thumb, and the other resting on his other palm.

He said, "Watch this. I can make it jump without moving my fingers."

The boy stared, not amused. The toothpick on Jim's palm began bouncing. The boy's eyes quickly widened.

Expanding his mouth, the boy exclaimed, "How did you do that?"

"It's an old Indian trick. Almost like magic."

Mr. Yoshimura inhaled sharply, and turned to look at his friend. "*There is a problem. The percentage of the late fee will triple after the six months of your agreement. I will speak with your new landlord about this. I know about American laws and I have an American friend who is a lawyer.*"

Relieved and assured, Mitsuru again bowed. "*I do not know how our community would survive without your special skills.*"

RUSSELL jogged up the road while holding the bag inside his coat; glad to live only a few blocks from the grocery store. Jack Benny's radio show had already begun, and he didn't want to miss the rest of the half-hour comedy skits. His cold nose dripped in the harsh mist; his foggy breath lagged behind his ears. The narrow street was nearly empty with the exception of a few parked cars. A Beagle-Shepherd mix barked and pranced at his heels. Its large, tan spots blended within its dirty white fur. Russell's family had the dog for a decade, always wandering the harmless roads, but never too far off.

"Down, Zasshu!" he panted, flinging his arm. "Go away! Go protect our chickens like a good mutt!"

Lights from the windows guided Russell to his home; given that darkness had dropped an hour ago. The constant drizzle had buried the yellow sun for many weeks. The weather behaved in its normal manner for the region, banishing strong light and a hope for dry socks and shoes. When he finally reached his house, jumping over the steps, he rushed inside to the living room. The couch and two cushioned chairs dominated the shallow room; surrounded by drooping drapes. A soft, lavender odor lingered in the room. His mother lay on the couch with beige lace doilies mounting the top sides. She hinged her arm over her forehead. Pink slippers warmed her tiny feet. Her long, black hair, with a few gray streaks, sprawled over a pillow. Above her hung a display of family photos, spreading from Japan to Washington; from the twenties to the forties; all hanging like guardians.

Lifting her head, she scolded in Japanese, *"Ah! Goro! Take off your shoes! Where is your mind?"*

Because Goro was his birth name, only his family didn't call him Russell.

Grunting, he returned to the front door to slide out of his wet shoes. Whenever he visited his friends' houses, he didn't need to remove his shoes. Wishing it was one of the many traditions his parents had left behind, he obeyed anyway. Dropping his shoes close to the door, alongside three other pairs, he said in English, "Mama, they were out of salt."

"*Nani*?"

Irritated, he repeated, "*Shio*. Salt."

"Oh, sawt."

Shaking his head, he pronounced, "With an 'l' mama. Salt. Sal-t."

"*Hai, I know!*"

She sat up, wheezing. Goro seemed to have the most problems recognizing his courtesies. Her oldest son never possessed this difficulty, and she thanked her dead grandfather for it. At least her oldest son's obedience would have made her ancestors proud.

"*Please put the things in the kitchen and get your sister to help me.*"

Russell asked as he walked to the kitchen, "Is Sadaye in the bath house with Papa?"

"*Nai, she is in her bedroom.*"

Russell was exhilarated when Sadaye returned home to take care of their mother, who was thankfully recovering from tuberculosis. Before then, as the last one left in his parents' house, he felt like a servant. Goro, get this. Goro, get that. Goro, be a man and do women's work. Since his sister had no children of her own, her duties as a daughter and a nurse conveniently merged to aid their challenging mother.

His mother looked up at him. "*Goro, why do you still have on your coat?*"

He grunted. "I didn't have time to take it off."

"*Where is your mind today, Goro?*" she demanded.

He mumbled, "Obviously not here."

"*What? What was said?*"

"Nothin', Mama. I'll get Sadaye."

After hanging his prized jacket in the hall closet, Russell thundered up the wooden steps with his mother's criticizing voice chasing him. He passed by watercolor paintings of Mount Fuji, Mount Rainier, and a family portrait from Japan; all painted by his father in his youth. His father no longer harvested his paint brushes, now harvesting the fields. He claimed he didn't have time for foolish hobbies because he was too busy supporting a family. That was more important.

Russell knocked on his sister's door, and announced, "Hey, Sadaye! Mama needs you in the kitchen!"

Before she could respond, Russell was already at the bottom of the staircase standing by his beloved radio. He twisted the knob, skipping the news, ignoring the war. A couple of weeks ago he snickered when President Roosevelt announced the unfolding plan about the Nazis aiming to hook their way through South America. Everyone worried. Russell knew it had to be a false report; an attempt to induce people to hate the Germans more. Like the Nazis really wanted to reap such a primitive place! For two years the anti-German propaganda gorged people's heads like thick syrup on fruit; sticky and sweet; deluding people's tastes. Nothing more.

He finally found his favorite radio station, *The Jack Benny Show*, and turned up the knob in the living room to hear static-tinted laughter and Jack's clever retort, "Well!"

* * *

MORNING sunlight splintered through the curtain, striking Jim's eyes. The unnatural glare forced him to wake. Blinking furiously, he groaned and turned his head away. The tall bookshelf loomed over him, full of English words and knowledge. He wished it would burn on the spot. All of the books were chosen by his father, and he hated being pressured to read each of them. Every day the thought of killing himself invited a sense of relief even if he lacked the courage. He focused on that damn photo across the room; a reminder of ancient honor- his great-grandfather. Each morning Jim had to look at it. The narrow eyes squinted back at him: Judging. Criticizing. Its rigid reflection was not prepared for the modern world. It had always been an eerie in presence: mythological in life; a phantom of nightmares.

Faint sounds traveled beneath the gap of his bedroom door. Every morning his father listened to the radio, drinking world news as if an alcoholic craving for more *saki.* Sometimes Mr. Yoshimura would share the information with his wife. Sometimes he wouldn't say anything to avoid upsetting her. Since the Japanese army instigated bloodshed in Nanking four years ago, harsh realities of war pervaded their consciousness. Like kites rattling in the wind, their nerves were constructed of thin paper; their security held by a fragile string.

Three knocks rang in Jim's ears.

"Jimmu," his father barked, opening the door. "Is time to wake up. Put on yur clothes an' help me change de oil in de car." He waited for Jim to acknowledge him. "You must get up now before Rose and Tom come over with good news, my son."

Jim moaned and rubbed his eyes. For once he would have liked to stay in bed longer without the chains of chores pulling him out. It was Sunday, for Christ's sake. Even God took the seventh day off at least once!

ROSE and Tom arrived mid-morning, bearing generous smiles. Almost giddy. Almost tipsy. Their arms wrapped each other, hugging their warmth before they sat down. Mrs. Yoshimura brought out her tea set, positioned the silver tray on the coffee table, and began serving the tea. Everyone anxiously settled in the living room, passing time with talk of the weather; patiently waiting for the news. Except for Jim. His expression was drained from spontaneity, inducing a lifeless smile. He pressed his back against the folding chair, and quietly watched his family from a corner; detached. Bethany nestled herself between both parents like a duckling that nestled in the sun. She bounced her hands on her lap.

Rose and Tom perched on the loveseat to face the family. Waiting for the chattering to cease, Rose smiled at Tom. Rose married her childhood sweetheart. She got married soon after she walked across the stage to receive her diploma, moving directly into her in-law's home. There she became a farmer's wife instead of a businessman's daughter. The day Rose entered Tom's house, she threw out all the rat poison, and continued to do so whenever she located a hidden bottle. Her in-laws thought she had acquired a touch of insanity, for what farmer didn't use rat poison to get rid of rodents?

"I have great news for all of you," Rose announced, squeezing her husband's hand. "I am going to have a child!" She bit her lower lip. "We're going to have a baby, if you can believe it!"

Tom included, "After a year of trying! We've finally been blessed."

Jim didn't care for Tom. He possessed no spine and complained repeatedly about wanting better recognition in the community. Since Tom was more of a disciple than a person in charge, his true achievement entailed marrying the daughter of an influential leader. In Jim's opinion, his brother-in-law was useless.

Mrs. Yoshimura scooped her hands to her lips, pinching her overjoyed eyes. "Ahhh!" she exhaled. *"A baby! I am going to be a sobo! Soon babies will bless this house with charitable prospects, and life would blossom as it should!"*

"This is such happy news!" Mr. Yoshimura nodded, rubbing the palms of his hands over his knees. "Such happy news."

Mrs. Yoshimura giggled. "*My mother used to say laugh three times! Once in praise. Once in promise. Once with purpose. Today is a good day for such a hospitable occasion!*"

Bethany asked, "Am I gonna be an auntie?"

"Of course, silly-bean," Rose replied. "Jim, what do you think? Are you ready to be an uncle?"

Jim glanced at his father who sat poised on the couch, across from him. His rigid face barely raised a grin, but his eyes flowed pride and delight. His bow tie fluttered with the movement of his throat.

"It will be an honor," Jim finally replied.

Mr. Yoshimura looked at his only son, and was disappointed at his lack of enthusiasm. "Jimmu, ah you not happy for yur sista's gud fortune?"

He couldn't force a smile. "Yes. I'm very happy."

"I do not undastand you," Mr. Yoshimura gruffly sighed. "In Japan, for dis occasion, everyone celebrates."

Jim bitterly said, "This isn't Japan, Papa."

Stunned, he spoke with fortitude and irritation. "In Japan, my fatha would beat me for speaking back."

Avoiding his eyes, Jim looked at his father's silky Western slippers. He knew how desperately his father wanted to breed a family in America, and someday show it off to his other family in Japan. To show *his* father that he was a man of importance despite his status as a middle son. Jim had never met his grandfather. The old photos revealed a harshness about him; almost inhuman. Jim never had any wishes to visit Japan.

"I didn't mean to disrespect you, Papa," he started, "I just meant- that things are different here." He then frowned up at his father. "Isn't that why you left Hiroshima?"

Mr. Yoshimura fluttered his eyelids like a moth caught in a net; unable to move forward or backward. Even though America provided magnificent opportunities, despite the chronic setbacks of being an *Issei*, Japan was first his home.

"One mus' never forget his birthright," he quietly admitted. "Dat is why I weow return home with a great fortune. An' you weow carry on the Yoshimura name. *Wakarimasu-ka*?"

Jim straightened. The ticking of the grandfather clock reverberated through the disturbing silence. Disagreements were rare and no one knew how to respond when one awakened. Jim wanted to tell his father to go to hell and walk out of the house; never to return. Vanish. Just like John.

"Yes, Papa," he said. "I've understood this since I was eight."

THE afternoon shaded a peaceful appearance as dusk blackened the gray sky. Russell laid his books on top of each other, and sat down at the empty dining table. He removed his gnawed pencil from his ear to continue to chew on it. The history and science books remained unopened while he tapped his finger tips. His mother and sister shifted around in the kitchen, talking and clanking, concentrating on cooking. His father napped on the couch with a Los Angeles newspaper, *Rafu Shimpo,* tented over his chest. Russell couldn't stand *not* listening to music. He knew if he turned the radio on his mother would be irritated. The radio, she claimed, diverted the mind. She couldn't understand that it actually motivated him. Jumping up, he trotted to the Victrola in the living room, picked a record, and returned to the closed books. Glenn Miller's "Sold American" bounced an upbeat mood.

"Goro!" his mother barked from the kitchen. There was no door to separate, or to even protect him. "*Are you working on your school work?*"

He grabbed a book and ripped it open. "Yes!" he said.

"*Is the music not distracting you?*"

"No!" he said.

"*I think it is distracting you.*"

His mother marched to the Victrola, stopped the record, and returned to the kitchen, ignoring his pleading eyes.

"*You must learn to be a better student, Goro!*" she stated. "*You must learn to study in silence, and hear your thoughts. How else do you plan to further your life if you do not maintain discipline?*"

"I plan to use my good looks," he mumbled.

"Ah!" she whisked, peeking through the doorway. "*No one is that attractive!*"

He smiled, and began to flick the pages backward. She stood for moment. Satisfied that he was at least pretending to be obedient, she returned to the messy kitchen. Boiling pots, full of noodles, leaked water down the edges. Sliced chestnuts and onions dispersed over the counter where Sadaye had chopped. Chicken, carrots, and snow peas sizzled in the pan. The cooking was conducted like music. An orchestra of pounding, clinking, and stirring chimed in an unusual rhythm. The aroma and steam filled the air like the *koto* harp soothing the soul.

Russell scanned the words, remembering very little. Minutes later car lights sailed through the window, over his eyes, blinding him for a moment and causing yellow dots to flutter around. Then the car lights switched off. He stood up to peer out the window. Faint street lights from the fading dusk outlined the vehicle and two heads. Russell continued to watch. No one left the car. They just sat- very still.

"I think Meito and Gerdie are here," Russell announced. "They might be fighting again. They're just sitting there."

Mrs. Hamaguchi and Sadaye emerged from the kitchen with their hands dripping water. They stared out the window.

"Maybe so," Sadaye remarked. "Maybe not. They're not moving at all."

Mrs. Hamaguchi wiped her hands on her apron, squinting. "*Do shimashita-ka?*"

"I don't know what's wrong, Mama," Sadaye answered.

They continued to stare out the window. Both women stood behind Russell, so he shifted to avoid having them literally breathe down his neck. The window wasn't designed to hold three grown heads knocking about. Feeling suffocated, he twitched and stepped back to escape. He wasn't *that* curious.

Mr. Hamaguchi awoke from his late nap. Crinkling the magazine when he sat up, he asked, "*Do shimashita-ka?*"

Mrs. Hamaguchi replied, "*Meito and the boys are here.*"

"*Then why are all of you staring as if the emperor of Japan just walked down the road?*"

"Because they're having one of their arguments," Russell said.

"We don't know for sure," Sadaye interjected.

"*Well, it is not polite to stare,*" Mr. Hamaguchi grunted. "*No matter who it is.*"

They reluctantly abandoned their posts. Russell sat down and took a book, although not actually reading it. Mrs. Hamaguchi followed Sadaye back into the kitchen. Two minutes passed. Russell began drumming his pencil on the table, listening to Glenn Miller in his head. Mr. Hamaguchi gathered loose newspapers and magazines, and piled them in a corner with the others that had accumulated over the week. Five minutes passed. Again Russell looked over his shoulder. Still no movement. Twice Mrs. Hamaguchi stood at the portal, squinting through the window, watching the sky darken. Slowly ten more minutes had elapsed into exhaustible time; each second carrying their curiosity into legitimate concern. Finally a car door squeaked; then shut.

Russell eagerly rose again.

Mrs. Hamaguchi scurried out of the kitchen and flung the front door open. Light harshly stained Meito's face, stopping him on the lawn. He appeared as though he had been shot; his arms limp at his side; his expression stung by pain. Russell had never seen his brother appear so overpowered.

"*Do shimashita-ka?*" his mother demanded.

"Oh my God, Mama," Meito exhaled, his thick brows almost touching each other. "My God. Japan bombed Pearl Harbor." Then switching languages, he repeated, "*Japan attacked America.*"

Moving to the front, Russell wanted to hear everything more clearly. Just an inch taller than his mother, he wedged between her and the door frame. Mr. Hamaguchi and Sadaye soon clustered from behind; alarmed.

Russell asked, "What's going on?"

Meito stared at him. "We're at war. America is at war with Japan."

Russell stepped backward; stunned. An odd mixture of extreme heat and cold collided together, and collapsed down his chest. He had sensed that America would eventually be drafted into war. Everyone did. The world had become too bloody for anyone to remain clean. But Russell thought it would be fought in Europe, not Asia. Pearl Harbor went ahead and changed everything.

Looking at his mother and father, as their faces spoiled with anxiety, he remembered the story of a German man living on Bainbridge whose house burned to the soil during the Great War. No one confessed to the arson, and therefore the crime remained unsolved. The German fled with his spirit cracked in half. He never returned. So then, what would happen to his parents? How would America deal with them? The country Russell knew and loved would fight against his parents' homeland. And his parents, without American citizenship, *denied* American citizenship, were now his homeland's enemy. He glanced at the dark window and, to his dislike, saw his own Japanese face.

CHAPTER TWO

Early December

MRS. YOSHIMUURA dropped the Seattle newspaper on the kitchen table. Tears smeared a photo of a Japanese man being hauled off by two FBI agents. His hands were cuffed in back while the tall men seized both his arms. Above the photo, the headline read, "JAPS UNDER FIRE-AMERICA PREVAILS!"

She uttered to her husband, "*Everyday in the newspapers Issei men all over are being arrested. When will they come for you?*"

Mr. Yoshimura couldn't answer.

"*What about our children?*" she persisted.

"*President Roosevelt will not do anything to our children,*" he assured his wife. "*They are Americans. The government might send us back to Japan, but then, it may not. Either way, Haruko, we must be strong for our children.*"

Jim had cracked his bedroom door to hear his parents during the late hours. He lay on his bed, watching the shadows streaming from the kitchen just before reaching the edge of his room. As his mother wept, he realized his ineptness to protect her; let alone to console her. He disliked witnessing her pain as shame reddened the Japanese community.

"*Wipe your face, Haruko. There is no need to start worrying ourselves until something is worth worrying about. We will deal with it as time unravels itself.*"

Bethany's small voice quietly intruded into Jim's eavesdropping. "Why is Mama crying?"

He saw her toes squirming behind his door. He whispered, "Go back to bed, Bethany. It's none of your business!"

"Why? I'm not a little girl anymore."

"Now, Bethany!" he warned.

"Now, Bethany!" she mimicked, returning to her room.

Jim sat up, brooding. The day after Pearl Harbor bled awkward feelings and tangled identities, thus destroying a fragile unsteadiness between the two. What would the public notice when he would walk down a street in his American jeans and jacket? Would they perceive him as an American? His eyes might slant their view. His features stood out beyond the typical-American veneer, and he knew he would be an easy target. The other day, Todd Smith stopped talking when Jim entered the classroom. Todd's mouth froze, no doubt guilty for saying something callous, or stupid. The others stood in the corner with sappy expressions. As if they could possibly understand the embarrassment. They never had experienced doors slammed in their faces while trying to sell tickets for the Boy Scouts, or being spat at for swimming on the same river bank with the McCoy brothers. They couldn't comprehend the ignorant sneers regarding their parents; parents who ate rice and seaweed, or wore *kimonos* and shared baths with other family members.

God, how he wished his brother were still here.

He slid his hand underneath the mattress to remove a stack of cards. It was the only object his father didn't burn or toss out. A long time ago, John had taught him the immoral game of poker, hiding the stack of cards in a shoebox; away from their righteous father. John used to say, "If you want respect, you need to work three times as hard as everyone else. But if you want to be equal in their eyes- that will never happen. That's why it's important you believe you're better than them. If you believe it, then it doesn't matter what they think!"

John had once believed it. But apparently it wasn't enough.

* * *

RUSSELL dumped his lunch bag in the trash before walking to school. Every week, for the past three years, he saved just enough money to buy the school's lunch, avoiding the interrogation of his peers when they asked "My God, what's *that* you're eating?" Jogging a few blocks from his home, waving at neighbors and friends, he stopped at Maria's house. Although it was out of the way, each morning he would leave early so he could escort her to class. All those months he continued to wait by the white fence; usually enduring her father's morning scowl from the window. Never once did he invite Russell inside. Russell couldn't determine whether this man disliked him because he was dating his daughter, or because he wasn't Filipino. Or both. Maria's mother, however, was a hell of alot more friendlier. She even baked him cookies on occasion.

As Russell waited outside the fence, he saw Maria's father standing in front of the window, sipping his black coffee; glaring. As usual, he offered no benevolent gesture. Feeling uncomfortable, Russell pretended that readjusting his leather book strap was more interesting; and yet, his glare wouldn't ease. Maria suddenly slammed the front door, but her father reopened it to yell at her in Pilipino. She shouted in turn; her cheeks flushed. Russell knew whatever it was between them, it no doubt was about him.

Closing the gate, she grabbed his arm. "Run!"

Together they bolted down the street with her father slamming the door. They swerved around the corner; their hearts rapidly beating. Although he already knew the answer, he had to ask anyway.

"What in the world was that all about?"

Maria lowered her head. She remained quiet for moment. “My fadda hear on de ah radio wha’ Japan do to his pe’po’ at home. He tank maybe you not so good for me.”

Angered, he vented, “I have nothing to do with what goes on over there any more than he does!”

“I know,” she said. “He bery worried about his ah mada an’ sista. Don’ take him serious, Rasso. He be scared.”

“Still, I don’t get it!” he flinched. “I’m an American! I’ve never been to Japan! I have no desire to go to Japan!”

Since he was eleven, he perfected the American accent, chose American friends, if their parents allowed it, wore the right clothes, joined the All-American Teams; everything in his control that was acceptable he pursued. Now Pearl Harbor ruined everything he had achieved, and he hated Japan for that.

“Man,” Russell continued, “it’s bad enough dealing with your dad on a normal basis. What about your mom? What does she think?”

“She ah not say much.”

“Figures,” he mumbled. “What about the Winter Dance? Can you still go with me?”

Maria slowed her pace with uncertainty wavering in her smile. “Oh, sure. My fadda, he blow off steam, don’ worry.”

“You mean blow-up! I don’t wanna be around when he starts setting off bombs!”

She laughed, wanting to laugh, wanting everything to reverse into normalcy. All week her father damned the Imperial Army and, for some odd reason, he perceived Russell with little distinction; that being related to them in some sort of fashion still tied an association by default. She was exhausted with defending herself but maintained her stance. It would only be a matter of time before her father would see what she saw in Russell.

Shaking her finger at him, she chuckled, “Be good! Don’ say bad tangs, Rasso!”

“I’m not! I’m being serious. I feel like sometimes I was the one who bombed Pearl Harbor. The way some people look at me . . .” he hesitated, not confident how much he should relate to Maria; afraid if he confessed too much she wouldn’t be amused by him any more. And now that her father began squeezing more pressure, he wondered how much longer she would last before she would break-up with him. One of his acquaintances actually had the audacity to tell Russell he could no longer eat with him during lunch. He said that his mom didn’t want him to hang around Russell anymore. No hard feelings, though, okay?

He glanced at Maria. “A lotta times I feel embarrassed, like it’s my fault for everything. And then I look at my parents. I see so much . . . regret . . . like they’re the ones who plotted the whole thing!”

Her smile withered as she squeezed his hand. “I know. I feow ashame I don’ speaka English good. You can. You can go to ah college. You can be any’tang. I weow ohways work in de field.”

Russell studied her hand. During the off-harvest months she had time to tend to her hands, dousing them with lotion and painting her fingernails. The warmth of her skin felt so comforting.

He looked up and asked, "Why do you like me?"

Astonished, she stopped to face him. "Silly question. Why you like me? You can ah hafe any girl in school. I'm nobody."

Russell held her other hand, and thought for a moment. "Because you're fun. But mostly, I think, is you're always optimistic. I haven't met anyone as enthusiastic about life as you." He watched her blush with a half-smile. Realizing that she never expressed anything unkind to anyone, or behind anyone, he needed to work on that sort of thing. "What about you?" he insisted, shrugging. "Why me?"

She continued to blush and stepped closer to him. Feeling his breath on her cheek, she whispered, "You hafe heart ana great huma. You like to ah help udder pe'po'. My Ma woulda say is bes' quality in men."

He caressed her chin, wanting to kiss her, but not so openly in this small town. His parents expected him to uphold proper conduct in public. And mostly he did. Mostly. He had cared for Maria for a while, except today he sensed a stronger emotion. Gratitude? Respect? Love even? That was a terrifying idea.

Stepping back, he said, "We better get to school. Find a parking spot."

She laughed. "Yes! When ah you going to buy a car? My feet hurt!"

"I was waiting for you to marry a rich slob so you can buy *me* one."

Her laughter fluttered like a strong wind rippling wet clothes on a line; strong yet invisible; invisible yet hopeful.

Mid December

MR. YOSHIMURA parked his 1935 Pontiac on a dirt road; a few feet from his house. Jim sat in the passenger seat, staring ahead. As usual, the conversation centered on Jim's schooling and his accomplishments. His hard work would expand opportunities not experienced by the *Issei* generation. Jim's fate was to be successful in America without the obvious discrimination binding him. Or so his father believed. Even after the seventh of December.

The front door swung open, and Bethany sprinted across the yard with her hands clapping. Her skirt revealed a freshly skinned knee. Mr. Yoshimura had hardly shut the car door before she squealed and shouted, "Papa! Papa!" She jumped into her father's arms, giggling. He smiled, hugging his ten-year-old daughter, rocking her back and forth.

Jim glared at his sister through the window. His father had stopped expressing affection toward him when he was eight.

Getting out of the car, he scoffed, "Aren't you a little too old to be doing that, Bethany?"

She scrunched her nose at him.

"Jimmu, you know betta dan to tease yur sista," his father warned.

Walking away, he replied, "Sorry, Papa."

"Such a welcoming!" Mr. Yoshimura exclaimed, patting Bethany on her back. "*Kore-wa taihen sukidesu*! I like dis very much, indeed!"

Jim tried to ignore his father's loving tone. His sister did not deserve his father's attention. She was too spoiled for a girl; always demanding recognition from adults as if she were so damn special. He walked up the stones that curved in a frown; beside the thick shrubberies. Along the border of the miniature fence laid the sleeping flower garden waiting for April's bloom. The white porch wrapped around the house like arms, clutching the hollow gaps, holding onto nothing. He entered the house. A smoke-filled aroma of seafood and fried rice drifted from the kitchen. The warm and dense seasoning of battered shrimp and cooking oils repressed the rooms. The hazy smoke blinded his thoughts, but his stomach ached as he inhaled the flavors deeper into his mouth.

"Mama, we're home," he announced.

He took off his shoes, meticulously placing them next to the front door. The staircase sat at the tip of the hall. He looked up. The old family photo had been replaced by a painting of Mount Fuji. His mother had turned paranoid about having another family photo taken in fear ghosts would disturb the living. It felt like some sort of betrayal. He remembered when his father removed the photo that still linked John's memory. Two days before the funeral. And no one stopped him. Jim wished he had grabbed it out of his father's hands to save it. All of John's photos were burned in the backyard. Without remorse it seemed. Today, not even dust recognized his brother; this shapeless memory. Jim knew he was a lot like John: moody, anxious, and shy, but he wasn't gifted, truly gifted like his brother, not quite excelling in every subject. John was a methodical one. Polished shoes. Ironed slacks. His books and records organized according to subject and size. Despite his odd, fussy habits, he enjoyed swing music and collected baseball cards.

Soon Bethany's laughter and his father's voice pierced his ears. Hearing them move up the path behind the closed door, he fled into the kitchen.

His mother enthusiastically declared, "*Kuchi-o akete!*"

"Why do you want me to open my mouth?" Jim asked.

The kitchen radiated like glass. A dainty round table was poised near the bay window as if posing for art. Lace curtains hung from the chiseled window frame. A bowl of pecans settled in the middle of the flowered tablecloth. His mother carried pride in her house; perpetually prepared for surprise visitors and thriving on their compliments.

She lifted a wooden spoon and blew on the olive liquid. "Try."

"What is it?" he asked.

"*Miso shiru.*"

"A bean soup, huh? I thought you didn't like bean soups."

"*Yes, but this one is very good!*" she answered in Japanese. "*Takagi-suma gave me her recipe. You must try it.*"

He grinned. "I thought you're not speaking to Mrs. Takagi. Didn't you say she was *yasiu* when she didn't buy your flowers at half price?"

"*Hai, she is very cheap, but I would not be such a good Christian if I did not forgive her.*" Mrs. Yoshimura erected her finger to testify her point. "*She is only jealous that I have the best garden on the island. So, come try this!*"

Jim walked to his mother and leaned down to taste the soup. She at least made him feel valuable by loving him without extreme expectations. Unlike his father, she would consistently ask for his opinions, and complimented him daily. He often wondered if his parents' marriage hadn't been arranged, who would she have married instead?

"Not too bad," he replied.

She suddenly switched to English. "Wha's wrong? Wha's missing?"

"I don't know, Mama," he shrugged. "I don't cook."

"Need mo' sawt, yes?"

He grinned. "Perhaps."

She smiled and patted his face. "*You are a good son. The girl you will someday marry will be just as fortunate!*"

Blushing, Jim shook his head. The hint of marriage wasn't exactly as enticing as the soup. Her optimism was more charitable than his own. Jim never had a girlfriend. For one reason or another, girls didn't seem to be attracted to him. Not that he wasn't attracted to them. After knowing what happened to his brother, and observing his parents' marriage, he convinced himself it was better being alone.

"*You better help your father and sister arrange the chairs for tonight's meeting*," she said. "*We have much to plan for the New Year.*"

ROWS of shoes bordered a wall beside the front door of the Yoshimura household. One of the unofficial committees, consisting of Buddhists and Christians, crowded Jim's living room. Both religious groups of the Nikkei community met in the same room only for special occasions, such as *the o-shogatso*, the New Year; otherwise they functioned on different terms. Wooden fold-out chairs were arranged between the sofa and loveseat. Jim, positioned next to his father, stared at the carpet. His father spoke of preparations for the New Year as cigarette smoke floated above their heads. Two Japanese paintings hung on the wall. The pictures discreetly illustrated the traditional court life of noble women in colorful flowered dresses. On the opposite wall centered a portrait of Jesus. A sour smell of pickled vegetables and steamed rice mingled among the flat stench of tobacco. His mother entertained in the kitchen with the other women. They savored in *ochazuke*; a treat of hot tea poured over rice eaten with preserved vegetables on the side.

Earlier Jim saw Tomiko enter his house with her father, and then withdrew into the kitchen with the other women. She kept her hair short; just above her jaw. When she wasn't in school or didn't have some sort of a special event to attend, she enjoyed wearing jeans, always wearing jeans. It didn't matter what she wore, Jim had always thought she radiated in anything.

"*So what will we do when the Emperor's Birthday arrives this April?*" one of the men asked. His black hair was unaffected by grey despite being in his mid forties. His small nose pointed down like a beak. Born in San Francisco, but raised in Tokyo, he was among the few *Kibei* on the island.

"*I do not know, Katsuji-san.*" Mr. Yoshimura replied, his tone remaining undisturbed. "*If we celebrate Emperor Hirohito's birthday, we might draw more suspicion on our community. I am not certain if we should take that chance this coming year."*

The man huffed, leaning back. Jim questioned Katsuji's objective to live in the United States when he constantly boasted about Japan's supremacy. If Japan was indeed the best nation known to man, as he often bragged, then why did he continue to stay on Bainbridge all these years?

"*How can anyone be so dishonorable and denounce the Emperor's birthday?"* Katsuji ranted. "*Your Christian beliefs have perverted your Japanese traditions! It is denouncing all things holy under the heavens! I am tired of always bowing down to the Americans because they feel superior to us! They fear us! They fear us because deep in their hearts they know we are superior to them! I am pleased that Pearl Harbor has awakened their arrogant, lazy minds! No more will we live in inequality!"*

Mr. Yoshimura blinked in shock. "*You are foolish! Making such claims will only propel you into prison, and I will not allow you to take the rest of us with you! I must ask you to leave my house!"*

Enraged, Katsuji jumped up and stumbled toward Mr. Yoshimura; his arm arched with a knotted fist as if he would sling his hand. He fiercely stared at Jim's father. Jim's father stared back, daring him. Katsuji grunted and unexpectedly smashed a lamp on the floor. Ceramic and glass dispersed on the carpet as the entire house shattered into silence. The men gawked at Katsuji; appalled he would behave so poorly. The women huddled in the kitchen, gaping behind the Victorian frame.

Jim was riveted. No one had ever disrespected his father before. Especially in his own home.

His father demonstrated control though his stern, immobile face. "*Baka*!" he snapped. "*You speak of dishonor? You are the one who has dishonored our community with your arrogance! Leave now! Or I will have the police lock you in jail!"*

Katsuji's eyes blazed. No one defended him while he stood alone in the middle of the room. He opened his mouth as if to say something; but instead, he marched off, grabbing his shoes and slamming the door behind him.

Jim tried to repress his smile. He covered his amusement with his hand, hoping no saw him. It was a treat to witness people lose their tempers. Many times he wished he could. What kind of liberation would that signify?

Tomiko reclined by the kitchen's portal, in front of the other women, crossing her arms. She looked at Jim. He glanced up, his smirk weakening. An uneasiness twisted his insides, causing his body to heat up. She had been watching him. And she had been watching him at school as well. At the age of sixteen, he had never kissed a girl. It was an embarrassing secret he wished not to tell anyone.

Bethany, without being asked, reached for a broom and dustpan in the kitchen to begin sweeping the mess, interrupting Tomiko's gaze. He sighed in relief. Mrs. Yoshimura promptly appeared with a teapot; equipped to refill empty cups. Steam swirled out of the spout. A series of polite gestures echoed throughout the room as she graciously accepted the compliments, smiling and bowing her head; her silver cross swinging under her chin. Her feet shuffled in tiny steps, implying delicacy like butterfly wings and flower petals. Once her duty was completed, she promptly disappeared back into the kitchen. Bethany followed her. Soon everyone relaxed and resumed business.

Hours absorbed the clock like soap absorbing water, lathering time into a smooth thickness. The men found satisfaction in the preparation for *mochi*, a potluck festival unifying friends and families for the *o-shogatso*. Smiles and bows were exchanged. Jim was responsible for returning coats that were stacked in the guest bedroom. Voices that flocked the living room sauntered outside, one by one, until quietness resettled.

Katsuji's name dispersed outside of the Yoshimura household among the crowd. People didn't impose discourtesy by not mentioning *his* name within the house, but the excitement of the afternoon was proper for gossip. If Katsuji had been drinking when he made his outburst, then all would have been forgiven the next day. Alcohol, as everyone knew, coerced people into doing and saying things they normally wouldn't.

Tomiko lingered in the doorway of the bedroom. Nervously rubbing her hands, she said, "Today was eventful."

Jim turned around, holding a minimal pile of coats in his arms. The guest room was small, and became smaller as he fidgeted. She walked to him, sifting through the remaining coats. Smiling, she tugged on hers to ease it out of his arms. Jim felt the pull teasing his body.

"You're quiet most of the time," she said.

He cleared his throat. "There are only few things worth talking about."

"And you choose your words carefully. But you're blunt in an honest sort of way." She paused, admiring his integrity. "I saw you grin at Katsuji. You have a strange sense of humor, you know."

His heart pulsated. He began to sweat. Ashamed for getting caught, worried what his father might think, his speech faulted. Rarely did he have difficulties speaking to anyone, but he found it more frustrating at that moment. Jim had known Tomiko all of his life, so why was he acting like a mute?

She winked. "See you in class."

"See you," he managed to mutter.

He explored her movements when she retreated to the front of the room. She smiled at him once more before leaving. It was funny how she called him blunt. She was equally as blunt; an unusual trait for a *Nisei* girl. And he liked it.

CHAPTER THREE

Late January

SADAYE declared, "We need to get going. Papa's expecting Goro at the store in an hour."

Kunio, only a year older than Sadaye, leaned back in his chair, squinting at the clock that presented mid-afternoon. His wife, Kay, stood up and began collecting the tea cups to wash in the sink. The visits seemed too short, too few, despite living so close. He had hoped for a better future for himself by moving to Seattle, as did their other sister, Chiyeko; but the struggles proved just as daunting as farm work. Employment within the Japanese community seemed scarce unless one was related to a business owner. Then outside of the community, he encountered excessive discrimination. Frustrated, Kunio was forced to work as a construction laborer, and his wife a maid. Sometimes he wished he stayed on Bainbridge; bought his own land even. At least he might have lived in his own house.

"Thank you for the hospitality," Sadaye extended. "Next month the both of you will have to come for a visit."

Chiyeko patted her six month old daughter on her tiny bottom. Setting the bottle down, sighing, she waited for her baby to burp. Her long hair, usually tidy, had strings loosely hanging out of her flowered scarf. She took care of three of her own children as well as babysitting Kunio's other two during the week. Since she didn't work outside of the home, everyone expected her to look after all the children. And yet she didn't complain. That was what families provided for each other: unconditional support.

"I'm sorry Tadao couldn't make it today," Chiyeko said wearily. "He's working the late shift again tonight, and needs the sleep."

"So does Mama!" Sadaye joked. "Her health is improving, but she gets tired easy enough."

Chiyeko chuckled. "If that ever was possible! Mama could never just relax."

Russell romped with his three nieces and nephew, all under the age of six, in the tight living room. Being the youngest in his family, he fancied being the oldest with his other siblings' families. He could also communicate with them more easily; not worrying about conversing in Japanese. Russell's older siblings spoke better Japanese than he could. The toddlers laughed as they playfully collapsed on top of Russell. He theatrically gasped and wheezed, as if his lungs were crushed.

Kunio unfolded a newspaper and rattled it. "Have you heard the latest?" He complained with sarcasm, "Apparently there are *Jap* spies cutting bamboo shoots to guide Jap planes for landing on the Coast!"

"Kunio!" Kay whispered, glancing uncomfortably at their children in the living room. The apartment's partially-divided walls were divided like domino sticks. "*Yoku nai!* Don't say such horrible things in front of the children!"

Russell stopped to listen while his nephew tugged on his leg, begging for his attention. The media indulged in foul propaganda, spreading outrageous stories like syphilis. The constant false alarms of Japanese subs and planes knotted people's terror. Now *all* lights were required to be hidden, or turned off at night. It had been an odd feeling to see darkness infesting the streets and houses. Street lights, head lights, flash lights; all boxed-up in a cave without echoes.

"*Okashii desu*," Kunio leered, scratching his cheek. "A funny thing indeed. In one day you become public enemy number one!" He stared at his sisters, a strange humor tightening his lips. "It took Capone and Baby Face Nelson years. Not us. It only took one day!"

Kay interjected, reseating herself, "Don't be over dramatic, Kunio. Sometimes I wish you weren't so pessimistic."

At his nephew's insistence, Russell grabbed Harry and flung him onto the couch. The girls then demanded that they be next.

Kunio barked, "Not on the couch!" He stood up at pointed at Russell. "Goro! You're a bad influence on my kids! Grow up!"

Russell rolled his eyes, restraining his irritation. He had difficulties getting along with Kunio who was too demanding; too bossy. He didn't seem happy unless he was miserable.

Russell groaned, "All right guys! Uncle Goro needs to get up, and go back home!"

His three nieces and nephew whined, begging him to stay. He wished Kunio would do the same.

WINTER'S breath followed Jim inside his father's store. Snow tumbled from his shoes, melting into puddles on the tiled floor. He enjoyed making deliveries, and volunteered whenever he could. Not only did it allow him to escape from his father for a time, but it also gave him opportunities to drive the car if the customers lived outside of town.

"Papa, I'm back!" he announced, removing his knitted gloves and cap.

"Ah, gud!" he replied from behind the counter, ringing up a customer, Mr. Sumida. "Da floor needs washing, Jimmu-san."

"Yes, Papa," he said.

A low rumbling pulsated the room. Jim looked out the large window; past the reversed letterings that read, Yoshi's Groceries. A black Ford Coupe cruised by; slowly; consciously. He didn't recognize the four men who stared at them. *At them.* It was beyond eerie. He watched the strangers until they disappeared. Relieved, he walked to the back to room to hang his coat.

"*The Japan today,*" Mr. Yoshimura expressed with remorse, "*is not the Japan we knew as children. She seems to have become angry, and does not want peace.*"

Jim quietly retrieved a mop and bucket, listening.

"*Ten years ago,*" Mr. Sumida resumed, "*I visited home. You are right. Japan is very different. My brother laughed at me when I spoke of simpler times. He said I was naive.*" He brooded and folded his chapped hands together. Then a discomfort crinkled his face. *"He said Japan is tired of being ignored by the Westerners, and that it is time to take what truly belongs to us. He also said one day Japan will be the most powerful nation in the world.*"

Mr. Yoshimura reached for a couple of bags. His brows merged in the center as he stated, "*Japan does not need to be so forceful. She will have to live with her conscience.*"

Jim noticed a Seattle newspaper lying on the counter. The headline read "THE YELLOW PERIL- HOW JAPANESE CROWD OUT THE WHITE RACE." Angered, he pitched the paper into the trash, and carried the bucket to a sink to fill it up with water. He was glad their local newspaper would not have printed such garbage. Mr. Woodward, printer and editor, had more dignity than that. A hell of a lot more!

"*Someone informed me,"* Mr. Sumida began, twitching the corner of his mouth, "*that all Japanese are going to be sent to prison camps."*

Jim turned off the water. Did he hear Mr. Sumida say what he thought he said? Prison for *all* Japanese people?

"*Tawagoto-san*!" Mr. Yoshimura chortled. "*Such nonsense!"*

But everyone recognized this harsh possibility. The FBI had been arresting *Issei* men all over the West Coast for months now. Ceaselessly. Even as close as Seattle. Then *Issei* bank accounts were currently frozen. No one knew for how long, including the banks. In the meantime, Jim volunteered to open a savings account in his own name, a non-threat to national security, and used it to deposit and withdraw the store's earnings.

RUSSELL walked beside Sadaye; securely; quietly. In the distance, grey clouds submerged Mount Rainier like sea foam; overbearingly; oppressively. It had been snowing. The busy street rattled and honked and clinked, tossing up fumes, congesting the Saturday lunch hour roads, shifting and stirring around corners, moving forward, and moving on one-way streets. People strode along the sidewalk, swerving to dodge each other. Although Russell enjoyed visiting the city, exploring through exotic shops, he hated the smell and noise of it all. He usually was contented living in the countryside.

Sadaye observed her wrist watch. "*Aku'un*!" she gasped. "If we don't hurry, we'll miss the bus. And if we miss the bus, we'll miss the ferry!"

"Well," he suggested, "why don't we take a shortcut through Madison Street?"

She slowed her pace. "I don't think so."

"Why not?"

Sadaye had lived in Seattle for two years, and knew what places to detour around. Knew what businesses to avoid. Knew the districts that didn't favor their kind of people. Or the Chinese. Or any other groups. Goro experienced minor racism, fortunately, sheltered from the world's wrath so far. Yet, she didn't know how to explain this to her brother.

She finally replied, "It'll be uncomfortable going down that way."

"Don't worry," he grinned. "I've gone through that way with my friends. We'll just walk faster!"

He yanked on her arm, crossing his eyes. She chuckled and timidly followed him. Hopefully they could walk through that section quickly and without difficulties. But she doubted it.

AS Jim hauled the bucket and mop to the front of the store, the black Ford Coupe rumbled at the entrance again. Jim felt very uneasy. He could see their eyes glaring, hating, aiming directly at them. The one in the back seat rolled down his window. His dark-brown hair was slicked back. His smooth face was polished with malice. Jim stiffened. All he could do was watch. Leering, the stranger flung a brick through the store window. A high-pitched shatter exploded. Shards of glass soared in the air. Jim jumped back. Mr. Yoshimura and his customer ducked. The brick skidded across the floor, anchoring at Jim's toes.

A howl echoed in the street, bellowing, "Go back to Japan, yella bastards!"

The driver squealed his tires. Smoke chased from behind while the strangers hooted. Jim rushed to the front door, crushing over the broken glass, and grabbed the brick. He felt his veins biting, his heart punching. Standing in the middle of the street, he arched his arm to throw it back. To throw it back at those bastards. The car turned a corner and vanished, but their cheers continued to echo beyond the houses and trees. People gathered outside, wondering what happened; gawking at the webbed hole as sharp as knives; gawking at Jim with a brick in his hand.

BUSINESSES connected the long block from hair salons to pawn shops; restaurants to bars; a bank to a flower shop. Russell and his friends had passed through this route once before. He couldn't understand his sister's dread. Even if the area was specially arranged for blacks. Some people stared; although most seemed disinterested, passing off glances. Sadaye focused forward, squeezing her purse under her arm; tightening her brows together. Russell jogged at her side with his hands inside his pockets. He had no idea his sister could stride that quickly in heels! Halfway down the street three teenage boys ensued from behind. They whispered among themselves, and sniggered loudly. Russell peeked over his shoulder when they started in.

"Hey!" one barked. "Ain't it past your curfew?"

"Man, don't you know Jap curfew is at eight, stupid?"

"How you know they Japs?" the third chimed. "Could be Chinks!"

"Cause they ain't got no card wrapped 'round their neck like Chinks!"

Russell and his sister sped-up their pace. The block felt as though it expanded like rubber: Pulling. Wobbling. Stretching. And time seemed to stall. The identification card the boys spoke of was designed to separate the Chinese population from the Japanese. Only the Chinese were allowed to wear these cards in the cities. Easier to flush out the enemy. Soon Russell began regretting taking this path.

"Don't you Japs know this ain't your town?"

"Yeah! What the hell you doin' here? You lost or something?"

"Hey!" the third insisted. "I'm talkin' to ya! Hey Japs, you deaf?"

"Maybe they don't speak no English."

"Hey!" yelled the other. "No speakie Engrish?"

They laughed and howled. Sadaye clung to her brother's arm, shaking. Russell felt a sickening knot cramping inside his stomach. His sister wiped off her tears. He touched her cold hand, trying to comfort her. Wanting to punch them in their stupid mouths, he bit down the urge, not wanting to upset his sister more so. Suddenly the boys triggered into singing "You're a Sap Mr. Jap." Russell and Sadaye swerved around the corner, leaving Madison Street. The boys burst into laughter, waving to them, shouting "G'bye Japs! Don't come 'round here no more!"

REALIZING he was being watched, Jim dropped the brick, trembling. He stared through the ragged hole and met his own disbelief reflecting in his father's face.

He asked, "Are you alright, Papa?"

"Yes, yes!" he replied, his hands shaking. Now he had to scrub out money to replace the large window. As if he didn't have enough worries! He watched the crowd move closer, cautiously parading forward, whispering to each other. It was the biggest excitement since Bob Nelson got his hand cut off at the mill six years ago. Jim studied the black tire marks left behind. Exhaling, he turned around to return inside, but his heart wouldn't stop pounding. It was a mess. Broken glass everywhere. It looked as though a grenade had hit the window panel.

Mr. Yoshimura angrily whispered, "*Such a disgrace!*"

"*Hai, a disgrace,*" Mr. Sumida agreed. "*Americans do not want us here. They never have, and now they can finally have their way. I fear they might shoot us for revenge from what our Imperial Army is doing.*"

"*Forgive me, but I will disagree,*" he replied, skittishly glancing at the chaos. Sweat formed on his forehead, unveiling concerns for an uncertain future.

Jim wondered how his father could not get furious. He should be cursing and demanding justification. It certainly was his right! Instead, his father calmly retrieved the broom and began sweeping. He swept as if cleaning-up the shame.

What else could they do? The violence of the world had ultimately stretched to their island and they became, for the first time, touchable.

Late February

"THOSE Jerrys and Japs don't know what they got themselves into!" Leo boasted in the hallway. The morning snow dissolved into his thick coat and hair. Four other football players gathered around him to talk of glory. "I could kick all of their asses with one hand tied behind my back! Before ya know it, Hitler will be wearin' a skirt and singin' an octave higher once we're done with 'im!"

A chorus of laughter reverberated down the hall. Students sauntered, weaving in and out empty classrooms, chatting with friends. A moldy odor mixed with perfume and cologne suspended in the air. Dampened shoes squeaked on the tiled floor. Jim tried to ignore Leo and his stooges. Each was an idiot. They had difficulty understanding much more than scoring and swaggering insults.

"Hey, Jim! I have a question for ya!"

He looked up. Leo stood beside him with his cronies trailing behind. His belly was as broad as his shoulders, and his chubby hands as massive as cement blocks.

"Is your old man in cahoots? Ya know, has a lot of connections, right?"

His chest tightened. "How do you mean? Connections to what?"

"You know, Japan. I heard he has relatives in the Japanese military. Is it true?"

Jim's breathe faltered. This subject was considerably touchy. He had two uncles in the Japanese navy and a few cousins its army. Being aware of people's ignorance and paranoia, it was best to say very little. His words could easily be misinterpreted. Last week he and Bethany watched a George Tobias movie, *Double Identity*. The opening newsreel exposed American marines running and crawling in between the long Pacific grasses, clutching their guns. Dead Japanese bodies were scattered in lumps as if mutilated rag dolls dumped to the side. He had wondered if any of those bodies could have been one of his relatives. A thought that made him ill. And while these images glared in front of them, the announcer's sonorous voice growled in their ears, "Those dirty little Japs."

Jim asked, "Why do you want to know?"

Leo flipped his head sideways, showing off a smirk. "See, what did I tell you guys? Once a Jap, always a Jap! Just what General DeWitt's been saying all along!"

Jim saw Russell walk behind Leo's back, observing curiously. Russell momentarily bridged his gaze over Leo's shoulder, linking eye contact with Jim. He appeared concerned, narrowing his brows, loosening his mouth to say something; yet he closed his lips and continued to walk by.

"Isn't your grandmother Austrian?" Jim blurted. The back of his neck tingled.

Leo glared at him and sneered, "Yeah, so?"

"Doesn't that make your family Nazi?"

The smirk crumbled from Leo's face. He hissed "Sonavabitch!" and slammed his elbow into Jim's jaw. Jim's head snapped back. His glasses flew off his face, sliding on the dirty floor as he toppled down, landing on his ribs, gasping. For a moment his head felt like it twirled in the wind. His hands started to shake with fury. He snatched his leather strap with books and flung it toward Leo's fat face, but whacked his fat belly instead. Leo ripped the strap from his hand and hurled it up the hall. He clutched Jim by the collar, tossing him against a row of lockers like a bundle of laundry. Jim again gasped. This time the pain punctured his entire body, and he felt as though his back had been crushed. People in the hallway just stood; watching and gaping. Leo persisted to smash him against the lockers until Russell slipped a half-Nelson, seizing the bully's neck, forcing Leo to let go. Jim slid down. Russell refused to unfasten his knuckles, squirming from behind, coaxing Leo to move apart.

Russell asserted, "Are you done?"

Leo flinched and huffed. "Yeah! Lemme go!"

Two teachers bolted out of their classrooms; their sharp heels clattering through the hallway. Russell finally released Leo. The teachers were stunned when they approached, finding Jim slumped over and Leo swaying from side to side to calm himself. They began to question Leo first. Russell spotted Jim's glasses and hurried to retrieve them.

Kneeling, he asked, "What did you say to him to make him so mad?"

Jim stared at up in disbelief. How strange Russell behaved. He stopped Leo from beating him, and yet defended this moron.

Wheezing, he demanded, "Why do you assume it was my fault?"

Russell hesitated before responding. "I know Leo. Even though he's a friend of mine, he could of put you in the hospital."

"And I would have sued him."

"Oh, really? What would that accomplish?"

"Satisfaction," he smirked.

Russell glanced up at Leo who continued to speak with the teachers. He heard Leo remark something about Jim calling him a Nazi. No doubt Leo made the first insult, although pissing him off only compelled matters to worsen. Readjusting his knee to the floor, he asked, "Are you alright?"

"Why do you care?" Jim snapped.

He frowned. He realized Jim wasn't going to thank him for helping out. "Because I have nothing else better to do. Can you at least stand?"

"Of course!" Jim awkwardly mounted to his feet; annoyed that Russell rose with him as if he were an invalid.

One teacher turned to face Jim. Her penciled eyebrows and tight lips quivered. "Well," she said. "What do you have to say for yourself?"

He glanced at Russell. "Why do I have to say anything?"

She grimaced. The teachers then concluded that both Jim and Leo needed to go to Principal Fuller's office, letting him decide the proper punishment. Russell took hold of Leo's arm just before he walked off to follow the teachers.

"You didn't have to do that! Jim's half your size."

Leo betrayed a mocking smile. "So are you."

JIM sat upright with his hands resting over his knees. He browsed around the office through a cracked lens. His glasses slightly tilted on his nose. He thought Leo should pay for the repair, but understood nothing would be done about it. The office was compacted with one tiny window, a few chairs, wood paneling, and stunk of ointment. He had never been in there and felt a bit nervous; yet he remained calm; nearly motionless. The secretary appeared almost in her sixties. Her darkly rounded glasses contrasted with her pale, wrinkled skin. She wore a bleak dress with white ruffles around her collar and wrists. The dress had to have been at least twenty years old. She tapped the typewriter like rain hitting water; swiftly and in tempo.

The principal's door opened. Jim looked up. Leo ambled out of the office and gestured his hands as if breaking a stick. He then winked at him as he sat two chairs apart. Principal Fuller emerged at the door and summoned Jim to enter. Jim gracefully stood up, ignoring Leo who slouched like a walrus on a beach.

Fuller said, "Take a seat, Mr. Yoshimura."

He closed the door while Jim seated himself in an upright position, waiting.

"This is very unusual coming from you," he began while sitting behind his desk. His receding hairline arched in a semicircle, exposing aging spots on his bare forehead. "Normally, you're very quiet. Reserved. Respectable. I don't understand it. What possessed you to call Leo a Nazi?"

Jim kept silent. Avoiding eye contact, he stared at the desk, observing the long ruler that lay straight across from his knees. He knew Fuller had already made up his mind about who to punish.

The principal stared. "Why won't you say something?" He waited for an answer. When nothing evaded from Jim's tongue, Fuller grumbled, "I don't understand your people at times. You leave me with no other choice, then. Extend your hands out; palms up."

Jim clenched his teeth. He began breathing rapidly while advancing out his arms. Being reprimanded like a child offered no real solution. His problems were no longer the inconveniences of adolescence. They were adult problems that were being handled as if quick punishment would rectify everything. Principal Fuller rose from his squeaky seat and stood beside Jim. He didn't appear angry; just irritated. Then he smacked Jim's hands. The sharp pain hit like lightning tearing his flesh, leaving it raw and throbbing. Each swat on his palms only infuriated Jim. As each swat reddened his skin, he quietly counted, holding back his pain. Then Fuller stopped. Twelve steady lashes in all. He stood erect; perspiration blotting on his wrinkled forehead. His breathing became deep as if he jogged up a flight of steps. Jim refused to blink. He refused to let his hot tears blister down his cheeks. His painful heaves hissed out of his flared nose. He sniffed and quickly brushed his fingers over his stinging eyes and watery nose.

"Now I'll have to call in your father and explain your behavior. As a respectable member in our community, I'm sure he'll be disappointed in you." The principal hesitated, pinching his lips. "Your people have been so peaceful. I just don't understand."

MR. YOSHIMURA remained quiet during the drive home from school. He was embarrassed. Anyone who bred disobedience embarked a bad name for the rest of the family. In Japan, if he had done the same, his father would have given him the beating of his life. An undisciplined son marked disorder not only in the family, but for the rest of society as well. Here in America, where individualism was highly prized, it relinquished opportunities for insubordination. He aspired to teach his son to respect authority, never to challenge it; otherwise chaos would transpire. Without patience, harmony would decompose. Examining his son, he couldn't recognize the source of his anger. He had a good home, a family who encouraged him, a moderate amount of money, and better advances for greater education. Jim's life had a bounty of privileges. Mr. Yoshimura certainly didn't have these same fortunes in Japan, nor did he receive the same support from his father. Because he had not been the oldest son, he was often ignored if not beaten for something he did wrong. He still had the scar on his neck since he was a boy; a welt from an iron rod used to shuffle coal in the stove.

Squeezing the steering wheel, the whites of his knuckles cried out. "Yur motha is very upset. Very upset!" he snapped. "*Learn to control your emotions, Jimmu. I am very disappointed in your behavior! Do you not care about this family?*" He paused momentarily; thinking; concerned. "Wis war in our passage, we mus' be stronga an' betta dan those who see us in da wrong way. You weow make it much worse when you lash out!"

"Yes, Papa. I know," he mumbled, looking out the passenger's window. He felt as if piles of stones filled his insides.

"Jimmu, in two years you weow be attending a university. Perhaps, it weow be betta if you leaf da Wes' Coast. Attend school in da East."

"Yes, Papa. I will."

The slushy morning concealed authentic beauty, hiding the promise of spring's bloom. As war surrounded them, Jim doubted if a true spring would arrive. How could his father be so goddamned naive? The outside world blew a forceful wind through their island, quickly tearing down their home. They would be standing in rubble. And what would they do about it? Nothing. It was his father's way; this submissiveness.

Mr. Yoshimura drove up the graveled driveway. Turning off the vehicle, he sat for a minute; his chest rapidly fluctuating. Jim heard his father's intense breathing as if he had been slashed open by a bayonet. The ticking of the car controlled their silence. Jim stared at his house while his mother stared back at him through the window. She tapped her fingertips on her chin; worried.

"Get out!" his father yelled.

Startled, Jim instantly obeyed. Mr. Yoshimura marched directly in front of him. He didn't look at his father, though seeing his temper tremble on his shoulders. Jim's palms continued to sting from Fuller's impact with his welts visible and coarse. He wondered if his hands would scar. Suddenly his father turned around and slapped him.

"It is very impor'tant you keep the Yoshimura name honorable!" his father commanded. "*The purpose of this family beats within your chest! You must not let your emotions destroy it!*"

Jim glared at his father. A nauseating lump soured in his stomach. His eyes glazed with scalding tears; his face flushed with hate. He wondered if his brother had felt this intensity just before he swallowed the poison. Flexing his hands, he thought about actually flinging his fists, wishing to hit back with such ferocity it would actually kill his father. His mother swung the front door open and stood on the porch. His father looked at her, twitching his muscles. Jim instantly severed loose from his father's control, running up the stone steps, fleeing past his mother. He darted up the stairs, and slammed his bedroom door. His arms shook. He pivoted in his room, searching for something to unleash his fury. He spotted the old photograph hanging on the wall. Knocking it down, he then smashed the antique glass with his foot. His mother abruptly opened his door. Horrified, she masked her gaping mouth with her hand. Jim moved his foot. A sharp blaze of guilt cut his face.

"It fell when I slammed the door, Mama. I'm sorry."

The lie was an obvious one. And it sickened him. His mother had always been his greatest supporter, so the need to deceive her seemed more insulting than stamping on his father's traditions. Witnessing her disappointment proved more painful than his father's hand.

Mrs. Yoshimura stared at her son, disbelief crumbling. Why would he commit such a sinful act by destroying valuable property? What was happening to her son? A fight in school, and now mutilating his ancestor's memory? How much shame could one family endure? And once Mr. Yoshimura discovered the damage, she feared he would make the same mistake as with John.

Footsteps thundered up the stairs. Jim cringed, dreading his father's reparation. Although Jim had been punished with the occasional scolding and additional chores, he knew this time would be different. Jim just didn't make his bed smooth enough. He just didn't forget to rake the leaves, or forget to organize his homework according to subject matter. He defaced his father with broken glass that damaged the family photograph.

Mr. Yoshimura reached at the portal, huffing. When he saw the shattered picture, his cheeks drained from color. He coarsely demanded, "*Do shimashita-ka?*"

Glancing at her son, Mrs. Yoshimura replied, her voice shaking, "*The picture fell when I slammed his bedroom door.*"

Shock replaced his anger. "*Why would you wish to slam the door?*"

She hesitated before answering, nervously grinding her fingers, avoiding her husband's infuriated glare. "*Because Jim did not take off his shoes and brought mud into our house.*"

Mr. Yoshimura stared at his own feet, embarrassed to find that he too still wore his shoes. Sliding his feet out, his temper sifted like sand struck by waves. As his rigid expression thawed, he began to reveal an awkward, child-like regret. And at that moment he realized he should never hit his son again. He had made a promise to himself years ago that his last son would not inherit his weaknesses. Confused and unable to catch his senses, Mr. Yoshimura wobbled back down the steps, clutching his shoes. No respectable man wore filthy shoes in his own home.

Jim gawked at his mother. She lied for him. He had never known her to directly lie. Sometimes she embellished to create excitement in her monotonous lifestyle. John had inherited her flair for storytelling. The trust and admiration for his mother overwhelmed him. He didn't know how to reveal his gratification. She glanced at him, her hands still quivering. She began leaving his room; then stopped.

"*It is your obligation to clean this mess.*" She rubbed her forehead and curtly sighed. "*But if you do something disrespectful again, I will not have the strength to protect you.*"

"I understand, Mama," he said. "Thank you."

She slightly nodded and walked off.

CHAPTER FOUR

Early March

LARGE, wet snowflakes had tumbled in the fog all morning long. Russell's shoes sloshed over the ground while he followed his father, heading toward the police station that was only a couple of blocks away. As his father clutched the sword case to his chest, Russell carried two hunting knives in their oak boxes. He knew his father would be giving up more than their sense of security. The *Samurai* sword had been in the family for three generations. And all morning long his parents had argued about the sword. His mother insisted there were some things not worth surrendering to preserve family honor while his father insisted that by not obeying the law they would lose their honor.

When they arrived at the station, other *Issei* and *Nisei* men stood in line, clinging to their belongings that were now regarded as contraband. The dullness of the walls captured echoes of a clicking clock. A typewriter tapped annoyingly; endlessly. It dinged, hesitated, and continued tapping. The small room condensed low murmurs into a tunnel, narrowing each man's utterance into submission. The three officers appeared uncomfortable; as if plucking feathers off live chickens. They spoke quickly, quietly, and avoided looking at the men's faces as much as possible. Each man gave his name, despite the fact that the officers knew every last one; and each had to turn over his possessions, completed by signing a form.

Russell couldn't understand any of it. Outsiders could hurl a brick at a neighbor's store window and not get caught, yet every Japanese person had to turn in what *could be* considered dangerous weapons as if *they were* the outsiders. Guns. Knives. Dynamite. Binoculars. Shortwave radios. Sure, technically they could be dangerous if used carelessly, but everyone else on the island possessed these items, too! Were they also standing in line to give away their protection? Then to top things off, a curfew had finally been issued on *his* island. And they were forbidden to leave the island. Nevertheless, his faith in Roosevelt did not splinter; it could not chip. He had to believe that proving one's loyalty would award trust and respect in the long run. As his father believed. He had to; otherwise, what was his purpose in life?

"Next please!" one of the officers announced.

Mr. Hamaguchi slid his cases forward. The officer, who was in his mid-thirties, opened them, counted, and scribbled on a white form. Reddish tints shined through his brown hair under the hair wax where he molded it perfectly like Clark Gable. His thin, rectangular mustache likewise mirrored that of movie stars. Russell knew him well enough. Once a month the officer would come in to have his hair trimmed by his father, always contributing a tip. Even when business slowed, he kept his monthly appointments and left his tips. Russell understood that Officer Dandridge had to perform his responsibilities. Just as his father had to perform his.

"How are ya, Russ?" Dandridge asked, carefully lining the cases on the counter.

"Fine," he politely answered.

"Think you're able to beat my cousin this year?"

Russell grinned. "I always beat Alex, sir."

Dandridge snickered. "True. Very true. But tell him that!"

"Did you find out who broke the window at Mr. Yoshimura's store?"

The officer reached for the longer case. "We're still not sure who broke his window. Don't think they came from Seattle. We waited at the dock all day for the car." He glanced up. "Never showed. We think they came up North; through Poulsbo."

Exhaling his annoyance, he replied, "Can't save the world from itself, I guess."

"No, I suppose not."

The officer flipped the case open. A three feet sword shined under the lights: its sharp arch frowning at the officer; its carved handle displaying tiny scars from battles that occurred centuries ago. The handle twisted like a vine, but was indented where human fingers could hold it. Dandridge had never seen one before.

"Whoa," he said, finally looking at Russell. "Is this one of them Samaru swords?"

"*Samurai*. Yes, it's a *Samurai* sword."

Dandridge scratched his nose and cleared his throat. He inspected both Russell and Mr. Hamaguchi while pushing out his lower lip. "I can't take this," he said, shaking his head. "Isn't this a family heritage thing?"

Baffled, Russell answered, "Ah, yeah, but we were told to turn in all weapons."

He leaned closer to Russell, tilting his head and tapping his finger on the sword. "I think this might be an exception. I'd feel bad if we took this."

Mr. Hamaguchi began questioning his son in Japanese, wondering what problem existed with the sword. Russell translated best to his ability.

Mr. Hamaguchi stared at the officer, struggling to say, "You take. You take."

The officer closed the case and returned it to Mr. Hamaguchi. Mr. Hamaguchi slid it back to him, urging him to submit it.

"No," Dandridge replied, pushing it away. "Russell, tell your father we don't need this. It's okay. Really."

While Russell again translated for his father, his father persisted by pushing it back, speaking to his son in his language.

"My father says he wants to obey the law," he clarified. "That's why he's giving you his sword. He wants to cooperate. He doesn't want trouble."

"There won't be any trouble if he doesn't give us the sword. He can keep it. Tell 'im that," he asserted, easing it forward, but Mr. Hamaguchi slapped his hand on the case.

"You take," he again urged.

Dandridge sighed. "Russell, please tell your father we don't take family heirlooms."

Russell became frustrated. Despite the officer's sympathetic gesture, if no one would take the damn thing, then he would!

"*Papa,*" Russell began, "*he does not wish to take an heirloom. He has respect for the Samurai sword.*"

Mr. Hamaguchi blinked a few times, and then reached to retrieve his sword.

"Sank you ah bery much," he said, bowing his head; his voice cracking as he tried to blink away his tears.

"Alright," Officer Dandridge remarked. "Just sign here and, for the love of Mike, please go home."

Mid March

JIM arranged the canned goods on the top shelf. His father's store remained quiet; with the exception of cars trickling up and down the road; their sounds rumbling through the windows. Sometimes he would stop and look out the spotless glass, wondering if the same thing might happen again. He was alone. When the squeaky door opened, hitting the bell and forcing a cold wind to trespass, Jim leapt back. Taking a breath, he walked down the aisle. Tomiko stood at the front; her cheeks flushed from the walk; her hair messy. She held a piece of paper in her right hand. He noticed both of her hands were trembling.

Standing at a distance, he asked, "Is there something I can help you with?"

She glanced at him; although kept her eyes on the paper. Slowly unfolding it, she tried to smooth out the crinkled areas by rubbing it. "I um, need a few items for dinner." She paused, now rolling the edges of the paper. Her face crinkled. Finally looking at him, she asked, "Is your father still here?"

Puzzled, he replied, "No. He's making a delivery." He crossed his arms and stepped closer. "Tomiko, what's wrong?"

She gasped and covered her face. "I'm sorry! I can't believe it!" She again gasped. "They took my father! They just *took* him! Without a warrant!" She removed her hand to directly face Jim. "They're coming for yours."

Jim briefly stopped breathing. He knew it was coming. But then, everyone knew it was coming. The events that led up to this day seemed to be a reactionary countdown. Since Pearl Harbor, *Issei* men had been arrested all over the West Coast. General DeWitt and others had poisoned the media with hatred for the Japanese, yet it was the media which swallowed it up like opium. The paper frequently bragged about the arrests of potential spies. Germans and Italians, as well as Japanese. Tomiko's tears flowed. She instantly embraced him, sobbing over his shoulder. Stunned, Jim let his arms dangle at his sides. The warmth of her body against him electrified his blood. For months he imagined what she might have felt like in his arms. And now, with her tears soaking into him, he wished he could comfort her in some way. Finally raising his arms, he gently patted her back, not knowing what else to do.

RUSSELL sprinted down the hill; his arms hissing back and forth like a saw tearing into a tree. He ran for over two miles. Running on dirt roads. Running on paved streets. The afternoon became late in the hour as a gray dusk slowly tumbled behind the cedar trees. A harsh disbelief sliced his body, bleeding his mind to a rhythm of denial. It couldn't be true. It couldn't be true. His legs flew faster. Wind blurred his vision. His mouth grew dry. His father would be there. Home. Safe.

MRS. YOSHIMURA tightened her apron. The fat noodles boiled in a pot while fish sizzled in a pan. She ignored the doorbell to continue to stir the noodles. She heard Bethany's voice greet the callers, but couldn't hear who entered because of the sizzling. Moaning, she wasn't in the mood to be interrupted tonight. She turned off the stove and walked out of the kitchen, wiping her hands on her apron. Two men, dressed in dark trench coats and hats, stood in the middle of the living room. Bethany rushed to her side, hiding behind her dress. Mrs. Yoshimura didn't know these men and quickly became alarmed. Their buffed, black shoes revealed no cracks from years of being worn; no thick mud from miles of walking. Their business-like shirts and vests indicated a means of wealth not too familiar in Winslow. In fact, they appeared like Hollywood gangsters: polished and organized. One stood slightly taller than the other, and more fierce. A detectable source of resentment infected the corner of his lip. He held a picture frame with a recent photograph of her family.

"Special Agents Thornburgh and Miller from the Federal Bureau of Investigation," the taller man announced, flipping his badge, and slithered it back inside his coat to reveal his holstered gun. He thinned his eyes as hobbled over her husband's name, "We're looking for Toshi-yu-ki Yoshi-mura. Where is he?"

RUSSELL'S feet hit the front porch; his hand reaching for the door knob. "*Papa*!" he gasped. "*Papa dodo desu-ka?*"

His mother, seated on the couch with her hands folded on her lap, replied, "*He is here, Goro. Please, shut the door*!"

"On the radio," he wheezed, "I heard on the radio . . . at my friend's house . . . that the FBI are arresting . . . *Issei* men." He shut the door. "*Mama is it true?*"

A stranger emerged from the kitchen, cloaked in a trench coat and broad hat. Staring at Mrs. Hamaguchi, he snarled, "Who is this?"

Bewilderment layered in her eyes as she shifted to look at her son; then at the man in a dark hat and coat. His shiny badge had distracted her when she answered the door. His hasty English barely understood. But she understood one, pivotal thing: they were going to arrest an innocent man.

"Who," he aimed his finger to Russell, "is this?"

"Ah," she exhaled, searching for English words. "He mayason."

"He's what? Speak English, for crying out loud!"

Feeling more intimidated, she shyly replied, "Mayason."

"What?"

"Her son!" Russell snapped. "Can't you see . . . she has . . . trouble speaking?"

The outsider curled his mouth upside down. "You'd think she would learn at some point. She's been in our country long enough to know better."

"Try learning Japanese . . . an' see how well you do!"

Mrs. Hamaguchi scolded, "*Goro! Do not be so disrespectful!*"

"I'd watch my mouth if I were you!" he angrily threatened, pointing to Russell. "Sit down and don't leave the premises until we're finished. We're in the middle of conducting a search, so don't answer the phone, and don't answer the door. Do *you* understand, *Jap*?"

"WHERE'S your husband?" the taller agent demanded. "Are you hiding him?"

Mrs. Yoshimura nervously glanced at both agents, although making sure to avoid eye contact. A woman never directly looked into the eyes of authority. "He not ah here now."

Tilting his head and tugging at the tip of his hat, he sarcastically asked, "Then where can we find him?"

She didn't answer. While rubbing her hands, her heart felt as if she had been running from a wild pack of dogs. Mrs. Yoshimura didn't trust these men. They had the power, and she didn't have any protection. The tall agent paced around her; his height soaring above her head. She felt his breath on the back of her neck and heard the creaking of his leather shoes. He leaned into her ear.

"Are you sure you're not hiding him, Missus? We can turn your home upside down without a second thought. And if we find him in a cellar, or some other sneaky little place," he paused to glance at Bethany, "your little girl will have to be put into foster care."

Mrs. Yoshimura nervously began patting her face. The idea that her family was being sliced apart caused her to feel nauseous. If her husband would be deported back to Japan, what would happen to her family? How would they survive? Horrified, she didn't know what to do.

The agent stopped in front of her, crossing his arms, glaring down. "Where is he? Huh? Your lack of cooperation will only make matters worse."

Bethany meekly answered, "He's at the store,"

"What store, Sweetheart?" the other agent asked, smiling. He appeared to be fifteen years older than his partner, and more patient. And yet his smooth face also seemed deceptive, as if suppressing his ambitions through stitches of courtesy.

"His store. Yoshi's Groceries," she replied, figeting.

"In town, Sweetheart?"

"Yes. On the main street."

"Thornburgh," the other agent announced. "Go ahead and retrieve our suspect, then come back here. In the meantime, I'll look about this place. Alright?" He winked at Bethany, still bearing his white teeth.

THE agent barked, "I said sit down!"

Russell obeyed, not attempting to remove his jacket, although he did remember to remove his shoes. He heard Sadaye's voice in the kitchen, interpreting for their father, answering the other agent's questions. They didn't dare move from their places. Suddenly knocking at the front door startled the family. The fierce agent glared at Russell.

"No visitors! Get rid of them!"

Russell stared at him and quickly moved to answer the door. A middle-aged woman, who was a friend and neighbor, stood on the porch. Her long hair was braided into a bun. She appeared worried.

"Oh, hello, Russell!" she said. "Is your sister home? I heard on the radio the FBI is finally rounding up Japanese men . . ."

"Mrs. Frey," he interrupted, "this isn't a good time. She'll call you back."

The woman looked as though he had slapped her. She blinked a few times, then whispered, "Are they in there now?"

Russell nodded. "You'll have to go. She'll call you later."

Before she could reply, he closed the door. He felt so humiliated.

"Lock the door!" the agent barked. "I don't want any more interruptions."

Reluctantly, he again obeyed. He felt the stranger's stare blister his face. Still breathing unevenly, Russell returned to his seat. The other agent walked from the kitchen and delivered a sharp nod. It was the signal. Russell's body radiated heat and sweat while he sat in stillness; watching them swarm in and out of rooms as they took letters, postcards, and scrolls. All and anything written in Japanese. They inquired about their family in Japan who might be in the military as they tossed pens, envelopes, phone books, and other personal items out of drawers. All of which landed on the carpet, making an incredible mess as the invaders' shoes walked all over their belongings. The fierce one reappeared in the living room, holding an oak case. He twitched his jawline like a wasp after a sting. He marched toward Russell and shoved the case under his chin.

"Why wasn't this sword turned to the police? You people had specific orders this month to turn in *all* weapons!"

Russell jerked backward, and looked up. Now what was he planning to accuse them of? Overthrowing the government with an old, dull sword while bellowing out *banzai*? A butcher's cleaver proved more dangerous, so why wasn't he claiming the kitchen set just as a treacherous as his father's sword?

"Well, we did," he cautiously replied. "But Officer Dandridge told us they wouldn't accept it because it's an heirloom."

The agent heaved in disbelief, thinning his eyes. “Do you think I’m stupid? You’re going to have me believe that your local police force didn’t accept this weapon because it’s an heirloom? As if they didn’t enforce the law?” He moved the case away from Russell and leaned on one leg. “Boy, you must think I’m easy to try and pull that kind of wool over my eyes. You people think you’re so damn clever.” He shook his head. His face suddenly darkened underneath the slanted rim of his hat. “I lost my brother at Pearl Harbor. We’ll see how goddamn clever you goddamn Japs really are!”

“Armstrong!” the other agent snapped, frowning. His arms were heavy with paper. “Maintain your focus. Remember our objective.”

The fierce one winced. Russell didn’t budge. He could smell the bitter cologne reeking from the agent’s skin. If the agent really wanted to, he could strike at Russell without consequences. Never in his life had he experienced such ruthless prejudice and animosity. Russell had been taught to respect people in higher authority; never to question their judgment. Today that he found difficulty not wanting to challenge this search. Not wanting to challenge this angry man. They didn’t reveal a warrant of any kind, so was this search even legal?

Armstrong finally stepped back, and sat the oak case beside the front door. Then he continued to pillage their home.

JIM gave Tomiko a glass of water. The back office maintained a musty odor from the constant dampness. She took a few sips. Her hands were still shaking. Without touching her, Jim hovered his palm over her hair, wanting to stoke her. Realizing how foolish her must have appeared, he pulled away. Shuffling to the opposite corner, he stood stiffly with his hands properly at his sides.

She set the glass on the desk, and asked, “What will you do when your father is gone?”

Staring out the doorway, he felt a sense of relief. If his father were to be deported, Jim would finally experience unconditional freedom. But he couldn’t tell her that. By keeping his thoughts minimal, she would not think less of him. She would not think less of him because she would not know him.

“I can run the business blindfolded,” he replied. “In fact, I could have done this even at the age of twelve.”

“You’re not like the other boys. You’ve always had a sense of confidence and direction. And you don’t care what other people think. I admire that.”

Jim blushed. He tapped his fingertips over his thighs. Most people thought those qualities were annoying. It amazed him why Tomiko would think otherwise. With her optimism, he figured she would be interested in someone else.

“I don’t know what we’ll do,” she admitted. “What if our fathers are deported?”

He sighed, not knowing how to answer. She was truly scared. “Like with everything else,” he began, “I guess we can only wait.”

The front door squeaked, bumping into the bell, and closed. Jim walked out of the backroom. Mr. Yoshimura removed his hat and strode toward Jim; his heavy footsteps thumping on the naked floors. Jim said nothing, although he recognized that his father had already heard the news. His wire glasses tried to conceal his growing wrinkles. Jim stepped aside.

His father was surprised to find Tomiko beside his desk.

"Tomiko-suma," he said, slipping out of his coat. "I am sorry, Dear, but no one is allowed back here." He peered at Jim disapprovingly. "Jimmu, you know da rules."

"She was upset, Papa. I thought she would feel more comfortable in the back."

Mr. Yoshimura hesitated, and closed his eyes. He nodded. "Yes. I see."

The front door opened again. Jim noticed a tall stranger in a black trench coat standing motionless. His odd emergence seemed like a phantom lurking in the shadows. Jim instantly knew. This would be the last time he would see his father. And he felt glad.

CHAPTER FIVE

Late March

OFFICER Dandridge felt sick when he walked around the town, stapling the announcements on telephone poles. He carried the batch of paper as if hauling a satchel of manure. People watched him, puzzled by the civic announcement printed in thick, black letters. Beneath the word "NOTICE," the next set of dictations began with "All persons of Japanese ancestry. . . will be evacuated. . ." Rumors about sending the Japanese to camps finally reached on shore; wrapped in a box; compliments from the West Coast Defense. Dandridge had called the local newspaper editor, Mr. Woodward, to let him know that morning, although not knowing what good it would do. A single letter of protest couldn't stop the forces in motion.

* * *

RUSSELL watched two men carry off the last of his father's barber chair into a truck. He stood behind the large window which read, "Barber" on the top, "Laundry" on the bottom. The only object that remained in the store was the front counter. Everything else they sold. The chairs. The register. The dryer. The baskets and hangers. Even the cheap pictures that hung on the walls.

"Well, Goro," Meito mournfully announced, "I think we're done here."

His brother stuffed the meager cash inside his wallet. He had no other choice but to sell their father's possessions at a quarter of valued price. It was better than nothing. And since no one knew how long they would be gone, or whether they were allowed to return home, or whether they would find other means to earn money to pay storage or mortgages, they sold what they could just to get by.

Russell felt helpless. And angry. And overwhelmed. Within the last three months his life had suddenly been controlled by chaos. Nothing made sense. And he couldn't believe that the president, of all politicians, would allow it. Roosevelt fought for the New Deal programs. He fought for the minorities as well as the common man. How could he allow this to happen?

"Goro?" Metio asked. "Are you ready to go?"

Russell had been embarrassed by his father's store most of his life, wishing it upheld more dignity like Yoshi's Groceries. He had believed that cutting other people's hair, or doing other people's dirty laundry was considered inferior work. A subservient role. There were times when some of his friend made fun of his parents' position. But now witnessing to the stripping down of his father's thirty year struggle, the thought of losing everything splintered his insides. His parents labored until their fingers bled. Bought clothes for their children instead of for themselves. Trying to save just a dollar every month. All of their efforts now meaningless.

"I guess I am," he muttered, and reluctantly walked out of the door.

* * *

MRS. YOSHIMURA locked her front door and slipped the key under the "welcome" mat. Her tan coat, with mink fur wrapped around her neck, sagged to her ankles. She wore a new black hat that fanned out above her forehead. Two metal pins were pierced in the back to secure it. Her gloves matched in color, each revealing two buttons at the corners of her wrists. She bent down to pick up her suitcase; the same suitcase in which she had brought from Japan to America exactly twenty-one years ago. It seemed to weigh more than a thousand pounds instead of twenty. Black and white images of war flickered in Mrs. Yoshimura's mind. Shattered buildings that were rotting in between smoke. Homeless people who stood on crumbled roads. A child whose face smeared in soot, crying on a doorstep where half a structure remained. All of these moving portraits she had seen at the movies for nearly three years suddenly appeared real. Too real. They themselves were now the refugees: a family without a home. Just like the black and white portraits. She turned around to look at her children. Rose and Tom were dropped off by a friend an hour ago. Bethany tightly held Rose's hand. Jim had his back facing their house while he stared down the dirt road; all waiting to be picked up by the military.

Mrs. Yoshimura placed her hand on her son's shoulder. "*Shikata ga nai*," she faintly said to him, trying to convince herself more than anything. "*Shikata ga nai*."

Jim narrowed his eyes. Did she know how ignorant she sounded? It can't be helped? That life was a series of helplessness? Her traditional beliefs forged clichés, holding onto empty wisdom and false hope. This proverb claimed no comfort, no answers, and certainly no stability. General DeWitt finally got his way. A lesser version of Hitler. And Roosevelt let him. As if the opposition was vigorous! Bigotry proved to be a staple in American diet; easily swallowed; easily ingested. His mother eased her hand down his back.

He stepped off the porch and bitterly said, "We'd better meet them at the cross road."

Each family member had dressed in traveling clothes as if going on some sort of holiday. Each carried a suitcase for the occasion. Each had tags pinned to their coats; their identity replaced by numbers. At the end of their long driveway, they stood in the wide open, expecting a military truck to arrive at any moment. Anxious and worried, they waited in muted stillness. Waited to board the ferries to reach Seattle. Waited for the unknown. Rough grunts, from grinding gears, began reverberating through the tall, thin trees. Then a line of army trucks appeared; one after another; slowly migrating down the road like olive-green beasts. And Jim's family was positioned right beside their path. Oddly each truck began passing them by, spitting out exhaust as they loudly rumbled. Jim counted four vehicles while he tried to flinch away the pollution. For awhile, it seemed they were being ignored; as if they were going to be undisturbed. Finally the fifth one stopped in front of them, dragging a trail of mud from behind.

A soldier jumped out of the passenger side. "Need some help?" he volunteered.

"Thank you," Tom replied, reaching down to pick-up the suitcases.

"Shu-wa t'ing."

Jim noticed the soldier's funny accent. He spoke similar to James Cagney, or so Jim thought, but looked as if he had just popped out of photograph from the Great War. His bowl-like metal hat had a strap underneath his chin. He wore tanned spats and a dark olive-green trench coat. Jim leaned to his side to peek through the window, discovering a bayonet-rifle standing upright on the seat. Suddenly two more soldiers sprung out from the back, carefully holding their rifles with both hands.

"Don' let dem scares ya. Deys only followering ordas."

Tom inquired, "Where are you from, if you don't mind me asking."

"Jersey. We're da Jersey Guard."

Tom glanced back at Rose, baffled, as if asking her, *Why send reserves from the East Coast? Are all the West Coast Guards used up?*

The other soldiers trudged to the rear where they yanked down the squeaky tailgate. It was full of people around the Winslow area. Mrs. Yoshimura gawked; stunned to see people she knew shrinking in the dim background; sitting like statues. She started crying.

Rose reached for her mother's hand to squeeze it. "*It will be alright*," she assured. "*Everything will be fine, Mama.*"

The soldier without his weapon, appearing no older than twenty, observed Bethany nervously staring at their rifles. He felt sorry for them. He really did. Bending down, he asked Bethany, "Wha's you-wa name, Honey?"

Startled, she jerked to look up at him. "Bethany," she murmured.

"Bet'any, huh?" he smiled, swinging his arms behind him, hiding his large hands. "I gotta niece by dat name. Small woirld. Dey call me Jerry," he winked.

She blushed and smiled as he stood up. Tom grabbed each suitcase and slid it on the floorboard. People started shuffling around to make more room in the small, crowded space. Four children were forced to relocate onto the floor. Tom then hoisted Mrs. Yoshimura and Rose onto the truck.

"Bethany, you're next," he said, motioning forward.

"Lemme help," Jerry insisted.

Jim watched in irritation. He couldn't understand why this man behaved in a pleasant manner when they were in the process of being being thrown out of their homes. Naturally he would be in a better mood; he wasn't losing a damn thing. And did this man actually believe that by continuing his chummy act that it would alleviate the embarrassment? The pain? Bethany fell for his act, allowing him to lift her up. Jerry then turned to look at him. Before he could say anything, Jim lunged into the truck and sat next to Rose. There was no way in hell he would let that man touch him. Tom thus followed. Instantly the other two soldiers jumped back inside, slammed the door shut, and secured the pin back in the hole. Locked in like damn cattle. The friendly one withdrew.

Everyone remained quiet while staring at the floor. No one could look at each other in the eye. Just like a funeral, Jim thought. He scanned the area to detect how many people he knew. Katsuji, the one who made a scene at his father's house, sat next to his wife on one side, and his elderly father on the other. His face clenched unspoken rage, constraining stiffness around his mouth. Jim then noticed Tomiko sitting in the back corner. Crossing her arms, she bent her head to the side, trying to conserve her tears. He wanted to console her, but unfortunately he could do nothing. The tall, fruitful trees, which use to shelter the island from the outside world, now pushed them into the muzzle of a rabid hound.

"PARK dem trucks ova dare!" a sergeant yelled, furiously pointing to his left. "Ova dare, dipwads!"

Russell thought the scene looked a bit comical. First of all, he had never comprehended how many Japanese lived on Bainbridge until that day; perhaps around two hundred or more; all gathering at the edge of Common Dock. Friends and neighbors mixed into the crowd, mending their farewells, yet saying very little. What could be said? That the government was wrong? That in the middle of a global crisis everyone should protest instead of uniting? And of course there were the soldiers who carried their bayonets over their shoulders as they marched through the crowd. Some of the officers stood aside, separately watching and barking orders. Five or six photographers swooped from nowhere and circled around to exploit their misfortune. Russell worried that once they disappeared, and the press would lose interest, very few people would remember them at all.

A rumor poured over the crowd about Mr. Sumida, a middle-aged mill worker, who hung himself late last night. When his wife found him, she must have snapped into hysterics which caused her to overdose on sleeping pills. The military found both their bodies in the bedroom that morning. A captain removed the man from the rope, laid him beside his wife, covered them both in a sheet, and called the local police to patch up loose ends. Someone mentioned that the captain had tears in his eyes, uttering, "This ain't right. It just ain't right."

Russell was numb. He knew Mr. Sumida. His father use to give him haircuts on a regular schedule. It just seemed unreal. That it had to be happening to someone else. He turned to his mother who sat on a suitcase, staring beyond the bridge at the quiet waters, trying not to cry. He hated Japan for bombing Pearl Harbor and wished, for a moment, that he could have been born without a Japanese face. If Japan hadn't been so goddamn greedy then he would be graduating from Winslow High School next year. He could continue his wrestling. But now who knew? His future was arranged by the collision of fear.

Meito, his brother, pinned the large, white tags on his twin sons' coats. (Joe and George weren't identical twins. Joe was an inch shorter, skinnier, and his face was slightly longer than George's.) These large labels had printed numbers, which tagged them like livestock. Gertrude, Meito's wife, held a handkerchief in her hand, occasionally brushing away her tears.

Meito gently stroke his sons' coats and said, "There. That wasn't so bad, now was it?".

Russell's other sister, Masako, who was two years younger than Sadaye, emerged from a car off the side of the congested road. Her husband, Osamu, opened the passenger's side, clinging their infant daughter. The driver, an elderly white man with a double chin, also got out of his car. He was their landlord, as well as a friend. Masako and Osamu expressed their farewell, straining to reserve their tears. Chiyeko, Kunio, and their families had departed the day before. Somewhere in Oregon; they've been told. Chiyeko and her husband owned their house, now empty and vulnerable to looters. Like so many others up and down the Coast. Despite friends promising to look after her hallowed home, no one could stop the potential violence.

Yesterday, Russell walked for miles; aimlessly; misguided. He followed the dirt roads, choosing a direction without any real decision, only following a path without true guidance. He had reached the southern part of the island, passing Port Blakely, passing Pleasant Beach, ending his journey at the small shore, and wanting to never forget the scent of his cedar trees. Seattle rose from the horizon, stretching its skyscrapers above the sea. It actually was very close. But beyond Seattle rose a hostile world: a world he wasn't ready to accept.

"Russell!" someone cried out, breaking his thoughts. "Hey, Russell!"

He turned around to see who called his name. Dave and Maria jogged down the dirt road, passing by parked cars and military trucks. Relief and an overwhelming sense of gratitude soared over him. He recognized who his true friends were. School was still in session, and despite the threat of expulsion, Russell's friends skipped their classes to see him one last time.

Dave shook his hand, and promised to take care of his dog, Zasshu. His curly hair frizzed from the wind and humidity. His light brown eyes glazed over. A genuine sorrow stained his face. Russell couldn't say anything. His throat tightened and his mouth became dry.

Then Maria held Russell's hand. She asked, "Can I ah talk to you?"

Nodding, they walked off to the side; hand in hand. He looked at her, studying her perfect features; her thick long hair; her red lips. The army tuck's fumes trailed in the background like foul perfume. Every so often an officer would snap an order to his men, silencing the crowd that encircled the dock. A ferry waded in the water; attached to the bridge. The light rain began to weep again, seeping into their skins. Russell didn't want to unlock her hand.

She leaned closer and said, "I be sorry I nod talk with you las' week. My fahda is nod unda'standing." Curling her fingers around his, she bent her head, biting her lip. "I miss you. I miss you forevera." She lifted her chin and sighed. Her large dark irises encircled intimacy. "I love you, Rasso."

Russell gazed at her dark, oval eyes; her bronzed skin shimmering in the rain. My God, she was beautiful. He would miss her silly laughs. Her enduring cheerfulness. Her encouragement. His chest ached as if his body had been slammed on the floor, knocking out all of his breath. He would never have dreamt of leaving Bainbridge Island. He imagined marrying Maria someday, owning his own business of some sort, and growing old here. How could he leave a home and people he loved? Now, because of the war, who really knew if they would return, or if they were allowed to return.

Releasing her hand, he slipped out of his varsity jacket. The cold moist air sliced through his long-sleeved shirt.

"Here," he said. "I want you to have this."

She stared at him; uncertain. He leaned forward and kissed her, caressing her cheek with his free hand. She still tasted of peppermint. Unbinding her lips, he whispered, "I love you, too."

She began to weep, covering her face with her hand. Russell tried to blink his tears away. Glancing at his mother and Dave, who seemed to fade in the mist and fog, he guarded his cheek next to hers, rubbing the back of her neck, struggling to soothe her.

"It's alright, Maria. Don't worry. I'll be back." He draped his jacket around her shoulders and kissed her forehead. Muttering, he managed to say, "I'll be back. I promise."

* * *

FOR two days, and two nights, they traveled on a passenger train where the constant "ping-ping-ping" rhythm pinched their anxieties. Rumors crept about the train, slicing everyone's throat one by one. No one knew if they would remain in the United States or be shipped off to Japan. No one knew if the *Issei* men would be allowed to unite with their families, or kept as prisoners of war, or shot for every American who had been killed by the Japanese military. And could they actually be eaten alive by these large mesquites that inhabited Manzanar, the place where they were being sent to?

THE squeaky door shuddered when the bus driver pulled the latch. Jim, who sat in the first row, jumped out. The need to get out of that congested bus overpowered his composure as he struggled with the urge to yell. The trip covered a thousand miles, provoking tiredness and irritability. And then Rose, in her delicate condition, constantly vomited during the trip. Some of the soldiers gave her motion sickness pills or crackers; unfortunately none of it worked well.

Within the hour their sleeping quarters hung in a pungent odor. Rose offered a pattern of apologies, feeling guilty for the smell. Jim couldn't handle it, and couldn't handle her agonizing moans. He spent most of his time in the lounge area, shuffling cards in his lap. By the second day, Russell unexpectedly sat down beside him and began playing poker. Jim never questioned him why, or visa-versa. For hours on end they spoke about nothing but the game, playing mostly in silence. And when they finally reached a small town called Lone Pine, the sun began to bow while they were being transferred to buses. Some of the townspeople stood and gawked, whispering among themselves and pointing. Jim felt as if they had mutated into circus oddities.

Tom, Rose, Mrs. Yoshimura and Bethany sluggishly followed him out of the bus. Mrs. Yoshimura muttered something about forgetting to water her plants and started to cry again. Jim watched the rows of white army buses appear from the desert horizon. With the shades drawn, which had been the case throughout their journey, and the sky converting to black, no one could see their watches, and therefore not knowing the time of day. Darkness etched the sky, preserving silhouettes underneath the tall light poles. People spilled out of the open doors like fish in a factory. Men, women, children, both young and old, tumbled onto the foreign ground. The ground was surprisingly soft. Like sand on beaches. Wind greeted everyone with force, pushing and pulling them as if a bully on a playground. Their coats didn't protect them from the unfamiliar chill. Confusion and uncertainty saturated people's faces. But something else was apparent: acceptance. Calm acceptance like stale breezes just before the storm.

"Where's Lily?" some woman shirked, a chilling panic severing the wind. "Lily! Where's my little girl!"

Jim searched for the woman who shouted in the middle of the chaos.

"*I have found her!*" a man shouted back in Japanese. "*Do not worry, sister!*"

Jim could barely see above people's hats and scarves. Barbed wire fencing stretched far in the distance, fading into the blackness. Two wooden watchtowers stood over them at the gates, rising fifty feet. Their erected presence instituted an eerie feeling with soldiers angling their bayonets downward. Jim saw the sharp edges gleam high above him. Searchlights, perched on each wooden rail like a one-eyed owl, prowling its for prey; waiting. A row of armed soldiers stood in front of the opened gate; along the fence. The soldiers' faces were concealed in the dusk's obscurity, but he certainly could see their hands clutching the rifles. No doubt they had their fingers wrapped around the triggers hoping for an opportunity. Jim shook his head. Unbelievable. Where the hell would they go if they tried to escape? Who knew exactly where they were other than in a desert in California? And it wasn't as though they could simply blend in the crowd. Pretend to be Chinese perhaps? Or Korean? No one in America liked Orientals in the first place, so what goddamn difference would it have made? The entire circumstance was a cruel joke; like a game of pin the tale on the donkey. The government was the tact on the tail and the Japanese people were the asses getting stabbed. And yet the joke still lingered in sheer irony that night: out of all the nights to arrive at this so-called relocation camp, it happened to be on April Fool's Day.

"START a registration line!" a soldier bellowed, standing on a platform and pointing to his left. "Start a registration line right here folks! Begin here!"

The Hamaguchis gathered in a circle. Russell carried his mother's heavy suitcase. She refused to allow anyone outside of family to take it from her in fear that her dishes might shatter in a stranger's care. She wasn't about to give up her most prized china set when they reached Lone Pine, arguing with a soldier who tried to remove it from her hands. She brought her set all the way from Japan as a wedding gift, and there was no chance she would let someone else handle it! Sadaye darted in between the dispute, promising the soldier they would comply with regulations once they arrived at camp. Aggravated, the soldier mumbled off, "I'm just trying to help, for Pete's sake!"

Mrs. Hamaguchi covered her nose to protect herself from the wind and sand. She counted what was left of family to be certain everyone was present. Because the buses filled immediately they had to ride separately. Relieved that her children and grandchildren remained together, she let her eldest son lead them into the long line.

Russell followed his family, feeling a thick numbness as he scanned their surroundings. So far he hated it. No forest. No sea. Being caged like criminals. His twin cousins, Joe and George, began whining, wanting to return home, not understanding why they had to travel a lengthy distance just to go camping. Dressed in their Sunday suits, their wrinkled pants and jackets swallowed the sand in between the crevasses. Russell thought that they appeared like small hobos who woke up one night not knowing where there were. Gertrude and Mieto snapped at their six year old sons to be quiet. He could see shame scuffing over their eyes; a strong sense of guilt for not explaining the real reason they were there.

"JIM," Tom said. "Over here!"

The Yoshimuras huddled together, gripping hands as if links in a chain to keep from separating. Jim walked to them, but refused to hold hands. Only women and children clung to each other for support. Although it was his duty to replace his father's position in his absence, he didn't think that carrying their hands was necessary. He planned to take care of his mother and sister, so he wished Tom, the jackass, would stop acting like he was head of the Yoshimura household. Ever since he married his sister he had been tip-toeing outside their house; waiting to enter without invitation.

"This way," the soldier on the platform repeated. "That's right, folks! Keep movin'! Keep it orderly!"

Families began to merge into a line, drifting toward an enormous metal building. The searchlights traced over their heads, sometimes glaring directly in their eyes. Hundreds of shuffling feet whispered in the open where no one could hear them for miles. Barracks were camouflaged behind fragile layers of light. The wide paths rolled out emptiness. A young man, pleasantly dressed for travel, remarked out loud, above the buzzing murmurs, "Is this it? Someone's got to be kidding me!"

Mrs. Yoshimura shivered, wondering where the trees were. There were no trees to shelter them against the sharp wind that threw sand into their faces. All her life she had known trees; but now she was thrown in a place where the land was stripped from beauty.

"*If there are no trees*," Mrs. Yoshimura said, "*then how can I grow a garden?*"

Tom touched her shoulder. "*We will find a way, Mama*."

"*Mr. Yoshimura will be so very disappointed!*" She dipped her head into her hand and continued to cry softly.

THE Hamaguchis waited outside for nearly an hour, hardly speaking to each other, watching the dark digest their silhouettes. Russell's other sister, Masako, who carried her two year old daughter, leaned against her husband, Osamu. Masako looked a lot like Russell and Sadaye with her rounded face and small nose. Her thick hair, tightly tucked around her face like sausages, had loose strands weaving in the air. Ruth, her only child, could have passed for a Japanese version of Shirley Temple. She sucked her tiny thumb, hiding her dimples and closing her eyes. Osamu enjoyed bragging about his daughter's appearance and insisted that Masako curl their daughter's hair just like the little actress.

When Russell and his family finally entered the registration building, five Caucasian men, wearing white shirts and colorless ties, sat behind two desks. Thin piles of paper were slightly cluttered next to a few scattered ink pens. In the opposite corner, a heap of luggage arched against the naked wall. Soldiers proceeded to bring in more suitcases, and flung them on top of the disorganized stack. Brown and black suitcases mingled with flowered and plain sacs. People prodded through the massive lump like ants, searching for their belongings. Meito and Gertrude began tugging at the bottom of the luggage stack, grunting and quietly swearing. Osamu drilled in the middle. Russell just grinned. The tags that were pinned on their coats flipped and twirled like circus dogs. For the last two days nothing humorous offered any relief; however watching his brother and in-laws waddle around as if they were fat geese, he couldn't stop grinning.

"Why do we have to?" a little boy whined. His blue cap and denim overalls mismatched in hue. "I don't wanna!"

His mother, buttoned-up in a printed dress, replied, "Because we're required to. Everyone has to get their shots. So we don't get sick."

Russell stared at the corner where people were receiving vaccinations. An elderly woman almost fainted; caught by a younger man with his sleeve rolled up. He carefully moved her to the floor, allowing her to lie down. She rocked her head back and forth, rubbing her hand on her face, moaning. Directly across the corner other people were holding numbered signs under their chins, waiting to have their photos taken like prisoners.

Masako lightly swayed side-to-side, humming a lullaby to her toddler in her arms. The twins became more restless and tired. Their feet turned sore for they weren't use to standing still for some length of time. They started to pinch each other, at first giggling at their fun, then once the pinching developed into pain, they pitched their fists into hitting. Mrs. Hamaguchi grabbed both their wrists and scolded them in Japanese. Not knowing the language, the twins stared at her as if she were a lunatic and tried to squirm out of her grip.

"Goro!" she demanded. "*Please take one of them! They are upsetting me!*"

Russell took George's hand and moved four feet apart from Joe. Everyone was irritable. No one slept well for over a week. Not since the evacuation notice. And the train ride was something else. The seats were hard.

The sleeping quarters were as tiny as their outhouse turned sideways. The food was served in meager portions. Yet above it all, the New Jersey guards were remarkably friendly. They were polite in assisting families, and tried to keep up morale by singing popular songs. One of them, Jerry, was especially helpful to Sadaye. He gave her notes, aspirin, and the last of his Hershey's bar. He even nicknamed her "Sadie." Russell's mother didn't like it one bit. She had a more difficult time tolerating the flirtation. Whenever he appeared, she sternly told him, "Sadaye gud Jap'nese gir-ow'." Sadaye kept assuring her family that she was only flattered; nothing more. Russell wasn't so certain. She accepted his address with a smile.

Sitting his mother's suitcase down, Russell released George to massage his aching hand. His palms bore a reddened tattoo from lugging his mother's dish set all this time. After he intensely rubbed his curled fingers, trying to rub out the stiffness, he turned to grab hold of George. He wasn't there.

"Oh, shit!" he hissed.

Russell quickly scanned over the heads and hats. There were too many people! He abandoned the suitcase and merged into the cluster. All the familiar faces from home blended together, and yet he couldn't find George. If he started calling out his cousin's name, his mother and brother would then know he lost him, and they would become furious. Suddenly, out of the corner of his eye, he saw a soldier clutch a child's arm. George started to cry as the soldier pushed him away. Angered, he plowed to the front of the building.

"You didn't have to do that!" Russell stated, frowning at the man. "He's only a kid!"

The soldier's face mirrored a shape of an apple with a pungent cleft in his chin. His blue eyes swelled out of the narrowness of his brows, glaring sharply as if sun rays scalding over a sea. His sandy hair mixed with darker streaks. A flashlight balanced inside the loop of his belt. Turning around, Russell gently placed his hands on George's shoulders for reassurance.

The soldier pursued Russell. Leaning down, he snarled, "Turn your back on me again Jap, and I'll kill ya!"

Russell instantly grabbed his cousin's hand and moved elsewhere. A sickening sensation throbbed inside his stomach. Glancing backward, he wanted to see if the soldier was serious. He stood rigid at the entrance door; his chest shoved forward like Napoleon, his left arm bent and partly hidden behind his back, his bayonet perched at an angle. He probably meant what he said. Feeling uneasy, Russell looked away. He hoped not to see him anytime soon. As he guided George, he made his cousin promise to not tell anyone what had happened.

THE Yoshimuras carried their baggage to one of the desks, and watched the man wearing glasses forage through their belongings. Each of their left arms was sore from the two injections they had just received. The clerk touched their clothes, their underwear, their photo album, and took Tom's camera and Mrs. Yoshimura's sewing scissors, claiming them as contraband. All they could do was watch. Then he dispensed a pamphlet.

"Numbers two-fifty-three and forty-nine will take block six, barrack fifteen, apartments B and C," he informed Tom, referring them as numbers instead of by their names. "Each block has lavatories for both men and women, a mess hall, a recreation hall, and laundry facility. Read this pamphlet carefully. It'll tell you all you need to know about living here. Next, please."

Annoyed, Jim demanded, "If we have any questions or concerns, who do we speak to?"

Exasperated, the man heavily sighed, "I don't have time to explain everything. You'll just have to figure it out. I imagine you're a bright boy."

Becoming more irritated, Jim insisted, "It's dark outside. What if we get lost?"

"The camp is designed precisely. You can't get lost. But if you do, ask one of the guards for directions. Next, *please*!"

SILENCE guided the Hamaguchis through the camp while everyone followed Meito, each hauling their bags and suitcases. Lamp posts provided streams of illumination, although faded easily into the sullen night. All the buildings were identical and stretched vertically. White strips attached to the barracks to display block numbers were scarcely visible. It was difficult to determine when one block ended and another began; Russell, however, pointed out that the larger gaps between the buildings had to indicate the division. At a crossroad, Russell's family branched off after saying their good-nights to each other. Russell watched Masako, Ruth, and Osamu drift off to their new residence while the rest of them entered one of the side doors. The room consumed shadows like a parasite. And it was as frigid as a cooler. The sweetly fresh pine wood overwhelmed their noses, making their stomachs a bit queasy.

"Wait here," Meito said. "I think I see a light bulb." As he slowly wandered through, he stumbled into something hard. "*Jigoku ni otosu!*" he cursed. "God! What is this?" He padded his fingers around a cold rectangular object. "I think it's a stove! A *tenpi*."

He stood up, swinging his hand in the air. Soon he felt a dangling cord and yanked it. What he saw infuriated him. Shells of bare wood supported the structure, depriving the walls of sheet rock. Half inch gaps in between the wooden floor and walls indicated weaknesses and flaws, and Meito questioned whether the barrack could stand to fight against the wind. Two naked light bulbs hung from the wooden ceiling as if heads in nooses. Miniature grey stoves, which looked like tin cans with erected pipes, sat on the right and left sections of the long building. Ten army cots, with dark green blankets folded in a square on top, were lined beside a wall. Twelve empty windows followed each other on one side and seven windows shared two doors on the opposite side. Two more doors were positioned at opposite ends of the hundred foot barrack.

Gertrude gasped and shook her head. Seeing no walls for separating the room, she bitterly remarked, "What are we suppose to do for privacy?"

Sadaye stared at the cots and said, "We don't need that many cots. We only need seven."

Russell gawked at the barrack; appalled. No walls. No furniture. No kitchen. No radio. What kind of place was this? It looked like some sort of solitary confinement. He walked over to one of the cots and pressed down. It felt firm; rigid. No pillows. No mattresses. Everyone frowned; except the twins who were more interested in the stoves' bellies by swinging the doors. Gertrude slapped both their hands, and complained about their unruly behavior.

Meito removed his hat, brooding over their bad luck. He sold his twenty acre farm, not knowing if he could afford the taxes without income, in exchange for this? He left his house, his possessions, and his pride for an empty space in the middle of nowhere? If he had known it was going to be this disgusting he would had loaded his shot gun and fought like hell! But no. He packed his bags instead, feeling obligated to protect his family. He knew his actions would embarrass them by provoking the authorities and possibly making things worse. A good citizen never defied leadership; even if the men in charge were terribly wrong.

Gertrude shrieked. She began to gag, her face turning red, pointing to George. In between his fingers George held the tail end of a scorpion. Meito flew to his son, dropping his hat. He instantly grabbed the scorpion and catapulted it out the door. Then he sprinted to the door to slam it shut.

"That was a big no-no!" he barked, his voice trembling. "That was a very dangerous creature! When you boys see it again, run away! Do you boys understand?"

Horrified, both nodded their heads, not fully comprehending why their father hollered at them. George started to sniffle. Gertrude went to him, draping her arms around her confused son. She rocked him back and forth, telling him that everything was alright, and that Daddy didn't mean to yell at him. That he was only protecting them.

"Let's see if we can get some sleep," Meito wearily sighed. Turning to his mother, he spoke in Japanese, "*Mama, do not worry. The sun will rise higher tomorrow.*

~PART II~

City in the Sierras

CHAPTER ONE

Early April, 1942

ROSE held Bethany's hand as they walked beside their mother. The raw light revealed frost on the roofs and shrubs; a faint fog released through their nostrils. The two borders of giant mountains placed the camp in the middle of its link. No one had the courage to use the latrines last night, not trusting the unknown darkness. They followed the wide, unpaved road, feeling sand creep inside their shoes, hoping to find the lavatories. Seeing two more women strolling in the same direction a few yards apart, Rose discreetly chased them. Four long lines exposed forty or so people who stood impatiently beside porta-potties for both the men and women. Bethany whined. Her bladder pained her to the limit of inducing tears. The wait only would torture her even more. Rose scanned the area. To her left she saw men enter a building with towels. To her right women were doing the same. These buildings had to have showers. She also noticed some men, whom she didn't recognize from her home island, had grown scraggly beards; very heathen-like. Not to mention that their clothes were wrinkled, and were filthy as if seamen stranded ashore. Three of these men, ranging between their twenties and thirties, casually moved over to the women's section to position themselves right in front of the open windows; staring; leering.

She gasped, "I don't believe it! They're a bunch of peeping Toms!"

Mummers sifted through the women's lines, but no one protested; afraid to speak out. Five of the Bainbridge men angrily stepped out of the latrine line to directly march to the three strangers. The Bainbridge men poked on one of the bearded man's shoulder.

"Where your manners?" one demanded. "These women are family!"

One of the bearded men only smirked. He glanced at his two friends, and finally replied in Japanese, "*It has been awhile since we have seen women. We had volunteered to arrive here last month. Our apologies.*"

"Well, find some other hobby, buddy."

The bearded men smiled and slowly strolled away; their eyes sidetracking to each window they passed. The Bainbridge men waited until the others merged with their own group once more before returning to their lines. Two of them stayed behind. Just in case. Rose, although feeling a little relieved, continued to stare at the unruly men. During the registration line last night she had heard that a group of men who volunteered from Los Angeles had entered the camp before them. A month into their internment had left them soiled.

She rubbed her rounded belly, worrying that her first child might be born here. She hoped they would move to someplace better by then. This had to be temporary until the government figured out a better plan. It had to be. These primitive conditions were barely acknowledged as civilized, so how could the government expect them to thrive in this environment?

RUSSELL walked alongside his brother, Meito; each dragging an empty potato bag. That morning everyone picked up one of these scratchy, smelly bags and had to walk a mile out of the camp border to stuff straw inside. These were to be used as mattresses. The two brothers continued to walk in silence. What could really be said? That they were thankful to be treated like outcasts in a land so foreign to them they might as well have been exiled to a foreign country? Plus, just beyond the eastern mountains, lay Death Valley. Now that was a comforting impression: death. Why name a valley "Death" if it didn't live up to its name? And why dump them there if they weren't expected to survive?

BETHANY sat on the crunchy bed made of straw, and wrapped her arms around her mother. She squeezed her, hoping to bring back life in her, hoping her mother would then embrace her like she always did when she felt scared. But she didn't.

Bethany asked, gently shaking her mother's shoulder, "Mama? Are you alright?"

As the afternoon frayed into ragged threads, Mrs. Yoshimura stared out the window. Dead, bony trees scattered between other barracks down the block. Rose tried to comfort her by telling her that since there were trees it was a sign she could grow a garden here. Not here, she thought. Without rain, her plants would die in this forsaken desert. Were they all also abandoned here to die?

"Yes, fine," she finally replied, squeezing her young daughter's hand. "Fine."

Mrs. Yoshimura lingered inside her memories; unaware of her daughter's warmth. It had been nineteen days since Mrs. Yoshimura's husband had been arrested. She had never been independent. Her father had provided for her until she married Toshiyuki. Their families knew each other through the vegetable market in Hiroshima. She began writing to him when she was twelve under her father's guidance. He encouraged her to write to this lonely stranger in Hawaii. He was a good man, her father told her. He would be grateful to receive any news about his homeland to ease his homesickness. Write to him about your cooking, he often encouraged. Five years later, Toshiyuki proposed marriage. By that time he migrated to Seattle; away from the sugar cane plantations to study in a university. She reluctantly accepted, insisting that she should finish a higher education first. Her father was outraged, believing that she was ready to move out of the crowded house. Being seventeen she was ripened for marriage.

For the only time in her life she did not recoil from her father's demand. She realized that once she married and had children, she would never have another opportunity to gain knowledge. Her father eventually agreed, with the understanding that her education would suffice to her husband's needs. After she graduated from a two year girl's school, she left her home to marry a man she never met. She felt divided and frightened. She was not a brave woman, but her father's sense of duty overwhelmed her doubts. Learning very little about the Western culture, Haruko knew adapting would be difficult. She would have to change her clothing, speak a perplexing language, possibly drive foreign cars, and raise her children without her family's help. During the ship's journey, she sobbed every night inside a hollow room.

Being forced from her home a second time, another piece of her spirit cracked. Starting over exhausted her optimism. Both adjustments stole her trust from authoritative men; whether her father, her husband, or government officials. She had never been allowed to think for herself, and now, she still didn't know what to think.

Late April

WIND rippled through the residents' clothes, trembling and fluttering, day after day. It creaked and popped the barracks like old ships lost at sea, flinging waves of yellowish-brown sand with pebbles up in the horizon. Dust confined the people from fresh air, strangling their lungs, stinging their eyes, intruding inside their quarters. Every day women swept their wooden floors to rid of the sand, and everyday sand erupted through the inch-wide gaps. The nightmare of prison slept with Russell's family every night. Living at the end of the block, they had a window's view of the barbed wire that stood seven feet tall, linking five prickly wires around the camp. On a clear day, when the wind behaved in a mild manner, they could see two watchtowers at opposing ends. The reddish-brown Sierras contrasted with the bluish-gray mountains of Mount Williamson. It was a delusion of freedom as both sets of mountains stood outside the fence, further fencing in Russell's family inside the desert.

The barrack remained stripped of solitude. Two flimsy blankets suspended down the ceiling that weakly divided the building in half. At night they hung their sagging coats over the windows. Russell, his mother, and Sadaye settled in the back portion. Meito and Gertrude took the front half. Joe and George constantly bickered during the days, staying inside the depressed barrack under Gertrude's supervision. She feared that if her sons stood too close to the fence, then the guards would shoot at them. Yet, when the boys lingered indoors, everyone else fled outdoors to avoid the twins' squabbling.

Russell went to the makeshift post office earlier that day, standing two hours in line to see if they going to continue to collect letters from their father in Montana. He was surprised to have picked up a letter so soon from his other sister and brother who were staying at an assembly center, called Puyallup, in Oregon. Although they wrote that everyone was doing well, the adjustments were very difficult. What irritated Russell while he reading the letter, he noticed that it had been sliced opened then resealed. Black lines were marked over certain sentences.

As the day wore on, Russell left his barrack a second time to rummage around for lumber.

Wandering around, he watched children race down the block, screaming and laughing. They tossed a yellow ball, yelling, "You're it! Get the Jap!" Even in camp the word "Jap" instituted an evil form; the true enemy. They were American, no doubt, but they were also American who happened to be of Japanese origin. Russell understood the complexity. Growing up he fought to prove how American he designed himself to be by joining the boy scouts, joining little league, joining wrestling; always joining.

He passed by a group of volunteer construction workers; all camp residents. So far, the only white faces Russell had seen worked at top positions such as the hospital, administration office, and the military. The volunteers dug a long ditch outside one of the bathrooms. Their black hair had turned almost blond from the sand. A handful of these volunteers came from Los Angeles. Most were in their twenties and thirties, wearing suspenders, Levis, or brown work pants. Some even wore the traditional Japanese leather boots that curved all the way up their calves, nearly reaching their knees. Those who were older even wore the traditional Japanese caps to shield their eyes from the sun. Russell assumed they were just now completing the sewage system on the south side. Rumors of more residents arriving the following month put urgency into finishing the camp. The camp looked as bad as ghettos he had seen in photographs: basic, raw, dirty, poor. And it also held a cozy quality comparable to Sing-Sing.

Suddenly a man shouted out in Japanese, "*Do not lay the shovel under my feet, Soichiro-san! Are you trying to kill me?*"

"*Watch where you are walking!*" sprang the rebuttal.

"*There are too many men crowding the ditch! How am I to pay attention to my feet, idiot?*"

"*By looking down, fool!*"

Grinning, Russell dragged the burlap sack behind his feet. A thin trail of sand followed his heels, hissing. The few shards of lumber that he found throughout the camp only allowed for one night of heat. Frustrated, he browsed around the border of the wire fence hoping to find more loose wood and nails that everyone else in camp had carelessly overlooked. Lumber became more precious than gold. People used it to build furniture, as well as heating their quarters. The other day his mother attempted to build a chair while using her iron as a hammer. Once she finished, she gathered every family member to show off her accomplishment. With a large smile on her face, she sat down for the demonstration. It loudly snapped, and she fell sideways.

As he continued his search for scraps of lumber, he had already passed by the military campsite on the east side of the camp; next to the highway. For the time being, these poor bastards didn't even live in barracks. Ironically. As an alternative they resided inside tents that resembled the Arabic style he had seen in movies. Tall and pointy on the top, pale in color, and shaped like a pentagon. All that was missing were camels and a harem!

He stopped. His stomach gurgled and moaned. Although he'd eaten lunch only two hours prior, he felt as if he hadn't eaten since yesterday. Russell was used to snacking off and on during the day, but this three times a day restriction irritated him. He craved creamy vanilla ice cream, freshly cooked rice that was wrapped in seaweed and raw fish, limp noodles, sweet strawberries, and fried shrimp. Instead, the canned mini-weenies and spam, burnt baked beans, soggy hash browns and runny eggs provided a bland consistency for each meal. Plus, the white cooks believed that just by dumping fruit or syrup on rice it would be considered as dessert. Idiots. The mess halls needed Japanese cooks who knew what the hell they were cooking! A young *Nisei* man, who had been sitting near the Hamaguchis, loudly criticized that the meals were just like the army before Uncle Sam kicked him out. He was only a corporal, and after General DeWitt declared *all* Japanese Americans as a threat, he and many others were kicked out in order to be picked up for evacuation like everyone else. Even sick people were hauled out of hospitals to be relocated to these camps. One man actually died during the extradition after they took him just two hours following his surgery.

That day Russell noticed a white lady wandering around and taking photos of the camp. Rumors about Dorothea Lange had to have been true, then; otherwise what other crazy *hukujin* would want to take photos of this shitty place? He watched this slender woman, dressed in bell bottoms with her hair pulled back in a scarf, click away. When she looked at him and smiled, he turned around to walk in a different direction; too embarrassed to have his image preserved in these humiliating circumstances.

He continued to walk for another fifteen minutes before finally stopping. As soon as he stopped, he stared past the fence and noticed a few scraps of wood lying between the sage bushes. His skin began to fry and his insides tingled. Should he dare? He quickly glanced about to see if anyone was watching him. Peering to his left, he could barely see the watchtower. The tower was tiny in the distance; surely the guard wouldn't be able to see him as clearly. Russell scratched his nose, debating. There had to be an abundance of lumber past the fence. He could retrieve as much as he liked. He scanned the area for the flimsy patrol that was supposed to circle the camp and keep people in order. During his search, he had only run across two. Besides, he was on the opposite corner from their quarters. Swinging the bag over his shoulder, he slowly walked toward the boundary. If his mother knew, she would have a heart attack, and then ask her ancestors' for forgiveness for raising such a disobedient son. He breathed faster and faster. Against his own better reasoning, Russell spread the wires apart and slid through, leaving the bag beside a post.

Russell began collecting lumber; carefully moving around the maze of bristly brushes; wrapping his arms around the priceless goods. The sage bushes, more or less like thick tumbleweeds, rose from half a foot to three feet high. For a moment, he could walk anywhere without repercussions. The flat, bare surface, perhaps a mile before touching the snow-covered mountains, invited him in. Behind the mountains were genuine towns; places where he could order a malt; see a movie; go dancing. Anyplace but here. The feeling of false security satisfied his need to escape.

Suddenly a crackle hit the air, and something whizzed by his shoulder.

"Shit!" he cried out, jumping backwards.

Another crackling sound popped in the distance, and something else spat at the sand three feet from his shoe. His heart choked. Dropping his loot, he sprinted to the fence. A third bullet pursued him, scratching his shoulder. His muscles painfully tightened. He stumbled through the sharp wire, ripping his jacket, fleeing from aim. He ran quickly and he ran without thought. The wind continued to whiz past his ears. Minutes evaporated. When he finally he stopped, his breathing was heavy; his sweat dripped over his brows. Unexpectedly, his arms and legs weakened like pudding, and he leaned against a building for support. He looked at his hands. They violently shivered. Russell didn't believe any of the guards would actually shoot. So far he had no real reason to worry because the Jersey guards were exceptionally kind. And anyway, it wasn't as if any of his people were sentenced as hard core criminals. There were children here. How could anyone shoot at innocent bystanders? Who would shoot at *him*?

He touched his right shoulder, feeling the sting. The bullet sliced his jacket and checkered shirt, revealing a scratch. Jesus Christ! Did the bastard intend to kill him? Russell closed his eyes, trying to recover his composure. He then felt the drafts enter through his jacket. One tear fluttered near his right biceps and another at his rib cage. What a stupid attempt! Stupid! Stupid! Stupid! He could have been killed. And all for what? Wood and nails? Except that his family badly needed it. Mortified, he privately swore that he would never tell a living soul. But what the hell was he going to tell his mother about his jacket? He certainly couldn't tell her the truth! Stripping out of his jacket, he wadded it into a ball and would think of something.

Three blocks up, a crowd of people swarmed the area where they thought they heard the shots. Rumors already flowed down their tongues, filling their imaginations with excitement. Someone saw a boy running from the fence.

"Is he hit?"

"Is his wound fatal?"

"Who is he?"

"Where is he? And what was he doing outside the fence?"

"Did he actually think he could escape?"

The rumors rushed to Russell within minutes as people traveled up and down the street. A sergeant, stocky and slightly pudgy, darted past Russell to the crowd. Once he arrived, he ordered the group to disperse immediately and let the military assess the situation. As his hands launched in the air, demonstrating his authority, people reluctantly moved away. Russell slid his fingers through his dirty hair. He took deep breaths to command courage, and began to walk, tossing his jacket inside a trash barrel. The need to see his sniper grew into a personal quest. What kind of an asshole did it take to shoot at an unarmed man? One leg slowly swung after the other, yet the more he thought about the shooting, he sped his pace. If he had been hit. If he had been fatally injured. The *ifs* stung his chest, bloating out hot tears. He had to know. He had to see the bastard's face.

Passing by the scattering crowd, Russell strode toward the watchtower. He started to shake again. The closer he came to the tower, his nerves loosened and he wanted to turn around. Maybe it was best not to know. Once he knew, he probably couldn't look at this soldier straight in the eye whenever confronted. Despite his doubts, his legs resumed at forward march.

He finally halted. A few people stood underneath, trying to hear what was being said between the private and major. The private explained that he had seen an escapee, shouted his warning like he was suppose to, and then executed his duty as a final result. Biting down on his tongue, Russell gazed upward. At first he had difficulty viewing the guards' features with the sun glaring in the background. The major then informed the private that when his shift was over to come see him and fill out a report. As the major climbed down the ladder, the guard shifted his stance and stared directly downward. Russell stopped breathing. Hundreds of invisible needles pricked his skin. He couldn't believe it. It was that soldier who threatened him at the registration room.

"Callis!" the major barked. "Next time use one bullet! We're in a war goddamn it! Don't waste 'em on these people, for Christ sake!"

"Yes, sir!" he sneered.

The major tensed his mouth and said, "I'm warning you, Callis." He continued to climb down the ladder. "You people move!" he ordered, flinging his hand as if shooing flies away. "There's nothin' to see here! Go! Unless you want me to take you in!"

Everyone, including Russell, promptly scurried like a broken set of marbles, cracking into many directions. Russell obeyed his shadow by following it up a street. He thought about one of his wrestling matches just before the evacuation. Two students from a different school were chanting "Kill the Jap! Kill the Jap!" He grew angry, turned, and jogged in front of his shadow. If he was going to survive this camp he needed to stay ahead of his own fear.

Early May

JIM crossed into another block, wanting to be as far away from Tom as possible. They had been bickering for over a month about everything- from the arrangements of the barrack to who should preside over the Yoshimura's finances. If Tom didn't stop assuming the authoritative role then Jim wasn't sure when he would just snap. Trying to shake off his anger, he followed three tumbleweeds bouncing in front of him like a pack of dogs. Thick trails of dust swept from behind. Turning around, he watched more buses prodding through the gates, unloading more Japanese people from Los Angeles and dumping their luggage outside the registration building. This was occurring on a weekly basis.

These Los Angeles people seemed different to Jim. Their skins were darker; a golden-bronzed tone and had more wrinkles than the people he knew from Bainbridge. They also spoke with an unfamiliar dialect in both English and Japanese. Some of them even stared at him as if he was a peculiar site to see. Perhaps he appeared upper class compared to many of them. He wore slacks with a white shirt and leather jacket. His pale skin, which easily stung under the sun, may have appeared more white. His hands were clean; polished even. As thousands more piled into camp, it became a noisy place to live. People gathered in groups, circling around barrels with homemade fires, gossiping, bragging, complaining. He could hear couples arguing as if in another room. Sometimes having sex even. Radios boasted out baseball games and music lingered in the air. Voices resonated in the snug area like a busy restaurant.

Just across from the entrance, two rows of vehicles, (twenty-one total,) wasted under the desert sun. These cars were brought in by the evacuees who refused to give up their transportation. Some were able to drive outside of camp on work furlough between the two towns. The wind had already begun stripping away the paint, leaving the cars defenseless. On the border of the highway and entrance, a wooden sigh, spread out like animal skin, publicized "MANZANAR WAR RELOCATION CENTER." Two military stars endorsed its dominance at the edges of the word "WAR."

During the tedious days Jim rarely thought of his father. Despite his miserable situation, and despite the crippling boredom, without his father's piercing control he felt an impression of freedom. And that was hopeful enough.

Mid May

RUSSELL turned his head to stare at the darkness, watching the streak of yellow light hitting its mark on the dividing blanket. The searchlight crawled over the wall, nibbling at the shadows, and stalking just beyond his toes. Russell's space swallowed him, digesting him, and at times he felt as though he couldn't breathe. Callis' face persisted in his dreams. And throughout the day, he found himself constantly looking in every corner. Just in case. Russell tried to elude his nightmares by sleeping very little. Often he would lie awake, listening to his brother beg for Gertrude's attention. Usually it ended in frustration and petty arguments the next day. That night, he heard them kissing; the rustle of their body movements; their awkward breathing. Suddenly they stopped.

"*Naze desu-ka*?" Meito whispered.

"Because everyone will hear us."

"Everyone's asleep! We'll be quiet as mice."

He pursued kissing her, but she softly grunted and rotated on her side.

He curtly sighed, "How much longer? Another two months?"

"Shhh! You'll wake the boys!"

"We can't go on as if we're already dead, Gerdie! We have to keep living!"

"Oh, really?" she muttered. "And what kind of life is this?"

Frowning, he glanced around their barren environment. Burlap curtains. Cots with straw mattresses. Unpainted walls. Naked ceiling. It wasn't a real home. And could never be. Stroking her shoulder and neck, his irritation subsided. "We have to make the best of it. Don't let it beat you down."

"We have nothing, Meito! You understand? Nothing! Nothing but sand and filth and . . ." she hesitated, choking. "No privacy. . ."

Her sobs were then broken into short gagging like someone who was drowning. Meito tried to console her by kissing her brow and telling her that everything would fall back into place.

Russell closed his eyes, shutting out the glare on the blanket. Maria never returned his letters. At first he wrote a letter once a week, then twice, but as he felt more isolated and lonely, he wrote one every day. Nearly two months had decayed as the sandstorms and construction of the camp progressed, and yet, no letter.

"We haven't lost everything, *koibito*," Meito gently said. "I have job. I can get furniture from Lone Pine. One of the *hakujin* drivers at the mess hall also owns a furniture store. He'll help out."

Meito continued to kiss Gertrude's face, wiping off her wet cheeks with his thumbs, smiling at her. Soon she responded with a grin, allowing him to pursue. They began to make noises again.

Russell glanced at his mother and sister who continued to sleep in the darkness; their faces as rigid as pebbles. He wondered if they were truly asleep or pretended in order to elude the embarrassing moment. Within twenty minutes, Russell squeezed the pillow over his ears, straining to muffle his brother's moans. The rhythmic squeaking of the cot lingered sluggishly, than gradually increased in speed. Russell replaced his thoughts on Maria, wondering if someone else was caressing his hand over her body. That could be the reason why she had not written. How could she betray him? Especially under these circumstances?

The creaking cot penetrated his mind and he couldn't stop thinking about Maria. The brawny smell of Pear Soap on her bare skin. The agility of her thighs. The warmth of her breasts. Dammit, he was going nuts! Jumping from his bed, Russell quickly slipped his shoes on and exited out the side door. Cold air instantly forced hair on his arms to prickle; cooling down his torrid blood and heart rate. Under the streetlight, he could see his breath transpire from his lips. The rows of barracks glowed from the blushing moon, making the block seem more cramped. Not knowing where he should head off to in the middle of the night, he decided the latrines would offer a destination. People were allowed to roam the camp; just as long as they weren't escaping from it. Rubbing his arms for heat, he trotted up the block. Once he arrived, he was shocked to see a long line weave outside from the latrine. Everyone, except him, wore coats.

An elderly man, who had thick bifocals resting over his pug-like nose, turned to Russell and remarked, "*I thought there would be no line at three in the morning. Apparently everyone else believed the same thing.*"

CHAPTER TWO

Late May

SADAYE eased the thermometer from under Russell's tongue. Squinting at the red line, she crinkled her brows and said, "He needs to go the hospital. His temperature's at a hundred and five. I can't do anything for him here. We don't have anything!"

Russell didn't like the expression on his sister's face. Her uncertainty and worry only induced a sense of panic. He detested hospitals each time his mother had to go to one. The smell. The sterile environment. The possibility of dying. And he didn't trust this camp's hospital. Sadaye, who worked there, had complained that they were always running out of something; that they were understaffed; that things were often not sanitized because there wasn't enough soap and hot water.

Gertrude grabbed both her sons by their arms and squeezed them to her chest. Looking at Meito, she asked, "You don't think he's given it to Joe and George?"

"I don't know," he replied. "Just keep a watch on them."

Mrs. Hamaguchi began patting her son's face, hoping for a quick cure. Coping with her own illness for the last five years diseased her confidence. With scarlet fever, measles, and the whooping cough spreading throughout the camp, she had good reasons to worry. Sadaye took Russell's hand, gently pulling him up. She turned to Meito, silently asking him for help. He promptly responded, wrapping one arm around his brother's ribs, and gently removed him from the bed. Together they slowly walked to the door.

"*I should have known*," Mrs. Hamaguchi sighed, shaking her head. "*Today my eggs broke open before I had a chance to sit down to eat. I knew it was not a good sign.*"

Russell rolled his eyes. He imagined his mother swimming in yolk and praying to her ancestors. In fact, he could smell the vague odor of sweet incense. Her favorite ancestor was great-grandfather, Minoru, who had one good eye and one dead eye. It had been damaged during a typhoon when the fishing rod poked his eye out. Since then, he claimed to have seen visions. Together his great-grandfather and mother could sail the yellow seas and predict bad signs.

THE afternoon wind pushed against Russell and Meito, making their journey across the camp more difficult. They followed Sadaye and their mother who strode arm in arm, wearing scarves over their hair. Each step exhausted Russell. His flimsy muscles ached and his head spiraled. Pelts of sand stuck on his sweaty forehead. Time halted, paralyzing his ability to clearly think. By the time they arrived at the steps of the hospital, Russell's collar and arm pits were absorbed in perspiration. He saw his father standing behind a window, smiling at him.

"Why's Papa here?" he groggily asked.

"Papa?" Meito echoed, puzzled. "Goro, he's not here."

"I just saw him!"

"I think you're just seeing things."

Sulking, he muttered, "I know what I saw."

They walked up the steps, entering one of five barracks that were designed for the camp's hospital. Russell browsed the place. Beds, covered in white sheets, were positioned in two straight lines beside the bare walls. Half of the beds held ailing people inside the brown blankets like cocoons. An odd smell of rubbing alcohol and pine sap exhumed the large space. Russell again searched for his father. Some fathers were already being released from Montana, so why not him? But then, why would his father be at the hospital before seeing his family? Was he sick, too? Searching over all of the men's faces, Russell couldn't find him. He simply couldn't be found. Still lost. Still hidden.

Russell was literally being dragged to a separate room because the strength in his legs was gone. In this room at least there were four walls and a door for some privacy. Meito carefully sat him down in a chair. A white doctor, in his late twenties and with brown hair, poked a thermometer inside his mouth. The young doctor stepped backward to make sure he wasn't too close; perching his right hand on his hip.

He gruffly ordered, "Nurse, I need you to take these people outside of here. This is a restricted area. You know that!"

Sadaye attempted to translate the doctor's command to her mother, but her mother angrily interrupted. She insisted that she remain, and demanded how could he send her away when her son was very ill?

"What is she saying?" he curtly asked, looking at Mrs. Hamaguchi as if she were a child.

"She wants to stay, Dr. Huey. She's upset and worried."

Dr. Huey sighed out of aggravation. He walked to the corner and turned to face them at a distance. Crossing his arms, he clicked his tongue and said, "If he's contagious, then he'll contaminate everyone in this room. I don't want an epidemic spreading throughout this camp and get blamed for not controlling it!"

Meito glared at the doctor. "If my brother is contagious then we're already infected, so what's the point of all of us leaving? We leave and infect the camp anyway."

The doctor squinted. “I didn’t think about that.” Dropping his head, he began grunting. “Alright. You need to stay here for a while, but *don’t*,” he warned, raising his finger, “bother me. And please, *be* quiet.”

Sadaye struggled to control her temper. Doctor Huey certified himself to be an impatient and indifferent man. Often he couldn’t remember her name or even the other nurses’ and doctors’ names. Mostly he found difficulty pronouncing them, and therefore stated their professional titles instead. Nurse! Doctor! For the time being he was the only white doctor at the hospital who was in charge of all the other *Nisei* doctors; despite their experiences. He also got paid a regular wage whereas everyone else was paid no more than nineteen dollars a month.

“What does his temperature read?” the doctor asked.

Sadaye glanced at Huey who stood in the corner with his arms still sewn over his chest.

She removed the thermometer from her brother’s lips. “It’s a hundred and six.”

Huey lowered his chin, moaning and rocking his head from side to side.

“We’ll have to retrieve water from the washing room. I doubt the water will be cold enough to bring down his temperature, however. And we’re out of aspirin! Jesus! I went to medical school so I can be drafted to work in a dump like this?”

Sadaye wanted to tell him off. What did he truly know of misfortune? He still had a home to return to in Connecticut. His parents were safely tucked away in the comforts of their own house. And even though he was employed to work inside the camp, every night he could pass through the wire fence and into his own exclusive housing in another town. He had a real bed, a real furnace, a real kitchen, and a private bathroom. His complaints about his quarters couldn’t compare to hers.

“I can get ice from the mess hall,” she steadily declared.

“Ah, good thinking. Have one of the other nurses help you.”

Russell felt as though he would fizzle into ashes. The misery of his skin scalding underneath his damp clothes began to ignite insanity. Suddenly he began to unbutton his shirt. “I don’t care what you do!” he asserted, slinging his shirt off. “Just do something before I die!”

Sadaye sped out of the room. She grabbed another nurse by her arm, and together they raced to the mess hall on the northwest side of the camp. The doctor momentarily left the hollow room. Russell leaned back. The room rattled like a roller coaster; jilting his head from side to side; up and down; around and around. Voices circled near his ears, but he couldn’t understand; like foreign languages. He closed his eyes, feeling his body dropping; his mind fading. Where was Papa? He could hear his droning voice. He could hear him telling Russell not to spend all his money in Seattle. Not to buy too much candy. Be home by five. Then an unfamiliar voice intervened. A shadow standing beside his father’s shadow. The shrill voice rang in his ears, “Turn your back on me again, Jap, and I’ll kill ya! I’ll kill ya! I’ll kill ya!”

Russell shouted, yet no one heard him. He felt himself weeping heavily and uncontrollably. He felt himself murmuring, wanting his father to protect him. His father stood right beside this bully, and yet, did nothing. He did nothing. Why wasn't his father protecting him? Why was his father lurking like a coward? A coward? And was Russell just like his father? Also a coward? Russell cried out; pleading; sobbing, "Don't! Don't kill me! Please don't kill me!"

Sharp pain quickly woke him. Million of needles pierced through his flesh.

"Goro!" Sadaye shouted. "Goro! Look at me!"

His muscles shriveled in piercing pain. "Oh God!" he screamed. "What the hell are you doing!"

"You were hallucinating."

Russell looked down. He sat naked in a tin tub full of ice and water. He began shivering. "How. . . much . . . longer?"

"Five minutes or so. You're safe now. No one's going to kill you," she gently smiled. "I promise you that."

"I wouldn't. . . be . . . so sure!"

HALF an hour later, Russell fell asleep on the hospital cot; loosely tucked under the covers wearing the thin, grey gown. His temperature dropped, although his body was left weakened. Mrs. Hamaguchi sat beside him in a creaky chair with her hands containing her tears.

* * *

DAVE opened his porch door, holding a tin bowl of dog food, calling out for Russell's pet, Zasshu. Light rain draped the gray sky with a slick mist. His backyard overflowed with luscious greenery and blooming cedar trees. The closeness of the tall trees had always provided a sense of security. Feeling a chill, he zipped up his varsity coat and stepped off the porch. The rain softly drummed on his baseball cap, and patted his face. His curly, brown hair began to frizz in the moisture at the back of his cap. He continued to call out for Zasshu. His father, who also had curly hair and brown eyes, sat inside the screened area; drinking a fresh-brew of black coffee and reading *The Bainbridge Review*. The publicist and editor, Mr. Woodward, had been printing letters from a former high school reporter, Tomiko, about her experiences in Manzanar. For the last two months Mr. Woodward reminded everyone on the island not to forget their neighbors by printing weekly articles about them. While reading the articles, Dave's father was learning about the harsh, desert conditions trapped in between two mountain ranges. And about the low morale in camp.

"Hey!" he exclaimed to his son, Dave. "Russell's sister is mentioned in the paper today!"

"Is that so?" he hollered back. "What for?"

"Well," he moaned. "Not good. She's the one relating bad news. A mother died during childbirth." He loudly sighed. "Poor gal. Fortunately no one we know."

Dave moved into the woods, whistling and clicking his tongue. Layers of mud clung to his shoes. His rolled-up slacks were dampened from the persistent drizzle. He began to worry. He hadn't seen Russell's dog since early yesterday.

"I hear poor Mr. Woodward isn't still losing his subscribers," Dave's father resumed. "People don't feel comfortable he's printing these articles from Miss Tomiko. That and showing sympathy for our Japanese friends." He sighed in annoyance. "People are so ignorant, I swear! Our economy dropped nearly half since the evacuation!"

"I know, Dad," he moaned, in no mood to listen to another long speech about how many of the strawberry fields were rotting this year.

"People tend to forget who made this place manageable! They put their backs into it!"

Dave advanced into the woods. He continued with a desperate shouting and whistling, hoping to draw the stupid mutt from the bushes and trees. If he couldn't find his friend's dog, he would never forgive himself. He promised to take care of it until Russell returned home.

Then he stopped on top of a fresh growth of grass. "Oh Jesus!" he said.

The Beagle-Shepherd mix lay stiff on the ground. Its legs folded to his belly. Its eyes sealed. It looked like a fawn that had been starving for its mother's milk. Dave bent down and rested his hand on its neck, making sure the feeble animal was indeed deceased. He slowly shook his head, not knowing how to tell his friend. Russell loved that dog. He grew up with it, knowing Zasshu since a toddler. Maybe he should wait until his friend came back; when things would be better.

Removing his hand and exhaling regrettably, he muttered, "Couldn't you of at least waited until *after* the war?"

CHAPTER THREE

Early June

JIM lay in a distant state, trying to ignore the ticks that bit his skin. He rubbed his eyes with both palms as if to scrape out his frustrations. The idleness stabbed his mind, inflicting severe boredom on a maddening scale. His daily activities consisted of standing in line, eating three times a day, using the toilet right after, and staring at the light bulb in his barrack. He wanted to hit something. Or to break apart his bed made of straw. Or rip down the fence until his hands bled. If he ran beyond the fence and they shot him, he couldn't care less if he lived or died.

He threw a booklet across the room. Staring at the words awarded him a headache. Having nothing better to do, Jim had read and reread and reread this stupid booklet entitled *Questions and Answers for Evacuees*. It was designed to explain the function of Manzanar. They were allowed to organize committees so as long they weren't anti-American. They could place their belongings in storage, free of charge during the war. Weapons, short-wave radios, cameras, and Japanese books were considered contraband items. But most importantly, Manzanar *wasn't* a concentration camp; it was an "assembly center," administered by the newly formed government branch, the War Relocation Authority, or simply as the WRA.

Jim glanced at his two sisters lying on the same bed. Rose read *Little Women* to Bethany; her back resting against the wall; her left hand holding her head while she clutched the book in the other. Bethany lay flat; one arm folded across her chest; the other dangling over the edge. Both had their shoes off. Both exposing stained socks.

"Bethany," he asserted. "How many more times do you want that book read to you? You should know it by heart!"

She grimaced at him. "I like the book!"

"Just leave her alone," Rose groaned. "She's not doing anything to annoy you today."

Rose's stomach rolled outwardly; showing off her six month pregnancy. She wore oversized men's suspenders and checkered shirts because the donation store only had a few maternity dresses left after many other pregnant women scavenged through. Also, since her feet began to swell, and women shoes were scarce, she had been slipping into her husband's worn shoes. Feeling self conscious, she painted on lipstick and rouge everyday to flower out her femininity. Despite the daily compliments Tom gave her, she convinced herself that she was the most unattractive woman on the block. All she was missing was a clown hat and a big red nose!

"It's not the point," he replied. "She's in the fourth grade. She should be old enough to read it on her own."

"Maybe. But I enjoy reading to her. So just drop it."

He glanced around his barren environment, hating every goddamn thing about it. Vaulting from his bed, he declared, "I've got to go!"

Startled, Mrs. Yoshimura asked, "*Doko-e*?"

"Does it matter where?" he snapped, slamming the door behind him.

Instantly he covered his nose and mouth by pulling up his shirt. The windstorm tugged his body back and forth with the late afternoon sun warming his back. He pushed forward, heading toward an empty building near the mess hall. The only privacy he knew in this shitty place. The green buildings, dull and rickety, were cloned from one block to another. He chased the outlines of the buildings, counting them, memorizing the numbers like landmarks. Turn left after the fifth barrack. Turn right after the seventh barrack. Everyday he followed the same route to the mess hall. It unwelcomely became as familiar as home. Wooden power-line poles towered over each barrack. Sometimes a tree or shrubbery would add diversity to the landscape. Or sometimes an outsider's truck. Rows of trenches followed every block as if snakes hiding in the shadows. The trenches made a mismatched puzzle on the desert floor; dangerous for wanderers in the night. Still, he had to be careful even during the day because his vision was often blurred by yellowish-brown sand.

When Jim finally entered the vacant building, the dim light fed his sullen mood. He heard the wood creak, competing with the desert's grains that pounded against glass. The curtainless windows provided etchings of light. No one knew whether this building would be transformed as another administration office, or a school, or a place for entertainment. It just remained empty. Waiting like everyone else. He couldn't believe how everything, the construction, the community, and people's spirits stumbled into chaos.

Inspecting the spacious room that was four times as large as his barrack, a face moved out of obscurity.

"Hey," Russell said, "I thought I was only one who uses this place!"

Dumbfounded and disappointed, Jim stood motionless.

"Goin' crazy, huh?" Russell continued. "Yeah, me too." Staring out the set of windows, watching nothing but shields of wind and sand, he joked, "Whadda say we steal a truck and barrel the hell outta here? It'll be my treat. And if we get caught, all we'll do is claim insanity. It's definitely justified." Returning to look at Jim, he waited for acknowledgment. A reaction. A pulse even.

Frustrated by his hopeless silence, Russell stepped forward and tried something else. "I've got the latest edition of *Life* magazine. It's the victory battle of Midway. Interested?" He tapped the curled magazine on his own chest. "You realize the sooner it's over, the sooner we can go home!"

Although Jim didn't want to be here, he didn't want to go back, either. It was a graveyard of memories. He dreamt of how to escape them, to find a place where he could start his life with another beginning. Without John. Without his father. At times the pain was so stiff he felt as if he were mummified in a morgue.

Sighing, Russell persisted, "Wanna borrow it?"

Jim stared, debating his true motive. He couldn't understand why Russell kept this friendly facade. There were others he could befriend. Why him?

"It's too dark to read in here," he flatly replied.

Russell flashed an inspiring grin. "Not if you got a flashlight."

Extending the magazine to Jim, Russell waited until he cautiously accepted it. And Jim, so he wouldn't have to carry on conservation, began reading. Russell then leaned against a window and scratched his nose. He was a little uncertain how to ask, but his curiosity persevered. It was something his Winslow classmates had always wanted to know; although they lacked the courage to ask out right. Some questions were meant to be asked in private. And there they were. In seclusion. Having nowhere else to go.

"Can I ask you something personal?"

Jim peered at him. "It depends."

"Do you even like girls?"

He gawked at Russell as if he had just grown a third arm. "Yes. What the hell are you implying?"

Russell shrugged, looking down. "Well, no one's ever seen you with a girl."

He fidgeted while his cheeks blazed in embarrassment. Why would Russell even ask such a stupid question? "No one's seen me with sheep either, does that make me a shepherd?"

He grinned at the amusing correlation. "No."

"You had chickens back home. How do I know you weren't doing something funny in the coop?"

"Sorry, man," he chuckled. "I'm only asking."

"What the hell do you expect with that kind of question? And what about you? Do you like boys? I know you spent a long time in the locker room."

"Hey!" Russell barked. "Watch your mouth! I said I was sorry! You don't need to get smutty!"

Jim bit his lip until it grew numb. He had difficulty breathing. Russell lacked the maturity to understand. Life was more complex than just dealing with dances and girls. It also meant responsibilities and consequences. His father had taught him well on those points.

"I'm only going to say this once," he slowly began, unsure if he could really trust Russell, but he had to defend his reputation. "My brother, John . . ." he stopped. It had been four years since he said his brother's name out loud and it felt strange- like being lost at sea for a lifetime, and not knowing what to feel after rediscovering land. "John had dated Tomiko's sister. He lost his focus and got her into trouble. You know, in the family way. It's not worth it, Russell, I'm telling you. Until I'm much older and ready for marriage, I'm not concerned with dating. And that's only *if* I want to consider marriage."

Russell's anger faltered. He truly felt sorry for him. Anyone who intertwined that kind of logic to deny simple pleasures in life had serious problems.

"Okay," he replied. "I won't bring it up again."

THE few hours receded to suppertime, surrendering to the loud gong. The sand storm finally became fatigued, leaving behind gentler breezes. As the sun barely clung to the horizon, it still dropped its fire onto the desert's ground. Private Callis tugged on his tan uniform as he stood up to change shifts. Guarding the front gate was as exciting as watching cows take a dump. The small, square building, which resembled a goddamn pagoda, perched near the highway. Few vehicles passed in and out. Visitors who mostly drove down from Los Angeles, or truck drivers delivering packaged meals. Sometimes local farmers would come inside searching for laborers. He had been bored, goddamned bored ever since he was assigned to this godforsaken place. And it wasn't fair. All his friends were fighting for their country. And what in the hell was he doing? Babysitting a bunch of Japs. As far as he was concerned, all of them should have been deported on a volcanic island. Relieved that his shift was complete, he decided to take a stroll through camp.

RUSSELL swung his flashlight beam across the room, making sure that rattle snakes or scorpions hadn't managed to sneak in while they were still there. His neighbor had recently been bitten by a rattler when he reached for his boots underneath his cot. Fortunately the venom was treated in time, but he nearly lost his purple, swollen hand.

Abruptly the front door sprung open.

Jim and Russell jumped. An MP stood in the doorway; poised with his legs spread apart in an assertive manner; one foot in front of the other. His rifle pricked out from his back where it was tightly strapped on his shoulder.

"You boys shouldn't be in here!" he barked. "Where the hell did you get that flashlight? You know it's contraband!"

Russell felt the back of his neck singe like thin slices of pork on a pan. When his family arrived in camp, the man who searched through their things didn't mention whether his flashlight was considered illegal or not. Inhaling, he nervously responded, "I'm sorry, I didn't know."

"Lemme have a look."

He reluctantly walked to the soldier. He feared that any sudden movements would have been interrupted as either hostile or insubordinate. Keeping a four foot length, he extended his arm out, bearing his flashlight. Then glancing up, he recognized the soldier. It was him. He was the watchtower guard who shot at him. Becoming more alarmed, Russell stepped back a foot. His stomach muscles tightened. He knew he wasn't in a position to rationalize with an unreasonable ape.

Callis snatched the flashlight. He flickered the light directly into Russell's face, blinking as if he might have recognized him.

"It looks like it belongs to the military. Did you *steal* this, *boy*?"

Avoiding eye contact, he said, "No, sir. I had it since Boy Scouts. It has my troop number scratched at the bottom. With my initials, G. H."

Callis leaned forward, sharpening his lips. "Are you a cunning Jap? Do you think yer smarter than me? How do I know you just didn't scratch this yesterday?"

Russell thought before he answered. "Because the scratching is worn down."

"You *are* a cunning sonofabitch!" he retorted. "I'm gonna keep this and do an investigation. If yer truthful then you have nothin' to worry about. But if I find out yer up to somethin' no good, then I'll make sure you and yer people get the chair."

Russell wished the front of the building would collapse on top of the racist bastard. Or a sandstorm would suffocate him and abandon his body in the middle of the street for everyone to see. This soldier's existence made him ill.

Reclining backward, Callis twisted his attention to Jim. "What cha got in yer hand, Jap?"

Jim maintained calm, trying not to panic. He knew this soldier was on the prowl. "It's *Life* magazine, sir."

"Lemme see!" he ordered.

Jim cautiously handed it to him. Callis seized the object. He attentively explored the cover of the magazine; adoring it; caressing it while still holding the flashlight.

"I shoudda been there," he mumbled. "I would of made a difference there. I could of killed as many Nips as I needed to. Vengeance is mine, sayeth the Lord." He looked up. "Isn't that right? Americans need to revenge?"

Jim directly stared in his unsettling blue eyes. "We're Americans, too."

"Like hell you say!" he spat, hammering Jim on the forehead with the flashlight.

Jim tumbled sideways, falling to the floor. An immediate pain gashed throughout head. Warm droplets of blood trickled on his nose. Feeling dizzy, he remained on the ground, trying to resist the impulse to tear the rifle off the MP's shoulder and shoot him. Jim had never known what it took to hate until that moment.

"Bunch of yella heathens! Cowards!" the soldier bellowed. "Tell yer friends an' family that us Americans don't take no shit! You think Pearl Harbor is a victory? Pearl Harbor will be the biggest mistake you'll ever make!" He kicked Jim in the stomach. "Now, get the hell outta here!"

Russell instantly grabbed Jim by the shoulders and guided him out the door. Callis pushed both down the steps behind their backs. Landing on their stomachs, Jim felt his glasses fly off his face. Gasping for air, they quickly rose to their feet and attempted to run. Jim pressed his hand over his forehead to keep the blood from falling down. His sharp tears felt like they could gash open his cheeks; marking pain; enduring the humiliation.

"Let's go to your place," Jim muttered, wiping the blood off his nose with his sleeve. "I can't face my family right now. Not like this!"

Russell felt helpless. "Sure, Jim. We'll do whatever you want."

"And we can't tell them what happened. They're scared enough as it is."

Russell understood his concern; the same reason he hadn't told anyone about the shooting. He then realized they now shared something in common.

Mid June

"DID you sleep alright last night?" Russell asked, sitting down with his breakfast tray.

Hundreds of voices knocked about each other, scrambling up to the low ceiling, rivaling against the clinking of tin trays. The mess hall imitated the barracks with its bare ceiling, wooden floors, and bowl-like chandeliers; however it was twice the size, spreading only 40 feet by 100 feet. Rectangular picnic tables sat in line. Like everything else, they were assembled in a military-organized structure. The stench of sausages and hash browns embossed the room. The older generation had difficulty eating American meals, for they were used to rice, noodles, and seafood.

Jim answered, "I really didn't sleep."

Even without his glasses, which he never found since that day, Jim could somewhat see. He told his family that he fell in a ditch and hit his head on some loose lumber. He picked up his powdered milk, swirled it around, watching the tiny clumps spiral like a dust devil. How he missed his mother's home cooking. He yearned for fresh vegetables, fried dishes, boiled eggs, and soy sauce. This crap they were consuming denied genuine taste.

"You should of gotten orange juice," Russell suggested. "At least it's real."

"But it's watered down," he muttered.

Other Bainbridge boys gathered at the table, complaining and joking about the food. They came from all over the island: From Winslow to Battle Point to Port Madison and Port Blakely. Everyone ate apart from their families, migrating toward a perception of independence. They ignored their mothers' grievances concerning the breakage of family. For the first time in their lives they acted as kings, withdrawing further from their families and their traditions.

"The other day," one boasted, "I found a fingernail in my soup."

"Bullshit, Sam! I'm getting tired of your stories!"

"Really, Ikki? I'm getting tired of you!"

"Put a lid on it!" Russell snapped. "Can't a guy eat in misery without you two bickering?"

Sam flung his hands in the air, and declared, "I was just repeating what I heard- that's all! Just tryin' to add some excitement!"

Sam and Ikki were cousins who used most of their energies arguing. They looked nothing alike, making their genes defy the laws of nature. As far back as Russell could remember they constantly competed in every possible aspect. Grades. Sports, Jokes. Girls. Anything and everything.

Sam asked, "Russ, gonna join the wrestling team again when school starts?"

"I dunno. Maybe."

Russell let the glass slide down his fingers, bumping the table. A wave of milk spilt over, landing on his greasy hash browns. The last thing on his mind certainly didn't deal with wrestling.

Ikki stared at Sam across from the table, squinting and chewing. He leaned forward and said, "And where are we going to school, smart guy? In the backyard?"

"We already have a camp newspaper! There's a building for that! Why not a school? We gotta have a school."

"What we got and what we need are two different things, fat-head. What I need is my own room. What I got is you!"

"What I need is a car! What I got is you!" Sam rebutted.

Jim sighed, somewhat amused. They weren't exactly the key figures in proving higher intelligence. He watched Russell continue to bayonet his food, not eating. He noticed the lack of sleep began to exhaust Russell, making him more irritable and quiet. Russell had confided in him about the other two disturbances with that particular soldier. Jim was equally unnerved. He often fantasized about sneaking into one of the delivery trucks, hiding under a blanket and allowing the driver to take him outside of Manzanar. Once he reached Lone Pine, twelve miles away, he planned to wait at the train station. Don't look anyone directly in the eyes. Wear sunglasses to hide the obvious. Then at the station, he wouldn't have cared where it routed him. The idea was to get the hell out of there.

"Hey, Russ," Sam snickered, jabbing his elbow into Russell's arm. "Hey, here they come!"

Glancing at Sam, Russell turned to see who everyone else, except Jim, was staring at. Two Japanese nuns, with their black crane-like hats, strolled past them as though they were pigeons, carrying their trays of food with chopsticks lying on top. With the quick steps of their feet, the slight bobbing of their heads and their tiny delicate faces, they appeared very bizarre. The notion of Japanese nuns seemed as weird as lizards with feathers.

"*Ahiru*!" Sam whispered, and softly quacked like a duck. Some of the boys sniggered at his joke.

Russell ignored him. Following the nuns were orphaned children, varying between the ages of six and seventeen. While they paraded down the aisle in rows of two, from short to tall, each walked in disciplined form. They sat six tables down from Russell's group, usually occupying four tables at a time. The orphans arrived last month with more piling up through the weeks. There was one girl, about fifteen or sixteen, who attracted everyone's wandering eye. Her hair was pulled up at the sides and coiled on the top, leaving the back to succumb over her shoulders. Her pink lips and cheeks radiated under the dull lighting. The daintiness of her nose and mouth appeared like an artistic doll. Her white sweater gently lay over her well-blossomed chest. She often peeked down at them as she walked by, but displayed no reaction to their smiling upward at her. One of the Bainbridge boys even asked for her phone number. Most everyone laughed at the irony. No one had telephones in camp except the military and administration.

Russell continued to stare at the girl, watching the back of her skirt swing from side to side. He said, "I wonder who she is."

"She's an orphan," Sam replied. "She carries bad luck. They say her parents died of disease. She may be very pretty, but she's *warui*. I wouldn't go near her."

Ikki asserted, "That's because nobody wants to get near *you*! And how do you know about her, oh mighty Sam who holds such great wisdom?"

Annoyed, he defended, " 'Cause I asked one of the those orphans, wise guy!"

Russell again shifted his attention to Sam. Bothered that he would say such an ignorant remark regarding illnesses, he flatly said, "My mom had TB. Doesn't that make me bad luck?"

Startled, Sam blinked. "No, because your mom's still alive."

Throwing his fork at Sam, Ikki chided, "You're an idiot! Why would you say something that?"

Flinging the fork back at Ikki, he yelled, "Stop picking on me! You're getting on my last good nerve!"

"Or what? You'll do what?"

Russell flipped his tray over the table, knocking his milk down. The boys ducked as food exploded like a grenade splattering over their shirts and table.

"Goddamnit!" he roared, shooting straight up on his feet. "Am I going to make you two wear diapers? Or do you need a pacifier!"

The entire mess hall fainted into muteness. Jim was completely stunned. He never would have speculated that Russell could embrace such a temper. It reminded him of the only time when his father released his fury on John. John had acted dishonorably and received welts from their father's belt. Within a week, John killed himself.

Russell stomped away from everybody, abandoning his place. The orphan girl finally looked at him, grinning as he marched by her. He glanced at her as she sat down at her table. He heard his mother's voice trailing from behind, calling to him, insisting on knowing what had happened. As his footsteps boomed, people launched their gossiping. They needed to gossip. It was the only entertainment they were allowed to control. He opened the door and left his baffled mother in the dark. One way or another, he planned to flee this godforsaken desert. He would flee and return home to see why Maria neglected her promise.

RUSSELL wandered around the camp, trying to shave off his frustrations. His clothes absorbed his perspiration, making him stink similar to a wet dog. After the morning incident he, he needed to be alone to think. If he dealt with his mother, he would have to deal with her constant questions and criticism. Instead, he watched the three o'clock wind draft a twelve foot dust devil; a structure of a tornado. The brown funnel, near the highway yet beyond the columns of green barracks, almost appeared like smoke; like a dirty phantom of the Sierras. He tripped over an uneven spot on the ground, nearly losing his full balance. Swearing out loud, he searched the area to see if anyone was watching him. Only a handful of people roamed under the furious afternoon sun. The ground boiled, prying the heat to rise above his feet. Many stayed inside with the windows or doors opened for oxygen.

He then noticed a small group of teenage boys kicking a bottle down the blistering sand as they loudly spoke with a mixture of English and Japanese. They marched their worn shoes in a disorderly fashion as if defying discipline. Three out of the four had cigarettes loosely dangling in their mouths with their black hair slicked backwards. Their honey skin had been toasted in the Californian sun. The dark brown bottle clinked and rolled, clinked and rolled until one of them, who wore tattered army boots, harshly kicked it and sent it flying to the street light, crashing into pieces. Another mimicked a siren warning, cupping his hands and thrusting his head upward. Soon the others joined in by wailing high fluctuating pitches.

"Here come the Japs!" the one who broke the bottle shouted. "Look out boys! They're droppin' beer bottles! Don't walk barefooted 'cause you might cut your feet and bleed ta death! This means war!" He stopped walking and started imitating President Roosevelt. "We are- in grave danger. Pearl Harbor- though we don't own yet- was attacked! Though small in size- we know- it's not the size that counts- but how we use it. We are self righteous people. We deserve to win this shitty war! Whether hostilities exist outside of our God -blessed- nation or- exist within- we could use more! So help us God!"

The leader began walking again, following the others who had already turned around to walk backwards while they listened. The boys clapped and whistled, mocking a well-fed audience who cheered for a well-roasted speech. The leader began to fearlessly sing with the others loosely joining:

"My country tis of thee!
Sweet land of bigotry! Of thee I sing!
Land where my father's died!
Land where the gov'ment lied!
From every mountainside, let internment ring!"

Russell geared his aimless wandering to trail behind them without any intent other than to satisfy his curiosity. He regarded the teen's performance as an amusing masquerade. His absurdity imitated their country's absurdity. The existence of concentration camps were really disguised as "relocation" camps. Or "detention" centers. Democracy denied. Having their loyalty doubted and citizenships revoked. And doubting whether America even deserved their loyalty. Abruptly the gang halted, rotating to face him.

"Hey, *omono*, are you following us?" asserted the one who made the speech. His cigarette flopped like a seal on a beach when he spoke.

Embarrassed, Russell replied, "No."

"Seems to us you are."

"I'm just walking," he shrugged, somewhat glancing at the boy. "No crime in it."

"Where to?"

"Nowhere."

Peering at Russell, he insisted, "Did Shig's gang put you up to this?"

Russell crossed his arms and proclaimed, "I don't know them."

"Oh, really?" The youth also crossed his arms, staring directly at him. "Prove to us you don't know him, *omono-san.*"

Russell thought he was missing a screw. Plus, what they hell did *omono* mean?

"You have three seconds to defend yourself before we pound on you."

"What for?" Russell demanded.

"Two seconds."

"You're out of your mind!"

"One second."

"I don't know them! Who *is* Shig?"

"Too late," he smirked. "Pick a god and pray."

Russell's adrenaline pulsated a nervous strain through arms. "If you're gonna fight me, for whatever stupid reason, than you do it- alone! Not with your gang!"

The youth laughed, his cigarette falling out of his lips, shaking his finger at him. The others snickered, rattling their shoulders in muted humor. Russell felt as if he had just sat on a whoopi cushion.

"No," the boy began, "no, you don't know Shig. One of his gang would of tried to take all of us out! The smart thing would be to challenge one-on-one. Unless an idiot dies, he won't be cured, right?"

"You're out of your gourd!" Russell sputtered in irritation. Humiliated, he walked away while the boy continued to laugh.

"Hey . . . wait!" the boy managed to yell, trying to stop laughing. "Don't get so sore! I'm only joking! It's only a *jodan . . .* a *jodan*!"

Russell tried to ignore him. Quickly the youth jogged to his side.

"Hey, no harm done." He waited for Russell to say something. "Listen, I'm *Shig*."

Russell studied the boy who could be no older than seventeen. His broad mouth had cracked from the arid climate, yet, he seemed genuinely safe; hardly dangerous. He had a narrow forehead that showed-off his apple-shaped face and a smile that opened mischief.

"The name's Russell," he said, extending out his hand. Dizziness tingled inside his head. The sun gnawed on his exposed skin and he wanted to sit in the shade. His hunger faded as the heat forced him to sweat more and more. He neglected eating lunch as well as breakfast that day, now regretting it. His thirst fiercely craved for another stop at one of the water pumps.

"*Konichi-wa,* Russell-san!" he greeted, shaking his hand. "We're from San Pedro. How about you?"

"Bainbridge Island. Next to Seattle.

"Holy shit!" he exclaimed. "That's a helluva way from here!"

"Yeah." Russell paused, feeling weak. "By the way, what does *omono* mean?"

Shig gaped at him, astounded. “You don’t know what it means?”

“No,” he replied.

Snickering, Shig rolled his tongue over his salty lips. “What kind of Jap are you?”

Irritated, hating the ignorant expression even in mockery, Russell asserted, “First of all, I’m an American and I don’t like being referred as a *Jap*! And you should know better! Second, I only know basic Japanese.”

Shig’s burly smile dimmed, withdrawing into seriousness. “We’re all American, *omono*. I don’t mean no harm by it.” He inspected Russell, outlining his motive. “*Omono* is slang for wise guy. Come on! Met the rest of my gang! We call ourselves the *Yogores*!”

Russell figured that Shig’s gang would hardly be classified as “roughneck gangsters,” yet he considered the irony humorous. For one thing, they were too casual and clean-cut. More like a duplication of Mickey Roonies than gruff thugs, with the exclusion of Shig who wore army boots. Besides, when he imagined gangsters, Humphrey Bogart and James Cagney entered his mind. In fact, so did the FBI.

He followed Shig where the other three stood in front of a dried spiny tree.

“This is Bruce.”

He had a wide face and elephant ears. Russell shook his hand.

“This is Ralph.”

His face was young, as if a toddler with his eyes remaining close to his short nose. Russell also shook his hand.

“And this loser here is Hanabusa, but we call him Hank.”

“Hello,” Hank said, jiggling Russell’s hand. His thick black hair wildly soared above his head while his glasses flashed in the sun. His mannerisms seemed more subtle than the others, displaying no smile and averting direct eye contact.

“So,” Shig said, “What brings you to the Sierras? On vacation?”

Russell chuckled. “If so, then it’s the longest damned vacation I’ve been on!”

“How do you like the service? We hired armed guards to keep out trouble makers.”

“They’re real jewels. Couldn’t of asked for a better prison system.”

“Thank you, thank you!” he bowed, swooping his right arm to his stomach like a circus performer. “We thought the watchtowers and machine guns would add an extra-homey feeling. All my idea! I thought about hiring the Gestapo, but who really wants to hire the Gestapo? Then I thought- the military’s the military. And since General DeWitt is already acting like Hitler, all I had to do was pay off the president. Easy money,” he winked.

Russell placed his hand to his forehead, squinting, trying to squeeze out the dizziness. The burning of his sweaty skin refused to cease and he felt awfully nauseous. He heard about people catching heat stroke.

“Hey,” Shig said. “Are you alright?”

“Not sure.”

He studied Russell. “I think we need to get you inside.”

Russell stepped forward, then blacked out. The boys watched him collapse on his backside, somewhat surprised. Sand clung to his sticky body as the wind and grit hustled over him.

Bruce said, "That can't be a good thing."

CHAPTER FOUR

Mid June

JIM ambled around the cluttered store, picking up used clothes, used magazines and books, and other out-of-date items. He wanted to find a gift for Russell; a book perhaps while he rested in bed for the remainder of the week. Three months in camp and Russell was bedridden for a second time. The store proved to be another transformed barrack: a makeshift thrift shop, like a mangy three-legged dog on the side of the road. Like everything else; rehabilitated, misshaped in the structure of war, and smelly. Most items in the store were donated from nearby townspeople and other white people who felt sorry for them, endorsing their Christian duties, relieving their guilty conscience. And there were so many ragged black Bibles stacked on a square table.

He grazed over the magazine pile, sifting through recent *Reader's Digest* and *Life* subscriptions. He was foraging for information about the war. With only a handful of radios and outside newspapers, it was difficult to know what was happening regularly in Europe and the Pacific. Their local newspaper included brief news about the world, but focused mostly on insignificant camp events; marriage and birth announcements, restricted politics, goals and achievements of the community. The camp director made certain nothing more was mentioned. To rally up the "Nips" would endanger his disposition.

Jim came across a *Life* magazine with an attractive woman on the front cover, smiling, her legs crossed and hands lying in her lap, wearing an engagement ring. Beside her, in a frame, was a photographed soldier. In between the woman and the photograph laid a human skull. Squinting, still without his glasses, he could barely read the bottom inscription which stated, "G.I. sends trophy home to sweetheart of a Japanese skull." Disgusted, Jim flipped the large magazine over. Who in their right mind would ship a human skull as a gift?

"What happened to your glasses?"

Startled, he looked up. Tomiko stood near him, her hair growing longer, and now pulled back by a red bandana. Her white blouse was yellowed from the sand, wrinkled, and flaunted her slender neck. Her slacks tightly squeezed her curvy thighs, revealing three large buttons. Underneath her sweat eluded a sweet perfume. Jim stepped backward and ducked from direct eye contact. Each day he noticed Tomiko standing at the latrine line in the morning, wanting to speak to her, yet never knowing what to say. Not only that, but one evening in the showers, as he glanced through a crack in the wall of the women's section, he saw her nude. Even though there were frequent complaints about men peeping through the windows, nothing was done about it. Sometimes women would run outside and smack the men with wet towels. But since that night, he consumed her image on a daily basis.

"I lost my others. I do have another set on order. Should be in within a month."

He shuffled the magazines. Slumping forward, he tried to think of something else to calm him. Jim's heart continued to strike at his chest like a boxer, faster and harder. His skin became more heated and his mind dehydrated any clever thoughts, leaving his tongue bloated. He spoke like a six year old. He couldn't understand why his mind and body reacted this way. It provided no logic. Usually his composure carried stability, and yet, he felt like an idiot.

Discouragement subdued her smile, and she looked away. She couldn't understand why Jim showed no interest. Because he was so different, she was intrigued. His stern silence, his intelligence, and especially his extreme loneliness. She had hoped to lift his sadness, cutting out his isolation. Apparently he thought she was a waste of his time. Or maybe the rumors about him not liking girls were true.

"See you around," she said.

"Sure."

Jim admired her stroll as she turned and moved to the clothing section. He should have said more. Relief and disappointment swirled in his gut. He should have said a lot more. Languishing over his indecision, he withdrew to what he felt most comfortable with: books. Most of the books proved insignificant; popularized novels about romance or murder mysteries; many at least twenty years old. Sifting through the tattered piles, he found a more recent novel, *Of Mice and Men*. He had read it a few years ago and it possessed him. Although Jim liked the unusual relationships linked by loneliness, it was Steinbeck's depressing story that nourished him. The simple tragedy about ordinary migrant workers who had nothing in common but the air they breathed. The first time he finished it, the ending shocked him, severing his fear and pain in two. Who had the right to take life and under what circumstances? Was death truly cruel or justified mercy? Grabbing the book, he decided this would be the one.

Rattling his pocket, the dimes and quarters chimed in discord. It was more than enough. He began to feel more normal. Walking to the front counter, he glanced at Tomiko again, exploring her dainty posture. When she glanced at him, he coughed and turned elsewhere. Idiot, he thought again. Don't be such a coward. After he paid for the book, he drifted toward Tomiko, swaying through the tables. Standing beside her, he held his breath. She looked up at him.

Beaming, she said, "Is there something you want to say?"

"Ah," he choked. He stared at her neck, trying to avoid staring at her breasts. Clearing his throat, he continued, "My sister, younger sister- is putting on a recital. Flute recital this Saturday. At the Presbyterian Church." Nervously grinning and shaking his head, "She's really not that good, to be honest. But, if you would like to see, I mean hear it anyway, I'll be there. I have to be there."

She smiled. "Are you asking me out?"

Finally looking at her, he said with a frown, "I think I am."

RUSSELL examined the book as if he were examining a rotting carcass. The cover had a coffee stain and a cigarette burn. The picture exposed two skeleton trees, and two shadows of men walking down an unpaved path. Looking up at Jim, who seemed pleased in his solemn manner, Russell bled a smile. If he didn't have to complete a book report for a grade, he didn't see the purpose of reading, unless it was a comic book like Superman, Buck Rogers, The Batman, or Johnny Law. Nevertheless, he appreciated the thought. Especially coming from someone like Jim.

"Thanks," he said. "You didn't have to get me anything, you know."

Jim half-smiled. "Well, I knew you would be bored out of your mind, so I figured this will help ease your pain."

Russell heard his twin cousins, Joe and George, playing outside through the open windows. Their hyper voices overlapped the mild whistling of the wind. They pretended to be soldiers, one an American, the other a Nazi, rotating their roles in an endless cycle. His mother and brother were rarely home. Mrs. Hamaguchi had been volunteering at the hospital's nursery, or organizing an *Issei's* women's committee, or helping the elderly. Sometimes Gertrude would assist when she wasn't overpowered by her depression. And Meito bounced back and forth from the mess hall to clearing land on the south side of camp and back to the mess hall. When he returned at night, his exhaustion immediately drowned him into sleep. The occasional moments Russell saw them would be during the meals and at bedtime.

Flipping through the pages, he remarked, "I've never read this book. Is it any good?"

"The ending will shock you."

"That's what I need. A shock in my system!"

"After throwing that fit in the mess hall, you've already shocked everybody else's system."

Russell snorted out a chuckle, agreeing without a doubt.

Jim walked to one of the windows; next to a hand-crafted stack of shelves with Japanese ornaments. New white lace curtains hung from each window like pheasants after the hunt; wings spread; light jabbing through the gaps. He removed a handkerchief to wipe the sweat from his forehead. God, how he hated this intense heat!

Plucking the end of the drapes, he asked, "Where did you get these curtains?"

Russell leaned over his cot, reaching underneath his bed. He stopped, and winked. Lifting a thick catalog, he extended it towards Jim.

"*Sears Roebuck*," Russell bragged. "The summer issue."

Stunned, he took it. "How did you get a recent copy?"

"Don't tell the FBI.," he began, playfully lowering his voice, "but we smuggled it in!"

Jim knew his mother would love to check over a fresh catalog. "When your family's done, can we borrow it?"

"Borrow it now," he shrugged. "Just bring it back by the end of the week."

He slowly nodded. "Thanks. I'll do that." He again wiped his dripping face. Looking up at Russell, he finally asked the question he had been meaning to ask. "I'm curious," he began, attempting to swallow in order to lubricate his parched throat, "that time we played cards on the train, why did you choose me? Don't you have other *Nisei* friends?"

Russell achingly sighed, closing his eyes. Those few days on the train were one of the worst memories he harbored. Not that anything really happened. It was what the journey signified: being ripped out of one's home, hemorrhaging from the heart, and then thrust into the unknown like raw meat into a lion's den. It was the unknown that he hated. That unknown was just as excruciating as any other experience he had since being dumped inside this shit hole.

Opening his eyes, he answered with a hollow tone, "Because you rarely talk. And I didn't feel like talking to anyone."

Jim half smiled. "Listen, I'm going to take a shower. I'll be back later on tonight when it's cooler."

Russell stared up, completely shocked. "Really? First a gift, later on more company," he paused to raise a brow. "Are we friends?"

"Well now, I wouldn't get carried away."

"Wow. I didn't know you had a sense of humor."

"I don't," he grinned.

Heading to the side door, Jim waved and slipped out. As soon as the door shut, a truck reverberated on the street with its gears grinding. The truck yielded beside Russell's barrack; trembling; humming. A door squeaked open, then shut. The gears again shifted and rumbled forward. Russell eased from his bed, relocating to his window, seeing a 1919 Ford car cough up dust under its tires. He strained to see who was dropped off. All he spotted was a moving shadow jogging away from the wind and dust. It halted. Russell moved to another window and observed a man, with his head bent, hiding under a dark hat. The slope of his chin bore prickles, revealing that he had not shaved in a couple of days.

Russell said, "Someone's out there."

"Who is it?" Gertrude asked, pushing aside the hanging blanket from her side of the room. Strings of her hair pried from her uneven loop tied by a scarf. Bubbles of sweat glistened on her forehead. Her flowered dress hung around her once chubby hips. She had lost weight, dwindling down two sizes.

"I don't know," he replied.

Still feeling weak, his legs wobbled as he shuffled to the door. When he opened it, the man lifted his head.

"Papa!" Russell shouted.

Mr. Hamaguchi glanced down. He couldn't liberate a pleasing smile. Russell teetered down the stairs to embrace his father; almost losing his balance. Relief and joy overwhelmed him. His father only patted him on the shoulder.

"Papa, why didn't you tell us they released you?" he asked, stepping backward.

Mr. Hamaguchi's voice had weakened when he spoke. "*I did write. I wrote three weeks ago. I waited two hours at the front gate, and no one arrived.*"

Puzzled, and feeling a bit guilty, he said, "We didn't get the letter, Papa."

Joe and George emerged from underneath the barrack, their dusty bodies appearing like gingerbread boys dipped in gritty-yellow flour. They ran to their grandfather and clutched at his waist. Gertrude surfaced at the door frame, astonished.

Welcoming him, she exclaimed, "*Papa-san! Yoku irasshaimashita Papa-san*!"

Stroking his two grandsons' backs, he bowed his head, blinking away the swelling tears. The three and a half months in Montana ripped at his remaining youth, leaving it to bleed in a ditch. His imprisonment devoured his dreams as he waited for a mock trial to scrutinize his loyalty, forcing him to age twice as fast. More grey hairs outlined his despair. Without his store, his strawberry farm, or his home, his destiny as a father and husband dissolved like sugar lumps in hot tea. It didn't matter anymore. He no longer held worth.

Early July

THE military guards and internal police patrolled the camp as if walking barefooted in a slippery ravine. Rumors of rebellion wondered around. Fourth of July touched the evening sun with a cynical glance over the mountains. To the north, fireworks from the town of Independence quietly shrieked and mocked its name. To the south, Lone Pine could not be heard since the distance was greater; but nearby farmers released their celebration, cracking color in the dim sky.

The Hamaguchis and Yoshimuras gathered to watch the fireworks beyond the compound. Children lit the neighborhood with flaring sparks; galloping down the unpaved streets; tracing the darkness, laughing and ignoring the tensed adults. Some chased tumbleweeds between the trash cans and alleyways. Chains of people linked up the street; sitting or standing beside the two rows of green barracks. Other blocks dwindled within the dusk, evaporating into the air after the day's smoldering heat. The women united to the right side while the men assembled to the left. They spoke of nostalgia as if it were a forgotten art form that descended from an ancient century. Their words lingered like incense, honoring pleasant memories.

Russell ached in silence. Holidays normally brought excitement. The towns celebrated as if Manzanar didn't exist. Perhaps that was the best course, leaving them in peace. Although their denial meant the denial of genuine freedom. Wishing he were elsewhere, wishing he could sit on shore with Maria, he looked past the barracks to stare at the highway. It was profanely close. He could almost sip the gasoline from the vehicles that sailed by. A truck, hauling a group of whooping teenagers, had the radio blaring. Swing music fueled his body. God, how he missed it! How he missed *having* a radio! Turning back around, he twirled a miniature American flag between his fingers. If only they could acknowledge him as an American.

"That's the real problem," Tom said, folding his arms and leaning on one leg. He resumed the conversation with Meito; his voice droning like a fly's hum. Russell barely listened; not really giving a damn. "It's too dry out here, Meito. If we had fireworks, it might catch the barracks on fire. Wouldn't that be a misfortune?"

Meito snickered. "Right. Because we have so much to lose here."

Tom stood by Meito and Osamu, yet having his back turned on Jim. He grew a mustache, struggling to appear more distinguished. Anchoring a job in the administration building, Tom operated as a liaison between the *Issei* and *Nisei*, attempting to heal personal and political differences. Jim had told him he thought his job was a farce because the division between the two generations could not be united. Tom disagreed.

Mr. Hamaguchi sat in a handcrafted chair. In his right hand he clung to a Pepsi bottle with homemade *saki* simmering inside. He refused to groom himself that day, allowing his uncombed hair to mingle in the wild wind, and a rough face to soak the sand. Mrs. Hamaguchi endured the embarrassment. Unclean, uncouth, a laggard in a chair, he turned out to be a slob. With an illegal still hiding in their barrack, stinking the quarters like a skunk, gossip of his alcoholic nature brewed throughout the block. She could no longer look at her husband without tasting resentment.

Jim kept his guard on the *Nisei* and *Kibei* men wearing a white band, attached on their left arms, with the initials IP ridiculously stamped on like a badge. Even though they worked with the military, upholding an abstract ideal of honor as the internal police, they could never be in charge. They were nothing more than lackeys for both the military and the administration. The captain of the police station was white, for Christ's sake! As all the men in true authority were *lily white!* Jim would rather be crucified then lower his principles to accommodate the government's superficiality.

Tom continued, "I did manage to get in the sparklers, though. I knew the kids would love it!"

Joe and George, wearing shorts and jackets, chased Bethany in the street with the sparkling sticks. She pretended to be afraid as the boys laughed at her short screams. Her hair matured at a longer length, bracing over her shoulders. Little two-year old Ruth, her black curls bouncing like popcorn, waddled to catch up with the boys, giggling when she was able to touch them. The women of both families cradled their time by comparing their children. How smart and attractive they were. How talented and obedient they were.

Russell finally said out loud, "It doesn't feel like the Fourth."

Meito twitched the corner of his mouth and sighed. Cramping his brows together, he replied, "We should of organized a parade. If we're still here next year, that's what we need to do."

"*Ah, so desu-ka?*" Mr. Hamaguchi scoffed.

Surprised by his father's pessimistic remark, Meito asked, "*You do not believe so?*"

"*It does not matter what I believe! It matters only what they believe!*"

"*It does matter, Papa. Even a little bit.*"

"*I said it does not matter,*" he mumbled.

Osamu crossed his arms. His broad face and modest cheek bones sprouted wrinkles from the hot sun. In his mid-twenties, he looked older. His quiet temperament rarely announced his presence in a room. Nodding his head, he encouraged, "Things will get better. They certainly can't get any worse."

Mr. Hamaguchi bent his bottle to his mouth and swallowed. Rolling his tongue over his lips, he briefly closed his glassy eyes and stood up. Grunting, he shuffled back into the barrack, hiding from the world.

Russell glanced at his father, ashamed as neighbors stared at the stumbling man; leaning and whispering to each other. How could his father degrade himself like that? Especially in front of everyone they knew! When, or if they returned to Winslow, the respect he cultivated would be spoiled. Who wanted to have his hair cut or laundry washed from someone whose breath stunk of *saki*?

"Don't worry, Goro," Meito said, Russell's shoulder. "This is temporary. He's going through a lot. Give him time."

Russell looked at his older brother; uncertain. His father's condition scared him. It worsened as the two weeks aged. He babbled about nothing. About his boyhood. His many uncles. His dog that drowned in the sea. That Meito really wasn't his son. Stories that did not connect. Stories that crisscrossed and overlapped people and dates. If they were abandoned in this shit hole for years to come, the years might burn their father like a roasted pig in the grill.

"Hey, Jim," Russell announced. "Wanna go over to Ikki and Sam's place? Play checkers or something?"

Jim sighed, not really in the mood. Opening his mouth to reply, he hesitated. "Wait a minute. Didn't you have a flag up earlier?"

"Yeah, sure enough! Someone took it. In between lunch."

He chuckled. "That's strange. Who would want to steal the American flag? It's not like we need it! Celebrating freedom behind a fence? What's wrong with this goddamn picture?"

Tom snapped, "Watch your mouth, Jim! If the FBI got wind of your opinions they might do worse to you."

"Like what? Throw me in a prison camp in the middle of a goddamn desert?"

Feeling uneasy about where the argument could drift off to, Osamu interrupted, "Did anyone see who took the flag?"

"Nope," Russell answered, also concerned about changing the subject. Despite what anyone might truly feel under their skins, it was best not to say anything obscene against the government. "In broad daylight and everyone's blind. Must be the wind 'cause apparently no one saw a damn thing."

Jim detached a smile. "Maybe *The Shadow* did it."

"Yeah! Who knows what evil lurks in the hearts of man?"

Tapping his temple, he echoed, "*The Shadow* knows."

Meito grinned, and said, "I wish he'd tell me! I want my damn flag back!"

Russell snickered. Slipping his hand into his pocket, he glanced down the street. At the curve of his eye he saw a group of men marching. He looked again. Katsuji steered the trail, having five followers. In his right arm, he carried an American flag balled up like a basketball. Russell poked his brother. "What in the world is going on?"

Meito turned. Squinting at the group, he mumbled, "Now what the hell does he want?"

The men, who Russell recognized as workers from his mess hall, were all *Kibei.* Their English was not much better than his Japanese. As they passed by the children, they stopped directly in front of Meito. Katsuji's sharp features became rigid as steel. His slender face built a beak-like nose, trimmed mouth, narrow brows. Slinging the flag on the ground, next to Meito, he leered. The children ceased playing and ogled at these men. The women yielded their chattering. Staring. Worrying.

Katsuji barked, "Oy! You drop frag! Pick up!"

Meito ground his teeth, breathing unevenly. The muscles in his arms coiled like a rattler ready to strike. Glaring at him, he asserted, "Is *that* my flag, Katsuji?"

He didn't respond, but continued to leer. Pointing down to the flag, he again demanded, "Pick up frag!" He watched Meito stand, testing his control. Then converting to Japanese, he inquired, "*What is wrong with you, Meito-san? Are you not a good American boy? Why do you not pick up the American flag?*"

Meito spat with a sting on his tongue, "Go to hell!"

Katsuji's grin shriveled. He stuck his hand in his pocket and removed a box of matches. Rattling it, he winked at Meito. Both men stared at each other, waiting to see who would execute the first action; not believing either of them had the moxie. Everyone watched in grim awe. The shrilling and popping of firecrackers resumed to strike the horizon. The colors that surrounded the camp stained the dusky sky like wounds, bleeding downward.

Russell scanned the area for the police. The internal police and MPs were now conveniently absent from view, and the guard in the watchtower wasn't paying any attention. Returning his attention to Katsuji, he examined the box and the flag.

Russell exclaimed, "If you burn the flag, you'll go to jail!"

Meito pulled his younger brother aside, and he ordered, "Stay out of it, Goro! It doesn't concern you!"

Angered, Russell shoved his brother. Meito raised his palm, giving him a silent warning. Russell quietly obeyed; but blinked furiously.

Replacing his stance, Meito said, "Do it! Do it, you ungrateful bastard!"

Stunned that Meito would challenge him, Katsuji opened the box and lit the match. Leering as if to say this was his last chance, he picked up the flag with his boot. The match's smoke lingered in the chilly air; defiant and absurd. Suddenly Katsuji's fire ignited the flag and he dropped it to the ground. Some of the spectators gasped and criticized, yet no one stopped him. Smirking at Meito, he pitched the box directly into the fire. Seconds later, it erupted. A large flame roared, and sulfur corrupted the air with a powerful stench. Meito jumped back and called Katsuji a damned fool. One of the spectators shouted in Japanese, "*Hi! Hi!*" while some of the women cried out. The children ran to their mothers, hugging at their waists.

The watchguard finally ripped his attention from the sky. Aiming his bayonet toward the raging flag, people scattered like guppies. Katsuji and his men scurried off, laughing and mocking. Ignoring the nervous guard, Russell swiftly threw sand over the orange flame. Soon Meito and Osamu joined, subduing the fire.

Jim shook his head. It was only a matter of time before something more serious would transpire. Two military police and three internal police ran down the street toward their circle. Recognizing one of the MPs, Jim sunk his head and slowly headed to his barrack.

Callis stared at the charred American flag, completely horrified. "What the hell just happened?" he demanded. "Are you Japs crazy?"

Russell looked up. Panicking, he fell back. There had to have been about sixty military police throughout the camp, why did he continue to encounter the same one? Did someone up above have a warped sense of humor or what? Callis' chiseled features tightened when he recognized Russell. Grabbing at his shirt, the muscular soldier tugged him upward. Despite Callis' height, Russell was more robust. Flipping his hands above his shoulders, as though surrendering, Russell did not dare look Callis directly in the eye.

"Did jew do this? Huh? Yellow heathen!"

"I would never do something like this!

"I think ya did."

Callis bulldozed him backward between two trash barrels. Russell tripped, crashing to the ground. He quickly covered his head with his arms for protection as the barrels tumbled on top of him. His mother cried out "No!" while everyone crippled in disgust and shock. Osamu grabbed Meito's sleeve, propelling his weight against his brother-in-law's chest, preventing Meito from hitting the MP.

"It wasn't him!" Meito cried out. "There's witnesses who can testify to that!"

Callis squinted. "Then who in the hell did?"

Russell pushed the barrels aside, and painfully rose to his feet. His hands shook. He heaved for breath. His cheeks flushed from fear and rage. How he wanted to cram the asshole's head in a headlock and grind his belly so far in the sand that his back would snap in two! Assault him in front of everyone; especially his mother!

Callis stomped to Meito. Glaring down at him, he insisted, "Who the hell did, I said!"

Russell stared at his brother, wondering if he would actually expose Katsuji. They were already accusing Meito of being a spy, associating him with other *Nisei* who worked for the government. They were also convinced that

Meito allowed the white drivers to sell their food to the black market. Informing on them would only encourage their motives and make his life a lot more difficult.

Meito divided his lips, hesitated for minute, and at last replied, “I don’t know who he is. It’s too dark out here to see anything.”

Callis leaned into his face. “I don’t believe you. You Japs cover up for each other. You stick together like flies on shit. I could arrest you now for withholding information.” Pointing to Russell, he yipped, “You, too! Yer already in enough trouble! I remember *you*!”

“Callis!” The other MP interjected. He appeared younger behind his freckles. “If this guy doesn’t know, then he doesn’t know! Not everything’s a conspiracy!”

He yelled, “They desecrated our flag, goddamnit! What the hell is wrong with you? Are ya turning yella, too?”

The young man stiffened his back. “Losing your temper and beating on these people isn’t going to help! We’ll do a proper investigation, by the book, and get to the bottom of this!”

“They don’t go by the book! How do you justify that, *Palmer*?”

Walking to Callis, and forcing him to move apart from Meito with the palm of his hand, he simply said, “There are children present. How is violence going to justify their faith in the system? We’ll find this guy who burned our flag. We’ll find him- just- calm down first.”

Callis shifted his stance, flexing his shoulders like a boxer in a ring. Snorting, he shook his head and then sniggered, “Boy-oh-boy! You’ve got yer priorities all messed up! These Nips should be boiled for what they did at Pearl Harbor! Sneaky little bastards!”

Lowering his voice, Palmer contended, “I don’t blame your German ancestry for the war! So don’t blame these people for theirs!”

Shocked that Palmer had brought it up, he dragged a step back. Although he didn’t saying anything, he lipped the words, “Fuck you,” and walked toward the front gates a few blocks away.

Palmer held his breath and counted to five, resting his hands on his hips. He surveyed the area; watching the people watching him. He smiled weakly, trying to hold onto what trust they had left. Turning around, he swept his arms over his head and shouted to the watchguard, “We got it under control, Murphy! Put down your rifle!” When the watchguard complied, he then walked to Russell and gently rested his palm onto Russell’s shoulder. He asked, “Are you alright, son?”

As the soldier stood beside him, Russell realized that this MP was only an inch taller than himself. His head spun from the fury that had knocked the wind out of him. Embarrassed that all eyes were on him, and angry that his family watched him be victimized by that brute, he wasn’t sure how to discern what just happened. Plus, this sympathy that Palmer displayed was almost unfamiliar. He remained amazed by the control Palmer seemed to have over Callis. And relieved. Rubbing his eyes, he inhaled a few short breaths to recuperate.

"I'll live."

Removing his hand to scratch his chin, Palmer replied, "Tough bird, eh? What's your name?"

"Russell, sir."

One of the *Nisei* police asked, "What do you want to do with the flag, sir?"

He chewed on his lower lip. "How hot is it? Can you touch it?"

"Yeah, it's pretty much cooled down. Take it for evidence, then?"

"That's what I'd do." Returning to Russell, he carefully studied him. "Did you see who did it?"

Russell looked at his brother who appeared calmer, and then looked at his mother who wiped her tears from her face, refusing to sob out loud. Sadaye kept her mouth covered, shaking her head and likewise masking her tears. Rose circled her swollen belly with her hands as if tracing an invisible armor for her unborn child. Gertrude hovered over her sons, guiding them inside the flimsy security of the barrack. Everyone thought the same thing: How could someone burden oneself with such hatred?

"No," Russell finally answered. "It was hard to see much of anything."

"Are you sure? You know, I can't help you if you don't help me, Russell. That's just the plain facts of life."

He lingered in silence. He would love to spill the beans, and yet he understood that turning into a stool pigeon would harbor stronger consequences. For himself. For his entire family.

Palmer tilted his head, patiently waiting. "Was it Saburo Maruki?" He paused, struggling to investigate Russell's expressions in the dim light. "Choichi Okamtoto? Katsuji Sakata?" Russell glanced up. Eager, Palmer saw recognition. He lowered his voice and repeated, "Was it Katsuji?"

Russell blinked. "There were five or six men, and it was too dark. I couldn't see any of them, so I couldn't say."

Palmer sighed in pure frustration and readjusted his helmet. "If we don't catch this guy, he'll do more harm. I'm just trying to keep this camp peaceful. I'm not your enemy, Russell."

"But I'm yours," he bitterly began, "otherwise we wouldn't be here!"

A genuine shroud of regret rustled over Palmer's face. "If war made sense, then I would be out of a job, son."

CHAPTER FIVE

Mid July

THE first pond was designed at one of the mess halls so people, while waiting endlessly in line, had at least something to admire. Thus, Tom decided to build a pond for his mother-in-law, and bought seeds so she could at last plant a garden. After that, two of Yoshimura's neighbors had decided to do the same. Then, like chicken pox, everyone in camp caught the epidemic.

On some level everyone had become accustomed to their new life. They grew accustomed to the rattlesnakes and scorpions by looking in their shoes and dresser drawers first before poking their flesh inside dark holes. They accustomed to the grit that imposed itself inside their cluttered homes and in their meals. They even became accustomed to water tasting like rusty metal. That week, however, a hundred laborers, both men and women, returned from Idaho after harvesting potatoes. With some money in their pockets and blisters on their hands, for two months they lived in freedom; even if temporary. Despite their additional wrinkles, scars, and aching muscles, it was better than coughing out sand and wishing they were elsewhere.

Now they would have to learn to readapt again.

* * *

RUSSELL studied the ivory envelope from New Jersey. The foreign letter came from a Jerry Roth whose neatly printed handwriting was addressed to a Miss Sadie Hamaguchi. He frowned. Jerry? Who in the hell was Jerry from New Jersey? Glancing around the newly sheet-rocked post office, a musty odor combined with human sweat and pinewood, he fought to think who Jerry might be. The woman behind the long counter, perhaps in her early twenties, stared at him; perhaps wondering why he continued to stand in the same spot. The clock in the back of her ticked as if wasting time. A line trailed behind him, waiting forty-five minutes instead of the full two-three hours time. The lunch hour was nearly over and she was the only worker stranded in the mid heat. Her slim eyes seemed dull; bored. A rattling fan blew from the side of her short neck, forcing her hair to stick to her cheek, waving like a spider's web flapping in the wind.

He looked up at her. "I suppose you don't know a Jerry Roth from New Jersey."

She blinked, hardly amused. "I don't get paid enough to know. Or even care to."

He grinned and walked outside, passing by the line of sweaty people, gripping his clammy hands around the few envelopes. Jerry. The name sounded familiar. Then it struck him. Jerry from the evacuation! The National Guard. Russell stopped. He squinted at the ivory envelope again. If his mother knew a white man was writing to one of her daughters she would collapse on the floor, beseeching mercy from her ancestors. So for the sake of protecting Sadaye, he walked under a barrack's shade and slit through the envelope.

My Dear Sweet Sadie,
I'm glad to hear from you. It's been two weeks. There's really not much going on this side of the country, just the usual stuff. We've been practicing and practicing for the unexpected. You never know, you know. I'm glad to hear you're doing fine under the circumstances. Maybe someday I'll get to visit. Maybe some day you'll get to leave. Sorry if the letter is so short. I'm stuck with guard duty this week. I miss your smiles. I never met anyone as graceful as you. Please continue to write. Until then - Jerry.

Russell refolded the letter. She should know better than this. Instead of meeting his friends at Sam and Ikki's barrack, as planned after he retrieved the mail, he strode halfway across the camp to the hospital where Sadaye resumed her shift. The two-mile walk exhausted his throat, compelling his tongue to feel like sandpaper. He trudged up the steps and into the building, begging for water. Another nurse quickly aided his request, guiding him to an empty bed where he sat and perspired. He felt dog-tired and was inclined to sleep. The hospital was half full; usually elderly people whose bodies withered from the heat or food poisoning. The young nurse, in a white apron and cap, returned with a warm glass. He guzzled it down anyway.

Gasping and wiping his chin, he asked, "Where's Sadaye?"

The nurse lowered her trimmed brows. He thought she looked pretty with her smooth complexion.

She asked, "Are you one of her brothers?"

"Yes!" he wheezed. "I need to talk to her. It's important."

She abandoned him as her bulky shoes boomed on the wooden floor. Russell felt uncomfortable. He hated hospitals. He hated the smells of alcohol, urine, and pine. From the corner of his eye, he recognized Dr. Huey who was examining a patient's chart four beds down the aisle.

"Hey!" Russell proclaimed, waving at Huey, measuring the doctor's indifference by challenging it. "Remember me, Doc?" The doctor ignored Russell as he persisted to study the chart. "Dr. Huey!" Russell announced, irritated. "How's it going?"

Finally, and reluctantly, the brown-headed doctor turned his head to look at him. He flabbily smiled, nodded, and returned to his own world. His smile revered distance. Even the pellets of sweat appeared cleaner than everyone else. It must be nice to have a private shower, Russell thought, rather than bathing with hundreds of strangers each day; providing that the pumps would work that day. Russell then saw his sister walk toward him. Her black hair was reeled in the back; under a hair net. Her fading lipstick made her rounded lips look pale. A troubled expression showed through her fatigued eyes. She dropped her hand on his shoulder and hunched over.

"Goro, why are you here? What's wrong? It is Mama?"

"You have some explaining to do."

Tipping a brow, she said, "Excuse me?"

"This!" he plugged the letter under her nose. "Who's Jerry?"

She grabbed the envelope to inspect it. Angered, she vented, "You *opened* my letter?"

"Better me than Mama!"

"You little jerk! You had no right!" She glanced around to see who was watching her. Kneeling down, she whispered, "I'll kill you! This is none of your business, Goro!"

"A *hakujin*!" he snapped. "Are you crazy?"

Angered, she defended, "He's different."

"How do you know? How do you know he's not just feeling sorry for you?"

"Knock it off!"

Russell glanced at Dr. Huey who pretended not to be interested as he flipped the paper; his eyes twining back and forth. Ignoring him, Russell leaned nearer to his sister. She smelled of iodine and baby powder that it almost overwhelmed his senses, causing a slight dizziness. He slumped back.

"You have no business getting involved with a white guy! Like there's not enough problems in our lives, Sadaye! Or should I call you, *Sadie*?"

She jumped to her feet. Her cheeks became parched as her lids fluttered. She was attracted to Jerry's generosity. His sympathy. His sense of humor. He knew what it was like to be discriminated against because of their names; because of their heritage. She was rather surprised that her youngest brother, who fought so hard to fit in, would criticize. She never spoke harshly against him when he kept joining clubs where people either rejected or tolerated him. When he was dating a Filipino. When he articulated less Japanese in their own parents' house.

Her voice quivered. "Go home, Goro! This isn't the place!"

"How serious is it?" he demanded. "I mean, you've only known the guy for a couple of days! You think that by writing letters it's gonna be somethin' more?"

"Don't tell anyone! There may not be a reason to upset them! So just go home!"

Russell watched his sister walk off, leaving him flustered and helpless. What was she thinking? Idealistically, he really couldn't care less whether her new boyfriend was white or not, but they were living in a detention camp, for crying out loud! It was obvious where everyone stood between the barbed-wire fences.

Late July

MEITO attended the Fair Employment Practices Committee for the first time; made up entirely of mess hall workers, farmers, firemen, and other professional groups. Ted Tanaka, a *Nisei* man in his early thirties and who was properly groomed, stood up behind a long table. Beside him sat seven of his men, staring confidently out at the committee. The daily disappearance of sugar and meat was an increasing problem. Meito's kitchen crew was overwhelmed by people's criticisms and grievances, as were the other mess hall staffs throughout the camp. Rumors swarmed like locusts about white drivers selling these valuable commodities on the black market- with some of the *Nisei* getting paid on the side. Something had to be done. And quickly, otherwise Meito feared a protest would agitate the military. After witnessing how some of the military police managed the Fourth's situation, he sorely lacked the trust.

But that wasn't all that troubled him. He suspected a few *Nisei* of informing on each other for scraps of respect and favors from the administration. Or for the FBI. The same kind of G-men who had pillaged their homes and forcibly dragged their fathers to Montana. Katsuji and other *Kibeis* only became additionally outraged by the unfairness and betrayal, thus blaming anyone in their warpath. And for some stupid reason they were accusing Meito, too. Just because he was responsible for signing the delivery papers didn't imply he was in cahoots with the white drivers, or the administration.

Meito leaned on the wall, about midway in the room, along with a line of curious bystanders; Tom included. Windows were splintered open to allow the drafty night breezes to participate, attempting to cool the crowded room. Two fans awkwardly rotated from side to side, competing with Ted's voice. Sweat, smoke, and musty cologne collided in the air, pushing out the faint pine odor of the exposed wood. He noticed Katsuji sitting near the exit; away from Ted's clique who overshadowed the front. The sight of Katsuji irritated him. Each day proved more challenging as he tried to avoid Katsuji. It was like trying to avoid a barn cat in a barn.

Ted predominantly spoke Japanese; randomly tossing in English. At the end of the table, a young man wearing a crisp, white shirt, promptly scribbled on sheets of paper, recording the minutes of the meeting with Japanese characters. At the end of the week, someone else would translate the words into English for the camp director to read, to evaluate, and to conclude the suitability. Just like a judge in a juvenile court.

"*Before I forget*," Ted expressed, folding his fingers and placing his hands in front of him. "*I would like to take the time to thank all people from Bainbridge Island. If it were not for the men and women who helped finish the construction of the camp, volunteered at the hospital and mess halls*," he exhibited a broad smile, "then we would be in worse shape today! *I am not saying that the people from Los Angeles and Terminal Island performed less, that's not my point, I am saying the Bainbridge people complained the least!*" He chuckled with a few others who followed. "*The Bainbridge people have proven their loyalties and support. Again, domo arigato.*"

Although Meito felt flattered, a compliment toward his people who were greatly outnumbered by the Californian Japanese, he knew Ted was a politician. These Californians were more aggressive in private as well as politically. Perhaps because they endured a heavier strand of bigotry, dealing with violent anti-Japanese groups and segregation all of their lives, their attitudes were not as amicable. Even some of the Hawaiians seemed more crude; racially mixed with the natives, or Chinese, or Filipino. Not to mention their dialect was short and vulgar; a pigeon language unaccustomed to Meito and his folk. And their peacock-style marches displayed a confidence he lacked. Quite honestly, he had never fully felt comfortable around them.

Katsuji remained silent, listening to Ted's speech about the disappearance of the meat and sugar, and how everyone should unite instead of pointing fingers at one another. Part of the problem was that each man present was not an *Issei*. Only one *Kibei* among the clique, and he was only a secretary. The Japanese American Citizen League, compiled strictly of *Nisei*, regulated the committee. Despite their intentions about supplying more jobs, seeking equality in America, Katsuji felt he and others were often overlooked. The advantages the *Nisei* embodied resided in both education and succeeding past the language barriers, thus leaving the *Issei* and *Kibei* floating off shore; far from the mainland. And the *Nisei* outnumbered the others like cluttered sea shells on the beaches. Aside from dealing with racism outside the Japanese community, Katsuji was outraged by the prejudices within. His father was an important leader in San Francisco at one point. He organized the fishermen's union for the Japanese when the Union itself rejected them. He organized the funding for a Buddhist temple. He even organized charities for families who lost their head of household and had no way of supporting themselves. He was tired of the hypocrisy and needed to voice his opinions.

"*You speak of unity,*" Katsuji scornful began, rising to his feet, "*and yet you do not care about the Issei or the Kibei! You will not let my father and his friends be in charge in your committee! Nor us! I expect it from the WRA, but not from you!*"

Meito watched Ted sigh apprehensively. The room teetered in absolute silence as the crowd stared at their leader, wondering how he would handle the agitator. The justice that Katsuji demanded did merit a clear explanation. To deny the *Issei* authority, who affirmed control before the war in their own communities, did seem a bit insulting. The *Issei* men had already forfeited their pride when they lost their homes; a place which identified their roles as protectors, leaders, and businessmen. But today, because of a war that spread beyond Europe and bled into Asia, everything was turned upside down.

Ted tapped his fingers on the table. "*You know that the Issei cannot vote therefore they cannot govern. It is the law. I do not have the power to change it. Not now, anyway.*" He cleared his throat. "*And you know each member was elected by a democratic vote. How the results came to be was decided by the*

Nisei as well the Kibei on each block. It is unjustified how you accuse us otherwise." Readily alternating into English, he asserted, "End of discussion!"

Meito lowered his head. He knew the statement wasn't entirely true. The names inside the committee were carefully selected by Ted's group, and then voted by people with citizenship.

Katsuji thinned his eyes, slowly shaking his head like a lion that statically flapped its tail. He angrily persisted, "*You and your men only care about your ambitions! The War Relocation Authority and administration can suckle on pig tits! We do not have to follow this absurd law! We have our own laws! In Japan, your action would be considered dishonorable!*"

"*We are not in Japan!*" Ted snapped, nailing his fist on the table. "*If we are to be taken seriously in America, then we must abide by American laws!*"

Katsuji kicked his chair back. The crowd jilted. Ted's men bounced to their feet, stationing behind the table. Katsuji's temper displeased many of them, for it was not appropriate to lose control of oneself in public.

Meito strengthened his back and crossed his arms; waiting. He also knew Katsuji and his men had already infected a cavity in the community, decaying solidarity which they desperately needed to preserve.

Katsuji shouted, his elbows arched like claws, "*I have followed the American laws, and look where it has put us! You are a bigger fool than I thought if you believe your loyalty means something to America!*"

"Get out!" Ted yelled, flinging his index finger. "Get the hell out!"

Katsuji hesitated, glaring at Ted. He looked around the frowning crowd, seeing that they wished him to leave. Mulling over his next tactic, he then studied Meito, who resisted blinking as he stared directly back. One of his men, Saburo, younger and more stocky, rose to whisper into his ear, then readjusted his stance, watching Ted.

Returning to Ted, Katsuji asserted, "*If you were a wise man, Tanaka-san, than you should acknowledge us! We are not done discussing this!*"

Katsuji reluctantly withdrew. Eight other men followed him, displaying stern, embittered guises; quietly strutting their defiance. Once they shut the door, Ted's men cautiously re-positioned themselves, sitting with their chins high in the air and tugging out their arms as if they had just swung a punch.

Ted announced with a flimsy grin, "Well, let's get back on track, shall we!"

THE meeting lagged for three hours, presenting promises of further investigations, more meetings, and yet accomplishing nothing. Meito felt like he had been picking strawberries all season only to realize that there were a hundred more acres to complete. After shuffling a few complaints around with the other men outside, he began to walk back to his apartment.

"Meito, how do you think the meeting went tonight?" Tom asked, reeling at his side like a worm on a fishing rod. The streetlights pursued their backs, tracing the profile of their features.

Glancing at Tom, he grunted, "*Kachi ga aru*! A real waste of time, you know."

"Well," he shrugged, "everything has a starting point. Even if nobody goes anywhere."

Meito chuckled at the fruitless expression. "If nobody moves, then how do you know it's a starting point? Without an end there can't be a beginning."

Tom blinked. "Got me! Hey, listen," he chirped, brushing his mustache with his fingertip. "You work with Katsuji, right? In our mess hall?"

"Yep," he remarked, looking up at the stars. Without the moon that night, the sky yielded in obscurity. He wondered what Tom really wanted.

"We think he sent Ted Tanaka a threatening letter."

Clenching his thick brows together, skeptical, he asked, "Who's *we*?"

"The committee. He showed some of us the letter."

Meito gnawed his lip. Tom wasn't a representative of the committee, having no tangible clout, only being an observer like himself. But then, assuming he was no one of real importance, how did Tom gain access inside Tanaka's circle?

Sighing, he inquired, "And what makes you think it's Katsuji?"

"You saw what he did to your flag! The threat he made tonight. He's a dangerous element."

"Dangerous element?" Meito chuckled. "Where did you pick up that kind of language? Sounds like something the FBI would say."

Tom nearly tripped. Then regaining balance, he grabbed Meito's arm, and advanced forward. "We could use your help, Meito. Anything you could tell me about Katsuji would be helpful."

Staring at Tom, baffled and annoyed, he said, "Sometimes he doesn't wash his hands when he cooks. Is that helpful?"

He released Meito. "I'm trying to keep this camp safe. I don't have an easy job, you know. It would be nice if you helped out."

"Well, there's only so much we can do. But if I think of anything else, I'll let you know."

Meito readjusted his hands in his pockets, and walked off. He would be damned if he was going to get caught in the middle of things.

Exhaling his frustrations, Tom returned to Tanaka's group who all stood outside, smoking off-brand cigarettes. Tom glanced at Meito one more time, and shook his head, shrugging.

Ted flicked his cigarette, peering at Meito, suspecting his reluctance. Why anyone would want to protect Katsuji was beyond his reasoning. Ted had his priorities justified and he didn't need ignorant people criticizing him. He didn't invest ten years of his life to achieve political importance just to be intimidated by someone like Katsuji. And he didn't graduate from Berkeley with a PhD just to be sneered off by someone like Meito. Puffing, he spoke of starting another charter and calling it the Manzanar Commission for Self-Government.

Early August

RUSSELL said nothing more as Jim struggled to keep up with his friend. Trying to find a new image, Russell wore a tan cap and sunglasses, appearing similar to the heroes in his comic books. Shig even gave him an extra pair of army boots. They hustled across the alley, passing by Joe and George who held sticks and rocks in their sullied hands. Jumping over his steps, Russell rushed inside his barrack, ordering Jim to shut the door. A pungent odor hit them. Glancing at the brewing still, Russell winced. Shifting through the drooping blankets, he stood beside a coffee table. On top of the table perched a sheeted, rectangular object. Jim cautiously followed Russell's steps, but paused in front Sam and Ikki; each slouching over another bed and drumming their feet on the floor. Russell rushed through the barrack to shut the all the curtains, then returned to his friends.

Hovering his hand above the object, he eagerly asked, "Are you ready?"

"Yes!" Sam declared. "We've been waiting forever!"

Russell plucked off the sheet and revealed a radio.

Squinting, Ikki asserted, "Where the hell did you it?"

"I found it!"

"But where? Radios don't exactly grow on trees!"

Suspicious, worried, Jim frowned. "Where did you get the money to buy it?"

Sliding his sunglasses off, extending his proud grin. "Don't worry about it."

"You did buy it, right?"

"And I told you not to worry about it."

"Jesus!" Jim said. "How stupid can you be? If you get caught you'll be in serious trouble!"

Russell glared at him and snapped, "Are you planning to tell?"

"No," he defended. "The point I'm making is that someone *else* could tell."

Ignoring Jim, he turned the knob, passing over static and country music until he found a Big Band station. Bunny Berigan's song, "All God's Chillun Got Rhythm," skipped the trumpets, guitar, and drums like crickets skipping in grass.

Smiling, Russell claimed, "There you are, boys! Modern technology at its best!"

Sam excitedly said, "Man! I almost forgot what swing music sounded like!" Jumping to his feet, he turned to Ikki, bowing and propping up his hand. With an amusing grin, he asked, "Can I have this dance?"

Ikki gave him a disgusted look. "Go piss on yourself!"

"Yeah, I love you, too!" Turning to face Russell, he persisted, "How about you?"

Russell squinted, unsure. The image of two boys dancing simultaneously looked extremely odd. It certainly didn't seem natural. Lifting a brow, he muttered, "In front of everyone?"

"There's only four people here!"

"And none of 'em wear a brassiere. Get the picture?"

Sam groaned and tugged at Russell's arm. "*Higai moso!* It's not like there any girls to ask right now! It's just a dance! Not marriage!"

Russell groaned, debating. Browsing over Jim's and Ikki's dry expressions, he could see that they really could care less. Clapping his hands, he said, "What the hell! You only live once, right?" He pushed the table into a corner, anchoring the radio so it wouldn't fall over. Standing upright, he announced, "I'm leading."

"Why do you get to lead?"

"Because I'm stronger than you."

Sam fidgeted. "That ain't right. Whoever asked first should lead."

"If you want to dance, I'm leading, Sam. It's up to you."

He slowly groaned, twisting from side to side. "Fine," he conceded. "But don't tell no one you were leading!"

"I'm not telling anyone I'm dancing with you in the first place!"

Sam reluctantly offered his hand and Russell reluctantly took it. Tilting backward, hoping to the beat, Russell see-sawed his feet and shoulders, and then spun around. Sam pecked like a pigeon. They twisted their hips, spun again, leapt, and swayed. Soon a woman singer joined the buoyant music, her cheerful voice vibrating through the circular speaker. Jim and Ikki stared uneasily, relieved that the curtains were closed so no one else could see them dancing together.

* * *

RUSSELL continued to wear his cap and sunglasses while eating his rice. Obtaining the radio was the best trophy yet. His family, although stunned and a little concerned, also seemed a bit more optimistic. And relieved. Now the outside world could enter into their world, and they felt less isolated; more normal. And because of this, the crowded mess hall didn't bother him that evening. Often he felt like they were ants scurrying around while they carried food back to the hill. It was an endless cycle: waiting in line for over an hour clutching a tin tray, waiting, ogling soggy rice or dried chicken, or mushy peaches or fried bologna, still waiting in line, finding a table to sit at, then waiting again until the next time.

The Bainbridge boys yapped as they chewed. Some sniggered at people who tired to eat fried bologna with chopsticks because the bologna kept slipping out like slimy fish; otherwise news of the war drenched their imaginations. Despite the Allies' defeats during early summer in North Africa, Russia, and the Atlantic, they still were inspired to be a part of the action. To achieve true victories for both America and their families. To prove their loyalties. That would be a great thing.

Russell changed the subject and boasted, "Hey, you guys know my brother-in-law, Osamu, just joined the patrol, right?" Each nodded. "Well," he continued, snickering. "Last night he and his partner heard these noises coming from an empty building." He smiled widely, cracking his dried skin. "They found a couple going at it standing straight up!" A chorus of laughter sprung up from his story. Laughing deeply himself, Russell tried to pursue his speech. "They were . . . they all were sooo embarrassed . . . Osamu could only give them a warning! The girl left her . . . her slip and garter belt behind!"

They laughed for a few more minutes before they could continue to eat. Except Jim. He found no amusement in it.

"You shouldn't talk about someone else's privacy," he criticized after everyone yielded their laughter.

Annoyed, Russell peered through his dark glasses. "Don't be such a bluenose. Why not?"

"You just shouldn't, Russell. It's disrespectful and immature." He poked at his food. "And I have to say I don't like this change in you. You're acting like a hooligan. Where did you find that ridiculous outfit anyway?"

Lowering his fork, he demanded, "What difference does it make?"

He pointed behind Russell's eyes. "And why don't you take off those sunglasses? We're inside for Pete's sake."

"Because I don't have to, Jim, that's why. And what's with you today? Are you on the rag or something?"

Chuckling circulated around the table. Hurt, insulted, Jim stood up and grabbed his tray. "I'm trying to tell you to be careful, is all."

As he walked away, Russell felt a little guilty. Jim really didn't deserve that snide remark. The next time he ran into Jim, he would apologize. The boys at the table resumed their swaggering. Their amusement riveted on insults and fantasies, having little else to compensate their idle time. Without chores, farm work or school work, pranks and games repaired their boredom. Sometimes when one of them looked away, another would pour salt all over his tray, or everyone would scoop food off his plate and onto theirs. Other times, they counted to three and shoveled food in their mouths as fast as they could, the champion winning either cigarettes or loose coins. The game that day began with each picking out a pretty girl and bragging about how they were going to ask her for a date. Take her on a night out on the town. Show her a real good time. They laughed at their own jokes, knowing they couldn't go anywhere.

Sam faintly punched Russell's arm, and asked, "Hey, what about you, Russ? Which one?"

He lifted his chin as if a nobleman ready to pronounce his engagement. Pointing to the table where the two nuns sat, five tables down the aisle, he replied, "That one."

Sam gawked. "*Chikusho!* Are you crazy? A nun!"

"No, you idiot!" he snapped. "The girl in the pink blouse *next* to the nuns! Look!"

Everyone leaned their bodies to left, peering over a manifold of heads. The orphan girl, with her hair coiled up at the sides, had her back facing them. Every day, three times a day, she sauntered by them, her pleated skirt flirting as easily as her hips. Sometimes she would glance down, sometimes not, and rarely did she smile. No matter how many times they insisted she tell them her name, her pink lips remained sealed. Her aloofness indicated arrogance. There was nothing worse in a *Nisei* girl than her own pride.

"Why her?" Sam asked. "She's *diseased.* I told you she's bad luck!"

"That's a dopey *nihonjin* superstition!" Russell vented. Tugging on his cap, he proclaimed, "Sam, there comes a time in your life when you need to let go of Japanese traditions. How else do you expect to make it in America?"

Sam placed his hands behind his head as an odd grin squirmed below his nose. He said to Russell, "I betcha you don't have the nerve to ask her out. And betcha she rejects you like cow manure! Can't even come close to popping her cork!"

Russell cracked, "Like you would know how!"

The others chuckled, jiggling their shoulders, their cheeks stuffed with food.

"Okay, wise guy! Make fun all you like. The point is she ain't on your level!"

Ikki swallowed his rice and turned to Russell. "Weren't you dating Maria back home?"

Russell leaned back, irritated. It had been over four months since his arrival and still nothing from her. Not a letter. Not a note. Not even a damn postcard! As the weeks dehydrated his body in the heat, he stopped writing. He knew his letters were reaching Bainbridge because Dave Lundberg occasionally wrote back; sometimes sending him baseball cards, Wrigley's gum or packages of cookies. Out of desperation, he asked Dave if Maria was in fact dating someone else! Now, he just waited. The uncertainty was killing him. She had to have been kissing some other guy, letting his hands skim over her curves like a serpent through water; rippling; beckoning; dipping.

Angered, Russell grumbled, "A long time ago!"

Sam shrugged, "What did you expect? She's there, you're here. *Shikata ga nai*, man!"

"Yeah," he replied, his tone drained of faith. "Things can't be helped, alright." He stood up. Forget all this crap of not doing anything. The boys ogled at Russell; mouths slightly severed as he marched toward the orphan tables. Ikki muttered something about losing his mind. No one should prance as they please in front of strangers without proper introductions, especially in front of Japanese nuns! Not only was it impolite, but also contemptuous.

Russell strutted, indicating confidence despite a nervousness twisting his neck. He halted at the end of the table. Reclining to his right foot, his arms arched at his hips, he looked directly at the girl who sat directly in the middle.

Clearing his throat he asserted, "Hi, there!"

All heads spun, including the two nuns and the girl. Staring at him as if he were an invader, their eyes marveled in distrust and bewilderment. Russell awkwardly shifted to his other foot.

Inhaling, he persisted, "We were wondering," he nodded at the stupefied girl, "what your name is."

One of the nuns, her discreet face fortified under her sable-winged hat, gracefully rose. Her silver cross glistened with her movements. She appeared to survive in her late fifties. A thin golden ring retired on her left hand; next to her smallest finger. When she spoke, her voice softly flowed and with a poetic rhythm.

"*My son, you are more than welcome to join us, however, this is an immodest approach. You have embarrassed us.*"

The girl covered her grin, suppressing her amusement underneath the nun's prudence. Removing his sunglasses, he apologized in Japanese. The nun gently angled her head, smiled, and delicately bowed; closing her eyes. Russell unskillfully returned the bow, fumbling over his ineptness to be just as graceful, irritated that he should respond in an old tradition.

"*Perhaps*," the nun continued, "*you would like to attend our services tomorrow afternoon. You may bring guests. Everyone is welcomed.*"

Befuddled, Russell curled his lips. Looking at the girl again, who finally loosened her hand away from her grin, he said to the nun, "*I will think about it.*"

Russell promptly returned to his table, feeling like he had been flipped over and pinned in a wrestling competition. Sliding his sunglasses back on his face, he plopped down. Dreading the sneers from his friends, the harassment began, ricocheting from one boy to another, down the line.

"Shot down, huh?"

"You had a better chance with Jimmy Durante!"

"Can I borrow your sunglasses so I can run 'n hide, too?"

"Maybe you shou'da asked one of the nuns instead!"

"When are ya gonna ask me out so I can make my confession?"

He nodded repetitiously, allowing his friends' taunting to go through its cycle. The sooner the better. Then he thought about his mother. She would have been outraged if she knew he was considering attending church, even if his intentions meant only to get a girl's name. She didn't trust Western religions, viewing them as hypocritical and confusing. When a band of Jehovah Witnesses dispersed Bibles five years ago, she accused them of stealing a human being's essence; an offense to Buddha. They goggled at her as if she had fled from an insane asylum; white-belted jacket and all. Sadaye quit translating when they accused Mrs. Hamaguchi of devil worship.

CHAPTER SIX

Early August

CHIYEKO licked the envelope and pressed it shut. Her circular face and small eyes sagged under the single light bulb. She heard children's laughter and shouting men behind the thin walls after a morning drizzle. The bare line of windows caught whiffs of the Oregon fairground. Loose wood and puddles assembled in the camp; similar to old photographs of the American frontier. To some extent, it bore the cliché of a booming mining town. Primitive with no indoor plumbing. Very little organization of any kind. Politically. Socially. The sharp difference being that the law was enforced by the military with search lights, wire fence, and loaded rifles.

This was Camp Harmony

Her husband, Tadao, slept on the cot up-right, slumping against a wall as one leg hung over the edge, still clinging their napping toddler in his sheltered arms. His hair slunk over his right brow. His wrist watch ticked in idle time. Everything was packed again; their suitcases full like clams with water and grit. She jiggled the fountain pen and wrote the Manzanar address on top of a wooden box with stenciled letters POTATOES. This would be her last letter from this empty place. Tomorrow everyone would be sent to Idaho at a more permanent location. Perhaps better circumstances would evolve. It made no sense to her why they was shuffled from one camp to another unless the other one were better; otherwise it would be a waste of the government's time and money. She didn't mention any of her concerns in the letter. Between censorship and keeping a strong tone for her parents, she wrote about simpler things. The weather. Her three daughters' good health. The new move.

Chiyeko sniffled and wiped her wet cheeks. She had never been separated from the rest of her family. Usually the distance was only a ferry ride apart. Yes, her brother Kunio and his family were also there, yet it proved crudely adequate. It appeared as though her daughters were going to grow up missing the close family bond. She unfolded a handbag full of recent letters.

Letters from home. From California. From Montana. Someday the family had to be united. This couldn't last forever.

* * *

MRS. HAMAGUCHI pierced a long pin in her hat, mounting it over her spiraled bun. Her freshly ironed blouse, chalky colored and stain free, glared under the ceiling light bulb. She slipped into her thick, bronzed shoes and brushed dust off her lengthy dark skirt. She was alone with her drunken husband. Walking to the radio, her heels clunking, slightly agitating the flimsy walls, she lowered the sound. The newscaster delighted in the towering sales of war bonds, for patriotism was on an ultimate high. And even though the economy was stronger than it had been in over a decade, the rationing of gas limited people's traveling status. So much for summer vacations this year folks! Ha! Ha! Also the rationing of sugar, meat, nylons, rubber supplies, and canned goods was one of the ways to support the boys over there! Everyone must do their part to win this war for Uncle Sam!

She ignored the news, not completely understanding English in the first place. She looked at her husband who buried himself behind cylinder tins and tubes. His belly revealed an empty bottle lying between his legs. She felt cheated. She didn't submit her photograph twenty-eight years ago to age in humiliation. Breaching her fate by sailing away from Japan, Mrs. Hamaguchi arrived in America to marry someone *not* prearranged by her family. After five years of straining to keep her relations, her family never returned her letters; and so she stopped trying. She figured by their standards she no longer existed. Only desperate, scandalous women served as picture brides. Not to mention that it was her second marriage. Her first husband died in a brutal storm, leaving her with nothing but hostile in-laws and expectations of marrying his younger brother. She had just turned seventeen when she fled. It didn't matter anyway. She descended from a family where all girls burdened the house, and she knew her absence had released a blessing.

Mrs. Hamaguchi remembered the last conversation she exchanged with her mother. She had just purchased a new Western dress, pale blue with a black belt and shoes to match, and decided to cut her long, thick hair. Proud of her modern appearance, being so young, she was also terribly frightened. How foolish she must had seemed! Her mother arrived at the dock, with two of her uncles, wearing the traditional flowered kimono. Her uncles looked so plain in their rural apparel: white shirts wrapped around their chests, baggy pants, *geta* shoes with white socks. Each clashed against the Western suits and colorful dresses of the city people. Her mother cried when she saw Setsumi's beautifully butchered hair.

"*How could you do such a thing?*" her mother demanded. "*Now your new husband will think he will marry an unfeminine woman! What kind of bad luck will you bring into your second marriage? You are already a spoilt woman.*"

Angered by her mother's lack of sympathy, she defended, "*I will marry a modern man, and so I must be a modern woman, okasan*!"

Her mother concealed her tears with both hands, hiding her fragile mouth and eyes. Setsumi thought her *okasan* had aged too quickly with disappointment. She knew her action would make it more difficult for her younger sisters to find suitable husbands. Her shame would carry on a legacy throughout Okinawa. But she had believed that someday she would return home with a rich husband and heal the family's name with great honor. Why couldn't her mother understand?

"*Do not worry, obasan,*" Setsumi encouraged, trying to inspire her own fears into confidence. She hadn't slept last night in the hotel room, listening to the city of Makurazuki's rumbling cars and people's echoing voices. She had never stayed in a city, and felt both excited and scared. "*I had prayed to our ancestors for good fortune, and this morning, I found money on the dock.*"

Her mother delicately wiped her wet cheeks. Looking at her daughter for the last time, she placed her trembling hand over Setsumi's belly. Gently padding it, she asked, "*Does your new husband know?*"

"*Nai,*" she whispered. "*I will tell him after the second wedding in America.*"

"*May the gods smile on you favorably.*"

Setsumi bowed to her mother, then bowed to her uncles who stood at a distance. They didn't say good-bye. They only bowed in turn. As she walked onto the ship, restraining her tears, she didn't want the gods, or her mother, to see that she could be making a mistake. She couldn't undo the mock marriage already arranged in Japan to allow her passage to America. What was done had been done.

Mrs. Hamaguchi stared at her husband once more. She tried to accept where fate had taken her, but all she could feel was anger. Before leaving the cluttered barrack, full of small furniture, a wooden couch blanketed with a flowered sheet that sat beside water bowls, shelves, winding clocks, and beds, Mrs. Hamaguchi took a Japanese translation book. She met Mrs. Yoshimura outside who also dressed in her formal clothing, carrying an English dictionary. They appeared as if they were ready to attend church or a temple, clean and trim, and not to an English class.

An evening wind bristled tiny pebbles into their shoes and through their clothes. Fortunately the camp began to molt its fractured form, healing its thick zigzagged ditches and its incomplete barracks. People appreciated the safety of not falling into trenches at night when rushing to the latrines. The two women strolled down their block, chattering, wondering exactly when school was going to start for their children. The promise of schools eased their minds. They knew education was the only commodity that guaranteed their children's success. Even if in an internment camp.

Mrs. Hamaguchi said, "*I worry for my son, Goro. He no longer eats with family. He is always running wild about the camp. And he is not clean much of the time. I fear that he is becoming distant.*"

"*Hai,*" Mrs. Yoshimura agreed. "*Even my son Jimmu is also not himself. He is often angry. He and Tom bicker most commonly, or they do not speak to each at all. What are we to do? My husband cannot discipline because he is still absent. I do not know what to do. How will my only son grow into a man?*"

Mrs. Hamaguchi yielded. She could provide no answer because she felt the same way. People ambled up and down the wobbly road, balancing their feet on loose sand as if walking on feather pillows. Reviewing the numbers on the barracks, Mrs. Hamaguchi realized they were lost. Each building indicated a place of residence, displaying flower beds, wooden lawn chairs, trash barrels, and fire extinguishers hanging on most buildings. The two women had passed by the Buddhist temple and a couple of churches, each revealing wooden signs that stood in front of the green buildings that advertised their services. They even passed by *The Manzanar Free Press*, yet they could not find a double structure barrack as directed.

Tugging on her friend's sleeve, she said, "*I do not believe the English class is in this block.*"

Mrs. Yoshimura replied, "*That is the direction Kazuko-san told me.*"

Annoyed, she uttered, "*Maybe he does not know how to give directions!*"

"*Do not be so harsh, Setsumi-suma. He is in his seventies.*"

"*I knew I should have asked the teacher!*" she brooded, sliding the book at her waist side. "*Why should our class have to move to another place?*"

"*Because there are too many students and not enough space.*"

"*There is never enough space!*" Mrs. Hamaguchi complained. Rotating in a circle and studying the unfamiliar block, she exhaled, "*Ten thousand people. Ten thousand people are living in a square of three miles.*"

Sparing a grin, Mrs. Yoshimura rubbed her friend's shoulder. She shared the same frustration: feeling congested as if a group of goldfishes swimming in a small pond. Nonetheless, she accepted her fate like everything else. Fighting against it only provoked madness.

She humorously asked, "*And how is this different from Japan*?"

Mrs. Hamaguchi thought for a moment. Smiling, she admitted, "*I am not sure!*"

"*Let us ask around. Someone will assist us.*"

She nodded. "*Hai, you are right. I must learn to be more patient.*"

Glancing at her side, Mrs. Hamaguchi saw nine boys, all in their late teens, trudging toward them. Their dark blue jeans, dusty and crinkled, were rolled inside out at the bottom of their battered shoes. A crude layer seemed to peel from their scarred skins, each smoking rough-made cigarettes in their coarse lips. The shortest one was the oddest looking one out of the group. His high forehead and small chin tormented his roaming left eye.

Mrs. Yoshimura instantly stepped closer to her friend, feeling uneasy. When the gang stopped in front of the older women, establishing their territory three feet apart, the two mothers tightened together. The shortest one removed his cigarette and spoke with gruffness. He was only an inch smaller than the two women.

"*Oba san,*" he mocked, insulting the respectful title. His Japanese dialect resonated a harsh sound. "*You look lost. Maybe we can help, oba san.*"

Not trusting him, Mrs. Hamaguchi quickly stated, "*No! Thank you for asking.*"

Tensed and confused, Mrs. Yoshimura countered, "*Yes, we are lost. We are searching for the English class.*"

Mrs. Hamaguchi fidgeted, aggravated at her friend's lack of sense about those rough boys. She kept her eyes away from theirs, avoiding any direct confrontation. She had been educated by those kinds of people before, in Japan, a certain fishermen clan dwelling on the far edges of the island. They were like sharks, slippery and crude who enjoyed circling their game. They honored their own laws.

The short boy stuck the cigarette back in his mouth, inhaled, then blew into the women's faces. Smirking, he remarked, "*Why spoil your time with learning English? My oba sans, no one can train old dogs with new tricks. As it is said in America.*"

Raising her translation book to her chest, Mrs. Hamaguchi nervously replied, "*It is not a concern to you.*"

She clutched Mrs. Yoshimura's arm and moved away from the circle. The women started to trot. The gang followed at their heels. They panicked, trying to run faster. The short one jumped in front of the mothers, laughing, wheeling his cigarette as a stop sign. The other eight encircled them like gamblers in a rooster fight. Some of the boys poked the women; testing them; taunting them; sniggering at them. Mrs. Hamaguchi looked around to see if anybody would help them. Others seemed just as afraid of the gang while no one offered to step in. The bystanders swiftly withdrew from the street; into the alleys, or inside their barracks. Angered, she couldn't believe her own people refused to rescue them. And she wondered where the patrolmen were. Suddenly she swung her book in front of the boy. Astonished, he leaped back. Leering at her, he began laughing. He jeered at her meek attempt to protect herself, ridiculing the form she used by imitating her girlish swing. The other boys cackled.

Embarrassed, and even more agitated, she asserted, "*Does your father know what kind of yogore you have become?*"

His face fell. When the others promptly stopped their laughter, he said, "*My father is dead. He shot himself on the day of the evacuation.*"

Flabbergasted, both mothers didn't know how to respond. Suicide was only considered worthy when a man sacrificed himself to his country, not to his own vanity. The philosophy of the old Shogun, now transformed into Shintoism, was not designed by women. Every time a man made a mess, women were left behind to clean it up. After living in America for over two decades, both mothers no longer believed in every aspect of Shintoism.

Changing tactics, Mrs. Hamaguchi gently said, "*I am very sorry to hear such news. I am certain your father was a very honorable man.*"

"*He was an honorable man!*" the boy spat. Crimping his lips, he sneered, "*But then what does a woman really know of honor?*"

Trying to hold her outrage, for she didn't like being insulted by someone more than half her age, Mrs. Hamaguchi answered, "*It is a burden we must carry.*" She gracefully bowed, displaying her submission. Raising her head and finally looking at the boy directly, she politely asked, "*May we pass by you? We now know that we have imposed and wish to apologize*."

The boy squinted at her; thinking; calculating. Taking another puff, he exhaled to his side, away from her face this time. He grinned. "*That is much better*," he said. "*Everyone should know their place. Oba san, you have my permission to leave*."

Both women bowed and quickly scurried. Unlike Mrs. Hamaguchi, Mrs. Yoshimura had never experienced harassment from her own people. Growing up in a quiet, merchant society, then relocating to Bainbridge, she was lucky to live in peace. Not saying anything, her hands quivered. She followed her friend back to their barracks, straining to keep herself from crying hysterically

Mrs. Hamaguchi fastened her mouth, not wanting to express what she truly thought. How could those boys justify their power and deny basic respect? They were nothing more than the manure that clung to the bottom of her shoes. She considered filing a police report; but then decided not to. What would the police actually do? Warn them? Tell them not to harass people again? Besides, if no one cared, hiding like mice, than why should she care?

RUSSELL smashed his fist into the sheetrock, puncturing a hole beside one of the shelves, making it rattle. Startled and disturbed, the Hamaguchis braced the late evening's deterioration. Meito grabbed both his brother's arms and pushed him down onto a bed. Hunching over him, Meito strained to calm his brother. Sweating, Russell twitched. He wanted to protect his mother, but learned that protection was only a hallucination. Surrounded by a barbed wire fence like goddamn cattle! Machine guns aimed at their hearts. *Nikkei* people mugging and harassing each other. Where was the goddamn fairness?

Meito professed, "Goro! What's wrong with you? You can't destroy the wall! That doesn't help Mama!"

Russell said nothing as his right hand throbbed. He could sense the storm of his blood spiraling. Stiffly breathing, he turned his head and stared at a watercolor picture of the Sierra Mountains. The rough paper slightly wrinkled and slouched at the corners. His mother had painted it, stylizing her blues and purples. She discarded the watchtowers and fence as if painting freedom. As if painting a paradise.

"Goro!" Meito persisted. "Don't let anger control you! It won't do any good, *ototo*!"

"Then what the hell are we suppose to do? Take it up the back side?"

Squeezing his arms, Meito curtly whispered, "Watch your mouth, Goro! Not in front of the women and my kids!"

"I'll kill 'em! Swear to God!"

"Enough! That's enough!"

Russell felt his brother's hands clenching his biceps more furiously; more painfully. Russell's muscles prickled like thorns. His outrage tore open his eyes, raising feverish tears, strangling his throat. No one, but no one would ever touch his mother again! Rolling his shoulders, he prodded his arms between his brother, breaking away. Meito snatched his brother's wrists.

"*Jigoku ni otosu!*" Meito cursed. "Calm down, Goro!"

Without thinking, Russell yanked his brother forward, forcing him to lose his balance. He elbowed Meito in his chest and flipped him over. Lying on top of his older brother, he pinched his knees in the middle of Meito's shoulder blades. The squeaky springs shuddered, jolting the mattress.

Gertrude reached for her two sons, gasping, tugging them to her thighs. She buried herself and her sons in a corner. Sadaye covered her mouth, shaking her head, unable to speak. Mr. Hamaguchi, through his glazed eyes, could only watch.

Meito launched his chest to his side, plunging Russell to the floor. Russell grabbed his brother's belt with both hands and pulled down his pants. The front end of Meito's shirt barely covered his privates. Meito instantly covered his crotch with his hand. Stunned, Russell blinked a few times.

Mrs. Hamaguchi ran to Russell, slapped him on his head, and fiercely scolded him about his irrational behavior. Russell began to laugh. Meito swiftly and clumsily plucked his pants up.

Ignoring his mother's criticisms, Russell managed to chortle out, "Why don't you- put on- some underwear?"

Embarrassed, he rose to his feet, adjusting his belt. The side seams were split. As his cheeks flushed out redness, he retorted, "I had boxers on, *baka!* You pulled them down, too!"

Russell laughed more loudly, falling on his back. His mother stared at him as if his brain had slipped out of his ears. Everyone else didn't know how to respond. Their family had never physically fought against each other before. The stress of camp only seemed to have prompted the worst in people; even among brothers.

Meito slowly snickered. He couldn't believe that his little brother had just yanked down his pants in front of everyone. It wasn't exactly like he had something new on display! Bending down and extending out his hand to Russell, he said, "Come on! Get up, you boob!"

Russell continued to laugh, relaxing his arms over his bouncing belly. Struggling to subdue his convulsions, he rubbed his face. He felt as though he were on the tip of a blade, ready to slice apart his sanity

"I'm sorry," Russell softly apologized.

Meito simply grinned, patting his brother's back. Then seizing Russell's jeans, he yanked them down. Mr. Hamaguchi and the twins laughed instantly while the women exhaled their astonishment and disapproval. Nodding and smirking, Russell retrieved what was left of his pride to his waist.

Mrs. Hamaguchi stepped backward, kneading her knuckles like dough, wondering how she could have raised such insolent children.

Meito asked, "Feel any better?"

"Tons," he said, tucking in his shirt.

"And you're not gonna start trouble?"

"No, not me," he said, averting his brother's stare.

"Look at me!"

Russell leveled his gaze directly at Meito. He stood a foot shorter than his eldest brother. Glancing at the cavity in the wall, his regret sagged inside the void. He massaged his aching hand, his strong bones fumbling in weakness. Turning his attention out one of the side windows, the western sun, dark orange like a tangerine, veiled itself behind the windy dust and met at the pointed tip of the mountains. The horizon hemorrhaged across the thin clouds. Russell observed the tragic charm, admiring a beauty cursed by the desert. He hoped for rain. Everyday he prayed for relief. He hated the bitter sun and the barbaric blue sky. Like a poisonous snake, beautiful in color but deadly to its bite, Manzanar became his enemy. Tensing his jaw, his anger leaked through; dripping; crushing,;recasting his optimism.

Meito saw it. It disturbed him, and he did not trust his brother's judgment. "Promise me," Meito insisted. "Promise Mama! You won't do anything stupid."

Dismissing a sigh, he responded with a salted tone, "Cross my heart. Hope to die."

CHAPTER SEVEN

Mid August

RUSSELL asked, "Are you sure? I mean, this isn't your sort of thing, Jim."

Folding his sweaty handkerchief and stuffing it in his jean pocket, Jim glanced at the group. He left his glasses in his barrack, not taking a chance on shattering his second pair. He impatiently rubbed his brow for the fifth time. The late afternoon heat faintly peeled back, spiraling mirages into the acrid wind. Sam and Ikki were the other two Bainbridge boys who stood among the San Pedro clan. Everyone was covered in sand and dust, appearing like migrant workers in the Dust Bowl. When Russell had asked for help from the other Bainbridge boys at breakfast, they withdrew, dismissing their obligation, except Sam and Ikki. Jim wanted retribution for his mother's honor. And to also outsource his rage. Shig's gang simply agreed because they had nothing else better to do. So, between Russell's and Shig's groups, each fortified eight bodies.

"For the last time, yes!" Jim exhaled. "I'm sure! I'm not made of paper!"

Shrugging, Russell remarked, "The thing is, I've seen you fight! Don't expect me to visit your grave."

"And I won't visit yours!" he snapped.

Rumors about the Terminal Island gang rippled throughout all four corners of camp. Their reputation as a ruthless and violent league, defeating other gangs and prevailing over territories, induced remote concern. As long as riots didn't rift through the camp, the military tolerated them, not really wanting daily involvement if they could help it. But the internal police had a true challenge. Sometimes they would arrest certain members, if they could catch them. Usually the gang dispersed like rabbits through the broad alleys when they arrived with their sticks and handcuffs. Too much space among the barracks and in the streets averted the possibilities to hook one.

Shig kicked the ground; the tip of his dirty boot piercing the earth, leaving a hole.

"*Koun-o inorimasu!*" he announced, beaming. "Mark of good fortune."

Ralph, Bruck, and Hank, all wearing plaid shirts and stiff jeans, had their hair slicked back. They grinned at each other. Accepting the mission compelled purpose, excitement, and escape from tedious boredom. The plan consisted of conquering the Terminal Island gang just before dinner. Sam and Ikki felt unsettled and fidgety. They hadn't experienced gang combat before, only engaging in individual fist fights from time to time, usually among each other. They thought about gangster movies with Tommy guns and daggers and prison flicks with James Cagney. What did they really know of violence? Even though knives were contraband material, who knew if the other guy didn't possess one anyway? Their only defense pivoted around their own fists.

Slapping Russell's shoulder, Shig announced, "Don't worry. I know the type. Those guys from Terminal Island only *think* they're tough. They're no better than strays pissin' on trees." Causally tipping to his side, and crossing his arms to elevate his confidence, he persisted, "No doubt we'll just make arrangements at first. You know," he shrugged, "make the rules of how 'n where 'n when. What to use. Have guys keep a lookout for the cops."

Surprised, Jim asked, "You've done this before, then?"

Smirking, he replied, "Hell, yes. I was born in Little Tokyo. Only lived in San Pedro for the past year." Raising his brows, he sneered, "Don't tell me you two are a pair of virgins."

"I'm ready," Russell affirmed, ignoring the remark, suppressing his nerves. He felt excitement drumming as it often did right before his wrestling tournaments.

Raising both hands in the air, Shig mocked, "*Banzai*!"

"Put your arms down, dammit!" Russell sputtered, thinking of Private Callis who was unleashed in the camp. "You'll liable to get yourself shot!"

"*Banzai*!" Ralph responded in jest. His youthful appearance revealed the closeness between his eyes and short nose. Shig echoed another Banzai.

"*Banzai*!" Bruce blurted in turn, whose elephant ears jabbed out of his wide face. Then Hank echoed his *Banzai*; his soaring black hair wild in the wind; his round glasses shimmering in the sun. Soon the San Pedro youths laughed at their own meek imitations of the Japanese military. They comprehended very little of Shintoism, and could actually care less.

Jim stared at the San Pedro clique, doubtful about their abilities. This was the first time he, Sam, and Ikki had met them. Russell had only known them for a month. Leaning into Russell's ear, Jim muttered, "Do you really trust them?"

"Yeah, sure. Why not?"

Frowning, he shook his head and stated, "You worry me."

Bored, Ralph moaned, "Sooooo- where are they?"

Shig removed a cigarette and match from his shirt's pocket. Lifting his boot, he flicked it. "They're watching us," he said, inhaling the cigarette and dropping the match. "Let them. Pretend you're relaxed." He drifted toward Russell, and brushed his boots as if tossing aside his worries. Offering each of the Bainbridge boys a smoke, Sam was the only one who accepted. "So, Russ," he casually continued. "Carrying a torch for anyone back home?"

Russell hesitated before answering. “Her name’s Maria.”

“Maria?” His voice hoisted a pitch. Intrigued as if talking about something forbidden, he inquired, “A white girl? An Italian?”

“No, Filipino.”

He coughed in disbelief. His face wrinkled when he exhaled the smoke. Snickering, he said, “What? What the hell for? They’re nothin’ but a lazy, filthy group!”

Russell flinched in disbelief. “Excuse me?”

“It’s true, Russ,” he maintained. “I’ve worked along with ‘em most of my life. Their skin’s darker than us. You always have to keep telling them how to do their jobs over and over. Nothin’ sticks in their heads! They’re *shiranai.* And they smell! I tell ya, it’s better being Japanese then a Nigger or a Pino!”

Overhearing the conversation, Ralph hollered, “Hey, Shig! What’s the difference between a Filipino ana snake?”

He clapped his hands and said, “Oh, I know this one!” Transforming into W. C. Fields, he said, “A snake- can shed its skiiin!”

Russell tasted a sickened anger expanding inside his stomach like molded yeast. Out of all the insults and jokes he heard against his own people, he thought it bizarre that these boys lowered themselves to another form of racism. Feeling superior sliced away dignity, leaving behind a false sense of wisdom.

“That’s the biggest crock of shit!” Russell argued. “How does this make you better than the *hakujins*?”

Peering at Russell, puffing at his raw cigarette, he scoffed, “How does dating a Pino make you better than me?”

Russell pushed Shig. “Jackass!”

Flicking his cigarette, Shig pushed Russell. “Asshole!”

Russell grabbed Shig’s right arm with both his hands. Yanking his arm, Russell looked like a hawk flipping its body over once it caught its prey from the sky. Shig flopped on his gut. Quickly roosting on top, Russell scooped his arms over Shig’s neck; through his armpits. He pinned his knee in Shig’s back, making his arms immobile; his forehead being toiled into the sand. This would have been as illegal move if it were a real match.

Russell demanded, “Say you’re sorry!”

“For what, dammit!” he wheezed. “I’m the one on the goddamn ground!”

“For being an idiot!”

Ralph and Hank grabbed Russell, trying to yank him like a tick on a cow. They choked his neck, tearing his collar as they tugged. Russell squeezed tight, refusing to let Shig go, demonstrating a message. He wasn’t a feather that could easily be plucked off. The bystanders rushed to the side line, dissembling in the shade, looking away. They shied from gang involvement. Russell finally released Shig. Ralph and Hank threw him to the ground as Shig leapt up to kick Russell in the knee.

“Jesus Christ!” Shig panted, rubbing the rear of his neck. “What the hell’s your goddamn problem?”

Leaping up to his feet, he attested, "Have respect! Apologize for calling my girlfriend a Pino!"

Glaring at Russell, he lowered his hand from his tender neck, breathing coarsely. He realized he had truly offended him, although he couldn't comprehend why Russell would care so much.

"Sorry, *omono*!" he resentfully vented. "I didn't realize you gave a damn!"

"Shig," he began, the wilting hot air and powdered earth drunk his body dry, "you can't say those things. You sound . . . just as ignorant. I'm surprised! You know what it's like to be discriminated against! We're better than that!"

Shig jerked his head and bit his bottom lip. He thought for a minute, exhaling out his anger. Extending his hand to Russell, he said, "Listen, life's too short to be petty. We're on the same side for cryin' out loud!"

Russell studied him. He wasn't convinced that Shig proposed absolute sincerity. There was nothing more repulsive than a bigot. With everyone staring at him, weary and anxious, he shook his hand and nodded.

"You have one hellova head lock there, Russ! You wrestle?"

Unfastening his hand, he replied, "I used to."

"When school starts, you should try out."

"Maybe. I dunno. I don't think it matters much anymore. What about you? Do you wrestle?"

Shig chuckled, raising his palm as if testifying. "I'll stick with boxing!"

Russell bent his bruised knee to his stomach; flexing; massaging. He started to walk in circles, shaking out the ache. It wasn't new, the bruises. Between sprained muscles and internal abrasions, his past matches taught him to be quick and to endure the pain. He had to admit, though, Shig had one hell of an impact! Of course the steel-toed boot inflicted more sting than the kick itself.

Swirling dust flung in their faces, catching grit on their sticky skins. Ralph and Hank hooted and clapped. Sam swore out loud. After Russell wiped his eyes, he saw eight figures moving down the wide street; their bodies rippling under the hot sun. One by one, Russell's friends stared at the figures that streamed closer, merging with the yellowish wind. The drifters began revealing their features. Masking their immortality. Embracing the pellets of sand like bullets.

Sam, standing beside his cousin and rattling his bony leg, asked, "Suppose that's them?"

"Well, it ain't the Queen's army!" Ikki snapped.

Jim squinted. Without his glasses, he had one hell of a time deciphering faces. The leader, steering the gang, was short and waddled like a goose. His stubby legs slightly bowed. His feet flapped. Jim turned to Russell and said, "That has to be him. No one else can be that ugly."

Shig uttered, shaking his head, "Pigs. A buncha *butas*."

"Too bad I eat pork," Russell joked, trying to flatten his nervousness.

"Fry 'em up on a skillet. Watch 'em sizzle," Shig said.

The short one halted at five feet apart. His gang curved around him, protecting him. His high forehead, small chin, and wandering right eye fractured charm into pieces. Russell inspected each gang member, all wearing blue jeans with the bottoms flipped inside out. Some had acne scars. Their lips were cracked; hair mangled and greasy; their hands were rough as dead bark. Stiff scowls gripped their faces as if gripping shark's teeth. Jim was right about one thing: no one else could be that ugly.

The short one walked closer, squinting at Russell and Jim who stood in front of the line. He pinched his mouth; observing.

Russell remained quiet, wondering what the hell he was planning.

"So," the short one began in English, his dialect emulating the *Issei.* He lightly tugged on Russell's torn collar. "I think maybe you looking for fun. Or maybe looking for new territory to own." He clicked his tongue and switched to Japanese. "*Women should never be out by themselves. Who knows what sort of trouble they will find themselves in. Even dogs have better sense.*"

A cycle of chuckles jostled around the gang; audacity heaving through their muscles; spitefulness through their pores. Russell instantly tightened. Clenching his knuckles, he directly peered at leader one who stood a few inches shorter. He could take him out in a heartbeat. What was so intimidating about this guy, anyway?

Shig sneered, "If dogs have better sense, then how is it your mother gave birth to you?"

The short one jerked to stare at him. Shifting his jaw he slapped Shig's face. Pointing at him, he furiously asserted, "*Do not confuse my mother with yours, little girl!*"

Russell pivoted around and promptly seized Shig's shoulders to prevent him from lurching forward. "Not now!" he warned, pushing his weight against Shig's chest. "It's my fight!" Shig rammed his steel-toe boot in the ground. Huffing, he pulled back and cursed, flinging his arms out, glaring at the short one. Russell turned to face the boy. "You," he barked, "need to apologize! You had no right to bully my mom the other day!"

"Ohhh!" he leered, boosting his brows. "So da dog has hona!"

Russell slapped his smirking face. "Do you, *shojo*?"

A red imprint surged on the short one's cheek. A brittle delirium shaped his anger as he squinted; calculating. An unpleasant calm probed between the two. His regulated emotions were unfamiliar to Russell, and he wasn't sure what the boy's next move entailed. Even in wrestling, Russell could speculate his opponent's ensuing moves. But this one was as foreign to him as much as the Japanese Emperor himself.

The short one stiffened his back. "You don' know who you fucking with." Fluctuating his jaw, his eye darting, he persisted, "*I can break your neck in half, and watch you die in pain!*"

An uneasiness surged Russell's heart. There was something appalling about his threat; a distressing sincerity. He shifted his left foot back and crossed his arms. "So can I," he asserted.

The boy spat at the ground, barely missing Russell's foot. Leering as if a brace clutched his skull, he said, "I don' think so. You too soft." He reached for Russell's torn collar once more, but Russell snatched his wrist, choking it. The short one swiftly twirled his arm free. He uttered something unfamiliar to Russell. A Japanese curse perhaps. Or just rotten profanity.

"I know this place," Russell announced, his blood assaulting his sweaty skin. "On Block Five. It's an empty building. I'll kick your ass there, little girl!"

Jim flinched at Russell. Surely he wasn't talking about that building on that night in which Callis had attacked them. Surely he wasn't *that* stupid.

THE empty barrack filled quickly; absorbing body heat; absorbing sixteen bodies. The street lights flickered on despite the sun's persisting glow. Murmurs shuffled on opposite sides, subduing the scuffle of feet. Cigarette smoke began filling the air. The evening light punched unswervingly past the sharp edges of Mount Williamson. A reddish streak scraped across the sky like bleeding cuts. Jim began to have doubts. He didn't realize revenge involved so many people. He thought it would be more one-on-one rather than lugging gangs around like suitcases. And what if it really got out of control? Would it mean that someone might die? Or would the police arrest everyone? Thrust them in the stockade? He glanced at Russell who showed no fear, no worry, and that worried Jim. Wrestling validated one thing, but actual fighting proved more precarious. How could Russell look so astonishingly calm?

Russell stretched his arms over his head, and bent to touch his toes. He repeatedly watched his opponent directly across who likewise stretched his limbs. There was something odd about him; almost inhuman. His movements quickened like whips when he flicked his arms. Russell had never seen movements as sharp and precise. The muscles on his arms were better defined as if flawlessly carved. Russell knew he didn't have time for doubts.

"What do you think, Jim?" Russell asked, shaking out his hands. "Is this guy puttin' on a show or what?"

Shig interjected, "He does look skilled. But that could be just for show."

Jim stared at Shig, unimpressed. "How would you know?"

Lifting a cigarette to his lips, he bragged, "I've had my share of fights! That's how I know!" He puffed and blew smoke into Jim's face. "What about you, tough guy? Ever scarred those pretty-little-hands?"

Coughing, Jim waved the smoke away from his eyes. Flustered, he turned his back, not interested in getting into a pissing contest with Shig. He observed the gang across the way, evaluating their fixed stances like strategic makers. An excitement crept between their lips like a dirty secret as they stared at Russell. Did Russell truly know what he was getting himself into?

Shig continued, "Just pull some of that wrestling stuff on him, Russ. You'll have the upper hand!"

Jim grabbed his friend's arm one last time. Tugging him aside, he reclined into his ear and whispered, "Russell, you've never seen him fight! You don't know what he's capable of!"

Straining back, irritated and not in the mood for skepticism, he quipped, "That's the best part! Didn't you know that?" He freed his arm. "Listen, Jim, I asked you if you were sure about this. You said you were. You said you weren't made of paper. I don't need this right now! If you're gonna flip your wig, do it elsewhere, because I'm kinda busy right now!"

Russell took a few short breaths to clean his worry and wash out any tension from his expressions. To look calm and in control; if not ready to rip off a foot. His opponent unbuttoned his white shirt, stained from sweat, and handed it to a friend. His face remained angry, hard, like a gothic statue.

He chipped a cocky smile. "*Today you will always remember my name: Shikami!*"

Russell pretended to yawn and unbuttoned his shirt. His undershirt revealed the desert's blemishes and his sweat. He gave his striped shirt to Jim, winking with confidence. Glancing at Sam and Ikki, who stared at him, concerned, he smiled broadly. Turning to look at Shikami, Russell envisioned him harassing his mother, cursing in front of her, touching her. His grin fell, transforming into anger. The son-of-a-bitch was going to pay. Russell felt his skin heat and muscles tighten as he imagined in great detail of all the pain he planned to inflict.

"Ralph," Shig declared, pointing his cigarette toward his chest. "Go outside an' make sure no one's peeking through if you know what I mean. We don't want any unexpected surprises." He then glared at Shikami. "I suggest you do the same, *shojo*!"

"Is ohready done!" he grunted, insulted. "One on each side! *I am no fucking idiot! Unlike you, little girl!*"

Shig clenched his jaw and flicked his cigarette. "When you're done with him Russ, lemme break his goddamn neck!"

Russell jumped to the burning cigarette, twisting it with his shoe. Snapping at his waist side, he barked, "Are you crazy? Do you want to start a fire?"

"Sorry, man," Shig shrugged, somewhat embarrassed.

Russell gave Shig one last scowl as if reprimanding him. He then walked to the middle of the barrack, not removing his eyes from his opponent, his shoes rumbling the floor. Shikami in turn sauntered to the middle, his chiseled grin unmoving, his arched legs severing the gap between his knees. Russell curved his shoulders like a badger, opening his palms, guarding. Shikami twitch in reflex, then quickly dropped to the ground and swung his leg. Russell instantly fell on his back. Shikami's gang jeered. Jim had never seen anyone sweep across the floor with one leg as if a spinning top. Russell didn't even see it coming.

Shig nervously lit another cigarette.

Russell regained his breath and thoughts. For a moment everything was blurred. Shikami paced to and fro. Gesturing him to stand. Leering down at him in amusement. Russell waited until his foe's ankle came into reach and twisted it with both of his feet. He tripped, but recovered his balance. Russell rolled and hurdled to his feet.

Shikami affirmed, "Funny! Ohmos' clever!"

Russell realigned his position, rocking on his heels, his hands hovering at his waist. He waited for Shikami to attack first in order to asset his strengths, and then hit at his weaknesses. Shikami bent his arms like boomerangs. Russell thought it was very odd. What form of fighting was he applying? Suddenly Shikami's hand flung at one side. Russell blocked it. And then blocked his other hand. Soon Shikami hit his chest with his elbow and coiled around to kick Russell's ribs. Russell fell sideways; dazed and breathless. He lunged back up and tried to catch another swinging kick that whacked him in his eye. He again fell down. Shikami rigidly snapped to attention; arms hooked; knees flexed; gently swaying like a leaf.

Sam gnawed his knuckles. Jim rattled a leg, ready to aid Russell. Ikki closed his eyes and uncrossed his arms. None of the Bainbridge boys had ever seen any of those maneuvers.

Shig noticed their dumbfounded expressions as he blew out his smoke. He said, "I suppose Russell doesn't know Judo or Karate."

The three stared at Shig.

Sam replied, "My brother saw it once in Seattle."

"Doesn't help Russell though, does it?"

Russell shook his head to wiggle out his dizziness, ignoring his throbbing eye. He quickly rose. Out of the corner of his good eye, he saw another flashing kick. He swiveled his arm, jointly grabbing Shikami's ankle and thigh with both hands and flipped him like a flapjack. Shikami landed with his hands on the floor and bounced up. He spun around, propelling his wrists like axes as Russell ducked twice but still was stricken with a sharp impact. He tried to hit Shikami a few times, slinging his fists like a bag of rocks, but was clogged each time by stinging blows. Shikami then grabbed Russell's flinging left arm, twisting it, breaking his wrist. Russell dropped to his knees, crying out. Tears blurred his vision while pain blurred his mind.

Shikami's gang clapped and cheered.

Jim leapt forward, yet was barricaded by Shig who grabbed his shoulders.

Driving him backward, Shig asserted, "This ain't your fight! You start now and everything's gonna get ugly! You wanna be responsible for that?"

Yanking Shig's collar, he yelled, "I don't want to be responsible for Russell's death!"

"You're not responsible! It's his deal!"

"He's my friend, damnit! He should be yours, too!"

Shig shoved him into a wall. "He is, you self-righteous prick! *Jigoku ni otosu!* "

Jim clutched Shig's elbows and spat, "You go to hell!"

"Stop it!" Russell hollered, turning his body toward his friends. "Just stop it! Kill each other on another day, will ya! I ain't dead yet, for Christ's sake!"

Jim and Shig looked astonished, briefly staring at Russell. Jim pushed Shig away and circled to the side, furiously blinking and panting through his nostrils. Shig slapped his hands over his chest as if proving a point. Glaring at Jim, he moved in between Ralph and Bruce.

Russell held his breath and fluttered his lids. He pretended to pass out, flopping on his back, sprawled like a star fish. His chest continued to heave; his skin continued to sweat. Shikami clapped his hands, holding his palms in a tight victory, rattling his wrists. He too was short on breath.

He boasted, "You see! He not las' for fifteen minute! He is a *konchu*! A weak bug easy to squash!"

His rigid face leaked a careless confidence as he strode around Russell. He leaned down, one knee on the floor, and squeezed Russell's cheeks with one hand. Insisting with a larger, more satisfied grin, he muttered, "*My grandmother has better strength than you, little girl!*"

Russell opened his eyes. He seized his opponent's undershirt with his good hand and flipped him over, wrapping his legs around his neck, squeezing his throat. Gasping, Shikami attempted to punch Russell's ribs without real effect. Russell clenched his muscles, thereby fortifying his ribs against significant pain. The room plummeted into complete silence. No one moved. A rambling truck reverberated through the cracks, slinging dust and pebbles from behind, hitting one of the windows, startling a few. Russell pinched his athletic legs even tighter and listened to the boy wheeze. Without realizing he had lowered his broken wrist towards his hip, Shikami managed to seize it and twisted it. Russell yelled out in pain, his reflex squeezing tighter. Both lay on the floor; strangling and twisting; grunting and howling; waiting for the other to faint first. Slowly, both their strengths drained like quick sand as minutes maintained a sluggish motion. They panted; each feeling the narrow control of killing and dying at the same moment. It was only a matter of time, and time was an entity worth wasting.

"Jesus Christ!" Sam burst. "Someone do something!"

A gong faintly echoed down the street, announcing supper. People roused from their barracks, streaming like ribbons to one of the mess halls. Children's laughter mocked the flippancy of the situation. And still no one moved.

The side door suddenly opened. One of Shikami's members yelped, "*Gunjin*!"

Russell and Shikami instantly released each other. Boys promptly fled the barrack as if fleeing a sinking ship. Jim ran to help Russell rise to his feet. One of Shikami's pals did the same, reaching under his arms to lift him. For a second Russell peered at the choking boy whose neck revealed redness and wrinkles from his jeans. Both knew it wasn't finished. The interruption of the prowling MP only postponed the end. Shig followed Jim and Russell out the back door, blending with the dispersing supper crowd. Russell glanced back and saw one soldier with three internal police officers trot to the scene. When the men finally arrived, entering the empty building, they discovered nothing of importance; not even traces of blood. One of the officers, however, did find a cigarette still burning.

"Russell," Jim announced, walking briskly right beside his friend. "You need to go to the hospital."

"So close!" he sputtered, mulling over the lost opportunity. "So damn close!"

Russell scanned the area in hopes of finding Shikami. No signs. He had evaporated like water. But that was alright. He would put Shikami in the hospital; broken, bruised, and crying for his mother. Russell knew exactly where to find him when his wrist would be completely healed.

CHAPTER EIGHT

Late August

ROSE flipped the damp rag over her forehead, desperately wanting to ease the hotness and soreness of her worn-out body. Her flushed cheeks glowed in dullness. Moaning again, feeling her skin stick to the sheet, she would scream each minute if she thought it would do any good. Any day now, she told herself. Soon it will be over. But worries of something going horribly wrong throbbed inside her head. She wished she could leave this camp and give birth in a real hospital. Rumors of babies dying unnecessarily infected her anxieties.

Mrs. Yoshimura brought another cup of herbal tea. She encouraged Rose to drink it every hour to quicken the birth, but so far it only managed to quicken peeing into the bucket more frequently. Standing in the latrine line had been too painful for her; not to mention that the line was always too long, so she thought of another, more accessible, outlet.

"*Nai Mama!*" Rose whined. "*I can't! I can't! If I drink one more I'll give birth to a watermelon!*"

"*When I was pregnant with you,*" Mrs. Yoshimura said, sitting down on a chair across from the table, smiling, "*I drank this special tea. Within days you decided to come out!*"

Bethany, wanting desperately to be part of the woman's clique, moved from her bed to the floor beside her mother. She carried her *Little Women's* book like a trophy. She would be eleven in a few weeks; just shy of maturing into a little lady.

"Mama," Rose exhaled. "I'm dying here!" Converting to Japanese, she pleaded "*Please Mama, no more tea!*"

Mrs. Yoshimura was insulted. How could Rose deny her the pleasure of taking care of her? During her pregnancies, she had no family to support her or offer advice. She was alone. Isolated. Her husband worked while she swam in loneliness, discomfort, and tending to demanding children.

"I'll drink the tea!" Bethany declared, jumping to her feet.

Mrs. Yoshimura stood up and snipped, "*Do what you think is best, then!*"

She moved to her own bed to lie down. Closing her eyes, she began sniffing, sipping in her tears. The desert's chill scraped off the mountains once the burning sun settled. She tried very hard to make her daughter's pregnancy as comfortable as possible; yet, in turn, she refused her! She would never have exhibited the audacity to refuse her mother back in Hiroshima. It simply wasn't done. Sometimes she wished she had never left Japan. The confusion of the foreign language and culture not only bound her into seclusion, but her own children were ungracious and gruff. How could they be good Japanese children when Americans indulged these undesirable traits?

The toddler on the other side of the barrack giggled at her mother's silly humming noises. The nightly boredom perpetuated like a fluttering moth bouncing off the lantern's light. The senseless flapping of their complaints droned on. Masako, Russell's sister who ended up sharing the same barrack with the Yoshimuras, played with her daughter. Her brimming hums broke the monotony, implying a secure and normal life. Ruth's laughter bloomed louder and louder as if performing until she shrieked and began giggling over again. Osamu sat in chair, reading *The Manzanar Free Press*.

Bethany reached over the table and sipped the warm tea. She sat on the chair and took a few more swallows. Smiling, she cheerfully said, "This is really good, Mama! You do make good tea."

Rose rolled her eyes. "Mama, it's not like I don't appreciate your thoughtfulness, I'm just really full. *Wakarimasu-ka?"*

"*Hai*," she sulked.

Bethany retained an upbeat tone. "So, are you gonna have a boy or girl, Rose?"

"A girl. My stomach is up high. See?" She reached for Bethany's hand and laid it across her bloated stomach; just underneath her breasts. "If I was going to have a boy, it would be low, down here," she dragged her sister's hand over the lump, and paused it just above her hip.

"Ohhh!" she giggled, still clinging to the saucer. "How did you get so big?"

Rose glanced at her mother, searching for a suitable answer. Sighing, she replied, "I drunk lots of tea. That's how babies grow!"

The door suddenly opened, startling everyone. Tom jumped in and quickly latched the door shut. His mangled hair settled in the calmness of the barrack. A yellowish-brown stain seemed to bleach the darkness of his hair. He smiled broadly.

"I've got great news!" he announced. "We're being allowed to feature movies!"

Bethany perked up. "Really?"

"The administration has yet to decide which empty building to use, but," he stretched his smile even further, "we've got entertainment!"

Masako lifted the quilted blanket, peeking through. Her shoulder length hair was tied in a blue bandana, exposing her bangs. She asked, "Why did the administration wait so long?"

Tom walked to his wife, bent down, and started rubbing her rounded belly. She glared at him, yet said nothing.

"Red tape," he answered. "You know how things are. Pretty soon we should be able to get the newsreels as well." He turned to look at his mother-in-law. "*Is that not happy news, Mama?*" Turning to look at Osamu who glanced up from his reading, he continued, "Finally, we'll be able to watch the war! I feel so out of touch with the outside world. I thought Winslow was bad!"

"Dear!" Rose snapped, grabbing his hand. He stared at her. "Please don't do that anymore! It's very uncomfortable."

"I thought you liked it," he pouted. "You never mentioned it before."

She released his hand and flipped her rag. "That's because now I'm ready to explode."

Offended, he stood up and mumbled, "I'll say!" Turning around, he said, "Great news, huh, Bethany?"

Masako asked, "So what's playing first, Tom?"

"*The Letter.*"

Masako pinched her brows, and groaned. "That picture is two years old. I've already seen it."

"Well," Tom replied, "it's better than nothing."

* * *

THE lights flicked off. Someone in the back clapped and hooted, however was quieted by a whisk of hushes. Tomiko chuckled and folded her hands on her lap. A sluggish speaker slurred, then loudly boasted the extravagant music from the back. Jim glanced at her and dropped his hand to his side, carefully reaching toward Tomiko. At first she pretended not to notice, but her hand steadily fell to her side. Exotic scenery of Pacific palms and ferns lacquered the silver screen. Asian servants in white cloth leisured during the nightly introduction. Jim found her hand and slipped his fingers through hers. A shot thundered. Some people in the audience stirred, watching a man tumble out of the open door, wearing a casual suit. Another shot rippled. Bette Davis chased him in a sumptuous evening gown, aiming the revolver: shooting, shooting, shooting.

Tomiko's eyes widened; her lips splitting in awe. Staring at the screen, she watched the houseboy, who really was in his late forties, dash out of the plantation's villa when the two detectives arrived. Jim's hand lingered in between hers, and he experienced difficulty concentrating on the movie. The warmth of her hand ensued fantasies of brushing her neck, her legs, her lips. He began to enjoy the evening out, enjoying the escape, even if for a couple of hours.

JIM and Tomiko strolled on the soft ground, guided by the lights and the sky's pastels. He loosened her hand, not indulging in public affection. Tomiko was disappointed, yet reserved her feelings. A half moon glossed the violet twilight. Jim spoke very little, adding a comment now and then during her lively chatter about the movie. He often gazed at her neck, wondering what her skin tasted like.

Occasionally he surrendered a series of modest smiles, but kept a distance of three feet between them. Tomiko unexpectedly grabbed his hand and squeezed his palm. His blood thundered out of his brain.

"I'm not ready to go home, yet," she declared. "What about you?"

"Yeah, sure!" he awkwardly replied.

She pulled him off the main street and between the barracks. He eagerly followed. They maneuvered in and out of the shadows as if being chased, seeking privacy. Tomiko enjoyed the game while Jim enjoyed the chase. She found a shrubby tree beside a man-made pond and sat down. Folding her naked legs to one side, leaning on her hip, she erected her arm for support. Jim laid his knees down, sitting on his heels, his hands properly displayed over his lap. He continued to watch her, unable to concentrate. She started to reminisce about the better times in Winslow when she would run through her father's strawberry fields and hide in an empty tree stump. Or the time when she and her sister used to sneak the radio into their beds late at night. With things being so different, she had hardly the time to feel happy.

When she spoke of Kiyoko, Jim thought about his brother. He remembered the times when Tomiko's sister came over their house to study, or eat Sunday dinners. After John's death, Kiyoko disappeared, only returning home for Christmas. Rumors about her going away to a "mothers" home coursed through the island. If Kiyoko did have that baby, and did not terminate the pregnancy as other sets of rumors implied, then there would have been a part of John still living today.

"What are you thinking about, Jim?"

He drew back, realizing he forgot that Tomiko sat beside him. "Not much."

She nibbled her lip. "I doubt it. I've never known you to *not* be thinking about something. You always have this . . . this intrigued look. Like you're searching for answers."

He tipped his brow. "Is that what I look like?"

"You do to me, anyway," she answered, rubbing her knee. "So, what were you just thinking?"

He frowned, knowing it would be wise to not tell her. He didn't want her to think less of him. "I just . . . I just would like to . . . thank you for coming to the movie with me."

Tomiko raised his hand to her cheek, gently rubbing it. She could see his chest heave, anticipating, and yet she knew he would be too shy to pursue. Leaning forward, she kissed him; her lips weightless, flushed, moist, and moved leisurely over his. She then moved back, opening her eyes, wondering if she was too bold.

Stunned and aroused, Jim stared at her. Suddenly, he kissed her without thinking, holding onto her lips as long as he could.

* * *

RUSSELL peered at Jim, who couldn't stop grinning. Chewing on his salted ham, Russell lowered his cast onto his lap to make the minor throb from irritating him. His bruised, swollen eye began to change colors again; softening, appearing less offensive. His ribs were still sore, but at least he was getting used to it. They stopped talking about the fight as if old men tiring of their wives. The drawl was bit of a disappointment. No winners meant no victory. And an absent victory was not worth bragging about, so the Bainbridge boys began chattering about baseball and football from previous seasons to alleviate their boredom. Russell pitched in a comment or argument concerning the best player. Jim kept quiet, privately grinning. Russell scooped a lump of mashed potatoes and flicked it to Jim's forehead. Jim slung the lump on the floor.

"What the hell is wrong with you?" Jim snapped.

Russell laughed as the others chuckled. He replied, "I'm trying to bring you back to earth! Where've you been?"

Wiping his sticky forehead with his fingertips, he retorted, "What's it to you?"

"I gotta know!" he winked.

Grunting, Jim glared at his immature friend. "Believe it or not, Russell, I don't have to tell you."

Russell dramatically propelled his head back as if he had been slugged in the chin. "Oh! In the throat!"

A chorus of snickers and chuckles reeled up the row. The afternoon sun's glare broke through the line of widows, landing on the boys' trays, over some of their shoulders. The heat gorged their skins like on oven; their sweaty shirts absorbing boredom as if absorbing blood.

Sam, across the table, pointed his fork at Russell and said, "I hear someone's gonna put a swing band together."

Ikki, who sat beside his cousin, jeered, "Oh, God! I hope you don't try out!"

Offended, he leaned to his side. "Why not? I can play the trumpet!"

"Because I've heard you play, dopey! You're not that good."

"That's just your opinion, dopey!" Sam vented.

"A swing band," Russell interjected. "That would be swell. We need something else other than listening you two argue over the meaning of life!"

"I *can* play!" Sam mumbled, and engulfed a mouthful of peas.

A clatter of trays ruptured through the mess hall, followed by a brief moment of silence. Russell and his friends swung their heads around to look at the front of the line. No mess. A shout and a retort bellowed from behind the kitchen. Then nothing. Everyone began talking as if the sound was only a passing fart.

Ikki said, "At least once a week those guys in the back are droppin' stuff. You think they'd be more careful."

A young boy, about the age of ten, walked up to Russell's table. His navy shorts and striped shirt were clean and properly ironed, although his socks and brown shoes were covered in dust. His neatly combed hair revealed wild strands that had been let loose by the wind. A silver cross lay over his buttoned chest. He stood beside Jim, curling his lips. Everyone at the table hindered from gossiping and revolving food in their mouths just to stare at the strange, little boy.

Jim presented a half smile. "Can I help you?"

The boy looked down and wiggled his feet. He held a piece of paper in his hand. "I'm supposed ta give a note to him," he pointed to Russell. "The one with the black eye."

Russell straightened his slouching position as if awarded a medal. Leaning over the table, he grabbed the folded paper directly over Jim's plate. "Thanks, kiddo!" he boasted. "Who's it from?"

"From Naomi."

Resettling himself, he asked, "Who's that?"

The boy turned to look at the table where the two winged nuns sat; four tables down the aisle. He pivoted his tiny stance and rolled his reluctant eyes. "My sister!" he sighed with embarrassment. "She's the one wearing the pink blouse. If she got caught she would havta say fifty Hail Mary's!"

The Bainbridge gang all glanced at the girl who's back faced them. She pretended she wasn't being watched, casually twining her legs, slightly arching her neck and flipping her long hair to briefly show off her polished skin.

Sam declared, "She's the one who's always ignoring us!"

"I thought," Ikki began, "you said she's *wari*. Bad luck."

He paused. "Well. She is."

"Then why should you care? Are you stuck on her, wise guy?"

Sam cramped his brows together and twitched the corner of his mouth. "I'm not," he defended.

Russell opened the letter and quietly read. The boy fidgeted as he waited. "Tell her, yes," Russell finally answered, folding it. "That's not a problem."

The boy responded with making an odd, discomforted face and returned to his table. One of the nuns delicately bent down to the boy's shoulder, inquiring as she glanced at Russell's table with concern. The boy shrugged and packed potatoes in his mouth to avoid further inquisition. The middle-aged nun studied the Bainbridge boys with apprehension, tapping her small finger over her bottom lip. The boys darted her eye contact.

Sam eagerly asked, "What did it say?"

Russell stretched a smile. "She wants to meet me outside in about fifteen minutes. Any of you lug heads gotta watch?"

"I do," Jim said, nodding. "I'll keep you informed."

Another clattering of trays shattered through the building. Shouting punctured past the swinging door. Threats of ripping arms off reverberated in mixed Japanese and English. The door slammed open, and Katsuji, wearing a stained apron and white cap, thundered to the mess line, bumping into the servers. Meito followed, wearing his uniform, yelling out his defense. Katsuji smashed his chest into Meito's, arguing about the loss of meat, accusing him of stealing it. The three servers, who appeared no older than twenty-five, pried themselves in between the scalded men and yanked them to opposite corners. Katsuji insisted that Meito was an *inu* for the government, just like Ted Tanaka; and Mieto insisted that Katsuji was a misinformed idiot.

Russell immediately sprinted to his brother's side. Standing behind the counter, he watched Katsuji's movements. Meito panted; his cheeks reddened; his muscles flinching. The server, who was shorter, had clutched his hands around Meito's arms; grimacing; sweating. A white man in his early thirties with light brown hair, who wore sharp slacks, polished shoes and a starched shirt, emerged out of the kitchen. Russell recognized him as one of the administration leaders who made trips around the mess halls in camp to oversee them. The man braced his legs in the middle and began pointing.

"I've had it up to my eyeballs with you two!" he barked. "This is beyond ridiculous! If neither of you two can find a way to work together, then I have no other choice but to fire you both! Do you get the drift here, fellas?" Then poorly attempting to speak Japanese, he questioned, "*Ah-na-ta-no sha-shin-o toht-teh ee'ee dess-ka?*"

Meito looked at him as though his tongue fell out of his mouth. Russell and a few others snickered. Puzzlement crept on the man's face as he turned to look at Meito.

"What in the hell did I just say?" he demanded.

"You asked if you could take our picture."

"You know, it's one of your buddies who's been teaching me."

Meito grinned. "Then I suggest you stop taking lessons from him."

The man perched his fists on his hips, slightly grinning. "I think you're right." He turned to Katsuji. "You've given me more heartburn than my own children! This is your final warning, for the both of you!"

The man glanced at Russell, his hazel iris revealing worry and irritation. He stood like a general in the army; a stance as rigid as a wooden fence. All that seemed to be missing were sun glasses and a cigar. Russell studied Katsuji who swayed in the corner, behind another server, wrapped in grease and white. Returning to the steamy kitchen, the man slightly nodded at Meito, acknowledging his respect. Russell maintained his tensed muscles. Katsuji shoved past the server and pounded the swinging door as he returned back to his duties. Meito patted his friend's shoulder, showing his appreciation. He eased to his younger brother.

"Goro," he said, his voice drained. "Go back to your table. There's nothing you can do here. Thanks anyway."

Russell was more than ready to fight again; more than ready to regain his pride; more than ready to knock Katsuji in his place. But, instead, he replied, "Sure, okay," and reluctantly walked back to his group of friends.

"What the hell was that all about?" Sam asked.

"They're needing someone to blame, so they're blaming my brother."

Jim remarked, "Katsuji needs to be relocated elsewhere. He's nothing but trouble."

Russell began to eat quickly, remembering that he was supposed to meet the girl of mystery outside. Soon the boys resolved in trivial conversations again, ignoring problems they knew they weren't directly linked to. Besides, girls and war provided more benefits in their lives than petty problems of the camp.

Watching Russell shove the food in his mouth, Jim remarked, "You better slow down before you choke. No matter how fast you can cram it down, it still tastes like shit."

He smiled and slowed his pace. With a mouthful, he asked, "Is it time yet?"

Jim twisted his wrist to look at his watch. "No. You still have five minutes or so."

Russell glanced at the table with the two nuns and the girl. "Sam," he said, swallowing his last bite. "Do me a favor and return my tray. I don't got time."

"Sure Russ. No skin off my *shiri.*"

Pushing his empty tray forward, he stood up and winked. He then slid through the aisles and out the door. Removing his cap from the seat of his jeans, he flipped it and tugged it over his loose hair. The hot wind greeted him as usual with grapples of sand stinging him by forceful twists. He slipped his sun glasses out of his shirt's pocket and tried to protect his eyes. Leaning against the corner, he folded his tanning arms and waited. Within a minute, she came out. Her long hair flew up like crow's wings as she shielded her hand above her perfectly sculpted brows. Smiling at him, she walked past him into the building's shade. He followed her.

"You seem to keep yourself busy," she said, pointing to his cast.

Grinning, he replied, "If you only knew."

"I'm Naomi. Naomi Sakamoto."

He glanced at her skirt that tightly squeezed her hips, then up to her eyes, passing by the outlines of her bra straps. "Russell Hamaguchi."

"I told the Sisters I went to the latrines." Her soft smile revealed an embarrassing form. She began coiling her fingers around some of her wild strands of hair. Her pink mouth delicately parted, showing off her white teeth. She pivoted and reclined in between the row of windows. Tilting her head, she continued, "My parents gave me a French name. They thought it sounded as pretty as a bird's song." She lightly chuckled. "That was one of my mother's better stories."

"What happened to them?" He paused, realizing his rude behavior. "If you don't mind me asking."

Her expression remained serene as if settled by shallow waters. "Will it bother you knowing my parents died of illnesses?" She looked at him. "Most everyone feels I'm bad luck. It's just stupid Japanese traditions."

"I know," he stated in confidence. "I don't believe in Japanese superstitions. They're a waste of time."

Naomi smiled and bent her right leg over the other. Russell noticed how smooth her firm legs appeared.

She said, "Most *Nisei* boys won't approach me. It's bad enough I'm an orphan, but Catholic, too. Why did you approach me?"

"Well ah . . . for one thing, I don't care if you're Catholic or Jewish or from Mars." He pushed his sunglasses up his salted nose. "Besides, out of all of us at the table, you smiled at *me*. So, I wanted to know your name."

Bundling her hand over her elbow, she laid her arms across her chest. She unlaced another smile and tapped her finger on her lip. "I thought you were a little different. I couldn't figure it, but thought it."

Russell awkwardly slid his hands into his pockets and rocked on his feet. Her flattery pleased and embarrassed him. She was different from Maria. It was almost more appealing. Maria was such a polite, indirect sort of gal who relied on proper traditions and worried what her father might do to them if they were ever caught. This Naomi didn't seem as reserved. Perhaps with her being an orphan she acquired unconventional standards due to her unconventional situation.

"So," he continued, "where are you originally from?"

"Little Tokyo. But five years ago, once my father passed on, my brother and me were moved to Bakersfield. That's where my foster parents took us. They are Catholic, you know." She shifted her stance, reclining her shoulders against the building while extending her feet out. The wind caught her blouse and blew inside, revealing shadows of her cleavage. "My foster parents fought to keep us from the evacuation. They even went to a lawyer. But he said he couldn't help. He told them just to accept it." She shrugged. "They were so sad."

"What about you? Weren't you sad to leave?"

"They're not my real parents," she asserted. "They're not even Japanese! What do they know what goes inside my head?" Her smile suddenly split, bleeding bitterness. She dropped her coiling fingers at her side, showing no signs of amusement. "They would like try to understand, but they think priests and Rose Maries can fix me. They really are very silly people."

Russell no longer noticed people strolling by like driftwood dumped by the storm's hostilities. The heat's mirage and dust faded them from focus. Naomi presented escape. Escape from boredom, from guilt, from this goddamned desert where they ate and slept with dirt, wondering if one of the guards may get trigger-happy. A place where his father soaked *saki* until he passed out on the floor. He hated Manzanar. This dirty, sticky, unproductive shithole.

"Suppose," he suggested, "we see a movie this evening. When it's cooler."

"I can't. It's Sunday."

Russell raised his brows, flustered. "So?"

She chuckled and began twining her thick hair between her fingers again. "It is the Sabbath. I can't do anything on this day. Don't you know about the Sabbath?"

He grinned. "Kind of. I know everything is closed on Sundays except movie theaters." She laughed, finally, following a smooth flow of giggles. "Besides," he continued, "I should be Buddhist, but my parents aren't all that religious, anyway."

"Well, I'm glad I'm not responsible for saving your soul!"

He chuckled, enjoying her company. "Then, what about tomorrow?"

She began to walk away from him, ready to turn the corner. Pausing, she coyly said, "I'll think about it."

* * *

JIM hopped his half-painted, white pebble over Russell's half-black pebble on a white checkered-cardboard. Retaining his glory, only his eyes gloated as he picked up two black stones to his side.

"King me," he said.

Russell curtly exhaled and reluctantly flipped Jim's pebble over, revealing complete whiteness. Jim had two more full stones than Russell. The light bulb shed dull shadows just under their faces. Two dresser drawers stood at both ends of Russell's bed, with the radio on top of one, close to the hanging blanket. The closed curtains radiated from the street light, indicating that it was only a matter of time before the searchlights cruised up the streets. Between the eight beds, three dresser drawers, and two tables, one round the other squared, Russell felt the space squeezing him like a tic.

Curfew crept at half hour away, sliding through the late summer's bright moon. The Dorsey brothers preceded a brief news account of Hitler's advances further into Russia and Japan's stalemate among the Solomon Islands. Gertrude's soft droning voice intruded past the blanket, her words moving over the tale of Brer Rabbit and Brer Fox. Joe and George stopped asking questions about why Rabbit would outsmart Fox when foxes were supposed to be smarter as they drifted to sleep.

CALLIS arrived first. He stood close to Russell's barrack, staring through an opened window, listening to the radio's music and faint chattering. Light from the window slashed across his rigid face at an angle, hiding his blues eyes, yet exacting his cleft chin. He squeezed his loaded bayonet. Wetting his lips, he impatiently waited for the other two.

SCRATCHING his head, Russell stood up, grinding his jaw side to side, and then plopped back down. "I can do this!" he affirmed. "I can beat you, Jimbo, I just know it!"

"You can keep trying, but so far I have no confidence in you."

Mr. Hamaguchi began to snore. The cot where Russell's father lay was positioned beside Mrs. Hamaguchi's mattress in an L shape, facing the corner. At the foot of his cot rose the bubbling handmade still, infecting the room with a sour stench. Jim felt sorry for Russell. Watching his friend's face crinkled as he kept glancing at his father, he decided to end the game. His cocky grin weakened and winning didn't seem as important.

"It's getting late," he announced. "We've been playing for three hours. Why don't we finish tomorrow?"

Russell's eyes flared. He shook his finger at him. "I knew I would wear you down! Give up now and I won't let you beg for mercy!"

Easing a smirk, he stated, "Oh, I never beg, Russell. I thought you knew me better than that."

"There's a time and place for everything, *omono*! Just wait!"

Loud knocks rattled the wooden door like paper. Everyone jumped.

"Police! Open up!"

Russell panicked. He sprinted to the radio like a rattler hitting its prey. Unplugging it, he swung it to the floor. Then tearing his bed sheet off, he covered the radio and sat on it. Jim watched Russell; amazed and disappointed. He had a suspicion that his friend stole the radio, but he had stolen it under the influence of Shig. From the start Jim recognized Shig's immoral nature.

Meito opened the front door, already barricading the military police with questions: Why were they there? What in God's name was going on? Didn't they have anything else better to do than harass them?

Footsteps pounded the floor. A gun poked through the hanging blanket. Immediately the blanket was pulled down and fell to the dirt. Russell stared at Callis, numbed, praying he wouldn't shoot him in front of his friend and family.

Callis' helmet glared under the light bulb, sinking his blue. He instantly recognized Russell, and revealed an executioner's leer.

Russell had to be cursed. Why else would the same asshole keep prowling into his life? Maybe his mother was right. Maybe bad things perpetuated until a person stopped committing bad things and cleaned up his karma. Like lying to his family. Breaking promises. Wanting to date a Catholic.

Strolling toward Russell, tightly gripping his rifle, he leaned directly into his face. "I suppose you don't know anything about a missin' radio, eh, Nip?"

Russell dropped his eyes and said nothing. The bully's breath smelled of onions and radishes.

Callis started opening dresser drawers and dumping the clothes on the floor. "Where is it? Where's the radio?"

He continued to fling the clothes out of the drawers, watching Russell sweat. Thundering to the still, he knocked it over with his boot. Glass shattered and alcohol streamed on the wooden floor, slipping through the cracks, skidding to Russell and Jim's feet.

Russell couldn't breathe. If he did, he feared Callis would knock him down for forming a sound. Mr. Hamaguchi twitched and revealed his glazed eyes. He stared up at the tall soldier; his lips cutting open his mouth, stunned, afraid.

"Ain't supposta have one of these!" Callis barked. He looked down at Mr. Hamaguchi, disgust molding his face. "This crap will kill ya!"

Private Palmer and Dr. Huey awkwardly entered the room. Both were stunned to bare witness to Callis' temper. Meito directly followed with his arms crossed, and chest boosted out like a rooster ready for a cockfight. His eyes enlarged when he saw the mess. Breathing unevenly, he bit the side of his cheek trying to control his outrage. Gertrude stood over sons, embracing the book as if a shield. Joe and George trembled underneath their covers; too petrified to cry. Russell briefly glanced at him. He felt as his bones were breaking with every blink.

"I heard the radio. I heard it outside, genius! I know you got it!" Thundering back to Russell, stomping over the clothes, he grabbed Russell's collar. Callis snarled, his veins emerging from his neck. "I'm speaking to you, asshole! Did you steal a radio? Did you steal his," he pointed to Dr. Huey, "radio, you little yella bastard?"

Palmer interjected, "There's no need for insults, Callis! And there are children and women present, so watch the language! We're here to investigate, not to scare these folks to death."

Callis twisted his neck to look directly at Huey, ignoring his partner. "Is this the one you've seen hangin' round the hospital, Doc?"

Dr. Huey nervously rubbed his hands, wishing he wasn't present in someone else's home. He would rather have the MPs handle the situation without his attendance, or would rather wait at the police station instead of disrupting a family. He felt their eyes jabbing him. He glanced at Russell, then looked directly at Callis and nodded.

Palmer placed his hand on Callis' shoulder, quietly pleading with him to remain calm, and gently tugging him aside. Unwillingly, Callis stepped back, his heavy boots manipulating the silence, dominating the peace. Resting one knee on the floor, Palmer allowed his other leg to establish stability while leveling his eyes to Russell. Without his rifle, he spoke with a firm and even tone.

"It doesn't concern me that you have a radio. I really don't care about that. But of course, shortwave radios are another matter." He hesitated, carefully watching Russell's expressions. "What concerns me is that you have somebody *else's* radio. We know you took it. You and Shigeru Matsuoka."

Meito snapped his eyes to his brother. "You said you traded the radio from someone at the hospital. You *stole* it?"

Russell avoided his brother's horrified expression, and felt a tremendous amount of shame. Even Jim's terrified look hacked at his soul. How did they know? Who ratted them out? Was it Shig? Or one of his members? Did they arrest Shig for stealing a radio from the administration, and then plea bargained with him if he informed on his accomplices? At that moment he wanted to kill Shig turning him in.

"Russell," Palmer persisted. "Do you understand me? Do you understand the implications of what you have done?"

Russell could say nothing. He slowly rose to his feet to remove the cover. The rectangular box, with thick knobs and a circular speaker, sat under the table's shadow. Callis sharpened his grin.

Women's laughter and feet trudging up the steps interrupted the tension. Everyone turned to the front. Sadaye and Mrs. Hamaguchi walked inside their home, then stopped. Their laughs were shattered when they saw two MPs infiltrating their space. Mrs. Hamaguchi instantly blathered out her panic in Japanese, believing they were there to take her husband away again. Her shrieks broke the disciplined tranquil, creating a reaction from Callis who swiftly grabbed Russell and forced him to his bed. His rifle clanked against the light bulb, smashing it, causing darkness to descend. He flipped Russell on his stomach, crushing his leg in between Russell's crotch. Snatching both of his wrists with one hand, he pulled him up as if trying to snap a twig in half. Russell cried out in pain.

Palmer seized one of Callis' sleeve and yelled, "He's just a kid, for Pete's sake! It's not like he murdered anyone, Callis! He's not going anywhere!"

Callis twirled his own arm free, glaring at his partner, not understanding how could Palmer defend these Japs. He reached for his handcuffs and clumsily snapped them over Russell's wrists; but the cast protected Russell's left wrist. Grunting and cursing for the usage of one hand, not daring to let loose of his rifle, he yanked Russell up like a bag of laundry.

Jim saw his Russell's hand change from pink to purple. The cuffs were too tight! They were too tight!

Russell's family watched in terror. One man's power was another man's anguish. They wanted to weep, but their tears were frozen. They wanted to defend, to fight, but their strengths were defined by strict codes of honor. They looked at these two young soldiers who seemingly did not trust each other and questioned their own value of trust.

Dr. Huey began to perspire layers of remorse. Breathing heavily, he grimaced, thinking, constantly glancing at Sadaye. She appeared stunned, bewildered, wondering why he stood in their barrack. He cleared his throat.

"Ah, gentlemen!" Huey announced, resting his hands over his waist. His voice slightly wavered. "Listen, I'm not going to press charges."

Callis jerked to look at the doctor. His rage and disappointment fired from his nostrils.

"It's obvious," the doctor continued, "he thought he needed the radio more badly than I do."

Callis protested, "That's not what you said last month! You said you wanted to find the sonovabitch who took your radio- from your office- and personally watch him get handcuffed and thrown in jail to rot! That's what you said!"

Huey glanced at Sadaye once more, exhaling with embarrassment. "Yes," he quietly admitted. "Yes, I did say something like it. But," he looked at Russell whose painfully terrified face wrought guilt, "I can't go through with it. His sister works for me. If I want her to perform well, then I don't want to be responsible for her resentment." He shook his head. "It's not worth it. It's just a radio."

Russell was flabbergasted. He figured out of all the whites in camp, Dr. Huey would be one of the first to hand over a blindfold and cigarette.

Palmer, crunching over the tiny shards, angered by his partner's irrational temper, interjected, "Better uncuff him, Callis. I'll hold your rifle for you."

Callis stood like an angry raccoon caught in a tree with his teeth grinding, and seeping a low frustrated growl from his chest. Unwilling to move, he hissed inside Russell's ear, "Next time I'll kill ya!" Then snapping to attention, he glared at Palmer who stared at him with great apprehension. Releasing Russell's wrists with his hand, he snarled, "You uncuff him! I ain't giving my rifle to nobody!"

Meito, Dr. Huey, and Sadaye stepped out of his path as he marched out of their barrack, slamming the door, swearing. The second light bulb concealed the other half of the barrack in bleakness. Mrs. Hamaguchi collapsed on Meito's bed and finally released her sobs, shaking. Sadaye rushed over to embrace her mother, letting her mother's head rest on her shoulder, repeating comforting words.

Palmer hated his job at times. Especially when he was partnered-up with Callis. Hardly anyone from their unit liked the son-of-a-bitch. And he felt sorry for Russell. The humiliation this kid must be enduring. Turning to look at Russell's hands, he slipped out the key and unbound them.

"You're lucky this time, Russell," Palmer said, keeping an authoritative tone, slipping the cuffs into his pocket. "But if I ever catch you doing something this stupid again, I will take you to jail. You seem to have a nice family. Don't break their hearts." He then ordered Russell to face him. He kept a harsh expression through the dimness, knowing if he revealed any sympathy, then Russell would not learn his lesson and would continue to meet Callis' malice. "I know this is your first offence," he continued. "Let it be your last." He turned to look at Dr. Huey who stood beside a stove. "Get your radio, sir, and then we can leave."

Dr. Huey awkwardly shifted his feet, and carefully walked to his radio. Russell sunk his chin, his eyes burning with shame as he shuffled to the opposite corner where his drunken father continued to sleep. Huey bent down to retrieve his possession. He tried to avoid eye contact; especially from the mother and Sadaye. Without speaking, he quickly exited with Palmer trailing directly behind. After the front door closed, Meito glared at his brother, heaving.

"Jim, you better leave," he commanded.

Jim nodded and rose from his seat. He looked at Russell, wanting to say something, wanting to ease the humiliation; at least to say good night. When he closed the door, he heard yelling swell from the weak walls.

"Are you just *stupid*?" Meito yelled. "What the hell were you thinking, Goro? Stealing?" His arms began to jitter with rage as he paced. "*Kokuhyo suru!* So stupid! So stupid!"

Joe and George curled their legs to their chest, afraid to breathe too loudly. Their father had never raised his voice to that level except once when they were caught smoking in the shed last year. Everyone else felt numb, and all they could do was watch Meito's anger inflate in the small room. Mr. Hamaguchi jerked again. He grumbled something underneath Meito's yelling, then passed out.

Russell wished he were dead. He never thought about how he could bring so much dishonor into his family. Abruptly, Meito slapped him so forcefully he plummeted to the ground, barely missing the stove's edge. Sadaye shrieked, telling him to stop. Horrified by what he had just done to his little brother, Meito wiped his face and barged out the side door. Russell thought his eyeball had popped out. Laying his hand over his heated cheek, he stumbled to his feet, and sat on his mother's bed. Wiping the streaming tears, he muttered, "I'm sorry. I'm so sorry."

CHAPTER NINE

Early September

THE countless sunsets revised its colors like seasonal chameleons and butterflies, molting pinks to orange, purples to dark blues. The western mountains continued its weather-tattered skeleton, sharply pointing to the heavens as if accusing the universe of injustice and ridicule. The two links of mountains bounced the sounds of vehicles riding the highway; bouncing the sounds of ten thousand voices walking through the sages and wind; bouncing the sounds of crying babies born inside the camp.

ROSE screamed, shaking the hospital's walls. Her labor had endured nineteen hours of sweat and the most pain she had experienced in her life. As if a butcher's cleaver was thrust in her back, and then continuously twisted deeper into her spine. Her face began to turn a soft shade of blue. Sadaye held her hand; her eyes tired; her mouth covered by white clothe, her feet aching. A different doctor, not Huey, but a *Nisei* woman in her late-thirties, pressed her hand on Rose's stomach. Her colorless coat was smeared with bloody. The doctor frantically moved to Rose's perched legs to reach inside with a forceps to retrieve the baby's head. The umbilical cord was wrapped around the baby's neck.

She charged, "Okay, Rose, now push again! Push harder! *Oshimasu*!"

BETHANY slid her arm underneath her mother. Rose's screams coerced the hairs on her arm to prickle. The waiting room still had fresh paint and paste from the sheet rock. Their seats were fold-out metal chairs that were sparsely spread like weeds. She was afraid her sister was going to die. Just like the woman in May. Just like John.

Mrs. Yoshimura stroked her daughter's hair not so much as to calm Bethany, but to calm herself. Fear of losing another child bruised her lungs as if a hammer had been pounding inside her chest; not her heart. Loose stands of hair webbed from under her hat. The late night had wearisomely turned into early daylight. She couldn't let her body rest.

Tom paced in zigzags, chewing on his mustache, counting his steps, counting how many times his wife screamed down the hall. Twelve this hour. Wasn't there a goddamn thing the doctors could do to make her feel better? To make certain her life wasn't in danger? To make her stop screaming! With him constantly scratching behind his head, he started to scrape against his skin, causing it to flake and slightly bled. He hadn't noticed.

But Jim had.

Jim sunk back into the chair, stretched out a leg, crossed his arms and continued to study Tom's nervousness. Not that Jim didn't worry for his sister, for he knew the hospital lacked a lot of things like everything else in camp, he just didn't see the point of acting out such emotions. Pacing wasn't going to make Rose's labor any easier.

SADAYE positioned both her palms on Rose's belly, pushing and grunting along with the expected mother. The doctor, whose mask now exposed blood spots, carefully pulled the baby's head out with one hand, using her other hand to catch the rest. Another nurse quickly unwrapped the twine-like cord around the baby's neck while the doctor swiped a baser and sucked the sticky substance from its mouth and nose. Its bluish body began to flow redness. A sign of normalcy. A sign of relief.

"How are you holding up, Rose?" the doctor asked, wiping sweat from her forehead with her gloved hand.

Rose's cheeks were pale. Her throat hurt a great deal. "Fine, I guess," she replied. Exasperated. Her voice rifting like a broken speaker. "How's my baby? How is she?"

The doctor turned the infant upside down and smacked its bottom. Within seconds, the baby cracked a cry. She smiled. Placing her hand under its head, she let the other nurse cut the cord.

"I'd say he's just fine," the doctor said. "*Omedeto Mama*! You have a new baby boy."

"A boy?" she meekly echoed, a little confused. "Not a girl?"

TOM halted as if he had been bitten by a horse fly. "She's stopped!" he exhaled. "She's stopped screaming." He paused. "Do any of you hear a baby yet?"

Mrs. Yoshimura and Bethany perked up. Straightening their backs, they watched Tom trot out of the room to search for the result. Bethany looked at her brother who hadn't budged, and didn't seem to be a bit concerned.

"Jim, what do you think happened?" she asked, attempting to shake out a response.

He looked at her, exhausted and irritable. "I don't know, Bethany. I'm not God."

"Why are you always so mean? I'm just asking!"

He turned his head, closing his eyes. "We'll just have to wait and see, Bethany. Like everybody else."

She curtly sighed. He was such a jerk. Sometimes she wished he would go away and never return. She didn't remember John being like that. In fact, she had few memories of her eldest brother. Once he swung her so high on the swing she almost fell out. But she loved it because he caught her anyway and made her laugh. All Jim ever did was try to make her cry.

"*Ano-ne!* Aren't you one of Russell's friends?" a female voice sprung in the room.

Jim opened his eyes. A pretty girl in a candy striper's uniform stood in the doorway. Her hair was neatly looped in the back. He recognized her. She was the orphan who ate at the same mess hall as Jim and Russell. Naomi, he remembered Russell telling him.

"Yes," he answered.

She walked inside, folding her fingers together, and hesitated a few feet from him. A silver cross dangled over the striped apron. She glanced at Bethany and Mrs. Yoshimura who blankly stared at her in turn.

"I'm Naomi."

"I know," he said.

She waited to see if he would say anything else, like his name. When a few seconds passed in silence, she pursued, "I'm wondering where Russell's been? We were suppose to see a movie last Monday and he never came. And I haven't seen him in the mess hall in a couple of weeks. Is he sick?"

Jim sighed, looking down at her bobby socks and two-toned shoes. He pondered revealing anything to her at all. Russell hadn't left his bed, except to use the latrine. His mother brought the food to him so he would eat something during the long days. He would pick at the food, drink some water, but mostly left it for the flies. He hadn't even taken a shower or combed his hair. Yesterday his mother sent for a Japanese doctor since he refused to go to the hospital. The doctor discovered nothing physically wrong with him, other than mild dehydration, and recommended that Russell should find a hobby, or a job to keep him busy. Instead he chose to sleep most of the time.

"No, he's not sick," Jim confessed. He raised his head again to catch her expression. She appeared a little apprehensive. "He's been . . . not himself. He'll snap out of it, I'm sure."

She flinched. "Is he depressed?"

"A little, yes."

"Why? What happened? He was fine when I spoke to him last."

He narrowed his lids in thought. What Russell experienced should be kept private. In fact, Jim didn't even tell any of the Bainbridge gang. Sighing, he finally replied, "I can't say for sure."

Releasing her hands, disappointed, she stepped back. "Thank you, anyway. Will you tell him I'm thinking of him? And he's in my prayers?"

"Sure," he nodded.

She frowned, not convinced of his sincerity. Turning around, she left the room wondering if Russell would indeed receive her message.

Mrs. Yoshimura sat up to stretch her legs and back. She strolled to her son and placed her bare hand on his shoulder. "*You should have been more polite to the girl, Jimmu,*" she gently expressed. "*But under the circumstances, I do understand.*" She bent down and kissed him on his forehead.

Voices, with a mixture of Japanese and English, vibrated down the hall. Jim shifted, slumping forward, resting his head between his arching arms. God, he was tired! Excited footsteps rattled down the hall and soon Tom appeared at the doorway.

"It's a boy!" he boasted with relief. "A healthy boy!"

Mrs. Yoshimura covered her wide smile with both her hands, squinting with joy. "*I have a grandson! I am a grandmother! How is Rose? Is she alright?*"

"Yes, thank God!"

Bethany jumped to her feet, clapping. "When can we see him? When can we see Rose?"

Tom walked over to his mother-in-law and hugged her. "I am so relieved, Mama! They are just fine." He then hugged Bethany. "We get to see them in a couple of hours. I'm a father! I can't believe it! A father!"

Jim felt numb. The word "uncle" seemed odd, foreign, as if an abandoned lifeboat drifting at sea. He knew he should be happy, exhilarated like everyone else, but the thought of bringing new life inside a detention camp disgusted him. What would be printed on the birth certificate? This phantom place that doesn't exist on the map? The name of a ghetto holding prisoners of war? Owens Valley used to grow apple orchards at the beginning of the century, however left to die after Los Angeles required more water to support the overpopulated city. *The Manzanar Free Press* featured a brief history about the reconstructed metropolis last month, as if justifying its purpose. Manzanar: Spanish slang for "apple orchard." Jim found irony in its identity. When Eve bit into the forbidden apple, the chaos and misery that ensued stemmed from an apple. Now that they lived in a place where they were surrounded by temptation and corruption, the name did justify purpose.

JIM reached down for the stool and dragged it to Russell's bed. The barrack was essentially empty as everyone had left for breakfast. The late morning rays eased from the lace curtains, declining from Russell's sheet, slipping away. Jim sat down. Mentally measuring the length of his friend's back, he watched for any movement. He then purposely scooted the stool, creating noises to somehow get his friend's attention. When Russell refused to respond, he began poking him. He reacted like a corpse.

"My sister just gave birth to a baby boy," he stated. "Tom named him after himself. What an egotistical jackass." He waited, tapping his fingers on his legs. "It was a difficult labor for her, but fortunately, everything turned out alright. There was a time when we weren't certain." Again he waited. Noises from outside the barrack replaced Russell's consuming silence. Getting irritated, he exclaimed, "How much longer are you going to feel sorry for yourself? So you screwed up! At least you're not in jail like Shig. Tom ratted him out once he connected the dots. Started with Bruce when he left behind his driver's license. In the office. What a genius!" he chuckled, trying to find a way to reach his friend. "Russell, listen. Be thankful. The men in administration weren't as forgiving as the doctor. Be thankful you're not in jail."

Russell couldn't live with the disappointment that assented down his brother's glare. That look. That permanent look. The outrage that surged from Meito's hand rifted his will into bits of grain. They hadn't spoken to each other since then, sifting through the hours with animosity. How could Jim understand that?

"Get the hell out," Russell grumbled.

Stunned, he said, "Excuse me?"

Russell exhaled, closing his lids as if preparing to die. His back ached from lying down for weeks. He knew his brother would never forgive him. Russell felt as if his life was jumbled in a garbage pile. He wished he had never existed. He mumbled, "You heard me."

"Russell, you've got to get up! Get out!" He waited for a response. "You're really beginning to smell bad!" he sighed, hoping Russell would do something. His friend's silence began to worry him. As a final resort, he said, "I ran into Naomi this morning. She's volunteering at the hospital. Did you know that?"

"I don't care."

"That's what I told her," Jim firmly remarked. "That you didn't care. That you'd rather stink up your barrack than go out with her." He paused, raising his brows. "So I asked her out."

"You did not!" he snapped. "You're full of crap!"

"No," he said, straightening his back. "That's what *you* smell like." He then yanked the pillow out from Russell's head and tossed it across the room. Standing up, he announced, "I'm going to lunch. It's been a long morning, and I'd rather eat than watch you piss away!" Russell didn't reply and only continued to lie in bed without his pillow. Walking to the side door, Jim looked at him, truly feeling sorry for him. "We can't let bullies like Callis beat us down, Russell. We need to fight back."

"Screw you!" he yelled. "And don't let the door hit you in the ass on your way out!"

Angered, Jim slammed the door behind him.

"GORO," Sadaye nudged. "Wake up."

He stirred, grunting, smelling steamed rice and spam. Sliding his cast arm over his eyes, he struggled to hide from the afternoon light. His sister proceeded to nudge him, calling his name.

"What!" he finally snapped.

"I have your lunch."

Flopping his body to the side, he muttered, "I'm not hungry."

"I also have a letter from Maria."

His heart jumped. It had been five months since he had any contact with her. "So?" he muttered.

She waved the envelope in front of his face, enticing his curiosity. He tried to ignore it. She continued to flap it until he finally gave in. Grinning, she walked over to her bed to lie down. It had been a long morning and she began to doze off. Russell tossed the envelope on the floor and unfolded the three page letter. He scrutinized the pages, clenching his jaw. It began with an overflow of apologies combined with her worries and endearments. She blamed her father for throwing away his letters, and not even telling her that Russell had indeed been writing for all that time. It was Dave who approached her at school and told her everything. Feeling betrayed by her father, she confronted him and that was when he confessed with great reluctance. He told her he was protecting her. Protecting her from a relationship that would never last. The distance was too far and who knew if Russell would ever return. But above all, he was protecting her from the enemy of his people. They were Filipino. The Japanese ruled over his family back home. He wasn't going to be responsible for his daughter's lack of good judgment.

"That bastard!" Russell cried out. "That arrogant sonovabitch!" He pounced to his feet, feeling a rip inside his chest, and kicked the stool over.

"What? What is it, Goro?" Sadaye jerked, a little frightened by his abnormal temper. She worried that someday he would lunge into real trouble if he didn't do something positive with his time. And this gang he had been associating with only made it worse.

"Maria's father!" he ranted. "All this time I thought she didn't care! That she stopped caring! He's been throwing away my letters! Like goddamn garbage!"

"Well, swearing isn't helping anything," she said, a bit annoyed. He kicked the stool again, forcing it to skid underneath his father's bed. Sadaye jumped to her feet, appalled by his behavior. "Goro! Throwing a tantrum is a waste of time! Don't resent Maria's father for his shortcomings! Work around it!"

Russell stared at his sister in disbelief. "I'm not the one with the hang-up, Sadaye!"

"I know, I know. It's just that . . . getting angry at something you can't control is useless. There are certain things that can't be helped."

Pacing, he spat, "Right! So I'm told!"

"*Yoku nai.* Don't drive yourself crazy over it," she insisted, brushing off the dust from her shoulders. "It isn't good at all, you know. You'll just drive yourself into an early grave."

He halted in the middle of the room, peering at her. "Oh, that's rich! Are you still writing to Jerry? I notice you keep getting the mail."

She frowned at him. "What's happening to you, Goro? I don't know you anymore! One minute you're calm, the next you come home with broken bones and bruises! You and Meito fight, then won't speak to each other! You're depressed, then angry, depressed and angry." She flipped her hands up. "*Do shimashita-ka?* Tell me!"

Russell crumpled the paper and slammed a chair into the table. "How should I know, dammit!" he yelled. "We're not supposed to be here! I should be worrying about next season's game, or whether Maria would want to go steady with me! I should graduate next year and hope to get drunk on prom night!" He slammed the chair again. "It's not my fault! Not my fault! What did we do to deserve this?"

Sadaye sat down and sighed. “Sometimes,” she calmly began, “sometimes the role we ask for isn’t what we deserve, or what we think we deserve. But fate will have a purpose. Is it fair? Nothing is. I’m not the *chojo* of the family. I’m not even the oldest daughter little alone the oldest- period. But Mama expects it from me because I’m still single.” She lowered her head. “Did you know I was engaged once?”

Russell hestitated, astonished. “No. When?”

“It would of been two years ago.” She paused, nervously brushing her uniform. “He was a doctor. Steve Hirami. The first time Mama had tuberculosis, I told him I would be gone awhile until she got better. I really didn’t want to go.” She slowly shook her head and bitterly chuckled. “Mama can be very persuasive. She made me feel so guilty that for days I couldn’t sleep. So I came back. Then Mama had a relapse. When a year passed, he stopped waiting for me. The next year, he married another nurse.” Her voice weakened as she shut her eyes. “Is that fair? That I should put my life on hold for Mama? Always for Mama. Always.”

Russell’s anger suddenly dispersed like water breaking through a cracked vase. No one knew that Sadaye had potential in marriage. He had always assumed it was her choice to remain single. He cleared his throat. “Why didn’t you tell anyone?”

“Because it wasn’t a good time. Mama’s illness was more important. Anyway,” she continued, reinforcing her voice and lifting her gaze, “I think maybe someone better will want to wait for me.”

“Like Jerry?”

She almost revealed a smile and smeared off her tears. “I think so. He really is a kind man.”

Russell thought for a minute, speculating the value of his sister’s judgment. People avoided interracial relationships because it was not only against the law in many states, but obviously safer. No harassment. No family rifts. Maria was different since she was at least Asian. The boundaries were less offensive to most. Except her father. He walked to Sadaye and sat beside her. She turned to look at him. Russell wondered if he appeared as worn out and as depressed as his sister. He then realized he wasn’t the only one who struggled with the adjustments. His father drank a lot. His mother emerged into all kinds of available classes: sewing and specialty cooking, although she already knew how, then there were painting and English classes, in addition to the tea ceremonies. His sister worked as many shifts as the hospital would allow. His brother, Meito. That was probably why he had hit him because everyone had become someone else.

“Well,” he said, “I won’t tell anyone- yet. If the time comes, I’ll let you do the honors.” He nudged her. “Just let me know in advance so I can jump state. You know Mama’s gonna kill you. I don’t want to be a witness to murder.”

She cradled her arm around him, briefly smiling. “I know. You’ll be the first one I’ll miss when I go to heaven.” She paused and began sniffing. “If your stench doesn’t kill me first. Seriously, Goro, and I’m begging you, take a bath today. Take a bath, change clothes, and go out tonight!”

Russell moaned his reluctance. It just felt like too much effort. And all for what? Where could he really go? If it wasn't that damned fence which kept them imprisoned, then it was the monstrous mountains and its gritty winds.

"I've come to terms with no longer feeling sorry for myself," she continued. "And so should you. Accept the things you can't change, but make the changes within yourself."

Squinting up at his sister, he mumbled, "Alright, Buddha."

* * *

EIGHTY-FOUR, eighty-five, eighty-six. Russell counted the people entering inside the building, keeping his nervous mind busy. He wasn't doing anything wrong. The movie would start in five minutes and he doubted that Naomi would actually show. He buttoned his brown jacket as the street light flashed on, spreading traces of artificial light. The evening sun slouched, granting the half moon to dominate the colored sky. Ninety, ninety-one. A faint trace of perfume fluttered his way. That was the same perfume Maria use to wear. He jerked his head to make sure she wasn't standing right beside him. *Stupid*, he thought. He was just being paranoid for no good reason. He figured he wasn't committing a wrongful act. It was just a movie. If she decided to show. Ninety-four. Noises from the building echoed outside. He worried it would be too tight inside; too damned crowded. Ninety-six, ninety-seven. He began gnawing on his lip. When he counted to a hundred and one, he'd leave. He felt dopey standing by himself when people were arriving in twos or threes.

The doors closed while people settled in the congested structure, shutting him out. He peeked through the window, as if a peeping Tom, watching the lights disappear and soon the reel flickered its silver magic. Maybe she was already inside. Maybe she changed her mind and would rather be by herself. He heard the muffled sound of music as the credits began. It was too late. Despite standing an hour in line to shower and clean up by borrowing one of Jim's refined slacks and allowing his sister trim his hair, it was just as well. This was a sign. He should engage his focus strictly on Maria. She did reaffirm her love for him. And he did love her, so what in the hell was he doing there? Stuffing his hands in his pockets, he started to walk away, considering how he should write his next letter to Maria; what to mention, what to not tell.

"Russell!" a girl cried out.

He turned around. Naomi trotted toward him in a pleated dress and black shoes. Her pink sweater clung just under her breasts. Her small bows shimmered under the light as her long hair bounced. Her red lips were fresh, ample. He was very glad to see her. Very. But he pretended to be uninterested.

"The movie house is really full," he said.

She halted closely to him, breathing unevenly from her jog. "Oh, it doesn't matter! I've already seen it three times."

"That good, huh?"

"I'm that bored!" she laughed. "The funny thing is my foster parents wouldn't allow me to watch *The Letter* the first time it came out. In fact, I wasn't allowed to watch movies- period! They think movies are *akushitsu*." She rumpled her nose in mock humor. "You know, filthy. So," she said, pivoting, swinging her bent knee as she tugged on her sweater, smiling, "what would you like to do instead?"

He unlatched a grin, wishing they could be anywhere but here. What else could they do? Watch old folk bicker and challenge each other in the community center as they played Magh Jung? Play hide and seek with the guards who might be trigger happy? One guard specifically.

I dunno," he shrugged.

Naomi hair swayed in the evening's breeze. "How about a walk, then?"

He thought for a second, mulling over the limited prospects. Her delicate neck displayed two small moles. For some reason he wanted to touch them, feel the imperfections as if testing the reality of her presence. He searched the crowded barracks from behind her; the off-green tarpaper dimming below the orange sunset. Everywhere he turned, they were surrounded by barracks. He returned to her perfectly shaped eyes; nice rounded oval shapes that weren't too small or too large. "Let's walk beside the fence," he remarked, stuffing his good hand into his pocket. "I'm tired of looking at the same thing."

MINDING the fifteen-foot rule, Russell and Naomi strolled along the barbed wire fence. The wooden posts, tall and rectangular, patrolled every short stretch, extending cords of sharp knots with braided strands like blistered piano strings. No music, though. The desert lacked the conveniences of civilization. Even joys of music and dancing. As strange birds and restless reptiles shuddered in the desert, their tuneless movements murmured in the shadows. Just pretending to walk outside the fence offered tiny pleasures of lost freedom. And to be so close. The temptation was undeniably there. Naomi talked about her dead parents and her lively brother. Russell barely listened. He couldn't help feeling guilty. What Maria didn't know certainty couldn't anger her. And what did she expect? Five months without hearing from her, then suddenly one letter? His body stung as if ice jabbed his skin, tightening his muscles. Once they had almost plunged deeper, after hours of kissing in the autumn woods, uninterrupted, but decided to wait. They weren't ready for the consequences.

"Russell," Naomi said, tugging on his arm, stopping. "What do you think?"

Crinkling his brows, he finally turned to look at her. "Think about what?"

"Right here!" she pointed past the barbed wire, directly into the shrubbery that appeared like short, fat, dying pine trees. "Want to give it a try?"

Shocked, he stuttered, "Wh-what?"

"I heard rumors there's a pond outside the North side of camp," she grinned. "See the shed way out there?"

He peered through the wires. An old, brown building, wooden and shaped like a box, squatted in the middle of nowhere. He had also heard that once a ranch had existed; now reduced to a small farm. A rumor that a fishing pond, perhaps a mile or two beyond the fence, provided moisture for the arid land. But since no one had actually seen the pond, it remained a myth.

"Yeah, I see the shed," he replied.

"Many times I dream of walking past this stupid fence. Even for a short time."

He rested his knuckles over his hips. He studied a few pedestrians ambling behind the barracks while he and Naomi stood closer to the fence. No one was watching. Even the erected watchtowers seemed uninterested in them, appearing like obscure figures in the dusk. Nonetheless the towers seemed as intimidating as nightly predators. Stepping back, he asked, "What are you suggesting?"

She placed her fingers over her lips, hiding a grin. She whispered, "How about a stroll outside of camp?"

"Are you serious?"

"It's getting dark. No one will see."

He could still hear the three bullets crackling, hissing, and the thunderous blow of his heart beating his throat. He could still feel the one bullet tearing through his jacket. He could still feel Callis' furious breath on his neck, scalding and fresh, his brutal words scarring Russell's ears.

"Do you want to get shot at?" he snapped.

"We'll be sneaky like field mice," she persisted, but an uncertain child-like voice tailed off after his harsh tone.

"You're crazy! I'm not going to risk my life just to look at a stupid pond!"

He marched away from her.

Jogging at his side, she gasped, "Why are you acting like this?"

He returned to the soft road, infuriated, frightened, rushing past trash cans and people; moving as far from temptation as possible.

Naomi, who was confused and offended, somehow managed to keep up with his pace. "Russell!" she demanded. "I thought you had courage! Besides, no one's watching!"

"I can't believe you're that naive!" he spouted. "Did you have all this planned out? Missing the movie on purpose so you could sneak out? Get shot at?"

She was a bit stunned. "No one will shoot at us!"

Russell stopped and grabbed her arm. "Sister, you must be out of your gourd! This ain't summer camp and those guards have real bullets! Didn't you hear about a shooting incident in April?" He frowned at her hollow face. She nervously shook her head. "That was *me* he was shooting at! I crossed over for scraps of wood and he shot at *me!* Don't you get it? We're target practice for these guys! They don't give a damn about us!"

Tears absorbed her eyes. She grabbed his wrist and pushed his arm from her. Wiping her cheeks, she angrily walked backward. He watched her run up the street, running like a wounded crane with its wings yanked apart. She turned a corner and slipped further into the center of camp. At that moment he felt incredibly stupid. Shutting his eyes, he rubbed his forehead. He knew he needed to apologize. Despite her naiveté, he shouldn't have exploded and insulted her. She hadn't done anything to deserve his anger.

Mid September

MR. YOSHIMURA read the letter from his wife; dated about a week ago. Sitting next to a small window, a dam of Montana mountains overlooked the sunken valley where his quarters existed. A rectangular room, constructed of wood and the military's lack of imagination, had been his residence for the last seven months. He was the only one there at that moment. Sharing the barrack with nineteen other *Issei* men, all waiting for the insipid trials to end and waiting to reunite with their families, Mr. Yoshimura maintained his patience. What else could he do? Patience was the only entity he could control.

He heard the men's voices murmuring from the court yard, surrounded by a wire fence and bored, young guards. Last month one of the guards had given an elderly man a mild heart attack, threatening him for not listening. It didn't even occur to the ignorant guard that the old man could not understand English.

He glanced out the window. The trees were quite beautiful as they blossomed their autumn colors of reds and oranges. And yet the mountains made Mr. Yoshimura feel so small; trapped. Sighing, he returned to his letter, seeing his wife's diminishing good humor. Her letters grew shorter. This worried him. Was it Jim? Certainly he hadn't preceded the same path as John. Jim was still young. John was too young.

How he missed his family. The idleness only made his ache more agonizing like gnawing hunger. Feeling a breeze across the room and scents of burning wood, he turned his head. An American soldier stood at the doorway, dark hair and eyes, and without his rifle. He appeared moderately young. His tan uniform was always crisp and clean as a good soldier should be. He maneuvered a smile at Mr. Yoshimura.

"I thought you'd be here," the soldier said, striding toward him. "Why aren't you in the yard enjoying this fine weather like everyone else? A hermit's life is no way to live, didn't you know!"

Mr. Yoshimura rubbed his eyes under his wire-rimmed glasses. He didn't button his white-collar shirt all the way to his neck, displaying his undershirt. Even his slacks were wrinkled. Today he was not interpreting for the military and politicians. He was tired. Very tired.

"Gud afta'noon, Captain," he replied. Standing up, he extended his hand to shake the soldier's hand. The soldier slipped out a box of cigarettes from his pocket and offered one to Mr. Yoshimura. Bowing his head, he graciously declined.

"You've been doing an excellent job, Mr. Yoshimura," he continued, lighting up an off-brand cigarette. Finding the name brands were not only expensive, but a real pain in the ass to locate in the black market. He exhaled a strand of smoke. "The trials been moving more smoothly with your help. Your cooperation won't go without its merits." Again he smiled. He slipped his hand into another pocket and offered a shiny black pen and a pack of stamps. "So you can continue to write to your family, and let them know how you're supporting America. They should be very proud!"

Mr. Yoshimura gazed at the gesture in front him. Despite that he had no more stamps and was using the last piece of writing paper, he couldn't accept the gift. Slowly the other *Issei* men began bitterly ignoring him. It was his duty to defend them from the lies, not to prolong the blame. In their eyes he had been assisting the accusers. What disturbed Mr. Yoshimura, though, was that they could not understand that he had no choice. If he didn't work with the Americans, knowing his special ability to speak English very well, they would ship him back to Japan. It was bad enough the government was already accusing him of engaged alliances to the Japanese Imperial Navy, not grasping the division between himself and his admiral brother, not grasping the division between politics and a simple family relationship. They ascused him of possessing Japanese documents, such as scrolls and letters from home. They accused him of endorsing a strong political role on Bainbridge. And they made him sit by the judge on a weekly basis to explain his defense over and over and over.

Mr. Yoshimura looked at the captain. "You ah a kind man, but I cannot take dis. You mus' undastand it is not because I do not wan' to." He paused, observing the empty bunks behind the American soldier, feeling the hollowness of his peer's respect. "I do not know how to say da reason without offending yur generous offa. But please, try to undastand anyway."

The captain scrunched his nose and inhaled deeply. Shaking his head, he dropped the stamps and pen on a square table beside Mr. Yoshimura. "I have to admit, I don't always get you guys. I know you're under a lot of pressure, though. I certainly wouldn't want to be in your position!" He paused, then winked. "I'm not giving you anything. Sometimes I leave things behind. It's a bad habit my wife's trying to break me out of."

Mr. Yoshimura blinked. He was stunned that this man exposed more sympathy than his own people during the last few months. At the trials, the captain often watched, sometimes with his eyes closed. The soldier strode back to the door, his thick boots pounding on the thin floor. He hesitated, tossing a two finger salute. Mr. Yoshimura again bowed, watching the man in the uniform shut the door; a trail of cigarette smoke still lingering. For a moment, he wondered if the soldier's gesture signified genuine respect or patronizing flattery. Either way, it felt good knowing he was still appreciated on some level.

* * *

RUSSELL'S arm itched. It irritated him that he could not scratch beneath his cast. One more month, then freedom. He followed Shig through the camp. Patting his pocket, he made sure he didn't lose the dollar he borrowed from Sadaye. The sand in their shoes rarely bothered them now, even when their socks filled up with tiny pebbles. A late afternoon wind pushed at their sides and stung their necks. A mild coolness rustled from the north, fighting against the last remains of the sun's warmth. They shivered. Winter seemed more than ready to make an early arrival.

When Shig and Russell reached their destination, Shig gently took Russell's arm and said, "I didn't want to say anything in front of your family, but I want you to know it wasn't me."

Russell stared at him, knowing exactly what Shig was referring to.

Lowering his voice, Shig continued, "I didn't turn you in. And I want you to understand even though Hank did . . . he's a little slow. He didn't mean to. They just kept hammering him until they made him cry."

Russell didn't blink while his friend explained. Breaking a smile, he replied, "Well, I was mad as hell at you. At first. But I realized it was my own damn fault. Shouldn't of done it anyway. At least my guy dropped the charges."

"We're good, then?" Shig asked, releasing his arm.

"How can we be good when we got caught like a bunch of dummies?"

Chuckling, Shig playfully slugged Russell's shoulder and nodded in agreement. He jogged up a set of steps and entered the front door, leaving Russell to close it from behind. Amazed to see barefooted men draped in white shirts and loose-fitting pants, Russell watched in awe. Twenty men were lined in five rows, wearing white head bands wrapped around their foreheads, mimicking their instructor's movements, shouting. Their arms snapped out their punches. They kicked high. The barrack shook. Again, repeating, punching and kicking, loudly and swiftly. Russell felt like he entered a secret society. He had never seen such a thing, although he knew that something like this did exist. Back home his community had supported the sportsmanship of Judo, and yet Russell thought it was a waste of his time. Anything Japanese, even before the war, he had believed it useless because it meant a further separation from being considered an American. Now he was living in a world he would have never imagined.

Shig removed his hat and shoes, placing them in a corner. Tugging on his friend's coat, he motioned at Russell to do the same. Placing his finger to his lips, Shig then motioned him to sit on their knees, hands resting on top of their legs. Watching the half hour of exercises in silence, Russell felt the hardwood floor burn his legs, tingle, and eventually becoming numb. The instructor, somewhere in his thirties, clapped his hands and bowed. Without saying much else, his students promptly retrieved a large straw mat from a closet and rolled it in the middle of the room.

Shig leaned into Russell and whispered, "Okay, this is where it gets really interesting!"

The students sat around the mat, their faces stern, waiting for the instructor to speak. The instructor glanced at Shig and Russell, his expression emotionless and difficult to know whether their presence was welcoming or a flat out annoyance. He spoke rapidly, harshly, almost grunting. Russell didn't understand half the words, wondering what dialect he was using. Most men in the room looked more like Indians than Japanese. Russell assumed they were descendants of Northern Japan. Two students sprang up and positioned themselves in front of each other. The instructor stood on the side, folding his arms. Russell thought the arrangement looked similar to wrestling. Easy enough. The students bowed and instantly stirred their footing. Their feet delicately crunched the frayed mat, and suddenly, one grabbed the other and flipped him, causing his opponent to crash on his back. He sharply gasped. Quickly, the other leapt up and arched defensively; his arms bent at his ribs. For a moment, they stood at rigid angles; staring. The other one grunted and propelled his hands forward, but was stopped and flipped over again. The instructor said nothing; only nodded.

Russell could only watch in absolute fascination. For an hour, he and Shig admired the Judo students exchange their abilities: tossing, arching, launching their open hands in quick strokes; grunting. The more advanced students lunged their arms and feet in a forceful type of dance. The slapping of skin on muscle jilted the barrack, lasting for a few minutes at a time. Russell felt their body heat. Sweat flew off their foreheads as they leapt and darted; spun and fell. At the end of each brief match, the instructor criticized, showing the more appropriate method, but complimented what they were doing correctly, revealing a crisp, firm smile. During this time, he sporadically glanced at Russell and Shig. When the lessons came to an end, the students rolled the mat and set it back inside the closet.

Shig bent to Russell and murmured, "Great stuff, eh? Too bad the rest of the world won't catch on. Can you honestly see white people doing that sort of thing?" He chuckled. "They won't even touch *sushi* or *tofu!* Boy, would I love to see that day come!"

Russell grinned. "I can't even see myself doing that! And I hate *tofu!*"

The instructor, standing at the opposite corner of the room, turned to look Russell. He began sauntering toward them, swaying like a seagull in the wind. His frame was modest compared to Russell's stocky built, but he stood nearly the same height. He narrowed his brows and huffed. Clicking his tongue, he continued, "An' where do both you come from?"

"Bainbridge Island."

"San Pedro."

As the instructor waved his two fingers up, indicating for the both to stand, Russell and Shig rose clumsily. Russell then noticed scars on the instructor's check and the bottom of his chin.

The instructor folded his arms and asserted, "*Anata-no namae wa.*"

"I'm Russell."

"Shig."

He again clicked his tongue. "Yes, yes." He hesitated in thought. "So why is Russell an' Shig inter'ested in this form of art?"

Russell cleared his throat. "Because I want to know how."

The instructor tilted his head, squinting at him in amusement. "*Desu-ka?* How to what?"

Russell glanced at Shig who looked down. He said, "To fight, of course."

The man slowly nodded. "I see. But what if I can't teach you?"

Wondering if this guy was either nuts or vain, Russell snickered. "Then I guess I don't learn!"

"I guess not!" Turning around, the instructor began to walk away. "You boys hafe ah good day."

Stunned, Russell gawked at his friend; confused as to what just happened. Shig only shrugged and displayed his palms out in hopelessness. Russell remembered the first day he tackled wrestling two years ago. The coach told him he was five pounds under weight and to return the following year when he gained more weight. Noticing that there weren't any Orientals on the team, Russell stuffed himself with noodles and water, and for extra insurance, tightly wrapped small bags of rice around his thighs; near his crotch. He returned an hour later, standing on the scale, insisting he was more than capable. His friend Dave had taught him all the moves six months prior and Russell knew he could perform, and perform it well. But now this instructor was passing the buck just because he didn't answer correctly?

Annoyed, Russell followed him. "Hey, wait! I want to learn!"

"*Honto-ni?*" he chuckled. "You hafe a broken wrist. You boys go home. Maybe anotha time."

Frustrated, he vented, "You're the only one in camp who teaches this kind of stuff! I can pay you! So what's the problem?"

Aggravated, the instructor stopped. His more experienced students also paused; curious. Sighing, he strained his neck to his side and retorted, "This kind of stuff? Do you even know what it is?" Turning around, he stared at Russell. "*Shiranai!* How can you learn? Yur sloppy manners ah shameful. An' it's about defense, not attacking!"

"That's what I need! I just need to know some things to defend myself. Like, what are the weaknesses? What can I look out for?"

"Yur back. Make sure it don't break when you fall."

Some of the students chuckled. They stood around them as if part of a tribunal event; watching; judging.

Shig tugged on his sleeve and whispered, "Come on, Russ. Let's blow this joint."

Russell didn't stir. He despised losing.

The instructor studied Russell's displeased reaction. He asked, "Who you fighting?"

"Why should that matter?" Russell deflected

"It mattas."

"His name's Shikami."

"Shikami, really," he replied, tipping a brow. "I hafe a nephew by that name."

Russell stared. He had to be pulling his leg! Surely what were the chances throughout the entire camp? After all, there were only ten thousand people! Leaning on one foot, he persisted, "Listen, I'm here to learn. I may be ignorant about a lot of things, but I can't help that. I come from a very tiny island. Chickens 'n strawberries is what I know! If you're gonna hold that against me, then maybe," he paused, playfully narrowing his eyes, "maybe I really don't want to learn from you."

The instructor slowly blinked. "Ignorance is not clever, nor is worth bragging about." He sighed, and sharply nodded. "Most of my students, myself included, began fery young. Much younger dan you. Yur skills will be clumsy at best. An' with a cast on! You hafe a wonderful sense of huma, Russell!"

The instructor began walking away again, heading to a corner where his coat and shoes lay. Russell's cheeks flushed and he breathed deeply. He glanced at the other men who had nothing else better to do than watch him beg. He felt stupid. Why should it be so difficult? Like some sort of an exclusive group at a ridiculous country club!

Shig tugged on his sleeve once more, but spoke loudly and clearly. "Let's go, *omono-san*. I know someone else who can teach you something worthwhile."

Clearing his throat, Russell remarked, "I was told to learn from an honorable man. I think I *will* go to another teacher. At least maybe he won't have shame teaching a backwards bum like me to be somethin' better." He turned around, and winked at Shig. If he understood anything Japanese from his parents, it was the impulsivity of honor. Walking to the front door with his friend following him, the instructor stomped his foot.

"*Tomaru!*" the instructor barked. Russell and Shig stopped and rotated their stance. "Don' think I don' know what yur doing! You are not dat clever. But if you foolishly insist, den I will hafe to put you on da right path!"

~PART III~

In Memory of Pearl Harbor

CHAPTER ONE

Mid September

THE single light bulb hung above Tom's head like a lynched pigeon. He stroked his mustache, staring at the black typewriter. A collection of paper settled beside his rested elbow, waiting for his translation, and then to rewrite it to Director Nash for that week. Despite the mundane repetition of his work, the privileges attached to his title elevated his prestige. He knew almost everything that happened in camp; more so than the camp newspaper, it seemed. All he had to do was record it and let the big wigs decide how to handle things. The last man who held this position quit. He told Ted Tanaka he didn't want to be a part of his group, giving into Katsuji's mob intimidation. That was when Tom eagerly volunteered. He wasn't timid. Besides, he was tired of assisting old people with their complaints and problems. They hated the food; the rice was always soggy because of the high elevation. They hated the living arrangements; men could always peek at their daughters any time of the day. They hated not being a part of the political committees; where was their respect?

Ted stood up, stretching his arms upward, yawning. The long building absorbed his sound like cold, crunching snow. His smooth face whittled a sternness, dictating righteous authority. In his early thirties, his name was familiar to every person in camp, both white and Japanese. It was his people who fixed Manzanar's obstacles: community spirit, clubs, schools, troublemakers. A complicated, thankless task he and his men embarked; very much like pioneers of the Great West, with a couple of exceptions. Such as living behind a guarded fence during a time of war. Nonetheless, he took it as a progressing adventure.

"Tom," he barked, lowering his arms and walking to him. "I need the Farmer's Union statements completed by mid-morning tomorrow. We're required to review it in case Mr. Nash questions some of the financial output. Need it soon!"

Tom slid his fingers through his hair. Looking up, he leaked a tedious grin. "On top of it, boss-man!"

Ted remarked, "*I enjoy hearing the sound of total obedience!*" He quickly turned around and pointed to another worker. "Ito! How's that list of radicals coming along?"

Ito, a chubby man with thinning hair on top of his head, readjusted his bifocals. His desk, which essentially was a square table holding another type writer and thick piles of paper, wobbled after thumping his palms on top. Clearing his throat, he replied with a soft voice, "*Each week you ask, and each week I tell you the same answer. It has not changed since the last time you asked.* Same-o, same-o."

Ted pricked his eyebrows together. "I find it hard to believe. Katsuji and Saburo are constantly on the prowl for new recruits. I wish the *Kibei* would leave gullible men alone!"

Ito vented, "*Ted, I am a Kibei!*"

"You're the exception," he swiftly replied, biting his bottom lip, embarrassed for forgetting. He briefly paced, then stopped. Annoyed, he tottered on his heels. "Are you sure, Ito? No one else on that list? Nash needs to be aware of such activities. The last thing we need is a riot, you know!"

Ito slowly raised his right hand. Exasperated, he said, "If I don't hear it from God, then I don't know nothin'!"

"Fair enough," Ted temporarily smiled. He turned around, again, studying Tom. "How about you? Turning in that gang was a big help, but do you know of anyone else?"

"I'm keeping my eyes open and ears peeled for others."

"That's good. Each of us knows that the preservation of Democracy is a great challenge. Even within." For a quick moment, each one felt uncomfortable. The harsh irony reminded them the downside of the system. Ted clapped and announced, "Tonight's meeting! Let's be sure we have ideas to raise money for our schools! I'll be damned if my nieces and nephews become illiterate due to incompetence!"

Early October

THE morning traffic streamed heavier than normal. People emerged from their barracks, escorting their children to school while teenagers trekked independently. The cool eastern sun nipped its rays at the tips of the mountains like bickering Blue Jays: fierce, stubborn, ostentatious. The Bainbridge boys felt the energy of the Blue Jay with the hope of change that morning. Except Jim.

Jim continued the conversation, "Then how is it that the truck drivers keep stealing our food by the load?"

Russell grunted in annoyance, in no mood to bicker today. "I've already told you. Meito has gone to the camp director many times about it. He told my brother that without a witness, there was no real proof. Since there's no proof, there's no crime!"

Jim furiously shook his head. For breakfast he had counted three patties of sausages instead of the usual four. Last month he also noticed the amount of meat appeared smaller each day. Tom had mentioned that the government was spending about twenty-nine cents for three meals per person a day. The rations proved already meager, but the theft inflicted further insult. Somebody was selling their meat to the black market.

"How can he," Jim persisted, "the camp director, the big chief, explain half empty trucks when they arrive in camp?"

"They're not half empty for crying out loud! Don't believe those stupid rumors!"

"The trucks are entering with a much lighter load. That you can't argue against."

He exhaled in frustration, "For the last time, the director can't do anything without evidence!"

"That didn't stop the FBI from arresting our fathers!"

Discomfort strained their mouths, tugging at their necks like leashes. No one liked to speak of that moment when men in trench coats and dark hats barged through their homes. Like a black cat sprinting in their path, like a single flower dying in a healthy garden, to openly speak against the government in public was taboo.

Russell continued, "All's the director said was that we need to be self-sufficient. That we need to grow our own gardens and produce our own livestock. We already began farming this year."

"In the desert?" he retorted. "How the hell are we supposed to harvest or even maintain food on this dried-up land?"

"It was fertile once," he sighed, tired of arguing. "No one's used it since is all."

"I wonder why!" He flipped his palms open. "Who wants it now? Los Angeles has all the water!"

Russell chuckled. "Not all of it! Otherwise we'd all be dead!"

"You know exactly what I mean, Russell! No need to mock me."

Sam slid a comb out of his pocket and began shaving off his dandruff. "Listen Jimbo, don't be such a sour grape! Not today, 'cause I'm feelin' pretty good. This here, everything around us, is only temporary. Like the stomach flu. Just gotta wait 'til you throw everything up to get back on your feet."

Jim stared at Sam, completely disgusted. Russell and Ikki instantly laughed. Sam had to snicker at his own absurdity. The five block stroll seemed longer with Jim bitching the entire way. Somebody had to do something to change the subject. No matter how stupid it sounded.

"Promise me," Russell snorted at Sam. "Promise me if you ever run for public office, you'll hire someone else to write your speeches. You really do stink at boosting morale!"

The high school was arranged on block seven, confiscating the entire block. Several ditches lined in between the barracks. Men in their late twenties and thirties occasionally glanced up as they heaved and slung their shovels outside the cleaved earth. The ditches appeared like WWI trenches. The Bainbridge boys ignored the workers and gazed at the luxury of available skirts. Back home, competition was fierce. Only a handful of *Nisei* girls surfaced within their remote reach; except now it was like plucking apples in an orchard.

Sam announced, rubbing his hands together, "Oh boy! Looks like it's gonna be a great year!"

"We'll see," Ikki flatly stated. "This is only the preliminaries."

The boys slid pieces of paper out of their pockets. A list of classes, crinkled and smeared from the typewriter's ink, linked their schedules to the row of barracks; numbers matching the classes on the outside of doors like real rooms. The dusty streets became the exchanging hallways.

"Suppose," Russell began, scanning the wide streets and barracks, "it's a lot like a college campus. You know, changing different buildings with different classes. That would be alright."

Jim counted, "Suppose it's more like a chain gain. Working in shitty conditions. That wouldn't be alright."

Russell playfully punched his friend's shoulder and grabbed the collar of his jacket like a hook. He grinned and said, "You're lucky we don't have the first class together, then. I'm really gettin' tired of looking at you every damn day!"

Annoyed, Jim pushed him, and rebuffed, "The feeling's mutual!"

Sam and Ikki chuckled, shaking their heads as they stuffed their fists inside their coat pockets. They were relieved to have Russell back. For a while they had worried about his shape of mind; worrying that he would surrender to suicide. They had heard about two men and one woman all of whom had faulted to such sickness since arriving at camp. One man who attempted to cut himself with a butter knife didn't quite succeed; nevertheless was taken to the hospital for evaluation. The woman actually died after digesting rat poison, abandoning her husband and three children. Her funeral was held outside of the wire fence where a small cemetery existed for those who died mostly from diseases.

Russell pretended to slug Sam. Sam pretended to fling his chin back in pain.

Smiling, Russell asked, "How 'bout you? Ready for Speech, Sammy?"

"Anything but another day lookin' at Ikki's ass in the morning!"

Ikki refuted, "At least people can tell apart my ass and your face!"

"Paper and glue sticks on you! All that slack slides off my back!"

Ikki rolled his eyes, extending a growl. "We're not in the third grade, *baka!*"

Sam puffed his cheeks and crisscrossed his eyes. Feeling giddy, his cousin's worst insults held little value against his ego. Attending school again contributed an opportunity to sit as far away from Ikki as possible! He was tired of sharing the same space, hearing him snore or mumble in his sleep. Everywhere he went, there he stood or sat or slept or pissed. They even shared the same friends, which made it nearly impossible to achieve absolute solitude. They shaped like a couple. Or worse, twins! Sam and Ikki. Ikki and Sam. Thank God they didn't share the same family features! At least that much!

"Well," Russell exhaled, "let the games begin!"

The wind fractured their circle into three routes; their feet were chased by pebbles of sand and dust clouds. Sam followed Russell, since they shared the same class while Jim and Ikki journeyed in different directions. A memory of Winslow High trailed behind their footprints like molted skins easily swept aside by harsh gravel. Russell hiked up the steps and opened the door. Shocked, he hesitated in the frame, gawking at the emptiness. He really shouldn't have been that surprised. Everything else in camp was like a rusty, broken-down car. But he had hoped that something would be different. That something would indicate a return to civilization.

Sam gently pushed him inside, shutting the door, trying to keep dust from intruding any further. He, too, gaped at the shallowness of the structure. There were no desks and no chairs. Students were scattered about like loose marbles. Some in pairs; gossiping; flirting. A blackboard hung at the back as if napping on a swing. An American flag saluted in the corner, angling sharply, cleanly, colorfully. It had been a long time since he bore witness to the American flag. Russell felt odd, displaced, and he had missed it. He missed feeling like an equal. A young woman, fair complexion with dark blond hair and hazel green eyes, stood near the precious board; her bony knuckles exposed as she began writing her name on the board.

Russell and Sam sat at the back of the classroom when they noticed another classmate talking to a girl. His hair was neatly slicked back, and he had a broad smile when he joked. There was something very unusual about him. Curious, Russell walked over to his new classmate.

"Excuse me," Russell began, "but I couldn't help noticing." The boy stopped flirting with the girl and looked up with a half smile. Russell continued, "You're not Japanese."

"That's right! Actually I'm Irish-Mexican."

Russell blinked in astonishment. "Then what in the heck are you doin' here?"

The boy shifted in his stance to lean on one leg. "Honestly, when I heard my friends were being sent away because of their ancestry, I thought, well, that's a load of bunk! The only thing I could think of doing to help out was to go ahead and get on that train with them. So, here I am."

Russell stood for a moment. "So, what- you just got on? Just like that? What about your family?"

"They're back in Los Angeles."

"Ah- don't they, you know, miss you?"

He nodded. "Of course. I let them know after I arrived. They were upset at first, but supported my decision afterwards."

Russell chewed his lip, trying to understand how it could be possible. "What about the officials? Didn't they notice?"

His broadened his smile, amused. "Honestly, they couldn't tell the difference. They assumed I was Japanese, too! Never asked any questions when I signed in. Took my photo, gave me shots, and boarded me up with family friends."

Glancing at Sam, he eased a grin. "What's your name?"

"Ralph Lazo."

"So, you even told them your name and they still didn't realize you're not Japanese?"

"Blind as bats, these white guys are. Blind and narrow minded."

THE fifth period approached surprisingly quick, tricking the clocks to tick faster, the minutes rushing along the curve. At the rate the classes ran, school would end by noon. Students obsessed with the clocks, staring at the black rims and white background, ignoring the teachers' lectures; their legs getting cold and numb from sitting on the floors. They had to focus on something. The rooms were literally empty. The teachers, who were predominantly white, predominantly women, taught with no books and in some rooms, no chalk boards. The students were left with either staring at the teachers or the clocks.

JIM, who sat in the front Indian-style, curiously glanced in the back. He saw Shig shifting his legs for comfort, wearing stiff jeans and those ridiculous army boots. His slick black hair was perfectly arranged. He noticed Jim. Jim turned away. He found difficulty trusting Shig on any level.

"*Konichi-wa!*" Shig declared, walking up front before class officially began.

Jim sighed, wishing he were elsewhere. "Hello."

Shig squatted beside him, and said, "I've been doin' fine, Jim, no need to concern yourself. How's life been treating you, *tomodachi?*"

He carefully studied Shig, wondering what he was actually up to. "Under the circumstances, I can't find anything more to complain about."

He snickered. "Ain't that the truth, brother! So," he paused, swallowing, flickering resentment through his lids, "Tom's your brother, right?"

"Brother-in-law!" he snapped. "I didn't choose him. My sister did."

"Life's funny that way, huh? Can't choose those in your family. But seriously, how close are you two?"

Jim clenched his jaw, and bent to the opposite direction from Shig. "What do you want?"

Shig glanced at the preoccupied teacher who erased the entire blackboard to start over for a new class. The chemistry teacher was a *Nisei* man, younger like the rest, clean-cut and dressed for church, except for chalk dust that stained his ironed suit and bow tie. Shig suddenly stood up, snatching Jim's arm, forcing him to stand and relocating him to the other side of the room. Eyes followed them, quietly snooping. Appalled, Jim flipped his arm free.

Shig hissed, "Don't bullshit me, man! What kind of group does Tom hang with?"

"Excuse me?"

"Is he an *inu?* A goddamn informant for the FBI?"

The whispering room plunged into absolute silence. Jim felt as though he had been punched in the stomach.

"What?" Jim gasped.

"You heard me." He stepped back. "Listen, if he is, I don't want nothin' to do with you! It's bad enough he turned us to the WRA . . ." he hesitated, reaching for composure, furiously blinking as he folded his arms. "I don't ever want to be asked those kind of damn questions again! Askin' which side we're loyal to! Askin' if we belong to a militant gang and plan on planting bombs on

U.S. soil," he choked as if his air was smothered by gas. "It was just a goddamn radio! Not fucking espionage!"

The teacher quickly pivoted around and clapped his hands. He exclaimed, "Break it up! Break it up! *So desu! Yoku nai!* Watch your language while in class, or I'll have to send you home!"

Shig leaned directly in his face. "You better ask Tom where his loyalties are! Not mine!"

He shoved Jim as he passed. Jim exhaled in disbelief. Wide eyes and opened mouths fanned the room with excited wonderment. Whispers eagerly whisked throughout the room. What the hell just happened? Why would anyone suspect Shig of something far more serious than petty theft? Had everyone lost their minds?

RUSSELL kept staring at the back of Naomi's hair, impatiently counting, waiting for the class to end to finally talk to her. His left foot rattled while he rolled his thumbs. She had ignored him from the beginning of English class. He probably deserved it. He traced an apology in his brain, thinking of different phrases to say, outlining particular words such as "sorry," "jerk," and "forgiveness." Mrs. Berlitz maintained her speech of what she expected from her new students, pacing from side to side as if raccoon deciding to cross a creek. She was a nervous woman in her twenties, constantly fidgeting her fingers, jilting on her heels. Her peaceful voice and large, brown eyes directed at each of her students. Sometimes she called some of the girls "dear" when asking them questions.

"Well," Mrs. Berlitz concluded, "I believe that should do it for today. I'm sorry the books haven't arrived yet, so tomorrow I'll read out loud, and we'll discuss it then." Again she awkwardly smiled, rubbing her hands. "Remember, I want each of you to write an essay about a favorite holiday memory. Papers and pencils are at the door. Pick them up on your way out. Thank you."

Students started shuffling to the door, seizing the items on the floor in two cardboard boxes. Russell watched Naomi walk by him. She didn't even glance his way. He followed her, trailing promptly out the door, down the steps. Trotting to her side, he began his pleading.

"Naomi! Listen, I'm sorry for acting like a jerk! It wasn't my best day!" He proceeded with her pace, moving and weaving through the dispersing crowd like a leaf on a windy day. He saw Shig at the corner of his eye and nodded his recognition, but did not falter from her side. "I had a lot going on and took it out on you. I'm really sorry! I didn't mean anything I said!"

She clipped a crude glance. "Is that so?"

"But you gotta understand that going past the fence is dangerous! I ought to know!"

"So that makes *you* the crazy one," she snipped.

He softly grunted. "What else do you want me to say?"

She slowed her steps, maneuvering like broken branches in a stream. "You hurt me. I thought you were better than the rest."

"I'm not perfect, Naomi. Even my own mother would agree!"

She finally stopped. He almost tripped, not expecting the sudden standstill.

"I thought you were less judgmental," she explained. "I get so fed up with everyone judging like old Japanese folks."

"Well, I know what you mean. I feel like we're actually in Japan! I've never heard so much Japanese in my life!"

She raised a brow. "Aren't there Japanese people in your hometown?"

"Yeah," he shrugged, looking at her, wishing for blue mountains and waters instead of being surrounded by yellow sand. All that yellow. All that crowded isolation. "But not that many *Nikkei* folk. I come from a small island."

She started walking again. He instantly followed, skimming past by other students.

He asked, "Are you still mad at me?"

"We'll see," she coyly answered. "I'll have to think about it some more."

* * *

JIM carefully studied Tom's movements. He could see his brother-in-law's silhouette sway on the hanging blanket. A new lamp glowed brightly in the night, out shining the exposed ceiling bulb. Thomas Jr. finally yielded his crying. Tom was unusually quiet. Jim could hear and even understand Osamu and Masaku's whispering on the opposite side of the barrack. He stood up from his bed, walking across the short path, passing Bethany and his mother.

Stopping, he said, "Tom, I would like to ask you a question."

Tom ceased his movements, surprised that Jim volunteered to speak to him. Ricocheting his glance between his wife, who appeared equally astonished, he stepped forward, moving the blanket aside.

"What is it?" he asked.

Jim lowered his voice. "I ran into Shig this morning." He paused, watching for a sign of guilt. Nothing. A cactus without its bloom. "I know he deserved to go to jail, but he told me something disturbing." Again he watched Tom's expression, wondering and despising Tom's ambitions. "He told me they questioned his loyalty. Where would they get an idea like that, Tom? You were the one who turned Shig's gang into the police. Exactly what did you tell them?"

Tom curtly sighed. "Shig's gang needed to be investigated."

"Why? They may be idiots, but that doesn't mean they're anything like Katsuji's group."

Frustrated, he tightened his fists. "We've heard them mocking America."

"So, who hasn't?"

"You don't get it, do you, Jim?" he snapped. "There are undesirables in this camp who want nothing more than to destroy everything we've worked for! We have to protect ourselves- and our children!"

Rose turned to look at the back of her husband. His unbuttoned shirt hinged at his sides. His socks revealed a dirty ring around his ankles from his shoes after trekking all about the camp. She began to worry. Since he had joined

Tanaka's group, he had become a bit more paranoid. And transforming into a different man.

Jim lowered his chin. "Then is it true? Have you," he stopped, wondering if he should pursue such a sensitive subject. "Have you been . . . spying . . . for the FBI?"

Tom's face suddenly reddened. Releasing the blanket, he glanced at his wife who stared at him, baffled.

"I don't have to justify myself!"

"Who are you loyal to?" Jim angrily insisted. "Our own people or the bastards who put us here?"

"I told you I don't have to justify myself to you!" he retorted.

Jim pulled the blanket aside to look at him. "People know about you, Tom. And I'm ashamed that you're even a part of this family!"

"Jimmu!" Rose gasped. "You don't mean it!"

Tom stopped moving. He blinked. All that he could do was blink. He couldn't look at his own wife and son.

Jim returned to his bed, feeling his mother's bewilderment pursuing him. He didn't give a damn. For all he cared, Tom should go to hell.

Rose watched her husband, uncertain what to think.

Swerving his back, facing directly into the wall, Tom removed his shirt, letting it drop to the floor. Bending over, he retrieved his plaid pajamas and hid his body inside. As a wife, she should support him. As a friend, she should advise him. No one in camp liked to be called a traitor. No matter which side a man stood.

* * *

GERTRUDE exclaimed, "Is that you, Meito?"

"Yeah, it's me. Who else?"

His footsteps shuddered toward the middle of the room. He said nothing to Russell who lay on his bed. And in turn, Russell said nothing to him. Resting his arm over his eyes, Russell wondered how much longer his brother would refuse to acknowledge him. It had been weeks. When Meito's footsteps stopped, he heard something heavy being removed from a wooden box.

Gertrude slunk past the slouching blanket to see what her husband was up to on the other side of the barrack. Her polka-dot dress betrayed an out-of-fashion design from the last decade; its ruffles waving like crumpled fans; its long sleeves sliding over her wrists. Since she had lost twenty pounds, she felt embarrassed wearing her original clothes that sagged over her changed body. Resorting to the salvage store, she had to buy old clothes that would at least fit her. She walked to Meito and kissed him on his cheek. Squeezing his hand, she smiled at the new piece of modern convenience.

Meito plugged it in. Music blared out. Startled, Meito turned the volume down. "I've Got a Gal in Kalamazoo" bounced its rhythm throughout the structure as if bouncing yo-yos.

Russell at first looked at his brother, then at the most beautiful thing he had seen in nearly seven months. A radio! Meito had brought back a radio! Its polished mahogany radiated in the light. The Cathedral arch rose a short distance, but was equally impeccable as the color. It appeared pristine. Like freshly acquired honey.

Stunned, Russell asked, "Where did you get it?"

Meito squeezed Gertrude's hand and kissed her on her lips. Blushing, she covered her wet lips with her hand, giggling. Meito grinned at her shyness.

"I bought it from the Sears catalog." Turning to stare at Russell, displaying a seriousness, he stated, "That's how it should of been done."

Embarrassed, Russell looked down.

George and Joe leapt from their beds as they laughed and clapped in their plaid pajamas; their naked feet dancing on the mismatched rugs. Meito snatched George and swung him around. Next he grabbed Joe to do the same. Both boys squealed and laughed.

George excitedly insisted, "*The Shadow!* Let's listen to *The Shadow!*"

"Yeah!" Joe hooted while his father placed his feet back on the floor. "*The Shadow!*"

Gertrude shook her head, her smile fading into concern. "No. It's getting late. It's your bedtime."

"Please!" the boys chirped in unison. "Please, Mama! Please!"

Meito said, "Let them listen to it. Let the boys stay up this once!"

She glared at him, resting her knuckles on her hips, leaning her weight on one leg. She hated when he rebutted her authority. It had been difficult raising two sons when he was often busy; often absent. And when he did finally show to play father, he often undermined her.

She snipped, "Why not? Just let the boys do whatever they want!"

A little stunned, he stepped back. "Is something wrong?"

"*Nai*," she exhaled, twirling her hands. "*Nani mo nai!* I'm going to get ready for bed!"

"What, Gerdie?" he asked, insulted. "What did I do wrong this time? Don't you want a radio?"

She shifted her stance. "Yes, I want a radio. But I also want the boys to respect me."

Meito blinked and glanced at his father as if silently pleading for advice. "They respect you."

"How can they respect me when all the time you tell them the opposite from what I tell them?"

He flicked his head sideways, disbelieving her accusation. "I do not, Gerdie! You're overreacting!"

She brought out her fingers, numbering them as she rattled a list. "What about the time when I told them not to go fishing in that silly little pond? You said yes and they were disappointed when they caught nothing. I had to deal with their disappointment- again. Or the time I told them not to get a dog before evacuation, and then we had to give him to a neighbor? Guess who stayed up late trying to comfort their tears? Or allowing them to buy too much candy when you know they get sick? Or letting them wear dirty clothes when you know I work so hard to keep clean ones around?"

"Why are you bringing this up now?" He glanced at his two sons who got nervous whenever they fought. Joe slipped his thumb in his mouth; his wide eyes staring up at him. Meito modified his words unfamiliar to sons. *"If you were upset with me all this time why did you not tell me? I'm only trying to make our sons' childhood more bearable in this goddamned place! It is not as though I have enough problems at work!*" He pointed his finger to the ground to prove a point. *"Everyday I encounter resentment from Katsuji and his clan; and sometimes I think I will go mad! I do not need it from my family, too! If I have offended you,*" he tossed his hands in the air and enforced his voice, "*then I am sorry! I will no longer have any say in raising our sons! Do you feel better now, Gerdie? They will not only respect you, but fear you! Is that what you would like*?"

Gertrude narrowed her lids while her cheeks flushed. She felt all her in-laws staring at her like owls fixed on a mouse's movement, anticipating. Not wanting to induce an uglier disagreement, she responded with silence and disappeared behind the blanket to lie on her bed and tried not to cry. Mrs. Hamaguchi walked to Gertrude's bed, sat on a stool, and began stroking her hair. Gertrude looked up, wiping her tears.

Meito pinched his brows, feeling fibers of remorse. He calmly ordered, "You boys better get to bed, too. Do as your mother tells you. No arguing."

George whined, "That's not fair!"

"That's too bad. Now scram before I kick some keisters!"

Joe giggled at his father's funny words and trotted back to his bed. George reluctantly followed, grumbling, wishing he were bigger like Russell and could do anything he wished.

Russell sat up, slumping over his knees, studying his brother. He wanted desperately to seek his forgiveness. He watched Meito revolve the radio's knob, skimming past country music and news until he found the station for *The Shadow*. He then leaned back in the chair, shutting his eyes, folding his hands behind his head. His broad face chipped aside his aggravation as he inattentively listened to the deep, cryptic voice from the speaker.

"Meito," Russell began, wiggling his fingers on his knees. "How much longer are you going to ignore me?"

Meito slowly sighed. He wasn't ignoring Goro to teach him a lesson necessarily, but more so feeling ashamed for hitting his brother in the first place.

"Not too much longer," he replied.

"I ask because," Russell paused, clearing his dry throat and trying to muster some nerve, "it's been a month and I don't think I can stand much more of it."

Meito flipped his eyes open. "Is that so, little brother?"

"Listen, Meito. I'm really sorry for what I've done. You've got to know that."

"I do," he said. "I do." Reclining forward, he suddenly slapped his hand on the radio. "Well, Happy belated birthday, Goro! I bought this for you!"

Russell stared at him. He must not have heard him correctly. Why would Meito do something like that after all the pain Russell had inflicted on their family? It didn't make sense.

"What?" he said.

Meito rested his chin over his folded fingers. He discreetly repeated, "I got it for you. Since I didn't get you anything for your seventeenth birthday, I thought I'd make it up now."

Russell sensed his throat swelling, making it difficult to utter a sound. He remembered a time when his brother repaired a pocket watch he accidentally broke, carelessly dropping it through his small hands. Instead of reporting it to their mother, Meito skipped a high school dance to mend it; mending Russell's terrified tears; mending family peace. The watch was an heirloom, or rather an antique trophy. Their mother's father took it off the body of a Russian officer during the conflict over Manchuria about forty years ago.

Russell looked at Meito. How could he tell his brother that loved him? That he was gratefully indebted? That if it weren't for him, Russell had no one else to look up to. When Russell was a child, he wanted to be so much like his eldest brother; firm; gracious; keen like Spencer Tracy.

Russell managed to whisper, "Thank you."

Meito glanced at his father once more, who shadowed a pleasing smile. For another hour they could be a complete family without worry, without a wire fence, and without Pearl Harbor tying knots at their ankles, reminding them of a close enemy at bay. Shedding a sincere grin, hoping Goro had learned his lesson, he replied, "*Itashimashite.*"

CHAPTER TWO

Early October

THE broadcaster's voice faintly rumbled in Jim's ears. He stood in a corner, watching his family, oddly watching himself when he was twelve. The red-headed doctor, Dr. Ellis, he remembered, who hadn't died of a heart attack just yet, looked at him, directly, as if he was the only one who saw Jim. The sheriff and mortician carried his brother's body down the staircase. The body was exposed. Jim didn't remember John's body being that small, fragile, almost the size of a twelve year old boy. As he sat on his father's reclining chair, watching the two strangers walk by him, ignoring him, the nauseating feeling returned. He thought he would vomit. Tomiko slowly walked through the hallway, wearing a white-lace dress; perhaps a wedding dress. Her belly arched outwardly like a watermelon. Jim looked at her. She barely glanced his way while she disappeared into his kitchen, holding something in her hand. Jim wanted to know if that was his baby she held. Or was it John's? He followed her. She sat down at the round table with a glass bowl of Morning Glories; next to the bay window. She began eating the petals and extended her other hand to give him something. He opened his palm and she dropped a dead canary in his hand.

"What's this?" he asked.

"Your brother wanted you to have it."

"Why?"

"He killed the bird for you."

He looked at the canary again. It was bloodied; mutilated. Appalled, he dropped it, and demanded, "Why would he do such a thing?"

Tomiko gazed up at him, chewing the petals. "To save you."

"To save me from what?" She didn't answer and continued to stare up at him. "From what, Tomiko?"

A hand rested on his shoulder. Startled, he turned around. John stood in front of him; pale; cold. He looked how he did at his funeral. But there he stood.

"John!" he exclaimed. "You're not dead!"

His brother wore a white short-sleeve shirt and dark slacks; wrinkle free. Smiling, he said, "Wake up, Jim. I need you to wake up. *Mezame saseru.*"

Jim slowly woke, hearing his brother's voice echo in his head. He couldn't remember where he was, staring blindly at the shallowness of the dark room. Ribbons of light straggled through the curtains. He rose from his bed and shuffled on the cold floor, feeling the air tickling his bare feet beneath the rugs and gaping holes. Bethany and his mother slept untroubled by nightmares; their faces smooth, almost limpid. The search light suddenly pricked in, glaring directly in Jim's eyes. He sat down. His body radiated heat against the chill. Someone coughed. Startled, Jim jerked. He saw a metal object flickering in the corner. And a man stood. Jim couldn't see clearly.

"Who's there?" Jim demanded. The man remained silent. Panicking, his voice inflated. "How did you get in here?"

He could hear him breathe. Jim sprang to his feet. His heart lashed in his chest and ears. The man stepped forward; his foot heavy like stone. Jim saw his blond hair and cleft chin. In his hand he held a bayonet with the angular knife attached at the top. His MP uniform emerged in the inconsistent light. Jim recognized him. Callis.

"Outside," the brute ordered.

Jim couldn't move. He couldn't believe any of this. Why didn't his family invest in a lock?

"I said outside!"

"Why?"

Callis pointed his bayonet at Jim's throat. Jim could almost feel the sharp edge pressing on his Adam's apple. He looked at his sister and mother who still slept. Briefly closing his eyes, he imagined in the morning they would wonder where he would be, wondering what had happened to him in the middle of the night. Reluctantly Jim shuffled to the door and opened it, allowing the freezing wind to stab his face and arms. A yellow moonlight soaked his clothes with a deathly cold sensation. A dog barked in the distance. Stepping out of his security, he began rubbing his arms, his bare feet sinking in the soft, frosty sand. Across the street, he saw a garden of morning glories. How odd. The frost should have killed them. Callis followed at his heels, arching his gun down to Jim's back.

Callis threatened, "Walk down the street until I tell you to stop."

Jim glanced behind him. "You can't do this. You have no right."

"I can do anything I goddamn well pleased! Yer nothin' but a fucking Jap!"

Tears burned his eyes. If Callis planned to shoot him, he refused to be executed in front of his family's barrack. Shivering, he began walking. He wondered if anyone would see them, if anyone would stop them, but the late hour secured people to their warm beds and the patrol watchmen to their quarters. He wondered what he might have done to provoke Callis. Or perhaps it was random. Jim never forgot the feeling of being hit by the flashlight and watching helplessly as Callis attacked Russell.

"Walk faster!" Callis ordered.

Jim watched his own breath puff from his nose as if he were some sort of enraged bull. Speeding his pace, he thought about running away. What could it hurt? At least he might have a better chance. Yet, where could he hide? Where could he seek protection? The walk strangely seemed short. They reached the edge of camp where the barbed wire fence divided them and the shed that stood outside of camp.

Callis said, “Go through the fence.”

“What?” he echoed.

“Go through the fucking fence!”

There were occurrences when a couple of people slipped out of the fence and were never heard from again. They were proclaimed deceased since there had been no other sightings. After all, how difficult was it to identify a pair of Oriental men in a region full of whites? And there was a lot of wildlife to clean up any decomposing bodies.

Jim turned around. “Why? So you can shoot me?”

“I can shoot you now,” he leered.

Jim hesitated. The fervent twist on Callis’ face only validated his insanity. Jim scanned past the fence, pondering his ability to outrun bullets. He thought about the rumors that a pond existed perhaps a few miles from there. A farm house surely had to be within the vicinity. Was Jim crazy for even considering such an attempt?

Nervously glaring at Callis, he affirmed, “If you’re going to shoot me, shoot me in the front. That way people will know I didn’t run. That way they’ll know *you’re* the coward.”

Callis lifted his rifle in between Jim’s eyes, gripping the trigger. “Your brother died as a yella coward and so will you!”

Jim gasped when he woke. His sweat stuck to his pillow when he jerked up. His arms shook and his chest ached. Wiping his hand over his cheeks, he stared at the corner, staring to make sure Callis wasn’t standing in it. His nightmares were increasing. They were increasing and he didn’t know how to purge them. Why couldn’t his dreams die just like his brother?

* * *

RUSSELL studied the letter again. He ignored the morning noises of his family: His cousin’s chatter about school. Meito and Gertrude discussing money and how much more they needed for this month’s storage rent back in Bainbridge. The shuffling sounds of his mother’s slippers. The silence between his parents.

Russell smiled. Maria had beautifully written five pages to him. Her English was improving. She wrote about home. The school play that she tried out for and received a modest part in *Brigadoon.* She missed him terribly and continued to wear his varsity coat every day. She even admitted that sometimes at night she would cry. All of it was unfair. Her father’s disapproval. The war that was so far away. She would never stop loving him. And she promised to wait.

Russell then thought about Naomi. He felt guilty. He truly liked Naomi. Her tenacity. Her sense of fun and adventure. Since he met her, he didn’t seem to miss Maria nearly as much. Especially at night. At night when he thought about

Maria's laughter, making his life simpler. It was her optimism and loyalty that had made him feel exceptional; more so than wrestling. But Naomi, she was different. She definitely was different.

* * *

POINTING past the fence, Naomi whispered, "Right here I think!"

The plump midnight moon radiated a transparent glow all over the dark desert. Russell gripped Jim's arm, tugging him backward. Tomiko immediately halted. They arched against a barrack, eluding the searchlights, standing thirty feet away from the wire fence. Both the girls wisely wore pants and jackets for the event. Russell wore his favorite grey sweatshirt with letters reading "Class of '44." Jim flipped up the collar of his brown jacket. A chill indulged the nightly breeze, testing each person's backbone. Their hearts clamored like loose pebbles under a truck's wheel. To be caught equaled a criminal's fate, yet the boldness deepened a lunatic's thrill. They had to try it. At least once. Russell knew what it meant far more than any of them, but he was drained from worry and fear. If he wanted to defeat this spiraling dread that controlled him, he had to cross that fence. If he couldn't cross Callis, then perhaps leaving the barrier served as a replacement. Not only that, but the lust for freedom was too tempting. During the prolonged months, which they were trapped like grimy vermin, he endlessly fantasized his escape. As did everyone else in camp. The thought teased him like a mouse's tail tickling a cat's mouth. They had planned to reach as far as the wooden shed, and if they felt even braver, they would search for the mythical pond.

Tomiko peered through the prickly thickets with its shadows hunting light. She sustained a faint voice. "I see it."

Jim raised his finger to his lips, irritably rumpling his brows. Tomiko glanced at him. Her hands were shivering. He noticed it and reached across to hold one of her frigid, clammy hands, then turned to look at Russell. Russell peered straight ahead. Again, Jim was amazed how he could manage to appear so damn calm! He felt as though his skin would tear apart with each step. He had never committed such a daring stunt.

Russell strained his head up, staring at the roofs of the barracks, waiting for the searchlight to dash across. Distant barking from a dog resounded through the vacant streets. Even a distant vehicle could be heard traveling in the quiet camp. Russell had insisted the four of them pair off, leaving a wide gap between each couple to avoid any suspicion from the guards, or the police patrol, or people making nightly latrine trips. If anyone was watching. As they approached the northern section, Russell directed them among the broad alleys of trash cans and gardens. His giddiness awakened adventure. Now, as he slightly slumped against a wall, his excited mind competed with his feverish body. He felt Naomi's soft hands squeezing his arm. He peeked down at her. She revealed a partial grin. Squeezing her hand, he looked up again.

"In a moment," he whispered. "It'll pass soon."

Five, six, seven, eight- the light leapt on the roofs like an owl in flight; one eye gleaming under the moon. It advanced beyond the closed windows and lumpy sand, skidding near Russell's feet. Then it swept up again into another block.

"Now!" he gasped.

He sprinted forward, hearing his own heart pulsate. Naomi quickly ensued, then Tomiko and Jim. Russell lifted the bottom wire with his arm in the cast, allowing his friends to roll underneath. Once they darted across the maze of sage bushes, he rolled under. Their feet could have been mistaken for a pack wild dogs as they crunched over the brittle shrubberies, panting nimbly. The shed, small and battered, leaned to one side. Cavities welcomed its neglect; its inevitable decay. Tomiko was the first to reach it. Relieved, she softly giggled her exhilaration. The remaining three hid in the back, out of sight from snooping surveillance. Breathing heavily, Jim reclined against the weary wall, next to Tomiko. Russell watched Naomi smile uncontrollably; her hair braided in a two links. The tender blueish radiance complimented her grace and curves.

Naomi encouraged, "Who feels like going a bit further?"

Grinning, Russell answered, "Need you ask?"

He began jogging parallel to the western mountains, as if heading to the town of Independence. Naomi excitedly chased his dusty tracks, stretching her arms up to the stars. Grunting, uncertain, Jim followed both with Tomiko at his side. Wishing he could hoot or shout or sing, Russell took off his sweatshirt, feeling the cold air slit open his joy through his undershirt. He jumped a few times, hands expanded, reaching for the infinite frontier. Jim thought he was deranged. After a few minutes, he starting heaving uneasily. His legs ached. His lungs were stinging.

"Wait!" he wheezed, curbing his trot to a tread. "Hey! Slow down!"

Tomiko instantly slowed at his side, not panting as badly. Russell looked behind. Surprised that his friend had crumpled as rapidly as burnt wood, he turned around to meet Jim hovering over his own feet, hands resting on his knees.

"Don't do that," Russell said, conserving a low voice. "You need to walk it out. If you do start to feel lightheaded, then put your head between your legs."

Jim straightened his back, and wobbled ahead, wheezing.

Concerned, Russell asked, "You don't have asthma, do ya?"

"No!" he gasped.

Strolling along, rather amused, Russell asked, "Are you really that out of shape? You realize these two gals can outrun you?"

Glaring at him, insulted, he remarked, "I suppose . . . you think . . . it's funny!"

"Not funny, no," he grinned. "Sad. I think it's really sad."

"Shhh!" Tomiko quietly asserted, grimacing. "Don't talk so much! Just keep moving!"

The four journeyed onward as if Louis and Clark. Their feet crunched on the new trail, sensing their fresh discoveries. As the distance expanded between them and the watchtowers, they began to feel relief, indulgence even. They had almost forgotten the sensation of wandering freely, without a crowd, without soldiers, without regret. Russell pulled his sweatshirt back on, his body heat now numbing from the late chill. He felt invincible, like the Lone Ranger defeating his enemies and riding off into the horizon.

Tomiko slipped her fingers into Jim's hand. Startled, he looked at her. Her short hair, tousled from the run, caressed her neck. The moon's radiance outlined her face; her lips. Jim wanted to touch her naked skin. He discreetly unfastened a smile, entangling his fingers into hers.

Naomi flipped up her jacket's collar and muttered, shivering, "I hope we don't run into snakes! I hate snakes!"

Russell joked, "Any different from inside of camp?"

She mischievously poked out her tongue.

"Careful," Russell mocked. "Snakes might mistake your tongue for food!"

"Very funny," she flatly remarked, shuddering a worried look.

Russell glanced at Jim who appeared as though he knew he was marching straight into quicksand. Sullen, rigid, nervous. Russell believed that his friend should learn to select moments like picking strawberries. Take the ripened ones and let the spoilt ones well alone. Russell then touched Naomi's hand, her cool fingers arching, allowing him fold into her. The further they walked from the fence, the closer he felt to a normal life. He smelled burning wood trickling through the cold breeze, perhaps coming from Manzanar, or the small town ahead, or even from a nearby ranch. It didn't matter. It reminded him of home.

The crunching of their footsteps replaced conversation. A delight. The mile stretched into two, then three. Hours forgotten. The moon switching sides in the distance. A shimmering passage deflected an odd distraction. They halted, marveling, repelled from exhaustion in the late, late night.

Russell leaned on one side of his leg, his voice creaked when he spoke. "There it is. How about that? It does exist!"

A bony tree, extending limbs under the hazy illumination, stood beside the pond; perhaps apprehensive to share its isolation. The four treaded toward the moon's reflection in the water, excited to have found a forbidden treasure. The pond was larger than the four had imagined; mysteriously enduring the arid climate. Russell wondered if it held any fish. He had heard there was also a brook that escaped down the mountains, and had heard that some men had snuck out at night to fish.

Russell let Naomi sit down first as she reclined against the splintering bark. Squatting close to her, he watched Jim and Tomiko settle across, readjusting their bottoms from the prickly shrubbery.

Naomi sighed, "This is nice."

"It'd be nicer if there was a clearer spot," Jim complained. "I don't know if I'm sitting on a bush or a porcupine."

Russell snickered. "Now you know what it feels like to be a pain in the rear end!"

Jim frowned, hardly amused.

Tomiko, sitting on her legs, "What do you guys miss the most about home?"

"The ocean!" Russell exclaimed. "I miss looking out the blue sea. It's so drab here, you know."

She persisted wistfully, "I miss the scent of strawberries. The sweetness. Even your clothes smelled like strawberries when spending a day in the fields."

"I miss my parents," Naomi said. "I miss them tucking me in bed. Going on picnics." She lingered her memories for a time, and everyone could sense her pain. "I miss what they look like."

"I am so sorry," Tomiko said with empathy. "I'm sure they're watching you from above, keeping you safe."

Naomi attempted to smile, and slowly nodded.

Then turning to Jim, hoping to raise the mood again, Tomiko invited, "What about you, Jim? What do you miss?"

Jim noticed all eyes looking at him, expecting a whimsical response to pass the time. The memories he clutched from his home island broke any fondness a person should retain. The disgusted knot that expanded in his belly since his brother's death putrefied until he tasted it in his mouth. The obsession with death almost made him swallow half a bottle of sleeping pills last summer. Bethany walked in his room, asking what he was doing. The bewilderment in her innocence filtered guilt, knowing what it was like finding a dead body sprawled in the attic. Instantly he told her to return the bottle to the kitchen, then ran into the bathroom to vomit.

Turning his head away from his friends, he bitterly replied, "I don't miss a damn thing."

Shocked by his assertion, Russell questioned, "Why would you say that, Jim?"

"I have my reasons."

Russell thought for a moment, trying to comprehend where his remark came from. "Is it because you miss your brother?"

"None of your business!" Jim snapped. "There are reasons you can't comprehend!"

Russell stared at Jim. "Oh, gee, I didn't think my small mind would offend you. I keep forgetting we're not equal!"

"That's not what I mean," Jim exhaled, turning to look at him. "I like to keep some personal things private."

"You still think you're so superior to everyone else," Russell affirmed. "Do you really believe you're the only one with problems? That you're *sooo* smart nobody can understand you? Trust me, you're not half as quick as you think you are!"

"And I certainly can say the same thing about you!"

Distressed about a fight, Naomi cheerfully interjected, "I can bend my fingers all the way back! See!" She quickly exposed her unique trick.

"Doesn't that hurt?" Tomiko asked, also wanting to avoid a fight.

"Not at all! I'm double-jointed."

Jim glanced at Naomi, then Tomiko. Realizing he had gone too far, he cleared his throat and thought for a moment's composure. His sleepless nights were making him extremely irritable and, no doubt, hard to be around. Tomiko began talking about the good old days again and soon Russell and Naomi joined in the frivolous chatter, each expounding further into the late hours of the night.

RUSSELL jilted. He opened his eyes. Looking at the eastern Sierra Mountains, a pink streak awoke in the horizon, stretching alongside the murky sky. Each star's glimmer weakened at the bottom. His body felt cold.

"Shit!" he blurted, "Oh, shit!" He twisted his body and shook Naomi who fell asleep leaning on the tree. She blinked and moaned. Jumping to his feet, he rushed to the other side of the stubby tree and jostled Jim and Tomiko. "We're screwed! Oh Jesus, we're dead meat!"

Panic stabbed Jim's stomach, tightening his muscles. The girls leapt to their feet, rubbing their eyes, rapidly breathing. The sun began to advance, seizing their nightly shroud, exposing them in its expedite light. They were at least three miles out, about an hour and a half away at walking speed, and just had under an hour of darkness remaining. Russell knew he could make it perhaps in half its time running, but he worried about the other three who weren't as fit. Jim especially.

"If we're gonna make it," Russell announced, "then we need to move now! Think all of you can do it?" He looked directly at Jim.

Tomiko asked, "If we don't, what will happen?"

Russell then looked at Tomiko. "They might . . . actually shoot at us. And they might put us in jail, too."

Jim twined his brows, growing more nervous. How could he have been so irresponsible? The thrill of slipping past the fence warranted foolishness, however to fall asleep confirmed complete stupidity. And they didn't have time to think.

"Let's go!" Naomi said, tugging at Russell's sweatshirt. "Being reprimanded by nuns is worse than going to jail! Trust me!"

Russell moved to Jim, settling his good hand over Jim's shoulder and encouraged, "You can do this, Jim, okay? Nothin' like your adrenaline pumping to motive you." He flicked a smile. "Just keep your pace. Don't force it. Breath in 'n out of your mouth. Got it?"

Jim anxiously nodded. Russell yanked on his friend's jacket, pushing him to run first. He then sprung after Jim's flight with the girls jogging at both their sides. The first mile sped by like a seagull in the wind, hustling against the ocean's breeze. Russell knew he could run more swiftly; instead he shuffled among his friends to keep encouraging them; their shoes chopping on the shrubberies established a rhythm. Russell thought about the rapid melody of "Sing, Sing, Sing" as their feet stomped like clattering drums.

Jim's certainty wavered. Even in gym class he barely passed the coach's requirements. His lungs burned, growing more painful as the minutes skidded across the flat landscape. Jim instantly slowed, nearly stopping, gasping.

Russell shouted, "Wait!" The girls, panting, halted a few feet apart from Jim and Russell. They could see a haze of blue blending nimbly in the grey sky. Their hope of making it dwindled along with the fading stars. Russell clutched Jim's sleeve, yanking him forward, huffing.

"Walk!" he demanded.

Jim stumbled, wishing he could fall dead and therefore ending the stabbing sensation in his chest.

"Walk!" Russell persisted, pulling him as he marched onward.

His arms flopping at his waist side, Jim wheezed, "I can't!"

"I don't care!" he snapped.

Whining, he protested, "You go!"

"Don't give in!"

Jim angrily seized Russell's wrist. "Let go!"

Tomiko and Naomi, confused and concerned what they boys were doing, swayed on their feet to keep their legs from cramping. Russell grabbed Jim's elbow, yanking him while he began to jog, forcing Jim to follow.

"If you get caught," Russell asserted, "I'll get caught! Then the girls! You want that?"

Jim trudged along, scowling, not having the energy to argue. Russell refused to unlock his grip. The girls waited for them to catch up then jogged beside them. Another mile evolved, chasing the shrinking moon toward the western mountains. Pink began to bloom in the eastern skyline. Russell continued to insist they reach to the shed. At least the shed. By the third mile, they could see a square shadow through the sun's faint radiance. Fatigued, breathless, the four ignored their aches as an excitable twinge of hope shoved them forward. If they came that far, then who knew? The watchtower lurked in the far distance. The searchlight disappeared as a blur of light replaced its ambition. The four ran faster to approach the battered shed. They could see nothing else but the small building. Heard nothing but the clamor of their hearts. Naomi bumped into Jim. Jim bumped into Russell. For a moment, they arched against the wall, trying to compose their sweaty backs and sharp breaths. Russell peeked around the corner, staring at the fifty feet ahead of them, surveying for any patrol. A person or two drifted behind the city of barracks; too early in the morning for the rest of camp life to rise. He then stared at the watchtower which appeared more like a toy tower. Even in the brisk glow when the desert could be seen by the eye, it could affirm trickery. Like waking from a stiff sleep and believing something moved at the corner of an eye.

Heaving, Russell whispered, "Coast is . . . clear!"

"Wait!" Jim gasped, falling to his knees. He found no supplementary strength. Once he reached the shed, he felt his bones crumble and desire to run fully broken.

Russell bent down. "Now!"

"You go!" he grunted.

"Come on!" Russell insisted. He glanced up at the girls, who looked scared, their hair reckless from the long jog. "Just pass . . . the fence! Then . . . collapse!"

Jim lifted his dizzy head. He knew he couldn't go much further, yet didn't want to be responsible for everyone else's demise. He nodded and painfully rose to his feet, droplets of sweat hitting the ground.

"Okay!" Jim replied. "Okay! Right beside . . . you!" He briefly studied the girls and continued, "Take Naomi . . . with you! Tomiko . . . follow!"

Russell peeked around the corner once more, extending his hand to Naomi. "Now!" he barked.

Russell ran with Naomi, his legs stinging, staring directly at the fence. Tomiko instantly traced their steps and glanced back. Jim slumped over. The sun's rays slashed through the mountain tips, sliding across the highway and directly into the camp. Russell hit the ground, pushing the bottom wire up. Naomi rolled under. He turned to look behind. Tomiko spun around and ran back to the shed.

Horrified, Russell hollered, "What are you doing?"

Naomi grabbed his neck and collar, yanking him forward. His arm snagged on the wire, ripping his favorite sweatshirt. "Guard!" she panted.

Panicking, he fumbled to his feet, scuffling away from the fence. Naomi snatched his hand; pulling; running. He darted across, but tripped and fell near the edge of one of the barracks.

For a second, he thought he felt a bullet stab inside his ribs. He looked up. An internal police officer stood in front of him. Blinking and refocusing, he realized the officer was his brother-in-law, Osamu. He carried a flashlight and wore a white patch on his left arm that had "POLICE" painted in black. Dressed in jeans and a brown, corduroy coat, he frowned at Russell and Naomi.

"If I didn't know any better," Osamu firmly remarked, "I'd think you two were up to no good." Crossing his arms and leaning to one side, he maintained, "Care to tell me why the both of you are out of breath?" They didn't respond. A guilty expression smeared on their faces. "I didn't think so." He then peered past the fence to investigate the shed. Russell finally rose, still holding Naomi's hand. They kept their eyes to the ground. Returning his attention to them, Osamu stated, "You two need to stay clear of the fence. I really don't want to know what you were doing. *Kiotsukete, kudasai.* This is a warning. Next time I may not be so nice, Russell. Don't make me have another conversation with your mother."

Stunned, Russell and Naomi blinked. They couldn't leave their friends behind.

"Scat!" he ordered.

Naomi tugged on Russell's arm, quickly walking away.

Panic and guilt drilled inside his chest. He couldn't believe it. He couldn't abandon them just like that. Without food or water. Without toiletry. For how long? Until it got dark? Until the camp fell into a deep sleep? What if one of them got bit by a rattler or stung by a scorpion? How could he help his friends? What were Jim and Tomiko going to do for the next eighteen hours?

CHAPTER THREE

JIM sat in a corner, next to the fractured door, wiping his moist forehead. A musty odor of wood and mold sagged in the air. The floor, collected of dirt and sand, bore tiny drifts of dunes with small rodent feet and reptile curves. Jim, breathing through his mouth, had already sealed his eyes. He desperately craved for water. The sharp prick in his lungs made it difficult for him to relax. His dried tongue irritated his throat. Perhaps accepting the consequences by walking out in the open would be far better than waiting in an abandoned shed with no water. Tomiko sat beside him and removed a canteen from her jacket. She opened it.

"Here," she said, raising it to his lips. "Take a sip."

He freed his eyes. "What is it?"

She smiled, readjusting her legs to lean on one side. "I got some water from the pond. As a souvenir."

Slapping his tongue, he swallowed a few times, not wanting to be selfish and drink all of it. He then studied her; amazed; puzzled. He asked, "Why didn't you go with them?"

"Because you shouldn't be by yourself."

He cleared his throat, awed that she would do such a thing. With the expectation of his mother, no one had ever extended that kind of selflessness. Ever. Not even his own father. He couldn't understand why anyone would take additional risks.

"You finish the rest," he encouraged. "I know you're just as thirsty."

She again smiled and drunk once. "I'll save the rest for later."

He chuckled. "Why? There's enough for a few more sips."

"Later is good. Patience is what makes us responsible."

Jim ruptured a series of chuckles, shaking his head at the steep irony. "If we really were that responsible, we wouldn't be in this fix!"

Tomiko reclined her back against the wall, staring at rotted holes where streams of light crawled through. Loose spider webs dangled in three of the corners. She hadn't realized how ridiculous she had sounded. She began to chuckle, slipping her hand over her mouth. Jim laughed more heartily, resting his palms over his bouncing belly. She laughed. They couldn't stop. It felt too good to laugh.

"I have to pee!" she abruptly confessed, gasping.

He resumed his hilarity, laughing uncontrollably. "So do I!"

"Oh, boy!" she cried. "What are we going to do? Can't go outside!"

"No! But if we keep this up, we won't have to worry about it much longer!"

"Tell you what," she proposed, "If you won't look, neither will I!"

"And we can't tell anyone!"

"Our little secret won't ever, ever, leave this shed! That's a promise!"

RUSSELL quietly closed his barrack's door. Darkness gushed from the secured curtains and he had to adjust his eyes to see where he was going. Carefully watching his sleeping parents and sister, he crept to his bed, stepping around the table. The stove's flame dwindled from the night's slumber; a faint crackle splitting like a twig. Last night's heat became the morning's chill. His mind sluggish, his body aching with exhaustion, he removed his pillow from his cover and fell into his mattress, closing his eyes. Slipping the pillow under his head, he needed to rest for a while before he figured what to do next.

Mrs. Hamaguchi rose from her pillow. Troubled and vexed, she slipped into her orange slippers and shuffled to her son. Her long hair drooped on her narrow shoulders; her grey streaks exposed. Bending down, she shook him and asserted, "*Where have you been, Goro? When I got up this early morning, you were already gone! Where were you?*"

He sprung his eyes back open. He hadn't prepared a story, thinking that no one would notice him missing. He even arranged his covers to appear as if his shape had been lying in bed during the night. How in the world did she figure it out?

"Uh," he began, his head hurting from the pressure, "the bathroom."

She twisted her mouth in disbelief. "*For five hours?*"

"Uh," he looked away, hating lying to his mother. Not small lies. They didn't count. Just the larger ones. "The line was long. I couldn't wait. So I went to another block."

She vented an aggravated sigh. Standing up, she remarked, "*If you are going to lie to me, than at least tell me something more clever. I am too angry to speak to you now.*" Her voice strained and tears swelled. "*I believed something had happened to my son! But why should I worry when he returns home after urinating all night?*" She flipped her hands and stared at the ceiling as if beseeching one of her ancestors.

Russell glanced up as his mother shuffled back to her bed. The guilt continued to accumulate. He had to think of a way to protect Jim and Tomiko from getting caught. He wondered how Naomi expected to handle it. No one else was supposed to know. Would she tell? Or keep silent as she had promised? Now appreciating how easily things could become complicated, he shifted to his side, staring at the wall. It was suppose to be a basic plan. Run past the fence, to the shed, to the pond, then return inside before sunset. If they hadn't dozed off by the pond, talking about insignificant amusements, then they all would have reappeared in bed hours ago. Safely.

A CYCLE of gongs rang throughout the camp, announcing the ritual servings of lunch. The sun hovered in mid sky, warming noon at a comfortable temperature. The radiant blue flaunted an unblemished view: no clouds and no strong wind flinging dust balls up into the horizon. Quietness settled between the two links of massive mountains. Jim awakened in peace. It had been a month since he woke without a crying baby acting as an alarm three to five times during the night. Fluttering his lids, he couldn't remember where he was at. Tomiko twitched. He looked at the top of her head, covered in pelts of dust. She also had fallen asleep, leaning on his shoulder where they sat. Rubbing his face, he moaned and stretched out his legs. She softly grunted, maneuvering, sitting upward. Her warmth electrified him and he felt an urge to touch her. Yawning,

Tomiko browsed around the shed, slowly recognizing her new surroundings.

Jim stood up to pop his spine into its proper place. And to resist his desires.

Brushing dirt off her pants, she asked, "What time do you think it is?"

Straining his arms for any kind of distraction, he replied, "I thought I just heard the gongs. Lunch-time, maybe."

"I have to admit, I'm hungry."

"So am I," he grinned. "I hadn't planned on a picnic. Have you?"

She smiled in turn. "No."

Jim continued to stare at her, remembering the few times they necked in alleys, and once in his barrack when everyone attended a Sunday afternoon feature. The sensation never left him. He dreamt about her almost nightly when he wasn't having nightmares. But now, without the usual interruptions, he feared he wouldn't be able to control himself. And he didn't like that. The last thing he needed to do was shame his family. Looking away, he quickly walked to the opposite corner and stood, crossing his arms.

Tomiko rose to her feet, wondering why suddenly he wished to be away from her. He always had an oddness about him, and sometimes it frustrated her. Whenever she believed they shared a closeness, sharing personal thoughts and embraces, suddenly he would become paralyzed and move apart from her, never explaining why.

She joked, "I could draw a line in the middle so that way I'll have my space and you'll have yours."

He flinched. "What?"

"I'm kidding," she replied more seriously. "It just seems you rather be over there. That's all I mean." She waited for him to say something. She continued, "This morning we seemed to enjoy each other's company and now," she glanced at him, searching for a confession of some sort, "and now, you look like you're in pain. I know we're in an awkward situation. But still."

Jim narrowed his eyes, confused. "Still what?"

Folding her arms, Tomiko began massaging her elbows. She wasn't confident if she ought to pursue the subject further. He was often pretty fickle about displaying emotions; especially tender ones. Funny, his father was like that, if not more stern. The *Issei* admired Mr. Yoshimura: his business, his education, his modest wealth on the island. The *Nisei* thought the opposite. Jim's father intimated them, rarely smiling, rarely complementing. Perhaps that was the reason both of his sons were a bit more complicated than most. She sat down again, extending her feet forward, exposing her mismatched socks.

Sighing, she asked, "So how long do you think we have to stay here?"

He peered at her neck; its perfect arch, smooth skin, down to the center of her chest. The buttons were small; perhaps easy to unfasten. Then he felt ashamed. Snapping back to her eyes, he responded, "I imagine till dark. It would be foolish otherwise."

"Perhaps you're right. Still, we'll have a lot of explaining to do. Everyone will want to know what happened to us."

"We'll think of something," he stated. "Even if we have to bend the truth a bit. To protect them, right? From worrying so much? They have enough to worry about besides us."

She uncomfortably sighed. "I usually don't like misleading my parents. On the other hand, if I can say very little, I'm better off!"

He nodded. "Exactly. That's it exactly."

Tomiko knew time would straggle like a dying crab dragging its body across the beach. Hoping the time with Jim would be fun, his moodiness killed it all together.

"I do remember," she started, glancing at him, "a time you use to smile a lot more. You must really miss your brother. He used to read me stories when he was waiting for Kiyoko. Did you know that?"

He closed his eyes. He started to breathe heavily, his skin boiling, and slowly the coil in his stomach became queasy. John used to read to him, too. Finding old books from yard sales, John collected Western stories. Their father thought these books were a waste, trivial, nevertheless tolerated John's collection of those silly American Westerns. At least the books increased his English skills. After John's death, his father burned all of them.

SAM exclaimed, "There he is! Wondered what happened to you this morning!"

Russell sat his tray on the table. Tired from arguing with his mother, hungry from sleeping through breakfast, he sliced an irritated glance at Sam.

"Where's Jim?" Ikki interjected. "Haven't seen him all day, either."

Glancing at the rest of his Bainbridge friends, who stared at him in curiosity, Russell wasn't certain if he should tell. Not that he didn't trust them, he just didn't trust some of their loose mouths. Like Sam's, for instance. No one disclosed any kind of secretes around Sam. Not that he didn't possess good intentions, it was just that Sam often didn't think before he spoke.

"No offense to you guys," Russell began, raising both his brows, "but he and Tomiko went to another mess hall. They didn't want their parents watching them."

Sam jeered, chewing his roll of bread, "Ohhh, I see. Gettin' pretty serious, huh?"

"I guess," Russell replied, grinding the clumps of his mashed potatoes with his fork.

The Bainbridge boys continued their gossip about sports and girls. Russell wasn't listening. He knew he had to speak with Jim and Tomiko's families, pretending they were somewhere in camp: safe. To alarm their parents would only make their situation worse. But if Russell devised such a plan, he needed some help. And he needed to speak with Naomi to make sure she hadn't spilled the beans. He again glanced at Ikki, wondering if he could confide his burden, wondering if Ikki wouldn't mind helping him lie about Jim and Tomiko's whereabouts. Perhaps Shig as well, if it came to that. The trickiest of parts would be explaining their bedtime absence.

When Ikki stood up, his tray empty of crumbs, Russell fiercely tugged him back down. Annoyed, Ikki stared at him. Russell leaned into his ear and bluntly whispered, "I need to ask you a *big* favor and you can't tell anyone!"

Reclining to his side, peering at Russell, he replied, "Yeah- what?"

"Outside. Not here."

TOMIKO ended her story about an alley cat with a laugh. The cat, ugly and mean, that had lived underneath her porch for a year, had been outsmarted by a squirrel. The squirrel, lean and flexible, managed to slip through its claws up a tree and through her gutter where the cat's head became stuck. Her father had to wear thick farming gloves to pull the cat out with its back paws furiously scratching. Jim smiled. He remembered hearing about that incident a few years ago. It seemed Winslow people never had enough gossip to recycle. And some stories lasted for decades when secrets were attached.

"I suppose," Tomiko chuckled more calmly, "you don't think it was all that funny."

Jim, sitting directly across from her, resumed his grin. He enjoyed listening to her chat. She was very different from him, in the sense that she appeared to enjoy life. Optimistic in many ways. She wanted to become a journalist and attend junior college for further skills. She had also hoped to buy land for her father so he could have something that was his own. She rarely spoke of her sister as if her sister were a phantom. Kiyoko. A name as distant as his brother's. Gossip routinely circulated about their siblings perhaps once a year. And that was another reason he wanted to escape from the island.

He finally replied, "Just because I may not laugh doesn't mean I lack a sense of humor."

Tomiko covered her smile with the tips of her fingers. She hesitated, fascinated by his formality. Earlier, she was agitated, truly agitated, but realizing her anger wasn't passing time any sooner, she began talking. About anything. And he listened. He honestly listened. She had not met a boy who didn't talk about himself, or about sports, or even about the weather. And he was so proper. Or at least he tried to behave as such. Already serious and determined at the age of twelve, his solemn manner often confused people; however she had known something extraordinary was hidden inside.

Dropping her hand into her lap, she declared, "You're weird, Jim! Simply weird! After all these years, I still can't figure you out!"

"You're not supposed to," he quipped.

She playfully bit her lip. "It would make my life less difficult."

He narrowed his eyes and sighed. "You're also peculiar."

"That's the best compliment I've gotten this year," she beamed. She was relieved he had transformed into a better mood. "Do you know the words to 'Night and Day'?"

Watching her, he relaxed, slightly slumping. A bizarre warmth nibbled in his chest and he didn't understand what the sensation implied. It was almost like lying in the late sun, surrounded by wild grass and crickets, waiting for the next wave of breezes. And yet the impression was far more heavy, more demanding and persistent. He couldn't stop staring at her.

"Not really," he answered.

"How about the tune, then? Want to hum along?"

He simply smiled. "I would rather hear you sing."

She blushed, lowering her chin. For moment, she nervously giggled but closed her eyes, easing her head up, and began to serenade him with her smooth, tender voice. As she sang, Jim forgot he was hiding out in a forbidden place, a barren place full of discarded people in the middle of the Sierras. It didn't matter that his father was locked away in Montana, enduring the trials. It didn't matter that his brother was dead, his memory like an old, fading photograph. It even didn't matter that tomorrow he might be sitting in jail, listening to his mother cry out in shame. He waited for the moment to feel Tomiko's warmth, her reassuring enthusiasm, her ability to make the universe vanish. It was only a matter of time before his own death, so he might as well indulge just a bit, regardless of what his father might think.

Tomiko stopped singing in the middle of the song. Her heart submitting to a whirl of intensities; a flourishing pressure in her chest. She wanted to be near him; to feel his warmth. Rising to her feet, she walked to him, a little nervous.

Watching her as streaks of light touched her body, Jim faintly asked "Why me? I'm not exactly Frank Sinatra or Fred Astaire."

She bent down, grinning modestly, caressing his cheek with her finger tips. "Because you're not them. Not even by a long shot." She paused. "I remember the first year of high school when we were in biology. When my grades were higher than everyone else's- except for you, of course. We were at an equal ground." She caressed his lips. "All the boys were threatened by me. And the girls just wanted to talk about boys. When we formed groups for study, no one wanted me to join."

Jim felt his throat tightened as his skin roast from the rapid lashing in his chest. God how he wanted to kiss her entire face, her perfect neck, her thighs. Each time he was with her, the sensation expanded more strongly, almost forcefully, and he felt his control drain as easily as sand through an hourglass.

"But you asked me," she continued. "*You* did. It didn't seem to bother you. That's when I knew you were special."

She leaned closer, her steamy breath stroking his mouth, waiting, inviting. Tracing his other cheek with her other hand, Tomiko sank her knees into the dirt with her eyes shut, kissing him. She marveled at how quickly he learned to respond, pulsating his lips, reaching around her back, massaging. Tender, she thought.

Jim marveled at how easily she allowed him to dip his hands through her blouse. Her skin blushed as warmly as roasted apples. He chased her neck with his mouth, shifting her, her hip curving into his lap. She eased her hands around his shoulders, through his gritty hair, removing his glasses. Pursuing his forehead with her lips, she slowly trailed his brow as he roamed down her chest. He felt awed. The salty taste on his tongue, the energy aching through his muscles, his mind fogged, and yet he wanted to please her. He wanted Tomiko to experience the sharp joy his heart consumed at that moment. Shifting her again to the ground, his legs over hers, she began to unbutton her blouse, exposing her brassiere, then exposing her bare skin. Stunned at first, uncertain by the proposal, Jim looked directly at her.

Whispering, he asked, "How far do you want to go?"

She curled her bottom lip under her tongue, breathing erratically. Lifting her head up to reach his parted mouth, kissing willingly, she briefly yielded for her reply. "Until the earth stops moving."

THE late afternoon sun tussled with the moon, both sides streaming ribbons of off-colored reds. Gentle winds spread the thin layers of sand across the ground; merging; bracing the wild spontaneity. A dizzy moan entered the barracks' roofs, quietly popping the windows, exhaling through weakened cracks. The autumn sensation aroused an unfamiliar experience from the summer's harsh heat: relief, delight, a new beginning.

RUSSELL frantically used excuses to abide more time for his missing friends. He saw them at one of the picnic areas. He saw them heading toward the movies. Ikki claimed to have seen them dashing off to another mess hall on another block. Both sets of parents began to worry for it was not like their children to be absent from home the entire day. Russell and Ikki tried to assure them that Jim and Tomiko just wanted to spend some time together, being Sunday, right before school. Tomiko's father didn't like his daughter roving all over camp without supervision. As the hours prolonged, his anxieties increased. Finally, he buckled his boots and started walking to search for his youngest daughter. He didn't care if Jim came from a good family. Jim was still a seventeen year old boy! A small-framed muscular man, Mitsuru was strong enough to break thick logs with a tiny ax, and Russell presumed that Jim would be no different than those splintering logs.

Naomi had volunteered to help with the illusion. She would claim she had spent time with Tomiko playing games at the rec. Despite that Naomi was reprimanded by the sisters, her bed obviously not slept in and her clothes horribly wrinkled, she was forbidden to wander by herself, confined to the orphanage, and would be forced to do a third of the laundry for the next three months. Russell, as a last resort, had to use Jim's eleven year old sister as a point of contact. Bethany was only agreeable with a promise that Russell would dance with her when the dance hall finally opened.

JIM sympathetically expressed, "I hope I didn't hurt you too badly."

Tomiko slumped in his lap, her back resting on his bare chest, wrapping her fingers around his hand. Her blouse held one button in place. The warmth in her chest prickled a bit, like easing into hot water.

"No," she replied. "You were very gentle."

Jim had already slipped back into his wrinkled slacks. His shirt, blemished from lying on top of it, loosely hung at his ribs. He brushed his fingertips through her hair, softly sweeping upward. He had never felt so calm before; so untroubled, weak even. Wanting to tell her every thought that passed, his entire body swam in her heat. Wanting to tell her everything, but he feared of blundering the mood and thus driving her away from him. Most of all he feared if she knew the thoughts that swelled in his head, she would instantly lose interest.

She curved her naked toes to tickle his naked feet. Surprised he didn't cringe, she plunged her feet over his ankles and dragged them into the middle. Giggling, she arched her head to kiss him. He responded quickly, reaching to her lips, embracing a while longer. Dull streams of rays entered past the holes, constraining the light, producing shadows. Their aching bellies yearned for food, however they ignored the discomfort. Unbinding her lips, Jim wished they could hide out for another night. Hide from the world for the rest of their short lives. Tomiko slid her fingers up his neck. He hoped she would never release him.

"It's getting dark," she stated. "Soon I won't be able to see you."

He smiled, drifting his other hand between her breasts. "It won't matter. I can still feel you."

Giggling, she playfully asked, "Is that all that matters?"

"Without my glasses," he joked, "I can't see too clearly anyway, so what difference does it make?"

She again giggled. Grabbing both his hands, she squeezed them over her chest. She had never felt so safe before. She believed that she would never feel secure in this world again. The world gone berserk, a butchery of consequences, and there they were, sitting in a decaying shed, left with scraps of promises.

Yearning, dreaming, she whispered, "I love you, you know."

Jim blinked a few times, flattered but scared. Certain words diffused unevenly such as love; small words his family never spoke. How could he repeat such an awkward phrase? He would be willing to dedicate himself directly to her. At least she knew it, and he was showing it, wasn't that good enough?

He kissed her forehead and said, "So now what?"

Pinching her brows, Tomiko wondered why he couldn't repeat those words. How could they have just shared a remarkable thing and Jim not be emotionally affected? Did he just not feel the same?

"I don't know," she replied, unfastening his fingers, her hand sliding down to the floor.

Realizing the disappointment in her voice, he reassured, "I guess we're going steady now."

"Yes," she murmured. "I guess so."

THE nightly moon lit the sluggish desert, pronouncing its dominance. People abandoned the streets while they settled for bed. Russell hunched over his bed, staring at the clock that ticked on his mother's dresser drawer. 8:41 p.m. He slipped a glance toward her way. She pulled a hanging blanket from one side to another and began undressing. His father snored as four Pepsi bottles lined beside his shoes, empty of homemade *saki*. Sadaye had not returned from the hospital yet, not usually until 9:15 or so. His two cousins were already asleep while Meito and Gertrude whispered about gossip they heard that week. Russell stood up. His shoes tied, his jacket bundled around, he walked to the door.

Stopping, he declared, "I need to go get Jim from the library, Mama. He said he would stop by later to return my school book and hasn't."

She halted, her silhouette frozen on the thin blanket. Displeased, she affirmed, "*You are not going out at this time of night, Goro! Tomorrow you have school and I still have yet to resolve your punishment.*"

He knew exactly what his mother would say. Sighing, he retreated to her and confided, "I didn't want to say anything, but," he cleared his throat, "I don't want Jim to get into any more trouble with Tomiko's father."

"*Nani*?" she snapped, not thoroughly understanding English.

Rolling his tongue, he persisted in fragile Japanese, "*Jim is still with Tomiko. They are at the library with Naomi. I do not wish for my friends to be in more trouble. Understand, Mama?*"

"*It is not your responsibility. You are not their fathers.*"

Annoyed, he said, "If we don't look after each other, than who else will?"

He marched back to the door and nearly slammed it from behind. Appalled, Mrs. Hamaguchi sputtered an array of criticism concerning his disobedience; her voice chasing him through the weak walls. Russell, ignoring her, nervously hiked through the darkness, pursuing the streetlights until he came closer to the fence. The searchlights overlooked the alleys where he skidded like a water bug, lanky, agile. Breathing heavily, he stood against the corner of a barrack, staring at the shed, waiting, contemplating. He wasn't even sure if Jim and Tomiko were still in the shed. And if they weren't, what happened to them? Were they safe? Or caught? Or had they simply disappeared? Minutes evaporated like hours, straggling his worry and guilt. When were they coming out? He heard his own breath. His heart ground into his ears. He couldn't think evenly. Should he check to be absolutely certain? He flinched. Maybe he should. Maybe not. Viewing the search light that flew across and overshot the roofs, he dashed to the fence. When he whirled under the bottom wire, Jim and Tomiko nearly toppled over his feet. Shocked to see them, Russell jumped up.

Jim allowed Tomiko to slide by, holding the bottom wire. He hissed, "Go, Russell!"

Russell instantly twirled through again with Jim following. The three darted like rabbits. Panting, they reached to the middle, away from the north, unharmed. Russell suddenly snatched Jim's arm and shoved him against a wooden barrel. Jim fell down, hitting his head on the tip rim. Tomiko gasped.

"Stupid jerk!" Russell barked. "What the hell were you thinking?"

"Dammit!" he replied, thrusting sand up to Russell, but missed as the grains faded into the dark. A faint cloud glimmered under the moon's beam.

"I had to tell people you two were at the picnic area," Russell proceeded, flinging his fingers out one by one to prove a point, "then at the movies, then with me and Ikki, and ultimately at the library- out of all places!" He turned to stare at Tomiko. "Even Naomi will say she was at the library with you two!" Backtracking to Jim, who continued to sulk on the ground and readjust his glasses, Russell asserted, "Tomiko's father was ready to turn you in for kidnapping, he was so upset! I told him I would personally see to it she return home soon!" Puffing, he traced his angry steps in circles. "You two are so far up the creek I don't know how the hell you'll paddle your cans back down!"

Once Jim's dizzy spell passed, he jumped up to his feet and pushed Russell. "It was your goddamn idea, genius! None of this would have happened if you hadn't talked all of us into it!"

Russell pushed back. "If you were in better shape you wouldn't of gotten stuck in the damn shed!"

A door flung opened from a nearby barrack, startling everyone. A middle-aged man, wearing only striped boxer shorts and black socks, harshly yelled, "*If you people do not shut up then I will be forced to smack your mouths! Leave now before I call on the police*!"

Out of quick reflexes, the three jogged up the road and suddenly, unexpectedly, started laughing at the wildly irritated man. When they finally reached their block, Russell gently settled his hands over Jim's shoulders.

"Hey, sorry, *omono*!" he said. "Lost my cool! You two really had me worrying, for crying out loud!"

Jim squeezed his friend's cheeks and seriously remarked, "It doesn't matter. We're all screwed anyway."

"Well, tonight we only managed to break the curfew. We'll see what kind of trouble to get ourselves into tomorrow." He turned to Tomiko. "Remember, you were at the library with Naomi, too. I made sure I chaperoned you two home." He squinted at Jim. "I really don't want to know what you two did for the last thirteen hours. The less I know the better off I am."

Waving, Russell wished his friends a good night and trudged up the steps to slip inside. Tomiko looked at Jim. Her laughter now thawed by doubt. Shivering, the rear of her bare neck chilled. She lowered her chin. Wasn't he going to say something?

Jim zipped his corduroy jacket. He returned his thoughts to the camp. How unfair it seemed. And oddly surreal. To be back. Noticing Tomiko, he walked to her and stroked his knuckles over her hot cheek. Leaning forward, he dipped a kiss just below her eye. “No one but you,” he assured.

She closed her eyes, smiling, relieved he had meant it even if he couldn’t say those particular words. She knew someday he would.

CHAPTER FOUR

Mid October

RUSSELL flexed his wrist, free from the itchy cast. The cast, which had been stained yellow and brown, and had his friends' signatures and clumsy drawings, appeared scraggly and useless. Dr. Huey tossed it in a trash can in a corner. Russell again flexed his wrist, delighted to finally get rid of the damned burden. Now he could complete what he had started with the Terminal Island gang. Shikami was right about one thing: Russell would always remember his despicable name. The room began conforming to an actual office with plastered walls, a varnished counter, a stack of magazines on a table, cabinets, and a calendar. Gradually the potent stench of pine was fading, not smelling so raw. Russell even sat in a wooden chair, not the lousy folding metal chairs that populated the camp for cheap convenience.

Dr. Huey returned to Russell's arm, sitting on his chair, gently squeezing his wrist. He asked, "Does it hurt when I do this?" Russell shook his head. "Rotate your wrist and tell me if there still is any pain."

Russell studied the doctor while he rolled his palm. Dr. Huey's brown hair needed a trim. His face remained pale despite the summer's repressive glare swelling against the bright sand. His skin surprisingly was almost untouched by the sunburns. Russell's tan seemed to clash against it. Curiously, Russell had never thanked him for what he did, and curiously, Dr. Huey had never mentioned the radio since that night.

"Everything feels in good place," Dr. Huey stated.

"Is it true?" Russell asked, staring at the calendar. Only twenty-one more days until Halloween. "Are you being transferred?"

Dr. Huey released Russell's arm. He looked at Russell, mystified. "Yes. Why would it matter to you?"

"Just asking, is all."

The doctor leaned back and sighed. Standing up, he announced, "Looks like you're ready to hit the road. I'm giving you a clean bill of health."

"Okay, thanks."

Russell unrolled his sleeve and buttoned his cuff. Dr. Huey plucked his chart from the counter and began to scribble. With the doctor's back turned, Russell quickly sat up and slid out a small box wrapped in newspaper. He dropped it on the corner as he quickly exited.

Dr. Huey flinched, staring at the box, not remembering seeing it before. Baffled, he stepped towards the slightly crinkled object. Picking it up, he gazed at his name written in pencil. Glancing through the doorway, realizing Russell had left it behind, he rattled it. He then placed his chart down and peeled the paper. Flipping the top up, he removed a pair of cufflinks. Stunned, he gazed at the gift. He wondered why Russell would do such a thing. None of his staff cared much for him, nor his patients, so this gesture came as a complete shock. A note was stuffed at the bottom. Removing it, the paper read a simple "Thank you." Moderately smiling, he slipped Russell's appreciation inside his coat pocket and securely patted it. He now understood. Out of the six months he had been there, at least something valuable came from his disappointing experiences.

RUSSELL jumped off the hospital's steps, almost gilding. Thumping on the soft ground, he jogged through the dusty streets. Some of the main streets had actual names, starting with First Street. Excited, feeling invincible, he swept easily from the west side of camp to the east, passing by roaming trucks and cars, strands of people, churches, and even a few established businesses. Thrift store. Barber shop. Dentistry. Typewriter repair and alterations shops. Poultry and hog farms were organized on the outskirts. On the other side of camp, modest factories produced clothing, furniture, and camouflage nets. Russell had been amazed that his camp could accrue that much within a six mile radius. Encouraged and regulated by the War Relocation Authority, of course.

He had finally reached a double size barrack not too far from his block. It was the same building where Callis had hit Jim and where he fought Shikami. How crazy had his life become? Panting, he trotted up the steps. Muffled swing music echoed through the door. Count Basie's jiving song, "The Apple Jump," energized him as he swiftly entered. His friends and other classmates had decorated the room with orange, black, and red strings dangling from the ceiling and twisting them to the walls. In the middle of the room, and standing on ladders, students lined Chinese red lanterns. Someone rolled a black rug on one side where the band would be playing that weekend. Few *Nisei* adults supervised as they stood at the side lines, watching. Sam's brother, a gangly young man who had a stuttering problem but adept with his hands, arranged the speakers and microphone. Seeing Shig and his gang taping the strings, Russell jogged towards them.

Slapping Shig's shoulder, he boasted, "I've got my hand back! Now I can really start some trouble!"

Shig turned around and playfully grabbed Russell's collar, shaking him. "Oh brother! Any bastard will do!"

Russell grabbed Shig's collar. "You oughta know!"

Releasing each other's grip, Shig announced, "I think it's time for a break!"

Trailing behind Shig, Bruce with his wide face and elephant ears, youthful Ralph with his eyes remaining too close to his nose, and shy Hank with speculated glasses, all wore dark jeans folded on the bottom. Russell followed them back outside. Shig slipped out a cigarette and a match. Striking the match with his thumb, he lit it and passed the match around.

"So," Shig observed, inhaling. "What ever happened to Jim and his dame?" He exhaled, cautiously peering. "What was so goddamn important you had to cover for him?"

Russell stared back, his heavy breath catching his sweat. He carefully glanced at the others, uncertain how much trust to invest in these guys.

"You know how it is," he grinned, trying to sound blasé. "Jim just wanted some privacy with Tomiko."

"Where at? It's not an easy thing to do."

Russell folded his arms, an impatience straining at the corners of his mouth. "You'd be amazed with a little imagination and a lot of determination."

Shig squinted at first, but suddenly ruptured into laughing. Swatting Russell's shoulder, he amplified, "Yeah, I just bet! If Jim's not careful, he'll put himself in a difficult position with the girl! So, how did the folks take it?"

Russell replied, "Jim's mom really didn't say anything. I think she was afraid to. Tomiko's father, on the other hand, ranted until he lost his voice! And she's forbidden to be alone with Jim from now on."

Shig continued to laugh in a hollow tone as if pretending to be amused. The other three sniggered. He tugged Russell aside and demanded, "How long have you been friends with Jim?"

Surprised he would ask such a question, he replied with an upbeat tone, "I've known him since kindergarten. Why?"

He took a puff and blew the smoke out of his nose. "Do you trust him? Or Tom?"

Russell carefully studied them, not fully comprehending what they were implying. "I don't see why I shouldn't."

Shig glanced at his friends who stared back with identical skepticism. Wind jostled a small tumbleweed between their feet, scraping against their dusty shoes. He said, "You know what I sometimes can't get. There's alotta *Nisei* who still have Japanese accents. Makes the rest of us look bad. Like we're fat-heads. Second class citizens. It's not fair." He took a puff from his homemade cigarette. "And then there's alotta *Nisei* who'd trade their dignity for any scraps of favors. You don't rat out your own people. Especially to the FBI!" Leaning closer to Russell's ear, he whispered, "Tom's an *inu*."

"What?" he snorted. "Who Tom? He's just a farmer!"

"If Tom's an *inu*, what do you think it makes Jim? Or the rest of his family?"

Russell gawked at him. How in the hell was he supposed to respond to that? He pushed Shig, and asserted, "I'm going back inside! You guys are full of shit!"

"As a friend I'm only warning you!" Shig advanced, watching Russell slam the door. Taking another puff, he mumbled, "Better know who your real friends are."

* * *

SATURDAY evening approached with enthusiasm. The street lights glowed in the faint darkness, chasing telephone wires attached to civic buildings. Giddy music echoed lightly throughout the northeast side of Manzanar, reaching to the edge of the quiet highway. Young people followed the beating sound. Escorts chattered. Clothes ironed and cleaned. Shoes polished. Those who made the three mile trek from the opposite perimeter who fewer. Those who lived closer swam out like geese. Russell had joined Ikki and Sam, Jim and Tomiko; all dressed in casual clothes; flexible for sporadic dancing movements. Naomi's punishment left Russell without a date. But then Ikki and Sam were also dateless, so it didn't seem nearly as bad. Behind them straggled Sadaye, with a friend from work, and Bethany. Sadaye and her friend chatted about high school sweethearts, reminiscing about a time before the war, feeling homesick. Bethany sometimes would laugh, wishing to be a part of their world, not truly understanding much of it. Tomiko listened while the boys spoke of football and war; her hands kept together. Jim maintained a distance, rarely speaking while Russell and Sam dominated the conversations with Ikki interjecting the occasional insult to Sam. Tomiko and Jim knew they needed to preserve a formal space in front of family and friends, not wanting to upset their parents more so.

The building dangled white Christmas lights around the roof, igniting attention. Inside people scattered about the floor in groups, circling and lining along the walls, observing and anticipating. Russell's group emerged through the door two at a time. They scanned the area. To their right side supported a long table with two punch bowls. To their left stood the band and singers. And there were only four *hakujins* who mingled in the crowd, including Russell's music teacher who swayed his finger to the beat. A man in his thirties with curly dark hair, his teacher tried to appear as if he were in charge of everything. Proclaiming to be sympathetic to the Japanese, he seldom listened to his students, often being too busy rambling about his hardships as an Italian-American.

A band of five men blared out their trumpets and clarinet, plucking a cello and rattling a drum set. Three attractive women, with ruby lips and thick false lashes, all trimmed in shiny blue dresses with long hair curled over their shoulders and spiraling on top, harmonized splendidly. Russell was ready to grab a girl, any girl, and ricochet off the music. The noise shook the floor and people's voices clattered against the horns and vocals.

Sadaye exclaimed to Bethany, "Ah, this is very nice! Look at the red lanterns, Bethany! And all those streamers! Aren't they pretty?"

Bethany tugged her skirt and brushed off the grit. She shyly smiled and nodded, not interested in the decoration. Nervous, this was her first dance. And from the looks of it, she was the youngest. She knew if her father were here, he would never had allow her to go, but since Sadaye guaranteed her mother to be the perfect chaperon, she was allowed. Glancing up at Russell, she wondered if he would keep his promise.

Sadaye slid out of her checkered coat. She announced, “Everyone give me your coats! I’ll have them hung up!”

Sam’s older brother, Earnest, suddenly jumped into the circle, startling Sadaye. He had been waiting for her between the door and refreshment table. His striped shirt and suspenders hung on his bony body like drapes. Anxiously smiling, he stuttered, “I’ll t-take ‘em for you, Miss Hama-Hama-guchi!”

Stunned by his abrupt presence, she politely thanked him and gave him her coat. Everyone else followed, piling the coats in his thin arms.

Sam sniggered. He knew his brother had a crush on Sadaye since the eighth grade. Both Earnest and Sadaye already had graduated in ‘39.

Raising his voice, Sam commented, “Well it’s good to see you doing somethin’ useful, Ernie!”

“Always a pl-pl-pleasure!” he replied, admiring Sadaye.

Sadaye casually returned his smile, but then turned her head in another direction. Bowing his head, his smile fading, Ernest walked off to a line of coat hangers and carefully hung the coats over the racks.

Russell revealed a large grin at Bethany and declared, “I believe the first dance is ours!”

She blushed and giggled, lowering her eyes. He gently took her hand and guided her to the middle of the room. He placed his hand on her dainty shoulder and molded her hands on the proper spots of shoulder and waist. Together they began swaying back and forth.

Sadaye laughed at her brother. “Always a flirt!” she said. “No wonder Mama worries so much about him!”

Sam and Ikki searched the room for potential partners, pausing on the pretty girls, passing by the ones they thought were less attractive. During their fruitless foraging, they found Shig’s group instead, and strolled around the dance floor to greet them.

Jim glanced few times at Shig whose glare nicked across the room. Annoyed at Shig’s ignorance, he announced he was going to retrieve a drink. Tomiko brushed her fingers on his wrist, telling him she would like one. He smiled and returned her quick caress. As he walked to the refreshment table, he frowned at Shig one more time to make his point. Quickly pouring the punch, he returned to Tomiko and began sipping.

Ernest reappeared, standing near Sadaye. His nervousness prompted his hands to hop inside his pockets, then at his waist, then around his chest, and back into his pockets, periodically peeking at her. She pretended not to notice, blinking hastily, feeling uncomfortable by his presence. He had always been an odd one, and she had difficulty carrying on a conversation with him. She moved closer to her friend and began chatting about anything that distracted her mind. The band. Work at the hospital. Anything.

The door opened, dispensing more boys and young men, ranging from sixteen to twenty-five years of age, most clothed in brightly colorful suits: amber, cobalt, burgundy, indigo, avocado, and crimson. Others were dressed in pinstripes. All displayed spats, two-toned shoes, mismatched vests with flashy ties, long chains attached from their belts to their broad pockets, and hair extending down their necks. Five of them wore large rounded hats. With baggy slacks and jackets that sharply pointed on their shoulders, their attire sprang charisma. Sadaye and her friend shuffled to the side, crowding into Jim and Tomiko. Shig only chuckled. He knew *exactly* who those clowns were; coming from Los Angles, coming from another society. Mexicans. Coloreds. Even their own people, although he didn't see the appeal. He had seen those types of people when he had stayed in L.A. for a while, visiting relatives.

Sam, his mouth gaped, expressed, "Don't they know it's not Halloween yet!"

Bruce, Ralph, and Hank snickered, rattling their shoulders, wondering how someone was that damned naive. Ikki, a little baffled, could not unfasten his stare on the flamboyant array. He had never seen such a display of boldness and defiance!

"They're Zoot Suits," Shig sneered, nodding in that direction. "They think they're so goddamn special because of those lame-brain outfits! *Nasakenai!* You know, a real shame!"

Russell repaired his rhythm to the music despite his gawking. Bethany slightly stumbled, not knowing what to make of those strange men who looked like comic book gangsters. To encourage her confidence, Russell softly swayed her toward the middle. Murmurs jaunted from one side of the room to the other, yet the band and singers preserved their focus.

One of the older members turned to face Sadaye and her friend, grinning, exhibiting a gold tooth. He asked, "Wanna dance?"

The friend instantly protested, "I can't dance! I have blisters on my feet!"

He then studied Sadaye. She held her breath and searched for Ernest. When she saw him, she replied, "I already have a date! But thank you, anyway!"

Quickly trotting away, her chin down, fists tightened, she snatched Sam's brother by the elbow and relocated him onto the floor. Stunned, Ernest neglected his footing while she tried to dance. Irritated and embarrassed, she ordered him to move his feet or else!

Jim, feeling intimidated, clutched Tomiko's free hand and pulled her apart from them; repositioning themselves in the opposite corner. He observed them deploying through the crowd in pairs. They exaggerated their strides: slowly, sharply, staggering with ease and inconsistent grace.

Tomiko bent into Jim's ear, and asked, "Do you know who they look like?"

Peering at them, he slowly shook his head. A couple of them found brave partners, jiggling and hopping to the music. Aside from their quick grace and outrageous maneuvers of flinging their arms and legs, their lack of smiles implied a determined seriousness; a purpose even.

Grinning, Tomiko continued, "Cab Calloway! Just like Calloway!"

"You know Cab Calloway!" Ikki vented at his cousin. He glanced at Shig as if sharing his aggravation. " He sung 'Minnie the Moocher'? Big smile?"

"Yeah, sure!" Sam replied, revealing a crooked grin. "Yeah! He's been in the movies before! I know who he is!"

The door again opened, allowing the streetlight to toss a streak. Glancing in that direction, Russell saw Naomi step in. Her red lips and shiny black hair descending down her shoulders radiated her charm. Slipping out of her jacket, her pink flowered dress with a pleated blouse fit snugly on her body. Staring at her, amazed and marveling how she snuck out of her punishment, he watched her hang her coat. A young man in a green suit, barely in his twenties with a smooth completion and cocky eyes, instantly approached. Nervously glancing about the area, Naomi shrugged and began dancing with the stranger. Outraged, Russell glared at them as they bounced to the tune. He stepped on Bethany's feet, but didn't hear her cry out in pain. Impatiently waiting for the song finished, he quickly returned Bethany to the side lines and patted her on the head. Keeping his eyes on Naomi and the stranger in the green suit, he didn't hear what Bethany said when he marched off. As Naomi twirled, her long hair flipping, her skirt flying to the top of her knees, Russell jumped back. Annoyed, he grabbed her wrist. She gaped at him, barely gasping. Pulling her to him, he stepped in between and slid off the side, hopping to the rhythm.

The green suit stood in shock. He rubbed his smooth chin, angered, and lurched forward to grab Russell's shoulder. Russell, seeing him, slunk his shoulder and skidded backward, switching Naomi's hands around him, away from the Suit. Then Russell pushed her further to the outer sphere of the dance floor while she skipped her feet to keep up with him. The suit chased them around the floor, lunging his hand to them, missing them. Russell's friends had been watching from the start, sniggering and laughing at the farcical hunt. The Suit became angrier; his lips bristling; his thick brows cramping at the dent of his long nose. Russell, surprised how keen Naomi could follow his sharp curves and twists, smirked at the other guy's clumsiness. She seemed to enjoy the game as well, giggling.

The other suits began to watch, chuckling along the sideline, encouraging their friend to catch the couple, telling him where they were going and how he should grab them. Soon people on the dance floor moved to the side to also observe, spreading more room for Russell and Naomi to leap and spin.

Sadaye pushed Earnest to her side to watch her brother. Awed by his velocity and grace, she had never seen him funnel like a leaf caught in the wind.

Russell felt cockier; savoring the attention; coaxing the crowd's cheer with clever moves. It was the same exhilaration he experienced at wrestling matches. He felt superior. Invincible. A god. Suddenly he stumbled. The suit had finally managed to clutch Russell's sleeve and yanked him back. Naomi stopped, stunned, breathing stiffly. The Suit then jumped forward and proceeded to dance; his slick shoes flashing under the lights; his quick feet leaping like birds on soil.

Shig laughed loudly, clapping his hands, and then shouted, "Go get 'im, Russell! He ain't got nothin' on you, *omono-san!*"

Jim folded his arms, feeling the embarrassment for Russell. And at the same time, when someone was too busy showing-off, often he got what he deserved. Jim glanced at Tomiko who revealed an amused grin. She returned the glance and leaned closer to him. But not too close.

Russell brushed his bangs out of his eyes; calculating; sweating; breathing. He already knew the Suit wasn't as quick. Outlining his opponent's contour and movements, Russell could determine the Suit's faults. Naomi maintained her quickness as if challenging Russell. She constantly glanced at him, dancing in circles while he stood motionless. Russell looked at Shig, winked, and trotted to the Suit, emulating the Suit's bounce, grinning. Whenever the Suit thought Russell was about to make a gesture, he tried to shift and swing. Russell maintained a distance, following, yet not attempting anything. The Suit became more irritated, wondering what Russell planned to do as he only followed and grinned. Naomi also shuffled in confusion. He looked silly just bouncing at her side and not even trying. Russell continued to follow throughout the song.

Infuriated, the Suit suddenly stopped and seized Russell's neck. Leaning into his face, he snapped, "What do you want, man?"

Russell fluttered his eyes. "Don't you know already? I want to dance with you, big boy!"

The Suit stared at him. Immediately he burst into laughter. At first he was ready to fight, exasperated from appearing like a damn fool around the floor, but he certainly wasn't expecting this! Releasing Russell's neck, he slapped his own knee. "How can I turn down a wicked offer like that?"

Russell, glancing at Naomi, declared, "I don't know how you could wear a hat like that!"

The Suit rolled his eyes and puckered his lips. "Don't be rippin' the threads unless you the Feds! This style is the most, man! A jivin' new line of hope an' prosperity!"

Russell squinted and tilted his head. He had never heard language quite like it. Except once. In a movie. He didn't think people actually spoke in rhyme. He wasn't convinced if it was entirely English.

Clearing his throat, he said, "What?"

The suit swept his finger tips around the rim of his hat. "The name's Kit. Kit Kitsune!"

Russell continued to squint. Unbelievable. The guy was a true comedian. "Your last name is *Fox?* Did you make it up?"

He wet his lips and narrowed his eyes. His humor slumped as he inhaled. "Don't tell me you never thought about tailoring your name to fit your profile, man."

Russell blinked. It was none of his business whether Russell had decided to change his name or not. What did he know about image? This Kit Kitsune appeared more like a girl than anything! Hair extending midway at the back of his neck. Flabby pants. Bold colors. Enormous shoulder pads.

"So," the Fox pursued, admiring Naomi, slipping his hands into his large pockets. "This *skato's* your date? Why was she left to drift alone?"

Naomi flinched in irritation. She hated being referred to as a skirt, or dame, or any other stupid label. She had a real name. That was one of the reasons she liked Russell. He showed more respect than most boys who tried to fit in by tossing out witless lingo. Japanese or English.

Russell again winked at Naomi, and asserted his attention at the Fox. "It's like this, *omono*. Let her choose who she wants to dance with. That way nobody's steppin' on anybody's toes."

Both boys turned to look at Naomi. The music swayed a lovely Jimmy Dorsey tune; perfect for a romantic mood. She eased a grin, flattery unveiling right in front of her, and she began to playfully tap her red lips. Shrugging, she pretended to languish.

"This is a very difficult decision to make. On the one hand, Kitsune is far more handsome." The Fox leered, reclining on one foot as if he had a Royal Flush. Smiling, she gazed at Russell's reaction. His shrinking face confirmed that he was not amused. At all. She flirtatiously continued, "On the other hand, Russell is a much better dancer." Extending her hand to Russell, she insisted, "So I pick you!" She quickly looked at the Fox. "Thanks for the dance, anyway. It was fun!"

Russell jabbed out his tongue and swung Naomi around to the middle of the room. The Fox exhaled in aggravation and muttered, "Asshole!" Shig's gang applauded and whistled at Russell. They couldn't believe his audacity, slipping away without a mark. Russell bowed his head in victory at Shig, beaming broadly. Some people peeked toward Shig's way, annoyed by his crudeness, but resumed their dancing or chattering.

Even Jim couldn't hide his smile, marveling how Russell snatched Naomi from another man's hand without starting a brawl. He then turned to Tomiko in her white blouse and tan slacks. He was glad she didn't feel the need to shellac her appearance; unlike every other girl in the room whose emphasis on clothes, make-up, and perfume to somehow repair their insecurities. Tomiko gently tugged at his hand, suggesting a dance as she glanced to the floor. Self-conscious for not truly knowing how to dance, he told her "Not yet." Disappointed, she bit her lip and said nothing. Realizing her frustration, he touched her hand and caressed her palm. At that moment he really wished they were elsewhere; privately; secretly. He would rather be dizzy from his short of breath than from the clatter of thumping shoes and piercing trumpets.

"The Woodchopper's Ball" launched instantly. Russell looped his hand around Naomi's back and sprang out a leg. She zigzagged her hips, holding tightly on his other hand and shoulder. Soon they kicked in harmony, bending their backs, flipping and hopping. Impressed how spontaneously they swung in fashion, Russell hadn't found a partner as skilled as Naomi before. Normally he would have practiced with Sadaye, who really wasn't all that shabby, but perfected certain moves with a wooden coat hanger. Naomi was literally quick and light. He flipped her again and she landed like a rubber ball. Wheeling her around, he bumped into the Fox again. Annoyed, Russell frowned at his opponent in avocado green. The Fox clung to another girl in a short skirt and painted nylons. The dark line extended from her heels to thigh; just under her garter belt.

Catching Russell's shoulder, the Fox boasted, "What scheme can your feet dream on this slick board, brother?"

Russell squinted, confused. He wasn't exactly sure what the Fox had said. "Are you challenging me?"

"You bet, man!" Then thinning his eyes, he insisted, "What's the game? Are ya up to it?"

Russell turned to look at Naomi. A slight trace of perspiration trickled on her forehead. Her cheeks glowed from the scurry. She truly was a splendor. Raising his brows, he asked, "How about it? Think we can outdo this joker?"

Lifting her chin, she playfully replied, "Need you ask?"

Russell snatched her hand and jumped to her side. Leaning to her ear, he said, "I hope you know the Lindy!"

"I know enough!" she beamed.

He spun her, her skirt snapping at her calves. Hopping and jittering, together they whipped their bodies in circles, slinging their chests back and forth. Quick, sharp, thunderous moves fanned out and compressed; fanned out and compressed. They barely had time to glimpse the Fox's maneuvers; the room whirling at their heels.

The Fox tossed his partner over his back, slung her forward through his legs, making her fly and bounce back to the floor. He then slung her backward through his legs, bending over as she jumped over him. People again drifted off to the side, creating a ring, watching.

Bethany giggled, covering her small mouth with her hand. Pointing to the Fox's partner, she remarked to Sadaye, "I can see that girl's panties!"

Mortified, Sadaye grabbed her finger and asserted, "Don't! It's vulgar!"

Bethany sunk her giggles, hurt by her brash criticism.

Russell, frustrated by the Fox's sudden display of flair, yelled out to Naomi, "Around the world!"

Naomi slung to his side. He grabbed her waist; she jumped and twirled like a Ferris wheel. He bowed down as she rolled over, linking elbows, hopping on his other side. He then slipped his hands in between his legs, catching her palms, sliding her underneath. She sprung up and caught his hand again, and they swung around; fingers in the air, wiggling. The Fox quickly snatched Naomi's free hand and jumped through, pushing her to the side. Russell gawked at the switch, angered, pausing when the other girl yanked him forward. People snickered. Shig laughed loudly. Russell looked at her. Small eyes. Plump lips. Flat nose. Almost pretty. Smirking, the girl twirled in a circle, showing off her garter belt, and then grabbed his hand again and pivoted him around. Glancing at his opponent and Naomi, Russell began to dance with the other girl, shifting to the beat.

Tomiko watched in awe, wishing she could be out on the dance floor, wishing Jim would have the courage to try. She glanced at him, his face seemingly not amused. What was he thinking?

Each couple patterned their steps and tosses, attempting to out burn each shoes. Russell, not satisfied with the girl, sometimes breaking beats, sometimes skidding apart because the girl often exaggerated her performance, quickly jumped in between Naomi and the Fox. Russell spun Naomi backward, and soon recovered their rhythm. The Fox lunged to the girl to retrieve his jittering poise. Lifting Naomi, Russell swung her legs to the right, then the left, then tipped her upward; her pink dress tumbling; her heels diving down and straight through his legs. She skidded on the floor, slightly humiliated, her dress exposing her thigh. Russell turned around, blinked, and reeled to her side, pulling her up. Swiftly they swayed, fanning out and compressing, fanning out and compressing, and finally stopped on the last note when she jumped on his leg, curving like a boomerang.

The crowd applauded both couples; delighted in the entertainment, feeling more at ease with the dance and the strange men in gaudy suits. For the first time in months, people felt normal, living in a normal place, war obscure in their thoughts. The excited evening, the magnificent band, even the cheap punch with rationed sugar, all seemed to erase the watchtower through the northern windows.

A moderate tune followed with the three women vocalists singing "Let's Get Away From It All." People began to dance once more, dispersing like fallen petals on water; drifting; trickling; circulating. The Fox, panting and grinning, walked to Russell and extended out his hand. Russell, breathing heavily, stared; uncertain. Nobody won. Or lost for that matter. But at least the Fox didn't keep his greasy hands on Naomi. Russell decided to shake his hand.

"Man-o, man!" the Fox claimed. "You two really know how to wax a floor!" He released Russell's grip, tugging on his vest. "Ain't too bad in those drabs, brother! Ever consider upscalin' your wardrobe?"

Russell chuckled, resting his knuckles on his hips. "When I get that drunk, I might consider . . . *brother!*"

The Fox bobbed his finger at him, streaming a grin. "When you do get that drunk," he looked at Naomi, "it won't matter if you're wearin' her wardrobe, if you know what I mean!"

Russell dropped his smile. He glanced at Naomi, who blushed and lowered her head. Glaring at the Fox, straining his jaw, he stated, "You're out of line. Watch it!"

"Only jivin', man," he replied, readjusting his large hat, staring directly at Russell. For a moment, his seriousness outlined a hidden determination. "Don't let her too loose if you don't want her to squeeze another goose! *Gokoun-o inorimasu!* You might need that kind of luck!"

Offended, Russell thought for a second. Leaning on one foot, he rebutted, "Why don't you stroll before I shove it up your hole?"

The Fox flared his eyes; stunned. Heaving his sharp shoulders as if boosting a menacing image, he slowly nodded. "Jus' an observation. But I'd be careful anyway, if you know what I mean." Smacking his mouth, he rolled his finger tips around his hat once more and explored Naomi. "It's been fun, sister. If you ever change your mind," he winked and grinned, then revolved around. Sweeping one foot out, dragging the other, sweeping and dragging, the Fox staggered back to his partner who glared at him in annoyance, glancing at Naomi. He fastened his arm to her hip and began rocking to the melody.

Russell knew he had to keep an eye on that slick one. Turning away from the Fox to look at Naomi, he wiped his forehead with the back of his hand. Both had a shiny layer of sweat tracing their faces. He gently rested his left hand on her waist, meeting her other hand midway. Not speaking, they swayed like two swans on wavy waters. Russell really wanted to kiss her. It had been a long time since he felt the subtle warmth of moist lips. He stepped closer to her, her heat twining into his skin, through his clothes. He could hear her breathing. Naomi touched his cheek with hers, closing her eyes. He squeezed her hand and massaged her waist. She smiled.

"*Jyubun desu!*" a voice harshly scolded. "That is quite enough!"

Naomi opened her eyes. Russell felt a firm hand pulling him from behind. He jerked to see who intruded. A woman in her mid-forties, with hair tucked into a bun and penciled eyebrows, frowned at him. He knew she was the home economics teacher; unmarried; an old hag more or less.

The woman persisted, "At least a twelve-inch distance between you both!"

Naomi instantly stepped backward. Her teacher was more intimidating than the nuns.

Russell squinted and strained his lips. What gave this hag the right to regulate his personal space? With everything being so damned crowded, his space regulated by the military or his parents, the last thing he needed was another Nazi poking her nose. The woman warily studied Russell, the lines on her face expanding like webs. She cleared her throat, lifted a brow, and strode back to the side lines.

Tomiko tugged Jim's arm, forcing him to the dance floor despite his stumbling reluctance. She tired of waiting. Smiling, she delicately encouraged him, telling him it was actually easier than he thought.

Every muscle in his body tightened and he could feel everyone staring at him, judging him. His ears transformed in redness. Why was she doing this to him? Did she want to humiliate him?

"Relax, Jim. All you need to do is rock from side to side." She placed his hands on her shoulder and waist and started teetering. Resting her hands on his shoulders, she maintained, "Like this. Just pretend you're rocking to and fro on a ferry boat."

Flinching, he scanned the room, wondering who was watching them. He saw Shig, Ralph, and Ikki dance with other girls from school, chatting, chuckling, enjoying themselves. Jim marveled at how naturally they moved without regrets. Without fear.

Tomiko softly grasped his chin. "I'm right here," she said. "Don't worry about anyone else. I only want to dance with you."

He revealed a half smile, slightly blushing. Two weeks had passed without a suicidal thought since that day. And it felt good to not think about his brother. Relief even. He began shifting his feet, moving at her pace, realizing it wasn't as difficult as he believed.

Sam awkwardly stood with Hank and Bruce, all fidgeting in the corner, longing for dance partners instead of lounging like goons. Staring wistfully at the pretty girls in the middle of room, wishing the pretty ones were dancing with them, the more homely ones lined up at the opposite wall. Just like them.

Sadaye sat down on a wooden lawn chair. She asked Ernest, for the fourth time, to retrieve punch, trying to keep him occupied. Brushing her loose hair strands aside, she began talking to her friend about the curious Zoot Suits, joking about their outrageous styles.

Bethany folded her arms, wanting to fit in, knowing she still was too young- yet too old. It didn't seem fair that Russell was dancing with that other girl. She didn't come from the same island. She certainly didn't know as much about him. That he liked vanilla ice cream. He hummed Glenn Miller's tunes more than the others. And that he was one of Winslow's most popular athletes.

Russell asked, "Wanna take a breather outside?" Naomi eased a grin and nodded. Inspecting the chaperons at the sidelines, knowing their defense, he continued, "I'll meet you there in a minute. I'll go first."

He squeezed her hand and walked off the dance floor to the rows of coat hangers. He glanced at his sister who seemed preoccupied with trying to keep Ernest busy. Russell smiled and shook his head. Poor Ernest. He was trying too hard to please Sadaye. If the guy only understood he was wasting his energies. Zipping his jacket, Russell turned to look at Naomi who ambled toward his way. He muffled his guilt about Maria. The last letter she wrote became vague, as if she were hiding something. But at the same time, was he being just as honest?

The streetlight glared against the front door. He leapt from the steps, the nightly chill embracing his bare neck and hands. A few other couples stood outside; whispering; nestling. Russell couldn't stop smiling. He felt alive. The millions of stars that sprawled above the two mountain ranges flattered the radiating half moon. He leaned against the wall, staring up, ignoring the wire fence at the edge of the highway. Echoes of the music muted through the walls. Russell tapped his foot and hummed along.

Naomi came out. She hopped down the steps and took hold of his hand. She whispered into his ear, "There is a garden they finished on the west side of camp. Hardly anyone should be there now." She tugged on his arm and they trotted up the street, slipping further inside the camp, disappearing, finding a secret spot.

A group of nine boys paraded down the street wearing starched jeans, rolled inside out at the bottom. Their hair slicked back. Their hands scarred like old men. Some inhaled roughly made cigarettes. Some chewed tobacco. The leader, short and muscular, waddled ahead. His roving right eye attracted uncomfortable glances from nightly strollers. Smirking, Shikami returned to the building he had fought in two months ago, now a place of entertainment, not a place for broken bones. He knew Russell had to be there. And if he wasn't, then one of his friends. Two long months eroded before he had a chance to finish his obligation. If his gang were to retain their respect, he had to finish Russell.

He marched up the steps and burst through the door. His gang spilled in like an overturned barrel of oil. They oozed among the crowd, clumping together, not spreading thinly. People had begun to recognize the Terminal Island gang, often avoiding the middle of camp if they could. Escaping the gang's glare, people looked down or turned the other way.

Shig stopped dancing. He glared at the gang, and stretched over to grab Ralph and Ikki. Pulling the two away from the girls, shoving them together, he declared, "They're here! Holy shit!"

Sam, panicking, tugged on Hank's sleeve and pointed to Shikami. Hank and Bruce stared at him; surprised, fearful. The fight had almost slipped from their brains like sand through cracks while school, girls, and news of war preoccupied their time. How strange it seemed to watch the gang disperse through their territory.

Jim felt a harsh tap on his shoulder. Annoyed, he turned around, releasing Tomiko's grip. Shocked to see Shikami sneer in front of him, he jolted backwards, his heart jilting. Then angered, Jim stepped in front of Tomiko, protecting her. He could smell a bitter cologne leaking from Shikami's chest.

"What do you want?" Jim snapped.

Shikami slit his eyes towards Tomiko, still leering, but returned his pounding gaze at him. Shaking his finger in Jim's face, he replied in Japanese, "*I remember you! I broke your friend's hand!*"

Jim harshly glared; the music now throbbing in his ears, his skin burning. "And I remember your neck being crushed."

Shikami clicked his tongue and sniggered. Setting his knuckles on his waist, the rest of his gang merged at his side, never truly deserting him. They formed a semicircle, elbowing dancers off, dominating their space. Tomiko became nervous, wondering what they wanted from Jim. Jim was not the type who mingled with trouble. She slid her arm through his, stepping closer to him.

Shikami demanded, "What is yur friend's name? Yur friend, da dog. By now his hand is betta, okay?"

Jim hesitated, squinting. "Yes. It's completely healed."

"Is he not here? What is his name, *shojo?*"

Again he paused. "Ask him yourself."

Shikami grabbed his collar and reclined into his face. "You fuck with me I can break yur neck!" Pushing his chest against Jim, he spat, "*Tell your dog I will meet him on block twenty-nine! If he does not show, then I will have to make a visit at his home.*" He unfastened his knotted clutch and stepped back. "I do know where he lives, you know! He has a bery pretty sista!"

Numbed that Shikami had been following Russell, Jim could only stare, his voice evaporating like boiling water. He had no real concept the velocity this gang possessed. Perhaps out of fierce pride. Or meanness. Or just harsh boredom. Jim felt Tomiko cramping her hands around his arm. He briefly thought about Leo. Even Leo's crudeness could not compare with the Terminal Island boys.

Shig intruded with Ralph and Ikki straggling along. Aiming face-to-face at the brute, Shig barked, "You ain't welcome here, *minikui!* The sight of you causes maggots to puke!"

Shikami twitched his jaw. Despite his composed muscles that surged like electricity, the thickness in his eyes leveled a peculiar glare. A moment cut through the animosity; a genuine distaste for one another lagged under their sweltering breaths. Bruce, Hank, and Sam shoved through. Shikami grabbed Shig's throat, grinding his thick calloused fingers into his windpipe. Ralph clipped his nails into Shikami's wrist, yelling at him to let go of his friend. Shikami smirked and unbound his vise. Shig gasped. People stared. The music instructor and another male teacher, a *Nisei*, punched through the crowd, rightly concerned. Positioning themselves in between the boys, the two teachers expanded their arms to motion the split.

The music teacher claimed, "This is a dance! Not a boxing match, boys!" He carefully studied Shikami, skimming from tattered shoes to oily black hair combed backwards. Peering doubtfully, he continued, "I'm afraid I'll have to ask you to leave. I don't think you boys really belong here."

Shikami fidgeted, looking away in sheer annoyance. Wetting his lips, staring directly at the teacher, he replied, "An' we don' hafe time to fool 'round." He crisply winked, mocking the man's authority. "Next time, huh, teach?" Turning to Shig, he announced, "*Next Sunday. Two hours after dinner. At the building where Judo classes are held. It will be empty then.*"

Twitching his head sideways, Shikami silently ordered his gang to follow him out the door. Satisfied with the delivery of his message, he waddled to the door; his bowed legs distinguishing his threatening conduct. Glancing towards Jim as he opened the door, allowing the chill to strike the crowd's backs, he flipped his collar and hopped down the steps.

The music teacher proudly smiled as if conquering Napoleon's army. He nodded, telling everyone to pursue their enjoyment, and returned to the punch line where he came. The other teacher rolled his eyes and uttered "It's a good thing I'm not Catholic, otherwise I'd have to worship him as a saint!" Shig and the others chuckled, knowing the music teacher's vanity very well, all having been exposed to it in class. The *Nisei* teacher crossed his arms and strolled away, shaking his head.

Saying nothing to Jim, Shig walked to the punch bowl to retrieve a drink for his throbbing dried throat. His friends followed, ranting about the commotion, slugging remarks about what they would do if they had been in Shig's position. Shig again glanced at Jim, still uncertain about his loyalties.

CHAPTER FIVE

THE late afternoon resided in peace. The wind finally fatigued from its persistence, enabling people to enjoy the outdoors. Radios echoed through thin walls alongside a cheering crowd from a women's volleyball match. Children ran through the streets. Strollers strayed from their blocks, searching for something to do within the dull compound. The movie house was full. The few shops were closed. An amateur play in the makeshift community building was still in the process of rehearsals. Jim's barrack remained quiet. Everyone was either at the movie or the volleyball game. He took Russell's toy car from the Monopoly board and set it in the jail square.

Grinning, he said, "This is the second time you've been in the dog house."

Frustrated, Russell replied, "I hate these cards! They really don't give you a chance to do good!"

"I'm doing well. I have a hundred dollars and counting."

"And I don't even have two bits to my name!" Glancing at Jim's iron piece, he murmured, "I should of been the hat. Seems to bring better luck!"

"Luck is only a frame of mind," he said, avoiding his nervousness about the confrontation with Shikami later on that evening. He knew Russell had to be equally as nervous, otherwise he wouldn't have been so agitated about the game. Normally his friend couldn't care less whether he was winning or losing in Monopoly.

GERTRUDE continued to drop her dresses onto her bed from the handmade closet; a darkly stained pine box. Frustrated, she tugged each dress at the waist. None of her dresses fit her anymore. She was too skinny! Without a sewing machine, refitting her clothes by hand proved a real nuisance. She had already taken them in twice so far! And buying new dresses either from the camp store or catalogs were expensive compared to the little income Meito brought home. Meito and Sadaye's incomes were the only resources that supported eight people. A total of thirty dollars for two families for the whole month. How were they able to rebuild their lives on Meito's fifteen dollars? Even when the Depression had fallen to its worst year nearly nine years ago, at least they were still bringing in fifty dollars more!

Gertrude threw a dress on the floor. She couldn't understand why Russell resisted looking for a job to help out. He was in good health; strong. There was farm work outside of camp this past spring and summer he could have taken. Or even construction work inside the camp. There was always construction.

She stood for a moment, clenching her fists. Looking around the barrack, it almost resembled a home. They finally had real mattresses. All of them. Even if used, and thankfully none of the mattresses harbored bedbugs. Dresser drawers. Shelves with thin books and ceramic animals. Curtains and throw rugs. A broom and ironing board in the corner. Her sons' drawings from school pinned on one side of the wall, showing their old home with green trees and blue waters. Zasshu, the family mutt. She closed her eyes to keep the tears from burning her cheeks. She heard her mother-in-law stuttering over English words, repetitiously, monotonously. It really was getting on her nerves.

She asked, "*Are you using the kerosene lantern, Mama?*"

Mrs. Hamaguchi stopped and glanced around her space. "*I am not. And I do not see it. Why?*"

"*It is getting dark outside and I would like to do some reading after dinner.*"

"*Perhaps*," she thought, tapping her bony finger on her mouth, "*perhaps Meito has misplaced it. He used it last night.*"

"Perhaps," she whispered.

Sighing, Gertrude opened her eyes and walked over to a window. Sweeping aside her loose tears, she stared out the street, beside her father-in-law who sat in a patio chair with a Pepsi bottle in hand, and stared at the western mountains. The sun was falling sooner this time of year. Dinner was near. Her husband at work. Suddenly, she held her breath. Where were her two sons? Panicking, she rushed out the door. She should never have let her father-in-law keep an eye on them in the first place, the drunk!

"Where's Joe and George, Papa-san?" she cried. "You were supposed to watch them!"

Mr. Hamaguchi squinted and slowly turned to look at her. His prickly face and glazed eyes bore little responsibility. He seemed confused. Wetting his lips, he sluggishly replied, "*They should be near*."

Angered, she began yelling out her son's names. They were not yet seven years old; too small to be by themselves; too young to use the best of judgment. Last week a woman was raped by one of their own people three blocks from where they lived. There were criminals loose in the congested camp. Loose! How could he be so stupid? Her shrieks rang in desperation. Soon, Joe and George jumped from behind their barrack, coughing. Stunned, relieved, Gertrude walked to them. Guilt smeared their tiny faces. They were up to something.

She scolded, "Stay out where I can see you both! You two know better than that!"

"Yes, Mama," they replied; their hands at their backs, their eyes as wide as raccoons caught rummaging through garbage.

She carefully glared at them. "What were you doing?"

"Nothin' Mama," they replied.

"I just bet," she murmured. Pointing at her side, she persisted, "Out where I can see you. Got it?" They nodded. Unsure, she folded her arms. "On second thought, the both of you get inside. It's getting dark anyway."

George whined, "But I don' wanna!"

"You've got games in there. Play those."

Joe immediately trotted up the steps, his brown socks slumping at his ankles, his knickers dusty from rolling in the sand. George fiercely frowned. He refused to move.

"Now!" she snapped.

He glanced at his grandfather, hoping for support, but he was falling asleep again. George huffed and griped, "It's not fair!"

"Now!" she yelled, grabbing his collar and pulling him forward.

He reluctantly moved, stomping his feet. Gertrude rolled her eyes and muttered up to the sky, "Give me strength!"

The boys resettled at their own table near their beds. Joe had already retrieved a box with a jigsaw puzzle of cowboys and Indians and spread it out. George sulked, slouching in the chair. Gertrude picked up her dress from the floor and began hanging her clothes back in the closet. She'd sew tomorrow. She didn't feel like it tonight. Glancing at George again, she firmly stated, "If you're going to pout all night then you'll go to bed early."

He whined, "I'm not pouting."

George reached across the board to play with the piece between his fingers. Gertrude tightened her lips, not in the mood to argue. Loudly sighing, she stopped and sniffed the room. Joe stared at his brother, scared, but George retained a rigid glare, silently warning him to keep quiet. He continued to put pieces together while Joe fidgeted, his young forehead crinkling with worry.

Sniffing again, Gertrude looked at her sons. "Do you smell something burning?" she asked.

Joe and George stared at each other without blinking. George said, "No."

She lifted her chin, sniffing. "I smell it. Must be coming from outside."

Mrs. Hamaguchi rested her palms on the English book and also sniffed. She remarked, "*I do smell something burning*."

Smoke climbed from the cracks of the floor, spreading like dust clouds. Gertrude gasped and jumped away from the corner where the smoke filtered through. She quickly grabbed both her sons' hands and yanked them outside. Mrs. Hamaguchi instantly followed. Thick waves of smoke pushed from underneath the barrack. Suddenly a flame flickered on the side as if wildly escaping, wanting to bite and sting. Mr. Hamaguchi opened his eyes. Turning his head, feeling the flame fan out, crackling and heating the desert air, he vaulted out of his chair, dropping his secret bottle. Joe began crying.

Gertrude shrilled, "Fire! There's fire! Somebody help us!"

A crowd gathered in the middle of the soft street, watching in horror and awe as the vehemence orange flame lit their faces. Instantly, seven men and two women began tossing sand into the fire, powerlessly, frantically. A couple of the residents ran with tin buckets, flinging sparse splashes of water from the meager pump. It was better than nothing. Mrs. Hamaguchi heaved, pointing to her decaying home, covering her shocked mouth. Not again, she wept. Not again. She had left her childhood home when she first married, then left her second home after her husband's death to flee to America. She had lost her third home when they were forced to leave because of the war. And now this? Now this? Why? Were her ancestors punishing her? Instructing her that she should reveal Mieto the truth? Or that she should had never left Japan and should have married her first husband's brother? Her fate deemed a harshness cursed by her former in-laws.

Russell sprang out of Jim's barrack. Horrified, he stared at the bright fever consuming his barrack. Jim chased him, bumping into him when Russell halted on the street. Feeling the panic, Jim worried the fire would skip over to the other barracks, including his. A breeze tickled the fire and the thirsty air would drink anything, including fire. The tight quarters would make chaos more tempting. What would happen if half the camp burned? Would they have to relocate again?

Russell suddenly gasped, "The radio!"

He ran inside the smoke. Jim and the rest of Russell's family stared, crippled, shocked. Soon Gertrude and Mrs. Hamaguchi screamed out his name, telling him to come back out. Jim held his breath. He couldn't believe Russell was that idiotic! It was only a radio, for Christ's sake! The residents who were assisting hesitated, stupefied that someone was that insane, nevertheless continued their mission. If they didn't stop the fire now, it would jump over to other homes, inflicting more damage.

Russell covered his mouth and nose with his shirt's collar. He was amazed how quickly the fire had infected his barrack, reaching, burning. The heat stabbed at his body and he felt as though his skin would instantly peel. His eyes stung and he choked. Coughing, squinting with watery vision, he pushed the table out of way and grabbed the radio. Yanking the cord from behind as he dashed to the door, he glanced at his father's still. *Shit!* He stumbled out of the door, sweat flaking from his forehead.

"Get back!" he yelled. "Get back! It'll explode!"

Gertrude trembled as she pulled her sons on the other side of the long street. How she wished Meito were there! She really needed his comfort! Russell's parents followed. Jim stared at Russell's dirty face and wild eyes. All he could do was stare. Russell snatched Jim's arm and forced him to move. Three residents ignored Russell's warning, perhaps not believing him, perhaps not hearing him. Standing twenty feet away, Mrs. Hamaguchi smacked the back of Russell's head, scolding him for being stupid. He cringed, but took-in her fearful frustration. He knew she was right, but at least he saved something. At least they could still have something left. The crowd expanded like poppy seeds blowing into a barrel of tar. Smoke staggered upward; rupturing; revealing its rage for miles. The entire camp understood. People driving on the isolated highway recognized it. Even the rural town of Independence saw a faint reflection from the crumpling sun.

Tom ran down the street, shoving people aside to reach to his family. When he saw it wasn't his barrack on fire, he exhaled in short relief. He squeezed Rose's shoulder and kissed his baby's cheek in her arms. Rose sniffled, wiping her tears off her scared face. It could easily have been her home. Tom hugged his mother-in-law and patted Bethany's head. He then searched for the Hamaguchis in the thick crowd and saw some making an attempt to put out the fire. When he detected them huddling in the middle of two other barracks, he strode over to offer them reassurance.

"I've contacted the fire department," he started, resting his hands on his hips like John Wayne. "We have an emergency phone there. We should get everything under control."

Russell bellowed. "There's a still in there!"

"A *what?*"

"A still! You know, for making booze!"

Tom's strong profile fell. He gazed at Russell as if he had been shot. "You're kidding me. It's illegal to have one!"

Russell rolled his eyes. "No shit! How is it you're the only bozo in camp who didn't know?"

Jim snickered. Tom had been so occupied with Tanaka's group he rarely observed his own surroundings.

Embarrassed, Tom glanced down. "Jesus! These people need to get away from it!"

Russell sat his radio on the ground and replied, "Yeah, I know!" He again snatched Jim's arm and urged, "Come on!"

Pushing through, Tom began yelling to the people to move further back. Soon, Russell and Jim echoed the warning, trying to swing their arms to propel the crowd behind the flames. The reluctant brood slowly shifted, too slowly, only a few wise ones listening and helped along. A thunderous blast. Glass exploded. Recoil of screams. Shards of people dropped to their knees. Black smoke punched through the desert's draft. A man's voice yelled, "Move back, dammit!" People spread like split water, evaporating into alleys and down the streets. The fire truck siren penetrated the terrified silence, rushing to the northeastern sector. Russell jumped up and looked around him. His hysteric heart pounded in his ears. Tom darted off. Where was Jim? Rubbing the sand out of his eyes, he frantically skimmed the messy area where splintered glass and wood laid.

"Jim!" he choked. "Jim!"

Jim crawled. Russell rushed to him, easing his friend to stand. The back of his white shirt revealed black tears and red scratches. Without saying anything, Russell guided him off to the side. An ambulance siren hollered on the opposing boundary, competing with the other shrill. It was almost like Manzanar was being bombed! Russell triggered into laughter. He couldn't stop himself. Leaning against a neighboring barrack, releasing Jim, he sagged his belly and laughed.

Jim, befuddled, feeling his back prickle with pain, thought his friend had just lost his mind.

He demanded, "What the hell could be so funny?" Russell shook his head, laughing harder, unable to speak. "What the hell are you laughing at, Russell? Did the heat scorch your brain?"

He rested his palms on his knees, gasping, aching. "Oh boy!" he wheezed. "Oh boy, you shoulda seen their faces! Boom! Ahhh!" He closed his runny eyes, shaking his head, heaving out his hysterics. The two sirens screeched in his already ringing ears. Both vehicles would be there very soon. He irrationally resumed, "I wish I had a camera for that one! Ka-boom!"

Jim cried, "Stop it, Russell!"

Russell sluggishly groaned, gradually regaining his composure. He watched the yellow fire truck speed up the street and abruptly stopped next to his dissolving home. The firefighters, all *Nisei* robed in slick flaxen coats and helmets, hurtled out of the truck. Two sprinted past by him, hauling the flat hose and quickly tied it to an outside pump near the showers. They dashed back, signaling the crew to proceed. The hose began spitting, the pressure weakened by restrictions of water used daily in the camp. Irritated, two firemen sprayed the best they could while others retrieved buckets of sand to toss. Volunteers emerged with shovels and buckets, aggressively struggling to put out the fire.

"We didn't mean to, Mama!" Joe suddenly wailed. George glared at him. "George knocked over the lantern! But I had the matches!"

Everyone turned to stare. Disbelief wrinkled their faces.

Gertrude bent down to her sons' level, resting her hand on Joe's knee, not blinking. She asked, "Where did you boys get the matches?"

Joe heaved, looking down, sniffing. He whispered, "From Papa's coat."

"Why were you in his pocket?"

Again he sniffled, rubbing his dirty finger under his ruby nose. "To get-to get," he stuttered, "to get some money."

Gertrude tried not to lose her temper, feeling her muscles tighten. Despite their young age, they should have known better. She sharply snapped, "You boys have no idea how angry I am! If you want money, you ask! If you're looking in anybody's pockets, you ask!" She bit her lip, tasting the dried sand, tasting her own failure as a mother. "And you certainly don't play with matches! How stupid! How so very stupid!"

Russell gazed ahead, numbed. At that moment it didn't matter who started the fire. He'd rather not think about it because it would hurt too much. He watched the structure collapse as the fire chewed everything his family had left. What they had left. At least he saved the radio. At least that much.

Worried about his friend's state of mind, Jim leaned into his ear and said, "Maybe you shouldn't fight today. Not after this, Russell."

Clearing his throat, he firmly replied, "I need to. I really need to."

THE early evening sun spread its wings over the Sierra city, flapping dust devils underneath. Shikami led his gang through the soft streets named after numbers and indigenous tribes. People's gardens went into hibernation, leaving behind stiff branches and withered limbs. Homemade ponds, likewise, were narrower; water being reserved for the upcoming winter and next year's harvests outside of Manzanar. A car rumbled by him. The driver was white. Perhaps a visitor. Perhaps an FBI agent. Shikami smirked, and waved to the outsider. The man looked at him, confused, then slowly turned into another street. Rumors of federal agents scouting about swarmed among people's boredom and worries. It was insulting enough to have their citizenship revoked, but for these trench-coat spies to flutter around like moths, hiding in closets and hope chests, it made their situation more disturbing.

Shikami's reputation had reached to all four corners of the camp, including a personal reservation on the administration's "special" list of mischievous activities. Breaking into the canteen store and stealing. Mugging at night. Preserving his territory in the middle of the camp through intimidation. He waddled along; his bow legs as strong as a rhinoceros; his muscular arms swaying; his blemished face as tough as goatskin. Eight of his gang members, with their hair slicked back, maintained a similar harsh expression, establishing their purpose. They were from Terminal Island. They were survivors.

RUSSELL waited with his buddies in the same building where he had been taking his martial arts class. He could still smell human sweat and faint bitter incense from the instructor concluding his class with a Buddhist prayer. The doublewide barrack was conveniently empty on Sundays. Bruce, Ralph, and Hank shared a cigarette as they passed it around, gossiping about baseball. Shig held his own cigarette, unwilling to allocate his nicotine. Ikki unraveled a piece of Wrigley's gum and began chewing. Sam and Jim leaned against the wall, quietly watching him chew and stretch. Russell felt confident. Within the last two months he developed his skills in Judo, jogged every morning just before school, and rebuilt his upper body with a hundred push-ups and sit-ups. Sometimes he practiced his wrestling techniques with Sam or Shig. He even impressed his critical instructor, using what knowledge he had from the old days and sometimes mixing wrestling with Judo. Both were very complimentary toward each other, and Russell found Judo and wrestling interchangeable.

Ikki looked out at one of windows, and announced, "I see them coming."

Everyone, except Russell, turned to face the line of windows to watch. The Terminal Island gang marched with distinction. The wide streets opened up valleys; their footprints freckled the smooth surface. Russell ignored the distractions: the windows, the sun, his friends' excited chatter placing bets. His concentration was more focused than he had ever experienced. In the past, despite the serious competitiveness he often proved to himself, today would be incomparable. He wasn't fighting for sport. There would be no rules. No protection from referees. Injuries would be more severe- if not brutal.

Shikami thumped on the steps, swinging the door open. Wind and dust flew from behind as he entered. He peered carefully at his opponents. Seven of his members aligned themselves near the door, crossing their arms over their chests, glaring. Another remained outside as a scout. Shikami then walked in front of Russell's friends; his muscular shoulders swaying like a battered ship on sea. His cocky grin elevated firmness. Confidence even.

He faced Shig first. "I know you, little girl. You think you tough?" He clicked his tongue, shaking his head. "*It will be fun to do you next, shojo.*"

Shig blew smoke in his face. Chipping a smirk, he replied, "Sorry *shojo*, I'm not a queer. Find someone else to screw."

He sighed, not removing his stare from Shig and suddenly spat on his shoe. Shig strained his jaw, trying not to hit him, knowing today was Russell's fight; not his. He knew Shikami was only testing him, and testing him wickedly.

Russell preserved a blank expression as he directly looked at Shikami. They stood horizontally from one another, silently arranging their positions, arranging their honor. Initially Russell had planned to protect his mother's dignity and the thought of some punk insulting her had scuffed his nerves. But since then, it developed into repairing his reputation. And repairing his value as a human being. The room became tranquil like snow fainting from the sky. No one spoke. No one shuffled their feet. No one even sneezed. Yet everyone fell in line for the first move.

Jim wished he had the ability to defend himself. Physically, anyway. If Jim encompassed the talent to fight, then he could help Russell. His father discouraged sports, believing they were too ruthless in a civilized world. Observing Shikami's smirk, Jim hated him. And he hated Callis. He detested bullies who manipulated their strength to feel superior. He remembered that Russell had admitted once being a bully himself, harassing a *Kibei* kid who wore glasses, had buck teeth, and spoke with a Japanese accent. Jim recognized the difference between people like Shikimi, Leo, and Callis. That wasn't power. That simply was self hatred.

Shikami paced around Russell in a circle. He knew what Russell had been up to. Learning Judo from his uncle. Clever and ambitious. Fortunately for Shikami, he had been familiar with the art since he was ten. And Aikido. Last time he only used a small portion since Russell knew nothing about it at all. This time he would be generous in his knowledge. This time he would put Russell in the hospital to fulfill his glory. Stopping in front of Russell, he declared, "Today, I weow break yur neck."

"Almost broke yours as I recall," he retorted.

"Only because you cheated."

"I thought that's how the game's played, *shojo!* "

Russell stepped back, adjusting his fixed stance; knees bent; arms loosely at his side. Shikami followed, his smirk as rigid as a knife. Concentrating, Russell allowed a few seconds to pass in between them. It was always difficult to determine who would make the initial move. Advantages and disadvantages equaled in motion, and all of it was dependent on each opponent's skill. This time he believed that Shikami expected him to strike first. To see what he had to offer. Shikami didn't even blink. Swiftly, Russell wheeled his hand toward his wrists, testing Shikami's reflexes. He sharply flexed, cutting into Russell's blow. Again Russell flung his other hand, encountering the expected jab. He continued the repetition, swaying like a brittle boat on stormy waters, pretending his ineptness. These first series of moves were not his legitimate abilities.

Irritated, Shikami made the first assertive move, thrusting both fists upward and downward as if holding a bowl, hitting Russell in the stomach, barely nicking his chin. Russell quickly gasped and revolved his arm over Shikami's head, grabbing his collar. Shikami slugged Russell's rib cage and swept sideways to stab his elbow into Russell's spine, nearly batting him to the floor. Russell twirled around, pain pinching in his front and back. Sweat began to prick his forehead. A couple of seconds elapsed. Their stares scattered bored resentment and fascination. This fight embodied an ancient tradition in a modern world, and so their silence respected it. Unlike the typical American boasting, their silence signified more self-control. Grinning, Shikami glanced at his gang. Bouncing, he punched to Russell's face. Russell seized his fist, twisting his arm, piercing his ribs with a series of punches. Shikami spun like a coin, again hitting Russell from behind with his leg. Russell slouched to the floor, yanking at Shikami's ankle who instantly collapsed. Infuriated, Shikami kicked Russell in his shoulder as Russell tried to lunge over him. Flipping up, Shikami caught Russell's advancing arms and swung Russell in a full circle, crashing him directly into his spiked hand. Russell choked and toppled down; belly up.

Jim held his breath. He heard Russell wheeze.

For a moment, Russell felt his throat swell and he couldn't breathe. Shikami slammed his foot into Russell's stomach, causing him to remain lifeless. His gang finally released a soaring cheer and laughter along with clattering claps. Sam starting chewing his fingernails, blinking incessantly. Ikki nervously hid his hands inside his pockets, chewing his gum more quickly. Jim jerked forward, but Shig plucked him back and snapped, "Not yet!" Jim glared at him. He pushed Shig, and then stood apart from everyone.

Russell sluggishly rolled over and painfully curled into a coiled leaf position. Shikami circled around him, slamming his fists in every weak spot. Provoked, Russell flung his fist at Shikami's ribs. Grabbing Russell's arm, he cut another spiked cleft of his flat palm into Russell's throat. He coughed, spitting out speckles of blood. Stunned he was bleeding internally, Russell tottered on his back, shutting his eyes, tearing up, feeling the room swirl with continuous slashes. Between the wheezing noises he was making, he could hear Shikami's discomforted heaving. This went on for several minutes, except it felt much slower and he felt stuck in this moment while tasting his own metallic blood curdling in his mouth after each hit. He saw Maria's face looking down at him, sympathetic and disappointed. Her lips parted as if to say something, then closing her eyes, his mother's face materialized. He heard her voice, despite her mouth remaining sealed, whispering to him, "*No son of mine is worthy of death because no son of mine is worthy of this life.*"

Russell opened his eyes. In an instant, he caught Shikami's propelling leg and yanked it. Shikami finally fell on his back, a grunt bolting from his mouth. Russell's adrenaline prevailed over his pain, inspiring him to jump on top of Shikami, clenching a loose leg and shoving it over Shikami's shoulder blade. He then knifed his knee into Shikami's other leg, pinning him down and squeezing his hand around Shikami's throat. Shikami gurgled, clutching his hands on Russell's tight grip, desperately wiggling. Russell felt his rival's strong muscles twitch underneath his own. Shikami slammed his fists back into Russell's ribs and began to spit up bubbles from his cracked lips. Russell grunted, tightening his entire body, but he did not budge. His mind and hand focused on his enemy's neck. The thought of breaking it inflicted a foolish satisfaction. The anger that mounted during the year bled through his fingers and all over this Jap's throat.

Shikami's gang gawked, watching their leader's face turn red then purple, watching him choke and sputter. Much to Russell's friends amazement, they equally gawked, too stunned to applaud. Everyone in that room started to understand that Russell could easily kill Shikami.

Jim realized Russell had snapped. That something else surged inside him; possessed him. As much as Jim despised Shikami, observing his death was not worth it, and Russell being responsible absolutely was not worth it.

Jim barked, "That's enough, Russell! Don't murder the bastard!" Russell didn't hear him. Jim darted to Russell and grabbed him. Much to his surprise, Russell felt like stone; heavy and rigid. He tried pushing his friend out of balance, but his pampered muscles lacked adequate strength. "Let go!" Jim yelled.

Sam quickly pounced into motion, helping Jim. Together they yanked Russell as if hauling a load of cement. Shikami gasped and rolled to his side, cradling his hand over his bruises. The marks were visible and indented. Russell became paralyzed. Jim and Sam dragged him into a corner while Shikami's group finally bustled around their leader to help him raise to his feet. Shig and his trio could only stand motionless. Shig carefully inspected Shikami's gang with their outrage glaring at Russell.

Shig mumbled to his friends, "This could get really ugly, boys."

Jim called out Russell's name several times. When he still wasn't responding, he slapped Russell. Several times in a row, in fact. Stunned, Russell jerked to stare up at Jim.

Jim asserted, "I told you shouldn't have fought today! Have you lost your goddamn mind?"

Russell breathed unevenly as sweat bristled down his neck. The tightness of his muscles suddenly weakened, and he began to shake. It felt odd. Like dreaming under a hot sun and not particularly knowing where reality lay. Guilt dripped through his thoughts, slowly comprehending his consequences. What he was capable of committing.

Russell feebly asked, "Is he alright?"

Jim glanced to his side, briefly seeing Shikami stagger. "I think he'll live. But Jesus, are you alright?"

He nodded. "I think so. I think I need to go home, though." After hearing his own words he realized he really had no home to go to.

Sam and Jim assisted him to his feet. Soon Shikami's brood surrounded them, barricading themselves with clenched fists and stout footing. Resentment soaked behind their dark eyes. Their rough skin, textured by sun and seawater, exposed years of hatred in one moment. A hatred they justified from years of defending against mobs and newspapers and politicians. Against the Knights of Columbus and Sons and Daughters of the American Revolution. Against the Chinese and Negroes. And now against their own.

Shig walked to the seven members, and tapped one on the shoulder. The boy turned around. Grinning, Shig mocked, "Is this a private club or can anyone join?"

The boy scrunched his nose and flexed his mouth. His stocky built appeared notably bulkier compared to Shig's modest size. He gripped Shig's sweatshirt collar, and pushed him into the corner next to Russell. Each gang member extended their arms, taking off their coats, removing pieces of articles that would hinder them. Shikami sat on a stool beside another member, lethargically recuperating. Ikki helplessly looked at Ralph, Hank, and Bruce at the sidelines, wondering what to do next.

Footsteps rattled the barrack. The front door launched open and the Judo instructor, Toru, marched inside with two other adults following. His brown checkered coat and dusty jeans disguised him an average laborer; not a reputable martial artist. His brown hat clenched just above his irritated brow. Stomping to Shikami, he fiercely frowned at his nephew.

Toru snapped, "*What has your mother told you about fighting, Shikami-san?*"

Shikami couldn't reply. With his voice crippled, his throat dried, he could only cough. His gang instantly diffused like liquid out of a broken glass, migrating apart from Russell and his friends. The two other adults, who wore thick slacks and long boots, projected their stiff expressions with authority while they guarded the entrance. No one would be fleeing just yet. And apparently their so-called lookout "scout" had mysteriously departed when the adults came into view. Shikami's uncle gently brushed his fingertips over his nephew's damaged neck. Grunting, he stepped back and carefully studied all the boys in his room. Without words, each avoided eye contact, avoiding blame.

The instructor barked, "Russell! Come to me now!"

Wobbling forward, still in need of Jim's assistance, Russell began to feel guilty. Guilty for misusing the art. And guilty for taking advantage of his instructor's hospitality.

"Russell," he maintained, "you hafe not been learning. Da first lesson is not to beat da shit out of yur opponent!" He then scowled at Shikami. "*And my brother, may his soul rest in peace, did not raise a disrespectful yogore! Do you not care that everywhere the police are always watching you?*" He then rotated to glare at Shikami's group who seemed more interested looking at their shoes than looking at him. "You boys hafe big mouths! I hear eferything!" Returning to his nephew and student, he continued his disgust. "Starting tomorrow, I weow teach both how to not kill each otha! If you disobey, den I weow not only report you to da police, but weow expose da shame to yur family!"

CHAPTER SIX

Late October

THE evening wind rattled the cluttered barrack. Men in their fifties to seventies assembled in semi-organized clumps in the community center. Games ranging from cards to Mahjong to dice kept their minds distracted that Wednesday evening; every Wednesday. Very few who could actually read English had brought newspapers, and then translated the best they could for their friends. Often they kept their political views about the war passive and neutral. Too many ears were present, and for the sake of their family and reputations, it was best to say very little. Local politics were a different matter, however, because they complained as much as they could about their lack of authority and how the *Nisei* continued to let the meat and sugar crisis climax out of control.

Mr. Hamaguchi slumped forward in a corner, crinkling his thick wavy brows and pitted face. He began watching the games to escape his wife's invariable nagging. (After his miniature distillery exploded, although it wasn't his fault for starting the fire in the first place, the fact that he was placed on the administration's list for behavioral misconduct ignited his wife into a rampage. Her choice of weaponry: her mouth.) Her displeasure only compelled his need to sip more from his bottle, needing to forget his failure: His failure as a husband, a father, and a complete failure as caretaker for his family. Jobs for the *Issei* were limited. Everything was controlled by the youth these days.

When he fled from poverty before his seventeenth birthday in 1909, Japan and China had just signed a treaty which granted Imperial Japan the opportunity to borrow Manchuria's golden railroad of the Orient, (four years after Russia and Japan fought for that golden expansion, and fourteen years after Japan made its first invasion to take the wealth without permission.) If Mr. Hamaguchi were a man of foresight, he should have seen how Japan's aggression would bleed into his life decades later, destroying it. The same foresight he should have used when his new wife arrived at the dock with another man's baby. (After Meito was born they moved from Oakland to Bainbridge Island to escape the gossip.) But he was a man of underprivileged judgment. When his friends boasted that the best kind of wife was a picture bride; a bride who didn't care if a man was wealthy or not because it was the promise of wealth that America supplied which would make a man's life truly successful, Mr. Hamaguchi dreamt of supple opportunities, a devoted wife, and many children. What did he get instead? A wife who loathed him, children who disregarded him, and all those supple opportunities he once thought possible now boiled inside a glass bottle. He was born with nothing and now it looked like he was going to die with nothing: karma playing out in full circle. He had to have done something terrible in his previous life to deserve this life.

Mr. Hamaguchi chewed on a stick of black licorice, attempting to hide the faint smell of alcohol. Although he was forbidden to construct another homemade still in his new barrack, he quickly befriended another alcoholic who already had one hidden in his barrack. He knew the rumors blended with the desert's breezes about him fermenting into a drunk; nevertheless, he pretended he wasn't one as long as everyone else pretended.

A record player had babysat the *Issei* men as if lulling them to sleep; only soft muttering contended with Bing Crosby's crooning voice.

"*Why do they insist we have to listen to that man whine?*" an elderly man grumbled, sitting behind a square table of Chinese checkers. "*We are not children! We are not invalids! We can choose our own music! If I had known this before the evacuation, I would have brought my own damn records!*"

"*If you had,*" his colleague bluntly replied, "*they would have taken them from you! They do not trust Japanese music, my friend. And even so,*" he grinned, "*I would have to take the records from you. You have no accountability of taste!*"

The other man scratched his wrinkled chin, sneaking a grin. "*It is a kind blessing that your mother is still alive. Who else would love such an ugly face, my friend!*"

His colleague laughed, reclining against the backing of his chair. "*Is it any wonder we are sixty-five and still bachelors?*"

Mr. Hamaguchi loosened a smile. He never could remember their names, however enjoyed overhearing their wit anyway. They were once teachers of a Japanese language school in Los Angeles. For forty years they taught reluctant *Nisei* the language of their ancestors only to become obsolete in retirement. Yet, a part of him was thankful that kind of school didn't exist on Bainbridge. For one thing, who had the time and money to invest into such luxuries? His children could blend so much more easily into American society without being regarded as deviant. Although it would had been nice if Goro spoke more Japanese at home. And why did he change his name? It was a good name; his grandfather's name. He was a brave war hero who died two months before his last son was born.

"*I do not wish to discuss it any more*!" someone spat, standing up from a table full of card players. The entire room turned to look at him, only Cosby's tune echoed in the background. "*You were not there! You do not have the privilege to disagree!*"

Mr. Hamaguchi recognized the loud man as his former neighbor on the island. Two weeks ago he returned from Missoula, the same place where he had been released merely three months prior. Yes, Missoula. A small town enclosed by the environment. Similar to Manzanar in that sense.

"*Toshiyuki Yoshimura is a good man!*" the other rebutted. It was Mitsuru, Tomiko's father.

"*I used to believe so!*" he sneered.

Mitsuru rose to his feet, standing directly across from the boastful man who disrupted the peaceful night. Everyone watched with a thrilling gaze; glad that the monotony chipped away their boredom. Including Mr. Hamaguchi.

"*I had been there, Choichi-san!*" Mitsuru defended, resting his knuckles over his stack of cards. "*Most of us had been there! You are not the only one who felt the humiliation of propaganda!*"

Choichi, wearing a vest and bow tie, huffed at Mitsuru. He scowled, "*Those trials are a mockery to our honor! And anyone who collaborates with it is just as dishonorable! Furthermore, how can you not even suspect that he might be an informant for them?*"

Mr. Hamaguchi stopped chewing. Choichi's statement tore open everyone's suspicious nature. Everyone might have thought it, but no one dared to speak of it.

Mitsuru's face deflected redness, his veins on his neck straining like rope. "*The only honor I doubt is yours! We should support each other, not accuse, otherwise we are no better than the rest!*"

Mitsuru inspected his peers around him, raising his chin, tightening his lips. No one spoke. Breathing deeply, he reseated himself and grabbed his cards.

Choichi grunted, hesitating. He quickly glanced around the room. He knew this wasn't the right time or the place. Exasperated, he flung out his hands as if tossing his anger aside and sat down.

The gossip immediately followed, devouring the excitement, theorizing who was right and who was wrong. Mr. Hamaguchi began chewing again. Blinking in thought, he also wondered if some truth accompanied Choichi's accusation.

* * *

TOM tucked the baby's blanket under his son's arms. He smiled broadly, proudly, and patted his son's thick, soft hair. My God, he was a handsome baby. No blemishes. Healthy. A pair of strong lungs that could curdle Hitler's blood! The walnut crib was a gift from Tanaka's group. They understood the importance of providing for family. Sighing, he glanced at his wife who lay with her arm over her forehead, her dress arching at her thigh. The doctor said it usually took a couple of months before she would recover. He realized how much he loved her. Sometimes, with life fracturing time and responsibilities it was easy to overlook her loveliness and his need to be tender, thoughtful, impassioned. Sometimes he would purposely focus on other aspects of life to keep from going crazy, that way he would irritate his wife less often. He walked over to Rose and lightly caressed her hair. His mother-in-law was attending one of her classes, who knew which exactly, just an interlude from monotony.

Rose opened her eyes and smiled. She shifted, allowing room for her husband to sit beside her. She could barely remember the last time they had privacy. Reaching up, she grazed her fingers over his mustache. She whispered, "When are you going to cut that silly thing off? You look so much better without it."

Annoyed, he stopped stroking her head. "I like it. Ted says it makes me look more dignified."

"Who are you married to? Me or Ted?"

He chuckled. "Have I been that neglectful?"

She quit caressing his mustache. "It's more than that. I think you value his opinion more than mine."

"Don't be silly. I've always respected your opinions."

"Then shave off your mustache, Tom," she insisted.

"Are you serious? Are you going to make a big deal about my mustache?"

"Are you?"

He heaved in exasperation and stood up. The political pressures made him worry for the safety of his family. Didn't she understand that? The Kitchen Worker's Union had circulated vicious accusations against the administration, against the WRA, against *Nisei* who they believed licked the heels of the FBI like dogs. Traitors, they spat out in public. *Inus*. Spies. Ugly matters Tom tried not to discuss in his home. It was the one sanctuary he wished to keep secure. These bitter, obnoxious men were too angry to establish a hopeful future after the war. They were only making it worse. Goddamned fascists! Japanese loyalists! And Katsuji, the flag burner, the leprosy of stereotypes for their people, who eagerly collaborated in the Union; a farce! But then what did he expect from someone who really wasn't an islander?

Shaking his head, Tom replied, "We're not arguing over something this small! *Bakarashi!*" He stepped to the door and opened it. "I'm going for a walk!"

Rose watched him hide in the dimming light as he slammed the door. Since he joined Tanaka's party, his stress greatly increased, and he refused to share any of his thoughts or concerns with her. He was different. More silent. More grumpy. He also seemed to care more about politics than his own family. She threw her pillow at the door, quietly cursing.

* * *

JIM knocked on the door. Breathing heavily after hiking all the way across the camp, he stared at a hilly lump lurching about hundred feet from the fence. Although he had been aware of the abnormal mass settled in between the two mountains, it appeared out of place. Even more so in the shadows of dusk. How did it even form? What sort of geographical mystery could create this reddish-brown rock shaped like an elephant's body? Like an island. Completely detached. Completely odd. Completely trapped.

Russell opened the door. Smiling, he exclaimed, "Well, it took you long enough! Half the day already wasted!"

Jim quipped, "No offence to you, but I had better things to do!"

"None taken! I would rather spend time with old people than you, anyway. Better complainers."

Russell released the door as Jim took hold of the knob, then after closing it he followed Russell to the middle of the barrack. To Jim's surprise, the barrack was already equipped with furniture and beds. He had expected Russell's new housing to be barren. Like everything else. Three beds aligned on the walls' sides with a sagging blanket covering Mrs. Hamaguchi's seclusion. There were two dresser drawers; one with a vanity mirror. Striped curtains matched the striped rugs. The other family who had once lived in that barrack recently relocated to a different camp to be united with their relatives, leaving behind their heavy belongings. And an actual wall had been constructed of sheet rock, separating the Hamaguchis from another couple; the Morimotos.

The Morimotos were Russell's new bunkmates who lived at the end of the barrack. They were well into their fifties, although they appeared ten years older. Their wrinkled hands bore bony knuckles; their eyes tucked under their lids. Mr. Morimoto still clung to his war uniform which he had carefully unfolded and hung on the wall to protect it from creasing. He was among the few *Issei* who were in fact given an American citizenship due to his heroism during the Big One. It was Morimoto's uniform which slowly revived Russell's belief in the American system. Belief that change was possible. That the Constitution could keep its original promises.

Jim asked, "Why didn't the other people take their stuff with them?"

Russell snorted. "How? They requested to be transferred to Topaz, I think, in Utah. They had no other way of getting there other than train! Try stuffing a bed down your pants!"

Sitting down, he remarked, "I suppose that still hasn't stopped you from trying, though."

"I don't have to," he winked. "My package is fine the way it is!"

Grinning, he again glanced around. "It's quiet here. Where's the folks?"

"My father's at the community center. My mother's visiting Meito on Block Nineteen."

The Hamaguchis had been spilt further apart. Meito and his family were relocated to another barrack. Sadaye eagerly agreed to move into the women's dorm. Russell knew why. She wanted her freedom! But Russell, who had one more year remaining before his independence, had to settle with living with his parents.

"So, basically," Jim inquired, "you have the place to yourself?"

Russell smiled. "Basically. So I invited Naomi and Tomiko to come over. But we can't be too loud or else the Morimotos can hear us."

Jim lifted his brows. He readjusted his seating. His heart began to beat faster. It had been weeks since he and Tomiko acquired privacy. He asked, "How long have you been planning this?"

"Tuesday," Russell replied, leaning on the table, resting his chin inside his palms. "No chaperones. How about that?" Russell retrieved a stack of cards from the shelf. "How about some poker until the girls get here?"

"Why not? I know how to call your bluffs."

He chuckled. "Oh yeah? Or maybe you think you got me figured, brother!"

Russell slid the cards out of the box and tousled it in one hand. Since April, he treated his boredom through whimsical tricks. Despite his small hands, they were strong and limber. In front of Jim, he tossed the stack with grace, flipping it from one palm to the other like a centipede. He continued his show by separating the stack in both hands and shuffled equivalently.

"That may be great," Jim humorously began, "but can you pull a rabbit out of your ear?"

"I might be able to pull one out of your hole!" Russell laughed at himself and pitched out the cards.

Jim shook his finger at him, squinting, grinning. "Anyway, how are things going with Shikami and your Judo instructor, what's his name?"

"Toru. So far I hate it." He grimaced. "All we've been doing is cleaning, or scrubbing floors, or sitting beside each other in silence." Placing the deck between them, he shuffled through his stack. "Toru said before we can face each other again we need to learn to be tolerant of each other. Or something like that."

Jim slowly shuffled his cards, his humor waning. "Do you ever think about what could have happened if I hadn't stopped you?"

He pinched his brows as he sighed out of frustration. "I'd rather not. But sometimes I dream about it." He then grunted. "That seems to be the story of my life!" Brushing his fingertips on his cards, Russell cleared his throat, wanting to change the subject. "Can I ask you a personal question?"

"You're already asking."

"Well, I didn't wanna ask in front of the other guys. I know you're kinda funny about these things." He briefly hesitated. "You 'n Tomiko . . . have you?"

Leaning back, he exhaled a long sigh, then flickered a quick smirk. "None of your business."

"I knew it!" Russell exclaimed. "That day you two were stranded in the shed! What was it like?"

"And I said none of your business." He pretended to be interested in his set of cards, but his grin continued to widen. "I am finding it harder to concentrate during the days. I think about her even when I'm supposed to be busy."

"Do you love her?"

Jim didn't answer. He felt the same, awkward sting vibrating inside as when Tomiko told him that she had loved him. It was difficult to pronounce. It was a coarse word that swelled in this throat and he simply couldn't vocalize it.

"Do you love Maria?" he asked instead.

Russell paused, sighing. "Yeah, but it's hard, you know. Trying not to think about her." He closed his eyes. "Please, do me a favor and don't tell Naomi. Besides, Maria will probably marry someone else anyway."

"What about Naomi, then? Do you also love her?"

Nervously laughing, he defended, "What kind of question is that? Geez! How in the hell did you turn this one around? You never did answer my question in the first place!"

A knock on the door startled Russell. He jumped up to open it. Tomiko and Naomi stood on the steps, their shoes covered in dust, their hair loose from the walk.

Naomi glared at him, and demanded, "Who's Maria?"

SADAYE said an early goodnight to her new set of roommates; clunking off her thick shoes; exhausted from the long sixteen hours at the hospital. The women's dorm smelled of lavender and sweaty feet. An ensemble of creams, perfumes, lipstick, and hair curlers unveiled beauty in its rawest form. Despite the rows of beds as designed by military men, she liked being a part of it, liked gossiping in the late hours, sharing forbidden secrets she could never tell her mother! Some of the women had their own trunks at the foot of their cots. Sadaye groaned as she lay down, holding a sealed letter from New Jersey. She smiled. After all these months, he still continued to write to her.

A young woman with a narrow face and large eyes walked to Sadaye; her silk robe untied and exposing a low cut gown. She sat on Sadaye's cot, shivering.

"Boy! It's always cold in here!" she remarked.

Sadaye looked up. She really didn't like this woman. She was too aggressive and perpetuated an unfavorable reparation. Any other woman associating with her often became equally condemned. No one in the dorm wished to speak with her; often ignoring her or reserving a bitter distance.

"I imagine so, Katie. I don't know why you're still wearing summer night clothes."

She shrugged. "Because I can! So, you had two visitors this afternoon. They seemed *very* interested. What have you been doing to these poor slobs to make them visit in the middle of the afternoon?"

Blushing, Sadaye replied, "Nothing. One works at the hospital. The other was a patient."

"Really?" she slyly nodded. "Gave them a bath, did we?"

Annoyed, she said, "I'm not that kind of a nurse, Katie."

"That's a shame. We all need a hobby of some sort."

"Yes, well, I thought it was illegal in most states."

Katie stood up. "Honey, thank God it's illegal in most states." She winked, and then pointed to the letter. "That's some correspondence you've got going. Isn't taboo to be interested in someone outside your own kind?"

Sadaye held her breath. She had only been there a week. How was it possible for her to know?

"Don't look so shocked, sweetie," Katie grinned. "I don't read your letters or nothin'. It's when you talk at night with some of the other gals. Who really can sleep?" She began to twirl her hair. "Take advantage of it. Who knows, he may be your ticket out of here. I'd buy that ride!"

Sadaye laid the envelope on her stomach, and stared up with annoyance and skepticism. "I couldn't do anything like that. To use people."

Katie's humorous veneer dropped from her chin. She bent down and firmly uttered, "You're a funny one."

"What do you mean?"

"Don't be so sure what you're capable of *not* doing. Modesty is a fake word, meaning you pretend to be one kind of gal when you're something more. You write to this guy because you can be someone else. Someone who's not tied down in Japanese traditions."

Sadaye quickly rose. "What if he likes me for being just me?"

"Don't you know he likes you because he thinks you're forbidden? You're not Eve. You're the apple, sister!"

RUSSELL chased Naomi through the street, apologizing, feeling like a monkey in an Abbott and Costello skit. He couldn't understand why. He had never felt like a monkey with Maria. But then, Maria was less flirtatious, less demanding, and a better listener. Naomi talked as much as he did, more on certain levels. But oh, man, she knew how to dance and kiss!

"What else do you want me to say?" he asserted, ensuing her track of dust. "I didn't mention her before 'cause I didn't think it mattered!"

"You're unbelievable! What am I? Someone to take her place until you go back home?"

"We may not go back home, Naomi!"

She yielded, crossing her arms, blinking in disgust. "So in the meantime, find a substitute?"

"That's not fair, Naomi! It's not like that."

She sprinted, her cheeks flushed, eyes submerged in tears. Russell ran beside her.

"Naomi, don't cry! Oh geez! I don't want to make you cry! Talk to me!"

She continued her pace, feeling embarrassed as people watched. The tightness of the barracks and bored people made it worse. She wished Russell would go away, just go away like everyone else. Maybe she should become a nun. At least the humiliation wouldn't repeat if she altered her focus on something more meaningful.

Russell resumed, "Listen, I like you very much!"

"But you *love* Maria!" she bitterly snapped.

"But I'm with you! You have no idea how much I think about you! You make my loneliness go away! You make it possible to wake up in the mornings! I don't want to be with anyone else, you see!"

Naomi halted, brushing her wet eyes, sifting her thoughts. "You should of told me. I had the right to know. I could of made the decision then."

He clenched his jaw, breathing heavily, worried. "So . . . tell me now."

She had difficulties looking at him. "Now I don't know."

He extended his hand forward, keeping his palm opened, untied. Naomi peeked down, breathing unevenly. She genuinely liked him, however, she didn't want that additional strain.

MUSIC from the radio muddled their sounds. Anxious, exhilarated, raw senses blushing again, Tomiko let Jim unfasten her brassiere. In an impulsive minute, once Russell left them, they braced, knowing it could be weeks, perhaps months before they could be alone. Swiftly, like eagles plunging the sea for food, for thirst, they toppled on a bed, forgetting the world. Forgetting their friends. Forgetting the old couple living behind the sheetrock.

THE street lights accompanied Russell and Naomi as they ambled in a muted state. Random gusts of wind flipped dirt in their faces. Echoing gongs rustled against the panel of barracks, announcing super. Russell had been too nervous to speak, fearing he would say something stupid and offend her to the limit of permanent breakage. Naomi had been thinking during this time. She browsed at other couples who dawdled in the yellow, sandy streets; some content; some doleful. They were near a public garden where a pond, more of a puddle than anything, and wooden log tarried in the haze. Russell followed her, passing a few barrels. He brushed off the sand for Naomi and then sat on the thick log beside her.

She finally spoke, "What's Maria like?"

Russell scratched the back of his head, tensing his brows. It was a little uncomfortable. "Well," he sighed, staring down at his feet. "She has a great sense of humor. She likes to laugh. And she's smart. Sometimes she helps me with schoolwork. Mainly math." He hesitated, unsure how much further he should relate.

"Is she pretty?"

"I think so, yes."

"Why didn't you tell me you have a girlfriend?"

He shrugged. "I don't know. It's not like I'm married or anything! But what about you? Don't you have a boyfriend back home?"

"No," she remarked. "Not really. Once people find out both your parents died from illnesses," she closed her eyes, feeling them burn, heaving unsteadily. She had to recover her sensibilities. Clearing her throat, she maintained, "They treat you like you're the one spreading disease. People are absurd, you know?"

"Isn't that the truth." He leaned closer to her and squeezed her cool hand. When she didn't oppose, he moved forward and curved his arm around her shoulder. It felt nice. "So," he continued. "What do you want?"

"What do *you* want, Russell?"

"Honestly, I don't know."

Naomi gently patted his hand that rested on her shoulder. She nestled her cheek on his chest and sniffled in the cold evening. The warmth of his body felt reassuring; nevertheless she needed his complete commitment. If he loved someone else, then it wasn't fair for either of them.

She whispered, "Then I'll decide for you."

TOMIKO asked, "Do you feel guilty?"

Jim streamed his fingers through her hair. They sat on a bed, reclining in the corner of the walls, her back bracing on his stomach. Their shirts and pants were clumsily buttoned; their shoes lumped underneath some chairs. He hadn't thought about guilt. Ironically it was the first time it didn't occur to him. But while he played with her rumpled hair, guilt gushed downward like a leaking barrel of liquor.

"No," he lied. If he engaged in doubt, then all of it would have been wrong. He knew what they did was beyond improper: The place. The time. He would be damned if he was going to embark on regrets. "You didn't feel guilty the first time."

Tomiko stretched out her legs and covered her flushed face with her hands. Grinning she, said, "I know, I know! But I think we should feel guilty!" She dropped her hands back on her lap. "I mean, we're told so. We graduate next year, for Pete's sake! Shouldn't we have waited at least after then?"

He began caressing her neck. "What difference would that make?"

"At least by then we could move into single dorms. Be more independent, I think." Jim smiled and kissed her ear. "My father!" she chuckled. "If he knew!"

His smile weakened, and for a moment he remembered how his brother had gotten himself into trouble. It was John's junior year as well. The regrets were now piercing him. Jim now worried about provoking identical mistakes. For a moment he held his breath. He would make this different. He would make this honest. "Why don't we get married?"

Tomiko gasped. She covered her mouth, blinking in delirium. "What?"

"Let's get married. Of course, we can wait until after graduation."

She couldn't speak. Her body rushed in a surge of excitement. Before she answered, she needed to hear Jim say it. Resting her palms on her neck, she finally voiced, "Tell me you love me, Jim."

He hesitated. "You know I do."

"Say it, then. I want you to say it."

The knot in his chest stopped just below his tonsils, hindering his words. Fumbling, he mumbled it.

Tomiko laughed, "Louder!" He repeated his mumbling. She teased, "I'm not convinced!"

"I love you," he said, feeling the knot pop out of his mouth, gone, insignificant, free. "I love you, Tomiko. Will you marry me?"

She turned around, giggling, and kissed him for a long period. The salt that lagged on his lips, she wiped away.

"Yes," she replied. "Yes."

He beamed, resting his palms on her cheeks, embracing her. His giddy feeling suddenly staggered, and he stopped kissing Tomiko. Worried about his father's reaction, remembering how his father lost his temper when John announced he wouldn't attend college because of Tomiko's sister, Jim whispered, "Let's not tell anyone just yet."

Disappointment stung her face. "Why?"

He paused, not wishing to botch the mood. "Not until I buy you a ring. I want it to be flawless. To make sure the engagement is respectable."

A soft smile bloomed in between his hands.

"That's one of the reasons why I love you," she whispered.

CHAPTER SEVEN

Early November

MRS. BERLITZ, Russell's English teacher, and Mr. Fiordi, the music teacher, stood beside the small bus as they counted ten students bouncing aboard. That Saturday the two teachers arranged for a field trip outside of camp, escorting those who had been selected in a box every weekend for that month. The camp director agreed, along with the two towns, making sure Independence and Lone Pine felt comfortable with the idea. No protests were publicly voiced. Surprisingly so. Jim submitted to Tomiko's wish to sit by the window. How odd it seemed to be excited riding a silly school bus lent from Lone Pine. The last seven months retreated into an insignificant life; much like the isolation of Bainbridge Island. As Tomiko squeezed his hand, he wished they had the bus to themselves. How he missed grazing over her bare skin. She looked radiant in her tanned slacks and checkered coat, all complimenting the natural flush of her cheeks; her lips. God, he craved to kiss her. Instead, he settled beside her, easing an aching smile.

Russell joked with Sam and Shig. Wearing a crackled leather jacket, cap, and sunglasses, he felt invincible like Flynn and Gable. Shig emulated the style. The last time they sat on a bus, the shades were drawn down and the bus drivers were cranky as hell! But there were no shades on this bus, and they were going to be openly seen. They hadn't completely disappeared. They still existed.

The twenty-some year old English teacher clapped her hands to gain their attention. Russell really liked her. She proved to be a kind woman, always encouraging even the dumbest of people in class. And she never referred to them as *Japs* behind their backs in the mess hall. Some of the white teachers presumed no one would be listening, or that they couldn't be heard.

"Okay people," she chirped. "Now remember some of the guidelines!"

Mr. Fiordi jumped up the steps, a large grin overstating his sincerity. Dressed in a suit, his well trimmed face and smooth hair presented a theatrical elegance. Mrs. Berlitz glanced at him, almost annoyed by his egocentric conduct.

"Remember, we are guests," she continued, "so stay together and in pairs. I know some of you brought money along, but for those who couldn't, the movie and lunch are part of the donation from the community."

"That's right," Mr. Fiordi interrupted, bracing his hands in a symbolic clasp. "It's important to recognize the unity. Everyone goes under hardships, and everyone works together to make life work. Just like music. Music is harmony. Harmony is unity."

Shig sniggered. "The meatball should jump in the lake!"

Russell and Sam chuckled. Mr. Fiordi squinted at the back, unsure what kind of remark was made at his expense.

Mrs. Berlitz resumed, "The minute someone acts out of place, there may be a chance that these little field trips will be canceled in the future. So please," she looked directly at Shig with his slick black hair and rolled up jeans, "please, be on your best behavior." She turned to look at the balding bus driver. "I believe we're ready to head out. Let's skiddoo!"

Both teachers seated themselves at the front, trusting their students to behave behind them. When the bus began moving, everyone jilted in excitement, barely fastening their patience, eager to feel the sun embrace their faces in absolute freedom. To reenter a normal life was more precious than sugar or meat. Four girls waved at people they knew, giggling. Russell wished they wouldn't be returning. In the spring, work furlough most likely would be granted again and he decided he would actually join despite the back-breaking farm work. Anything. Anything to get away from here for a while.

Shig pointed, "Look at those cars!"

Russell looked out the window, peering at the line of vehicles sitting off the perimeter of the camp's entrance. He forgot that a portion of Nikkon people had driven here on a voluntary notion. The cars' paints were stripped from the harsh winds, peeling easily from the sand's graveled nails. Despite their bruising and cuts, it hadn't rained enough to cause them to bleed out rust- as of yet.

"I feel sorry for the dopes who brought those up here!" Shig said.

The bus stopped at the front gate where two square brick structures stood twenty feet apart. The buildings had been designed by some of the residents and therefore fanned out Japanese style roofs. The wire fence did not protrude at the entrance, ironically enough. Two sets of military police were stationed at each post, young, bored. Russell watched them squint under the bright sun, leaning on one leg at a time, recognizing that they too wished they could be elsewhere. He grinned. At least that was something everyone had in common. Then he saw Callis in the building. Turning away, Russell pressed his shoulder against the window to hide his face. Jesus, the bastard was like a vampire! Everywhere Russell looked, there he was lurking in the shadows! The door opened and an MP sluggishly walked up the steps. Mrs. Berlitz handed him a permission slip. He stared at it as if he were illiterate, struggling over the unfamiliar names. Exhaling through his nose, he pinched his lips and counted the heads on the bus. Hurry up, Russell thought. God, hurry before Callis recognized him! He didn't dare look through the window.

Shig noticed his discomfort. He asked, "Hey, what's wrong?"

Russell mumbled, “Glance in the building! That’s the guy!”

Shig turned to look. “Really? The yellow headed guy?”

Sam also stared through. Callis tightened his jaw as he stared directly back, his sharp blue eyes blistering. Sam instantly looked away, feeling his hatred firing into the cavity of his stomach.

The MP on the bus returned the piece of paper to Mrs. Berlitz, not speaking, indifferent, and hopped off. As the door closed, he signaled the driver to pull forward. The bus rattled and advanced, spreading a path of rolling dust. Relieved, Russell briefly closed his eyes. Shig flattened his middle finger against the window, beside Russell’s shoulder, smiling down at Callis. The brute surprisingly didn’t shift as he glared up at his sturdy finger. Instead, he clicked his finger and thumb to his temple, mimicking an execution.

Russell uttered angrily, “You shouldn’t of done that!”

“Why?” Shig scoffed. “He don’t know who I am!”

“But he’ll remember your face next time, you boob!”

His smirk remained strong when he replied, “Fear is as deep as the mind allows.”

The bus hesitated before veering onto the paved highway. Jim frowned at the large wooden sign, ragged on the sides, still hanging on each pole like a skinned animal; next to the road to broadcast its existence: Manzanar Relocation Center.

THE town of Lone Pine proved no larger than Winslow. Perhaps a hundred people. Perhaps a bit less. A strip of turn-of-the-century buildings preserved the Old West: Basic. Horizontal. Wooden. Far better than hundreds of tar-papered barracks. Houses barely stretched far from the main street, huddling closely, protecting people from the harsh winds. A ragged Irish Setter trotted up the sidewalk. It had no collar, yet it pranced as if the town belonged to it.

The ten students gathered on the sidewalk, quietly chattering, making sure they weren’t loud or offensive. Mr. Fiordi expanded his arms out to lure his students’ attention, telling them to follow. The townspeople curiously stared as if witnessing a meteor shower. They had never seen Orientals in real life. Or black folk. Or even Mexicans, despite that California had once belonged to Mexico in another life. Lone Pine had been so far removed from the rest of the world, just a fraction off to Death Valley, who really wanted to come out that way? In fact, it had been over fifty years since any of them had encountered Indians in that region who were now either dead or relocated to some kind of Reservation. Only lost travelers discovered the isolated town. And there were so few. The townspeople knew because of their special location the government had chosen their highway to relocate these unfortunate folks. It became a bizarre arrangement by having a detention camp at a five mile distance. Nevertheless everyone knew they had a duty to perform in order to support their country.

The group began their outing by eating brunch in a local café. The fresh meal made them wish they could eat burgers and malts every day. The greasy meat, runny eggs, and soggy rice provided by the mess halls only made them wish they didn’t have to go back. At all. A middle-aged, brown-headed waitress with stained teeth, was a polite person. She didn't stare, assert comments, or treat them in a patronizing fashion as Russell and his friends had often encountered. It felt strange to be waited on. The extended months of internment had taught them to stand in line, wait for their food to be flung onto their plates, sit down with ample complaints, then return their plates and silverware to the sloppy chefs behind the counter. The system ran like a Ford assembly line.

Although they were grateful to leave camp, and were grateful when the waitress would call them, "darlin's" or "honey's," an agonizing uncertainty revolved in their minds which made them constantly alert of the public's reactions; constantly preparing themselves for the worst. They knew something had to be waiting for them right around the corner. Pearl Harbor had also taught them that lesson. And the events that followed.

Next, they were allowed to walk around and shop for about an hour. They were such a sight, a following of older children trailed at their heels. Russell thought it amusing. He really didn't care. It felt too good to breathe outside the cage. Mr. Fiordi attempted to shoo them away a couple of times like a band of stray dogs.

Reclining into Shig's ear, Russell quipped, "Doesn't he realize he's making a bigger fool out of himself by doin' that?"

Shig leered. "He's our protector! The Great White Hope of all hopes, *omono!*"

"He's not that bad, you guys," Sam defended from behind. He was tired of his classmates and friends making fun of Mr. Fiordi. Mr. Fiordi at least tried to care, tried to understand their troubles. He insisted, "How many white teachers do you know who gives a rat's ass?"

"You're missing the point," Shig said. "He *is* the ass!"

"I think you're the ass, *omono-san!*" Sam bitterly asserted. "All you ever do is put people down! Even the president! You ain't that special!"

Shig stopped. His sarcastic grin slid out of his teeth. Grabbing Sam's collar, he charged, "Neither are you!"

Russell spat, "Knock it off you two! You wanna take away what privileges we have? Grow up, I swear!"

Shig's irritation trickled off his arm as he released Sam. He huffed, walking off, "Man, I need a smoke!"

Resting his hand on Sam's shoulder, Russell asked, "You alright? Don't take him so serious. He's only blowing off steam, is all."

Sam stared at his friend, unconvinced. "He thinks he's superior, Russ."

He chewed on his lip, somewhat believing it. "Well that's because he lives in a place where he thinks he's the only rooster!"

Tugging on his shoulder, Russell guided him forward, chuckling. They passed by a war poster taped on a barbershop's front door, colorfully exaggerating a German in uniform. The cartoon bore a broad head with thick brows and small eyes; hunched over in darker tones. It looked non-human. Above the figure read in thick, yellow letters, "Attila the Hun on the Run!"

The three boys stopped in front of a five and dime store; cluttered with other people's things for sale. Books. Cloths. Shoes. Dishes. Sam and Shig, stood apart from each other and stared through the large spotted window. Russell jingled his pocket. Sadaye and Meito donated some money for his trip. He truly was appreciative because he didn't have to ask. They spared him some change anyway.

Four children, in between the ages of eight and nine, slowly walked toward Russell and his friends. Wearing overalls and high-tops, even the girl who appeared like a boy with short hair and a baseball cap, arched their necks up, staring at them in awe. Shig slowly turned to look down at the kids. Soon Russell and Sam also shifted to gaze over their shoulders.

The girl asked, "Are you guys from the camp?"

Russell and Sam glanced at each other.

Shig tensely squinted and remarked, "Yeah, so?"

She smiled. "That's nifty! I never met criminals before!"

"We're not criminals!" Shig snapped. He rolled his eyes and entered the store.

The girl widened her surprise, and stared at Russell. Sighing, a bit disappointedly, she asked, "You guys ain't criminals then?"

One of the boys interposed, "My Paw says you guys are spies an' that's why yer in prison."

"Oh, yeah!" said another boy, sheepishly. "You guys 'mitted 'S' sponges an' blew balloons with bombs. That's why you guys is in prison."

The girl persisted, "If you didn't do nothin', then why are ya in prison?"

Russell scratched his forehead, annoyed. How could someone explain the convoluted political beliefs to a nine year old? She probably thought kissing was still gross. Adjusting his stance, he replied, "It's like this, kiddo." He glanced at Sam again and winked. "The Nazi's been threatening us since the war began. And boy, were we scared out of our wits! You know how the Nazis are!" The children nodded. "Mean. Very mean! Thank God President Roosevelt stepped in to protect us! Moved us from our homes to here." He leaned closer to the gullible gang, and whispered, "Nobody knows we're here. So, don't tell, okay?" They children nodded, amazed, excited that something secretive entered into their dull lives. Russell grinned and opened the door. "I'm counting on you guys!" he stated. "Everyone's gotta do their part."

Sam avoided their eyes in fear he would automatically laugh and ruin the entire guise. He followed Russell into the store, snickering. The old clerk carefully peered up from *Life* magazine, watching the three strangers wander in his store. He laid the magazine on the counter and remained quiet. His fat bifocals expanded his grey irises into large coins. Russell glanced his way, past a pile of belts. The clerk seemed really ancient. He very well could have been a soldier during the Civil War for all that Russell knew! Shig ambled alone, as if hunting. The store offered a better selection of goods, it seemed, and therefore seemed that much more alluring for Shig. He began picking up pens, pencils, a couple of watches, pocket knives. Russell migrated to the dishes, scanning at the small selection, thinking about buying a gift for his mother. These dishes were so plain, however. He wanted something nicer to cheer her up. Standing in thought for quite some time, Shig unexpectedly grabbed his arm.

"Let's go!" he asserted.

"Wait!" Russell said. "I'm not ready!" He looked down at Shig's pockets, from his jacket to his jeans. They were bulging. Surely he didn't do what Russell thought he did.

"Suit yourself," Shig uttered.

He quickly exited the store and darted across the street, entering a clothing store. Mrs. Berlitz wandered by, peeking through the window to keep a check on her students. Russell was stunned. And infuriated. If Shig got caught again, he would sabotage their future. For everyone! It was bad enough they were under incessant surveillance, and yet to risk what decent reputation they had left not only proved reckless, but also confirmed absolute selfishness. It took Russell a long time before he understood this.

THE movie theater smelled of mold in an aging cellar. Scrawny in structure, the narrow aisles and wide screen pinched the creaky seats and sticky floor in the middle. Jim had missed sitting in a real theater. It would be an all day affair. Before the featured film, they would first watch cartoons, then newsreels, then the serials, and finally a newer movie that wasn't at least a year old. The large poster in the lobby enchanted a great comedic adventure. He heard about bandleader Kay Kaiser playing a major part in *My Favorite Spy*. More movies whirled around the war, glamorizing it, consuming it with a loyalist fever. As the lights dimmed, Warner Brother's logo lit the room; its music punching from the large speakers. Popcorn softened the musty smell. The theater was nearly full; comprised mostly of the young. A new episode of Bugs Bunny came to life. The funny accent reminded Jim of the Jersey Guards during the evacuation. Abruptly, an absurd miniature Japanese character with giant glasses and buckteeth entered the scene, dragging a long sword at his side. He spoke gibberish. Bugs Bunny became furious, aggressive, a side Jim had never quite seen before in the caricature while it snarled, "I'm gonna snip that Nip! I'm gonna snip that yella, cowardly Nip!"

Jim heard people chuckling from behind as they chewed on their popcorn. Glancing at Tomiko and Russell, their stiffness and lack of laughter indicated their self-consciousness as well. He rubbed his mouth, knowing that image on screen didn't represent him. Or his friends. And he hated how those images often perverted the way people saw them. They were American. That figure could never be them. Not ever. He had to close his eyes. A repulsion swelled in his stomach. He remembered the sheriff's and mortician's disgusted expressions when they carried John's body through the doorway. And that goddamned radio ringing in everyone's ears. Those men's faces never left his nightmares. They couldn't decipher the difference between his family and the Japanese on the other side of the world. They couldn't because they simply didn't want to. He began sweating. He had difficulty breathing. All day long he felt everyone stare at them. Stare and point and judge. All his life he felt it. And now this animation reminded him what America unquestionably thought of them. God, how he wanted the goddamn cartoon to end!

Tomiko noticed him squirming. Reclining to his ear, she asked, "What's wrong? Are you sick?"

"I need air!" he gasped.

Jumping up, stumbling over other people's feet, he bolted to the lobby. Startled, a pretty cashier stared at him; her maroon apron mismatching her red lips and nails. Glancing at her, he fled to the restroom. Mr. Fiordi emerged from the theater, concerned, and followed Jim to the men's room.

As Mr. Fiordi stood near the entrance door, one hand in his pocket, he asked, "Jim, are you not feeling well?"

Jim hid in the stall, yet unconsciously left the door open. He refused to answer his teacher, recalling Leo's smirking face at the principal's office. No one believed him. No one wanted to. That was just the habit of the world. This unjust world full of discrimination and belligerence. John understood it. He died because of it.

"Jim, are you not going to answer me?" Mr. Fiordi waited while Jim made a shuffling sound. Removing his hand from his pocket, he continued, "I'm not your enemy, Jim. I do want to help."

Jim answered in a harsh, flat voice his father often used when he was in no mood to be bothered. "Thank you, Mr. Fiordi, but I'll be fine. I just found the cartoon offensive, is all."

"I know that cartoon is offensive. But are you sure that's all that's bothering you? Nothing else?"

Jim wished he would leave him alone. What right did he have being this intrusive? What the hell did he know about anything? "Could you give me a minute, Mr. Fiordi? I only need a minute."

He sighed. "Listen Jim, how can I help you if you bottle up? How can anyone help you when you don't speak for yourself? Believe it or not, I've been noticing this from the beginning of class. It's not healthy. You'll make yourself ill."

Pinching his own arms, Jim stared at the floor. "Please, Mr. Fiordi. Only a minute."

He hesitated before he reluctantly retreated from the room.

THE late afternoon sun unraveled cloaks of orange, dimming the sky. The day spilled too quickly, and everyone knew the hour had sunk into the cracks. The bus hummed while the students chatted about their day, hoping their chats would block their dread of returning. Russell sat beside Shig who buried himself in the back corner. He hadn't forgotten what his friend did at the store. Angered, he dipped his hand in one of Shig's pocket, removing the two watches and several pens.

He hissed, "What in the hell is *this?*"

Shig grabbed the items from Russell, and asserted, "Are you crazy, Russ?"

"Are *you* crazy? Do you wanna revoke what rights we got so far?"

Shig stuffed the items back into his pocket. Frowning, he whispered, "Listen, man, it's only a few things we need. Just a few! I didn't rob a bank or nothin'!"

Russell furiously blinked. "If you got caught . . ."

"But I didn't, okay? So knock it off!" He leaned his shoulder blades against the window, carefully watching Russell. Releasing a grin, he persisted, "I even picked up some things for you."

"I don't want it!" he snapped. Russell glanced at the teachers who sat in the front, thankfully oblivious to their conversation. The two girls, who sat in front of them, also seemed oblivious, talking about the movie and boys. "Shig," he quietly maintained. "Didn't going to jail teach you anything?"

He squinted and leered. "Not a goddamn thing! Besides, what difference does it make? We're in a prison camp! So I figure bad and good are intertwined like rope, anyway."

Russell shook his head. He had never met anyone quite like him before. "You have more lives than any cat I know!"

"That's because I'm talented."

"I doubt it," he muttered. "Just remember, anything you do will come back on the rest of us! I wish it wasn't like that, but you know it is."

Shig looked at him with curiosity. "Since when did you start caring about stupid traditions? Weren't you the one who boasted about every man for himself?"

"No!" he snickered. "That was *you!* And you're the one always quoting Japanese sayings!"

He smirked and turned to look out the window. "Still, you said you wanted your independence. And how you hated anything you did, or didn't do, would come back to your family. You did say you wanted to be your own man."

Scratching the back of his neck, Russell explained, "Yeah, but," he paused, readjusting his position. "But you also don't disrespect your family. And what you do can hurt them." Leaning closer to Shig, he affirmed, "Listen, if we're gonna be friends, then you're gonna have to stop . . . this bad habit of yours." Shig glared at Russell. "I mean it, Shig," he continued. "I'm tired of worrying whether my mother will die of a heart attack because of me. Or who I hang out with. I want something more out of my life."

"And you think I don't?" he asserted.

"I think we need to keep our lives . . . clean, you know?"

Peering out the window, Shig fumed for a time. He thought Russell would be the last person to judge him. Since Russell had been attending those damn Judo lessons, he began to see less of Russell. And he was the one who introduced Russell to Judo in the first place.

Crossing his arms, Shig angrily answered, "It's not fair what you're asking of me. We have so little in our lives."

Russell settled his hands over his lap and looked over people's heads. "We can make it better. I've been thinking about working outside of camp. Earn my own money. Maybe find a sponsor so I can leave this place. You can, too, but you have to stop doing what you do," he warned. "If you get caught again, you know I'll get blamed, too, and then none of us can leave this goddamned place."

Turning away, Shig stared at the desert's shadows and its prickly shrubs. Everything appeared so abandoned and ugly in this ragged environment. Nothing to look forward to. Nothing to gain. Nothing but hostile storms from every direction. Deeply sighing, he vaguely replied, "When a character of a man is not clear to you, look at his friends."

Late November

KUNIO sloshed through the thick mud, carrying his two year old daughter, Clara, in one arm while holding his four year old son's hand, Harry, with the other. The unexpected Idaho showers withdrew the drought from exile, leaving behind large puddles and soggy clay. His boots quickly caked over. They were heading to the administration building to pick up coats for the upcoming winter. The desert's cold revealed its true nature during the mornings, and so the WRA had arranged the dispersal of old rejected military coats. Pea-coats, as everyone referred them to. They were pea-green in color and securely constructed out of wool. The camp residents were not prepared for that kind of cold since all of them came from the Pacific Northwest: Seattle. Tacoma. Olympia. Portland. Salem. Everyone was used to modest winters; although not completely unfamiliar with its bitter moments.

Kay, Kunio's wife, could not go with them, for she was in the hospital. She had become critically anemic since their arrival at Minidoka, often refusing to eat the mess hall food. She feared she would catch cholera, salmonella, and other illnesses. At Camp Harmony, she contracted constant diarrhea and had been convinced she had one type of disease or another. Kunio refused to let her indulge her antics onto their children and he compelled them to eat everything on their trays. Unfortunately, he couldn't persuade his wife to do the same. Now she lay at the infirmary with IVs rooted into her veins.

The mountains appeared drab in the horizon, not nearly as great as the ones in Washington, and certainly not as inspiring as Mount Rainier. These mountains were tinted brown and reached upward in a stout manner. He could see where the range began and ended. No mystery there. And the landscape was flat. No valleys. No canyons. Just a ravine where a young boy drowned that summer because he wandered off like an unleashed stray. And who was responsible for that incident? Not the parents who were too busy cleaning their home, making it more hospitable. Not the residents who ignored the boy swimming in heavy currents, too busy constructing the camp for themselves. And certainly not the MPs who watched the boy drown from their high watchtowers, too busy being bored.

Kunio thought about the rest of his family in Manzanar. Goro had a birthday two months ago. He felt a little guilty for not at least sending his brother a gift or card, but he had a meager amount of money and so much on his mind. The potato harvest was complete. His furlough income had ceased; however, he had to keep paying for the storage unit back in Seattle. It angered him. They were forced to leave their home by the government and yet there was no compensation for maintaining their property. Not to mention they still were responsible for paying taxes! His sister Chiyeko helped out with what she could, except she and her husband had three children to take care of and had their own financial strains as well. Since September, Kunio had been working odd jobs: carpentry, dish washing, janitorial. *Nisei* with fancy degrees got the good jobs. Desk jobs. And people like himself were left with the scraps.

"Daddy," Harry whined. "Daddy!"

Kunio stopped walking. He realized his son's hand had slipped from him. Turning around, he saw Harry wedged in the mud. His tiny body was incapable of popping out of the thickness. He began crying, holding out his arms for support. Kunio felt embarrassed for not noticing it sooner after his needless complaints. Returning to his son, and gently putting his daughter down, he pulled him out like a grounded weed, pulling him right out of his boots. Trying to comfort his children, who both were now crying, he held them close to his chest and uttered, "Everything's alright. Someday we'll go home. We'll all go home and be a real family again. I promise."

CHAPTER EIGHT

Early December

TED Tanaka yanked on the beaded string, clicking his light off. The late evening's darkness invaded his modest apartment; light hidden from his heavy curtains. He tugged his covers loose, and slid inside his bed. As a bachelor, he knew had been lucky to live alone. Since the construction of camp, he managed to find a private room after people were either transferred to other camps or fled, (with WRA permission of course,) to the Midwest and East Coast, therefore allotting a bit more space inside the compacted camp. It irritated him when others didn't take advantage of these opportunities; these transfers and furloughs, that were created by him and his committees. It irritated him when they exhausted their energies in bickering an invisible war instead of unifying. The pettiness that contaminated his community underlined an invisible war. As well as the pettiness that inflated within Manzanar's administration. Although he understood their frustrations with the conditions of the camp, the act of pointing fingers wasn't going to solve anything. Bridges weren't built by one hand nor were they built without organization. And how could the JACL convince the president, congress, and the military that the *Nisei* were indeed citizens worthy of trust if people like Katsuji infiltrated opposition? That and a growing number of *Kibei* chose to denounce loyalty for the United States, thus making it difficult for the rest to prove otherwise. Katsuji's influences had been infecting some of the *Nisei's* anger. Not very practical. Ted took an oath to protect the rights of the *Nisei*. Although he felt confident he knew how to defend them to the government, he struggled with knowing how to preserve them within his own community.

He sighed, his mind and body aching, yet feeling his own warmth quilting underneath his blanket, comforting him. Surprisingly, his neighbors in the next room were quiet. Tired from hours of debate and planning the future, he dozed off in the darkness, unaware of its intentions and its movements: The creaking of the outside steps. The shuffling of feet passing through an unsecured door; a passing murmur. Swiftly, fiercely, smashing fists awoke him. Unable to see, four hooded men in dark outfits fractured his face and ribs. Gasping, Ted lurched up, but fell to the hard floor. The pain slashed his focus. He couldn't think. He could barely breathe. He couldn't cry out for help. Stone fists became more fierce and rapid like a swarm of wasps. The loud scuffling rang in his ears. The prickly pounding bruised and cut his skin. He swallowed his hot, salted blood. The pain. The pain slowly faded as he floated up into the darkness.

MEITO opened the door, rubbing his drowsy eyes. His flannel shirt was partly buttoned; his slacks wrinkled from the sitting in a folded stack of clothes. An orange morning sun peeked over the mountain tips as if watching Manzanar, knowing that soon its red veins would be spilled onto the soil. Sadaye, insulated in an pea-green coat and nurse's uniform, stood on the stoop; her hands under her armpits. Her warm breath straggled in the drafty air. Her nose and ears exposed a ruby spirit.

Meito shuddered from the chill and grunted, "*Ohayo!* Get inside! What in the world are you doing here so early?"

She whisked through the entrance, her thick shoes clunking on the wood. She glanced down at the sleeping twins who cuddled closely on one bed. Gertrude tied her orange robe while stumbling into her fuzzy slippers. Sadaye shifted to the side, allowing her brother to shut the cold door.

She began, "I thought you should know."

He gazed at her, yawning, scratching his whiskers. "Oh, yeah? Is the world finally coming to an end? I'd hope to sleep through it."

"Katsuji was arrested last night."

Meito stopped scratching. "Really? I knew his big mouth would catch up to him."

Sadaye glanced at the twins, fidgeting, and whispered, "For beating Ted Tanaka to a bloody pulp! Ted came in . . . well, actually was carried in . . . on my shift last night. He almost bled to death."

Meito stared in stupefaction. He wasn't confident if Katsuji was truly capable of that kind of violence. Granted, he had a temper, but it resorted to tantrums rather than barbarity. Meito had figured him to be a classic schoolyard bully: pushing and swearing, yet when the pushing became overwhelming, he would back down. He usually backed down. Meito had known Katsuji for over fifteen years, as aggravating as those years may have been. Just because someone disliked a fellow, no matter if that fellow deserved to be disliked, it didn't convey absolute guilt.

He asked, "Are they sure? Was Katsuji positively identified?"

"Ted said so," she replied. "Because of the gravity of things, Katsuji was sent to another town. Independence, I believe they mentioned."

He shook his head. "It doesn't make sense. He doesn't seem the type!"

Gertrude imposed, "It does make sense, Meito. He burns your flag. An American flag of all things! He threatens you all the time. He's even threatened Ted! He's weak which makes him dangerous."

Meito twitched his mouth, afraid of what might happen next. The factions in camp streamed like electric volts, reaching from the mess halls and heading to the administration building. Essentially there were two powerful cliques: those who undeniably supported America, and those who undeniably wanted America to kiss their asses. The accusations transmitted with fluidity between these groups, and he was aware of the excuses and frustrations each harbored against each other.

He folded his arms and muttered, “Damn. This doesn’t look good. The anniversary of Pearl Harbor is tomorrow. I wonder what kind of *banquet* these people have in mind.”

SHIG boasted, “Done!”

His friends proceeded to heap clumps of hash browns, sausages, eggs, and biscuits inside their mouths, chewing sloppily, swallowing quickly. Like a military unit following orders, one by one, two by two, the boys slapped down their forks, gulped liquefied powdered-milk, and sprung to their feet. Ralph, Hank, and Bruce. Russell, Jim, Sam, and Ikki. An allied group of islanders and mainlanders. Rushing out the mess hall doors, ignoring sniped comments about their rude behavior from the *Issei* who still stood in line, they ran through the streets, tracking down another mess hall to invade. Their mission was to raid as many mess halls as possible before the kitchens closed.

They began this game two months ago as their appetites increased when the heat steadily vanished. Jim and Shig maintained a silent distance, compressing their animosities for the sake of their mutual friends. Perhaps from an outside view, the eight boys appeared like field mice rummaging for scraps left by farmers, but their intentions were well planned. Shig wore his watch, timing their movements, their pace, encouraging his gang for improvements. Last week they set a record of hitting four mess halls in an hour and fifteen minutes. Their girlfriends thought they were foolish, not understanding the proficiency it actually took, and the thrill it released.

THE afternoon sun stood between the two mountains, glaring down at Block 22 where two thousand residents migrated from the mess hall and into the fire break, impatiently waiting. The morning meeting proved frivolous, lasting only thirty minutes as discussions of a strike overpowered the discussion of Katsuji’s release. Osamu, who was only a week away from relocating to Maine after six weeks of red tape, sat in the vehicle with four of eight police officers; three of them white. The Chief of Internal Security, a middle-aged man with a pear shaped-body, led them into the mass. Osamu’s white band, nestled on his left arm, mirrored an impeccable strand of discipline; second best to a legion.

As they reeled two vehicles in alignment of the road, the crowd turned in their direction like pages in a book flipped by gusts of wind. Stunned by the overwhelming clot of agitated men, Osamu wished he and the other *Nisei* officers were allowed to possess wooden clubs like their white colleagues. They staggered from the cars; nervous; awestruck. The officers were asked to leave by an echoing chant of sharp phrases. Without protest, the Chief flicked his hand, commanding them to leave. Coils of dust blew into the mass, pressuring some to cough. The half-hour wait validated their dissatisfaction and some walked away while the others marched directly to the administration building. The three men who directed the long journey shouted for justice and shouted for respect. Each step they delivered only enhanced their outrage.

RUSSELL heard the shouts echo in his barrack. He had returned home to quickly change his soiled shirt. Surprised to see his brother sitting with their parents, he briefly greeted Meito while slinging off his shirt. Rummaging through the drawer, he glanced at his quiet family.

"What's wrong?" he asked.

Meito stared. "Maybe you should stay close to home today, Goro."

Poking his head and arms through favorite his sweatshirt, he said, "Why?"

"I've heard rumors," he began, leaning forward in between his parents. "Rumors about a protest. A massive protest."

Russell looked at his mother whose pinned hair revealed more gray and tired circles than last year. Then he looked at his father whose thinning hair above his forehead enhanced his age. He hadn't noticed it before. They appeared so different. So old. Distant.

"A protest," Russell repeated, unaware of Meito's implications.

Annoyed, he affirmed, "It could get ugly. Ted Tanaka was beaten last night. They arrested Katsuji. Now there's a protest for Katsuji's release as well as other complaints. You know, with the missing meat and sugar. The poor clothing for the upcoming winter."

"I see," he replied, thinking if he were to leave now, he could make it just in time for the football game Sam and Ikki were organizing on their block. All his friends were attending. He was wearing his lucky sweatshirt, so he felt confident that his team would beat the other. Russell darted to the door.

Meito barked, "Promise me, Goro, whatever happens, use your head! Stay out of the way!"

"Okay," he nodded.

Mrs. Hamaguchi suddenly stood, her palms attached to the edge of the table. "*Please stay home, Goro!*"

Russell opened the door, the shouts from a few blocks downward became more crisp. He smiled and said, "Don't worry, Mama. Nothin' really happens on Sundays."

THE football coiled in the brilliant air, competing with the wind that swept along like wagon wheels. Ikki caught it as he sprinted, however was knocked down by Ralph and Bruce. Shig's gang played against the Bainbridge boys, wearing grey sweatshirts with humorous black letterings, "YOGORES," on the front. The *Issei* didn't appreciate their irony, interpreting "roughnecks" literally and just as menacing. Their slick raven hair were messy from tumbling; dusty and reckless. Others from various districts of Los Angeles allied with Shig. The Bainbridge boys wrapped assorted bandanas around their right arms, distinguishing themselves from their opponents. A handful of the Manzanar athletes were from the high school team, looking for any reason to play. The purpose of these Sunday games defined equality among the classes; regardless of size and age.

Russell, slightly panting and sweating, slowed his pace along the sidelines of the road. He missed his original block. It was the place where not only his friends lived, but also it was conveniently located near the post office, canteen, auditorium, and fire station. Sam stood in a row of spectators, clapping and yelling. The residents of Second Street continued their routine of washing, cleaning, and returning from church. A rock garden, designed in a semicircle with wooden lawn chairs and molded shrubbery, appeared new. Even a small deck had been built to allure appeasement in the harsh conditions. An elderly man sat in a chair with his granddaughter on his lap, telling her a story in an old language she couldn't understand.

Slapping Sam's shoulder, Russell asked, "Who's winning?"

"It's been going back and forth. They'd get ahead, then us. Right now it's us."

"Great! Can hardly wait to pound on these guys!"

Russell flipped his bangs from his eyes, knowing he needed a trim. He thought about informing Sam about the crowd of men marching this way to the administration building, except the sound of the game's cheers numbed his tongue. He didn't want to spoil anything. Besides, the administration building was another block away; meaning the protest wouldn't intrude on their fun.

"Hey!" Russell said, tugging on Sam's sleeve. "Where's Jim?"

Sam cringed. "He and Tomiko went to the library! Are they nuts? The library?"

"Sounds like they want some privacy!" he laughed.

"But the library? Geez! Shoot me, why don't ya!"

"Be careful what you wish for, Sammy. Karma has a strange sense of humor."

Sam squinted and shook his head. Slapping Russell's shoulder, he laughed and continued to cheer for his team.

THE three leaders gathered at the entrance of their destination; their followers rolling around them as if a herd of cattle. Mr. Bridges, the Project Director and his assistant, Mr. Petty, had been anxiously expecting their arrival after receiving a phone call from the police station. Bridges, in his late forties and twenty years his assistant's senior, preserved a respectable stance as he walked down the steps. His dark suit and tie clashed against the crowd's work pants, and dusty coats and hats. Since his arrival at Manzanar, upon the personal invitation from his friend, President Franklin D. Roosevelt, his goal was to mend the broken trust between white Americans and Japanese-Americans. In order to regain this trust, he lifted the ban of not allowing the possession of cameras, he encouraged more work furloughs, and furthermore encouraged the development of local businesses.

Mr. Petty, his opposite, wore a leather jacket that nearly matched his hair color. Younger and more impatient, his sarcastic remarks built walls around the *Nisei* men they worked with. Mr. Petty's temperament made him unpopular and made Director Bridges' job that much more difficult.

The shouts dissipated with the afternoon wind; yet murmurs hummed like mosquitoes over a stagnant pond. Twelve soldiers immediately jogged across the front gates, and lined up firmly in the middle of the police station and administration building with their captain yelling out snappy orders. Four machine guns were perched on thick tripods, aiming into the crowd.

Director Bridges glanced through the mob, not able to see the metal boxes with long thin barrels pointing awkwardly into his direction. He knew the soldiers would not shoot while he still lingered inside. Worried about bloodshed, he continued to linger among the group, hoping he could talk with them peacefully; hoping the military would not have an excuse to fire. Police officers closely tracked at his sides. Bridges recognized the three leaders, having dealt with them since his arrival in camp a month ago, replacing the other ones who became fed up with the camp's politics. Walking further into the mob, with his assistant following in silence, Bridges took on the role of a diplomat: calm and determined. As he stepped closer to the leaders, their men stepped in front of him.

The Director lightly remarked, "I didn't realize I was this popular! Maybe I ought to run for president!"

Some of the men laughed. One humorously retorted in turn, "Maybe I could be yur right hand man!"

"I never turn down help!" he quipped.

Someone pushed Mr. Petty, bumping directly into Bridges. Angered, Mr. Petty jerked around to see who harassed him and shouted out, "Bastard!" A line of men reflected a smudged and contentious fortitude. The heat from all the bodies made the tip of his forehead perspire. His nerves twisted. He knew nothing good could come from this protest and wondered how many in the crowd were on the FBI's list. It was a long list.

Bridges asked, "So, what exactly do you fellows want?"

The oldest leader, a *Kibei* with glasses and a bow tie, responded, "De unconditional release of Katsuji Sakata."

He tightened his jaw. "You know I can't do that, Choichi. I can't do that because it's an unrealistic request. If I start bending the law then I would be responsible for lawlessness. And so would you."

"Katsuji is innocent, Mista Bridges," he bluntly remarked. His tone rang in harshness, and yet it remained even. "All we wan' is justice. Is bad enough my peopo' ah still waiting for trials for crimes dey not commit. Right ah now we hold you responsibo' for injustice. Dat is not unrealistic."

Bridges shifted on one foot, staring past Choichi's people. "My men have been working on his case since early this morning. We are working on justice, you've got to believe that."

"Justice," he chortled. "We see none. We taste none. Give us yur ah trust an' we weow trus' you in return. Give us back Katsuji."

Bridges flicked his eyes, understanding the longer they argued, the more agitated the mob would develop. "You need to have the crowd disperse, and quickly. I'm not committing to anything with a swarm of people around us. I'm not negotiating in this manner- but," he paused, glancing at the other two leaders, "if we were able to meet with chosen representatives, under a more stable environment, than I would be more willing."

"*Nai!*" somebody shouted from behind. "No surrenda! No surrenda!"

A chanting of *banzais* diffused. More men stepped in between their leaders and the directors, pushing them further apart; a communication gap swiftly eroding. It was a purposeful gesture. It was meant to intimidate the *hakujins*.

SAM stopped clapping. He tilted his ear toward the chanting. The noise sounded like it streamed down two blocks. He glanced at his friends, who seemed more interested in running and chasing the football than wondering what was going on. Other residents slowly begun to turn to the curious commotion, but didn't budge from their places. An uneasiness pinched their faces. Their curiosities were not as bold as Sam's. Biting his lip, he simply had to know, and darted to the vague dust cloud that rolled through his streets.

THE Director became annoyed. Their lack of cooperation signified a power struggle. He continued to walk through the crowd, listening to their demands, responding in short answers, promising nothing. Time lagged and not a thing was getting accomplished during his circulation. The front gates opened once more, detaching eighteen more soldiers with fixed bayonets. Then Mr. Petty fell. Looking down, Bridges saw his assistant rub the back of his head. He had been hit by something. Mr. Petty instantly jumped up and grabbed his assailant by his collar, shoving and cursing at him. The man shouted back, claiming dogs that pissed on their master's guests deserved to get kicked around. Two *Nisei* and three police officers plied their hands in between the two, yanking them apart. Bridges was outraged.

"Take *that* man to the police station!" he charged. "And Mr. Petty, refrain from agitating these men even more so! Dammit! We live in a civilized part of the world!"

He felt a portion of the crowd wave forward, toward the wall of soldiers, then backward. They were testing their limits. Some men were spouting at Bridges, calling him weak and ignorant. The clamor then swam to the soldiers, shaking their middle fingers at them, tagging them as "shitheads," "bastards," and "assholes" in both English and Japanese. The crowd again crammed to the line of the military; their outbursts blistering the cool air.

Choichi and the other leaders were alarmed. They had believed they could manage the crowd. It was apparent the harsh insults and disorderly shoving showed no confidence in anyone's abilities. Choichi pushed his way through the frantic structure of men in search of Bridges. Something had to be done before people became injured, or killed even.

"Mista Bridges!" Choichi shouted, waving his hand above his head. "Mista Bridges!"

Mr. Petty heard the cry, turning to squint at Choichi. He tugged on Director Bridges' sleeve, trying to divert his attention from other administrative personnel and police officers. Bridges had encompassed a meeting with white staff members to discuss physical enforcement.

Choichi finally welded his shoulders from the crowd. He asserted, "I again urge you to release Katsuji before it becomes ugly! We hafe ah decided to privately meet with police chief, commanda of military police, and you, Mista Bridges."

Bridges saw panic on his face. Nodding, he replied, "Yes, I agree. I know a place."

RUSSELL stopped running after Shig, who held the football, and listened to the shouts from the next block. Each team member, including the spectators, stopped to listen. Russell, panting and sweating, wondered if his brother had been right. What if a riot would overturn the camp? Would that mean looting? People beaten by batons and rifle butts like photos he had seen in newspapers? Then the thought delighted him. He had never witnessed one before. And it certainly would stimulate excitement in his dull life. Ikki jogged to Russell, resting his elbow on his friend's shoulder, breathing heavily.

Russell asked, "Think we should check it out?"

Ikki, his salty face dirtied from plunging into the sand, replied, "Nah! It ain't none of our business! Let the chowderheads figure it out!"

Shig jogged his way to Russell. "It's about time somethin' like this happens! Maybe now some things will improve!"

Displeased about politics, Ikki insisted, "We have more important things to worry about. Let's get back to the game."

Russell glanced around. "Where's Sam?"

THE Director shook Choichi's hand in a greeting, relieved they had agreed on something. Even if the agreement was temporary, it at least implied a truce. Mr. Petty's apartment, near the administration building, was adopted as a neutral place. Bridges, as well as his assistant and the commanders of both civilian and military police were present. Eight men covered the four corners; cigarette smoke stacking layers each passing minute, all shrinking the small room. One of the other leaders and a friend of Katsuji's, stood up. Saburo had been offended by the entire. Although Katsuji would be returned to the Manzanar jail within the hour, Saburo didn't want to agree, (but was voted out by his peers,) to Bridges' imposition of monitoring further public meetings or negotiations. Then, to make matters more insulting, Choichi suggested to *hunt* for Ted's real attackers. He was no better than the informants.

Punching his fist on the table, he ranted, "I do not undastand how traitors are praised an' heroes punished! Ted did deserve to be beaten! All informants should share the same fate!"

His dark eyes glazed with fierce intensity it prickled bumps on Bridges' arms.

Choichi uttered outside of the Director's natural language, "*But each of us did agree to the terms, Saburo-san. Remember your agreement. Do not shame us in front of these men. We will have our justice tonight.*"

Saburo glared through the two windows across from him. He saw his people eagerly waiting to hear their leaders speak; to hear how they would triumph over this despicable insult the United States had imposed on their good names. Not to mention the frequent harassment from the guards; one blond-headed guard in particular. Finally Saburo nodded and said nothing more in front of the white hypocrites. He had a large following; all of whom already had other plans and arrangements to enforce justice.

Bridges smiled, and then shook each of the representative's hands, including the reluctant Saburo. As they walked outside, greeting the thousands of men, Bridges asked that one of them translate the agreement. Saburo promptly stepped forward, allowing the director to speak first, however began his own version.

"*We are nearing our victory! Katsuji-san will be returned within the hour! And to show you my dedication to our people,*" he paused, smirking, "*I renounce my American citizenship! I renounce it because we are Japanese first and foremost, and we must never forget who we are*!" The men applauded in a feverish nature. As his speech expanded with his finger pointing to the sun, the crowd became more excited; thundered by the notion of their integrity. He continued, "*Therefore . . . therefore . . . we must finish our victory by returning to Block 22 first to show our strength by six o'clock tonight! Then we must walk to the police station and free Katsuji-san in the name of Japanese honor! In the name of our Great Emperor!*"

Sam watched the crowd loudly cheer. Their anger had quickly modified like lightening splintering a tree. He didn't understand much of the speech, only grasping a word or two. Something about victory and America and police station by six that night. If anything, it sounded as if another party would carry on.

Bridges, uncertain if Saburo remained true to their agreement, turned to Choichi. "Was the speech presented as we had discussed?"

Choichi refused to look at the project director. If he informed the director that Saburo had not only dismissed the terms, but elaborated his own political agenda, then Choichi would be considered a traitor as well, and beaten; if he were lucky. Five years ago, on a visit to Japan, a villager was arrested and hung for criticizing Emperor Hirohito. Although Choichi had pledged his faith to the Emperor, it didn't imply his faith to the radicals who misappropriated the emperor's name. Nervously glancing at Bridges, he weakly replied, "It was presented."

THE sun reclined with ease that evening, steadily gazing down at Manzanar. A peculiar lull sifted through camp just before the dinner bells; a harmony strained by patience. The drive around camp seemed to find a curious peacefulness for Director Bridges. Life continued as such. People were walking. Children were playing games. Church sessions were being held. A play being exhibited at the outdoor theater. Nothing out of the ordinary. Slowly circulating through the dusty lanes, Saburo's harsh voice and Choichi's vagueness persisted to impose his mind. Something didn't fit.

JIM held Tomiko's hand. They strolled from the library, which reeked of fresh plaster and old books, to a mess hall. They heard rumors of a protest earlier that day, but assumed the commotion had dwindled to a single flare. They had found a corner, hidden by shelves and tables, where privacy allowed a secure amount of secrecy. They spoke of wedding plans and a future not bounded by wire and day passes. Chicago or New York. Places so far from the desert it didn't make a difference which new city.

"Tomiko!" a girl cried out. "Hey, wait!"

They turned around. Naomi trotted toward them, surprisingly wearing the pea-green coat and a pair of slacks. Her vanity usually pirouetted in femininity. Jim grunted, not in the mood to deal with Naomi. He was annoyed by her. Russell had truly liked her and she dumped him like an tattered wallet.

Naomi smiled. "Do you mind if I eat with you?"

Tomiko glanced at Jim. She didn't object. She liked Naomi, but Jim, for one reason or another, didn't seem to. Tomiko knew he had better start liking more people otherwise his hermit lifestyle would force him to converse with trees. She returned the smile, and said, "Not at all, Naomi."

Jim cringed. Upset that Tomiko agreed without asking him, he released her hand and began walking away. Tomiko, stunned he would behave like a pampered child, and hurt that he would be so selfish, forced another smile.

Naomi, seeing her friend's disappointment, muttered, "What's his problem?"

She meekly replied, "Does it matter?"

THE dinner gongs rang in the camp, reverberating in between the mountains. Its chronic rhythm kept an incurable fate; a reminder of restrictions; an unjust cry. Camp residents poured out to their beckoning, wrapping scarves around their heads, buttoning coats, tying shoes, tugging on hats. Meito marched through the streets, searching for his brother. He had just quit his job at the mess hall, fed up with the Worker's Union bullshit, hearing about Saburo's infamous speech. The workers excitedly, and rather openly, spoke of it as if it were the Resurrection. Was that bastard so far gone on the fanatical side he simply lost all senses? Meito had to find his brother. He had to make sure none of his family was near the south side of camp where Saburo and his goons infested. Much to his surprise, the camp retained a calmness; for the time being. He thought about informing the police, although if someone saw him, then he would definitely be considered a spy. As if he didn't have enough problems! And surely they knew and were already prepared for it.

SADAYE jogged up the hospital's steps, chewing on preserved prunes. Striding by the rows of beds, over a third were full of patients, she went to the back to hang her coat. The cold weather inflicted the elderly more than anyone else; especially at night. She briefly gossiped with some of the other nurses, who spoke of the handsome unmarried doctors like high school girls. Then she walked to another ward, where the seven wards were detached and aligned in rows, to check on patients. Including Ted Tanaka, who slept. His left arm was wrapped in a cast; his ribs carefully taped. She felt sorry for him. His nose was swollen, his eyes were blackened, and he breathed with a squeak. Stitches circled the top of his forehead. The painkillers were working to a degree while his sleeping face wrinkled in discomfort. Knowing there was nothing more she could do for him, she continued her scheduled route.

THE five representatives approached the mess hall on Block 22 as previously agreed. The purpose of the second meeting was to affirm Katsuji's transfer. Much to the shock of Choichi, and the thrill of Saburo, the crowd had doubled in size, now extending to four thousand men. The other camp residents who carried on their dinner ritual quickly passed by the mess hall where the swarm of men stood, searching for other mess halls instead, trying to mind their own business. The street lights dimly flickered across the street borders like dying fire flies, spreading out in a connected fashion. The sun seemed to hide behind the mountains as quickly as possible. Bridges shut his car door; appalled. He knew Saburo had schemed this damned farce. He anxiously scanned the flood of men as if they were driftwood jamming along side of a riverbank. How were the leaders going to manage such a mob?

Choichi spotted the director. Dust ballooned from the men's feet, swaying in the breeze, maneuvering quickly and constantly. From the highway's perspective it appeared similar to a dust storm. The mountains siding with Death Valley, just beyond the highway, disregarded its other Sierra twin from the east where a gust of resentment festered. Choichi had the other representatives followed him as they reeled along the edge of the cluster. Bridges coughed from the dust and covered his mouth. Squinting ahead, Choichi and the other four surrounded him.

Choichi shouted, trying to compensate for the loud murmurs that harbored around them. "Mista Bridges! Glad you are ah able to come!"

Bridges extended his hand to shake Choichi's courtesy. Leaning closer to his ear, he replied, "Still think I should run for office?"

He barely chuckled. "Perhaps anotha time, Mista Bridges!"

"What in the world is going on, Choichi?" He glanced at Saburo whose rigid face mirrored the crowd's mood. "I thought we had agreed to more peaceful terms!"

Saburo sneered, "You said you did not want a meeting without yur presence! So, here we are! Wha's wrong, Mista Bridges? Do you not approve?"

"I don't approve of the attitude, Saburo!" he snapped. Returning to Choichi, he said, "Katsuji has been safely relocated to the camp jail. I wonder if you fellows had an opportunity to seek Tanaka's attackers."

A series of shouts interrupted the vulnerable meeting.

"Petty has been stealing our sugar!"

"Petty an' his accomplices are black marketers! Dey should be da ones in jail, not Katsuji-san!"

"I'm still waiting for my clothing allowance! I don't want my family to freeze to death!"

"My *obasan,* who is blind, can work fasta than the administration!"

Bridges barked, "This is getting ugly, Choichi! I don't like it one bit!"

The representatives skittishly looked at each other; all of whom had families. The brevity of the meeting remained a countdown to the moment of madness. They swiftly spoke together in Japanese and concluded their opinion.

Choichi announced, "We hafe confirmed our ah satisfaction dat you, Mista Bridges, hafe kept yur promise. Darefore, it is also in da agreement of da committee we should resign."

"*Nai!* " someone ranted. "*Chotto matte! Chotto matte!*"

"Nothing is resolved! Not a goddamned thing!"

Saburo leaked a gratifying smirk. He stared at Bridges who appeared flustered by the outbursts that pounded on his head. This was what it took to tear open the administration's eyes. He slipped his hand into his pocket and removed a folded piece of paper and gave it to a colleague, another *Kibei* in his thirties who had a mole on his eyelid. His colleague snatched it and darted down the line; just on the fringe of the crowd. More shouts ricocheted, demanding the unconditional release of Katsuji, demanding that informants like Ted Tanaka should be killed. Saburo's colleague grabbed a barrel full of charred wood and turned it upside-down. The black ashes bled all over the sand and floated in the air like smoke. He then jumped on top, unfolded several sheets of paper, and blared out names of informants: both men and women. The list exceeded over a hundred names. Tom's and Meito's names were printed on that list.

Exhilaration drenched the crowd in a drunken rage and another chant of *banzai's* infiltrated through the last barricade of peace. Then the mob began to split. Two more groups formed at the sidelines: one banding about seventy men; the other about five hundred. The groups broke and merged as easily and gracefully as sliced cheese. Amazed by their efficiency, Bridges had to wonder how long this revolt had been planned. Even General Eisenhower would have been impressed. A modest number of men removed hammers, kitchen knives, screwdrivers, and lumber axes from their coats, shaking the weapons above their heads and hats. Some, where they could find it, reached down to seize stones. Bridges turned to look at Saburo. He was conveniently absent.

A white police officer dashed to Bridges, his rounded belly jiggling against his leather belt with a baton swinging at his hip. Panting, he hollered, "Jesus Christ, sir! We got a goddamn mutiny on our hands! You better get the hell outta here!"

Infuriated, Bridges shouted to Choichi, "What in God's name is going on?"

Choichi blinked in dread, frantically drumming his fingers at his thighs. "I'm sorry, Mista Bridges! I don' undastand what day say! Too much noise!"

Bridges glanced at the police officer, but stared harshly at Choichi. "I think you know a helluva lot more than you let on!"

Choichi instantly dropped his eyes; ashamed that his people would behave profanely. He only wanted justice for Katsuji and to deliver better conditions for the mess halls. Bridges retreated to his vehicle, planning to drive back to his office and dispatch the dreaded phone call.

RUSSELL slapped his fork on the dining table and boasted, "Done!"

His friends slurped pea soup or quickly swallowed the dumplings. Ikki choked, but recovered as he guzzled the powdered milk down his throat. Shig and his gang, one by one, followed Russell's lead, slapping their utensils on the table to signify their skill. It was their second mess hall they conquered. Even though their stomachs might cramp during the run, it warranted no excuse.

"Goro!" someone hollered. "Goro!"

Russell looked up. Meito trotted down the aisle, passing by the rows of people peacefully eating their dinner. Baffled, Russell stood to greet his brother.

"What are you doing here? How did you find me?"

"I knew you'd be in this part of camp!"

"Why aren't you at work?"

Meito swooped over to his brother, out of breath from the rapid walking and jogging. The shouting from four blocks away resonated a curdling chill when he heard his name being called out. Not that it surprised him, Katsuji had always resented his higher position, although to hear it shot out in the open, in front of an angry crowd, made him shuddered.

He said, "We're gonna havta find another place to stay tonight. The family."

"What are you talking about?"

Meito glanced at his brother's circle of friends, and not wanting to create panic, he dragged him off into the middle of the aisle. Russell's friends strained their necks to listen. He said, "Listen, *ototo*, and don't argue. Beatings are going to happen tonight. I'm on a list."

"What list?"

Meito shuffled Russell a little further down. "A stupid list! What can I say? I want you to get Mama and Papa and bring them to the Catholic Church."

"But we're not Catholic."

"Shut up, Goro, and listen!" he snapped. Pausing for a moment, trying to decide what to do next, he continued, "I have a couple of friends I think we can stay with. Just do as I say and everything will be alright."

Russell nodded. A numbness circulated in his head and he thought about the crowd of men earlier that day who surged through the streets, shouting. He really didn't think they would turn on their own people. How could they? It seemed almost cannibalistic in nature.

Meito released his arm and turned to his brother's friends. He announced, "Once you boys finish your meal, go home and *stay* home! There's a riot ready to happen! Don't anyone of you get involved!"

The Bainbridge boys and Shig's gang gazed at Meito, contemplating the value of his words. Shig grinned and proceeded to eat as if he were deaf. Sam began to fidget, tapping his heel, excited, wanting to see. The others sat in stupefaction. No one dared to believe that a revolt could be possible.

Russell started buttoning his coat, worried that a group of men had already arrived at his barrack, harassing his parents. When Meito darted off, he chased him, catching his sleeve. He needed to know.

"Meito, who else is on that list?"

Meito crimped his brows. “I’m not sure, but,” he cleared his throat, “but, I believe they mentioned Tom. Jim’s brother-in-law. You may want to find a way to warn them, too.”

CHAPTER NINE

SADAYE gently rearranged a stack of pillows for an elderly patient who needed help sitting up for his dinner tray. Faint music from a radio swayed down the hallway, through the front part of the hospital. Most of the time she didn't notice the sounds, concentrating on changing bedpans, checking blood pressures and temperatures, or consoling people's loneliness. Sometimes she indulged in the idea of becoming a doctor herself, like the other female doctor, yet she enjoyed the more personal and frequent contact with people.

"*Are you comfortable, Yenuchi-san? I can bring more pillows if you would like it.*"

The man smiled, bringing out more wrinkles inside his crumpled face, his eyes nearly buried under his thickly wild brows. "*Hai. I am very comfortable, Miss. You are most kind and pretty.*"

She returned the smile. "*Thank you very much. What would your wife say if she knew you were flirting?*"

"*She has cataracts and bad hearing! Besides, I am too old to do much more, so I am harmless.*"

"*I find it difficult to believe you. You have more vigor left than you think.*"

He chuckled a raspy cackle, then coughed for a while. Trying to pat her hand, he insisted, "*Oh miss, don't give an old man hope! My ancestors already have a long list of unforgivable things I did in my youth.*"

She softly laughed and reached for a plate of rice. His shaking muscles constrained his adeptness to hold anything in his stubby hands. While she fed him with a spoon, she glanced out a window across from her. The horizon displayed a contradiction of light and dark, typical for that time in the evening. In the distance, beneath the collapsing sunshine, a dust cloud swelled in the street, escorting sixty figures. As Sadaye rose, setting the plate on the tray, she said, "*Excuse me, Yenuchi-san.*"

She walked closer to the window in Ward Three. From the hospital's view, they appeared inferior compared to the overseeing ranges of mountains.

But as they ensued, as their frames grew larger, the mass of bobbing heads and rumbling voices slowly became just as intimidating as the desert's peaks. These men were perfectly desperate: Desperate to seek revenge. Desperate to rebel. Desperate to enforce respect. And she knew why they were coming. She instantly rushed to Ted, her shoes drumming on the wooden floor. The elderly man squinted in confusion, but remained quiet.

"I need to move you, Mr. Tanaka! Do you understand?"

He muttered, "I can hear them, too!"

Ted wrapped his good arm around her and heaved his broken body up. She slumped under his free arm, carefully holding his wrist. The two shuffled across the long room like drunken sailors. She stopped, letting him lean against the wall and removed blankets from the bottom of an orthopedic bed. Quickly she helped Ted slip onto the bottom shelf. Once he curled into position, grunting in pain, she unfolded the blankets and draped them over his shape. She looked up at her elderly patient and placed her finger over her lips. The old man nodded. Sadaye then left the ward, jogging back to the front building where the crowd gathered. A few of the doctors and nurses streamed to the eastern side of the windows. The head physician, Dr. Greene, who replaced Dr. Huey two months ago, entered the arena. Frustrated and aggravated, the young man with glasses and freckles, wearing his long white jacket, paced in front of the double-framed door. He was a quiet man who often smelled of cigars and lotion. His calm nature often put people at ease while his polite manner never implicated a rashness. Sadaye even liked him.

"That's it," Dr. Greene declared definitely. "We're going to need some beefy support. I'm getting the MPs!"

Sadaye and two other nurses instinctively stepped through the doors and positioned themselves in front. The cold wind took away all her body heat. Soon she shivered, wrapping her sweater as tightly as she could. Her thick, white stockings did not protect her legs from the nippy sting. Her heart felt like it darted out of her chest and clogged her throat. She couldn't believe what she was doing. The other women were wives, mothers, having small children to take care of, and yet they also felt the need to protect those who were not family. A duty, more significant than a job, compelled them to stand in the cold and in front of a group of men. They knew these men would not beat them. To beat on a woman only signified their unworthiness as men.

The compacted mob flanked at the steps, demanding for Ted. Sadaye and her two co-workers shouted back their refusal in both English and Japanese. Binding their arms like links in a chain with Sadaye in the middle, the women braced in force; unmoving; fortified. One of the members of the group trotted up to them, smirking, his slick hair parted more on his left side. A mole perched on his right eyelid. His pants preserved ash stains from turning over the barrel.

"Let us by," he threatened.

"No!" one of the nurses declared. "This is a hospital! Not yur bulling ground!"

Agitated, he said, "Women have no understanding in politics. You should not mix emotion with official matters."

Sadaye affirmed, "Our policy doesn't allow solicitation. So I suggest you take your political beliefs elsewhere."

He leered at her, almost amused by her gesture. "Ladies, I suggest you move by."

"Ted Tanaka has already been removed," Sadaye resumed. "So it's pointless you even trying."

"I'll be the judge of that, Miss."

The third nurse, who was the eldest of the other two, interjected, "Does your mother know what you're doing? Isn't it a bit offensive she could have raised an insolent son?"

He glared at the third nurse, his mouth tensing with resentment. "*You need to leave my mother out of this!*"

Dr. Greene opened the door and walked around them. Straightening his back and folding his arms across his chest, he stood directly beside Saburo's colleague. "You boys can't come in here."

"It is not yur place to make demands!"

"Well, you and your men are not coming in! My hospital won't be molested just because you wish it!"

Sadaye scanned the crowd who eagerly listened, waiting for that moment. She saw knives and hammers in their hands. Horrified, she squeezed both her co-workers' hands, her heart pulsating like showers of hail. Surely they wouldn't dare. Surely it was only for show; only for intimidation.

The man argued, "We're not going anywhere until we are satisfied! Do you see what my men hold in their palms?" He hesitated to allow Dr. Greene to take a sturdy look. Smirking, he persisted, "I don't think I have to tell you what we are capable of doing."

Dr. Greene calmly returned his focus on the troublemaker. "I've known more original threats than yours. You believe you're clever? Stronger?" He carefully wet his lips and disdainfully voiced, "Turning on frail patients is a pathetic way to demonstrate your message!"

The man leaned closer to Dr. Greene. "It will be a matter of time before my men become more annoyed with you. Do you wish they burn your hospital down?"

Sadaye held her breath. The crowd increased its harsh murmurs, expressing shortness, expressing sarcasm. Their words remained in Japanese, ascending above Dr. Greene's comprehension. They stirred in a rippling manner; their bodies waving on a cove of sand. She envisioned the hospital entangled in a fire's slaughter with its thick smoke gagging ninety patients and forty staff.

Dr. Greene replied, "I'll allow *you* to search, and that's it!"

"Eight of us!" the man asserted.

"Unacceptable! I'll allow three, then."

"Six."

The doctor thought for a minute. "Five, and *only* five! And I will be present during this asinine witch hunt!

The man frowned. "Agreed," he reluctantly sighed, anxious to start the search instead of wasting more time bartering with the white man.

JIM heard the shouts echo not too far from where he walked Tomiko to her barrack. Rumors of a riot surrounded the camp with fear. The streets were unusually bare. He said goodnight to her, not kissing her and watched her slip back inside. Tomiko's father watched from the window. Jim waved to her father who nodded in turn. He walked to his barrack across the street, curiously listening to the bellows that trailed off to the police station. Katsuji's name crackled in air. Jim shook his head. Some people got exactly what they deserved.

Leaping up his steps, he entered his home. Rose, Bethany, Tom, and his mother sat at the table as if attending a wake. Shutting the door, he asked, "What's going on?"

Rose jumped to her feet, and charged to her baby in the crib. Her ruby scarf looped around her hair, mismatching her dull overalls. With tears in her eyes, she spurted, "Well, I'm not staying to find out, Tom! I'm not taking the chance of harming our child because of your pride!"

Jim took his coat off, concerned. "What harm?"

Bethany looked up at her brother. Her flushed cheeks indicated she was upset. "Russell told us Tom is on a list. That he might be in danger."

Exasperated, Tom flung his hand upward. "I'm not in danger, Bethany! *Mattaku nai!* How many times do I have to say it? Rose!" he pleaded, watching her frantically bundle Thomas Jr. "Rose! This is what they want. To control us by foolish threats. Nothing is going to happen!"

She ignored her husband. Russell was more convincing and realistic than Tom. She grabbed a small knapsack, stuffing it with cloth diapers and powdered milk. Mrs. Yoshimura clenched Bethany's hand, sniffling. The shouting only confirmed madness. How she ached for her husband to be there, keeping the family strong, united, not bickering with a fractured temperament.

Reaching for her coat, Rose exclaimed, "I'm going to the Catholic Church. Who else is coming?"

Bethany, her two braids tied together with a bow, looked up at Jim. He recognized that she was seeking comfort. All he could do was appear concerned in his bewilderment. He wasn't sure what to make of it. Rose's panic. His mother's tears. Tom's stubbornness.

Mrs. Yoshimura said, "*Just in case, I believe it would not be a bad choice to stay elsewhere. Of course just for tonight.*"

Tom sat on his bed. "I'm not going anywhere! No one is going to run me out of home! Whatever kind of home we do have!"

Rose quickly buttoned her coat, swung the knapsack on her shoulder and hugged her baby. She curtly sighed. "Tom, I love you. But you're an idiot."

Mrs. Yoshimura tugged on Bethany's arm as she stood up. She then plucked two coats for Bethany and herself from the long nails that poked from the wall.

"I'm also not going," Jim stated. He walked to the grey stove and fixed his palms over the heat. "I actually agree with Tom this time. I'm not going to run and hide just because some fanatics are blowing hot air. I only like to see them try."

Tom gazed at him, flabbergasted. All those months Jim had made it clear how much he despised Tom. He was speechless.

Jim resumed warming his hands, refusing to observe Tom's reaction. He didn't want to give Tom more room to gloat.

Mrs. Yoshimura began trembling. If something were to happen to any of her children, she didn't know how much more she could endure.

THE five men, who elected themselves for the hunt, covered in dirt and dust, tramped through the hospital wards with Dr. Greene at their heels. Patients gazed from their beds, worried, frightened, while these men plowed with purpose. They hovered over each male patient, making sure Ted didn't lay limp on the pillow. They probed through the seven wards, peeking in corners, peeking in closets and storage rooms, peeking in the latrines. Dr. Greene expected them to rummage like raccoons in garbage cans, flinging fits. Surprisingly they held a particular amount of control despite their frustrations and kept their search clean.

Sadaye wanted to follow along, however feared she would only provoke the men, making them more suspicious and possibly giving away Ted's secret place. Instead, she nervously paced the room, squeezing her hands, praying. The other doctors and nurses carefully watched the crowd, speaking very little.

An ambulance with four military police finally arrived at the front. Sadaye stared out the window, observing the crowd shifting around the building; these men trying to follow the search through the row of windows. She recognized one of the soldiers. Even though his head was covered in a helmet, his young face conveyed an earnest appeal. She had seen him twice. Both times this soldier had intervened with the other one; the more brutal one with callous eyes. She never did catch their names.

The soldiers marched up the steps and flung the doors open, rattling the room, shaking the floor as they carried their rifles. The crowd began surrounding the ambulance and tossed stones at it, believing that Ted was already inside. Sadaye instantly withdrew from the window, worried that they crowd would start hurling stones toward her way.

Palmer stood beside Sadaye, his muscles tightening as he glanced out the line of windows. "Miss, where is Ted Tanaka?"

She studied him, wondering if he would recognize her. No matter. She had other uncertainties in her mind. The mob outside in particular. She began to wonder if she should expose Ted directly out in the open. Like a sitting duck. She feared there weren't enough soldiers to defend Ted, themselves, and everyone else in the wards, especially if these enraged men decided to use their weapons.

"I'm sorry, but he's not here," she nervously lied.

He tilted his head in disbelief. "We were told he would be here and needed immediate assistance for his removal."

"He's already been removed," she continued conclusively, glancing at the abused ambulance, hearing clinks and clanks from the soaring rocks. "And from the looks of it, it was a good thing."

Dr. Greene aligned his position at the door. The five men were on a second scavenger hunt, baffled as to why they could not find Ted. And so was

Dr. Greene. Ted somehow, sometime, had been relocated for his safety and without his knowledge. The man with a mole on his eyelid furiously paced the room. He stared at the orthopedic bed with the sheets drooping over it. Sadaye's elderly patient watched from his bed, still not understanding what the disturbance was all about other than a beating from the night before. Saburo's colleague stopped in the middle of the room.

The man grunted and stomped off. The other four trailed behind his defeat. Sadaye watched the soldiers sprint down the steps, returning to the dented ambulance. The cluster of men began to gripe; their tone discharging resentment. Soon the soaring rocks transferred to the hospital. The rattling of the stones sounded like thick rain until a window finally broke. Stunned, Sadaye turned to see which window. A pile of shards spread on the floor like dead petals fallen from a vase. One of the nurses cried out in pain and warily pulled out a few pieces from her leg. Blood instantly stained her white stocking. Sadaye subsequently felt guilty for leaving her elderly patient who was in the same area where Ted hid. She dashed from the building to head back to Ward Three.

One of the men in the crowd shouted that they should divide into smaller groups to find the rest of the *inus*. The names he shouted belonged to other JACL leaders who had supported the evacuation. Sadaye had recognized some of the names connected to the camp newspaper and internal police. Then she heard her brother-in-law's name, Osamu Hayashino, being shouted out as she entered her ward. Panicking, she ran back to the building where Dr. Greene had his office and a telephone.

THE sun had completely disappeared behind Mount Williamson, allowing the swarm of stars to infiltrate the sky. Camp residents shut their doors and pulled their curtains together, hoping to keep out the disorder. Some had locks, but most hadn't worried about it before since they had very little worth stealing. Now many wished they had invested in locks to protect themselves from the radicals. The five representatives lead five hundred men, fused with boys whose brothers or uncles or cousins were swimming toward the police station in the frenzy. Saburo yelled the loudest about justice, hoping to recruit more for his cause. As the moon skimmed just above the other side of the mountains, mess hall bells vibrated throughout the camp, establishing one definite cry. These particular rings weren't announcing chow time. No. Each mess hall contained meetings regarding Manzanar's fate. The revolt inspired thousands to ultimately take control of their lives without being monitored by the military or the War Relocation Authority. These men spoke of dispatching their own forces in order to pursue the traitors in camp.

Shikami had joined his uncle, Toru, the camp Judo instructor, marching proudly, marching for the honor of the Terminal Island men who suffered more humiliation than the others. Not only did the FBI seize all of the *Issei* and some *Kibei* men hours after Pearl Harbor, not only did the military declare their island a threat and no one could leave under any circumstances, taking it over like Alcatraz, but his island had been the port where his people first emigrated. For sixty years the Japanese who entered California initially passed through Terminal

Island. It was the West Coast's version of Ellis Island: this port where men had waited for their fortune, many carving their names and poems on the walls. To be remembered. To preserve their significance.

OSAMU braced his fists on the window's ledge. Staring directly at the mass, he fought the urge to flee and to run to his family's protection. He knew Meito would take care of them, so, in the meantime he needed to wait at the station, keeping Katsuji locked behind bars as ordered. Osamu's white arm band still wrapped to his arm, and he hadn't planned on removing it until all of this was finished. Two of the five *Nisei* officers were fidgeting. Sweat began to leak from their foreheads, and Katsuji, who lay on the cot with his feet balanced against the bars, grinned at their uneasiness. The crowd's noise grew overwhelming as if locusts festering on some poor farmer's crop. The captain, a white official who had bit of a belly and slight baldness, stood next to Osamu, chewing on his tongue, contemplating.

"Jesus Christ," he said. "It looks like an ambush."

The two *Nisei* officers bolted out the back door, leaving it swinging in the breeze. Startled, the captain leapt to the other side to slam it shut. Osamu turned to exam the vacant spots. He tried not to panic.

"Goddamnit!" the captain shouted. "Now I'm down to three men! Even Custer had it better than me!"

The last two officers could only look at each other. None of them, except the captain, carried any protection; not even batons, which was an unfair requirement. What else could they do? The captain stomped to the phone to call Mr. Bridges and inform him of their pitiful situation. Dust and men's breath floated in the air, surrounding the tiny square building in a full circle. Katsuji finally rose to his feet, looking out the window, inspecting the marvelous protest in his favor. From the tip of the mountains view, it appeared as though a broad bull's eye was mounted in the center, waiting for flying darts.

The captain hung up the black phone. "We should get back-up here pretty soon, boys."

SABURO escorted the other four representatives to the front door of the police station and lined-up in an organized shape. Each crossed their arms, establishing their authority and stance. The harsh buzzing of the crowd perpetuated, and thus far no one reacted just yet. Their mission of freeing Katsuji resided in an armistice at the moment, trusting their leaders' capabilities and promises. The captain opened the door and allowed the five men to merge inside. Katsuji nodded his greeting to his friends while they entered. Osamu watched Katsuji. Katsuji returned to his cot and laid down as if on a holiday. He looked up at Osamu and winked. Annoyed, Osamu returned to the window. How could Katsuji not be bothered by any of this? This massive intimidation? It equaled a dangerous consequence: this indifference. To Osamu's left side, he barely saw a line of MPs swiftly formulating and extending from the front gate towards the station. Their lean bayonets bobbed with each trotting step. The sharp metal tops gleamed under the street lights, glistening like sets of teeth. The crowd quieted a little.

Twenty soldiers, including Private Callis, paneled their bodies and weapons along the border of the crowd. The project director arrived back on scene, determined to find a resolution. Manzanar was his responsibility, and he hoped to preserve an optimistic reputation not only for himself, but for the people he wanted to protect. The children. The citizens of America despite their transient circumstances. Bridges couldn't believe he had been lied to, bamboozled even, by the men he thought he could trust. He had to admit, though, he hadn't acquired much faith in Saburo from the first time he met him. The column of soldiers prevented him from grinding through their barricade. A lieutenant met the frustrated Bridges.

"Sir!" he forcefully began. His stocky structure startled Bridges. "Sir, we were ordered not to let you pass for your own safety!"

Bridges retorted, "But I'm expected at the station to conclude a meeting! Important people are waiting for me!"

"I'm sorry, sir! But that's not gonna happen!"

"I thought I was in charge!" he snapped.

"Yes, sir, you are! But we're in charge of your safety! How can you run a camp if something were to happen to you, sir?"

Feeling as though someone had pulled down his pants in front of everyone, he stepped back. This helplessness was not a familiar ground. In fact, it irritated the hell out of him. He knew he had to resort to the last tactic: declare martial law. Grinding his jaw, he trudged back to Mr. Petty's apartment where he could observe everything and evaluate his next move. The young lieutenant began shouting at the crowd to disperse. His shouts rang out in repetition and without success.

Osamu hovered at the window, intensely staring past his reflection and into the darkening crowd. The streetlights barely extended their gleaming limbs, barely touching their faces, mutating them into painted figurines. He couldn't see the soldiers but spotted their metal tips just beyond the horizon of men. Osamu closed his eyes and began praying. He prayed for the safety of his family. He prayed for a quick and bloodless resolution. He prayed for another day.

RUSSELL rattled his leg as he sat on the pew, frowning at the shiny Jesus that hung on the wall. He wanted the night to be over. The last hour only agitated him. He was bored and worried for the safety of Jim. And about his other friends who lived close to the police station. And he could do nothing. It wasn't in his nature to be idle. Meito brought their other sister, Masako, and her toddler, Ruth, to the church as well. Even Jim's mother and his two sisters, Rose and Bethany with the baby, sat at the front, quietly praying to the chipped wooden figurine. He glanced at his parents who were seated apart; lost, angry at each other, angry at the world. The priest, an *Issei* in his sixties, continued to stay in the box where a couple of people affirmed their confessions. Russell leaned forward and cleared his throat. He had to leave. He had to bring Jim here.

Knowing that Meito wouldn't allow him to do such a thing, he stood up and said, "I need to use the latrine. I may be gone awhile." He placed his hand on his belly. "Stomach problems."

Meito caressed both his sons' hair as they laid their head on his lap. He was waiting to hear from a friend about locating to another place. He cautiously looked up.

"Okay. But if you're not back in half an hour, I'm coming to get you."

SAM darted off to the side and stood next to a couple of trash cans. The faint smell of rotten eggs interrupted his excitement. Was that tear gas he smelled? His heart pounded. Sweat formed on his forehead, quickly clawing his face when the chilly wind blew by. His ears rumbled with the crowd's boastful insults. He recognized some of the men as they pushed forward, then backward, then forward like ocean waves. He recognized the clerk at the post office. Crewmembers who fixed broken streetlights and telephone wire that were damaged by the wind. And assorted faces from the various mess halls. These *Nikkei* men were relatively young, robust, and although they were not as tall as the soldiers, their strength intimated the inexperienced military. The soldiers appeared to be spooked despite that they they were the ones holding loaded weapons. Rocks flew in the air and one landed at his feet. He glanced across the street where clouds of dust veiled the block. He barely saw Director Bridges stare out of a lit window, shaking his head. Ikki's voice echoed in his mind: "Don't go to the station, dimwit. It ain't none of our business. None."

JIM read a book on his bed while Tom continuously stared out the window. The bare streets indicated a ghostly facade. For awhile the crowd seemed to have quieted, perhaps given up, but then minutes later their furious complaints escalated. Some triggered into singing traditional Japanese songs, professing their loyalties to the Emperor. Additional *banzai's* blasted in the sky. Tom began pacing again, then sat at the table and flipped through *Life* magazine. Jim remained calm. He strained to ignore the noises, reading and rereading the same sentences, turning pages in a sluggish manner. Soon they heard piercing voices outside. Abruptly their door flung open and three men raced inside. Jim tossed his book at one of them, hitting him on the shoulder. Infuriated, the man slapped Jim on the face, knocking him down. His new glasses flew across the room. Jim fumbled to his feet, but was smashed down by the man's boot. The other two propelled their fists into Tom, crushing him on the table. Tom loudly gasped, swinging his arm, missing. The two men tossed him on the floor and began kicking.

Jim pushed up yet was booted in the ribs. He couldn't believe it. How could these men violently attack their own kind? Wheezing for breath, his eyes watering from pain, Jim watched Tom crawl defenselessly, bleeding from his mouth and nose. The three men then turned their hands onto tearing their home apart. They knocked over the bookshelf, pitched clothes out of the drawer, ripped the curtains down, yanked off the covers and sheets, and flipped over the table and chairs, nearly striking Jim.

One of them spat, "*Let this be an example of what happens to those who are informants! Never spy on your own people!*"

The men laughed at their satisfaction and left with the door swaying in the chilly wind. Jim wearisomely stood up; his bruised ribs aching with every movement. He shuffled around, foraging for his glasses. Tom lay rumpled in the corner, wiping the blood from his nose that wouldn't stop flowing. He began crying. Jim stopped. Shocked, he abandoned his search and shuffled to Tom, shuffling through the congested mess. He sluggishly reached down for a bed sheet and dragged it to Tom. Sitting down, Jim extended it to him. Tom meekly grasped it, his hands trembling, and started wiping his face.

Jim said, "Lean your head back and pinch your nose. That should stop the bleeding."

The door slammed. Both Jim and Tom jumped. Staring wildly at the door, they realized the wind had maneuvered the door. Tom blinked and then chuckled at their false panic. His vision was blurred, but he could still see the violence splattered on the floor. He glanced at Jim, surprised by his sympathy, although not ungrateful. He had wanted his respect for the longest time and could never understand why Jim hated him so.

Footsteps creaked up the steps. Jim and Tom froze. Knocking pursued. They remained paralyzed as they watched the door open again.

Russell stepped inside. "Oh my God!" he vented. "What the hell happened?"

Jim grunted, "What the hell do you think happened?"

Russell trampled over the piles of books and clothes, stabilizing his balance on the chairs that were erected upside-down. When Meito predicted turmoil, Russell hadn't visualized to what extent. Shaking his head, even as he walked through the mess, he never expected this. He yielded and squatted to exam Tom's nose. "Anything broken, Tom?"

His voice cracked a nasally sound. "I'm not sure."

"Better have it checked out," Russell continued. "I'll help you to the hospital." He glanced at Jim. "So, now do you guys believe me?"

They remained quiet, embarrassed, bruised. Russell gently rested Tom's arm on his shoulder and lifted him. Tom groaned and released the bed sheet, letting it fall with his fresh red stains soaked into the material. They shuffled across the room. The cold air invaded the barrack with the door suspending out in the open. Suddenly Ikki popped up on the steps.

"Dammit, Ikki!" Jim gasped. "You scared the shit out of me!"

His frantic expression crippled his face. "Sweet Jesus! You guys alright?"

"We will be," Jim grunted, limping.

"Have any of you seen Sam?" Ikki quickly asked. "He didn't come home after dinner!"

Russell replied, "I haven't seen him since I left you guys at the mess hall."

"I've been at the library," Jim muttered.

Ikki closed his eyes and twisted his mouth. "That blockhead! I bet he's at the goddamn police station!"

PRIVATE Callis stood in formation, yelling with his colleagues while yelling at the thick mob to move back. He squeezed his rifle, his thick knuckles forming a fist. Beside him was another private who shared the same passionate and patriotic sentiments as himself, tightly gripping the cold machine gun. Only the warmth of their palms indicated the weapons' expressive energy. They watched the Japs stir like snakes rolling in the thickest pasture with their tails viciously rattling. Some were launching large rocks like grenades. Callis hated the brainless policy of not firing into the crowd unless ordered by his inexperienced lieutenant. He had at least five years more so than him. Just because his superior had a damn college degree which gave him the right to hold rank didn't mean he deserved respect.

Shikami flung his burning cigarette over the soldiers' heads. Smirking, he thought those *hitsuji* needed to wear their helmets instead of their soda-jerk caps. Their caps could catch fire. A wonderful echo of a Japanese song besieged the air. The unified words praised Japan's honor and the Emperor's divine spirit. Their singing repelled against the soldiers' shouting, shaking like thunder, falling like rain. Instinctively Shikami hurled sand into their betrayers faces. Other cries from within the crowd clattered among the dynamic singing, shouting at the military and calling them "boy scouts." Then Shikami's grabbed a soldier's bayonet and pushed the blond headed soda-jerk.

Callis, livid, lurched forward and knocked him to the ground. Trying to point his gun at the Nip, another grabbed at the butt, jiggling it.

The man scoffed, "Shoot it! Come on, boy scout! Shoot the damn thing!"

Shikami's uncle quickly dragged him inside the crowd; away from the line of fire if the soldiers decided to act out on their instincts.

A young lieutenant ran down the line and grabbed the *Nisei's* wrist. "Let go!" He demanded. "Let go you, idiot!" He then pointed his bayonet to the man. The man, stunned, instantly released it and stepped back. The lieutenant lowered his weapon. Breathing coarsely, he raised his arm and glanced at his men, six of whom clasped tear gas grenades in their uneasy hands. He dispersed another round of grenades to in an even number of eight men in-between; a half a dozen more than the last round. "Okay!" he hollered. "Now!"

The soldiers yanked the hooks out and slung the black objects, which were the size of oranges, into the hearth of men. An explosion of smoke blew out. Abruptly, the crowd cracked like glass, spreading out to the edges of the fumes. Dust instantaneously mingled from the stirring of flock of feet.

Russell and Ikki halted on the fringe of Block One, catty-corner to the police station, leaning beside another barrack that stood near the barbed-wire fence. They began coughing from the smoke and dust that whisked in their direction. Russell pulled Ikki to the ground and covered his nose with the collar of his shirt. Russell had been relieved when Jim decided to take Tom to the hospital, then planned to meet up with him at the church. He had implored both not to tell Meito where he had been, not wanting to cause more grief to his family. They reluctantly agreed. He knew his brother would check on him at the latrine which was the reason he found Shig as a back-up. Shig had a similar build.

SHIG huddled in the stall with a sports magazine and extra dollar in his pocket that had been provided by Russell. He also told Shig to wear a grey sweatshirt and blue jeans. Drumming his shoes on the floor, he hummed tuneless tunes. With his pants resting at his ankles, he waited. Meito, right on time, angrily passed by the line of men who bellowed their complaints at him for cutting in line when he entered the building. When Shig heard Goro's name being barked, he promptly covered his face with the magazine.

"Over here!" he replied.

Meito marched down the rows of exposed stalls. Uncertain as he stared at Shig, whose voice was slightly higher, he squinted and hinged his knuckles on his hip. "Goro?"

"Busy!" Shig blurted.

He blinked a few times, not quite convinced. "What's wrong with you? You sound different."

"I'm in pain, do you mind?"

Biting on his lip, he reclined on one leg. "I'll be expecting you outside when you're done."

Shig didn't reply. He had hoped Russell's brother would retreat. Listening to his footsteps walk away, he planned to flee. He had been caught once; he wasn't that stupid a second time! Zipping his pants, taking off the sweatshirt and abandoning his old magazine, he snuck by Meito by following behind a chubby man.

THE front door tore open. Osamu jerked. Two radicals, dressed in corduroy and checkered coats, darted inside. Osamu and two of his colleagues jumped forward, shoving the intruders back outside. As the three slammed the door shut, Osamu clutched a board beside a chair and inserted it into the metal slots. Perspiring, he turned to look at Katsuji who continued to lay on the cot with a smirk. The captain and the five representatives emerged from the office, perplexed. They had been observing the massive ring from the rear window, no longer discussing possibilities. Pebbles embarked on a shower of clinks. No one could say anything.

WHEN the smoke cleared, Russell jumped to his feet, coughing. He glanced at his wristwatch. It was nearing nine o'clock. The chill whittled at his cheeks, scraping out a redness. He then slumped beside the barrack. Scanning at the line of soldiers, perhaps forty, searching for Sam, the mob gathered around the soldiers, now encasing the military in a box, reversing their positions. Hundreds of men and boys now dominated the exterior, trapping the *hakujins* in the middle. A string of others drifted a hundred feet away from the jail house like loose change dribbling from a torn pocket.

Ikki desperately asked, "Do you see him? Can you find him?"

Russell curtly sighed. "I can't see very much! It's too dark! And everyone keeps moving around!"

"Oh, God," he gasped, thumping on Russell's shoulder. "Look!"

Ikki pointed to a Ford Coupe being pushed by four men. On the doors of the vehicle were labels belonging to the fire department. They were heading toward the police station just up the street.

SAM remained by the trash barrels across from the administration building. He felt safe lingering by a governmental structure. He felt important; something his cousin or anyone else couldn't make fun of. Knowing that someday it would be marked in history, he could tell his friends and future generations that he had been an eyewitness. They would respect him and he would no longer be the tail end of his friends' jokes.

CALLIS watched the crowd merge back together like diseased flies. He aimed his bayonet to his right shoulder and fired. His buddy panicked and discharged three rounds. The lieutenant jolted to his right. A Ford Coupe, with lights glaring at him, sailed his way. He heard his captain ordered him to shoot at the moving vehicle. Instantly, he bumped a private off the other sub-machine gun and fired seven times. The crowd splintered. Sharp cries of pain exploded.

RUSSELL seized Ikki's sleeve and both plummeted to the ground again. He held his breath and went numb. His heart shuddered with the gun shots. All his thoughts bled out of his ears. He tasted the dirt. Other gunfire shots crackled in the air. More piercing cries. The car crashed into an army truck instead of the police station. Smoke from the weapons fused with the trampling dust clouds. Ikki covered his ears with his hands. The moaning of wounded men was so close. It could have been him. Then the shooting stopped. It had only been a couple of minutes of damage. Silence ruptured, but Russell heard his heart. It seemed louder than the machine gun and it took another minute to clear its result.

MEITO shuddered. The rattling shots paralyzed his heart. Panicking, suspecting that Goro was up to something, he darted back inside. Outraged to find another man reading the sports magazine, he darted out of the latrine and ran to the opposite side of camp.

ELEVEN men and one boy lay sporadically on the desert's soil. Others who had been injured ran away, bleeding, knowing they could tend to their own wounds. Osamu and his colleagues immediately reopened the door to bring in some of the more critical casualties. The five representatives, numbed, stared at their bleeding friends. Choichi couldn't speak. His dry throat prevented him from uttering a cry. Katsuji finally rose to his feet and stared through the bars; his smirk departed from his shaken face. Realizing how dangerous a political belief could evolve, his regrets remained silent. Glancing away from the three men who laid on the floor, Katsuji watched Saburo slip out of the door.

RUSSELL was horrified as he stood up and began walking in a daze. He heard the wail of the ambulance rushing to the police station. Bodies were scattered around it as if dead leaves discarded by an oak tree. Some men were moaning. Ikki followed his staggering. There were more shadows than light. The soldiers redefined their position, aligning in two rows, waiting for their orders as a clean up crew. Russell saw Osamu scout out the area. He picked up his tempo toward his brother-in-law, not knowing how to feel, and only concluded he should help move the bodies at least. Behind a barrel, Osamu dragged a body directly under a street light. Russell stopped. Ikki stopped. The entire world became paralyzed.

"Oh, Jesus, no!" Ikki brayed. "Jesus, no!" He ran to Osamu and clasped his hands around Sam's face wih his eyes fastened. His breathing limpid. At least Ikki could feel his warmth; even a little bit. That had to indicate he was still alive. It had to. "Sam!" he shrieked. "Sam, can you hear me?"

Osamu whispered, his voice strangled by shock, "Let's get him inside."

Ikki grabbed his cousin's arms. All he could see was Sam's calm expression. He didn't notice that Russell had to take Sam when he couldn't. He sat there. He sat and saw Sam disappear. His vision then became unclear. Suddenly a knot severed his throat and he fell to the ground, sobbing, sobbing hysterically, sobbing to painful exhaustion. He told Sam. He told him. He wouldn't listen. Now the blemishes of blood on the sand told Ikki. They told him. And he refused to look. He refused to understand.

Russell helped Osamu mount Sam on the square table where his legs drooped over the ledge. His hands frantically trembled and Russell couldn't control it. Sam had two bullet holes: one in the cavity of his heart; the other in his leg. His complexion quickly whitened, surrendering all colors of the flesh. Remembering how to monitor the pulse from his sister, Russell clasped Sam's cool arm and pressed two fingers over his friend's wrist. Ikki's cries filtered through the door, antagonizing the siren's approaching howl. Russell cringed. Panicking, not feeling a beat, he readjusted his fingers all over his arm in hopes to find life.

Frustrated, he spat, "I can't do this, Osamu! You find his pulse!"

Osamu looked up. Despite the obvious, he checked for a quiver of any kind. The ambulance pulled directly in front, reeling dust into the building. Russell stared at Osamu, coughing a little. They knew. They knew once they touched his sagging body, but said nothing. Russell fell into a chair. He closed his eyes and heaved. He felt as though his chest had been fractured by a sledgehammer. Two MPs entered with a stretcher. They turned to Osamu and glanced at Sam.

One asked, "How's the kid?"

Osamu looked away. His voice crackled when he spoke. "No need to take him first."

THREE ambulances shrilled towards the hospital, howling under a black sky that began hemorrhaging stars. Sadaye and two other nurses darted out the front door. Dr. Greene followed. The flickering lights tore over the barracks as the vehicles charged down the murky streets. An hour ago, Ted had finally been removed from his hiding place. Private Palmer said he would be relocated outside of Manzanar, possibly to Lone Pine. She had heard the shots twenty minutes ago. She heard the machine gun thunder an echoing stutter, bouncing in between the monstrous mountains. Now the ambulances came. What kind of mess would it be? Only a few times in her career she had bandaged a bullet wound, but to see men shot like a flock of ducks . . . she really wasn't prepared for it. The boxy vehicles stopped in a line. Instantly, Sadaye and other nurses and doctors rushed to them. The rear doors flung open. More soldiers jumped off. Bleeding men sat and laid on the floor. Orderlies ran out with more stretchers. Stunned to see that much blood, Sadaye stepped back. Blood soaked their clothes and formed small puddles on the ground. Some were in their fifties, but most were younger. Much younger. Blinking, she let her instincts rebound and hopped inside. Three men leaned against the sides, squinting in pain. She examined one who lay horizontally and had been shot in his right arm and left thigh.

She asked, "*Sir, are you conscious?*"

He grunted as tears stung his cheeks. "*Hai! Those bastards had no right!*"

She lowered her head closer to him. The streetlight glared over half his face. She saw a mole on his right eye and immediately recognized him. She recognized him from the farcical search two hours prior, threatening to beat Tanaka, threatening to finish the job. Infuriated, she sat up. Jim and Tom had limped to the hospital, badly bruised with minor concessions. She suspected additional victims would trickle in during the night. It was the fault of this man who now lay wounded. This agitator and many others who stupidity threatened the lives of her family and friends. They broke some of the hospital's windows. They harassed the soldiers. She wanted to say, "Well it looks like they finished the job for you instead! Funny how karma work out, don't you think?"

Shifting to the door, she kept quiet. It wasn't in her place to make such a remark. Staring out at the chaos, doctors and nurses and orderlies leaping about, she glanced at the man with the mole again, glad he had been wounded. He got what he deserved. Turning away, she sprung off.

"Over here!" she blurted to an orderly, grabbing his arm. "I have one who needs to go next!"

KATSUJI was escorted out of the camp, moving back to Independence's jail. The two-lane highway hid in obscurity like a secret passage. Along the edges the sage bushes languished; barely seen under the sickly moon light. This time Katsuji's wrists weren't cuffed. There seemed to be no need.

MEITO, breathless, horrified, stumbled over the bullet shells. Tire marks and hundred of foot prints were being erased by the wind. A couple of soldiers stood by the police station, talking to Mr. Bridges. Some police officers paced in circles, shaking their heads. An ambulance waited by the station's front door, its rear spread opened, vulnerable. Two MPs hauled a stretcher with a body covered in a sheet. His pulse rung in his ears. Goro! He saw his brother's shoes. His motionless legs. Running to the body, he felt the world compressing time into a corner, compressing it to force a longer stretch between here and now. He nearly collided with the body. He would never forgive himself if his brother were dead. He couldn't imagine telling their mother. Flipping the sheet, he thought he saw Goro's face.

"Meito?"

He turned. He saw his brother rose from a chair, under a single bulb inside the station. An MP grabbed Meito and shoved him against the wall just under the wooden sign that poked above him.

The soldier shouted, "What business do you have here?"

Meito looked at the body again. It was Sam. By God, it was Sam. His relief lasted in a sigh. Osamu darted to his side and firmly stood face-to-face with the soldier.

"He's with me!" Osamu yelled. "He's my brother-in-law!"

The soldier, clinging to his bayonet with one hand and squeezing Meito's collar with another, continued to glare. His wedding ring flickered under Meito's nose. Meito looked into his hazel eyes, noticing his eyes fluttering nervousness. He then became conscious that no one wanted to be there. In the middle of the desert. In the middle of a war. The M probably had children as well. A family man like himself.

Osamu begged, "Please, let him go! He had nothing to do with the riot. I swear!"

Director Bridges walked over, his glasses slightly powdered from the Sierra's soil. Martial law was his last resort. He disliked enforcing it. He disliked it, but he wasn't going to be responsible for an outright mutiny. And if the other camps got word of it, all nine of them, what kind of outbreak would that inflict? From California to Colorado to Arkansas? As if there weren't enough hostilities! Japanese balloons floating all over the West Coast with bombs. One actually killing a family while on a picnic in Oregon. Nazi spies camouflaged in American communities. Even Errol Flynn was under suspicion. Then there were the race riots in Los Angeles. It was obvious that the war over there had infiltrated directly into here.

Bridges barked, "What's going on?"

"My name's Meito Hamaguchi, sir." he replied, looking directly at him. "I'm here to take my little brother home. That's all!"

Russell tightened in numbness. Sam's death hadn't settled in. Meito's presence was just an illusion. He wanted to go home. To Winslow. The very thought of home caused his whole body to ache.

Bridges tipped a brow. "Meito? Have I met you once before?"

"Yes. Last month. While you were touring all the mess halls. I used to be in charge of Block Three."

He squinted. "Used to be?"

"Yes, sir. I quit. I'm tired of the bullshit."

The soldier shuffled his stance, adjusting his grip on Meito's collar, skittishly glancing between Bridges to Meito. He waited for the project director's next command.

Director Bridges sadly grinned. "I don't blame you." He looked at the MP. "Let him loose, private."

The soldier released Meito and stepped backward.

Bridges knew everything wasn't resolved just yet. In fact, like most outcomes of storms, it was the clean-up that would be the most exhausting thing. And he knew it would be up to police and soldiers to find the rest of perpetrators and that, no doubt, would take all night long, if not all week long.

Osamu clenched Russell's sleeve and pushed him to his brother. Meito hugged Russell, tightly, feeling his muscles twinge as he squeezed his knuckles and eyes. His brother was alive. And not hurt. Russell could hardly breathe. He expected his brother to slap him for disobeying him again. He wanted to be slapped. To sense the pain. To awaken him. Instead, Meito held him, smothering his senses.

Russell croaked, "Sam. Did you see Sam?"

Meito unbound his arms and carefully studied him. His sweat had braced filth around his forehead and neck. His cheeks were flushed and lips were cracked. He whispered, "I thought it was you, Goro."

Russell dipped his head into his hand. It smelled of Sam's salted blood and awful cologne. Jesus! It was as though he were still here. He had known Sam all of his life. Seventeen years. Russell shoved his brother aside and kicked the chairs. His chest felt like fire ants gnawing inside of him, burning, throbbing. Ikki, who now sat on the cot where Katsuji once occupied, covered his eyes with his hands and bit his tongue until it bled. Osamu and Bridges watched in astonishment. Death of a youth was a grave sign for anyone. A devastation. A shame.

Meito grabbed his brother and forced him to sit down. "Don't fight it, Goro!" he declared. "Don't fight it! Let it pass!"

Russell blinked. He thought he had been slapped. He felt a stinging of some sort buzzing on his cheeks. Suddenly, he fell forward and began crying. Meito patted his brother's head and quietly cried with him.

December 7

TWENTY-ONE men were arrested during the night and quickly transferred out of camp, including Saburo and Choichi. Five more, out of the eleven wounded that were found from last night's shooting, were watched by the military police, waiting for the time they were fit to be relocated. More were wounded, but avoided going to the hospital for obvious reasons. Amazingly only two died that night. Beatings against those who were believed to be *inus* continued as well as raids to find secret meetings until the reluctant dawning of the sun. No one knew where in the justice system they were to be judged. Locally? Federally? Since the existence of the camps, like Indian reservations, these desert colonies allotted by the government suggested a paradox: They were not prisoners of war, but they were not free. They were not citizens, but they were not foreigners either. They existed on land owned by the American government, but were no longer a part of America.

JIM squinted up at the ceiling as he lay on the gritty floor. Wooden beams sprawled out like a spider's web. Around ten last night his family and Russell's family were removed from the Catholic church to the auditorium. There, Director Bridges had distributed a few MPs to guard people who feared they would be harmed. So far sixty people slept on the floor. The large building was similar to a train station. And cold. Jim flipped up the collar of his coat, covering part of his chilled ears. Drafts whistled inside the incomplete structure. Sunlight fell through the broad segment of windows. Some cots were dragged in, allowing those who had bad backs to lie somewhat comfortably. But no one could sleep. Up until one in the morning, each mess hall resounded series of gongs, reminding everyone of Sam. Jim still couldn't believe it. Only yesterday morning he and the others dashed in and out of mess halls for breakfast. Sam's death struck everyone who knew him like a whip. Especially Russell. All night Russell sat near the front door, staring at his feet. His jeans had bloodstains. His dirty shoes had tear stains. He hunched over his knees, sometimes smearing his wet cheeks with the palms of his hands. Jim understood. Unfortunately, he understood.

A rumbling of an army truck echoed outside, shaking against the quiet murmurs and random coughing. The gears squeaked, then slowly stopped. A door slammed shut. Jim rose to his feet. Something was going to happen. Russell saw a cloud of dust filter underneath the front doors and suddenly the doors opened. He gazed up and saw it was Palmer. The private glanced down at him.

"Hello, Russell," he said, nodding, and walked into the middle of the room. Raising his voice, he continued, "I'm looking for Mrs. Maruyama! Is she here?"

Rose groggily blinked. She heard her name being called out but thought she was dreaming. Lying on a cot with her four month old son, she slowly shifted to rise. Bethany and Mrs. Yoshimura began yawning while they sluggishly sat up. The Yoshimura women remained in a circle.

Jim studied the soldier, recognizing him as the nice one, and walked to his sister.

Palmer again inquired, "Is there a Mrs. Maruyama?"

"Yes," Rose answered, readjusting her baby who cackled and thus starting crying. She stood, panicking. "What's wrong? Is something wrong with my husband?"

Palmer marched to greet her. "No, ma'am. But I have orders to remove you and your husband from camp."

She was stunned. "What? Why?"

"For your safety, ma'am."

Rose turned to gawk at her family. "What about the rest of my family?"

He paused. "Sorry, Mrs. Maruyama. Just you and your husband. And your son, of course."

The idea of further separating from her family sprang more panic. Her baby continued to wail, his face shriveling and souring into redness. She automatically began swaying to calm him, although her nerves jolted Thomas Jr. Her voice became higher when she pleaded. "But why?"

Palmer sighed when he glanced at the rest of her family. He didn't like doing this. He had never agreed with the entire evacuation and its results. It wasn't his job to criticize; it was his job to follow orders.

"We need to leave immediately," he maintained. "Your husband is waiting for you in the truck. He's already gathered some of your personals."

Rose had tears in her eyes. It wasn't fair. It just wasn't. Why should she be the one to break away from her family? From Bethany? What will Bethany do without her? Particularly when her body started the change? Their mother never taught them. Rose had to figure things out by herself.

"Why can't the rest of my family come along?" she insisted under her son's wailing.

"Because," Palmer stumbled. He hated getting involved in politics. "Because, ma'am, they aren't on the *list*."

Jim looked at Rose. He didn't want her to leave. If anything, Tom should be the one leaving. She had nothing to do with the riot: A wife. A mother. A sister. She shouldn't be the one.

Rose shook her head. The damned list! What exactly did it mean? The FBI version? The WRA? Or the Worker's Union? Nobody trusted each other, that was the problem! No wonder everything whirled like a cyclone.

"Mrs. Maruyama," Palmer insisted, extending his arm. "We need to go now."

Bethany and Mrs. Yoshimura couldn't speak. What could they say?

Rose cleared her throat, glancing at the remains of her family, and stated, "I'll see you later."

They watched Rose and her crying baby follow the soldier outside. No one knew the next time they would see each other again. The government and military had a funny way of carrying out responsibilities. Russell's family split in half. One half in Manzanar, the other in Minidoka. Then Jim's family being plucked apart like feathers. Mr. Yoshimura was still concealed in Missoula. Now Rose and Tom were heading off to who knew where.

They heard the truck rumble, creak, and finally heaved away. Jim walked to the front doors, paused, and walked outside. His warm breath sailed in the breeze. The morning sun lit the sky with harsh colors. Rubbing his hands, he sniffed, watching the army truck leave the camp, watching it pass by him behind the fence and watchtower. Rose, Tom, and the baby hid inside the canvas. He would miss them, he realized. Despite how much they annoyed him, or how much he despised Tom's politics, Jim would miss them. And he didn't want to think about Sam. Everything was finally calm. He didn't want to feel anything.

Russell opened the door and stood beside him. His eyes were red and glazed. He didn't speak, only breathed, allowing his breath to catch the cold. Jim did the same. They stood outside until the breakfast gongs ceased from echoing. So, this was the first anniversary of Pearl Harbor.

~PART IV~

Go For Broke

CHAPTER ONE

Mid December, 1942

SNOW tumbled from the layer of grey clouds. Christmas lights and skinny pine trees began to ascend inside people's barracks as they tried to forget that awful week. Half of the camp laborers refused to work. They refused to work because they still wanted their complaints not only to be heard, but to have something done about them. And still nothing improved. Osamu and his fellow officers resumed their search for the perpetrators of the riot, splitting up more secret meetings, arresting more men by half a dozen. The military stepped forward and increased their patrol, allowing the Reno battalion to soar around the edges of camp with their winged bayonets fixed on their shoulders. It was now best handled by martial law. As for the prisoners who idled in Lone Pine or Independence, they would be dispersed to other camps or prisons, based on their behaviors and the crimes they had committed. And as for people like Tom and his family, the twenty-one transcendental *inus*, the WRA continued to contemplate their future while they sat in sixteen small, empty buildings inside Death Valley.

RUSSELL laid down. With his arm over his eyes, he stayed home from school again. His motivation dissolved like sand in water. He knew other people who died in the past, but none were his friends. They were just old. He could only imagine how Ikki felt. The sharp fire destroying emotions. Destroying faith. Russell should have looked harder for Sam. Sooner. When the smoke eased, just before the shooting, he had an opportunity. He had an opportunity and he kept his face on the ground instead. If he had been smarter, braver, Sam would be alive at this hour. The image of his friend's limp body consumed his shame.

The Morimotos, at the opposite end of the barrack, softly chatted about their two sons trapped in Japan. Their sons had been attending the University of Tokyo to learn business when Pearl Harbor interrupted their studies. They hadn't heard anything from their grown children in a year. The couple hoped they were at least healthy and safe; nevertheless suspected that they had already been drafted in the Imperial Army. They knew it would not be easy for their sons. American citizens caught inside a hostile island. It would not be easy at all.

Russell's parents sat in silence that afternoon. Mrs. Hamaguchi brushed her fingers through her son's hair across the table, worried for him. They had lost so much in a lifetime. And now a boy's funeral. Sighing, she returned to her lessons, stumbling over her English, slowly mumbling through the sentences, endeavoring to improve her skill with the alien language. Mr. Hamaguchi drank himself to sleep to avoid living.

Knocking rattled the Hamaguchi's door. Mrs. Hamaguchi looked up. She glanced at her husband, who appeared like a beached whale, then glanced at her son who didn't flinch at the unpredicted call. Grunting, she rose from her creaky chair to open the door.

Staring at a pretty girl on the steps, she said, "*Hai?*"

"*Good afternoon, Mrs. Hamaguchi,*" Naomi replied in polite Japanese. *"Is Russell here?"*

"Rasso?" she repeated, confused. "Oh! Goro!"

Mrs. Hamaguchi allowed Naomi to enter and then reseated herself, pretending to return to her lessons.

Russell swept his feet over the bed and awkwardly stood in front of Naomi; his heart unexpectedly alive; pounding.

"Why are you here?" he asked as if releasing his last breath.

She squeezed her fingers, leaning on one leg. "To see how you're doing. I heard about Sam." She glanced down. "I'm sorry. I really liked him."

Russell slipped his hands into his pockets. He didn't know how to respond. He hadn't dealt with this type of thing before, and didn't know the proper edicts. If there was such a thing. But he was glad she came by. He didn't realized how much he missed her until he heard her voice. Her voice could comfort a giant's rage. Clearing his throat , he said, "Yeah. Sam had a gentle nature about him. Always had."

Naomi looked at his face. His summer tan appeared to be fading. She also saw partial creases where his sleeve had been resting over his eyes. Since she hadn't seen his face in a month, she realized she missed his cocky grin. There were times his confidence made him more attractive, yet, oddly enough, he seemed older. As if he had aged a year in that passing month.

She continued, "Tomorrow's Sam's funeral. I wondered," she paused, peeking at his parents who were busy in their own world. "If you don't mind, I wondered if I could go with you."

Russell admired her. Even more so now. "Yeah, sure. I'd like that."

"I would like also to give my sympathies to Ikki. Can you take me there?"

TART incense enbalmbed Ikki's barrack, ascending to the ceiling as if lost spirits crawling to the chilled heavens. A table full of Japanese-like dishes, (fried baloney with soy sauce, ketchup soups, rice with plums and rice with spam, stir-fry with onions, canned peas, and hot dogs,) laid out partially eaten offerings from family and friends. The curtains were locked together, keeping out light. A layer of sand from yesterday's storm remained on the floor; untouched. Ikki had curled-up in his bed; covered by the army's wool blanket. His parents, aunts, and uncles crowded the slender space; shrouded by family photos. At the foot of Sam's bed, a wooden box balanced a Buddhist figure on its top with additional incense and Sam's favorite dish: *sukiyaki*. Soft murmuring honored his peaceful journey.

Ernest, Sam's older brother, answered the door. His baggy eyes indicated ashes of grief. Russell and Naomi shivered in the wind and thickening snow.

"Ru- Ru- Russell," he stuttered. "Nice to-to see you. Come in!"

Russell knocked his shoes on the steps to rid of the dirt and snow before entering. Naomi followed Russell to the middle of the room where heat extracted in circumference. Everyone kept their shoes on to preserve warmth. Not too long after arriving at Manzanar, everyone discarded the tradition of placing their shoes beside the door. The desert climate made certain customs unsuitable to uphold. The grey belly stove crackled its dominance in the dim compartment. It was a superficially raw box. But adequate. Like a cremation den. Russell introduced Naomi to Sam's family and gave his sympathies to them as well. He waited to speak to Ikki last, wanting more time with his friend. As he leaned down to touch Ikki's shoulder, Russell understood that Sam had been more like a brother to him. They were only a year apart and didn't know any different. Ikki remained motionless.

"How are you holding up?" Russell asked.

Naomi stood next to him, clasping her hands, patiently staying at his side.

Ikki coughed and moaned. He took a few heavy breaths before answering. "You know I loved him," he whispered. "Even when he got on my nerves. Which was always."

Russell's eyes began to blur. "I know."

Ikki hesitated, again taking heavy breaths. "I should of stopped him. It was my fault, Russell. It was all my fault!"

Russell stared at the back of his friend's head; a sting pulsating in his lungs. He had believed it was his responsibility. He was physically stronger than both. He had experience in handling tense situations. If anything, Russell was to blame. He squeezed Ikki's shoulder, wanting to say something clever, reassuring, but his confidence fell back when he swallowed.

Naomi bent down near Ikki's ear. She knew what it was like. The loss. The guilt. When loved ones died while the survivors lived; guilt replaced reason and unfairness. She was ten when cancer seized her mother, and thirteen when pneumonia consumed her father. Her youngest brother was seven when they were orphaned three years ago. Her relatives were either in Hawaii or Japan and could not afford to claim them, so the state of California installed them in an orphanage. A Catholic one at that. Not her first choice. Her father only converted to Catholicism just before he died because he thought to ensure the protection of his children, denouncing his old religion for a new one was the American thing to do and, therefore, would make it easier for them to be adopted. She couldn't understand why he didn't choose something else. Apparently her father didn't realize that Catholics were often discriminated against, too. Within twenty months, an Irish couple became her foster parents, and took her brother as well. They were decent people, except Naomi didn't like the food they ate: blood sausages for breakfast and haggis for dinner. Nor did she like trying to remember the names of all the saints, or being forced to incite confessions to an ancient priest who smelled like vinegar and ointment.

She said, "It wasn't any of your faults. Sam was at the wrong place, wrong time, is all. Mistakes are like tea leaves. You can only see them after the tea is poured."

Russell turned to look up at her; even more amazed by her. She also looked directly at him. At that moment, he felt a secure affection feeding his heart. It was similar to the love he felt for Maria. This strange and impeding warmth. He assumed after their break-up that would be it. They would reserve a friendly stance, although not really preserving a friendship. Now it was something else.

She maintained, "Don't blame yourselves because it'll just make you sick. And that's no way to live. When my parents . . . departed, I thought if I was a better daughter, not so selfish, then maybe . . . who knows. First I blamed them. Then I blamed myself. It's no way to live, trust me."

Ikki slowly shifted on his bed to gaze at his friends. Wetting his lips, he said, "Thanks."

RUSSELL escorted Naomi to the Children's Village. The early evening ceased to snow and allowed patches of sky to smile downward. They languid in their steps, dividing time and space into their own terms. Quietly chatting about other things, life back home, avoiding the war, avoiding the funeral, they slid into a fragmented heaven guided by solitude. The cold became more of an itch rather than an open cut. Or since they grew used to it, the temperature didn't infringe on their walk. An hour later, when the gongs announced dinner, Russell stood beside Naomi at a white picket fence that protected the orphanage. Lumber settled in the middle, and a swing set was in the process of being built. Glancing through the row of windows, seeing a nun looking directly back, he took her hand into his and cleared his throat.

"Thank you for everything," he began, wanting to kiss her. "You didn't have to."

She grinned, looking down. "I wanted to. I wouldn't of felt right if I hadn't." She then looked up. "I better get going. The sisters are very protective. Don't forget to pick me up tomorrow. I already have permission to go to the funeral."

Russell stepped closer, feeling her breath touch the side of his cheek. He nodded and grazed her long hair with his fingertips. The words almost fell out. He grinned, stepping aside, and said, "I'll see you tomorrow, then.

* * *

JIM watched Bethany pull the bed spread over her face. She missed Rose and the baby. It was evident. Recently she would lie on her bed, staring inside magazines as she sluggishly flipped through. The barrack was strangely peaceful. Without the baby's cries it now seemed barren. Jim listened to the dinner gongs drone against the sagging sun. The reverberating sounds were remnants of last week's confusion and loss. He wasn't sure if he could attend Sam's funeral. The image of his ashes being disposed like crumbled leaves in a bonfire made him queasy. Exceptionally queasy.

Mrs. Yoshimura finished folding the laundry, and carefully padded it down in the two wicker baskets. Layers of wire sprawled high across the walls, bowing from the damp heaviness earlier that morning. With the cold air, drying clothes took longer. She groaned and stood up from a chair.

"*I am so pleased I have completed this chore!*" she announced, stretching her arms upward. "*I only wish I did not have to carry the loads back and forth from the laundry house. My back is very tender.*"

Jim also stretched from the table where his battered books circled around his paper. He smelled the stale soap linger in the room. Usually the odor remained for a day, or a day and a half, depending on how quickly the wind intervened through the gaps. It wasn't the most terrible smell he had known, but it still agitated his nose. It reminded him of plaster.

"I'm not hungry, Mama," he stated, resuming to his books.

Bethany mimicked, "Me neither."

Mrs. Yoshimura crinkled her perfectly plucked brows. "*Nai*? You hafa eat! Make strong body!"

Jim glanced up. "Not with the food they serve us."

She examined her children. They resembled wilting buds from her prized garden back in Winslow. The sort of wilting that occurred after an unforeseen frost. The changes in their lives were too many, too sudden. She disliked not being able to cook healthy meals for her family and hated dining in a crowded, noisy building where she noticed families eating apart. She detested trudging down the street with heavy baskets of laundry to another crowded building where hot water was a rarity. And she resented the American government that continued to imprison her husband away from their family. Or concealing her eldest daughter in the unknown; unable to communicate with her and her grandson. Then Jim's friend, Sam, a boy whose only shame was not using his common sense.

Lately, and more often, she wished she had stayed in Japan. Hiroshima, her childhood home, at least offered threads of comfort. For years she and her husband had spoke of returning to Japan and had shared their dreams with their children. But he had never set a date for the event, defending his responsibilities to the Japanese community on Bainbridge Island. His name placed distinguished smiles on people's faces. The longer they lived on the island, the more reluctant he seemed in their desire of returning. She knew he feared that he would lose his status despite the money he had accumulated. He was not the oldest son nor was he his father's beloved son. She remembered her husband once, and only once, mentioning that if his father wasn't preoccupied with ignoring him, than he was occupied with beating him.

"*If the both of you refuse to eat*," she continued, rubbing her stiff hands, "*then I will bring something back. Neither of you will have impoverished stomachs! We do not come from a background of destitution!*"

Annoyed by her children's defiance, an unfortunate American trait, she grabbed her double-layered coat and brown mittens with a matching scarf and rubber boots, and headed out the door; ready for the approaching winter's brawl.

Jim looked at his younger sister again. He heard her sniffling. She had been crying under the blanket; however kept silent for their mother to show she was big enough to be left alone. He sighed and rose to his feet. By then, Bethany's whimpering intensified. He browsed among the books on the shelf, a small collection stacked like gaping teeth, and slid out Bethany's favorite story. Jim dragged a stool beside her head. Clearing his throat, he opened *Little Women* and began reading chapter one. Just as Rose had done many times to fill the hours.

Bethany ceased from crying. She slowly removed the cover and stared at her moody brother. As he read out loud, she didn't think it would be possible that he would think of others beside himself. Especially her.

Wiping her nose, she said, "I thought you hated me. You've always hated me."

Jim stopped in mid-sentence. He shifted his tongue in his dry mouth, peering at the wall where her crayon drawings hinged on tacks. The pictures were colorful, and actually quite good. He realized she had artistic talent despite her other attempts with the clarinet and ballet.

"I've never hated, you," he wearily confessed. "Hate is such a strong word."

"You told Tom you hated him!" she refuted.

He hesitated for a moment. "I don't hate Tom, either." Sitting upright, he finally looked at Bethany. How could he explain things so that she could comprehend? She was still a child. Her innocence and optimism weren't infected by his cynicism. For that he truly envied her. Even when he was her age, he inherited the bitterness from John. His younger sister was lucky she inherited Rose's personality instead. "Bethany, you've got to understand something first," he uneasily persisted. "I have a difficult time- showing my emotions."

"Not really," she quipped. "You just have a hard time showing more than one!"

He squinted at her. "I'm a little more versatile than that."

She rolled her eyes. "I've seen you frown and seen you snarl. You don't laugh. You sometimes smile. You're not that hard to figure out, Jim!"

"Well, thanks for pointing that out, Bethany," he said. "I'm relieved my eleven-year-old sister can see past my obvious flaws!"

She blinked. She wasn't sure how seriously she should take her brother. She began to giggle, then embarked on a surge of laughter.

Irritated, Jim stared at her.

"Oh, Jim!" she said, "you look like Papa when you get so mad!"

Offended, he asked, "Do you want me to go on or what?"

Laughing, she replied, "I pick what!"

Jim curtly sighed. Bethany's laughter faded, easing into giggling, then a smile. She looked up at her brother, the edge of his lips straining, his eyes narrowing. He really didn't answer her question. "If you don't hate me," she began, her smile straining along with his temperament, "then why are you mad all the time?"

Jim stroked the pages. He wished she would just leave certain matters alone. And yet he thought it ironic that he had asked John the same question when he was eleven. Jim remembered his brother always brooding, snapping at him, reading *The Last of the Mohicans* to him; occasionally. Life was more difficult for John because he was the oldest son and the responsibilities spiraled around him like barbed wire. Now that Jim inherited the responsibilities, he wished he could sever the link.

He finally replied in a hollow tone, "Sometimes that's the way things are."

"Then why don't you change things?"

Jim shifted his feet, extending one leg out, looking down into the book, his thoughts gyrating over the black print. Bethany was not only too young to understand, but she was also a girl.

She rose from her pillow and gently tugged on her brother's sleeve. He looked up at her. "Why don't we ever talk about John? I remember him. But sometimes it gets really hard."

Stunned, he slashed his glance down onto his wrists. He snapped, "Dammit, Bethany! Grow up!"

Hurt, she plopped down on her pillow and crossed her arms over her chest. She wanted to cry, but was afraid to. Instead she locked her eyes shut.

Feeling guilty, seeing the damage on her faultless face, Jim reached out and stroked her forehead. His silent apology only padded his superficial intentions. Removing his hand, he continued to read the first chapter out loud, repeating some of the sentences he already recited as if caught in a circle.

* * *

THE morning languished with clouds entombing the sun as snow crumpled down, continuously, settling on the hardening earth. Two families stood outside the fence, encountering Mount Williamson's spiny point that gazed down at the wooden and raw stone tombstones. The cemetery was small, only squaring out in the distance of a fourth of a block. Everyone dressed in black. Ernest held Sam's urn. Russell stood beside Ikki. Naomi stood beside Russell. Even Mr. Friordi attended the service; the only white person who did so. Muffled sobs defied the silence. Ernest then walked forward, ignoring the watchtower that overlooked that particular corner of the camp, confronting the East. He lifted the top and let the desert wind take Sam's ashes further east; toward the thick wall of mountains, away from the west; away from Manzanar.

Naomi reached for Russell's hand and slipped her gloved fingers between his.

Sam's mother broke into strenuous weeping as she watched her son's ashes flutter as if an eagle's shadow. Her fierce cries splintered the sky in half, dividing land and clouds, dividing heaven and earth.

Russell shut his eyes, feeling his throat burn.

Naomi's tears fluttered down her face. The loss of her parents still rested at every funeral she attended, and yet with war raging, she knew she would be attending many more.

Director Bridges had allowed this particular memorial service for family and friends only. Russell was like family. Bainbridge Island was like a bloodline of mixed breeds. How he missed home. He missed fishing on the banks facing Seattle. Or the sweet fragrance of the strawberry fields. Or sharing playful insults with his friends, trying to outdo one another. Dave continued to write letters and informed him about some of the changes or gossip of Winslow. More and more of Russell's friends were being drafted into the war. The lists of casualties flourished like weeds in an abandoned yard. This year Dave would be on the draft list. Russell wished he could do something. To fight. If he could fight, then Sam's death would have dignity. And he could restore his own family's name. And the rest of the world would respect them regardless of their race.

Christmas Eve

A RADIO faintly chimed Christmas music. Tom rapidly clinked the tin cup with a shaving brush, swirling the cream into fullness. The mirror belonged to his wife; a rounded metal piece with an adjustable neck. He lathered his face, including his mustache. Children's laughter vibrated through the narrow room; a decomposing shack with a cracked, wooden ceiling. He could hear his own son's contented gurgling. Eight cots were aligned along the two opposing walls. Suitcases were either tucked underneath the cots or sat at the foot of them. A scrawny pine tree stood in the middle with popcorn strings wrapped around it, and colorfully shiny balls dangling on the limbs. A golden tin star was perched on the top. Other than the tree, the room was completely bare of luxuries. At that moment, regular barracks seemed more appealing and cozy.

Four adults and four children crammed in one of sixteen buildings assembled around the Death Valley National Monument. The other sixty refugees were scattered in the remaining shacks. This was Cow Creek camp. The chill in the building was no different than the barracks. A soldier paced around the cold, dusty encampment. These abandoned shacks now became an asylum for those whose names were on the endangered list. Now their names were on a waiting list; waiting for another relocation. Perhaps to other camps. Perhaps to other cities in the Midwest or East Coast.

Tom hoped to move to Chicago or Detroit, any place outside of wire fencing and isolation. Three weeks ago he had put in a request, searching for a sponsor, searching for any kind of work reasonable enough to support his family. A clerk. A factory worker. He read that women and Negroes were allowed to build airplanes and tanks. He would be willing to do that. And Director Bridges personally promised the transfer. Glancing at Rose, who buttoned up her blouse after breast feeding, Tom saw her return his glance. They rarely spoke to each other since their arrival. He knew she blamed him for separating her from the rest of her family. And could he truly resent her for that? He was the reason they were there. He breathed painfully with bruised ribs and a black eye. Rose shifted the baby onto her shoulders to burp him. Tom then began scraping his chin with his razor. He wished he could give his family Christmas gifts to make up for their situation.

A chain of dainty chimes jingled from the outside. Baffled, Tom lowered his blade; his face half-shaved, including his mustache, and directly looked at Rose. She looked at the door. The front door opened and a soldier dressed in a bright Santa suit entered, carrying a fat burlap sack. He released a loud series of "Ho–Ho-Hos" while thumping on the floor as if he were a large man beneath the red suit of pillows. His creamy beard and curled mustache jiggled with the miniature bells wrapped around his bloated waist. The children squealed and clapped their hands as they ran to Santa. The delirium in their small eyes touched soft smiles on parents' faces. Because no one had the resources or conveniences to buy or make presents, each believed this year would end in complete gloom.

Palmer exaggerated his laughter, imitating the Santa he knew as a child. He tried to deepen his young voice when he spoke to each child; each of whom he personally remembered their names. Gently patting their heads, he set the sac down and began giving out wrapped presents. A group of his friends in his unit donated money to purchase toys for these children who were stuck in no man's land. The two towns likewise promoted the same for the rest in Manzanar. Although Palmer and the others were aware that not all Japanese and Japanese-Americans celebrated Christmas, but for those who did they had hoped it would make one night happier.

Rose finally looked at her husband. The soldier's kindness caused her fatigued eyes to blur. Sometimes it was easy to forget charity. It was easy to forget when charity drifted with the desert winds. Staring at his half-cleaned face, stunned to see his adorned mustache vanishing, she asked, "Tom, what are you doing?"

"What does it look like I'm doing?"

"What I mean is I thought you loved that silly mustache of yours. Why are finally shaving it?"

He wiped his blade on a towel that lay over his shoulder. Without using hot water, skimming the blade on his skin felt more like cutting. It burned a bit. And it bled a bit. He continued to carve off his mustache, letting the hair fall into a bowl over his lap. He knew Sam. He went to school with Sam's brother. Letting his guilt scatter into the shallowness of the bowl, Tom wished he could have changed the circumstances of the riot.

"I don't need it anymore," he replied. "I suppose I never really needed it."

Rose shyly smiled. "That's what I've been telling you for months. It wasn't really meant to be for you. You're not like Ted. Or his clique."

He studied her face. It had been months since he carefully explored the changes in her. Her trimmed hair. Her flushed cheeks. Her prominent smile. From the corner of his eye, he saw Palmer hand out presents to the children, but he didn't notice much else.

He mournfully responded, "I am sorry for everything. I promise to make things better. And I promise to be a better husband, too."

TOMIKO laughed as she securely clutched Jim's hand running down the street. He tugged her arm in another direction, hiding from public view behind a dense shrub. Their pea-green coats conserved their body heat against the sharp wind that slashed through. Jim wanted to give Tomiko's present in private, not to mention he wanted an intimate moment with her. He kissed her as long as the sun's rays yielded, just before the setting of the evening. Each day it became harder to say goodnight without aching. Once he graduated from high school and found a reliable job, he wanted to marry her as soon as possible. The nights were becoming unbearable. Then after they married they could move to someplace else other than Winslow. For years he conceived of traveling far from home. From his father's dominance. From his brother's grave.

She whispered, "I got you something."

"So did I."

Together they reached inside their pockets to exchange small gifts. He dressed her present in newspaper. She dressed his present in flowered cloth with green yarn.

"You first," she announced.

"I would rather you go first," he replied.

Smiling, she leaned forward to briefly kiss him again. "Alright, if you insist! By they way, I love the paper you chose. You can't get any more practical than this."

He grinned in turn. "I spared no expense."

"Oh, obviously."

Like a cat tearing into a couch, Tomiko ripped the paper in half. Staring at the black velvety box, she gently rubbed it. It was a jewelry box. Astonished, she looked at him for a time before pinching it open. Then she saw it. A golden ring with a speckle of a diamond. Quickly covering her mouth, her eyes became teary.

"I don't make promises I don't intend to keep," he said.

Shaking, she slowly removed the ring and slipped it on her left hand. It was tight, although something that could be easily fixed, and something so perfect she wasn't willing to tell him of the minor inconvenience.

He continued, "I know it's not much, but someday I'll get you a better one."

Breathing rapidly, she asked, "How could you afford this one?"

"I've always saved money back. I had planned to buy my own car, except," he cleared his throat, "this is more important."

She had known he was special. All he needed was having someone believing in him. No longer feeling the frosty wind, she proclaimed, "I love you!"

He smiled. "I'm glad somebody does."

Jim unwrapped his gift and looked inside. It was a silver tie pin in a shape of a Morning Glory. Picking it up, he studied the elegant piece. It looked familiar.

"This is wonderful," he said. "This'll be great when I get another suit. Thank you so much." He leaned forward and kissed her.

Moving back, Tomiko beamed. She expressed, "It used to be your brother's. He gave it to my sister when they first dated. I thought you'd like it!"

His smile fell. The only other thing he had of his brother's were those stupid deck of cards. His family dreaded remembering John. It released so much pain. And Jim could never forget his brother's face frozen on the floor. Shriveled. Rooted in anguish. And to have something that reminded him of John's affliction: this pin which connected both families to shame, how could Tomiko even consider such a bitter gift? Suddenly he became ill.

"I can't take this!" he spouted, giving it back to her.

"What?" she blinked, completely stunned. "I don't understand. Why not?"

Feeling dizzy, he dropped it. "Tomiko! Don't you know this is inappropriate?"

Tears began to swell. Her voice weakened. "Jim, why are you overreacting? I know how important your brother was to you. Why don't you want it?"

"You don't give back dead people's things! You just don't! Especially knowing the history between your sister and my brother!"

He felt his skin blaze. The dreams about John and Tomiko choked his breathing. None of it made sense. None of it could make sense. He didn't even know where he fit among any of it.

Angered, she retorted, "And what manual did you read that from? A guide for rejection?" She rose to her feet. Wiping the tears from her cheeks, she persisted, "Jim, tell me what's really bothering you? Why can't you accept this?"

"I've got to go!" he muttered, walking away.

Tomiko followed him, wanting to understand and was tired of him going into silence. She cried out, "You're not the only one who's hurting, Jim! I thought surely your brother was going to marry my sister! I miss him, too, you know!"

He snapped, "I don't want to talk about it!"

She stopped as her tears flared. Desperate, she blurted, "Did you know it wasn't even his baby? It wasn't John's baby!"

Jim tripped, nearly forgetting his balance. Not believing her, not understanding what she was implying, he blinked fervently. Hesitating for a moment longer, he walked back to her. The dull street light dimmed her face and all he could see was the brittle reflection in her dark irises. She began shaking her head, looking down.

"Nobody knows," she whispered. "Kiyoko didn't say anything about it until much later. But I doubt it would had made much of a difference."

Jim felt numb. His body and speech were paralyzed.

She continued with a quiet declaration. "I think your brother knew. This isn't easy for me to say." She bit her tongue as her hands trembled. "She was raped. She tried to kill herself. So my father sent her to Tacoma to get help for her. Far from the gossip. But she didn't have the baby." Tomiko's voice decayed.

Wiping the tears continuously from her face, she barely resumed, "She couldn't bear the thought of having it. So my father took care of that, too."

Jim stared at her, unable to think clearly. How could he react to something like that? John had to have known. Why else would he have felt the need to die painfully? To perhaps feel responsible even?

He finally said, "I didn't know."

Sniffling, she said, "No one knew. No one outside of my family."

Jim stepped closer, wanting to comfort her, yet feeling a tight strain in his stomach pulling him the other way.

She looked up, almost beseechingly. Why couldn't he just reach out to her? Why the reluctance? She had been patient, understanding his loss of a brother. Treading closer, she bundled her arms around him, holding tightly, wanting to feel the warmth.

He whispered, "Did she say who did it?"

"Yes."

Again he hesitated. "Was it someone she knew?"

Tomiko exhaled caution. "John's friend. Robert."

He backed away. "Robert Pope?"

"Yes."

Jim clearly remembered Robert Pope. The bully who slugged a rock at John's forehead. And Russell who guided John to Dr. Ellis's house for stitches. Robert Pope, who wasn't a saint by a long shot, nor a friend of John's, was also Leo Riley's cousin.

Outrage and hate bulged inside his veins like ripened, rotting yeast: raising; fermenting; spoiling. As far as Jim knew, Robert freely wandered about Bainbridge Island without punishment for his crimes; crimes he actually inflicted. So why wasn't *that* bastard behind a goddamn fence?

"I've got to go!" he announced, pushing out of her embrace. "I've got to be by myself!"

Stunned, Tomiko watched Jim run off in the distance and vanish through the row of barracks. Hurt, feeling rejected, she just stood there. She didn't know what else to do as she held both the ring and silver pin in the same hand.

CHAPTER TWO

Early Winter, 1943

RUSSEL rocked his cards from side to side. He was on the verge of beating Jim one more time. Jim couldn't bluff his way out of hell if he wanted. Yet Russell was more concerned with his friend's silent treatment with Tomiko. Naomi told him a little about the unexpected rift after talking to Tomiko.

Sighing, he announced, "Sometimes I just don't get you. I think you need to see a shrink."

Jim shuffled his cards, sorting his formation of clubs and diamonds according to value. He shifted in his chair, and snapped, "You don't need to *get me*, Russell! I wasn't brought into this world for your leisure."

Russell glanced at him. Jim was in one of his pissy moods. "Oh, that's obvious!" he quipped. "You were brought into this world to fuss at!"

"And what do you know?"

"I know you're spending the New Year with me instead of Tomiko. Why are you avoiding her?" He waited for a response. When nothing slipped from Jim's mouth, he pursued, "I'm telling you, man, go tell her you're sorry. Tell her you lost your head because of everything this month."

Jim thinned his eyes. "It's more complicated than that."

"Oh, geez!" he exhaled. "Listen, how can anyone understand where you're comin' from? You clamp up quicker than a new pair of jock straps! What the hell is so important in that head of yours that nobody can understand?"

Jim stared past Russell, staring directly at nothing. The flowered curtains sagged like a cheap dress; flimsy in texture; tacky in design. Cheap and vain. Trying to hide the clutter from the outside world. Lights dimmed. The newscaster's voice related the deadlock in Stalingrad between the Nazis and the Russians. The deadlock implied no outcome of hope. Or miracles as million of people were being slaughtered. He closed his eyes. He could still see John's deadly petrified face; which was the reason he didn't attend Sam's funeral. Jim couldn't. If he had, he feared he would crumble into imperfect pieces.

Clearing his tight throat, he said, "My brother died very young."

Russell lowered his winning hand on the table. He slowly nodded, knowing the pain Jim continued to bare. For the first time in his life, he knew.

"Yeah," Russell replied. "My parents took me to your brother's memorial service. It's bizarre how he had an allergic reaction to something he ate. Too bad Dr. Ellis couldn't find out what it was. It would of been nice to know. Bring some sort of peace, I think."

Glaring up at Russell, Jim admitted bitterly, "The doctor knew, Russell. He was helping to protect my family's reputation. Well, protecting my father's reputation anyway. Who cares what the rest of us think!" He paused to carefully study his friend, not sure if he trusted Russell enough to tell him, but he felt the need to tell someone. Jim was tired of pretending that his brother's suicide was an accident.

"John ate rat poison."

Russell stared. "What?"

"He chose. . . to eat rat poison. He went through convolutions. Died in the attic. Died in severe pain and completely alone."

Jim suddenly lost his voice. His eyes singed, then blurred. The sharp pain he first experienced when he was twelve returned in his stomach. Shaking his head, he dropped his cards on the floor and stood up. The room whirled. His ears clattered. He began gasping for air and he couldn't find room in his lungs to breath. Panicking, he felt as though his lungs had collapsed, or were submerged in seawater.

Russell jumped up.

"You need to calm down, Jim!" he said, resting his hands on Jim's shoulders and guiding him toward his cot. "Put your head between your knees and slowly take deep breaths. If not you'll pass out."

Jim obeyed. Yellow specks blotted his vision, diffusing like grease in water. He couldn't believe what was happening to him. Normally he could control his emotions. His abrupt breathing worsened the more he thought about it. The dizziness rattled his head.

"Jim!" Russell barked. "You need to stay focused! Focus on deep breaths. Inhale," he paused, waiting. Jim wasn't listening. "I said inhale! You're turning blue!"

Jim gasped.

"Now exhale."

Jim finally followed the instructions.

"Again!" Russell encouraged. "Inhale . . . exhale . . ."

Jim lowered his face into his palms, feeling his mouth dry out and eyes stinging. He removed his glasses and squeezed them in between his fingers. The dreams at night were rotting his mind.

Russell said, "You're gonna be alright. You'll be just fine."

He examined Jim, genuinely concerned. Rubbing his back in circular motions, Russell sat down beside him and couldn't imagine what it would have been like lugging that kind of torment around for four years. No wonder the guy was so botched up! Not only dealing with the death of his brother, but a suicide? It was one of the greatest shame any family could endure in a lifetime.

"This coming spring," Russell began, "I hear Idaho is looking for laborers. Maybe we ought to volunteer for work. Get out of here for a while. Earn our own money."

Jim's breathing slowly returned to normal. A type of relief toppled off his back. It was almost like opening a bottle of cola and allowing the fizz to ooze out. It was soothing to share that burden. That secret with someone else. And for the sake of John, his memory could be shared, despite the stigma. Exhaling heavily, Jim resettled his glasses over his nose and bent forward.

Jim continued, "Tomiko just told why my brother killed himself. I had always believed it was because of my father. Well, to some degree, he didn't help John. My father keeps pushing and pushing until you feel like killing yourself."

Russell lifted his brows. "Jesus. You really need a hobby." He paused. "I have to admit, I thought it was strange when John died and Kiyoko disappeared that same week. Was one of the reasons . . . connected to . . . Kiyoko?"

Jim glanced up at him. He didn't mind telling Russell about his brother's suicide, althoug he knew it wasn't in his place to reveal about Tomiko's sister. Looking down, he didn't know what else to say. They sat in silence for a while, staring at the floor. The wind whistled and wheezed through the cracks. Distant music from a neighboring barrack echoed.

"Do you mind me asking if it was because . . ." Russell hesitated to clear his throat, "because Kiyoko got pregnant?"

Jim only answered with a reluctant nod and remained silent for another minute. "Tomiko doesn't even know about my brother," he finally said. "She still thinks my brother died from an allergic reaction; like everyone else in this narrow-minded community." He moaned. "I can't tell her. How could I tell her something like that? She won't respect me or my family again!"

"And yet it's okay to tell me," Russell humorously began, "because I *never* respected you."

Jim exhaled in frustration. "It's different with you, Russell! You're not judgmental." He paused as he slowly shook his head. He wished he could simply disappear. "And the worst part of the whole situation is . . . it wasn't even John's baby. She was violated. And because she was violated she had an abortion."

Russell, for the first time in his life, had nothing to say. Too shocked to make a wisecrack to ease Jim's pain, he remained immobile.

"It's goddamn pathetic," Jim continued, "the way events play out. I wish I could have changed things."

Russell pinched his brows. He began breathing deeply, allowing all of this information to submerge. While he thought quietly, certain aspects of Jim's life began to clarify itself: Why he was so moody. Why he was so critical. Why he had a difficult time forgiving people.

Sitting upright, he said, "You're worried about Tomiko no longer respecting you, but she unloaded a lot of embarrassing stuff about her family, too. Don't you think she's just as worried? Don't you think she's trying to make sense out of all of this, too? She confided in you. And what bonehead thing did you do? Walk away. How do you think Tomiko is feeling right now? Aside from feeling rejected by someone she cares about."

Surprised, Jim turned to look his friend. "Growing up, I've always had this perception that you were just another dumb jock."

He chuckled. "That's okay. I always thought you were an uptight snob. Now that we know you're wrong about me, how are we going to change my opinion about you?"

Jim eased what appeared like a grin. "Thanks, Russell. You're the only real friend I ever had in my worthless life. Well, you and Tomiko." He closed his eyes and deeply inhaled. "I just don't understand why everything has to be so fucked-up."

Russell sighed, tilting his head in aching thought, fully understanding the wounds Jim endured. "Then I guess it's true what they say. It can't be helped."

"Can it?" he said, snapping his eyes open. "I *hate* that stupid Japanese expression! It implies *no* responsibility for your actions! The things that you do or don't do!"

"Well, uh, I suppose it does. But aren't you taking on more responsibility than you can handle? I mean, there are things we can control in our lives, but there are a lot of other things that are just out of our hands. You couldn't control the circumstances that happened to your brother. We can't control what happens in war. Can't control who lives or who . . ." he stumbled on the thought and cleared his throat to finish, "or who dies."

Jim sat upright. "You miss my point, Russell. I understand we don't have control over everything in our lives. What I'm saying is *after* these events take place, we have a choice what to do next. Take responsibility for the decisions we make thereafter." Suddenly, he stood up and began pacing furiously. "We really did have a choice to not come to this fucking place! Like that Fred Korematsu guy! Granted, he's in prison for *disobeying*, but he still made that choice! And I know there are others!"

"What's one kind of prison over another, Jim?" he shrugged.

As if Russell hadn't said a word, Jim persisted his ranting. "And do you think my father had taken responsibility in my brother's death? *Hell* no! What does he do instead? Burn or throw everything away that had anything to do with John! As if the poor bastard didn't even exist!"

"What! Really?"

"Because it's the Japanese tradition to not make waves, not to disturb the peace like the sheep that we are, we all flock together waiting to get our heads chopped off!"

"I don't think the Japanese military is really being all that peaceful."

"And here we are, stuck, because none of us had the balls to take the responsibility to stand up for ourselves! If I had stood up for John, then maybe he might still be alive today!"

"Ahhhh . . . what exactly are we talking about? The camps or your brother?"

Stopping in the middle of the room, he looked at Russell again. "Haven't you been listening?"

Dumbfounded, Russell stared back at Jim. "I'm not sure. You keep going back and forth."

"Ah!" he whisked in aggravation and finally sat down on a chair; his right leg rattling while he slid his hands through his hair. "Screw it!" he muttered. "It really doesn't matter now!"

Russell waited to see if Jim was done. When a minute had surpassed in peace, he said, "Jim, I want you to know I'm honored you told me these things. And as your friend, I won't abuse this trust."

Jim's leg came to a standstill and he rested his hands in his lap. "I know you won't. I think you're the only person who wouldn't."

"And Tomiko. Don't forget about your girlfriend."

He paused and quietly repeated, "And Tomiko."

"So now, go and tell her you're sorry. And tell her what you told me. She obviously trusted you with her family secrets, so you need to do the same, *omono-san.*"

Jim studied his friend in awe. Shaking his head, he remarked, "When did you get so smart?"

He snickered. "This last year I had a lot of time to grow-up. Not by *my* choice, of course," he winked.

* * *

MARIA sat in the middle of her bedroom with a scrapbook she began since the evacuation last year. Her thick dark hair was tied in a ponytail. Her long neck slightly arched while she snipped through *The Bainbridge Review*, cutting out the weekly printed letters that Tomiko habitually wrote to Mr. Woodward as he habitually printed them in his paper. Her record player gently vibrated Billy Holiday's dolorous mood. The smallness of her room was at least private; remote from her parents. The closing of her door opened freedom from her father. She kept all of Russell's letters and Woodward's newspaper articles of this internment place called Manzanar in her book. She wanted to understand as much as possible. Tomiko's words attempted to relate the experiences a thousand miles away from the lusciousness of her island, comparing the sea to sand, the glistening blues of the calm waves to the blistering yellows of the wind storms, the longing for moisture against the dryness.

She remembered the first time Russell asked her out. She remembered what both were wearing the day of the Strawberry Festival. She had on a colorfully striped cap matching her skirt and socks. Her two-toned shoes gleamed after half an hour worth of polishing. Her cream-colored blouse was sharply ironed and fashionably laced. Without her parent's permission, she borrowed red lipstick from a friend. Russell wore tanned slacks and a striped vest. She thought someday she would marry him, however her expectations had been disrupted by war. Unlike her father, she knew it was stupid to blame the Japanese-Americans for the cruelty that occurred across the ocean. It was stupid because her father should know better. They knew what it was like being harassed because of the color of their skin and the shape of their eyes.

Fortunately Dave had proven to be a dedicated friend to Russell. She would use him to send and receive letters from Russell. Although she suspected he was seeing another girl in camp, and the thought of it stung her, she still hoped he would fulfill his promise to come back home. Mario had begun to show interest in her. She agreed to attend movies and dances with him partly out of loneliness, and partly to please her father. When she started dating Mario, a boy who was also Filipino, her father started speaking to her again. She felt guilty using him, but then she thought as long as it wasn't all that serious, than what was the harm?

Mid January

DIRECTOR Bridges stood outside of the administration building; awkwardly close to the highway; reminding everyone that this road could lead them out of imprisonment. His long coat flapped in the stiff wind; his naked face reddening under the late afternoon chill. He squinted and shivered, watching a few stands of people dash across the primitive streets. In spite of the unfortunate riot, and fortunately the radicals were removed out of Bridges' hands, President Roosevelt had begun to have doubts about the camps. Bridges was friends with the President since the New Deal, and together they worked for the rights of the underprivileged. He knew Roosevelt had never felt comfortable about the entire situation. He and Biddle, the Attorney General. Words like, "concentration camp" or "prison camps" didn't pacify their conscience. Roosevelt initially gave the decision to Biddle, and Biddle gave the decision back to Roosevelt. No one wanted the burden, not to mention Eleanor had been angry with her husband from the start. Caught between the belligerence of Congress and General DeWitt, and between the belligerence of the Japanese military and the American public, Roosevelt played "spin the bottle" with these people's future. Politics. Now that should be a four letter word.

Flecks of grit rattled against his glasses. Understanding the depraved morality, Bridges had to think of something to change it. If some of these young men were going to fight in the war, they needed a good reason. Roosevelt had brought up the subject, after the enduring persistence of the JACL. A unit of *Nisei* Hawaiians were already in Europe, enduring the highest casualty rate for the army. Those men wanted respect for their people so badly they exploited their own blood. It was men like those fellows who made Congress take another look at the Japanese-Americans. And it would be Bridges' job to prepare these Americans for the occasion.

* * *

RUSSELL glanced at his Judo instructor who tossed coal into the two tin stoves, sullying his fingers. Russell aligned his shoes with a few others and walked across the room to help two other students, in their twenties, lay out the mats. Hauling the bucket of coal back into the corner, the instructor wiped his hands on a stained towel. Russell then glanced up at the clock hanging next to a painting of Buddha.

"Toru-san," Russell began, walking to his instructor in his dingy socks. "How much longer is Shikami not going to show? It's been a month."

Toru grunted as he scooped his fingers into a can of balm and rubbed it into his skin. He had been impressed with Russell's dedication; in spite of the circumstances. Knowing Russell had lost a friend last month, yet there he stood, wanting more out of life. Toru had hoped his nephew would extend the same devotion, but since the riot, he seemed to have lost all faith. Both Toru and Shikami were there to support the cause. Both had wanted to be a part of something greater than themselves in order to help make improvements inside the camp. Instead, everything got out of hand: Men were wounded. Families separated- again. And nothing improved.

"*Shirimasen*," he sighed and slightly shivered in the nippy air. "I wish I did know." Studying Russell, he professed, "You hafe a strong spirit. Maybe not ohways best judgment, but a spirit deserving a warrior's heart."

Russell revealed an embarrassed smile, and replied with a formal acknowledgment, "*Goshin setsu-ni*."

Russell had appreciated his father's stories about a great-grandfather who descended from the Samurai tradition; however, it was a tradition he knew little about. He didn't grow up in Japan or Japantown. In fact, his Japanese was just about as reliable as his parents' English. Manzanar was the closest thing to *Nippon* culture he ever expected to experience. The theater. Tea classes and ceremonial dancing his mother and sister were attending. Judo even. And there was a rumor that this spring a prevalent garden-park would be constructed featuring a pond, a bridge, trees, and exotic flowers. That would be nice.

He asked, "What about Shikami? What kind of spirit does he have?"

Toru languished before answering. "His spirit is strong, but distorted." He placed his hand on Russell's shoulder; seriousness always present when he spoke. "I know you an' my nephew only to'erate each otha. An' both show respect to me, *daijobu desu*. But is more impor'tent to confront probrems by yur mind first, den yur fist. Follow dis road- *kono michi-o itte kudasai. Hai?*"

Russell nodded. "*Hai*."

He released Russell and clapped his hands, ordering his students to begin their stretching positions. Russell had admired Toru for the last three months; even to the point of wishing Toru was his father. His father continued to drink until he passed out every night, constantly smuggling in *saki* from somewhere since he was forbidden to own another stillery. Russell couldn't understand it. The mumbling. The self-pity. His father frequently hid at the community center to avoid coming home; until curfew. It was as if his father was no longer with his family and might as well had stayed in Montana with Mr. Yoshimura. At least Russell wouldn't have to live with the embarrassing fact that his father was the known drunk on Block Eleven.

MR. HAMAGUCHI gazed over his own folded hands on the square table, then glanced up at his wife who poured hot green tea for Meito and Osamu. His cup sat in a delicate dish; steaming. Because he knew this family gathering was important, he didn't drink any alcohol. His wife continued to ignore him. Didn't she see that he was completely sober today? And that he shaved? Why couldn't she appreciate his efforts?

Osamu said first, "*This new tea set is very pretty, Mama. Masako and I knew you would enjoy this gift.*"

"*Domo arigato,*" she replied, grinning and bowing.

Osamu continued, "*I had wanted to tell all of you sooner, however, at the time it has been a difficult choice.*" He carefully glanced at his in-laws who looked at him with great concern. His mother-in-law slowly sat down, still holding her tea pot. Last night he already told his parents; which was wearisome as he tried to compel his mother to cease from crying. Masaku didn't have the heart to tell her parents, so he reluctantly volunteered to cease his wife from crying as well. He uncomfortably proceeded, "*Masako and I have found a sponsor in Maine. I have an opportunity to work in a fish mill. Next week we will be leaving.*"

Meito half-smiled; more envious than heartbroken. "Well, congratulations, Osamu! I'm glad you're able escape this place."

Mr. and Mrs. Hamaguchi appeared panic-stricken. This meant their family was splitting further apart; abandoning them for another place they didn't know existed. America was so enormous it seemed dreadfully easy to get lost in it.

Mrs. Hamaguchi gasped, "*What about Winslow? Do you not wish to return home?*"

"*Hai,*" he said. "*We would like to return home. But as of now, we need to find another way for our future. There is none here.*"

Mrs. Hamaguchi desperately glanced all around her barrack, feeling her heart beat as fast as a rabbit's careless bolt. Her long hair was neatly tied in her routine bun; her graying streaks as prevalent as the progressing creases on her middle-aged face. Still, she refused to wear glasses to advance her appearances.

She asked, "*How far is Maine?*"

"*About three thousand miles,*" Osamu steadily replied.

"*Yoku nai!*" she cried. "*You cannot take my daughter and grandchild from me!*"

Meito firmly interjected, "*Mama, isn't that a little unfair to demand? He is thinking about their future as well.*"

Her outrage trembled through her fingers, and tightened the wrinkles on her forehead. No one touched the tea cups, fidgeting around the table. Too many changes had occurred in one year. She knew once the first attempt to abandon her began, the others would follow. At this rate, she would be left alone with her husband!

"*Yoku nai!*" she maintained. "*Family should not dispose of family!*"

Meito heavily sighed. She rarely was an agreeable woman. "*It is not as though they are leaving forever, Mama. It is not as though they have left Japan to come here.*"

Mrs. Hamaguchi stared at Meito, shocked. Being a picture bride was something she wasn't proud of. She wasn't allowed to attend her father's funeral because of the shameful legacy she left in her village. She bitterly countered, "*Do not compare my departure to Masako's. The circumstances were very different.*"

"*That is my point, Mama.*"

"*If you have not lived my life, then you have no point!*"

Meito blinked, jolted by her harsh reaction.

Mr. Hamaguchi interrupted, "*Osamu, will you remember to write to us, yes?*"

"*Of course, Papa-san,*" he smiled. "*And we will also send many photos!*"

Mr. Hamaguchi leaned back in his chair and inspected his son-in-law. A nice-looking young man with a modest appeal. He had come from a hard-working family, and so Mr. Hamaguchi never worried about his daughter's choice. Although he hoped to remain together as a family, he understood his children were adults who needed their freedom.

Meito interjected, "*Mama, do you remember when we signed a petition to be removed from Manzanar? So that we can be relocated with the rest of our family in Idaho?*"

Osamu glanced at Meito, a bit relieved he changed the subject, and delicately sipped his hot cup.

"*A friend told me that the petition has been approved by the WRA,*" he continued, tapping his knuckles on the table. "*Sometime next month we will be escorted to camp Minidoka.*" He hesitated to analyze his mother's blank expression. "*Is that not good news, Mama?*"

She stayed muted and unwilling to budge.

Mr. Hamaguchi had hoped for change. Since his arrival in Manzanar, he began contemplating suicide; so perhaps this change would return some of his dignity. He remarked in his wife's place, "*Hai, good news! We did not have the chance to say our goodbyes at evacuation. This will make up for it.*"

Mrs. Hamaguchi slowly stood and brushed lent off her sleeve. "*Just because you have countered good news with bad news does not make me pleased.*"

Meito knew better. "*It will make Masako happy if you could at least pretend to be glad for her. She values your approval. If she is unhappy, then it is you who will cause her unhappiness. And perhaps a thousand years of bad luck.*"

She winced. "*You are only clever because you have a clever mother.*" She glanced at her husband who peered up at her. Acknowledging her wifely obligations, she reluctantly added, "*And your wisdom from your father.*" She sat down again, carefully mulling over her options while sipping her tea. The three men sat in patience waiting for her decision; as they should.

Late January

RUSSELL waited by the white picket fence. He had walked eight blocks from his barrack to the orphanage, hoping to walk Naomi to breakfast. Streaming snowflakes draped the horizon like powdered sugar. The snow was an odd, comforting feeling. It reminded him of home. In fact, the first time he kissed it was snowing. A *Nisei* girl in his freshman class. They had volunteered to decorate for the Winter Dance and ended up kissing underneath the bleachers. After that, the girl attended the dance with someone else. Crushed and offended, Russell had asked Tomiko out. He chuckled at the memory. They went to a couple of movies since then, although they never really did hit it off. Perhaps she had her eye on Jim even at that point. What for, Russell could only speculate the worst.

He shivered. His wool gloves itched; although at least resisted the biting chill. The front doors opened and a nun with her winged hat, buttoning her dull green coat, escorted the children down the steps. The children, ranging from kindergarten to second grade, were tightly wrapped in thick coats and gloves. Some wore red rubber boots. Others had long scarves and knitted caps. They excitedly chatted as another nun walked out, telling the children to stay in line. Russell moved from the gate. The two nuns suspiciously glanced at him, no doubt wondering why he prowled behind their shielded fence. More children poured from the front door, pacing in a systematic order. Another winged nun in a pea coat popped out. She recognized him. Russell saw the squinting recognition and looked away. His face was stained red from the lengthy walk and wait. Naomi slowly exited with the older group. When she spotted Russell, she smiled. The nun promptly stepped toward him, placing her hands inside her pockets. As a woman in her forties, her smooth skin beguiled her age. Her small mouth revealed a sturdy tactic. Standing on the opposite side of the fence, she cleared her throat. Russell finally had to confront her.

"*I have seen you a few times before, my son,*" she softly declared.

"I wouldn't argue against that, ma'am."

"*If you are truly interested in Naomi,*" she paused, examining him, "*then perhaps a more proper way of seeing her is by attending some of our sermons.*"

Russell flinched at that thought. He didn't realize he needed to cross the moat before he would be allowed to continue to see Naomi. He replied in his parents' language, "*I am Buddhist.*"

She grinned. "*I was also born Buddhist back in Japan. There are many reasons to find purpose in this life. A priest saved me from being sold into prostitution.*" She peeked at Naomi who lethargically walked by them, pretending not to listen. "*Who will be your savior?*"

He looked directly at the nun. "I do remember you. You made this offer before. In the mess hall."

She finally eased a smile. "*What kind of nun would I be if I do not fulfill my mission?*" Then swapping into Russell's natural language, she said, "You think about it, my ah son."

Slightly coughing and sniffing, he watched Naomi amble down the street. Glancing back to the nun, he said, "Yeah, sure. I'll give it a thought. See ya later, ma'am!"

Relieved to skip out from the inquisition, he trotted by Naomi's side. Glad that she chose to attend public school instead of being stashed inside the church for her education, he had also planned to walk her to class after breakfast.

"Good morning," Russell smiled.

Beaming, she asked, "So what did you two talk about?"

"Oh!" he chuckled. "I think she was hinting at you being my savior or something."

"Really? That's a big responsibility. I hope you're worth my time."

"Trust me, sister, I'm worth it!"

She laughed, her foggy breath lagging in the air as the flakes melted on their skins. One of the other nuns in the back of the line marched to Russell. Not amused by his fraternization, she tapped him on his shoulder.

"Young man, you shoulda nod be here!" she vented.

Stunned, he jerked to look at the huffing woman. Without missing a beat, he replied, "Then where should I be?"

"In de mess hall with yur ah friends! Dis is ah nod escort service!"

He glanced at Naomi who covered her inappropriate snickering with her gloved hand. Beaming shamelessly, he stated, "I'm sorry. I thought I was joining the choir!"

The nun pointed in a different direction. "Prease go! Be good boy an' go ahead!"

Russell turned to look at Naomi, both trying not to laugh. He shrugged, "Well Naomi, when God calls I better run to the hillside to keep warm with the sheep! See you in class." He then returned to the nun. "Thanks for being my savior."

Naomi couldn't restrain her giggles any longer. The nun, confused by his references and the girl's frivolous laughter, peered at Russell as he trotted elsewhere. She then turned around to Naomi; a scowl emerging from the prickly corners of her lips. "*You must control yourself, child! A young woman must always remain composed.*"

"*I know, sister,*" she answered, slowly evading her snickering. "*That's why I need food in my stomach. To keep me grounded and not float away!*"

THE line of people extended their usual distance, spreading like dropped yarn that continued to roll. Standing in the snow became just as much as a ritual as the wind and sun. They stood as their growling stomachs complained. They withstood the heat, and now the frost. Still standing. Still waiting. Waiting for that moment to walk out of camp. Without restrictions. Without permission. While the snow bleached the drab landscape and onto people's heads, children playfully dashed around, tossing miniature snowballs and sweeping snow angels on the ground. Many of the children, who were from the Valley, had never seen real snow before. It was a great adventure to them. And it was a simple enjoyment for the parents.

George and Joe chased each other in circles; their tiny noses glowing. Tediously wrapped in second-hand coats and caps, they waddled like fat geese. Meito and Gertrude watched them from the edge of the line, fatigued from the daily boredom, yet radiating tender smiles at their sons. Tomorrow would be their seventh birthday and suppressing their excitement proved an impossible task. Although Gertrude tried to explain why they wouldn't be getting any cake because of the sugar ration, which the boys really didn't understand, she would give them more presents instead. The thought of toys cheered their spirits. The entire family donated something; whether loose change or soldiers carved out of wood.

Russell felt something cold hit the back of his neck. A dissolving snowball soaked his collar and dribbled down his coat. Annoyed, he spun around.

Shig clapped his hands and bellowed a dynamic laugh. His predictable trio of friends were not far behind, chuckling along.

"*Omono-san!*" Shig boasted. "Haven't seen you in a while! Where you been?"

He smiled. "On vacation. Just came back today."

Shig passed the chain of people to stand beside Russell. The people, Gertrude included who glanced over their shoulders, anxiously watched Shig's gang, wondering if they would swindle in between the line.

"Vacation, huh?" Shig jeered. "I just bet! You and Naomi, right?"

Russell shook his head. "Not this time. It was more of a recovery time alone, you know?"

His humor dropped off. It had been eight weeks since that night. Looking away, he replied, "Yeah, I know. I miss him, too." And nothing more was conveyed about Sam. "So, Russell," he continued, leaning on one leg. "Is it true? Are your people gonna move out of here? Get away from us California heathens?"

Russell countered, "Well, the Bainbridge clan would like to go! But nothing is set in stone."

Meito sighed. Goro would have to face it sooner or later. When he informed his little brother about the transfer, he didn't take it well. He demanded answers as to why they should relocate, refusing to desert his new group of friends. Especially his new girlfriend. Leaving Maria was difficult enough.

"Good," Shig said. "Hate to see you go when things are just getting interesting."

"I plan to be here as long as I can!" Russell shoved a smile, wishing he hadn't lied. He wanted to tell Shig, yet he couldn't.

"Don't plan *that* far ahead, *omono*," he winked. "Life has a funny twist about things. After all, luck exists in the leftovers. See you inside, then?"

"Already have the reservations."

"That's my man! A man with a plan!"

Shig saluted, still grinning, and traveled to the rear of the line with his trio dutifully tailing him. As tempting as it was to cut in line, he knew his place.

BY MID-AFTERNOON the school's front doors uniformly opened. Students rushed into the snow, their shoes mashing over other footprints. Their chattering seemed to break apart the clouds, allowing the sun's rays to beam down on top of them. Carrying textbooks and notebooks, the students casually flowed as if their monthly routine hadn't been disturbed. Some still spoke about the day after the riot when several students locked their teachers in the classrooms or wrote obscenities on the chalk boards. School was canceled that day. Talk of the events in December was more exciting than the war outside of the barbed wire fence. It was more exciting because they saw it happen. Names like Hitler, Stalin, Mussolini, and Tojo were detached from their understanding. These foreigners meant little in their lives.

Jim saw Russell in the crowd. During the winter holiday they spent much of their time talking about the distant war and playing poker. Jim began to respect his friend as an equal. He also realized he hadn't maintained a friendship since his brother's death. For the first time in years he didn't feel lonely. Worried that Russell would reclaim his old habits and spend more time with Shig, Jim jogged across the street and tapped Russell on his shoulder.

"I didn't see you eat with Shig's gang this morning," he said. "I thought you would start hanging with them again."

He shrugged. "Wasn't in the mood, I guess."

"Well, are you in the mood for trying out chess this time?"

Russell gawked at him. "Sure. I'm also in the mood for dancing in my underwear." He chuckled at himself as Jim frowned. "Sorry, man, don't have that kind of ambition!"

"Chess is a good source for developing your mind," he insisted.

"So is oxygen. If I tried to play chess I know the stress would cut off my ability to breathe!"

Jim was more insulted than amused. It irritated him that Russell didn't even want to try.

"Hey listen," Russell continued, scanning the area for Naomi. "I'll catch you later. Right now I've got something else to do."

Stunned, Jim watched his friend scurry through the bobbing heads of high school students. He took Russell's gesture as rejection, dismissing him as easily as mismatched socks. Clutching his books, feeling his knuckles tense, he started to march off except that he saw Tomiko stroll with two of her friends drifting in his direction. She looked at him. For an instant, the urge to walk towards her soared more forceful than his pride. However, when her two girlfriends also look his way, as if already snickering at him, judging him, he turned around and marched against her approaching gaze.

Tomiko then stopped. She felt as though blades had jabbed her chest. Tears flared. Everything had changed after that day they both were trapped in the shed. She presumed what they had shared had embodied love. Why was he rejecting her? Maybe everyone was right about Jim, that he was too cold, too selfish, *too* Japanese. She had believed in him. Her friends turned around and asked what was wrong. Tomiko shook her head and wiped her tears off.

CHAPTER THREE

Early February

MRS. HAMAGUCHI dabbed her eyes with a handkerchief, sniffling, not wanting to let go of daughter. Masako rocked her mother back and forth in the embrace; her eyes shut; equally optimistic and disheartened about leaving her family. Last year, the idea of separating family would have been a cruel temptation; and the idea of leaving Winslow proved just as callous. But like pebbles in a pond, movement and repercussion of waves, certain things couldn't be helped.

Masako said, "*I love you, Mama! You will always be in my thoughts.*"

Russell held his niece's hand, feeling a sadness drilling a shaft in his chest. And envy. Ruth clung to her new doll, watching the soldier shuffle luggage onto the truck. All she understood was that they were going on another trip. Even though Russell may not have been as close to Masako and Osamu, knowing they had been there provided stability in his unsettled life. He enjoyed the prestige of having a brother-in-law who was internal police and sometimes shared bizarre stories about other people.

Mr. Hamaguchi hugged Masko, then Osamu. Meito stood next in line, along with Gertrude, the twins, and Sadaye. The departure encompassed quite a gathering. Russell wished he could flee with them, and it didn't seem fair. Every family member should be allowed their freedom at the same time. And that thought angered him. Between the sponsorship programs and the farcical trials in Montana, it seemed the government had its *own* conspiracy to break-up Japanese communities.

* * *

JIM crunched over the firm sand frozen by brittle snow. He walked around the camp with the school camera, taking photos of people and the landscape. When the second semester began, he decided to do something completely different with his activities. He wanted to preoccupy his idle time with a valuable hobby, and by joining the yearbook staff certainly appeased his boredom. Since the riot, certain restrictions were lifted; such as possessing a camera and being allowed to snap photos of the camp. In fact, Director Bridges had encouraged it.

Jim headed to the wire fence and stood still for a moment. His wool brown gloves were cut at the fingertips so he had the ability to operate the camera. He purposely stood in the same place where he slipped past the fence for the first time. The landscape had altered; influenced by the three passing seasons. He thought about Callis. Even though he hadn't seen the brute lately, nevertheless Callis continued to terrorize his dreams. Observing the tower, he raised his camera to his eye and began clicking several shots. Someday this fence would decay. And perhaps someday no one would want to remember their experiences in Manzanar. But this camera could. And these photos could persist through the years when history would neglect them. These memories would be stronger than Callis' existence.

"Up yours, you bastard," he mumbled.

Mid February

A YOUNG man, in his late twenties with dark hair and shaven face, wore a crisp military uniform. The tanned, angular design replaced the antique knickers and strapped boots. His hat was tilted keenly on his head; the dark rim glistening under the naked light bulbs. He proudly marched down the aisle; surrounded by a cynical crowd layered in dust and weather-beaten coats. Murmurs dawdled in the musky room. Director Bridges shook the recruiter's hand, exchanging polite greetings. The barrack overflowed like piles of gravel deposited beside unfinished roads. Men squirmed in their seats and anxiously aligned the walls. Rumors of a recruiting officer appearing in camp had to be seen in person. Some men had already been discharged from the army shortly after Pearl Harbor. The idea that Uncle Sam had changed its mind was a curious contradiction.

Sitting in the first row, Jim crossed his arms and stretched out his leg. Russell tapped his foot. Ikki, Shig, and a few other Bainbridge boys scattered within the next two rows; waiting.

Bridges raised his hands in front of him, fluttering them to gain everyone's attention. When the murmurs ceased, he cleared his throat.

"Thank you for coming. First, I would like to welcome a guest. Someone who's traveled from Arizona to be here tonight. Second, I would like for you gentlemen to hear out what he has to say before you pass on any judgment. I believe he has an important role to fulfill, and to present additional options for your future. Please welcome Staff Sergeant Posh."

"Pish-posh!" Shig sniggered into Russell's ear.

Bridges stepped down. The young recruiter jumped up to the roughly made stage and braced himself behind the podium. Coughs and sniffling applauded him. His alert smile jabbed at the crowd.

Jim instantly disliked him.

Russell began to imagine himself in uniform.

"Good evening, gentlemen," he asserted, a sharp nod saluting them. "I'm glad to see a full house. And so many able-bodied men. It's good to be here." His smile did not avert from the harsh frowns that advanced in the audience. "Tonight I want to inform you about the epidemic that plagues Europe and the South Pacific. To inform you about the shocking tyrannies that enslave half of the world. And to inform you about the importance of spreading democracy like the gospel itself."

"What about the lack of democracy here?" someone blurted from the back.

The tension of creaky chairs echoed in the stuffy room. A few coughs implied a popular consensus. The recruiter flinched.

Russell looked over his shoulder, searching for the man who made the criticism. As true as the outburst was, he wondered if it was necessary and wondered if anger would spill inside the camp like before. He was tired of the bickering. Tired of the gloom. Tired of feeling at fault.

The recruiter remained firm. "Democracy is a unified effect. We, as a civilized nation, must take the initiative to liberate victims from oppression and wickedness. It is our job to make the world a better place, gentlemen."

Jim's muscles tightened, and a blistering sensation heated his body. All of this was bullshit. How could the government justify its pathetic hypocrisy? In one year they were stripped of their rights, removed from public, and robbed from their individual identities. Everyone realized the farce the *hakujin* in uniform imposed: here he was asking for their help to free the Europeans from oppression, and yet the Japanese people were submerged in the thick of it in America.

"The reason it is our job because we have a responsibility to help our allies. It is our responsibility to preserve, to secure, to demonstrate justice. And it is our responsibility to take out Hitler, to take out Mussolini, and to subdue the Japanese military."

Shig squinted. The recruiter looked like an actor from Hollywood with his fresh uniform and charismatic face; angular at the jaw line with glorious blue eyes. Shig wasn't sure what to make of him. Or what he represented. Sincerity? Pretentiousness?

"Now some of you may have already heard of the 100th Division. A division comprising of Japanese-Americans from Hawaii. During the last six months they have proven themselves to not only be profoundly courageous," he paused and slowly scanned at the audience, "but also profoundly devoted, noble men. They have more than earned their respect in the U.S. military."

Ikki kept imagining his cousin with bullets in his chest. The bloodied vision never disappeared from his dreams. Day or night. He attended this meeting not so much because he was curious, but because he was scrounging for answers. He hoped to regain some sense out of this pointless situation. If the military hadn't forced them to this goddamn camp, if the military hadn't shot Sam– if only.

The recruiter upheld his primed stance, ignoring the curt sighs and grunts that periodically diffused. "Uncle Sam recognizes the importance of identity. We have seen your need to be unique, therefore we have arranged a separate regiment for you to celebrate your uniqueness."

"You mean segregation!" a man shouted, lunging to his feet. He appeared no older than the recruiter. "You're looking for volunteers to fight in a segregated army! Thanks, but no thanks, buddy!"

People again shifted in the creaky chairs, watching the agitated man stumble over feet and stomp out of the barrack. Jim was surprised that no one followed. He thought about it, except that he was sitting in the first row and didn't want that kind of attention.

"Yes, the regiment will be segregated," the recruiter calmly acknowledged. "But it is to your advantage. The camp you are in now is designed to protect you from the hostilities of the outside world. This newly formed regiment will be designed to protect your heritage. You men should be proud that you'll receive your own division in the United States Army."

Russell wasn't entirely convinced. And it was obvious neither was his brother, otherwise Meito would have attended. Although Russell had accepted social segregation, for he had experienced it more significantly in Seattle than on Bainbridge, Manzanar made him reconsider things. The isolation, the watchtowers, the riot: all of which redefined what it meant being Japanese in America. He wanted to find explanations. To seek hope. He wasn't confident if joining the military would necessarily provide meaning and resolution, and yet, what if it could?

The next half-hour hustled the young recruiter's zealousness regarding patriotism, obligations, and glory. His voice trumpeted through the stale room, attempting to break apart the grudge, and yet his tone didn't acknowledge the paradox. At the conclusion of his speech, a weak applause stiffened his smile. Uncertainty was more vigorous than faith. Director Bridges returned to the podium, shook Posh's hand, and made a few more remarks about democracy and how it each individual was responsible for it. Once all of it was over, the men leaked out the doors like thick, sluggish oil. They buzzed about possibilities and consequences. Some, who were friends with Ted Tanaka, argued for the greater good of the community if they volunteered. Ted and his men from the Japanese American Citizen League had been fighting for a year to prove their people's loyalty. It would be wasteful if no one took responsibility.

Ikki vented, "I can't believe the gall the government has! How the hell can we fight for democracy overseas when it's not being used here?"

"I think it could be something more," Shig remarked. "Like proving yourself to the whole world."

"Why should we? No matter what we do, we'll always be a bunch of Japs to them!"

"That's my point! Show 'em we're American. Show 'em we can be trusted and get the hell out of these fucking camps!"

They thought for a moment. Each knew it would be the biggest decision any of them would have to make.

Russell asked, "Do you think it'll be worth it?"

"Why the hell not?" Shig replied. "Certainly can't prove anything while rotting in here. If you don't enter the tiger's cave, then you can't catch its cub!"

"How can risking your life for a bigoted system be worth it?" Jim inserted. "I don't see how sacrificing ourselves will improve our future. Especially if we're dead! In fact, I see it as another way the government can reduce its *Jap* problem!"

Ikki bitterly remarked, "I'm not gonna risk my skin. I would rather kiss Tojo's ass than fight for something that has no meaning."

Shig perked up. "Where's your sense of honor, Ikki?"

He shook his head, irritated. "Honor has nothing to do with it."

"Honor is something that they can't take from us," Shig pointed. "Besides, it's the same life whether we spend it laughing or crying."

Ikki clenched his jaw. He explored the crowd of straggling men; each not knowing which direction to choose. He had never felt so misplaced before. And empty. A great emptiness that blistered in his belly.

Shig continued, "Look at it this way, Ikki. Honor makes a man. So again, where's your sense of honor?"

He glared at him. "Buried with Sam."

"Then you should do it for Sam."

"You asshole!" Ikki cried, grabbing Shig's collar and ripping it off. "Don't use Sam like that!"

Shig glanced down at his jacket. Infuriated, he swung his fist, striking Ikki's chin. Ikki staggered backward, and then dove into Shig's stomach; both falling onto the ground. They rolled in the dirt, hitting each other in their ribs and faces; grunting; heaving; bleeding.

"Stop it!" Russell yelled. He tried to pull Ikki off. His two friends were twisted like a pretzel; kicking and punching. The flowing crowd began to clog as the men watched. Some were amused, and some were annoyed by the lack of maturity.

Russell grabbed Shig's shoulders and suddenly an elbow stabbed Russell in the crotch. He dropped to his knees, gasping. Three adults lunged forward, yanking the boys apart. Their friends watched from the sidelines.

Jim squatted to Russell. "Are you alright?"

"I just got my jewels cracked! What do you think?"

He grimaced, "Why do you feel the need to get involved in everyone's business? You can't save the world, Russell. "

Russell wheezed, glaring up at Ikki and Shig who were being forced to the opposite boundaries of the circled audience. He couldn't imagine anything else being more excruciating than the sharp throbbing he felt in between his legs. But he didn't regret it.

"Somebody has to!" he grunted.

* * *

TOMIKO flipped through her used history book with the edges peeling and pages slightly yellowed from age. Despite the stove crackling with heat, her barrack retained a chill. Wearing a corduroy jacket and denim jeans, she also kept her shoes on to protect her skin from sand and the cold. She rubbed her hands for warmth. Soft, classical music from the radio fulfilled the quietness. Her father sat near the stove, reading the Japanese translation of *The Manzanar Free Press*, a feature that was recently permitted. Before the riot it had been forbidden. Her mother teetered in a rocking chair, hand sewing a quilt made from cheap cloth. A tiny shrine balanced in the corner on top of a short table. Burnt-out candles surrounded a miniature Buddha. Suddenly knocks rattled the door, startling Tomiko and her parents.

"*Dare desu-ka?*" her father asked.

"I don't know who that is, Papa." She rose from her studies and promptly opened the side door. Russell shivered on the steps; a crisp wind pushing from behind. The late afternoon sunlight lingered on the side of his face. She peeked over his shoulder to see if Jim was with him. When she didn't see him, she reminded herself that she should start getting used to Jim disappointing her. Returning her focus to Russell, she asked, "Russell, what are you doing here?"

"Can I talk to you outside?"

Stunned, curious, Tomiko stepped back, glancing at her prying parents. Understanding that it was no doubt a private concern, she told them, "I'll be right back," and reached for her coat hanging on the rack. Closing the door, she stepped down onto the white land and waited for Russell to speak. Strollers roamed the streets like tumbleweeds; usually guided by wind with spools of loose snow chasing at their heels.

"Let's walk around the block," he suggested. As they began moving, he affirmed, "Jim's been miserable, you know. He misses you like crazy. I can tell."

Tomiko arched her shoulders, hiding her hands inside her pockets, trying to stop the sting from burning her throat. She thought it was sweet that Russell cared, however it was obvious Jim didn't care nearly as much. His pride being more important. In that aspect, Jim was just like his father.

"I don't see how," she said. "He's too selfish."

Russell snickered. "I can't argue with that!" He paused, noticing her discomfort. "But he has a lot on his mind, too."

"Who doesn't? Everyone has problems. The difference is I don't let them bog me down."

"Yeah," he sighed, "but I guess some of us needs more help."

"How can you help someone who doesn't want it?"

Russell flipped up his collar. He knew Jim was one of the more difficult-minded people he befriended; yet there were moments of unselfishness. And moments of good spirits. Those were the times Russell had hoped the best for Jim.

"I think he does want it," he continued. "He just doesn't know how to ask."

Again Russell hesitated, peering at the western mountains in the horizon. Snow seemed to have lived on the peaks in a monotonous spell: Stationary. Solemn. Last year the mountain snow didn't start melting until June.

"There was this time when I pretty well gave up on everything," he soberly began. "I barely ate. I barely got out of bed. I had a real hard time adjusting to this place. Then Jim stopped by to see me." Russell eased a grin. "Man, he sure did rattle my chain! But he got me out of bed."

Tomiko slowed her pace. The first time Jim kissed her, the first time they made love, he had an instinctive gentleness. It was difficult to comprehend he could also be unfeeling and unresponsive.

Russell squeezed her elbow, stopping. "Listen, Tomiko," he delicately said, leaning closer to her. "Jim has never gotten over his brother's death."

"So he should ignore me?"

He lowered his brows. "What I mean is he's never gotten over John's *suicide*." He watched her draw back. "Jim didn't want to tell you because he thought you might think less of him."

She crinkled her brows. "How could he think that? Why wouldn't he tell me? I told him something very personal about my sister! Why couldn't he do the same? Doesn't he trust me enough?"

"I don't know what it is."

Her cheeks flushed as her eyes glazed. "I knew John well enough to already figure it out. And I know how hard their father can be on them, so it's no surprise. Jim's got to learn to trust people! I hate it when he . . . he . . . just disappears!" Trying to regain her anger, she curiously studied Russell. "Why are you telling me this?"

He shivered, and then shrugged. "Oh, I don't know. Maybe I'm tired of him being so cranky. And he really is, by the way. More so than usual. Or maybe," he grinned, "maybe I believe in second chances."

JIM opened his door. Russell stood on his step, hands pressed into his pockets, hunching and leering with a guilty intention.

Apprehensive, Jim asked, "What are you up to?"

"Are you alone?"

He hesitated. "Yes. Why?"

"Good. You'll have some privacy."

"What are you talking about?"

Russell moved backward and allowed Tomiko to walk in front of him at the bottom the steps. She grazed her knuckles together, nervously looking up at Jim.

Jim simply stared. He couldn't speak.

She began, "You never did explain yourself. I think I deserve an explanation. And an apology."

Jim chewed on his lip and nodded. He moved to allow room for her to walk inside. He watched Russell grin from the curve of his eye just before he closed the door. While Tomiko settled behind the table with his school books and a thin pile of paper, he stood for a moment, thinking. Just the wonder of her made him realize how he yearned for her. Her love. Her encouragement. Her wit. Her mouth and skin. She patiently sat as if waiting for him to say something fundamental that would repair the injuries. Rubbing his palms over his slacks, he breathed past his dry lips. Where should he begin?

Clearing his throat, he said, "Um, I am sorry I offended you."

"Offended me?" she echoed. "You didn't offend me. You *hurt* me."

He scratched the back of his neck and swayed side to side. "I don't know how to do this right. I don't know how to correct my mistakes."

Tomiko slid her hands forward. "Jim, this isn't a math quiz. The answers aren't right or wrong." She exhaled, wondering at what point in his life he regarded mistakes as unmerciful failures. Although she knew his father was strict, however much of Jim's anxieties had to come from his own ego. "Just tell me why you would believe I would think less of you. And since you're at it, tell me why you want to marry me. Is it because you want to or because . . . of what we had done . . . and you feel obligated to?"

Jim was paralyzed. He stared at her, unable to answer any of her demands.

She leaned back and looked away. "Say something," she whispered. "I don't like it when you have nothing to say."

His hands started to tremble. "I want marry you because no one else has made me feel good about my life."

"But do you really love me?"

He folded his hands together in hopes he would stop shaking. "More than anything."

She blazed up at him. "Then why did you walk away from me? *Twice?*"

His legs suddenly weakened. He quickly stumbled to a chair to sit down. "I think because," he flinched, "I know someday. . . you'll eventually leave me. I was giving you a chance to do it now instead of later."

Shocked, she could only blink. "I don't believe it," she finally said. "You honestly can't believe it!"

He didn't want to talk about it. A powerful dizziness and throbbing in his head and chest overwhelmed his sensibilities. His vision quickly concaved and instantly he dropped his head in between his knees. He tried to take deep breaths as Russell had instructed before. He felt Tomiko's hands holding him, although he couldn't see her. Like an explosion, he combusted into tears. Sobbing. Choking. The pain crushed his heart and he couldn't control the bleeding-like sensation. He felt embarrassed. He hadn't cried since he was twelve.

Tomiko nuzzled him, stroking the back of his neck while softly rocking him. She closed her eyes, empathizing with his grief as tears dropped down her face. She was glad she ignored her friends' advice regarding Jim. They told her he had no feelings. That he was too selfish and arrogant. That she deserved someone better than him. She continued holding him for what seemed like a moth's cocooning period waiting for spring. Jim sluggishly regained his composure. His wet face seemed to have closed the hollowness in his gut. Even for a brief time. Sniffling, he stood up to walk to a box of tissue to blow his nose. Tomiko quietly watched him.

"I can't stop wondering if John lived . . ." he stopped, trying to breathe normally. "If John decided to live . . . then maybe I wouldn't hate him so much. For leaving us." Looking down at his double-layered socks over his feet, he pinched his fingers between his nose. "Why do you even love me? That's the real question."

"That *is* a good question," she sighed, watching his face wrinkle in dread. Smiling, she said, "Underneath it all, I know what you're capable of. Always had known it."

Jim stared at her in awe. He thought no one else other than his mother could see possibilities in him. Certainly not his father. His father didn't see it- he simply demanded it without excuses. Clearing his throat, he asked, "Do you still have your ring?" She reached down her neck and slipped out a necklace with her engagement ring attached at the end. "Do you still want to marry me?" he asked.

"That depends," she replied. "Are you going to be completely honest with me?"

He took in several breaths. "I do love you, Tomiko. And I haven't stopped wanting to share a life with you. I'm just . . ." again he paused, his voice shaking. "I am sorry for any pain I caused you. I just don't understand why you want to be with me."

She rose and walked to him. Folding her arms around his neck, she whispered, "Because I do, Jim. Nothing more. Nothing less." She kissed him. "You're going to have to trust people. You seem to trust Russell. Now trust me."

Placing his arms around her waist, looking down, he whispered, "Do you still have your gift? I think I'm ready to accept it now."

"Yes. But I'm not sure if I'm ready to give it back to you," she smiled.

He lightly chuckled. "I deserved that." He then let out a forceful sigh and confessed with exhaustion, "I just don't want to end up like my brother."

"I know," she replied, kissing his forehead. "And I don't want to end up like my sister. Who wants to live with memories of forgotten people?"

Early March

THE two front doors opened and people leaked into the dusk. Another line paralleled beside the barrack, stretching out to the road. A new movie, *The Human Comedy*, had arrived that weekend, replacing the older one that preserved steady scratches. Sometimes overused reels would arrive in camp after numerous circulations through small towns; but this time Camp Director Bridges managed to borrow a fresh one from Lone Pine. A newly released motion picture at that. Some suspected Bridges' motivates once the saw it: the film was about excessive patriotism. Even the Chinese were in the mix, wearing army uniforms among each common soldier on the train. It implied that all were considered equal. And that was an obvious lie.

Naomi slipped her arm around Russell's elbow, smiling. Jim reached to hold Tomiko's hand. The four ambled that Saturday night as excited voices surrounded them. Even for a couple of hours, the sensation of an ordinary life felt great.

Russell said, "I like Andy Rooney. He's the only actor who's not taller than me!"

"What does that have to do with anything?" Jim snickered.

"A lot! If a short guy can do anything, why not me?"

Naomi laughed. "Only *you* would make that kind of connection!"

Jim humorously smiled. "It's just a movie, Russell."

"I'm not talking about the movie," Russell replied, tipping a brow. "I'm talking about his *career*. Seriously, he's the shortest entertainer I know who can make himself bigger than life, you know? It's just good to see other possibilities. More so for anyone else who's considered the underdog in America."

"Good point," Jim nodded. "Because we're especially the underdogs right now."

Russell squeezed Naomi's hand and continued, "Now, the dance doesn't start for another hour. I left a game of Monopoly at Jim's place. Because it's so close by. How does that sound, girls?"

Naomi chirped, "Sounds good!"

They walked in silence for a moment. The street lights beamed down on their shoulders and brightened their flushed faces. A breeze ricocheted between the two mountain ranges, composing a low, rumbling tone like distant traffic through a tunnel. Sometimes the identical tone occurred just before falling snow. Or when naked tree limbs rustled in the wind. The barren sounds resembled memories of home.

"Goro!" someone cried out.

Russell turned around. His friends yielded in curiosity. Meito trotted toward him, dressed in a suit and hat, while Gertrude irritably followed in high heels.

"I thought you might be here," Meito said.

"Why are you all dressed up? Going to a funeral?"

Meito frowned, not amused by his grim sense of humor. "We just got back from town. Remember Gerdie and me had a day pass today?"

"Oh, yeah. How was it?"

Gertrude scowled at Meito for leaving her behind, although quickly retained her manners, smiling and nodding at Goro and his friends. The sand in her heels tickled her feet. She wished she had brought another pair of shoes to change into. They would have to walk six blocks.

"It was nice. Really nice." Meito extended his arm around Gertrude's waist and kissed her on her forehead. "We ordered some catalogs." He widely smiled. "We're gonna have another baby in seven months."

Russell was stunned. He looked at his brother, then Gertrude. They were beaming. "Well, congratulations, man! Mama's gonna burst!"

Tomiko and Naomi echoed their best wishes almost in unison. Jim shook Meito's hand.

Meito resumed, "Yeah, had the catalogs sent to Kunio's place in Idaho. So when all of us arrive there next month, they'll be there already."

Naomi stared at Russell, confused. "I thought you said you weren't leaving."

Russell flinched. He hadn't planned informing her until it was absolutely necessary. Preferably the day before. He hated farewells. So far they forecasted unpleasantness and tears; not to mention the inevitable detachment of the heart. Who wanted to keep receiving "Dear John" letters?

He sighed. "Not yet."

She unlocked her arm and stepped back. "When were you going to tell me?"

Russell glared at his brother who only shrugged in turn. Returning to look at Naomi, he replied, "I don't know. Listen, can we enjoy the night without discussing this? I have everything planned. I want this to be perfect."

"Why?" she snapped. "Is this like the Last Supper or something?"

Meito interjected, "Okay, Goro, we've got to get going. But listen, the main reason I wanted to track you down was to let you know me and another friend of mine found a temporary part-time job outside of Manzanar. Some old farmer is looking for hands to scrape and repaint his house. Interested?"

Scratching his head, Russell glanced between his brother and girlfriend, feeling bushwhacked. No one could help him. Jim and Tomiko could only supply pity. "Yeah, I'm interested. Give me a chance to make my own money."

"My friend has his own truck he drove in from Los Angeles. Meet us at the gates right after school on Monday. I'll get your furlough pass." He gently slugged his brother's arm and winked. "Enjoy the rest of your evening."

Russell sarcastically replied, "Thanks a lot, big brother."

"You're welcome, *ototo*."

He watched Meito and Gertrude walk off, dust blowing behind their heels like powder. Trying to smile in order to clean-up Meito's spill, Russell reached for Naomi's hand. She jerked away.

"Let's play the stupid game!" she sputtered.

"Naomi," he began pleading. "Don't get upset. Let's not worry about it tonight. We'll talk about it tomorrow, okay?"

She peered at him, trying to restrain her anger. "You lied to me, Russell. What else is there to talk about tomorrow?"

"Oh, man," he groaned, spreading his fingers through his hair. "I don't want to leave! It's not fair that I should have to. The whole Bainbridge community wants to and I'm stuck with their decision. It's not like I'm eighteen yet and can legally make my own decisions."

Jim felt sorry for Russell. He acknowledged Russell's pitiful effort to cling to something that wasn't in his reach to keep in the first place. The misery that Jim felt during those difficult weeks without Tomiko was an experience he hoped never to repeat. What Russell must be experiencing proved just as difficult. If Russell truly held the same intensity as love. Since he continued to date Naomi, he had stopped talking about Maria.

Russell turned to Jim and Tomiko. "Listen guys, we'll catch up with you later. I need to finish this in private."

"Of course," Tomiko responded. "Take your time."

Jim nodded. He squeezed Tomiko's hand, grateful she chose to stay, grateful for his friendship with Russell. He owed Russell. Someday he hoped he would be able to return the favor. Tugging on Tomiko's arm, they strolled toward his barrack, knowing they would be alone. His mother and sister were attending a Japanese play and would be gone for at least a couple of hours.

Russell turned to face Naomi. "Do you want to go for a walk?"

She buttoned up her sweater, looking down. "I want to go home."

"Can I walk with you?"

"Suit yourself," she mumbled.

He pressed his fists inside his jacket's pockets, chasing her; confused; disheartened. Minutes lapsed with the fallen sun, allowing the stars to build a coldness between them. Music from a radio faintly followed them, balancing their silence. Russell finally began, "I have two more weeks left. I had planned to tell you on Monday."

"You should of told me as soon as you knew," Naomi scolded. "I feel like an idiot when I'm the last to know!"

"I wanted to keep things normal. If I told you sooner, it would made things weird."

"I'm not some floozy with peas for brains. Give me some credit!"

Russell pinched his brows. "That's not what I mean. A similar situation happened with my other girlfriend back on the island. I really like you, Naomi. I don't want . . ." He hesitated, uncertain how far he should reveal his thoughts. If he really told her how he felt, and then by the next month she stopped writing to him for one reason or another, he would feel like an idiot.

Naomi slowed her pace. She glanced at him and saw a grimace shrouding his familiar flair. "I really like you, too, Russell. But sometimes you assume what I want without asking me."

"What do you want then?"

She released a long sigh; the kind of sigh that liberated all fears. "I don't want to be your second choice."

"What are you talking about? Since I've been here, I've only been seeing you."

"Someday we'll all go home." She watched another couple stroll the street; arm in arm; whispering. She wanted that kind of security. "When that day comes, who will you choose? Me or Maria?"

He nervously chuckled. "The chances of you finding someone else is better than me getting back with Maria."

Within a few seconds, she stopped. "It hasn't been easy, you know. And I'm tired." Naomi closed her eyes to keep tears from swelling. She felt cold, alone, and suddenly realized it was better that he went away now instead of a year from now when he vanished for war. Knowing his character, he would volunteer for it. Not just to escape camp, but because it would mean something. He more than likely would die not just for America, but for America's respect. It was in his nature. Even when he pretended otherwise. She would rather be an ex-girlfriend than a widower.

Russell waited. Her delay encouraged him to step nearer and, ultimately, to embrace her. The heat of her body calmed his fears as if nothing would change; as if nothing had ever happened. She laid her head on his shoulder.

"I love you," She breathed. "But it's okay if you don't."

He clasped her chin and leaned down to kiss her. At that moment, he didn't care about the future. It didn't seem to matter that every time he cared for someone he was on the verge of leaving. Naomi's lips reminded him how good it felt to be loved. She placed her hand on his cheek, lightly kissing him in turn.

The blood in his body surged, clashing against his sensibilities, no longer worried what other people considered proper behavior.

He whispered, "I love you, too."

She kissed him. "Then let's make the best of what time we have left."

CHAPTER FOUR

RUSSELL had jogged across the camp to reach the front gates as quickly as possible. The early afternoon warmth draped from the sun, barely touching his shoulders. Meito and his friend leaned against a car covered in desert soot; perfectly lined with the other vehicles. The hood and top was scraped from a year's worth of harsh storms that peeled off the paint like claws. A small gas station had been constructed six months ago to accommodate commercial truck drivers and visitors. Very small. Only one pump. The military had their own on the north side of camp. Panting, Russell smiled at his brother. Dressed in stained overalls and dull sunglasses, Meito squeezed Russell's shoulder, grinning. The other man appeared to be the same age as Meito, except that he had a mustache which caused him to appear more mature. He was the same height as Russell, standing just above five feet. When he smiled, a tooth was missing on the left side.

"Goro, this is Bill," Meito said, tossing his hand in his friend's direction. "He's the one who set this thingamajig."

Russell shook Bill's hand. "Good to meet you, sir."

Bill snorted. "Sir? Jesus! I ain't in charge of nothin'! All I got is wheels, not a title."

Russell grinned, amused by his bluntness. Glancing at his brother, he said, "Well then, Bill, I'd rather be called Russell, not Goro."

"Nothing's wrong with your name," Meito grunted. "I never understood why you changed it."

Russell sighed. "Just to irritate you and no other reason. I feel so lost when I can't make your skin crawl."

Bill smirked and retrieved his wallet from his back pocket. Removing a thin green booklet of stamps, he said, "Okay, let's do this."

"What's that?" Russell asked.

Shaking the booklet, he replied, "This? This rations my gas. I get more of these when I find outside jobs. I also get more of these when I carpool other workers." He pinched his smile as if saving a riddle. "Uncle Sam operates in amazing ways. And so does the black market."

Stunned, Russell looked at his brother, wondering what kind of "friend" Meito had been socializing with. Meito pushed up his sunglasses and opened the passenger door. He motioned Russell to get in the back, saying nothing. After Bill filled his tank, he drove to the entrance, handing over their work passes to a soldier. The young soldier, bored, shuffled the paper briskly and returned them to Bill. Russell thought it was strange that despite Manzanar being surrounded by a prickly fence, no official gates were built at the entrance; just two sentries with guards. The soldier stepped back, signaling for Bill to continue. As they pulled onto the highway, Russell realized he hadn't seen Callis since the riot. Maybe the bastard was finally sent elsewhere.

EARLY evening slunk after the sun, dividing time and distance between the two mountain ranges; away from civilization; away from Manzanar. Sweat soaked Russell's collar and armpits despite the cold air. Scraping cracked paint off dried wood strained his muscles and patience. The tedious repetition made him appreciate his abilities to be better at other things. Namely sports. At least he would earn something for his effort. An elderly woman, perhaps in her late seventies, shuffled out of her modest house; a one and a half story home with a runty porch and leaky roof. Her back was humped. Her white hair was coiled in a trim bun. Her long black dress and laced shoes appeared forty years out of date. She carried a tray of square sandwiches. Her husband, geared in chest-high trousers and strapped boots, wobbled from behind, carrying a pitcher of lemonade. Meito wiped his sweaty forehead and smiled at the couple. Russell, relieved for a break, laid his scraper on a footstool. Glancing up the ladder, he saw Bill spitting at his side, and then slowly climbed down. A pile of paint scraps settled around their feet.

Meito joked, "Is it time to get rid of us?"

The woman giggled. "Same way of gettin' rid of coyotes. By feeding 'em!"

Bill chimed in, "Always been my method, Mrs. Johnson."

The elderly man cracked a smile, squinting through thick bifocals as his parched face wilted. He set the glass pitcher on the stool, beside the scraper. Russell liked this couple. They were nice folks who were nearsighted and courteous. When Mr. Johnson shook his hand earlier, he asked Russell whether Russell knew Lon Cheney because he looked just like Cheney. Meito had to explain to the young and confused Russell that Cheney was a silent film actor: a man with a thousand faces, however was best known for his Oriental roles.

Mr. Johnson announced, "I'll get some glasses," and wobbled back into his house.

Bill instantly plunged into the sandwiches and consumed two at a time. Russell and Meito took one each. Once Bill swallowed, he looked at Meito, crinkling his nose. He muttered, "*What is it about mayonnaise that the hakujins like so much? Unsalted rice has more flavor.*"

Russell only grinned.

The elderly woman blinked in bewilderment. “What, dear?”

Meito replied, “He said that these kind of sandwiches are his most favorite.”

“Oh!” she widely beamed, the narrowness of her eyes amplifying above her proud, swollen cheeks. “I can make more so he can take with him!”

“Don’t!” Bill insisted. “You been more than generous. It’s better you ration your food for yourselves. We get plenty at camp.”

Russell stated, “I’ll take some more! I rarely get enough.”

“Goro,” his brother warned, whispering. “Don’t take advantage of this woman’s hospitality.”

“What, dear?” she asked.

Raising his voice, Russell replied, “Sorry, Mrs. Johnson.”

She continued to beam. “Oh, you boys are so polite! I wish my boys were that polite!”

“Thank you,” Meito smiled and nodded.

“And you boys speak English very good.” She lowered the tray, her smile fading. “You must be grateful. And sad. Coming over from China to get away from those brutal Japs!”

Russell choked on the bread. Bill and Meito raised their brows and stared at each other; more perplexed than appalled. Mrs. Johnson was sincere in her remark.

Bill snickered, “*Does she not understand what kind of camp we come from?*”

“What, dear?” she asked.

“He said,” Meito began, fluttering his eyes and straining from withholding his laughter, “he said he is grateful for being here. Every day he is grateful.”

Russell triggered into a coughing fit. Meito swatted his back a few times. The stinging in Russell’s throat seemed mild compared to Mrs. Johnson’s outrageous statement. He wanted to laugh. So badly he wanted to laugh, and yet he knew how inappropriate it would look despite having good reason. Regardless of other people’s ignorance, sometimes it was more hilarious than watching the Marx brothers being chased by a gorilla.

* * *

JIM scattered his photos on the rectangular table. Some were out of focus. Some were too dark. He took photos of people walking around camp, the mess hall’s interior, the mountains, and even a hand holding pliers as if in the process of cutting the wire fence. Chemicals from the dark room hovered in the air. A corner of the barrack had been walled off with a small door as an entrance. A red light hung above the door to let the others know when someone was developing film. The other half of the barrack was reserved for the honors classes. Six other classmates looked over Jim’s display, telling him what they thought. Some liked his subject matter, especially the hand clutching the pliers. Some disliked his clumsiness with the focus and aperture. If any of his photos were to be considered for the year book, Jim would have to learn to improve the camera’s balance. He cringed when they spoke, remaining quiet, only nodding his head.

Their teacher, Mr. Chapman, peeked at his wristwatch. His dark wavy hair had been parted on the side, appearing like two uneven bread rolls sitting on his head. He enjoyed wearing suspenders and striped, colored socks. As a bachelor in his forties, students wondered if he had any interest in women- at all.

Mr. Chapman tapped on his watch. "Our guest should be arriving soon," he announced.

A student asked, "Is that today?"

"Yep. This should be a real treat. We should thank Director Bridges for making the arrangements."

Another questioned, "Well, who is he? You never told us."

Mr. Chapman grinned. "Only the best naturalist-American photographer in history!" He walked towards the door and scanned out one of the windows. His grin broadened. "Here he is, ladies and gentlemen."

He opened the door, greeting the guest. An odd-looking man in his early forties thumped up the steps and strode inside. His long face hid under his dark beard with flecks of white, as if a Viking. He had a sharp, crooked nose, (a legendary nose which had been broken at the age of four when he was flung into his family's garden wall, face-first, during an aftershock three hours following San Francisco's 1906 quake,) and a nose that contradicted his stoutly-rounded eyes. Dark brown like a bull. His mountain hat resembled nostalgic, Western paintings that proved just as historic. He was a tall, slender man beneath his corduroy jacket.

Mr. Chapman proudly announced, "Everyone, this is Ansel Adams."

They were stunned. Jim included. Until Jim began studying photography, he hardly knew of him; just some guy who took photos of Yosemite Park and New Mexico. Now he had come to understand Ansel Adams as an artist and environmental activist. Ansel was as famous in the photography world as Babe Ruth was in baseball. He watched Ansel walk to his cluttered photos, and carefully sifted through them.

Mr. Chapman continued, "Mr. Adams will be taking photos of camp life this year. This also means he will take an interest in our school lives. So everyone should feel comfortable and act normal."

Jim had never met anyone quite as captivating as Ansel Adams. When Ansel spoke, his soft voice discredited his rough surface.

"How long have you been taking photos?" he asked Jim.

Embarrassed by his inexperience, he muttered, "A month."

"A month? Is that so?" He looked again at Jim's photos on top of the table. "I'm impressed, lad. You have an excellent eye for composition. And your lighting isn't bad, either."

Jim stared at Ansel Adams; dazed. The other six students were also in awe. No one had expected him to walk casually in their classroom. They heard rumors that he might visit Manzanar to promote a positive image of the detention camps, especially after the riot; however, like all the other rumors, no one knew which rumor to seriously accept as true.

"I particularly like this one," he resumed, pointing to the hand and pliers. "It's an honest statement."

Jim finally responded, "Thank you. Half the time I don't know what I'm doing in the dark room."

Ansel smiled, spreading his thick mustache outwardly. "Nobody does in the beginning. It takes time to mature like anything else. And even then, you're still learning and improving." He winked. "Keep up the good work!"

Jim couldn't believe it. An authentic compliment from a famous person. Famous and immortal. He now wanted his own camera.

* * *

THE hours embroidered time from the tip of the sun to the tip of the moon. The prolonged, laborious Saturday ended with the Johnson's house being fully scraped and painted. It had been awhile since Russell felt pride in his accomplishments. They had finally finished as soon as the sunlight plunged behind the prickly mountains. Smiling, he wiped his stained fingers over his sweatshirt. His face and shirt were splattered with yellow paint, fusing with his sweat. He dipped the paintbrush into a bucket and swirled it. Meito shook and flexed his hands to release the numbness from hours of tediously gripping. Bill twisted his back to pop his bones, moaning.

Mr. Johnson emerged from the front porch, wearing his faded overalls and misshapen hat. His thick, knobby hands looked like dying tree stumps. Squinting, he wobbled off the steps and shuffled toward Bill. A coyote bawled in the distance. Mr. Johnson sunk one of his hands inside his pocket, removing a small wad of cash. Unfolding it, he counted the ones out loud. Handing six dollars to Bill first, he advanced his other hand to offer an amicable shake.

"Thank ya, Bill," he said. "Good job." Mr. Johnson then shuffled to Russell, giving another six dollars. "Thank ya, Russell. Been a pleasure." Coughing, he finally shuffled to Meito, extending the same pay and courtesies. "Meat-o, take care."

Russell snorted. All week long, the Johnsons maintained to call his brother *Meat-o*. Each time they mispronounced his name, Russell had to chuckle. That was why he chose to change his name; to save from embarrassing both himself and the other person. Meito politely accepted the Johnson's hospitality, never resolving to correct them.

BILL'S car rattled and squeaked on the bumpy highway. His headlights were dim, managing to flicker enough glow on the narrow, darkening road. Burly shrubbery prowled in the shadows, rippling from the headlights, ensuing too closely. Russell stared out the rear window, sensing an eeriness. The radio's static aired country western music. One of the few stations that could reach out that far. On clearer days, the sounds of Swing could be detected. He glanced at the back of his brother's head. Bored, he began to chant.

"There was a farmer who had a dog, and Meat-o was his name-o. M-E-A-T-O."

"Shut up, Goro," he snapped.

Russell grinned and continued, "M-E-A-T-O. . ."

"Goro, you're acting like a *baka*."

"M-E-A-T-O . . . and Meat-o was his name-o."

Meito moaned, slowing shaking his head in silent protest. Bill chuckled and inhaled his cigarette. He flicked his blinker, starting to slow down, and pulled into the drive. The broad wooden MANZANAR sign greeted them as usual, hailing them like a stranded motorist off the side of the road. The difference, Russell mused, was that it felt more like a trap. Once caught, it seemed hopeless to escape. The desert alone could kill a person. Bill parked his car at the first gate and rolled down his window. The dinner gongs echoed across camp. An MP strode toward him, clutching his bayonet in his hand. Russell thought it was odd. Normally, if the soldiers carried one at all nowadays, they would sling their weapons at their sides. Bill reached for their passes on the dashboard to give to the guard.

Bill smiled, exposing his missing tooth, "Looks like we made it just in time."

The soldier leaned down. The street light barely struck the loose ends of his blond hair, hiding his eyes, etching half his face. His shoulders swelled against the window, looming like a grizzly. Russell leaned forward to see his face. It was Callis. Holding his breath, Russell fell back.

Callis scowled, "It's past yer curfew!"

Startled, Bill looked at his wristwatch. "My watch says it's six o'clock on the mark. And the dinner bells just went off a few seconds ago."

"Don't smart-mouth me! According to my watch, it's six o'one." He glared at the headlights and spat, "And are you people *stupid?* We're in the middle of a goddamn war and you have on your goddamn lights? Turn them lights off!"

Bill immediately obeyed. He looked at Meito; worried; anxious. Russell knew this wasn't good. He scanned the area, hoping another MP would appear soon to distract Callis. The collapsing light gave Callis too much control. Like an invisible man. If no one saw what Callis was capable of committing, then he could do no wrong.

Callis barked, "Get out of the car!"

Stunned, Bill looked at him. "What?"

"Get out!"

"Don't do it, Bill!" Russell pleaded.

Infuriated, Callis pointed his bayonet directly at Bill. "Get out of the fucking car, now!"

Bill fumbled for the door handle and wobbled out of his car. He desperately searched the area for other witnesses, seeking help. The front entrance was as deserted as a condemned building. Russell and Meito watched with their mouths gaping, brows twining, hearts raging, unsure how far Callis would go. The sharp end of the bayonet knifed near Bill's throat. Russell saw the blade's glimmer sitting on top of Bill's shoulder. Cringing, he grabbed the tip of the seat.

Callis flaunted a spiteful smirk. "Take off yer pants," he ordered.

Bill blinked. His hands began to tremble. Wetting his lips, he meekly replied, "I don't understand."

Callis nailed the butt of his bayonet into Bill's forehead, breaking his skin. Bill collapsed to the ground; a stream of blood sinking into his left eye. Dust outlined his body and powdered his blood. Horrified, Russell watched Callis' smirk saturate the side of his dimmed face. Meito flung the door open and ran to seize the weapon with both hands. Callis snarled, slamming Meito on the hood, twirling his bayonet, striking him on his cheekbone. When Meito lost his grip, Callis pushed him, forcing him to fall. Meito twisted his back and slid off the hood, landing on his stomach beside Bill. Callis kicked Meito in the ribs, kicking in a furious rhythm. Without thinking, Russell rushed from the car. He heard his own heart charging a thunderous shout, feeling a voltage twitch his muscles. This would be the last time the bastard would abuse them. In a flash, he seized the bayonet and kicked Callis in the ribs with his knee.

"Sonovabitch!" Callis gasped. He flabbily swung his free arm around, sweat trickling off his forehead.

Russell sprung back, still clutching the weapon. He kicked again, jabbing his foot in Callis' gut and yanking the bayonet out of his hand. He jumped back to move away from his brother, needing the room. Callis lunged forward to seize his gun. Russell twirled, hit Callis on his head with the butt, and watched him stumble backward.

Touching his forehead, he glared at Russell. "You'll get the fucking stockades for this!"

Growling, Callis hurled his bare knuckles toward Russell, thrusting his boots into the sand. Instantly, Russell dropped to the ground, wheeling his leg around to blow out Callis' knee. At that moment, he was glad Shikami had given him the ambition to learn new fighting techniques. Callis toppled down in pain as dust stuck to his sweat.

Meito sluggishly rose to his feet, moaning, using the hood for support. Spitting out specks of blood, he squinted at Bill who continued to lie on the ground. He could scarcely see Bill's blood dribbling onto the sand. His eyes remained closed, but at least he was still breathing. Meito removed his corduroy jacket and ripped the lining out. Painfully bending down to examine Bill, he gently lifted Bill's head to begin wrapping the linen around his wound. Meito knew he would need stitches.

Russell quickly ran to the car, and pushed the weapon underneath. Meito looked at him. He didn't know what to say to his brother.

Russell asked, "Will he be alright?"

"He should be."

Callis stood up, stealing sand inside his fist. He hopped on one leg, panting like a dog. His hatred oozed from his perspiration. He had never expected these spineless Japs to hit back. Assaulting a soldier was just as offensive as if they had assaulted the president of the United States.

Russell turned to face him. Without his weapon, Callis was nothing. Since the first day Russell arrived in camp, this tormentor manipulated his bayonet as a sanction for his rage. Always gripping it in his hand like a cane; always pitching an arrogant sneer just at the tip of the metal blade. Russell realized he was crippled without it. A passing vehicle on the highway scratched its lights over Callis' stiff body. Russell carefully watched him, suspecting he would try something devious. He stopped hobbling just four feet apart. Russell braced himself.

Callis bellowed, "What did you do with my goddamn gun, you little prick?"

He strained his jaw and imagined shooting the brute in his crotch. "What do you think? I sold it on the black market!"

"Goddamn wise ass! We'll see just how fucking funny you are in the goddamn chair!"

Russell peeked at the savage's hands, noting that one was opened, the other clinched. In a ruptured second, Russell ducked when Callis slung and released the sand in his fist. Sharp grains pricked one of Russell's eyes. He felt a blow to his ear. Toppling to the ground, another punch stabbed his ribs. Russell instantly rolled and opened his competent eye. He rolled again, withdrawing from Callis' stomping foot. Russell hurled sand toward Callis, giving him a moment to spring back on his feet. Callis swung his arms and missed. Russell lunged forward, pounding him to the earth. It didn't matter if his opponent was larger, just as long as Russell was more agile. They coiled on the deserts floor, provoking dust to race inside their mouths. Coughing, they punched their limbs as if scorpions fighting for a brash kill. Bruised, gasping, they tangled their loathing for each other under a yellow moon. With Callis' inferior knee, Russell squeezed his legs around it while dipping his arms behind his neck and flipping Callis on his belly. He applied a full-Nelson and pushed his knee into Callis' back. The harder he wiggled, Russell purposely stabbed his knee further into the Devil's brittle spine.

"Let me go you yella bastard!" Callis sputtered, desperately flinging his arms for control. He began a tangent of vulgar curses; the one thing he could do.

Russell ignored him. He knew if he allowed his emotions to control his strength, like that last time he fought Shikami, he would be no better than Callis. There had been endless nights when Russell imagined pounding Callis to a bloody mush of skin. The temptation existed. But so did his future. He did, however, manage to stab his knee into the bastard's spine once more. His adrenaline carved into his muscles, pumping, flexing, durable. He felt invincible. And strangely he felt drunk. His hurt ear continued to ring, his muscles ached, and nevertheless he refused to release Callis. The awareness of conquering his tormentor proved more exhilarating than anything else he had experienced. It overpowered the sensation of winning his wrestling matches in the past. Even beating Shikami. Russell learned he could do anything. Anything.

Meito tightened the knot around Bill's head. Patting his shoulder for reassurance, Meito slowly rose and walked to his brother. Astonished at how well Goro handled the situation, he studied him with admiration. He then realized he could start worrying less about his little brother. And that was a strong relief.

Seconds later, another MP ran past the two posts. The street light chased his back, outlining his face into obscurity. Arching his bayonet at Russell, he shouted, "Release him, now!"

Russell swiftly unbound his hands, releasing the bully, and cautiously eased to his feet. The sharp end of the weapon followed him as he slowly moved backwards with his palms out, proving his innocence. The soldier stepped closer, halting a foot from Callis' wheezing. Callis rose to his feet, and rolled his shoulders to shake out the pain. When the other soldier's face emerged into the light, Russell recognized him. To some extent, he was relieved to see it was Palmer.

Looking at Callis, Palmer asserted, "What in the *hell* just happened? I was only gone for five damn minutes!"

"These goddamn Japs shanghaied me!" Callis blustered. "And stole my weapon! They should be shot for insubordination!"

Looking at Russell, he demanded, "Where's the weapon?"

He cleared his throat and remained calm. "I took the gun from him after he began beating my friend and brother." He nodded toward Bill's vehicle. "It's under the car. We were only defending ourselves, sir."

"Liar!" Callis huffed. "Bunch of two-faced savages!"

"That's enough!" Palmer snapped. "Go retrieve your weapon."

Palmer quickly surveyed the area, watching his hot-headed partner limp to the parked car. Glancing at the two men near the hood of the car, one lying on the ground, the other shivering in the chill, he knew Callis had provoked these people. However, without proof, he had no other choice but to assume his partner's story- for the time being.

"Found it!" Callis boasted and pointed his loaded crutch at Meito. "Raise yer hands so I can see 'em!"

Forced to play this ludicrous game, Meito glared at the brute, easing his arms up.

"Walk closer to the car," Palmer said to Russell, still holding his rifle as required by his duty. When he stood beside Callis, he irritably exhaled, "Exactly what the hell brought this on? There's never been an incident at the front gate!"

"They were late for curfew," Callis said. "And they had their lights on in the middle of a black out!"

Confused, Palmer squinted. "How late could they be?" he asked. "I left two minutes before curfew to take a leak."

"Sometimes that's all it takes," he sneered.

Palmer examined his partner's cockiness. "And some of us are better at taking advantage of that moment."

Looking over the two men on the ground, Palmer finally saw the wounded man with a cloth wrapped around his head as red blotches soaked through. He shook his head and grunted. It annoyed him that something as stupid as this could occur. Especially so soon after the riot. He had heard of other minor riots and accidental shootings from the other camps. The WRA had tried to keep the majority of these reports silent in order to preserve tranquility. Sometimes the press got wind of it. For the most part, it seemed that these camps were nothing more than phantoms: something heard of but not seen.

"We need to get an ambulance out this way," Palmer remarked.

"Why?" Callis snorted. "It's not at though they can't fend for themselves."

"Shut it!" Palmer snapped at his dim-witted partner, although maintaining his bayonet upright, even if not directly at anyone. "I have no doubt you provoked these poor folks!"

Russell calmly asked Palmer, "Are we in trouble, sir?"

He hesitated before answering. "I don't know, son. But it sure doesn't look good."

* * *

PALMER patiently sat, carefully observing the major who came out from retirement to assist running the camp. He was a man in his fifties with thinning hair and dark wrinkles from practically living under the sun. His rounded face looked odd sitting on his thick neck. The major had seated himself in front of a narrow window without curtains, revealing the soldiers' barracks in the horizon. The investigation was going on its second day. Hopefully a decision would be made soon. Callis sat beside Palmer who irritably shook his leg, waiting for the major to speak. Palmer had to listen to Callis brag about how he laid out two of the Japs; the third one gave him a real challenge. He claimed they were resisting arrest when they were late for curfew.

The major loudly exhaled, interrupting the silence. Palmer instantly looked at him.

"Having interviewed all the parties involved," the major began, "I would like to hear your opinion, Private Palmer. What about this charge against this boy who seized Callis' weapon?"

Palmer cleared his throat. "Russell Hamaguchi took it *after* Callis nearly cracked open a man's skull. Then Russell put the weapon out of reach by sliding it under a car. It's evident he had no intention of ever discharging the gun, otherwise he would have done so. He had the opportunity and chose not to use it."

Callis glared at him, however Palmer ignored the attempted intimidation.

"What about the breaking of the curfew?" the major proceeded.

"Sir, I would have to question it. I was gone no more than five minutes. When I looked at my watch, it was only a couple of minutes before eighteen hundred hours. You're looking at a fine line."

"But you weren't there!" Callis bellowed.

He sarcastically replied, "Convenient for you, isn't it?"

Outraged, Callis swung his body toward the major. "Sir! I know this kid's a troublemaker! Just last year he refused to tell me who burned the American flag! He stole a radio! And now this!"

"But if you look at his record, sir," Palmer interjected, "you'll know this boy is clean. As well as his family. He's just a small town kid who made a couple of bad choices. Nothing more."

The major gnawed on his lip and nodded while scanning through the paperwork he collected. He was upset about the situation. Director Bridges had been working with the military to reconstruct a stable environment for Manzanar.

The longer they dwelled at this place, the more convinced many became that these camps were awkward. Despite some of the undesirables, like Katsuji and Saburo and their gangs, the idea that children lived here as well didn't seem right. Yet there was very little anyone could do to change it. There was a war after all. And orders must be followed.

He said, "Well, it does look like his father got in some trouble while building an illegal still in their barrack."

Palmer sighed. "Sir, no disrespect to the rules, sir, but if you lost everything and weren't sure of your future, wouldn't that make you want to take a swig or two?"

Staring directly at Palmer, shifting his jaw in thought, he replied, "I'm not in a position to answer that, private. But I do understand your point." Taking in a long breath, he continued, "There's still this matter of a civilian taking a piece of government property. And a lethal one at that."

"Exactly!" Callis projected, slapping his hand on his knee. "The dumb bastard oughta be tossed in the stockades!"

Palmer squeezed his fists, wanting to slug his so-called partner in the chops. He shifted closer to the major. "Callis has a reputation of harassing these people. I've witnessed it on several accounts."

"Harass?" Callis snapped. "I'm just doin' my goddamn job, Palmer! You know that!" He leaned to one side of the chair, smirking. "Besides, I don't find trouble! It finds me!"

The major grimaced, scanning at the list of complaints and warnings from Callis' commanding officer.

"My point is this, sir," Palmer persisted, "the boy removed the weapon out of his own hands as well as Callis'. And when I found them, the boy had Callis in a harmless headlock." He glanced at his fuming partner. "Besides, the boy is under age. What purpose would any of this serve?"

"What the hell are you, Palmer?" Callis chastised. "A Jap lover?"

"Private Callis," the major warned. "Mind your manners. I find your language not only vulgar, but immature. This isn't boot camp."

Again the major flipped through his paperwork. Callis was on the edge of getting booted out anyway, which seemed wasteful. Healthy men were needed for victory and it would be a shame to toss them aside because they were less than perfect. All they needed to be was loyal- which was Callis' *only* saving grace. Yet, it wouldn't hurt if Callis was someone else's problem.

He lowered his paperwork. "Having reviewed everything, and under your sergeant's recommendation," he then looked at Callis, "I concur that your skills would be best served in the South Pacific. Therefore, I plan to put in an immediate request for your transfer."

Callis' color in his face deteriorated. He had heard horror stories about decapitation and mutilation of American soldiers. Not to mention the rapid diseases and foot funguses that the jungles infected the men with. And insects as big as rats that sucked on men's blood until left for dead. The Pacific never got cold nor ever ceased from raining. If hell had a direction, it would be near Japan.

The major half-smiled. “There’s nothing like a little combat to bring out morality in a man.”

Lowering his head, Palmer smiled. Once that satisfaction settled in, he looked up to ask, “Sir, what about the boy?”

The major grabbed a green folder and shoved all his paperwork inside. Without returning the look to Palmer as he stood up to stuff everything inside a metal cabinet, he replied, “The same applies to the boy. Let him enlist. Should do more good than sending him to Leavenworth.”

CHAPTER FIVE

Mid March

NAOMI refused to rise out of her bed. Wrapped in her blankets, she quietly cried into her pillow. Today Russell would be leaving. And she hated goodbyes. Most of the people she cared about left her for one unfortunate reason or another. Her parents. Some of her white friends after Pearl Harbor. Now Russell. She knew this was it. How could she compete with distance and his girlfriend back on his island? One day they all would go home, and Naomi would become nothing more than a fling. Because she knew she would never see or hear from him again, there was no reason for her to tell him goodbye.

ARMY trucks reeled into the camp like a fishing line, and parked in a uniform column. The Bainbridge people waited in their traveling clothes, as they had done so before. About fifty of their members were absent; already relocated to other places for work far away from the existence of the camps. Bitter sentiments from the first evacuation streamed through their hearts, pushing against the faint disappointments and sorrow left on their island. Yet the assurance of change revived their hopes. They would reunite with friends and family in Minidoka; their kind of people; untroubled by gangs and political belligerence. It would be as though returning to the solidarity of their rural island.

Russell sat on his suitcase. A part of him felt relief to cast off bad memories. Another part resented what felt like ditching Naomi and his other friends. He knew long-distance relationships loosened strong ties. He thought about Maria, wondering if she still thought about him, wondering if she even still loved him. Her school photograph remained with him, from two years ago when they began dating. He missed her. Her optimism. Her habit of tilting her head when she smiled and her long hair falling to the side. Her touch. Often her lips tasted of peppermint. And there was genuine comfort in her presence. He thought about the promise he made to Maria, about returning home. How completely naive.

Jim walked to him, weaving around people who stood and chatted. His leather jacket and shoes appeared new, but in actuality were rarely worn; saving for special occasions. Although relocation could hardly qualify as special. Jim glanced at the soldiers jumping off the trucks to start loading the luggage.

He adjusted his glasses and said, "I've heard it actually rains in Idaho. That would be a novelty."

Russell squinted upward, trying to constrain the sunlight from glaring off Jim's shoulder. "It drizzled several times so far since we been here."

He grinned. "When you can count on one hand the times it rained that's not a good sign. I've told you this land is all dried up and useless."

Sighing, Russell stretched his back. He scanned at the western mountains that had been part of their back yard for almost a year- in a manner of speaking. "There is beauty here. I have to admit, I've never seen such colorful sunsets. It's almost peaceful."

"Sounds like you're going to miss this place," Jim remarked, amused. "Did the sun fry your brain again?"

"You're not gonna miss it? Not even your friends?"

Jim crossed his arms. "The friends I do have are also being relocated to Minidoka. So, no, I'm not going to miss this place."

"There he is!" Shig boasted with a cigarette between his fingers. He emerged through the crowd with Ralph, Bruce, and Hank faithfully following. "There's our *eiyu!* Our *shujinko!* Our hero!"

Russell sprang to his feet, smiling broadly. His California friends swayed like willows who were being guided by the course of the wind. Extending his hand to shake his farewell, Russell was relieved they came by to see him off. For a minute, he had begun to worry whether they would show at all.

Shig was the first to reach for his hand. "I wish I could of seen it!" he continued. "You give me reason to live, *omono-san!*"

Ralph then reached for his hand. "You're the poster boy for all *Nisei!*"

Bruce was next. "My first born son will be named after you, Russell!"

Russell proudly turned to Hank, his ego beginning to swell. Shy, reluctant Hank flickered a smile and shook his hand, saying nothing. Russell wasn't offended. That was just Hank.

Although Jim was glad that Callis got exactly what he deserved, he also felt displeased by Shig's public swaggering. It was inappropriate, if not shameful. He asserted, "Russell was lucky the soldier didn't kill him."

"Yeah," Shig leered. "Too bad *you* weren't there."

"What I mean is that I don't see the glory of Russell's behavior. He was only protecting himself, thereby making it his right. Not his glory."

"Is there a difference?" Shig snapped. He thinned his eyes at Jim. From day one they had judged each other with intensive suspicion.

"Thanks a lot, Jim," Russell sarcastically remarked. "That's one heck of a compliment!"

"It *is* a compliment," Jim defended. "I only meant that your instincts aren't fueled by vanity. They're honest and pure."

Rolling his tongue, Shig puffed his borrowed cigarette and exhaled. "Then are you implying that mine aren't pure?"

"I thought the implications were already there," he flatly said. "And since you're *so* full of Japanese wisdom, isn't knowledge without wisdom like a load of books on the back of an ass?"

Shig strained his jaw and started to breath deeply. "Asshole! It's snobs like you that give the rest of us a bad name! No wonder the rest of the world don't like us!"

"They don't like us because of superficial hotheads like you, *omono-san!*"

"Hey! Knock it off!" Russell injected, stepping in between his two friends. "The last thing I want to do is kick both of your asses before we leave!"

Jim stepped back, grimacing at Shig. Shig had a natural talent for inspiring trouble. Not to mention his flippancy ignored respect for others. Jim was more than elated knowing that today would be the last time he would encounter Shig. Glancing at Russell, he said, "I'll see you later," and walked away.

Shig waved at him and sneered, "*Sayonara, omono-san!* And don't forget that even monkeys fall from trees, jerk wad!"

"Don't rub it in," Russell warned. "He has good intentions. Just like you."

Shig rumpled his face and circled his eyes around as if two marbles swirling in empty bottles. Puffing his cigarette, he asked, "So, where's your gal? Isn't she gonna see you off, or what?"

Russell eagerly scanned over the crowd, hoping to spot Naomi soon. She had promised to be there. Forcing a grin, he replied, "You know how girls are. It takes them forever to get somewhere."

"Don't I know it!" he snickered. "Got four sisters!"

Russell watched the soldiers quickly and efficiently shove luggage into the trucks, and then extended their hands to help people jump up. The train at Lone Pine would depart in an hour. Hustling nearly two hundred folks would require cautious speed and it was like ushering a bunch of turtles in a race. Two army trucks began to pull out of camp, passing the two sentries. Fumes trespassed through the wire fence, leaving behind a bad smell and taste. Some coughed and flapped their hands in the air to fan out the dust mixed with the fumes. Shig babbled about how much time his sisters required to primp themselves. Russell started to worry as he watched the trucks drive off on the highway, not really listening. What if Naomi didn't arrive in time? Surely she knew better to calculate the time it took to walk from one side of the camp to the other. He patted his jacket's pocket to make sure the small gift was still tucked inside. Meito jogged towards him; just one truck across the line. Gertrude and their two sons were getting ready to load; each appropriately dressed for travel with cleaned clothes and polished shoes. His parents, alongside of Sadaye, readily stood by the rear of the next loading vehicle.

"Goro, pack up," Meito announced. "We'll be leaving in five minutes. Say your goodbyes now."

Panicking, Russell stared at his wristwatch. He wasn't ready. Two more trucks pulled out of Manzanar, withdrawing on a paved road towards a hopeful future. Again scanning the crowd, he wondered why in the hell she wasn't there yet! Maybe it was for the best. He hated farewells because it usually meant an indefinite thing. Yet, was that really the point? Didn't Naomi have the integrity to see him off?

Shig grabbed his hand, shaking it one last time. "It's been swell," he said. "You're a good friend to have around. Take care, *omono-san*."

Ralph, Bruce, and Hank followed his gesture, expressing their own sincerity. Russell felt a burden falling into the cavity of his belly. Glancing at Shig's boots, he snickered at the scars and would always remember those old army boots that his friend never removed, expect to sleep of course. He then glanced at Shig's brood whose slicked hair and wrinkled jeans became their trademark. Russell would miss these guys: these *yogores* from San Pedro. He leaned down for his suitcase, yet hesitated. Turning to Shig, he asked, "Can you do me one last favor?"

"Sure, man."

Russell removed the small box wrapped in striped paper. "Give this to Naomi. It's only a necklace, but I think she'll like it."

Flinging his cigarette aside, he was sorry to see Russell go. "I'm sure she will. But I think you should of gotten her a watch instead."

"Why?" he humorously responded. "So she could say goodbye to someone else on time?"

Shig chuckled and carefully slid the box inside the lining of his jacket. "I'll make sure she gets it."

Russell nodded and finally picked up his luggage. It felt heavier this time. He spotted his parents and sister hopping into the mouth of the truck with the canvas folded at the sides. His brother had already returned to the other one across the way, lifting up Joe and George. Russell shuffled to the rear, periodically looking for Naomi. He couldn't believe she just wouldn't show at all. Something had to have come about. Something big. Maybe the nuns forbade her. It was obvious they didn't like Russell hanging around. Maybe she became seriously ill last night. Although measles, mumps, chicken pox, and diphtheria were better contained, outbreaks could still occur at any time. Or maybe she was even bit by a rattler or stung by a scorpion. The possibilities seemed reasonable.

Handing over his suitcase to a soldier, he leapt inside and sat beside Sadaye. More people piled in. The cramped area made the air stuffy. Soon the space was completely full with luggage resting at their feet. Russell stared past the heads and out at the mountains. It had been the strangest year he encountered, yet it nearly became a home. Despite the grit in their rice, the scalding heat in the summer accompanied with walls of dust, or the brittle cold in the mornings, he got used to it. As much as he hated it, the environment was responsible for their livelihood.

The flaps were dropped, pulling dimness over their faces, except for a stream of light escaping through the gap. A soldier shouted the go-ahead. The dusty truck creaked and shuddered, slowly moving forward. Russell should have felt excited, nervous even. He would be reuniting with the rest of his family after another long trip. One and a half days, he was told. Almost like the train ride just the year before. Curtains swept down, no doubt. Very little to do on the train. Trapped. Russell had stashed his deck of cards in his pocket, hoping to occupy his boredom. As he heard the thick tires cut onto the highway, Russell stared at his feet. The idea that Naomi didn't make an effort to say good-bye disheartened him. No matter what story he tried to convince himself with, he realized she simply had chosen to not come. He would never see her again. And she broke her promise.

* * *

FIVE white buses entered Minidoka, past the front gate with their brakes squeaking, their engines rumbling. A crowd of family and friends huddled in the wind, excitedly waiting as the evening swelled into a thicket of stars. Jim gazed through the speckled window, watching the transition into their new environment. Idaho's desert had been left naked. Distant mountains were barely seen in plain view. A mound was left on the surface like a tumor, hardly attractive. The soft, brownish ground left creases as if a sloppy bed in the morning and impossible to make each day. Clots of snow lingered in a disordered pattern, leaking puddles. A creek aligned beside the camp but curved away from the fence, almost instinctively. And as usual, towns were remote, out of reach, detached from this back road. Jim waited for the elderly man, who sat beside him, strain as he rose and tottered down the aisle. He even waited for his mother and sister to shuffle ahead of him. The ride wasn't long from the train station, yet he still wished he could be near Tomiko. She assembled on another bus with her family, pretending a casual distance between them as they had managed on the train. It became more difficult to maintain. This unnatural formality. Sometimes he doubted whether waiting until senior graduation was even possible. He had been thinking about his own independence and responsibilities as a husband. Having his own space with Tomiko. His own income. He already knew how to supervise a business and its bookkeeping. At least his father taught him a useful skill.

Bethany suddenly turned around when he stepped into the aisle. "I can't believe this will be our third home! I hope Papa can finally meet us here."

Jim strained his mouth, peering at his sister. She had started wearing braids as her hair grew out. Before, he hadn't noticed that she was actually getting a bit taller. Sighing, he replied, "Maybe. The government certainly is taking its time with him."

She blinked. "What do you mean? Do you think he did something wrong?"

"Who knows what any of it means." He looked ahead. "You need to go, Bethany. The line's moving."

Disappointed by his lack of excitement and just hoping to hope, she frowned and returned forward to exit the bus.

When Jim hopped off the steps, he studied the area more closely. It amazed him how differently the horizon could appear once freed from the narrow scopes of shaded windows. It looked uglier than he thought. Reduced from the lusciousness of his island to the brittleness of Southern California to the bleakness of Central Idaho, he would have never considered homesickness. Most of his life he dreamt of leaving Bainbridge, and now, he began dreaming of the cedar trees and strawberry fields. Excited shouts and laughter sprung from the crowd like poppy seeds in a late Spring rush. Reunions decorated the evening with color and radiance. Jim saw Russell and his family intertwine into the crowd, quickly reuniting with the rest of their large family. They bundled in an irregular circle, embracing, smiling, chattering: all thirteen of them. Jim glanced at his mother and sister. The two held hands in the crowd of families, watching others connect while they stood alone.

He felt envious of Russell. And perhaps on some level he always had. If anything bothered Russell, he rarely let it on. And then there was his expansive family. Brothers. Sisters. Cousins. It would be impossible to image loneliness being a part of their lives. Even within Jim's own family, he felt isolated. But Tomiko somehow made it better. He could at least find room to breathe in comfort. The idea of starting their own family seemed attractive. Perhaps having six or seven children to fill up the quietness he grew up with. Let them clutter their rooms. Let them wear mismatched socks, at home of course, never in public. Let them speak without waiting for their father to tell them when they could. Still, he knew the timing wasn't possible. Not yet. Although he knew people who married in their junior year, most often because they were *forced* to; having a diploma and maintaining composure needed priority. There were too many *Nisei* who only had either a sixth grade or eighth grade education. A rural existence made it too convenient.

RUSSELL was surprised how much his other sister and sister-in-law changed the he last saw them. Even Tadao, his brother-in-law. He remembered Chiyeko with long, wavy hair she normally kept up in a scarf. Now with short hair, tucked behind her ears, freckles surfaced on her once clear complexion, making her appearance different from Sadaye's. In high school, many people thought they were twins because they looked so much alike. Kay, Kunio's wife, aged more quickly and looked a bit older by a few years. The desert burdens hadn't been gentle to her, it was evident. Chiyeko's husband, Tadao, or more simply Tad, greatly darkened under the constant sun. Back in Seattle, he had worked in a fishing factory, seldom seeing daylight. But between roofing and plowing potato fields for other farmers, his muscles strengthened along with his exposed skin. Russell began grabbing the suitcases that were being lined against the bus. Kunio and Meito ensued once they finished their long-awaited greetings. The women continued to chatter, clinging to their young children or grandchildren, wiping tears from their faces. Mr. Hamaguchi helped Gertrude hold one of the twins, rocking Joe from side to side. It seemed peculiar to be united as if the year spanned a decade. Russell had forgotten how Meito almost towered over everyone. He had always been an odd duck in the family.

"All the arrangements had been made," Kunio announced. "After the folks sign in at the administration, we'll show you where you're staying." He smiled at his brothers. "It should of been this way from the start. Splitting up families is just wrong."

Meito said, "Well, we're together now."

Kunio looked at Russell. "You, Mama and Papa will be staying with us."

Russell hesitated and stared in quiet protest. He hadn't forgotten how often Kunio complained about him. Every time he would visit Kunio in the city, his brother would tell him to be a more mature role model for his kids. Then he would gripe about the water rings left on the tables if Russell neglected to use the coasters. Or gripe about not rinsing the glasses once he finished. Kunio had transformed into a fascist after he married and started raising his own children.

He asked, "Are you sure it's a good idea?"

Kunio blinked. "What a dumb question to ask."

Russell grunted and remained silent. To argue would be useless. Especially when everyone was in a good mood. And that would be *another* thing Kunio would hold over his head.

* * *

ROSE settled seven-month-old Tomas, Jr. on her lap while she sat on the Chicago tram. The rattling rhythm reminded her of the Seattle trips she took through the city. Sometimes not going anywhere, only observing the city from stop to stop, observing people. Being part of civilization again synchronized her sanity. The desert isolation, with storms that elevated scalding heat or throbbing cold, would fling anyone into a crazy fit. Even though she missed the trees and the fields and the calmness of her rural island, at least the spring's cloudiness and light drizzle pacified her homesickness. She wore a new indigo dress with fashionable pleats around her waist under her dark coat with a matching rounded hat. It felt good that she bought it from a store instead of a catalog. Excited, glowing, she was on her way to a hairdresser recommended by one of Tom's co-worker's wives. Although Tom didn't enjoy assembling parts for Boeing B-17's, he made good pay and was equally glad to be out of Manzanar.

She watched a man read a newspaper that covered his face and nearly rested on his lap. His crossed leg revealed a polished shoe flopping in the aisle. Even well-to-do businessmen were rationing their gas for the war effort, taking public transportation one to three times a week. Rose's pleasing grin staggered when she studied the front headline of the *Chicago Tribune*. The words "Savage Japs" encouraged her to hold her son closer to her chest and kissed him on top of his head. Although her three month stay in Chicago had been peaceful, the threat of being exposed inflicted her doubt. Her current friends didn't know about the camps. She and Tom certainly weren't going to bring up the subject.

A middle-aged woman, who sat beside Rose, smiled at the baby. "He's a darling," she cooed.

Surprised, Rose looked at the stranger, not sure how to react. "Thank you," she said.

"What's his name?"

Readjusting him, she smiled in turn. "Thomas Jr."

"Oh! That's a strong name!" Her large bright blue eyes radiated under the arches of her thin brows. Her narrow red lips and portly nose gave a real Midwestern sincerity in her mannerisms. She asked, "Are you Korean?"

Rose hesitated. She glanced at the newspaper again and only nodded.

"I thought so!" the stranger continued. "I have a knack for pinpointing people's nationalities. I'm rarely wrong."

Forcing a smile, Rose remained silent. It was better to allow a stranger to do all the talking because it just made it better to hide the pain.

CHAPTER SIX

Question 27: "Are you willing to serve in the armed forces of the United States on combat duty, wherever ordered?"
Question 28: "Will you swear unqualified allegiance to the United States of America and faithfully defend the United States from any or all attack by foreign or domestic forces, and foreswear any form of allegiance or obedience to the Japanese emperor, or other foreign government, power or organization?"

LARGE, wet snowflakes tumbled from the sky like fallen, wilted petals. Kunio stood beside one of the windows, frowning at the single roll of a mountain behind the fence. He clutched a piece of paper in his left hand, the black ink slightly smeared. His eyes were watery, his nose reddened from a cold. Draped in a thick robe and layered socks, he waited for his family to return from church. Coughing, he returned to his bed. He balled the piece of paper and tossed it across the room. It was delivered from a friend who worked in the administration office, passing out early notices to a chosen few. It was bad enough the military requested them to answer two stupid questions to determine one's loyalty; now the military was requesting volunteers to be codebreakers in the Pacific. Kunio had the ability to learn languages. He knew German, some French, and when he studied Japanese before his children were born, he advanced three levels in a year and a half in Seattle. Today the military was in search of those who could help break the Japanese code. He chuckled. The military should have thought of that *before* placing them into concentration camps.

RUSSELL excitedly jogged down the soft street, needing to tell everyone the big decision he had just made. His old shoes collected mud from last week's melting snow. Clouds hid the glaring sun and its lustrous sky. Russell thought it ironic. At first he hated Manzanar's dehydrated environment that preserved a blazing shine. Ceaselessly blazing. His tanned skin signified as proof. Since Idaho's atmosphere was moist, flat, muddy even, he shouldn't have missed the influences of Death Valley. Oddly he did. The way someone missed expressing their bad habits. But more than anything he missed the uncompromising beauty of the mountains. They were hypnotic, making him forget why he was there.

He held a folded piece of paper and knew it would improve his life. It was an opportunity to finally reclaim his worth. For a year he had been doubting his purpose; his existence even. When he was a wrestler, or the son of a business owner and farmer, or a dutiful friend, he knew exactly where he belonged. He was somebody. Trying to find his individuality in these camps where he looked like everyone else to the outside world, where he was classified as the enemy, Russell owned little confidence. In Manzanar, by choosing to fight another gang, choosing to fight one of his own somehow appeared as if he were different. A hope that the outside world would notice he wasn't just a Jap. Or a Nip. Or a foreigner. Russell was certain that by joining the army he would not only reassemble his confidence, but also redeem his family's name in American society. They were just as loyal as the next family. If they weren't, then why in the hell did they sacrifice their lives to dwell in these kinds of camps?

JIM frowned and handed the paper back to Russell. "Your parents aren't going to sign this. Either of them would be crazy if they did."

Jim continued to pound a miniature post into the ground, aligned with three others arranged in a square. For his mother's birthday, he would prepare a small flower garden bordered by a picket fence and rocks. Bethany traded her *Orphan Annie* books for a package of tulip bulbs.

Annoyed, Russell demanded, "How is it crazy?"

"For one thing, you're still too young. You're not even old enough to legally drink, little alone vote." He straightened his back, holding the hammer at his waist side, glancing at people strolling down the unpaved street. A mild wind cooled his heated face. "Secondly, it's bullshit. Fight for freedom overseas when none of it is being practiced here." He bitterly chuckled. "Jesus, Russ. Why do you even *want* to join a segregated army?"

"Because I have to."

"You don't have to do a damn thing."

Russell curtly sighed. "Look at it this way: It's more like when my father lost his first business. It was a residential hotel deal. Remember when people wanted Bainbridge to be a vacation spot? Tried to bring in tourism to make our community more money?"

Jim nodded, leaning on one leg. The cynicism across his face was as sharp as broken glass.

"Your father helped mine get a loan," Russell continued. "He was able to rent a two story house, fix it up, the whole works. Anyway, when the Depression hit my father had to give up most of his farm so he wouldn't pay land rent, to keep up with the mortgage." Russell again hesitated, looking down at the dirt, remembering his mother's nightly weeping that lasted for a year. Everything they had worked for on the land had to be terminated. His family's modest income dwindled to a scarce amount. Extra income was fostered by Kunio and Meito working odd jobs all over the island; before they got married. "My father couldn't live with bankruptcy," he explained. "There were times we ate only rice once a day and that was it. Sometimes nothing at all."

Jim squinted, sympathizing with his friend, sometimes forgetting about other people's hardships. The Yoshimuras were one of the few families who were able to sustain a fluent stream of money. Others had to supplement with gardens. But during the winter months, Jim could only imagine what the Hamaguchis had to do to survive.

Russell looked up. "My father tried again five years later when Roosevelt rebuilt the banks. He still had credit which was unusual, as you well know. He reopened another business. It was his second chance." Without blinking, he gripped the piece of paper more tightly. "I want my second chance. I want it so bad I can actually taste blood in my mouth."

Jim flinched, surprised Russell would be so passionate about something as shallow as joining the military. It was the military that had forced them to relocate. That had brought guns, cages, and sentries into their lives. And had made them feel like criminals. Walking to a pile of wood, Jim bent down to pick up several pieces and a can of nails. He asked, "Is that what you want? Blood?"

"It's just a figure of speech."

"Is it?" He returned to the posts, squatted, and began hammering again.

Russell flinched, irritated by his harsh judgmental tone. Biting his lip, he said, "You didn't answer the two questions for the army."

"That loyalty questionnaire?" He grunted. "Hell no. I tossed the damned sheet into the stove."

"You have to give an answer! How would it look if you didn't?"

Jim shook his head, adjusting his position. "Those people are nothing more than a mob of hypocrites."

"Then fight for your family's honor, Jim! Prove to the world we're not just a bunch of Japs! That we're American citizens. We deserve respect."

Jim tapped his fingers inside the can of nails, feeling the tiny pricks. He still hated the place. It wasn't much different than Manzanar with creaky barracks; desert winds being pushed down from mountain tops near by; a barbed wire fence that insulted their dignity. "If you think by joining the army will earn their respect," Jim chided, "than you're nothing more than an idiot."

"I'm an idiot! I had no idea you thought so highly of me!"

"I just don't see why you would want to squander your life. Have yourself killed for what purpose?" he shrugged. "While you may or may not get your brains blow out, the rest of us will still rot behind barbed-wire fences. And someday, if we are allowed to leave, nothing will change. We'll still be Japs to the world. Still the bad guys who bombed Pearl Harbor." He stopped briefly to look up at Russell. "And if you're dead, then you just wasted your talents."

Russell crossed his arms and took a long sigh. "I don't know why I need to explain myself to you. If you can't understand it now, then I have nothing else to add. Besides, do you think it's a wise thing not answering the questions?"

Jim stood up, still feeling the prickling sensation on his finger tips. "By refusing to play their little game is proving something. And it's my right to refuse. That's the only aspect of my life they can't control."

Rubbing the back of his neck, concerned, Russell leaned closer. "Do you realize by refusing you may *never* have a chance to leave these camps?"

"Yes," he said bluntly. "They can put me on another one of their stupid lists for all I care."

"What does Tomiko think about your decision?"

He looked down. "She's entitled to her opinion."

"That's not what I mean!" he chuckled. "If you two were to get engaged and she has a chance to leave. . ." he paused, carefully studying Jim, "how awkward is that? She's already put up a lot from you."

Jim flicked his eyes at him. "What are you suggesting, Russell? That she'll find someone else? Someone *better*?"

"That you have to consider her feelings before you jump on your high horse!"

Jim swung his back around and began pounding a post. "What do *you* know?" he snapped. "We're already engaged!"

Russell stood motionless. "What?"

"We're keeping it quiet until graduation." He turned to another post and banged it with the hammer. "I do plan to talk to her about it. But in the meantime," he stopped, breathing heavily. "I'd appreciate it if you don't blab our engagement to anyone."

Russell pinched his brows together, not diverting his gaze from Jim's sharpness. "I don't get it. I thought I was your friend! Why wouldn't you tell me?"

Although Jim knew his brother was not at fault with Kiyoko's pregnancy, it still bothered him not knowing if his father understood. And it continued to bother him knowing who was responsible for inflicting pain on everyone while he flew around free as a jaybird. Because the two families shielded so much disgrace, indiscretion somehow provided a way to endure it. "It's complicated," he replied.

"Everything's complicated with you. It doesn't have to be, you know."

Jim knelt to sift through the raw pieces of wood. He muttered, "I wish that were true."

"And I wish you would trust me and you give me more credit." Russell paused to see if Jim would respond. When he kept his usual silence, Russell shook his head and asserted as he walked away, "Yeah, see you around!"

* * *

CHILDREN chased the tumbleweeds in the naked streets, laughing, shouting, and pretending the brittle balls were real toys. Joe and George seemed happy to play with their cousins Harry and Clara, who were at least a couple of years younger. Harry leapt like a frog after his sister, and Clara squealed with her dirty pants and socks. A few other children from the block joined in the game of hunting for tumbleweeds, although they were not allowed to actually touch them. Not only because the stiff weeds could hurt their little hands but also because their mothers didn't want to pull twigs out from their clothes and hair.

Gertrude and Kay sat in homemade lawn chairs, beside a dead garden that Kay had once attempted to grow. The infertile land rejected the meek stems before the tomatoes had a chance to survive. Draped in second-hand slacks to keep their legs warm and flowered scarves to keep their hair in place, they gossiped about their neighbors. Who made the loudest moans at night and how often. Who argued the most, evidence of a discontented marriage. Knowing which husband would sneak out or return home late, swaggering with fulfillment from another woman. There was one young couple in particular, the Nakazawas, when Mrs. Nakazawa would frequently have bruises on her arms; sometimes on her face. Whether in the mornings or evenings, Mrs. Nakazawa's screams would cut through the streets until Internal Police intervened. She would always proclaim her husband's innocence, and thus continued to endure his torment. Gertrude and Kay were grateful the Hamaguchi men were respectful, gentle, and devoted to their family.

Kunio carried a duffle bag over his shoulder as Russell followed from behind, lugging two duffle bags at his backside. Because Kay remained anemic, Kunio insisted he would perform the rigorous chores. Russell unwillingly agreed to help him with laundry, knowing if he refused Kunio, he would suffer a languished sermon about obligation and responsibility. Despite hating the idea they were the only men who stood behind the washboards as women snickered at them, choosing temporary humiliation over constant guilt should pay off in the long run. After all, he shared the same space with his demanding brother.

"Are you feeling better?" Kunio asked his wife, dropping the bag on his foot. "Did you finish eating some peanuts like the doctor said?"

She sighed, looking up. "Yes. I'm not completely helpless."

He reached for her hand. "Just get stronger for the children."

She didn't reply, merely squeezing his hand. Even though she appreciated his help, he never asked her. He never asked her if she wanted to give away their cat when they moved to Seattle. He just did. He never asked her if she wanted to marry him. He just said, "Let's go ahead and do it." She did love and trust him, but he assumed too much without asking. Unfortunately he caught that trait from his mother.

"So, Goro," Gertrude chimed, "how do you like doing laundry?"

"I don't. And I don't like being surrounded by old women."

She chuckled and winked at Kay. "Surely they all weren't old."

"Anyone ten years older than Goro is *too* old for him," Kunio remarked. "They can't flirt with him because it would be considered illegal."

Russell rolled his eyes, not amused. "Next year I'll be old enough to get into another set of trouble."

"That's not funny to joke about," Kunio scolded. "Consequences teach fools to know better. Don't be so careless."

Grunting and straining his jaw, he replied, "We just spent the last two hours trying to ignore being laughed at by old women. The only thing I've learned today is not to do it again. Otherwise, that would make me a fool a second time."

Kay and Gertrude glanced downward, smiling. To perform a woman's duty in public was indeed a brave act. Sometimes bachelors could wash their clothes without judgment, but a married man or a boy still living with his mother presented a different matter.

Kunio pressed his brows together and twitched the corner of his mouth. "Papa owned a laundry business for crying out loud! What's the difference?"

Russell snickered, "We don't get paid for doing it! At least cash gives a man dignity."

Swinging the bag over his shoulder, Kunio marched up the steps and slammed the door. Russell and his two sisters-in-law flinched.

Russell grinned widely, "I sure do hate it when he's wrong!"

Late March

PAPER scraps furnished the square table with patches of color. Bethany and her three friends sat at chatty attention, cutting out presidential silhouettes for their class. Lying on her bed resembled the first American flag with stars and stripes pasted on cardboard. A history book sprawled beside the flag; its pages dingy from years of sticky fingers. The room reeked of gooey-sweetness and diligent giggles. Mrs. Yoshimura poked the belly-stove with a rod iron. The forceful draft whistled through the wooden voids, bringing in more dust and chill. Although everyone bundled in their sweaters, the coolness became a stubborn familiarity, like a reoccurring rash. She smiled at her blossoming daughter and returned to ironing clothes. The children's laughter stuffed her emptiness, ignoring the sorrow of missing her grandson and husband. Her home felt somewhat settled that afternoon.

Jim entered at the side door. The girls disregarded his presence as they continued giggling and gossiping. He glanced at his sister's friends, frowning, and pounded his muddy shoes over the mat. He had retreated for an hour and a half walk, hoping to come back to find them already gone. Instead he found them exactly as he had left them.

Squeezing past Bethany, he muttered, "Even the tortoise would have won the race by now."

"Just 'cause you ran off doesn't mean we're racing," she quipped.

He grinned, impressed by her evolving wit. Her friends, however, still had a long journey ahead of them. Shuffling to his bed, he reached for a book on a wall shelf and pulled a blanket on a rope across his space. It seemed silly to pretend that additional walls existed, and that the shrilling voices could fade; but at least he couldn't see them. Slipping out of his grimy shoes, and then falling on his straw mattress, he began reading. Or at least attempted to read. His ears somehow persisted in listening to the drama of eleven-year-old girls. Who had crushes on boys. Who shared lunches together. Who passed notes to so-and-so. Jim consistently squirmed with each squeal. After ten minutes, he couldn't take much more of it.

"Alright!" he snapped, yanking his thin barrier open. Startled, they all shuttered into silence. Mrs. Yoshimura looked up, equally jolted. "You girls have been working on this project for over two hours! What have you accomplished?" No one answered. Bethany pointed to the uneven paper flag.

"How do you girls expect to accomplish anything with all this yammering?"

"*Jimmu*," Mrs. Yoshimura interjected. "*Allow Bethany and her friends to finish at their own pace. They are enjoying it*."

"And yet they've accomplished nothing, Mama." He examined each girl. "No offense, but none of you knows how to organize. You girls lack the discipline."

Bethany snickered. "You sound just like Papa!"

Jim flexed his jaw, and moaned in pure aggravation. He was nothing like their father. It disturbed him how his sister could be so damn ignorant as to imply such a comparison. Wrapping his arms across his chest, he asserted, "What is the purpose of this assignment, Bethany?"

"Um," she stumbled. "I think it's to um- show all the presidents and how the flag's changed."

He squinted. "And why is this important?"

"Um," she shrugged. "I dunno."

"Didn't your teacher explain it to you?"

She blinked. "Yes."

"So why is this important?"

Speechlessly pleading for help, her friends glanced away. Feeling abandoned, she meekly answered, "Because the teacher said so."

He sighed. "If you can't understand the goal of a project, then no wonder you're not finished. You have no sense of purpose."

One of Bethany's friends remarked, "We're only in the fifth grade."

"It doesn't matter. If you're old enough to talk about boys. . ." he stopped and cringed. Jim couldn't believe his youngest sister had been initiated on the matter. "You girls need to focus on another set of goals." Heading to them, he picked up Bethany's history book and laid it on the table. "Despite living in these camps, we have to pretend democracy works. We have to pretend freedom exists for all of us."

Mrs. Yoshimura reverted to ironing the clothes, trying to overlook her son's complaining, not wanting to worsen their circumstances by speaking openly.

"Slavery ended almost eighty years ago," he continued, "yet segregation exists all over the country. In the South. Then there are Indian reservations. And of course, there are Chinatowns or Jap Towns in all cities. These camps, for example. Now the military wants us to volunteer in segregated units."

Embarrassed, Bethany groaned and plunged her face into her hands. Her friends stared at him as if his set of brains had popped out of his head.

"Do you girls realize segregation *is* the result of democracy? It's the majority that always rules. Of course they don't teach you this in school." Flipping through the pages, he continued, "So then, how should you present your assignment? What do you think the purpose is?"

"I have to go home," one of girls mumbled.

"Me, too," another chimed.

Bethany raised her head, revealing her flushed cheeks.

"Sorry, Beth," the third remarked. "My parents want me home soon."

Horrified, she watched her friends quickly grab their belongings to skip out. She gazed up at her brother, tears swelling, feeling completely humiliated. "How could you do this to me?" she cried. "How could you be so mean?"

Puzzled, he defended, "I was trying to help."

"It was my project! My friends! And you ruined everything!"

"I didn't intend to scare off your friends, Bethany. I thought you needed some guidance because I got tired of you girls not talking about your project. Do you see?"

"I didn't ask you!" She yelled, standing up. "I didn't ask you, bonehead!"

"Bethany!" Mrs. Yoshimura gasped. "No bad names! Is bad mannas!"

"That's not fair, Mama! Jim said bad things against America and you didn't get after him!"

Mrs. Yoshimura nervously glanced at her son. She felt helpless. Her children were becoming more crude and outspoken as the months evolved into another harsh year. She had hoped that by moving to Minidoka family life would unify, that soon her husband would return home, that Jim would find a constructive purpose. Thus far, he developed an increasingly hostile mood. His complaints grew louder and more frequent. She feared he would do something he would later regret.

* * *

RUSSELL appeared interested in an open book, *Odyssey*, required in his literature class. The evening equaled in calmness; with the exception of a rattling roof provoked by an early wind storm. Lying on his cot, he constantly glanced at his mother who sat at the table with Kunio and Kay, playing Gin. He was waiting to relate his big news at some point, although knew his mother would not be as joyous. His father sat in a wooden lawn chair, listening to the world news. With his eyes shut, Russell wasn't sure if he was continuing to listen or had just fallen asleep. Beside his father, a flowered sheet hung to separate Harry and Clara's room. Every once in awhile, one of Russell's cousin's would cough. Kunio made sure his kids went to bed early. Better for the growth of their brains, he would tell Russell.

Closing the book, he decided it would be best to go for it. A couple of days ago he had passed his physical. Next month they would be shipping him off to boot camp; somewhere in Mississippi. Afraid someone else would spill the beans before he had a chance to personally warn her, Russell didn't tell any of his friends. Not even Jim. Not that he didn't trust Jim. It was obvious no one could crack him open. Russell already understood how Jim felt, so what would be the point?

Casually walking to his mother, he stood over her shoulder, easing his hands into his pockets. The dangling light bulbs slightly swung from the creaking beams. There were times Russell believed the ceiling would fly off in Manzanar. Fortunately it didn't. And fortunately he hadn't heard of it actually happening. It was one comforting thought during his entire experience there. Hopefully it wouldn't happen here either. He looked at Kunio and winked his code. Kunio would back him because he had also enlisted without telling her. This would be the night.

"Who's winning?" Russell asked, pretending to be interested.

"So far it's a tie between Mama and Kay," his brother replied.

"Then Mama's been catching on."

Mrs. Hamaguchi irritably rubbed her cards and tipped them closer to her chest. "If wan' pray, den sit. Udderwise, do ah not stand ober my ah back."

He raised his brows and grabbed a chair beside her. "Your English is improving. When did this happen?"

"You be too busy," she complained, sighing and organizing her stack. "Ohways gone. Ohways too busy for fam'ry."

He remained quiet. The only opportunity he spent time with his family was at night; just before bed. He didn't know what happened in their daily lives much more than they knew what occurred in his.

"So, Kunio," he began, slowly reeling out his objective. "Did you get a chance fill out that questionnaire?"

He squinted. "I did."

"Did you turn it in to the administration?"

Shaking his head, grinning, he repeated, "I did."

Mrs. Hamaguchi moaned and shifted in her seat. The women and *Issei* had a slightly different questionnaire to mark; provided by the WRA. When Kunio had translated it to her, she became outraged. It basically asked her and her husband to disown what citizenship they had left!

"*Those two questions are silly! And thoughtless!*" she criticized. "*We cannot have an American citizenship, but if we denounce our Japanese citizenship, then we are without a country! How can they put us in this situation?*"

Kay muttered, "I think it's meant only to draft *Nisei* men. The rest is a front. Making it look like it matters for the rest of us."

"Women can join WAC," Russell claimed.

"Just means we get to do more cleaning! At least we get paid for it," Kay smiled.

"Sadaye joined," he persisted. "That's not a bad idea, right Kunio?"

Kunio hesitated, looking at his wife. She already knew he signed up for military intelligence as a translator and code breaker in the South Pacific. Few were actually chosen based on their abilities and credentials. He had made arrangements that if anything should happen to him, Meito would take care of Kay and their two small children if he returned home in a body bag.

He finally replied, "It's all about commitment."

"Sacrifice, you mean," Kay said, fanning her cards.

Mrs. Hamaguchi inspected her children, fearing they were conspiring. First of all, Goro rarely volunteered to sit near her, especially when she was playing a game he considered dull. Secondly, she noticed that Kunio and Goro were *not* bickering.

Russell found a splinter in the wood and started tugging it backward. "I've heard great things about a *Nisei* regiment winning purple hearts all over Europe. I think they're all from Hawaii."

"*You are too young to join the army*," Mrs. Hamaguchi declared. "*You need to wait until you are eighteen.*"

Russell glanced at Kunio, surprised she had detected his plan that quickly. He hoped his brother would help thaw the brittle news to her. "I'll be eighteen in five months. What's the difference?"

"*In five months, you should be better prepared*," she insisted

"*Will you be pleased to know I have enlisted, Mama?*" Kunio asked on cue.

She blinked, and momentarily stopped breathing. Russell wasn't sure how to interpret his mother's reaction.

"*If this is what you need to do,*" she said. "*If you and Sadaye show support for this country, then it becomes the same responsibility for the family, too. This probably is a wise decision under the circumstances.*"

"I've already enlisted, Mama," Russell blurted.

She stared at him. "*Nai! I signed no such agreement!*"

"Papa has. I only need one signature from a parent."

Flabbergasted, she turned to stare at her napping husband. The static noises emerging from the radio saturated her ears, flooding her heart. She couldn't believe they made this decision without regarding her concerns. How could they engage in this act of betrayal? Slapping her cards on the table, she asserted, "*You cannot go!*"

Russell jerked backwards. "It's a done deal. Can't tell the army you changed your mind." He paused, thinking about a different approach. Lowering his head and voice, he altered languages. "*I asked Papa first because you were not here to ask.*"

Mrs. Hamaguchi glared at him, insulted he would mock her intelligence. "*Goro, I may be a simple housewife, but I know when my children are fibbing.*" She quickly pushed the table away from her, nearly squeezing Kunio. "*I will speak to whoever to undo this mess! You have no business going to war!*"

Mr. Hamaguchi snorted as he woke. Rubbing his eyes, he browsed around the room, realizing the tension that surged through. It wasn't difficult to calculate. All he had to do was look at his wife.

Russell crossed his arms and protested, "But Mama, you just gave your blessing to Kunio! Why not me?"

"*Because you need to finish school first! Because you are my youngest son! Because I say so!*"

"You're so stubborn!" he cried. "I have to do this now, right now, or I'll miss my big chance to make something of myself! I can always finish school later!"

She stood up, her face tightening, her muscles weakening. "*How can you finish school if you are dead?*" Her last few words cracked as tears flared out. She gasped and stumbled to her cot. Sitting down, she placed her hand over her mouth, trying not to fall apart in front of her children. Even if they were all grown.

Russell felt as though she had slapped him. And he felt dumb. He had been ready to defend his choice, convinced he was finally a man. And that integrity and honor were his best alibis. What he hadn't been prepared for, however, was watching his mother cry. He would rather see her angry than in pain.

Kunio clasped Kay's hand, quietly reassuring her.

Mr. Hamaguchi rose from his indoor lawn chair and walked to his wife. He missed her. They rarely spoke to each other despite living in such cramped quarters. Sitting beside her, he nestled his hand on her shoulder. She yanked away.

"*This is your fault!*" she sobbed.

He laid his hands together on his lap, sighing. "*This is not easy. I have lost much in a short amount of time. How can I continue to be a husband and father if I have nothing to give? If I have nothing to control?*" He looked up at his two sons, pleased about their loyalty to the family and to the country they were born in. Mr. Hamaguchi recognized their sacrifices meant bettering not only their own lives, but for their children's' lives after the war. The reason he agreed to sign Goro's enlistment paper was to insure hope for the future. That was the prospect for the *Nisei*. His had already passed. "*We should be proud we have raised strong children,*" Mr. Hamaguchi resumed. "*Their minds are following what we have taught them. It was our duty to raise them. Now it is their duty to fight for their homeland.*"

Stunned, impressed, Russell had seldom heard his father reveal earnest guidance.

Mrs. Hamaguchi brushed her loose hairs from her bun aside, sniffling. Looking down, she bitterly muttered, "*Goro had five more months left before going to war. Why did you take that from me?*" She then jumped up and grabbed her coat. "*I am going to stay the night with Meito. I am done talking to you!*"

THE mess hall rumbled voices off its walls, competing with the clinking of trays and utensils as if a disorderly symphony being directed with no tempo, no concord. The afternoon sunlight dove through the row of naked windows, flowing over people's faces; agitating them. Jim settled between Russell and Ikki while the rest of the Bainbridge clan discussed baseball. On some level Jim favored the company of being around people he grew-up among; it certainly retained a familiar security. Yet, at times, he wished they were a little more worldly; a little more conscious. Their conversations usually revolved three categories: sports, Nazis, and girls. They continued to speak as if nothing in their lives varied. Not about the draft. Not about the causes and effects of December's riot. Not even about their future. Their thoughts seemed nothing more than a static droll. Suspecting it was more of an avoidance approach, as if by not talking about these subjects would somehow abstain them from pain, it continued to bother Jim that it didn't seem to bother them. Although he had been noticing Ikki sitting quietly, swiveling an empty fork between his fingers, not engaging himself with the superficial chatter.

"What do you expect," one of Russell's friends argued, "when players like Ted Williams, Bernardino, Buddy Lewis, and Rigney enlist? There's nobody good left!"

"Like hell!" Russell boosted. "They keep the best ones on the field! You think they'll let Tobin and Cap Anson go off to war? There's different ways to fight and show patriotism. Like what the President said. America *needs* team spirit to beat Hitler! "

"But that still doesn't answer why we need women players," another friend contended. "Isn't it bad enough they're working in factories? Do they really need to take over baseball, too?"

"Are you kidding?" Russell grinned. "You mean you would blow a chance to look up girls' skirts? Give me a ticket! I'll let them sign their autograph just about anywhere!"

Laughter coursed around the table. The relocation to Idaho hadn't made a difference in their lifestyle. As far as they were concerned, they could be miserably amused at any place. Jim and Ikki, however, were not as equally entertained.

Jim blurted, "How can any of you ignore what's been going on? Has anyone else considered *not* answering that stupid questionnaire?"

The Bainbridge boys glanced at each other, avoiding Jim. Ikki stopped his swiveling.

"Don't any of you think it's insulting?" Jim persisted.

Russell joked, "I find this meal insulting! Honestly, who thought this beef could ever pass as a cow?"

A few boys chuckled with food in their mouths. Jim became more agitated.

"After all this time," he huffed, "after having our rights pissed on, don't any of you find it hypocritical? How can we support a democracy when it's nothing more than a goddamn lie?"

Russell began fidgeting. "I know the system isn't perfect- far from it, but to say it doesn't mean anything? That it's a lie?" He flexed his knuckles as he shook his head. "You have to believe in something, Jim. You have to find a way to make things better. I can't imagine what it would be like to not believe in something."

Jim rotated his body to confront Russell. "How can we have faith in a system that has destroyed our faith?"

He glanced at his friend, and firmly replied, "Only if you let it."

"Jim's right," Ikki interrupted. "If they can't trust us, then why in the hell should we trust them?" He impaled his potato with a fork and mumbled, "Bunch of two-faced bastards! If these goddamn camps didn't exist, Sam would still be alive!"

Everyone disconnected into silence. Sam's name hadn't been blatantly pronounced in months. To survive these conditions would require to not think at all. They could talk all they want, talk and joke and complain- just as long they didn't have to remember.

"I heard FDR has been encouraging night games so war workmen can attend," one of the boys timidly announced, trying to change the subject. "You know, for morale."

Ikki flung his potato on the floor. "Jesus Christ! Doesn't anyone give a damn!"

He leapt from the bench, flipping over his tray, and stomped out of the building. Jolted, the boys sat with confusion; unable to reassure Ikki; unable to reassure themselves. Jim knew what it was like to lose a family member, and knew the pain didn't lessen as people often said. It didn't lessen because there was no room for forgiveness.

Picking up the tray and scattered vegetables, Russell encouraged, "We'll get through this. Hell, if we can manage bad crops and no money," he paused to smile, "then this ain't nothing, *omonos!* This will be the only time in our lives we'll get free food. And we don't have to worry about rent. Really don't hafta work if we choose not to."

"Yeah, a real dream come true," another chimed, taking Ikki's abandoned beef patty from the table and dropping it on his tray.

"The surface isn't that clean," Russell said.

"Compared to what? The kitchen in the back? The last time these forks were shiny was when I saw pigs fly!"

Some snickered.

Jim brushed aside some of the peas and carrots, exasperated. "I was trying to hold an important discussion, but you people don't seem to take life seriously."

"We can take anything that's dished out," Russell sighed, dumping food particles into the tray. He sensed Jim was in one of his moods. "And we take life serious enough, don't worry."

"But do you agree this questionnaire is a pathetic way to draft us? Now that they're needing more men to fight, they're scraping at the bottom of a barrel."

"Boy, Jim," Russell jeered, "you sure do know how to inspire."

"Dammit, this is exactly what I'm talking about!" he snapped, standing up. Narrowing his eyes as the noises from the mess hall gritted against his nerves, the rumble throbbed louder in his ears. "Russell, you can't joke about everything! You dismiss everything so easily and you end up looking like a clown! Why do you think for the longest time I thought you were one of the biggest fools?"

Everyone grabbed their trays and scooted to the edges their seats as if dividing the Red Sea. People nearby turned to look at the dispute. Russell squeezed both ends of the tray, retaining his urge to whack Jim's face with it. Breathing unevenly, he sharply replied, "I can't believe you think so little of me! I thought we were friends."

Jim blinked, surprised Russell misinterpreted his intentions. "My point is you're not stupid, Russell. But I fail to understand why you sometimes *act* like it."

Remembering his Judo instructor's guidance about control, about tolerance, he thought before he reacted. "And what about you, smart guy? You're moody. You complain more than my mother ever did! And your sense of humor is lousy! Jim, despite your good days, you're one of the most selfish jerks I know!"

"Oh, I'm a selfish jerk? When did you do anything without worrying how people judge you? Or how your actions have consequences for the rest of the family? For years you've stripped off your Japanese heritage and embarrassed your parents from lack of discipline!"

"I know I'm not perfect, but I do have respect for others! Think about it Jim. If *you* respected other people's opinions, then that would make *you* less of an asshole!"

Jim slammed his knuckled onto the table. "You're the asshole if you think the government isn't going to screw you when you bend over! So go! Leave everyone behind! Go be such a great war hero! Joining the army won't make your eyes look any less slanted!"

He glared at Jim for a moment before responding. "That was low. Even coming from someone like you."

"Someone like me?"

"Yeah. A spoiled . . . little . . . brat."

Clenching his fists and breathing heavily, he yelled, "You can go straight to hell, Russell! As far as I'm concerned, we were never friends! Just stay out of my life! Leave me the hell alone, you lunatic!"

Abandoning his tray and his place at the table, Jim walked away. He figured it was best. After all, they had nothing in common, and Russell was betraying their friendship by aligning with Uncle Sam. The very same democratic "uncle" that betrayed them and their families. Not only that, Jim wasn't going to stay around to watch Russell's body being dumped into the ground when he came back from the war.

Russell stood dumbfounded. He felt as though Jim actually stabbed him in the gut. Infuriated, he yelled across the room, "Jim, you can screw yourself on your way out!"

"Hey!" a man shouted, rising from another table. "There are women and children present, so watch your language!"

Brushing his hand through his hair, embarrassed, he confessed, "Sorry! I'm sorry, sir. It won't happen again."

The audience slowly returned to chattering and eating, unaffected by the afternoon's commotion. Dizzy, befuddled, Russell slowly swiveled as if an explanation would drop from the ceiling. In spite of all the favors he did for Jim, covering for him that time he was stuck in the shed, or patching up things between him and Tomiko, or even allowing him to be his friend in the first place, Russell couldn't believe his fickleness. His ability to reject. Just like that. Just like *that*.

CHAPTER SEVEN

Mid April

THE overcast smeared streaks of rain over the flat horizon, concealing the plump mountain. For two weeks its grayish shadow became fatigued and deficient of all colors. The environment's complexion remained a familiarity for the community, descending from the Pacific Northwest; with the exception the solace of the ocean. The Bainbridge islanders were closer to home. It offered a bit of hope. A bit of relief. The rains, aside from gloom and large ponds all over camp, had announced opportunities. Fresh harvest allowed people to escape isolation and idleness; despite the progression of the desert colony. Local newspapers became less interested with these camps' affairs while the war's progression favored the Allies: Victory with the Battle of the Bismarck. The falling back of the Japanese from the Yangtze River. And the ousting of the Germans from Africa. Everyone knew they were going to win. It was inevitable. And with that would come absolution. Finally.

RUSSELL helped his sister carry bags from the Co-op store. Sadaye had asked him since he was the only one who didn't seem busy at the moment. As a favor for their mother, they bought rolls of fabric and yarn, green tea, and packets of paper and pens. Sadaye clutched an umbrella, trying to protect her WAC uniform against the drizzle. Russell couldn't care less. The walk was fairly short, and by the time they returned, he would have to change anyway. Although his raincoat provided some coverage, his jeans and head were drenched. Not only from the drizzle, but also from sloshing through what seemed like narrow lakes. The moisture even shriveled the barracks' tar paper like skin saturated in water. Despite the spring rains which continued to flood, a part of him felt comforted by it. He had missed the rain a great deal.

Sadaye looked distinctive in her navy-blue uniform, entailing a skirt, a blazer with a tie and cufflinks, a miniature hat, although her yellow galoshes struggled to uphold her refinement. And Russell thought the square hat amusingly resembled a toy French officer.

Glancing at his sister, he had to ask, "So, are you still writing to Jerry from New Jersey?"

She conserved a quietness before answering. "No. Deep down I knew it really was a matter of time. Just as well, I guess. We come from completely different backgrounds. I can't help think sometimes . . ." she stopped, revealing discomfort in between her brows. "I sometimes think I may not find anyone. I'm twenty-three and have no one in my life. Soon I'll be an old maid."

"Maybe it's not your time just yet, Sadaye. Maybe you're supposed to do something big first before you get married."

"Like what?"

"I dunno. You're real good at being a nurse. Maybe you should be a doctor. You've got more brains than me! Why not?"

She lowered her chin and leaked an aspiring grin. "A doctor. I think I'm too old to go to college. That's a long time, Goro. And besides, we can't afford it. Where could we get that kind of money?"

"Aren't there loans or something?"

"We have no collateral. We don't even own a car anymore."

Russell peered at the ground, pinching his lips, thinking. "There has to be a way somehow. I know at Manzanar's hospital there was a woman doctor. If she could do it, I don't see why you can't. Besides," he turned to face her, "look at Mama and Papa. I don't want to get stiff in the hands picking strawberries. Or break my back doing other people's laundry. We can do more with our lives."

"A doctor?" She permitted the idea to linger in her ears. "I've always wanted to be head nurse, but I hadn't thought about going beyond it."

"Well, think about it," he smiled.

She peered at her brother, grinning. "Well, that's one heck of a boost. When did you get mature?"

"Ahh!" he whisked. "Who says I actually am?"

She laughed. "I suppose it is still a work in progress!" When she finished laughing, she said, "Thanks, Goro. For listening. And not telling Mama about Jerry. You've been a good friend."

Russell was speechless. He would have never conceived that his older nagging sister would regard him as nothing more than a nuisance. Flattered, he exhibited a grin.

"Oh, hey!" she said. "I've been meaning to ask. Is Jim alright? I haven't seen him come by this way for a couple of weeks now. He's not sick, is he?"

Russell crinkled his nose in disgust. "In the head, maybe!"

"What?" she chuckled. "Why would you say that?"

Grunting, he shook his head. "We got into this really big fight. He's all upset I joined the army. Because I don't agree with his opinions, his royal highness has decided to end our friendship!"

Tilting her head in disbelief, she remarked, "So, you two aren't friends anymore? It's because of that dim-witted questionnaire, isn't it?"

"I guess!"

Sadaye remained quiet for a moment. "I can see Jim's point. How much more pain can a person take? And this loyalty thing they're passing out only makes it worse. As if by answering *yes* or *no* will make the government feel better where to put us next. As if our loyalty can be measured by a piece of paper." She paused to glance at her brother. "I know you're angry at Jim right now. Remember he's lost his brother, his father, and now he's losing you, too. Don't let one stupid fight end your friendship."

Russell grimaced. "Just because we hung out together doesn't mean we were friends."

Smiling softly, she remarked, "Just make sure you say goodbye to him before you leave."

"When pigs fly!"

Sadaye walked up the steps of the barrack to open the door. Holding a small damp bag in one arm, she clumsily managed to fold and shake her umbrella, then hesitated before entering. "Seriously, Goro. Don't let this fight be the last exchange of words you two have before you go off to war. You'll regret it."

He looked away and said nothing. Following his sister inside, "Happy journey!" sprang unison. Russell jolted. His heart pounced in his throat. Completely stunned, he gazed around to discover all of his family crammed in his barrack.

Kunio stepped forward to take the bags and said, "They got me twenty minutes ago!"

Sadaye poked him. "Did you really think I enjoyed your company enough to come with me to the store?"

Breathing again, the warmth of their body heat ceded Russell's shivering. He stumbled into laughter, shaking his head. "I don't know what to say!"

Meito emerged from the group. "Well little brother, this is yours and Kunio's golden moment. May good fortune bless you both." He looked at Kunio. "And may you both come home in one piece."

An uncomfortable muteness quivered through their bones.

"*Let us bring out the cake!*" Mr. Hamaguchi exclaimed.

"*Keh-ki*! *Keh-ki*!" George repeated, one of the few Japanese words he knew.

Gertrude, who was four months pregnant and now showing it, removed the glass from the conjoined plate, revealing a chocolate clump that sat on a table. Clara and Joe instantly clapped and squealed. Since they had been in the camps, they were denied sweets and pastries of any kind. Anticipating the joy, they hoped another relative would go off to war so they could have another chance of cake.

"Mine!" Harry blurted, his little fingers brushing the bottom of the frosting.

Kay grabbed his hands. "No, Harry!" She knelt to wipe them clean, blushing. "You have to wait your turn!"

Everyone chuckled, not too concerned about the cake's defect while Gertrude started slicing. Chiyeko assisted in the distribution, circulating plates after Gertrude placed slices along with forks. Tadao, Russell's brother-in-law, scooped a piece of cake into his mouth and instantly made a sour face. Others imitated soon after biting into it, including the children.

"Gertrude, no offense," Tadao began, "but this cake is missing something important."

Gertrude glared at him. "If you've forgotten sugar is rationed. So I found a recipe that uses a substitute."

"How can you substitute sugar?" he asked, completely disappointed. "I've been looking forward to this cake all week."

Chiyeko scolded her husband. "Beggars can't be choosers, Tad. You could be a bit more considerate, and just get used to it."

"That's been my problem. Getting use to everything," he muttered.

Gertrude slammed the knife on the table, her lips straining. "I did the best I could with what I got! I'm sorry for ruining the party!"

Tugging on his mother's dress, Joe encouraged with chocolate smeared on his mouth, "I like the cake, Mama. You're a good cook."

Chiyeko gently placed her hands over Gertrude's shoulders, squeezing tenderly. "Gerdie, the cake is fine. Let's just have a good time today. Don't worry about the cake, alright?"

"I've never had any objections about your cooking," Meito included. Frowning at Tadao, he stated, "I think someone owes my wife an apology."

With each person staring at him, Tadao nervously fidgeted. Russell thought he looked like an infant bird that fell out of a tree; twitching; helpless; expecting to die.

"I'm sorry, Gerdie," he said.

She sighed and nodded her forgiveness. The unpleasantness subsided, allowing everyone to fuse into chattering and avoiding the cake. Russell observed his family while they tried to sustain a natural spirit, pretending war wasn't on their minds. They talked about mundane events: school, flower design classes, softball, harvest opportunities. He would miss them. And their boring conversations. Not knowing if this would be his last privilege standing among them, he carefully remembered each face, hoping his memory would stretch clearly over time.

Mrs. Hamaguchi struggled to move toward the front where Russell and Kunio remained, bumping into her large family. She carried two white scarves with layers of red, horizontal stitches. The idea of sacrificing two sons in one month had never settled well with her; however, she had to accept why they were doing it. For honor. For family. And she began missing her children, both so handsome, so healthy and respectable, she wished they had an opportunity to know their grandparents back in Japan. Their aunts and uncles. Their cousins. Raising her children without the rest of her family proved both liberating and heartbreaking. No criticism also included no support. Yielding to her sons, all three circling collectively, she fluttered her eyes to reserve her tears. Meito, Kunio, and Russell stopped talking, waiting for her to speak. Mrs. Hamaguchi's tongue seemed disoriented; muted. Looking up at her sons, she gave Kunio and Russell the traditional scarves.

Kunio asked, "What are these, Mama?"

Clearing her voice, she replied, "*This past month I went around the blocks inviting friends and neighbors to sew a stitch. It is customary acquiring a thousand stitches for good luck.*"

They were dumbfounded.

"You sought out a thousand people?" Russell asked.

"*Hai*," she nodded.

Russell studied the special scarf, completely awed. "Mama, this is unbelievable!"

Kunio leaned forward to kiss his mother on her cheek. "*Domo arigato*."

Following his older brother's lead, Russell likewise kissed his mother. Feeling inspired, he didn't think she would ever approve. Linking the scarf in both hands, he envisioned her trudging all over the camp, in the rain, in the wind, seeking a thousand blessings. Her extraordinary dedication not only conceded her approval, but also her love. Not that he ever doubted her love as a mother, except now he truly appreciated it.

Early June

MID EVENING deluded the sun's rich pigments, allowing the half-moon and its dark cloak to sag over the horizon. A salty breeze vanished from the sea, reminding Maria of her emptiness. Wrapping her arms around her chest, she ambled out of the small theater with Mario beside her. Both quiet. The newsreels about the war only inflicted more emptiness. As the year stretched into another, the island seemed to shrink while boys left Bainbridge to possibly die. Yellow ribbons began to decorate her neighbor's doors, glaring brightly behind trees and mailboxes. A third of her classmates were gone. And more were in the process of leaving.

She glanced at Mario. He was a decent-looking guy who had no scars on his face. She didn't mind that. His lighter skin revealed prestige, unlike hers, indicating a true catch. Her father certainly had supported her choice this time. Unfairly so. Mario had graduated last year, but decided to wait until the draft snatched him for the war. Which it now had. He suddenly took her hand. Startled, Maria flinched. His hand felt cold, sweaty, and slightly trembled. He veered her away from the path, away from the meager trickling crowd, nearer to the wall of trees. He then coiled his fingers in between hers and stared without blinking. She remained quiet; indifferent.

"We hafe been dating for long time, now," he expressed. "I know you don' lofe me, Maria. But one day, I hope you will."

She looked down, ashamed for using him to please her father and to pass her time. Sadly, Mario knew and yet he persisted anyway.

Kneeling on one knee, he continued, "Maria, before I go to boot camp, will you marry me?"

She jerked her arm, except Mario refused to release her. Angered, she gasped. Her heart drilled against her lung. Feeling cheated with this promise, she thought about Russell and his promise. Recently she acquired a letter from him, informing her that he had volunteered and would be sent to Hattiesburg, Mississippi. She wished he hadn't. At least the camps guaranteed he would live. But now, he would have a fifty-fifty chance of dying. All this time she hoped

Russell would return home. And now, she may never see him again. So unintentionally, he lied about returning home. She began crying. Mario suddenly rose to embrace her and she instinctively locked her bones, restrained her breath. Yet, much to her confusion, the warmth of his body tricked her mind and body. The familiarity reminded her how greatly she needed to be loved. And to love in turn. Her choices were narrow with only a few eligible boys of her kind. Unless she moved to the cities. Unfortunately, the only valuable skill she possessed was harvesting. Maria cherished the lasting bonds that supported the island and hated the transient lifestyle of migrant workers. She would never do that again. Not for herself. And not for her children.

Reluctantly embracing him, she whispered, “Yes, I marry you.”

Early July

JIM positioned his hands over his knees and kept his back upright when he settled in the wooden chair. Someone closed the door, shutting out the typewriter’s rhythm, making the small room shrink. It had been sectioned off from the entire administration building. Examining the two men in short-sleeve shirts and ties, who sat behind a table with columns of paper near their elbows, he knew this meeting would be a waste of his time. He heard that for those who either withheld from answering the loyalty questionnaire, or answered with at least one “no” were given a second chance to amend their ways. Some in fact did. Like Ikki, which greatly disappointed Jim; changing his mind as though changing his dirty underwear. A half-glass of water sat between the stack of papers and the edge of the table. Despite that all the windows were unlocked and gaping like yawning lions, and despite that a series of fans were rotating, the early afternoon heat still forced everyone to sweat.

One of the men, a balding and unappealing individual, started, “Are you Jim Yoshimura?”

“Yes.”

The man skimmed down a piece of paper, then lifted it to skim another one. “It appears you have refused to answer questions 27 and 28.” He looked up. “Why?”

“They’re degrading questions. First of all, how can I fight for a country that preaches on freedom while I’m imprisoned?”

“This is not a prison, boy,” the man interrupted. “It’s a relocation center.”

Jim frowned. “How about detention center? How about custody? Confinement? Incarceration . . .”

“That’s enough!” he snapped, his thick brows twitching.

Jim paused to notice the disdain on both of their faces before resuming.

“Secondly, I don’t appreciate you implying that I never was loyal to America in the first place. I was born and raised here. I know no other country.”

“Then there shouldn’t be a problem defending your country,” the bald man said.

“I’ll defend my country the day my country defends *my* rights.”

The second man remarked, “You know these camps are offered to protect you.”

"It's a concentration camp! Who's really getting protected? My family and friends are treated like criminals. Look at the barbed-wire fence and sentry posts. Look at the soldiers carrying guns around innocent children!"

Both men were straining in silence before the second one cautiously replied, "To make sure the civility of the situation remains . . . civil. I don't need to explain further, young man, so I advise you to move on."

Jim warily stared at these two bureaucrats. "And finally, I also don't appreciate the situation my parents are in. They have no citizenship here, but if they denounce Japan, then they'll have absolutely *no* citizenship. They'll be without a country! What will happen to them after the war? Will *you* guarantee their protection?"

A disturbing stillness advanced in the room, hovering in the heat like a swarm of wasps. The balding man shuffled through his papers; sighing; sniffling. Jim didn't trust those papers, knowing these men could use the ink as another form of artillery. Anything could be written on those pages to justify this polite interrogation. If the FBI didn't have a reputation of misusing the information they gathered, then his father would have never been arrested, nor would Jim be sitting in a hot, little room defending himself.

"You have some relatives serving in the Japanese military," the grumpy, bald man continued. "Is that correct?"

"I guess. I never met them."

"It looks like your father had also served in the Japanese navy."

Jim flexed his knuckles. He could see where they were taking him. "Over a quarter of a century ago."

"But now your father is being detained in Missoula for treason. Is that correct?"

"Those charges are false!" he asserted, feeling his heart lashing.

"That's what his hearing will determine," he chided. "And, up until the war, he had lingering connections to Japan."

"His family's *from* Japan. What do you expect?"

"So are you saying *your* loyalties are likewise are with Japan?"

"How can that be possible?" he retorted. "I've never been there!"

"The apple usually doesn't fall far from the tree, does it, boy? The FBI has been monitoring your father's correspondence for the last ten years."

Jim was flabbergasted. He knew they had been watching his father since Pearl Harbor; however to have been spying on him for a decade? There was no war at that time! Or had they been anticipating it from the start? When the Japanese military first invaded Manchuria? Exactly where was the connection?

"This is a grievous state of affairs," the bald man grunted. He glanced at his quiet partner and rested his hands over Jim's file. His impatience dripped out of his pores. "How can we be sure your loyalties aren't linked with your father's? Your reluctance to answer these questions can only make us conclude to one thing. Frankly, your attitude offends me a great deal, boy."

"Stop calling me *boy*!" Jim affirmed. "You're not accusing me like a child so treat me with some respect," then he sarcastically emphasized, "*sir*."

"You're right," the bald man said. "You're not a child. And yet you're not a full-grown man, either." He leaned back and cracked his knuckles, looking at his partner to carry on.

Jim realized both were presenting an act. Almost bullying him into submission; this forceful burden they were trying to impose on him.

The second man leaned forward and drank the rest of his water. Setting it down, he announced, "Today we're giving you a second chance to do what's right. To make things right. To take your responsibilities as an American, and as a man. I think that's more than fair, really. Don't you?" He flickered a smile. "Now then, how do you choose to respond to questions 27 and 28?"

Early August

WIPING sweat from his forehead, Russell jogged through the bare, broad alleys as mud stuck to his heavy boots from the afternoon thunderstorm. He shouted his greetings to his fellow buddies. All *Nisei.* This section of boot camp had been "reserved" uniquely for them; however that was nothing new and therefore required little transition. Camp Shelby, like all things military, equaled in design to that of Manzanar and Minidoka. But only in design. The absence of women and dance halls made the stay less accommodating. Like joining a monastery. Without tranquility, of course. Compliments of an abrasive drill sergeant. The climate, on the other hand, denied its victims sympathy. The cotton uniform absorbed his perspiration, forming soggy patches along the sides of his upper body. Although the evening sun had doused its afternoon fire, humidity idled in the air: clammy; congested; unbearable. As if the swarms of blood suckers weren't aggravating enough. Or the millions of gnats. Or the shrilling pulsations of locusts droning with the crickets. It was a foreign, exotic land of its own.

Rushing inside his quarters, Russell carried a stack of letters; eager to read news from both homefronts. He plopped down on his cot, instantly undoing all his buttons for air. A weak breeze panted through the windows, struggling to trail behind a couple of fans. Most of his bunk mates were stripped down to their boxers and undershirts; their dog tags hinging around their necks. Leaning over his knees, ignoring the odor of sweaty feet and mildew, he shuffled the envelopes, choosing to read Maria's letter first. He had been speculating why it took so long for her to reply. No doubt her father slowed down their only means of communication. That or bureaucracy. While he tore the edges, someone slapped his shoulder, startling him.

"Goddamn, it's miserable in here!" Shig boasted.

"Do you mind?" he snapped. "I'm busy and would like some privacy!"

Shig sat across from him, unbuttoning his sweaty shirt. "The only privacy you'll get is when lights are out and you're under your sheets, *omono*."

He glared, not amused. Unfolding the single sheet of paper, he began reading.

"I hate wearing uniforms," Shig interrupted, slinging his shirt on his cot.

"Not my fault," Russell muttered, squinting at the letter. "You volunteered like an idiot."

"I don't mind the cause. I just hate the conformity."

Russell looked up, completely annoyed. "Shig, can't you wait 'till I'm done? Don't you have anything else better to do?"

Insulted, he sprung to his feet. His pants drooped, like many others whose military outfits were customized for taller men. Anyone under five foot three seemed virtually engulfed.

He defended, "All I'm saying is, with these uniforms, we look like a bunch of sissy Boy Scouts. Look." He yanked his slacks. "They barely fit us!"

Russell curtly sighed. "I've been waiting to hear from Maria for two and half months. Now that I have, you wanna talk about how you look?"

He narrowed his eyes, revealing dark, moist sags underneath; tired from the relentless heat; tired from the mundane exercises and practices; tired from wondering when Sergeant Stockwell would tell them they were ready to fight overseas. They were encroaching on twelve weeks whereas everyone else was being trained in half that time. It aggravated him recognizing how the government continued to mistrust them. Despite answering favorably on the questionnaire. Despite volunteering.

"It's probably a *Dear John* letter anyway," he retorted, walking off.

Frowning, Russell returned to the letter. He knew she would never do that to him, even though there were times he dwelled in doubt. As often as he thought about her, he knew, deep down, she was exceptionally faithful. Unlike Naomi who never said goodbye. Never wrote. But after he rushed the first two lines, the third one made him cease from reading. He had read enough and didn't need further explanation. Folding the letter and slipping it back inside the envelope, he reached for another instead. He let Meito's words distract her last words, "I have married someone else . . ." Pretending to smile, he assumed the news from his brother could erase Maria's lie. Gertrude had another baby, a girl, Amelia, who was born six weeks earlier and had to be transported to another hospital for additional care. Fortunately Amelia was strong natured and would be returning home soon.

Shouts suddenly punctured the dense air. Russell looked up. Everyone turned toward the windows where the shouting ensued. Rising to his feet, Russell strode across the room to peek over the men's shoulders. Stunned to find Shig yelling at one of their bunk mates, he watched in confusion as the two circled each other like roosters in a pen.

"I'm the *stupid* one?" Shig projected, knotting and hitting his fist against his own chest. "At least I can speak real English, you ignorant sonofabitch!"

Roku, a muscular Hawaiian with a narrow frame and bronzed coarsen skin, bellowed, "You *kontonks*, all alike! *Kontonks* tank so much better dan us! So priv'rieged!"

"Go back to the islands where you *buddaheads* can stop making the rest of us look bad! Jesus Christ, you guys eat like a bunch of pigs! It's disgusting!"

He yanked Shig's undershirt and ripped it. "Better go home! No prace for rittle boys!"

Shig swung his hand to pop Roku's ear. Instantly they scrambled into a downpour of soaring fists. Russell began to run out of the barrack when Sergeant Stockwell abruptly cracked an order for him to stay inside. Stockwell, a burly man with red hair, freckles, and a thick neck, stood outside of his living quarters. Baffled, Russell stared at his first sergeant who marched from the back and out the door in his full uniform. By then, the men's faces were practically pressed against the windows; gawking. Russell managed to squeeze in between.

Stockwell barked, "Yawl pull fuckin' apart right now!"

As if both were struck by lightening, Shig and Roku leapt apart as ordered. Slightly bleeding, bruised, dirtied, they gasped at attention, avoiding Stockwell's furious glare. Ashamed, breathing heavily, both kept their heads lowered.

"What in God's name inspired you Japs to get so goddamn pissy?" he snapped

Shig teetered on his feet, adjusting his stance. Hating how his sergeant would spit out the derogatory slang as carelessly as spitting tobacco, he gripped his anger and calmly explained, "Sir, I was taking a smoke, sir, when Roku asked for one. I told him I didn't have any more. He called me *baka*, sir. You know, stupid."

"He be lying, sir," Roku defended. "He ohways hiding cigarettes for himself. Nefer share, dat one don't."

Stockwell shook his head, thinning his eyes and positioned his hands behind his back. "As far as I'm concerned, both you Japs is stupid. This regiment don't have no room for fussin'." Again he hesitated, refraining from blinking, stretching out his discourse; thinking.

Russell strained to hear what they were talking about, trying to shuffle closer to one of the windows. Everyone knew Stockwell barely stomached training them. Because of it, they had to take excessive measures to prove that they were far and beyond the best of their kind.

"But if need be," Stockwell continued, "ta teach ya Japs unification, for the next two weeks yawl have extra duties which will require *both* to perform togetha." He revealed a tight smirk. "That means for the next two weeks you will be required to strip and wax floors. Pick up every single article of trash. Expect to clean every toilet in this here battalion- with a toothbrush! And anything else my brilliant mind can think of." Stepping closer between Shig and Roku, he insisted with a flat, belittling tone. "An' next time you Japs is fussin', not only will you get tossed in the brigs, not only will you get an article 15, but you fuckin' both will get stuck preformin' extra duty for the rest of yur goddamn pitiful time here! Is that goddamn clear?"

Shig and Roku resentfully stared at their sergeant, understanding they could say zilch about his coarse contempt. Instead, both responded with a sharp, "Sir, yes, sir!"

CHAPTER EIGHT

Mid September

MEN'S voices swirled around Mr. Yoshimura, tightening the cramped space that shoved lines of cots and shelves and enclosed the radio's music with creaking wind. To the left side of his cot, a Shinto monk from Oregon slept beside him. On his other side, a rancher from California shared the similar condition despite his wealth. Two months ago Mr. Yoshimura had been relocated to another detention center in Santa Fe, leaving the blistering winters of Montana. Not understanding the reason, he graciously accepted the move in good faith. What else could he do?

He tugged on his charitable suit given to him by Quakers who organized visits and care packets for the *Issei.* He was stunned and touched by their generosity. They were the single group of *hakujins* who made an effort on the *Issei's* behalf. Since his confinement, since the espionage accusations, his Winslow friends began believing the lies. When he tried to appeal his imprisonment and asked for their help as character witnesses, some wrote to the Board of Directors, insisting he remain behind barbed wire. They began remembering the times he held secret meetings at his house. Other times missing church- a clear sign he truly didn't convert to Christianity and therefore remained loyal to Shintoism, therefore loyal to his Emperor. They were disturbed at how much Mr. Yoshimura understood American laws and the banking system. And his interference with the community's ability in handling the strawberry festivals. They knew he was up to something. They had always known.

Only one supported him. But one wasn't enough.

He bent down to retrieve a round mirror and comb, making sure his appearance was up to par. Rose and Tom finally received permission to visit him, traveling from Chicago, bringing his grandson whom he had never met. Two and a half years had elapsed since his arrest. The tedious, mundane hours infected by boredom nearly drove him into insanity; but it was his hope of reuniting with his family that kept him patient. It would be his faith in the system that would ultimately define justice. Faith was all he had left in that narrow, overcrowded barrack.

* * *

THE squeaky door shuddered. The bus driver, with receding hair and moles, stared at them; unsure. Their uniforms, ironed and polished, identified them as clean-cut American men, and yet their small, oval eyes and raven-black hair confused the driver. It was obvious he had never seen Orientals in the South. Russell hiked up the muddy steps first and dipped the coins into the slot. Shig followed, smiling and greeting the stunned driver who gaped with unforgettable perplexity. The pack of passengers, both white and black, stared with odd curiosity as if gazing at a phenomenon. Russell hesitated while he squinted at the segregated seats; equally stunned. Even though he tolerated being a part of a segregated unit, because his skin was considered more white, he would be sitting almost as an equal with the rest of the world.

Shig tugged at his elbow. "Come on," he whispered. "Don't keep the driver waiting."

Feeling a tightness in his belly, Russell settled next to an elderly woman. He tried to ignore her desperate shuffling to the window to move apart. Shig sat beside a young boy who tried not to glance at Shig on a constant basis. The bus spat and jerked. A quivering of jolts complied with the forceful shifts. The eerie quietness lingered for a minute or so before people resumed their chattering. Russell rotated to look in the back once more. He encountered a bizarre sensation of sitting in a section with the *hakujins*. With them. He had spent the last year living apart from them. Looking through the speckled windows, Russell remembered when Shig had harshly professed it was better being Japanese than a nigger. He found no justification in that remark. He could anything be better? Better than what? And he found the remark as ugly as the dead bodies he had seen in the newsreels. He then turned to look at the frightened woman next to him. The four inch gap repelled a measurement of distrust.

"I'm sorry, ma'am," he said, relocating his right leg onto the aisle. "Am I taking too much space?"

She shook her head without looking at him, clutching her purse against her chest. He wanted to test her, wanting her to acknowledge him as a human being and not some damn foreigner.

"I've never left the West Coast before," he began. "It's been real nice seeing other parts of our country." He paused, hoping for a positive sign. Her shallow eyes stayed latched to the outside, trying to snub him. Russell shuffled closer to her, taking away an inch. "For instance, I would of never thought I'd visit the South. Read about it in history books. Seen pictures. But it's great seeing the real thing in person. I guess joining the military gives you an opportunity to travel." Again he paused as if anticipating a miracle. She couldn't ignore him the entire time. "My mother made a special scarf for me. A thousand stitches. She found a thousand people wishing me good luck. People who we barely knew."

The woman closed her eyes, biting her lip. She was listening. She definitely was hearing him, but what was she thinking? Was he finally getting to her?

"There's nothing I wouldn't do to keep my family safe," Russell advanced, pressuring her to acknowledge his worth. "There's no greater cause, don't you think? To protect family. To have freedom. To keep it." He steadied his gaze on the woman. "Nobody can take that from us, ma'am. Not without a fight. Do you have any sons fighting overseas?"

She slowly opened her eyes and loosened her hands, allowing her purse to slide down her chubby stomach. Her gray eyes filtered tears. Russell knew he had retrieved something valuable.

"Yes," she murmured. "One son an' three grandsons." She turned to look directly at him. "So young. So young, ma babies. One dead. Two missin' in action. Lord cannot bury ma loss an' yet each night I pray for peace." She lowered her head as tears rubbed down her wrinkled cheeks. "You boys come back home safe. For yur mamas. Come home alife."

Russell looked away. He hadn't expected the old woman to expound her pain in his lap. He wasn't certain what to do with it. Glancing at Shig again who was equally amazed, he unexpectedly reached for her hand to hold it for a moment. She sniffled and placed her other hand over his. He couldn't speak. How could he? While they quietly sat, the moment lasted longer than he intended.

She removed her hands and said, "Well, my stop is a'comin'."

Seconds later, the bus jerked to a halt. Russell stood and allowed the woman to pass, nodding a smile along the way. She reciprocated the smile and teetered off the bus. Shig moved to sit beside him.

"Did you see that?" Russell excitedly asked. "How about that? Who said miracles can't happen!"

Shig chuckled, one of the few times he had nothing to say. It dumbfounded him the manner in which Russell handled the situation. Through his own encounters in the past, to confront whites to alter their attitudes was unthinkable. Perhaps during the time of war, people made certain exceptions. Women and Negroes were working in factories up North. Even Mexicans. He heard that somewhere in Detroit women were actually getting paid as much as men! Despite the protests, the factory owner didn't budge. But the real test would come *after* the war whether things had truly changed or would return to normal.

Two more passengers boarded: a young white woman in a flowered dress, and a black man in uniform. Russell observed the corporal who appeared as though he might have been part Indian as well as having African descent. His cheekbones signified a sharpness, his jaw line long, and his eyes were more of an oval shape. Back home there were a few American Indians who continued to live on the island, trying to sustain what land they had left. Russell didn't know what happened to the rest. He just never thought about it. The corporal walked the aisle as if he were heading toward the rear, letting the woman settle first, but then stopped four seats down. Russell watched him gnaw on his bottom lip, his eyes focused, determined. He could see that this man was about to do something. Suddenly, the corporal sat in the empty seat, across from Shig.

"Hey!" the bus driver hollered. "You can't sit there! You know da rules!"

The young corporal's face remained firm while he crossed his arms. He declared, "I got da right to sit chere!"

"No, you ain't!" the driver advanced. "You betta get on before you cause real trouble!"

Russell watched the soldier's resistance; awed by his convictions and boldness; admiring his reserved composure. Not moving. Not yelling. Just saving his dignity.

"Boy, don't make me call da police!" the driver warned.

The corporal only blinked. The bus driver twisted around to look at him directly, scowling, and ultimately heaved out of his seat. He marched to the young man to stand over him. Russell thought the driver was about as threatening as a twig. He was skinny, barely rising above Russell's height, but people knew the type of authority he conveyed. It wasn't the driver who instituted intimidation; it was the law he represented. The driver grabbed the soldier's arm and yanked upward.

The soldier flipped his arm loose and asserted, "If I got da right to wear dis uniform, den I got da right to right chere!"

People at the rear of the bus remained quiet; anxious; afraid. Russell strained his neck to look from behind, seeing apprehension overshadowing their faces: ironically the same pattern of harsh doubt and exhausted hope he had seen in the camps. Observing the irritable mood ar the front, with passengers groaning and shifting in their seats, the bus was literally divided in half.

"It don't matta, boy," the driver sneered. "You still a nigga an' you belong in da back!"

"At least give him some respect," Russell interrupted. "He's defending our freedom for crying out loud!"

The driver blazed at him, eerily reminding him of Callis. The corporal gazed at Russell with wonder.

"Tain't yur concern!" the driver snapped.

"Go ta the back you stupid nigga!" someone yelled.

"Stop was'ing our time!" another mimicked.

The shouts began in pairs, then merged into chaos. Russell remembered the time he and Sadaye took a shortcut through a colored district in Seattle. Although a group of boys had harassed them, and that humiliating sensation never quite diminished, it couldn't have been as overwhelming as this poor soldier's ordeal at that moment. The shouting rang in Russell's ears like cannon fire. He felt helpless. And if he were to physically jump in, would that endanger his chance to fight overseas? To prove his loyalty? To re-establish honor for his family? He turned to Shig for support. His friend uncomfortably folded his arms across his chest, looking down at his shoes. When the driver realized the soldier wasn't giving in, he left the bus to return minutes later with a police officer. The officer, a tall man in his late thirties, towered over the corporal with his baton hinged at his waist. The crowd suddenly quieted; a sense of righteousness putting their minds at ease. In the back of the bus, people watched in horror, anticipating bloodshed.

The officer ordered, "Get up, boy."

Blinking intensively, the corporal again gnawed on his lip. "I got a right to sit chere like any otha American."

"Law says otherwise. You in enough hot water as is. Ain't too smart, is you, boy? " A smirk tarnished his clean appearance while he wrapped his hand around his baton. "Are you jus' waitin' to get lynched, nigga? Is that what you wan'?"

The soldier closed his eyes and exhaled deeply. Russell understood the desperate struggle the young man was trying to achieve. It felt desperate in the same way a survivor wanted to live.

Slapping the soldier several times, the officer then resorted to hitting him on the head with the baton. Shocked to be so close to brutality, in spite of his own experiences, Russell jumped to his feet.

"Don't!" Shig warned, grabbing his arm and pulling him back down.

The officer seized one of the corporal's wrists and jerked him up. Bleeding from the forehead, the soldier stared at the lawman; his muscles tightening; his mouth chilled; his eyelids shivering from rage. Everyone knew if the soldier struck back he automatically insured his own death. The officer finally handcuffed him, setting off a series of sighs in the crowd, and dragged the wounded soldier off the bus.

"Alright then," the bus driver chirped. "Let's get da show on da road!"

While the driver returned to his place, Shig leaned toward Russell and whispered, "Do you still believe in miracles?"

Early November

KUNIO believed Camp Savage had an ironic appeal: a name marking paganism, fierceness, wildness; yet in truth it was a school marked by discipline, obligation, and one hell of a crash course in Japanese. He survived its intensity that was expected from him, along with 5,000 others who passed unswervingly; the majority coming from Hawaii and the West Coast. And more were enrolling. Next week after graduation, his unit, the 25th Infantry Division, would be shipped to Australia, and then Guadalcanal. Their purpose: working for military intelligence in an attempt to intercept codes, to interrogate prisoners, and to pretend to be one of the enemy. They were the MIS: Military Intelligence Service. As a result, they learned how to understand the Japan's military language known as *heigo,* and learned to read and write Japanese as well, something that Kunio hadn't done since junior college. So for six months, six days a week, he had been baptized with the *Issei's* culture, ironically enough. For years his embarrassment and reluctance to learn his parent's heritage had troubled him, like his other siblings. Trying to please their parents while trying to belong to American society defined an intricate balancing act. No one knew which way to fall when they lost their balance; a choice each would rather not decide; this unfairness to choose one over the other and not both.

Now the circumstances were unique, to put it mildly. The government needed him. It needed him to be both. And that validated the best damn reason for his future and the future of his children.

* * *

TOMIKO wiped the wetness from her cheeks with a handkerchief. Jim reached for her hand across the table. Her parents sat in the room, reading, trying to supervise their courtship as much as possible. Her father never truly forgave the incident in Manzanar when she didn't return home that night. Since then, he enforced limitations when and where she could see Jim. And Jim aspired to earn back her father's trust by investing time with her family. Including her ten-year-old brother who was already tucked in bed.

"Tomiko, why does this surprise you? You've known how I felt about these camps, and you've agreed with me."

"But not to the point of being sent to a disloyalty camp!"

"First of all, you know I'm *not* disloyal. You know labeling me as disloyal is load of crap just because I refuse to answer their stupid questions! They have *no* right to ask those questions; especially since they're the ones who *took* our natural born rights from us! They took our American citizenship, and then expect us to bow down and thank them for giving it back to us!" He paused to regain his composure. "Look, I'm not the one who's forcing this ridiculous transfer. This isn't my fault."

She withdrew. "No, but you had a choice."

"That's unfair, Tomiko. They're the ones who made the decision in the long run."

"Why couldn't you just play along? We're not loyal to . . ." she stopped to glance at her parents, then leaned forward to speak quietly, "Japan. Why are you doing this?"

He flinched. "How can I respect myself, or you respect me if I change my morals just like that? Like some sort of flake?"

"So you think this is matter of respect?" she resentfully muttered, leaning backward, folding her handkerchief. "Where was your respect when you couldn't tell me you were leaving? You knew for five months!"

Gnawing his lip, he didn't know how to respond. Guilt punctured his face, and he felt like he had been cheating with another girl. Tomiko was complicating his principles. It wasn't as if his silence had been entirely dishonest. He was trying to protect her, knowing how upset she would be. Observing her parent's attempt to overcompensate their eavesdropping by rereading the first lines of the newspaper, he stood up from the table and sat directly next to her.

"Come with me. I love you, Tomiko, so much I can't sleep. I lay awake wanting to be near you. Come with me. We can get married at the other camp, I'm sure."

She ceased from breathing. Feeling her parents' discreet watchfulness and feeling Jim's warmth, she also felt entangled between two uncertainties. "I love you, too," she whispered, reaching for his hand and squeezing it. "You should of told me sooner, Jim. You should of trusted me enough to tell me first. But how can I trust you if you won't do the same?"

He wished they could be alone so he could kiss her. It had been an extensive amount of time since they experienced privacy. "You're right, Tomiko. I'm sorry."

"I want to marry you," she maintained her whispering, "but I don't want to go to another camp. I don't want to eave my family and friends behind, again. Besides, some of those men are violent at Tule Lake. That's not fair to me, either."

He angrily fidgeted. "So you won't come with me?"

"Jim," she sighed, "you can't expect me to make a decision tonight!"

Snapping his back upright, he jerked his hand out of Tomiko's bond.

"Jim, I don't want you leaving mad. You take things too seriously, sometimes."

"How else am I supposed to take things?"

She rose from her seat and turned around to speak to her parents. "*Please excuse us, Papa. We will finish our disagreement outside.*"

Grabbing his arm, she pulled him out of her barrack. As the sunset spilled its orange pigments, it kindled the dull hazy horizon to appear beautiful. They stood beside a miniature rock garden encircling a puddle that was designed for a pond. Idaho's soil couldn't flower a regular garden; only having enough nutrients to grow potatoes, and nothing else.

Crossing her arms, she continued, "You can't get mad at me. I'm not the one leaving. Do you realize how much this hurts?"

"I don't see why you can't come with me."

"Because, Jim, do you understand once you're at that place- you *can't* leave? Ever? Not for work! Not even for a day in town!"

He flexed his brows. "How do you know this?"

"A cousin of mine is a secretary for the administration. She knows what goes on inside the WRA."

He paused. "What else did she say?"

Tomiko dropped her chin. "They've been stacking up the military there. They're going to treat it like a *real* prison. I'm afraid it'll be worse than Manzanar." Her voice became fatigued. Last year's riot remained fresh as did the memory of Sam. "I can't be a part of that, Jim. I can't. And it hurts me more knowing you will be."

He relaxed his arms, realizing how selfish he had been behaving. "I'm sorry, Tomiko. I shouldn't have put that kind of pressure on you."

She stepped into his embrace and held him as long as she could. "I'll wait for you," she said. "When the war's over, it's you I want to marry."

He closed his eyes, trying to withhold his tears, feeling his throat swell and burn. He wanted to tell her he wished he didn't have to leave. That he was terrified. He feared if he told her, he would fall apart. And he knew he wasn't in a position to indulge in such a weakness. Particularly before relocating to another prison.

New Year's Eve

"MAMA," Sadaye began while unfolding a blanket on top of her mother. "*Why do you not have a doctor come visit you?*"

Mrs. Hamaguchi continued to cough, her nose reddened from the damp cold, her cheeks flushed from fever. The last three months she felt some sort of flu spoiling her strength. First it started mildly, and then became worse with the falling temperatures. Relieved that everyone would be spending their time at Meito's apartment for the New Year, Mrs. Hamaguchi hoped to recover soon.

"*Oh, Sadaye, I only have a little cold. What else can the doctor do? Tell me to take more rest? Besides*," she smiled after she coughed jaggedly, "*I have you to take care of me*."

"*Hai, Mama,"* she sighed exhaustively; somewhat irritably.

Sadaye turned around to reach for a wet cloth in a ceramic bowl. The worry and irritation were as visible as water in glass. Not that Mrs. Hamaguchi didn't experience the same worry. She hated hospitals. The sour odors. The painful shots. The doctors and nurses who spoke too quickly, like hummingbirds, keeping her scared and feeling stupid. Barely speaking English, she had never been so lonely. At least here, she could be near her family, her friends, her community, and yet, she didn't trust the camp hospital. The lack of resources reinforced her apprehension.

Sadaye fixed the rag on her mother's forehead, her brows straining from doubt. Two years ago her mother contracted the same symptoms, taking an extensive amount of time to be rehabilitated. The chilled humidity was not gentle to her health. Knowing that, Sadaye didn't understand why she refused to see a doctor.

Abrupt knocking rattled the door, startling both women. Rising from the chair, Sadaye walked across the room, passing by colorful paper ornaments. Kunio's children had decorated the barrack with sticky links of paper chains and sloppy origami animals which hung from the ceiling. Meito's twin sons also helped create chaos for the New Year while their grandmother smiled at their eagerly messy attempts. Then the children went over Meito's to decorate his quarters. Opening the door, Sadaye smiled at her older brother. Meito, wrapped in a thick coat, scarves, and mittens, stood on the steps, holding a tiny brown paper bag, his breath looming like a ghost in the bitter night.

He exclaimed, "I thought you two might want some *mochi* for tomorrow's celebration!"

"Well, how nice! Come in."

He thumped his shoes on the outer step before entering and gave the bag to Sadaye. Heading to the pot belly stove for warmth, he said, "The kids can't wait for their special money. They keep pestering us, begging and whining." He paused to look at his mother. "*How are you feeling, Mama?*"

Her coughing hindered her from answering. "*I am feeling better*."

He glanced at his sister, unconvinced. "Why don't we fetch Dr. Sato just in case? He's only two blocks from here."

Sadaye removed several rice-ball cakes out of the bag and sat them on a plate. "That's not a bad idea."

Moaning, Mrs. Hamaguchi protested, "*Nai!*" but an onslaught of coughing made her realized otherwise. "Okay!" she gasped. "Go, go!"

"I'll be back as soon as I can," he replied, quickly leaving.

While Meito shut the door, Mrs. Hamaguchi jolted to her side, pressing her face into the pillow, coughing hysterically. The jolting stabbed her entire body, nearly paralyzing her. She felt her throat scalding. Once her fit passed, she turned over, moaning, wheezing. Wiping the side of her cheek, she then felt warm liquid. She stared at her bloodied fingers. Panicking, she sprung up and gawked at chunks of blood on her pillow.

Sadaye was equally horrified. “Oh my God, Mama!” she gasped.

Mrs. Hamaguchi didn’t think her illness would return. Believing her previous sins had been redeemed, almost dying the first time, she feared that perhaps her second chance was on some sort of loan. Without her father’s forgiveness, and the forgiveness of his ancestors, she knew how her karma would end. Descending to her knees, she prayed to her ancestors in hopes she hadn’t infected her children and grandchildren.

CHAPTER NINE

Mid April, 1944

MUSIC trumpeted through the wide open doors. The Andrews Sister's "Boogie Woogie Bugle Boy" greeted Russell and Shig as they jumped off the army jeep. The bumpy ride extended up a private dirt road and curved down at a broad driveway. Some had arrived earlier; others arrived in jeeps or trucks or by way of hitchhiking. Mr. North's ranch resembled a photogenic plantation. White columns and a fanning veranda glowed from the lit windows. Weeping willows surrounded the mansion; green shutters darkened with the rise of the moon and chanting crickets. The structure stood more narrow than Russell would have suspected. He remembered Scarlet O'Hara's mansion appearing roomier on the big screen, folding out its flanks like the White House.

Shig exclaimed, "Boy, who would of thought we'd get invited to a place like this!" He reached in his uniform for a cigarette and lighter. He began puffing. "Do Southerners know how to be hospitable or what?"

Russell yanked his cap to his right side. "Yeah, but we've also seen their *other* side of hospitality."

They nodded at their buddies who trotted up the steps. Russell thought everyone looked stylish in their tanned uniforms; apart from the usual fatigues. Mr. North, a local business owner out of Hattiesburg, made it possible for the *Nisei* regiment to fit in a place where they were neither white nor colored. He personally donated his time and money in hosting some sort of USO function for the 442nd. Russell was moved by this stranger's generosity. He had experienced very little of it since the war began.

Shig exhaled and smiled. "Well, *omono*, ready to go fishing?"

"Don't you mean dancing?"

He wet his lips and continued to smirk. "You can dance. But I'm *fishing*!"

"What about your *new* wife?"

"What about her?"

Russell awkwardly chuckled. "You're married! You shouldn't be even considering anything like this!"

"Hey!" he snapped. "I don't judge you! So don't judge me!"

"Like hell you don't judge me!"

Shig peered at him and laughed. Slapping his hand on his Russell's shoulder, he asserted, "Say it tomorrow if you have something to say! Come on, let's burn a hole in this joint."

Russell had to snicker. His friend was something short of being curable. The music engaged high spirits and it would be a shame to break the mood. They jogged up the wooden steps. Standing at the entrance was a man in his forties who was dressed in a gray pin-striped suit. He wore a yellow ribbon on his left side.

Smiling widely and extending his hand, he said, "Thank ya for comin'!" Russell took his offer. The man looked directly at Russell's eyes and eagerly shook his hand. "I am Mista No'th; yur gracious host for the night." Mr. North reached to shake Shig's hand. "You boys enjoy, now."

When his hand was released, Shig asked, "Mr. North?"

"Yes, young man?"

"Do you think it's kind of . . . funny . . . your name is North, but you live in the South?"

Mr. North nodded, chuckling. He then winked. "Neva crossed ma mind."

They walked through the portal and entered a burly lobby-like room, surrounded by deer heads and outdoor oil paintings. The side doors were shut. The walls were coated in soft amber. In front of them loomed a staircase that ventured after the music to the second level. A few *Nisei* soldiers paced themselves up the polished wooden steps. Shig tugged at Russell's elbow and excitedly followed. The staircase looped around, broaching toward a secluded dance parlor. They saw glimpses of women skipping and bouncing to the Lindsey. Chairs lined the corridor with a couple of soldiers sitting and chatting. Russell and Shig paused at the threshold of the parlor. The rectangular room expanded like a bowling alley, shouldering a veranda at the end with opened glass doors to welcome the breeze. Large mirrors hung on both sides of the walls, reflecting the two chandeliers glare. Music and heels thundered in the room.

A young man, racial mixed with light brown skin and slick wavy hair, sat behind a Victrola and boxes of records. He was also dressed in a pinstriped suit. Next to him dwelled half-empty a punch bowl on a table, supporting paper cups. Russell counted four chaperones; two women and two men, each appearing no younger than their late fifties. Sixteen women, all taken, danced in the center. More soldiers leaned against the walls, bored and without the companionship of women.

Shig rumpled his mouth and grunted. "Damn. Should of brought my own fishing pole!"

"It's a good thing you didn't," Russell grinned. "Would of been too small, anyway."

Shig glared at him. "Hey, man, there ain't nothing wrong with my *pole*!"

Russell snickered and ambled off to the side, causally sliding his hand into his pocket. Shig followed. They wandered toward the punch table and stood like ogling sixth-graders attending their first dance. The young record-switcher leaned over and removed a 78 without looking. He glanced up at Russell and Shig, and rose to swap records. Russell watched the women. Some were considered attractive. Some much more plain with only lipstick promoting their beauty. Some were vigorous dancers; others only knew a few moves, keeping their rhythm simple. He missed Naomi. He remembered the time they propelled on the dance floor as if two heated popcorn kernels. That was a good night.

The women switched partners. Soldiers who bordered against the walls jumped in, forcing the remaining ones to retreat to the boundaries. Russell turned to say something to Shig, but he was already on the floor, waving goodbye. The music began and the cycle continued. Russell sighed. He poured himself a non-alcoholic drink and reclined on the wall, eying Shig closely. As much as he wanted to be a part of the exhilaration, he wasn't going to foolishly grab any available woman on the floor. He wasn't that desperate.

"Dere's a seat, if you wan'."

Surprised, Russell looked at the record-switcher. "What?"

"A seat," he said, pointing to a chair behind the table. "Is yours if you wan'."

Russell shrugged. "Why not? I don't look any prettier standing." He mindfully seated himself, still holding a full cup, and extended his hand over his chest. "The name's Russell."

"Earl Ray," he replied, shaking Russell's hand. "Gud to meetcha."

Russell sipped his red punch. "So, this is some important job you have."

"All hell would break loose if nobody change da records. Same sung repeatin' itself. Bad for morale."

"And bad for the war effort."

"Yeah, dat, too," he groaned and slumped forward, wrapping his fingers together, peering down at his feet. A few moles were visible on his neck.

Russell asked, "So, what's Mr. North like?"

He grinned. "Tain't all bad. Some folk is jus' different. Been workin' for 'im for five years or so. Got a brother in Tuskegee." He rotated to face Russell. "He a flyer for da army. Usta work 'round Mista No'th's yard, but had passion in book learnin'. Mista No'th saw potential in 'im. Help pay for his books when he wenta college."

Russell lifted his brows and sipped his punch again. "Wow. What a tyrant."

Earl Ray chuckled. "Yeah. Even got me dis suit for tonight." He paused and leaned closer to Russell. "Can I ask you somethin'?"

"As long as you're not asking me dance."

"Fair 'nough," he smiled, but soon his humor slid out of his lips. "Wha's it like? Bein' Japanese, I mean. Bein' part of a Jap unit?"

Russell tapped on his cup and squinted ahead. He watched Shig hop and swivel with a white woman who possible painted two lines on her legs, presenting an impression of nylons. Everyone appeared to be having a great time. Or at least on the dance floor. How could Earl Ray even ask such a question? How was Russell suppose to respond?

"I don't know," he flatly replied.

Earl Ray scratched his chin. "Lis'en, I only mean," he stopped. Russell gulped his beverage until he emptied his cup. Earl Ray sighed and scooted his chair nearer. "Lis'en, my brotha's unit is segregated. All my life, I ain't known nothin' else. I jus' wanna know if is da same for you people."

Russell looked at him. "Why do you want to know?"

"I gotta believe we have a chance. If you can do it, we can do it, too. Den da world knows change is a'comin'."

Russell clicked his tongue, slowly nodding his head. His still had family and friends left behind in prison camps, segregated from society. He thought about Jim. And the last disturbing words he stated. There had to be purpose. Russell needed to believe it, too. Then he recalled the Negro soldier from the bus. Even in his distinguished in uniform, the corporal was beaten and arrested anyway. The uniform didn't guarantee his equality. And that worried Russell. What if, in spite of his efforts, nothing would change?

Earl Ray lowered his voice, "Ten years 'go, my cousin was lynched. I was jus' twelve. Saw his body swanging in da tree."

Stunned, Russell asked, "What for?"

His face crinkled like a dried leaf scorched under the desert's sun. "For lookin' at the mayor's daughter. Jus' glancin'. Da mayor was affiliated with da hooded men." His sharp tone cut through Kay Kaiser's melody, maiming the festive mood. He gnawed on his bottom lip and straightened his posture. "You know, Mista No'th's given me hope. If weren't folk like him 'round here, I woulda given up long time 'go. Wheneva I hate da whites, Mista No'th makes me reconsida. Know what I mean?"

Russell again nodded. People like Dave, Mr. Woodward, and Officer Dandridge. Then there was Palmer, Mr. Bridges, and Ansel Adams. All had proven confidence for transformation and that transformation was possible. After Sam's death, he thought about giving up. It would have been easier to feel his skin burn against the fire rather than feeling his tears burn against his heart.

"Gotta change records!" Earl Ray exclaimed.

He turned around to yank another one from the pile and hovered his hand above the needle. Russell again thought about Jim. He felt sorry for his friend. The idea of not sensing any sort of hope must be the worst kind of hell.

Kay Kaiser was quickly replaced by Billie Holiday.

Earl Ray winked at him. "Ain't nobody singin' betta truths." Russell rose his empty cup in a silent toast. Earl Ray continued, "Mista No'th is one of da few whites who like Miss Holiday. Got a collection of her an' Duke Ellington."

Shig trotted across the narrow room; breathless; perspiring. He glanced at Earl Ray. Light skinned Negroes were not much more refined than the darker ones, in his opinion. He remembered each incident when they mocked Shig, embellishing shoddy Oriental dialect, insulting him with names. And that was before the war. "Hey Jap! The las' time you did my laundry you didn't get out the stain! Where's my refund?" "Hey you, don't you know we ain't got no room for your kind? Go back home an' make your damn noodles elsewhere!" It was bad enough the whites felt superior to him, but the Negroes, too? He wrinkled his nose.

Earl Ray caught it.

"Hey, *omono*," Shig panted. "Why aren't you on the floor?"

"If you haven't noticed, the men outnumber the women."

Shig rested his knuckles on his hips. "Yeah, well, let's move to the other side. Might have a better chance."

Russell detected something funny about Shig. He seemed discomforted and fidgety. Russell had already understood Shig's prejudice against non-Japanese people. Instead of giving in, he decided to be nonchalant about the situation. "I doubt that will help," he replied.

"Come on, Russell," he pleaded. He flinched when he looked at Earl Ray. Then shifting to Japanese, he urged, "*Russell, let us move elsewhere. This is not our place.*"

Russell grinned. "Oh, I'm sorry." He stood up. "Shig, this is my new friend, Earl Ray. Earl Ray, this is my old buddy, Shig."

Earl Ray extended his hand in front of Shig. Shig glared at Russell, straining his jaw. The annoyance in his dark eyes was as lucid as water. Quietly grunting, he reluctantly shook Earl Ray's hand.

"Okay," Shig said to Russell. "Let's go."

"How about some punch?"

"Not thirsty."

"You just got done dancing."

"I'm not thirsty."

"But you're sweating like a pig."

"Not thirsty!" Shig snapped.

Russell sighed. He had higher hopes for Shig. "It won't be my fault when you die of dehydration before Italy."

Shig nervously glanced at Earl Ray once more, rattling his leg. "I'll meet you outside when you're done," he announced and strode out to the veranda.

Embarrassed by his friend's behavior, he said, "I'm gonna have to apologize on behalf of his mother."

"We all got mothas. All da apologies jus' gonna make 'em go inta da grave."

A young woman, with soft freckles and reddish-brown hair, sauntered to Russell. Her ruby mouth unfolded like a thriving snapdragon. Her hips swayed in her polka-dotted dress. Her cleavage glowed under the lights. She browsed over the punch table to Russell to the records. Halting beside the Victrola, reposing her stance on one leg, extending her hip out, she smiled up to Earl Ray.

"Do me a fava," she said, wetting her lips. "When this song is ova, next song play 'Sing, Sing, Sing.' I like 'em long and energetic." She then looked at

Russell. "Yur the only one I hadn't danced with, yet. Right now I need ta take a breatha ou'side. But wait here 'till then. Okay, Darlin'?"

Russell was stupefied. "Okay."

"Ohright, then," she smiled, and sauntered to the veranda; a breeze stroking through her thin dress.

Earl Ray shook his head, snickering. "Boy, I hope you got life insurance. You gonna need it!"

Russell pinched his brows. "What do you mean?"

He didn't answer, still snickering, and sifted through the collection. Shig stood by the door, lighting another cigarette. His uniform appeared buffed against the outside darkness. Even the moon's glory seemed obscure in the horizon. Shig extended his disapproval at a distance. Russell retrieved drinks for himself and Earl Ray. If Shig was going to sulk, let him. After a few minutes lapsed, Billie Holiday's voice was replaced by an outbreak of drums. The woman promptly emerged out of the darkness; her ruby lips arousing Russell's interests. He smelled a faint sweetness straying from her skin. Taking his hand, she led him to the depth of spontaneous movements: rapid, vigorous, pulsating. The fleet of drums drove their feet to shuffle, bounce, and slide. Trumpets punched along with the rhythm. The true challenge of the song implied stamina for the active beat was notorious for lasting eight long minutes. Russell was surprised how graceful the young woman twirled and flipped. And it felt so natural. The strain of her muscles matched his almost in unison; as if they had been dance partners before. He knew she enjoyed spinning her skirt the way she would snap and swivel her hips. Not that he had any complaints. Glancing down, he saw that she wore authentic nylons. Not many women did now-a-days.

They proceeded to skip and wiggle with the brash song; with everyone else on the floor. Russell seemed able to ignore the small crowd, fastening on his own breath and the woman's heat. He felt liberated. Before Manzanar, before Minidoka, he didn't appreciate his freedom. At that moment, dancing in uniform, dancing with a beautiful woman, he realized the shortness of his time. Within the next month or so, he might be dead. He appreciated the sparing moment as if a second chance. As the song approached the end, Russell managed to swing her from side-to-side; her fingers tightly clasped around his neck; her face so close to his. She landed perfectly on the last note, and then it was over. The eight minutes seemed to have had been slashed in half. Some of the other women were exhausted and walked off the dance floor to sit down. The changing of partners began again. Russell smiled at the young woman. She beamed like a firefly carousing in the humid night. Her perspiration tempted the moon outside, so Russell stepped back to avoid it. He chuckled with her giddiness, breathing deeply from the rapid Jitterbug.

Earl Ray switched records, arranging a slower tune, but not too slow to discourage the GIs from holding the women too close. The four chaperones stretched their necks to make sure space between the sexes was proper. Russell noticed Shig returning to the floor with different partner. He continued to sulk.

"Yur a good danca," she grinned, brushing unleashed strands of hair away from her face.

Tugging his waist coat down, he replied, "You definitely can hold your own! Thank you for the dance."

"Ma name is Lou Anne."

"Mine's Russell."

"Russell," she cooed. "I like it. Has a strong, earnest sound to it."

He grinned, nearly blushing. "Thank you, Lou Anne."

She grasped his elbow just before he walked away. "Walk with me on the veranda, Russell. I'd like to take a smoke."

He nervously glanced around the room, watching anyone who might be watching them.

"Come on," she playfully insisted. "Yur really not all that shy."

His footing stuttered, but he followed her as he past the record player and a line of soldiers standing like fence posts. They stared at Russell, some smirking, others envious at his opportunity. One of the male chaperones gazed at them, his arms crisscrossed over his chest. Lou Anne snatched her purse lying on a table with other purses. The fresh breeze alleviated the stuffiness from the crowded room. A few other mixed couples lingered on the balcony, talking about triviality: movies, music, the weather; anything that abstained from talking about their deployment to Italy. She slipped her hand inside her purse, retrieving a sterling-silver cigarette case and matching lighter.

Russell said, "That's pretty fancy. It's a good thing it's not made from tin, otherwise you'd have to donate it for the cause."

She smiled after exhaling. "I *am* the cause. 'Sides, it was a parting gift."

"From who?"

She patted the tip of her tongue to remove some of the loose grains. "From some poor Yankee needin' a little compassion. Jealous?"

He boosted his brows. He began suspecting her occupation, however decided to have fun with it anyway. After all, he might not get another chance.

"Oh, yes," he joked. "After just that one dance, I've fallen madly in love! How can I compete with a fancy present like that?"

She laughed. "Yur a crack pot! I bet girls fall at yur feet!"

Russell shrugged and rolled his eyes. "Yeah, me and Clark Gable."

He gazed down, away from the Southern belle at his side. The robust weeping willows seemed to have ballooned in the darkness, appearing more intimidating beneath the moonlight than the sun. A marshy smell, blended with perfume and cigarettes, blew under his nose. He never acquired a comfortable feeling in this state. It seemed haunting; like the boogie men existing in dark corners of one's bedroom.

Lou Anne declared, "Right here, honey! I'm right here. Where did you go off to?"

He continued to stare into the trees. "I think of *Gone With the Wind* whenever I look at the scenery."

She sighed out of irritation. "Ya Yankees think alike. No imagination!"

Amused that she would refer him as a Yankee first, he turned to look at her. He was flattered that she would connect him along every other soldier. His features detached from the enemy.

"Mississippi is the second furthest I've been away from home," he confessed.

"I've met some boys where this is the first time they left home." She maneuvered a bold smile and tickled his chin with her finger tips. "So, where was yur first time, honey?"

He stiffened. "California."

"California!" she excitedly repeated. "Eva been to Hollywood?"

Russell had to step back. "No."

She squinted and took a puff, coyly swaying her shoulders to emphasize her cleavage. Glancing through the window, the male chaperon peered at him. As if warning him. As if condemning him. Although Russell knew Mr. North had a compassionate reputation, he wondered about the *other* people. He stepped backward, trying not to stare at her chest.

"What's wrong, sugar?" she said. "I don't bite."

"That's not what I'm worried about."

"What then?"

He stopped, bumping into the edge of the balcony. He thought about the soldier on the bus. Russell had become familiar with Southern justice. Clearing his throat, he replied, "Getting lynched."

She gawked at him. Suddenly she crackled into laughter. "Oh, honey!" she gasped. "Lynchin' is for niggas only!"

Her sense of flattery shattered him into disgust. Her carelessness provoked an ugliness in her stunning appearances. It was almost a perfect night. He almost felt that he belonged in her world: this world he had always wanted to be a part of regardless of consequence. Anger jabbed at the brink of his tongue, but he walked off, returning to his unit. He knew he didn't belong on that veranda.

She asserted from behind, "What's wrong with you?"

Russell didn't answer. He reseated to talk with Earl Ray, extending a third cup of punch to his new friend.

SHIG remained quiet during the ride back to camp, holding an off-brand cigarette near the cracked window. Russell sat in the middle, staring at the dark road surrounded by towering trees. It was the closest thing that reminded him of home in a long time. The driver, a local elderly man in denim overalls, obliged to giving them a lift outside of Mr. North's property. During the extended ride, their speechlessness was overlapped with mountain music. Russell and Shig had never heard it before and weren't sure what to make of it. The high fluctuation of voices competed with the squeaky bouncing truck. It differed from the Country-Western music they'd listened to in the past. At least the music suspended the awkward tension between the two friends. When they arrived at Camp Shelby, Russell and Shig echoed their thanks to the old farmer. Other soldiers began trickling in; many tipsy from cheap beer; a few others tipsy from a satisfactory night in the red light district.

Shig headed to the light pole to lean against it, watching Russell wave goodbye to the old man in the dust. He peered at Russell, not understanding him.

Crickets and locusts loudly chanted in the mist, muffling out the men's electrified chatter and laughter.

Russell glanced at Shig and began walking toward their barrack.

"What's with you?" Shig asserted.

He stopped, puzzled. Too tired to argue, he said, "I don't know. Why don't you tell me?"

"Why were you talking to that Colored?"

Russell snickered, shaking his head. "That really bothers you?"

"You know everyone has their place. We may be below the *hakujins*, but remember we're also above the Coloreds."

"And the Filipinos?" he retorted, squinting.

"Exactly!"

"Yeah, I remember having this conversation before!"

Russell shoved his hands into his pockets and strained his jaw. He walked away, recalling the time Shig stupidly called Maria a "Pino." And that asinine joke. *What's the difference between snakes and Pinos? Snakes can shed their skins.*

Shig bellowed from behind, "Never forget your place, Russell! Be proud where you come from! Don't screw it up!"

Russell hopped up the steps and yanked the door open. Slamming it, he removed his hat and charged down the aisle to his bed. His bunkmates jerked and stared curiously, yet maintained from prying. Unbuttoning his jacket and loosening his tie, he was sick of all the stereotyping, name calling, backbiting . . . among his own group of people little alone from others. The Hawaiians, *Buddaheads*. The mainlanders, *Kotonks*. What irritated him the most was how a friend of his, someone he trusted, could be so racist. Then he thought about Jim: judgmental and dismissive; insecure and stubborn. Although during that year Russell seldom gave Jim another thought, lately he had been reflecting on their dissolved friendship. If Jim wanted to play that half-witted game, so could Russell. When he sat down on his mattress, and started unfastening his laces, Roku stepped in front of him.

He said, "Russo, you wait before taking shoes off."

Confused, Russell looked up.

"A telegram for you," Roku somberly continued. "Sarge has it for you."

Russell held his breath. He knew the news couldn't be good, otherwise, why a telegram? He stood up, his laces flopping on his right foot as he rushed toward the front. He thought about his mother, then his father, or perhaps one of his cousins. They were so small and accident-prone. And the camp was full of hazardous elements. Walking at the end of the barrack as the men in his unit watched him, he halted at Sergeant Stockwell's room. Swallowing, he knocked without realizing his hand trembled. The wooden floor creaked and the door opened.

"Hamaguchi," Stockwell grunted, wearing his sleeveless undershirt and military boxers while his dog tags roped around his thickly freckled neck. He moved aside to allow Russell to enter his small space. "Sit down," he ordered as he reached for a tawny piece of paper at his desk. Russell eased onto a stool, preserving a stiff calmness. Stockwell sat in his chair. “This arrived while you was out,” he said, handing the telegram to him.

The fat letters nearly bleed into the paper, a sign of carelessness or stinginess. He read the words, but didn’t allow them to collapse through his consciousness:

This is not an easy message to send -STOP- Mama passed away early this morning -STOP- Her funeral will be held in three days from today at Minidoka -STOP- Travel safely -STOP- Meito

Russell continued to stare at the paper, unconsciously rubbing the corners. He felt nothing. Not the humidity that submerged his uniform. Not the fan that scratched a breeze on his face. He did feel the noises that dulled his ears: The loud insects. Men’s chattering. The squeaky fan. He heard and felt his heartbeat, however.

“I’m real sorry for yur loss,” Stockwell consoled, massaging his bare chin, blinking. “I made the cawl. Tomorra pick up yur week pass.” He sighed and leaned back into his rickety chair. “Don’t like this kinda news so soon to deployment. Tain’t good for makin’ the best judgment in combat. For anybody.”

Russell cleared his throat, trying to keep his voice normal. “Thank you.”

As he rose and rigidly walked out of Stockwell’s room, the last thing he wanted to do was to expose his weakness by falling apart, especially in front of Stockwell. He’d be damned if he allowed himself to do such a thing. Not here. Not before going to Italy.

CHAPTER TEN

MR. HAMAGUCHI knelt at the front of the Buddhist shrine, trembling. The morning hour still hung darkness in the frosty horizon. His nose and cheeks were flushed from a long, roaming walk. It was at the last minute when he saw lights pull from its windows, trapping him in his footprints. Although he had preyed at home sometimes, he hadn't chosen to enter a temple since he left Japan thirty-eight years ago. He barely remembered entering the Buddhist temple in Manzanar after the fire. He knew *saki* had been cheating him from his memories. Two monks left him alone while they swept the floor, and dusted the shelves and scrolls. Ordinarily they wouldn't have granted anyone permission to enter before their preparations, however, the despairing look on Mr. Hamaguchi's face made them reconsider. And since they hadn't seen him there before, they understood it was a visit he had needed for quite some time. The faint, tart scent that floated in the room from yesterday's burning incense reminded Mr. Hamaguchi of his childhood. A season in his life when he experienced no pain. No struggles. He was the fifth son of a farmer. And he had so many relatives surrounding his existence. When he became a young man, he thought he was better than his family because he possessed enormous visions. Just like Goro; which was one of the reasons he let Goro leave. He thought he would grow as a wealthy businessman in an American city and return home with silk clothes.

The first grim omen came after he stepped off the ship in San Francisco. A group of protesters infested the harbor with large signs and rotten tomatoes, violently shouting and throwing insults at him and his shipmates. There were no police officers to protect them. Years later, with blistered hands from wandering through other people's fields, he had no home, no family. Women, (*good* Japanese women who weren't *baishunfu*, promiscuous,) were either married or back in Japan. He had worked and saved for a decade before he contemplated a wife and family. Those were the loneliest years; until recently. At that point, he knew no woman. A friend of his had informed about picture brides, bragging how they could have any pick of the litter. Modern men find wives this way, Fujita-san, they told him. It shows people you have money and power. Looking through the pile of photos, it was then he chose his wife. He liked the spirit in her eyes. If only he had really known. A day later he paid for her passage and eagerly awaited her arrival.

That was the second disappointing omen.

It didn't bother Mr. Hamaguchi that she was a widower; perhaps it made him more curious because she would be more experienced. What had upset him was finding out, at the docks, that her belly poked out like a bloated whale! He couldn't believe she carried her dead husband's baby without informing him in her letters! Appalled, he immediately wanted to send her back, except there was no refund. She cried in his presence, confessing her former miserable life and how abusive her in-laws had been to her. Utterly embarrassed about the emotional scene she made, he grabbed her hand and dragged her to the courthouse for their marriage license. He had to save face somehow. He then promised her he would not tell their future children about this shame. A year later, they moved from San Francisco to Bainbridge Island where they were able to sustain their secret while establishing a suitable life together.

Mr. Hamaguchi opened his eyes to appeal strength from the icon. Despite the roughness he and his wife endured in the beginning, genuine love managed to thrive. How could it not after twenty-eight years? He didn't know how much he cared for her until the doctor sent him that shocking telegram. Her passing gouged such a fierce pain in his chest, he believed his ribs would crush his lungs. He again closed his eyes, feeling the tears swell and burn. He muttered, "*Forgive me for my past faults. And forgive me for my faults I suspect I will repeat.*"

MEITO kissed his two sons on their foreheads, whispering good-night. He pulled the blanket across the suspended rope as if closing a bedroom door. His baby daughter slept in a cardboard box on the floor, but she comfortably laid on top of a pillow and was gently tucked in warm blankets. Gertrude stood behind an ironing board, pressing his suit for tomorrow's funeral. A bowl of water sat at the end of the board. Dipping her fingers into it, she flicked droplets on the suit and propelled the iron in circles. Her black dress hung on a coat rack, along with Joe and George's small suits. She left the radio on, insulating the painful silence as if keeping the mind warm for tomorrow's cold.

Mr. Hamaguchi hunched over a spare bed, holding a half-empty bottle. Alcohol dwelled at the bottom, mixed in with a soda. Tonight he wanted to stay with Meito instead of Kunio. The promise he had made with his wife could now be cremated along with her spirit. Not that he intended to disrespect her, but Meito had the right to know.

* * *

EASING pins into her hat, Mrs. Yoshimura glanced at her daughter who was buttoning her coat. Bethany's hair sagged in braids. Her dark galoshes barely matched her dark dress. She must have grown at least a couple of inches. Her old dress now rested above her knees; and that was the only black apparel she had to wear to a funeral. She then glanced at her son who laid on his cot, reading.

Annoyed by his behavior, she announced, "*It is your obligation to attend the wake, Jimmu.*"

Sighing, he closed the book and looked up at his mother. "I realize that, Mama. But I can't explain to you why I can't go."

Bethany glanced at her brother and rolled her eyes.

"*Jimmu,*" Mrs. Yoshimura persisted. "*The Hamaguchis are close friends to the family. How can you be so indifferent?*"

"I'm not." Rising to his feet, he began pacing. "Mama, it's just that . . . that Russell might be there."

"*I should hope so! He is her son!*"

Jim shook his head. "You don't understand. We're not friends anymore."

Mrs. Yoshimura ceased from pinning her hat and lowered her arms.

"Why?" she asked in English.

He grunted. "Because . . . because he made his choice, Mama. He chose to abandon his friends and family for the conceit of glory. He would rather risk his life for scraps of the government's respect that he'll never attain. He chose to become the white man's lackey over the value of anyone's friendship. It was his choice to end the friendship the day he joined the army, not mine!"

Exasperated, she walked to him to stand directly in his path. "*Whatever the cause might have been, whatever the disagreement, it cannot be as feeble as either of your tempers. And if so, the fault is not within the friendship, but within your pride. Too much pride can ruin any relationship. If you haven't learned that from your father, then I cannot teach it to you.*"

THE jeep's tires knifed through the mud, pelting rocks and chunks of wet dirt. A soldier drove with such concentrated purpose that he furiously beeped at everyone who stood in his way. Russell clutched the seat with both hands while his balanced stumbled from the sharp jerks. His heart knocked about his chest. If he missed his mother's funeral just because some of the assholes who refused to offer him a ride at the train station . . . he didn't know what he was capable of doing. A sour knot had been swelling in his stomach for days; expanding; spoiling. He had wasted three hours trying to find a lift. People were apprehensive; mostly not wanting to deplete their gas to drop off a foreigner miles from their town. Ultimately a police officer volunteered to drive him to the camp. He only volunteered *after* complaints were made against him. At that point, Russell was on the brink of losing it. But now, at least someone gave a damn. Whenever he thought about giving up on the world, one person would repair his resentment. This soldier didn't even blink when he asked for a ride at the front gate, after the police officer just dumped him there.

When they slid beside the Buddhist temple, Russell was surprised to see a crowd of people honoring his mother. Not just family. At least eighty other friends from the Bainbridge community. Ikki and his other group of pals. All turned to look at him; their faces reflecting grief. It was an odd impression of home. That one year seemed like a decade. His friends changed without changing. Time held no reality. He then looked for Jim, hoping he would at least pay his respects.

Meito leapt from the door and darted through the crowd. His black suit revealed acute pleats down his new slacks. His slicked hair glittered under the sun.

"Goro!" he panted. "Jesus! We were wondering if you were going to arrive at all!"

"So was I! You think the postal service is bad! I would of had better luck with the Pony Express!" Russell turned to shake the soldier's hand. "Thanks. This really means a lot."

The soldier nodded. "You bet. And I am sorry for your loss."

Vaulting off the jeep, Russell hugged his brother for a moment and followed him inside to finish the memorial service. He glanced at his friends who nodded their recognition and he nodded in turn. As they entered the rectangular temple, he immediately smelled the collection of bitter-sweet incense. A bald, middle-aged priest read from the *sutra*; his gentle voice consoling; his orange robe elevating unity. People sat in rows, patiently waiting while one person at a time knelt at the alter. Each person would fold his hands together, bow, draw an incense stick towards his forehead, then unite his incense with the smoldering one in the urn as an offering. Once kindled, he would set aside his incense, bow again, and stand up to allow another person to repeat the custom. Although this tradition had been preserved, the revealing of Mrs. Hamaguchi's body in a casket was altered. Her body had already been cremated. Another urn that contained her ashes balanced on an end table across from the alter. That was not traditional. It would have been considered disgraceful under normal circumstances, but since her body was diseased, Mr. Hamaguchi thought it sanitary to have her cremated before the wake and funeral. One of his wife's friends had criticized him for not allowing anyone to pay for her toll in her afterlife. She was angered that now Mrs. Hamaguchi couldn't cross the River of the three Hells without the paper money placed in her casket. He had bitterly replied, "*What makes you think my wife would have been able to cross over in the first place?*"

The rest of Russell's family sat at the front, quietly crying, sniffling. Russell looked at each of them who, for a moment, seemed so distant and unfamiliar. He hesitated in the aisle as Meito resettled by his wife and children, and stared off to the side, his thick brows grinding. Something else was bothering him.

Russell then realized Kunio's absence. Leaning down to his father, he whispered, "Where's Kunio?"

Mr. Hamaguchi cleared his throat. "*He is not able to make it. He had been sent to the South Pacific. We do not know exactly where.*"

Stupefied, he asked, "Doesn't he know about Mama?"

"*Meito wrote a letter to his unit. I do not know when he will receive it.*"

Russell couldn't imagine how Kunio would feel once he got that letter. Not being able to attend their mother's funeral probably would leave him feeling helpless, guilty even. At least Russell made it. Barely.

As another person completed her respect, Russell took one step forward to make his offering. His father suddenly grabbed his arm. Russell looked at him. Extending his other arm with a string of beads and an incense, Mr. Hamaguchi whispered, "*You take these.*" Instinctively Russell complied. Walking to the altar, he knelt on the cushion, holding the dark beads between his folded palms; the stick between his fingers. He glanced at a wooden tablet inscribed in Japanese, assuming it was dedicated to his mother. The priest's voice fanned in the air like soft winds rustling through leaves. Russell somewhat understood what the priest was reading, and for the first time, he felt an influence of spirituality. The years of his parents' teachings about Buddhism rarely affected him; often he ignored them. Guilt surrendered to his pride which was full of ignorance. If only he had listened. If only he had been more selfless.

Igniting his incense and setting it aside, the tears began to prick out. For over three days he refused to cry; especially in front of strangers. He wished he had the chance to tell his mother how much he loved her and let her know he was sorry for the countless times he disappointed her. Wiping off his sweltering tears, quietly sniffling, he bowed and stood up in pristine uniform. He would make his mother proud of him. He would.

MEITO'S barrack had been converted to a place of ceremonial gathering. The month long ritual would allow friends and family to continue honoring Mrs. Hamaguchi with food and conversations. Incense would blister throughout the days and nights, consuming the crowded area like a moldy greenhouse. Gertrude bumped around people to offer them tea. Joe and George sat on their bunk, playing with toy soldiers, wrinkling their suits. Meito held his infant daughter in his arms, swaying her to sleep while talking to both of his sisters, Sadaye and Chiyeko.

Mr. Hamaguchi stood beside the table that contained rice and vegetable dishes, not able to eat. He just stood helpless. Appearing unconscious. Appearing nothing more than a thin, aging man. Russell, his eyes limp with exhaustion, scarcely listened to his brother-in-law, Tadao, drone on about harvesting potatoes that year. He gazed over people's heads, hoping to find an empty bed to fall into; except each bunk was modified as a makeshift bench. Early tomorrow morning he would have to leave everyone again, returning to Mississippi, and then heading off to Chesapeake Bay for deployment. And that would be it. Next month he would be in Italy. He felt extremely lucky to see his family one more time. To say his goodbyes one more time. Just in case.

Startled by a nudge, Russell turned to spot Tomiko. Tadao politely stopped talking.

"I'm sorry for your loss," she said.

"Thank you," he slowly nodded and looked behind her for Jim. Disappointed, he cleared his throat and inquired, "Are you here by yourself?"

"Well, I'm with my parents, but if you're asking about Jim," she paused, biting her lips. "I'm sorry. I think he really wants to be here, but for some ridiculous reason, his pride is getting in the way."

Russell softly squeezed her shoulder. "It's alright. Some people can't help it."

"You've been a good friend to him. It bothers me how he pushes people away. Especially those he cares most about." She sighed in aggravation. "I can't explain it."

"Tomiko, you don't have to," he replied. "I admire your patience. I ran out of patience a long time ago."

She glanced down. "Do you know he's being sent to Tule Lake by the end of this week?"

"Tule Lake? Isn't that where they're sending the troublemakers?"

"He's not a sympathizer to the Japanese Empire," she defended. "Stubborn, but hardly dangerous."

Russell shook his head. "I knew his arrogance would get him into trouble."

Pinching her brows, Tomiko kept quiet. It would be inconsiderate to argue with him at his mother's wake. Instead she hugged him and said, "You be careful in Italy. Hopefully I'll see you again." She released him and walked to the front door.

Russell watched her leave. Didn't Jim realize how fortunate he was to have someone like Tomiko? And it wasn't fair. As irritating as Jim was, the jackass still managed to hold onto a girl. He wished he had a sweetheart to say goodbye to. Boot camp wasn't exactly the ideal place to find steady dates. And especially in the South. Turning around, he shuffled through the crowd in search of an empty seat. Exhausted, he wanted to nap somewhere. Anywhere. On a cot. In a chair. Even on top of a table. It didn't matter.

Sadaye unexpectedly tapped him from behind and said, "There's someone here to see you, Goro."

Grunting, he followed his sister, who still wore her tan military uniform, to the front of the room. There stood Jim. Russell first believed he was hallucinating. Looking at his sister to make sure she saw him too, she encouraged with a flicker of a grin. He returned to stare at the sullen face that hid behind those intimidating glasses. Sadaye merged back into the group. Speechless, Russell didn't know what to say. Many times he had planned to tell Jim off. Tell him that his head was too small for his brain. Or that he had the personality of a rotting carcass. Better yet, just smack him around. He was an easy target.

"You're lucky I'm too tired to knock your block off," he finally said.

Jim narrowed his eyes and asked, "Can we talk outside?"

Russell crossed his arms. "I dunno know. Can we?"

"I don't want to say what I have to say at your mother's funeral, which by the way," he hesitated, yielding his temper to express his empathy, "I am very sorry. I liked your mother. She was a good woman." Russell only nodded. Jim glanced at a Buddhist shrine that perched in the area where Mrs. Hamaguchi used to sleep. "There were times she told us what she thought when we least expected it."

"And I grew up with it."

"Believe me, I know what it's like!"

Russell studied Jim, unsure what to think about his intentions. If Jim really cared, he should have attended the wake along with his other friends. There was nothing like a funeral to determine one's true friends. Swerving to the side, he snatched a bottle his father had left on the shelf and swallowed. He figured, what the hell. The strange, bitter taste forced his face to shrivel while it burned down his throat. Setting it back, he began gasping. Once he regained his composure, he announced, "Okay! Now I'm ready!"

Shocked, Jim asked, "Since when did you start drinking?"

"Since now," he grinned, feeling a fantastic warmth tingling through his veins. Never experiencing alcohol before, he had wondered why it appealed so strongly for his father. The difference between the two was that Russell wouldn't let it take control of his life.

As they stood on the unpaved street, lights extended a steady glimmer. Without the moon, the artificial glow passed on a sharper blackness, disregarding the massive stars which soared freely. Jim and Russell stood beneath the divided boundary. Between land and sky. Between each other.

Jim started, "So, tomorrow you're actually leaving for Europe."

"Yeah. And next week you'll be back in California."

He pivoted, feeling anxious. "It'll be an interesting comparison."

"That's you in a nutshell, Jim," he said resentfully. "You've always been an interesting comparison. I *bet* the entire farm Tomiko's the one who told you to see me. You're too *damn* arrogant to do it on your own! She should get a purple heart for putting up with you."

"Actually I came on my own account."

"I guess I should kiss your feet then!"

Jim felt as though blistering tar had been dumped over his skin. He began shaking and wondered where Russell's animosity came from. It wasn't like him. And it was a bit intimidating.

"You really owe me an apology," Russell asserted.

Jim studied him. The light seemed to photograph Russell's uniform and face in position of trust. And dignity. Jim had to admit that his tanned suit posed a striking characterization for him. With his stocky build and earnest ambitions, Russell flattered the uniform.

"I am sorry. . ." he began and squinted at a trash barrel inching out of an alley. "I don't know why I allow myself to get so worked up. At that point, I become someone else. It's like nothing else mattered, and that's not the case." He hesitated, flustered by his own ineptness. "I used not to be like this. For some reason these camps seem to bring out the worse in me."

Russell gently punched Jim on his shoulder. "I doubt it. I remembered when you tried to attack Leo." He faintly snickered. "Man, that took some balls. I've never even stood up to that guy."

"That's because you wanted to fit in."

Russell eased his hands into his pockets, slowly nodding, wishing he could hear his mother scold him one more time. For anything. It seemed funny how Jim mimicked her criticism, oddly providing some comfort. She never understood Russell's need to desperately belong, consistently nagging him to support the few Japanese functions that were available on the island. She had believed that by disregarding his heritage indicated he disliked a part of himself. And maybe she was right.

"I still think you're making a mistake," Jim insisted. "Volunteering for the army won't change things."

Russell irritably flinched. "I already know your opinion, so give me a break, will ya?"

"It just bothers me you would put your life on the line. Europe isn't our problem. Those countries can't take care of themselves. They don't understand the notion of democracy any more than we do. Besides, you're the only friend I have and for you to run off and get killed . . ." he stopped to swallow, trying to suppress his throat from burning. Not willing to unmask himself, he coughed a couple of times to grip his emotions. "Don't you think you'll be more useful on the home front, anyway?" he continued. "Don't you think it's more important to use your brain instead of muscle?"

Russell was dumbfounded. Jim rarely gave the impression he cared at all. Yielding a grin, he said, "You've missed me."

"No, I didn't!"

"Don't worry," he snickered. "I'm not gonna ask you to marry me!"

He briefly smiled and returned to his serious nature. "Again, I am sorry for your loss. I do know what it's like when it's your own family. And no offence to you or anyone else, I hate attending funerals. No good can come from them." He paused and decided to extend his hand. "Against all odds, I do wish you luck. And yes, someone here will miss you, if not me."

Russell took his hand, shaking it. "Thanks," he said. Then, without thinking, he pulled Jim forward, hugging him. "I'll be seeing you soon, Jim. You take care."

At first Jim was shocked. In his experiences, he had never embraced another who was the same sex. Not his brother. Not even his father. It simply wasn't done. Under these special circumstances, however, he proceeded to reach his other arm around Russell's back. It didn't seem justifiable. First of all, not having the time to relate his regrets. He had wished he had behaved more civil towards Russell, in spite of their differences. Secondly, it was bad enough thinking about saying his farewells to Tomiko, his mother and sister within a week, but also to a friend. A friend whose worth exceeded his brother's memory.

Jim expressed, "You take care of yourself, too, *omono-san*."

~PART V~

Restitutions

CHAPTER ONE

One Year Later

A SPIKED peak that stood alone from the other bluffs survived the desert's turbulent atmosphere, withstanding the wind storms, the scalding summers and frigid winters, the camp's division, and the enforced nightly raids which finally ceded. The bullies, the extremists, the *Sokuku Kenkyu Seinen-dan* who wore grey shirts and white bandanas around their foreheads, and the well intended *Daihyo Sha Kai* who unsuccessfully struggled for equal wages and safer farming practices, all had been deported to other prisons. After many of them had already been deported there in the first place. By now, Tule Lake was half-empty. Like the other nine internment camps that were scattered past the western sun. In early January, the Supreme Court rescinded its own decision to intern those who proved their loyalty, granting them conditional freedom. Unfortunately for those who were left behind were still categorized as dangerous elements. The troublemakers. The outcasts. Educated men and women whose skills and motives were considered dubious. Without American citizenship, whether denied or revoked, they remained concealed in the program.

JIM had relocated his Underwood typewriter near his cot and window. Sitting in a corner of the barrack, he continued hammering the heavy keys. Three stacks of paper, one blank, the other two doused in ink, laid on his keenly arranged bunk. A young man, slender with a short nose and rounded eyes, zipped through the front doors, aiming toward Jim. Carrying a shabby leather briefcase covered in dust and dried mud, he slapped Jim's shoulder.

"*Konichi-wa Jimmu-san!*" he said as he flipped the top and withdrew a folder. "I have the latest notes."

Irritated, he complained, "John, I told you I don't like you hitting me."

"*Higai moso*," he scoffed.

"I'm not paranoid. I just don't like you touching me."

Glancing at the stacks of paper, John frowned. "We have an office, you know. It looks silly using your bed like a desk."

"I accomplish more without distractions."

"Some might accuse you of being eccentric," he joked.

Jim ceased from typing. He looked up at his colleague, who ironically, owned the common name as his brother. In the beginning, Jim compared and criticized his colleague to his brother. Not that he thought John was particularly an unpleasant guy, just immature, despite being a couple of years older than Jim.

"Relax, Jimmu," he maintained. "Being eccentric is a compliment. It means you don't compromise yourself. Here," he transferred the folder to Jim. "It's already been translated to English. We need a typewritten copy to hand over to the administration."

Last year Jim joined the committee on Block 29, helping to organize educational awareness and promoting Japanese values. Although they had to separate themselves from the *Daihyo Sha Kai* in order to avoid the stockades and the military's nightly raids, they continued their interests and responsibilities outside the functions of the co-op.

Skimming through the paperwork, he grumbled, "When are they going to stop treating us like misbehaved children? We don't need chaperones in every aspect of our lives."

"Don't you know politics are as risky as sex?"

Jim winced. That horrifying night when he and Tom were beaten on the eve of Pearl Harbor's anniversary continued to invade his nightmares. As if his dreams weren't already afflicted by phantoms. His brother. Callis. Even Shikami and Katsuji. And last spring when he arrived, violence had overshadowed the camp, repeating the accusations of spies and incessant beatings, echoing Manzanar's mistakes. Ultimately the chaos excelled into a murder of a co-op leader. Unsolved. The fluke that saved these reports from being printed into the American public was the conquest in the South Pacific. It daunted Jim ever wanting to get involved in politics; and yet, with nothing else better to do since he graduated high school two years ago, he volunteered anyway. Then he began to like it. He enjoyed disagreeing with others, supporting his arguments with research and facts. Some of the fellows were attorneys who allowed Jim to borrow their prized law books. And he also enjoyed editing the weekly transcripts, advancing his skills, asserting other options toward his future; other than mathematics. But above all, he felt valuable. He was helping to strengthen his community.

"Well, John," he said, shuffling the folder underneath others on top of his cot, "I should have these done by this evening."

John inspected the piles, curious, and reclined down to sift through the third one he didn't recognize from their block meetings.

"What are you doing?" Jim snapped. "You'll botch up my system!"

He took the top layer, squinting, reading. "Is this some sort of journal?"

Jim leapt up. "Put it back!

"*Matsu*! *Matsu!*" he retorted, spinning around. "I didn't know you could write!"

"It's nothing like that, John! Don't be an ass and put it down!"

Ignoring his plea, John stepped into the aisle to read without interruption. Jim stumbled forward, but halted when John immediately flashed his palm. Removing his glasses, he pinched his fingers between his eyebrows and groaned out of embarrassment. How could he have been so stupid as to expose his personal articles so carelessly? He had been working on some ideas earlier that morning, however he didn't consider anyone would actually be that goddamn nosy.

John turned around, holding the paper with both hands. "I'm surprised. I didn't think you had this sort of thing in you."

Jim didn't reply, not knowing how to excuse his inadequate writing. Instead, he replaced his glasses and crossed his arms, acting as though he didn't care, wishing he could disappear.

"I especially like this passage," John resumed."'Exiled, shamed and damned like bastards, we stare through these barbed wire fences, our eyes, our eyes betrayed by this world; our eyes behind belligerence.'" He looked up, slowly nodding. "This is some potent stuff. Harsh and honest." Stepping back, he returned the sheet to Jim. "Too bad the rest of the world doesn't want to hear it."

Jim meticulously straightened his stacks, straining his jaw. They remained to be burdens: these secrets. Whether inside his family or inside any society. Theses burdens felt identical to Siamese twins, sharing traditions like a vital organ. If they could be disjoined, these secrets and traditions, the possibility of one surviving without the other seemed pointless.

"Did you read about Ansel Adams? The photographer?" John asked.

Intrigued, Jim resettled on his chair, turning half-way around to answer. "He visited Manzanar when I was there. I actually got to meet him while he was taking photos of the camp."

"Really? What was he like?"

Slowly grinning, he replied, "Unique. Not at all what you suspect."

"Well, you then know Adams wrote a book to go along with his photos. I believe he called his book -um, called it . . . *Born Free and Equal*. I guess it's about us and the WRA and how we work together to move forward. Or something like it. Anyway, like it matters much. People have been using his book as fuel for their bonfires across the country."

Jim sighed and leaned into the back of his chair. "Is that really so surprising?"

"No," John admitted, "I guess it isn't. But you still can't help it. Hoping that someone outside of these camps will listen."

"Listening hasn't been the problem. It's giving a damn."

Remaining quiet for a moment, John tapped his finger on his thigh. "Well, the best we can do is rebuild our community. Rebuild it in such a way that a force stronger than the government can't break it down."

"Oh really?" Jim grinned. "What's stronger than the forces of the government?"

John lifted his chin and asserted, "Civil disobedience. You just watch and see what happens when we move on after this war."

"And you think civil disobedience is the way?"

"Yes, I do. It'll be an entire movement that'll involve all underprivileged races."

* * *

THE classroom echoed like a pebble clinking down a hill in a tin can as the teacher's footsteps rattled the floor; her arms folded; her skin reeking of waxy soap. Bethany tried to focus on her test about the American Civil War; however when she skimmed the room, with two-thirds of the seats abandoned, she felt lonely, envious. She ended up celebrating her fourteenth birthday with only her mother. It wasn't fair. Most of her friends were elsewhere. Freed. Enjoying a normal life while she was stuck in this dumb camp with her mother. Her mother who couldn't leave because she was an *Issei* while her father was stuck in another prison camp. And Jim also. It was beyond embarrassing. To have two of her family members accused of betrayal and disloyalty. Although she understood their innocence, nevertheless rumors made it awkward to explain their situations. Even to her friends who were in a similar predicament because, what if, and that was a big what if, some of the accusations were true? Jim had harsh opinions. He was never happy anyway. And obviously her father wasn't trying hard enough to reunite them. He had always made things happen. Why not this time?

Bethany began erasing her answers on the paper, pushing, squeezing, tearing through. She had written to Rose about living with her in Chicago, except that Tom didn't know if they could handle the baby and her at the same time. Then the idea of deserting Mrs. Yoshimura braced extra concern. With Bethany gone, who else would keep their mother company under the conditions? She stopped and stared at the rip. Appalled by what she had done, she quietly began crying. Her teacher turned around, perplexed, and walked over.

Resting her hands on Bethany's shoulders, she asked, "Goodness, child, what on earth brought this on?"

Humiliated, feeling the remaining eyes gawk at her, she sniffled, "May I please be excused, Miss Warner?"

Her teacher knelt beside her. "If I excuse you, you'll have to take a different test."

"Okay," she murmured.

Rising to her feet, she took Bethany's hand, glanced at the seat and noticed the blood stain, and then led her outside. Since the barrack had no hallways for privacy, the outside provided a substitute. Miss Warner removed a handkerchief from a side pocket of her dress and handed it to her. Bethany thanked her, blotting her wet cheeks.

"Bethany, from one woman to another, I think I know what's upsetting you." Miss. Warner tilted her head, partly smiling. "I do think it's best you have this conversation with your mother."

Bethany gaped at her teacher, wondering what she was talking about.

"First go to the school nurse and tell her you'll need a spare napkin. Afterwards, go home and I'll see you tomorrow."

Sniffling, completely confused, she studied her teacher as though she misplaced her brain. "I don't need a napkin, Miss Warner. I didn't spill anything."

She softly bit her lip. "Yes, dear. I'm afraid you did."

* * *

NIGHTFALL seemed to have knocked out the moon in the skyline. Tule Lake allowed its street lights to escort the few nightly wanders. Those who roamed about drifted with the tumbleweeds and scorpions that seemed to have stalked their shadows. The desert's solitude continued to alienate them from the dissolving war. Although everyone knew armistice would take place, their future remained uncertain. Jim, bundled in a corduroy jacket over his flannels, carried a two-by-four while stumbling down the wide alley. He rarely used the latrines during the night, only when he had no other choice. He had never felt comfortable straying alone in the darkness. Some of the men he knew on the block had been beaten for political differences, others mugged for their shoes or nickels they towed in their pockets.

Yawning and rubbing his eyes, he flinched to clear his vision and scanned around his surroundings. Silence whispered through the barracks. A buzz tingled inside his ears. He gazed upward, admiring the openness not layered by pointy tree. The giant cosmos compelled him to feel small, dizzy, an impression he hadn't experienced before. Or an imprint he overlooked in the past.

Suddenly he halted. He widened his eyes, staring in disbelief. He had heard rumors, yet instinctively scoffed at them. Jim wasn't superstitious. Nor was he easily spooked. He had concluded the stories of phantom-like flames glowing over the barracks existed in people's imaginations. Many assumed that since Tule Lake was an old Indian burial site, the iridescence had to be lost or angry spirits. Jim didn't know what to believe. It could have been the Northern Lights, except that they weren't multi-colored as he had witnessed before back home. Or perhaps the gleams were a military experiment, but what would be the purpose when there was supposed to be a blackout? Or he was simply dreaming, walking along only half-awake. Regardless of the explanation, the serpent-like glow remained hypnotic. Then it dissolved as if clumps of sugar into water, fading into the blackness. Scratching his head, he had to admit, he had never encountered something as bizarre as this. He wasn't sure whether this implied some sort of miracle or hallucination.

Relapsing into reality, he proceeded his nightly journey. Once he finished, more awake by now and for the first time being the sole person at the latrines, he began to walk back to his quarters. To his left side he noticed a silhouette behind one of the street lights sparking a cigarette. The man was of a stocky stature; his features obscured by the shadows. Jim squeezed the rectangular club and increased his pace. He glanced over his shoulder. The man began to follow. Staring ahead, he steered to his barrack at the end of the block. The soft ground seemed to hinder his speed, and yet, the chill strengthened his adrenaline. To his right side another man darted out of an alley. Instantly, Jim swung his club at the intruder. The other man jumped and attempted to grab Jim's weapon. Jim continued to strike the attacker who kept dodging and pivoting. The stocky man seized his club from behind and punched his ribs. Gasping, Jim dropped to his knees. His face was hit. Falling back, he clutched sand in his fist and flung it upward. He heard one of them cry out. The other kicked his leg. He grunted, but refused to shout out his pain, not giving them any satisfaction. He flung two more fistfuls of sand and stumbled to get up. Another kick cracked his ribs, disabling him. Wheezing heavily, he was pulled up to his feet. The pain stabbed his side, causing him to sweat. He squinted. With his vision blurred, his head whirling, he clutched the man's wrists one last time. There was a hesitation.

"I know you," the stocky man said. "Sure, sure, I know you."

He released Jim. Jim supported his hand over his injury, trying to recover. He readjusted his glasses and stared until his focus returned. He recognized the roving eye which belonged to Shikami.

"I don't believe it," Jim uttered, his pain coinciding with each breath. "I thought I'd seen you around. At those *Sokuku* rallies. I thought they had relocated you to Texas!"

He smirked. "Can't catch what can't find."

Jim, despite the torment, straightened his back to overshadow Shikami. He glanced at the other man whose skin absorbed the dirt into his wrinkles, appearing as if half-masked.

"So," Jim said, his hands shivering, his voice hoarse. "What the hell are you planning to do with me now?"

Shikami hesitated while positioning his knotted knuckles over his hips. "Yur friend, Rasso, is it?" Jim nodded. "Yes, Rasso. Few can ah challenge me. Earn my respect. He is ah good fighta, yur friend. I figura Rasso is da type to not be sent here. Dutiful to his stupidity. Thinking America is honorable. But you," he lifted his brows. "You, I be surprised. A loyal friend to Rasso."

"Well, you certainly lived up to your stupidity!" he quipped. "Beating up people for no damn good reason! It just means you're a bully. A weak, insecure bully!"

His course face stiffened. "*What do you know about weakness, eh little girl?*" He advanced his face directly into Jim's, his breath reeking of fish and onions. "*Do you think you are smarter than me because your English is better? What do you know about my survival? What do you know about defending myself from the hajukins?*"

"And beating up your own people improves your survival?"

Shikami stepped back, huffing, blinking as if he had been slapped. "You ain't my goddamn peopo'! You ain't from my island!"

Jim realized he got to him. "I know how hard it is living in two worlds. And for Christ's sake, we're both put in these camps for the same goddamn reason!" Shikami looked away from Jim, his facade becoming less abrasive. Jim pursued, ignoring his own discomfort. "Listen, I'm tired. Tired of watching our own people attack each other instead of using that energy to defend our rights. I'm tired of living in fear. And most importantly, I'm just really tired." He shook his head, peering at the other man behind Shikami. "I had wanted to go back to sleep, but now I'll have to go to the hospital."

Shikami frowned. "You know, in Manzanar, my brother was shot at. He survive but can't use his arm, no way, no how. Useless."

Jim steadied his gaze and tone. “A friend of mine was killed in that riot. I understand hatred more than you give me credit for.”

Shikami blinked at Jim.

“But,” Jim continued, “hatred accomplishes nothing. And it eats you alive. And that’s no way to live.”

Folding his arms, Shikami relaxed his demeanor. He again remained quiet for a while. Perplexity broke off his cockiness, revealing a genuine vulnerability, shame even. Averting the other man’s scrutiny, he stepped backward and stared down at his feet.

“Why did you two attack me?” Jim asked. “It’s obvious I’m not carrying anything valuable at this time of night. I don’t think this is even your territory.” He cleared his throat, trying to suppress his anger. “I want to know why.”

He narrowed his eyes and shifted his jaw. “I can’t say.” Looking up, he inquired, “What yur name?”

Jim hesitated, trying to analyze the dual nature of Shikami and questioned why Shikami didn’t finish him off. For some curious reason, despite Russell being his adversary, Shikami respected Russell. So perhaps by respecting Russell he somehow respected Jim.

“Jimmu Yoshimura,” he finally answered.

He flickered a grin. “*Jimmu, eh? Like the legend of Japan’s first emperor?*”

“A coincidence.”

“Or karma. Maybe someday you too be a leada.”

He closed his eyes in pain, grunting. “Not with these broken bones.”

Shikami tilted his head, thinking. “I’ll help you to da hospital, Jimmu-san.”

“And will you stop beating people up?”

A smirk appeared after he glanced at his silent partner. “Nobody quits smoking in one day. Same ting.”

CHAPTER TWO

Late April

AN EARLY morning drizzle had receded, leaving muddied tracks over the snow for the convoy to pursue. The sun finally made a dim appearance by late afternoon, hiding behind streaks of clouds. Hiking up a dirt trail that deemed impervious to modern civilization, often traveled by horse-drawn carts and bicycles, Russell and Shig walked apart from the two non-*Nisei* Infantries; the 42nd and 45th. Sent as scouts for their combat team, they stalked alongside the modern rigs that were heading toward Munich; although they were on a different mission. Four other scouts from the 522nd were also canvassing the terrain, scavenging for German soldiers and their booby-traps. Nothing could thrill Russell more knowing that they were on the verge of conquering the birthplace of the Nazi party. He couldn't believe it. Wandering uninterrupted into the bowels of Nazi Germany. Years ago when he used to watch Hitler's control swell like a tumor on the newsreels, it seemed unreal because of the vast distance. The language. The clothes. The black and white reflections on a flat, chalky screen. When he used to believe his little island was protected against the world's hostilities. Now it felt odd, watching the newsreels that pointed at *them*.

Only four months away until his twentieth birthday, he realized if he lived through the remainder of war, he would need to complete his high school diploma. Fatigued, he continued to march with Shig; their helmets angled, concealing their bushy hair growing past their ears and down their necks. With prickly chins, uniforms soiled in mud and stained from mortar residue, they must have looked like a sorry pack of wild dogs. Russell could smell, and sometimes taste, whiffs of gasoline that the tanks and jeeps discharged. Odors he became accustomed to as much as his own. And his buddies. And the artillery's powder during battle. Surviving ten uninterrupted months of combat after combat after combat, Russell had never been so damned proud to serve among the most dedicated group of men. When the officers barked, "Go," they charged in unison without blinking. One mission; one heart. Everyone understood they had nothing to lose, but a hell of alot more to gain. In that course of time, Russell had been awarded two Purple Hearts and promoted to Corporal. Shig acquired one Purple Heart and moved up to Private First Class. Likewise, they also transformed as a pair of talented marksmen. The rest of the 442nd Combat Team had been divided between France and Italy, assisting the 100th Battalion, the first *Nisei* combat team from Hawaii. If it hadn't been for the Hawaiians and the Japanese American Citizens League's persistent letter writings, Russell would never have had the opportunity to do his part.

After an exhaustingly prolonged year, the white officers had stopped calling them *Japs* or *Nips*. Since the *Nisei* regiments maintained the highest casualty rate on both sides of the American theaters, they ultimately earned respect from celebrities like Bob Hope and Frank Sinatra who publicly praised them, and generals such as MacArthur and Eisenhower who had underestimated them. Every once in awhile Russell thought about Stockwell and whether he had altered his attitude regarding the *Japs*. If Stockwell abided any ration of honor, he would have to realize the color yellow was only skin deep.

Underneath his uniform the scarf with a thousand stitches remained secured, although slightly torn from bullets' slices. His old and fresh wounds marked his accomplishments; or better phrased, marked his luck. He was lucky his wounds weren't fatal. Unlike his other buddies. Unlike Roku. Twice the military threatened to ship Russell back home, once with Shig, but unless the surgeons amputated a limb or pronounced him dead, he hadn't planned on leaving just yet.

He glanced at his friend, concerned about his condition. Men had been hospitalized from excessive dehydration and illnesses. Aside from snipers, booby-traps, and prostitutes, viruses and infections were the next deadly problems on the list.

"How's your stomach? Getting any better?"

"It has to be," he replied. "After five or six trips, I don't think I have anything left!"

"I'm surprised these K-rations don't give everyone diarrhea. Just looking at our meals resembles it!"

Shig grinned. "Maybe we should write poems about our ordeal. Something like . . . 'If roses weren't red, and if violets weren't blue. . .' "

" '. . . then our shit don't smell like roses, too!' " Russell finished.

They chuckled. With their feet tender from marching since daybreak, minds numbed from sleeplessness and boredom, at least joking, even at the crudest level, provided some sort of asylum.

"Seriously, Shig," Russell continued, his smile withering. "Have you seen a medic yet? It's been going on for a couple of weeks. You can't do your job if your health is poor."

He moaned in protest. "I outlived hundreds of bullets. I doubt my diarrhea is just as risky."

"Not unless you pass out. Won't do me any good if I have to lug your heavy, unconscious ass around."

Squinting, Shig thought about the consequences of endangering other men's lives, especially if he were unconscious and he could prevent it. His recurring headaches and wobbling denoted signs that his body needed rest and nutrients. "Okay," he agreed. "Once when we meet up with the others, I'll take care of it."

BY MID-AFTERNOON they entered a quaint village undefiled by air raids. Russell found solace in its isolation; buried in thickets of trees. The multicolored houses, which were stacked on dense hills and bridged together like ivy vines, had to be at least a couple of centuries old. He had always fantasized about traveling through Europe and visiting ancient towns. The countryside made it easier to forget the war. Its beauty mellowed the harsh brutality that surrounded them; inflicted from fire and explosives, blood and death. In an odd way, despite the cultural differences, the mountainous hills, the cleanliness of snow, the seclusion from the world reminded Russell of Bainbridge. With the exception of hunting for SS men. The residents, however, were not as hospitable while Shig and Russell promptly explored the narrow village. The locals began closing their shutters, locking their doors, moving off the stone roads and hiding indoors as a handful of Americans began invading their village. No German soldiers were found out in the open. In fact, most of the residents remained sheltered, staring down from their windows. It was obvious they detested them.

"Dachau's a friendly town," Shig remarked.

"Yeah, remind me to pick up a postcard for later."

Trudging on another muddied road, which took them outside of Dachau, they found a spot overlooking a prison camp. From a distance they could easily see a double-layered fence, prickly and twisted, impounding thousands of thousands of people in gray-striped uniforms and dark, rounded caps. Half were without coats or real shoes; if any. A concrete ditch ran in front of the barricade, as if a primeval moat. Thick, white watchtowers were positioned at all four corners. They could also hear people dying. The prisoners' moaning resounded above the pines. Removing a pair of binoculars, Russell surveyed the camp more closely. He saw their faces. Young men who looked twice their age, and children, some no older than seven, supported each other from shoulder to shoulder. Their large eyes sunk into their skulls. Teeth were missing in their hysterical smiles as they watched the Americans travel toward their way. Their skins barley gripped over their knotted fists. Like half-eaten chicken legs.

Russell couldn't refrain from staring at the rawboned individuals; these ravenous men whose howling continued to rage. Some men were dragging themselves toward the towering front gate. A thick chain and lock had been wrapped at the iron portal; just below the words "Arbeit Macht Frei." Russell only understood the word "frei," which translated to "free." It had to be a sick joke. Then maneuvering his magnified view around the bulky entrance, he spotted heaps of parched bodies aligned beside roasted barracks.

"Christ almighty!" he exhaled.

"What?" Shig asked.

Russell handed the binoculars over to him. Shig scanned the vicinity, equally appalled. "What the fuck were these Krauts planning?"

Questions bombarded their aching heads, and they didn't know where to begin asking; other than why. They vaguely knew about these camps, what the newsreels identified them as labor colonies where political prisoners were incarcerated. And barely a decade ago, when Charlie Chaplin poked fun at Hitler with his first movie, *The Great Dictator*. Chaplin had also mentioned these concentration camps before *his* exile. Then the reports vanished from public. Ironically the same time their people had been interned.

Shig glanced up, but returned to the binoculars. "Where the hell are the guards? Did these fucking cowards just take off?"

Russell grabbed his rifle from his shoulder and carefully aimed it at the lock. Releasing his safety latch, he squinted. "Of course they did. They knew we were coming for them. And they know they're in deep shit. Because who knows what evil lurks in the heart of men?" Holding his breath, he pulled the trigger. He missed. Squeezing the trigger again, he saw his target drop on the cement floor. Lowering his gun, he tapped his forehead and he proceeded, "*The Shadow* knows!"

Shig grinned, handing over the binoculars to Russell. "Come on, *omono!* Let's take a peek 'round back."

They hiked down the hill, passing by a couple of tanks and jeeps that steered to the gate and saluted to officers. A putrid stench rose above the ground. As rotten as death on battlefields during the summer months. As moldy as open infections. As pungent as human waste. That and a burnt odor; like after bonfires. They had never seen, or smelled, anything of this intensity. Soon shouts from inside the camp launched more shouting in different languages; but all sounding something like "Americans! Americans!" Thousands more began to pour out of the remains of the barracks. Men and boys crammed against the barbed wire fence, waving and saluting, weeping and smiling compulsively. Their hysterical cries echoed like no other clamor. Not like that of cannons or aircraft. Or like the roaring cheers at a baseball game. The cheering grew incredibly thunderous that Russell had to cover his ears, surprised to experience a shrill louder than motor fire. There had to be more than 30,000 prisoners to generate that much noise.

Russell and Shig walked along side of a row of white, two-story houses with red roofs across the camp. Carefully sculpted rose bushes embroidered their gentility. Multiple windows met the spiraled fence. What an incredibly insane view. To live in luxury only yards apart from misery. To purposely watch people starve to death. An SS soldier stood behind one of the pristine windows, smoking a cigar, waiting. Infuriated, disgusted, Russell resisted the urge to shoot the bastard through that distant window. Instead, a couple of American officers entered his house and pushed him outside at gunpoint. Just off to side was another building constructed of brick; long and narrow with a chimney stack pointing up to the sky. Returning to the haunted faces, Russell spotted a boy, perhaps nine or ten years old, wrapped in a filthy blanket with torn scarves around his feet. The boy appeared more malnourished than the other children whom Russell had seen begging from the Americans. Reaching into one of his pockets, Russell retrieved beef jerky and cautiously walked to the boy at the end of the ditch. He knelt and held out his stick of beef. The boy stared at it, amazed.

He suddenly smiled and thanked Russell in either German or Polish; Russell couldn't tell the difference, nor could he hear the boy from the blaring excitement. Two more children stretched out their dirty, bony hands. He searched through his other pockets to retrieve a Hershey's bar. Breaking it in half, he gave the pieces to the older boys who swallowed it with only a couple of bites.

Shig stared in astonishment. He rummaged through his pockets and retrieved a tin box of Spam. Opening it, he extended the persevered meat out in the open. A man quickly grabbed it, nodding and thanking him repetitively and then swallowed it with his fingers.

At that moment, Russell had never felt important enough to influence other lives. His friends died striving to repair freedom for their families back home, and for those who were under Nazi occupation. It was inexplicable. This feeling. This delirium mixed with tears. The months of strenuous work across Italy to France to Germany had meant something. Inspired by an honorable force. Something larger than himself. It didn't matter he was an American. Or Japanese-American. Or that he had won military awards in a segregated unit. Or that his love-life was in the dumps. He was a part of a drum. A rhythm. A unity. No matter how ugly. How cruel. There was something worth saving that day that would transfigure the world. And he was an element of that force.

Rising to his feet, Russell followed Shig, heading toward the backside of the bleached houses. There was supposed to be a train track the Nazi used to ship cargo. It was also their job to pinpoint the exact location and set up arrangements for confiscation. Slowly the thunderous cheering began to recede in rippling waves, leaving Shig's and Russell's ears in a ringing state. Russell glanced at his wristwatch, realizing they needed to hurry along. Treading beyond a row of trees, they did find an extended line of box cars sitting on the cold tracks, abandoned. Other American soldiers canvassed the area, sniffing alongside of the wooden cars like hounds. A rotting stench oozed through the gapes, becoming unbearable. Russell didn't want to know what was behind the doors. He stood in one spot, staring. It had better be dead cows. And that was why people were starving. Shig grabbed the latch and nodded to him for assistance. Reluctantly Russell helped him slide it open. Horrified, repulsed, they gawked at a large mound of stiff, rotten corpses. Bones exposed over half-corroded skins. Eyes sunken if not gone. Lips shriveled over missing teeth.

Russell couldn't breath.

The mound seemed as massive as Mount Rainier. There had to be hundreds dead. Discarded openly. Vainly. Russell fell back and vomited. He had seen dead bodies. An endless reservoir of corpses. But that was expected during war. After a while he became accustomed it, as everyone else had to. Even after seeing his first, killing his first, and doubting whether he could continue, none of it compared to that heap of shriveled, decaying corpses trapped in those boxes.

Shig instantly covered his nose and blazed at the site as if he had been stabbed. He turned away, crying. His disbelief could not have been matched by anything else he had seen or heard during that year. Missing limbs. Gutted stomachs. Crushed skulls. Men bleeding to death at his side while he continued loading up the canons. These prisoners were civilians. They weren't the enemy. They weren't trained to defend themselves.

Embarrassed for vomiting, Russell stumbled off. He had been stupidly comparing his experiences to this gruesome camp. But how could he? Measuring his personal ordeals to these people somehow counterbalanced what bigotry represented. Not to excuse the violations against his civil rights; however the violations against these prisoners went beyond the violence and hatred he had known. Or could ever know. And for that, he was relieved he and his family lived in America. Even with its imperfections. At least his country wasn't killing them off like diseased rodents. At least they had their health. Still possessed a little bit of money. Had food that didn't need to be sold and bought on the black market just to survive. And at least they could return to a homeland that hadn't been destroyed by bombs. If this war could reconstruct anything, then it should reconstruct what remained human.

Early May

DOWNTOWN Kansas City was besieged by a kaleidoscopic of confetti, honking vehicles, and an enormous cheering crowd. Music rung in between the tall buildings while people danced on the sidewalks and streets. Germany finally surrendered, following five and a half years since the invasion of Poland, the Blitz, and the threat of Nazi expansion to the rest of civilization. Optimism grew into fever, resilience into pride, and a belief that righteousness had crushed the world's vices. Just as President Roosevelt had prophesied before his unexpected death. Applauding continued to boom throughout the busy terminal, levitating to the high ceiling like a singing choir. The exhilaration had gushed inside the train station, supported by newspapers, radio, and people's infectious chattering.

Meito stuffed four tickets inside his coat as he walked back to his family. His excitement leaned elsewhere. Not to underplay his relief that the war was settling down; but after two years in two detention camps and ten months between the Kansas-Missouri borders, he was more than ready to go home. Even though his sponsor was a pleasant man, a Presbyterian minister who provided a carpentry job for him and a maid position for Gertrude, it wasn't a strong enough reason for them to stay. Meito smiled at his wife. She wore a new polka-dotted dress, feeding their year-old daughter with a bottle of rationed milk. Joe and George, now ten years old, swung their bare legs over the bench, staring at the electrified crowd. Their tan knickers and white shirts were also new. George's bow tie was crooked, but then Meito's level of concern just wasn't there.

He leaned down to kiss Gertrude's forehead and sat beside her. "We're all set."

She pressed her sculpted brows. "Did you have any trouble getting the tickets?"

"No," he sighed. "I think they don't care here. Or they don't know the difference. I guess this is where ignorance is actually a blessing."

Gertrude didn't feel comfortable. "Do you think we'll be welcomed once we're back home?"

He rolled his tongue. "I don't see why they'll oppose."

"They didn't oppose the evacuation," she bitterly remarked.

"Neither did we."

They allowed the surrounding noises to divide their awkwardness. She resumed, "I'm really scared, Meito. What if they don't want us back? What if they start calling us bad names or throwing bricks in our house? What if the boys get into fights at school? We have children and a baby to look after! How can we protect them?"

Meito shifted his body to directly face her. "We rarely had troubles with our neighbors before. We're lucky to be from such a small community. I would be more worried about living in Seattle than Winslow." He gently caressed her ear while easing a grin. "We'll be okay."

Gertrude languished for a few moments, not confident about her husband's casual manner. "What about our folks? They're still left behind in those camps and we're still at war with Japan. What do you think will happen to them?"

He looked away. He couldn't provide an answer. Without American citizenship, the government guaranteed nothing. And the Pacific battles could take as much as two more years despite the fact Japan was losing. No matter how exceedingly slow. Like an ailing tortoise with a strong shell. In the meantime, if President Truman sensed a threat of any kind, or used the *Issei* as a means to exchange them with American POWs, then that would be that. His father and Gertrude's parents would be gone. The military could also transfer Goro there, right beside Kunio, and more bloodshed would drain on both sides. It was hard enough having the rest of his family scattered across the Midwest and East Coast, further away from home. The new president had better find a way to end the war, and to end it quickly before his family would completely erode.

* * *

SHIG and Russell were sent to scout through the slaughtered city to begin American occupation. They had visited one of the Nazi headquarters that once hung its broad flag at the entrance. By the time they arrived, a massive bonfire incinerated the flag while Russian soldiers were shooting at the iron eagle. Other Allied soldiers, the Brits with a few of their colonial affiliates, the Africans and Indians, also helped to tighten Austria's perimeters.

"You know, I've been thinking," Russell announced.

Shig snickered. "Don't you know it's mutiny when grunts start thinking?"

He flicked a grin and continued, "I've been thinking about going by my birth name."

"Why?" he blinked, a little puzzled. "You don't like your nickname anymore?"

"It's not that," he said, moving forward. "My parents named me after my great-grandfather. He was a *samurai*, you know."

"Really?" he grinned. "I had no idea I was in the company of such greatness!"

"Knock it off, Shig! I'm being serious," he lightly warned, smiling as he readjusted his rifle. Something grand and humbling emerged in his harrowing experiences. He remembered legends of the *samurai* his father narrated: legends of family glory and honor. He considered themselves to be the new warriors. There seemed to be a connection between the two eras and two empires. Russell felt it. And no doubt others in the artillery had felt, too. If they hadn't, then they probably wouldn't have accomplished what they had accomplished.

"So," Shig proceeded, "you want me to start calling you- Goro, is it?"

"That's the plan," he said, and slowed his pace, frowning. "I haven't been a very good son," he continued. "All those years I wasted arguing or ignoring my mother. About how she spoke. The food she cooked. Her life stories growing up in Japan. I was so selfish."

"What brought this on suddenly? It's a beautiful day. The war's over. You're still single and can have any girl you like!"

Russell moaned, glancing at the gutted buildings. "Tomorrow's her birthday." He abruptly halted. "I can't prepare her favorite dishes. I can't make a boat for her spiritual journey. How can I be a better son when I can't honor her in her custom? My parents wanted so much for me and what I have done for them?"

Shig squinted at the blue horizon concealed by rubble and smoke, then backtracked to Russell. Releasing a long sigh, he expressed with empathy, "I know this must be hard right now. Especially today. But you got to believe that you *are* a good son *and* a good soldier. Don't let your guard down by letting your guilt get to you." He paused, fumbling for an appropriate expression. "Whenever things seemed impossible, my father would tell me: 'If you fall seven times, you stand up eight.'" He again paused and placed his hand over Russell's shoulder. "That's the best advice I can give you." Russell nodded, wiping his eyes. "Besides, your father's still alive. Make it up to him."

"God!" he murmured. "Some sap I became!"

"Better a sap than a lunatic," Shig remarked, half-smiling. "Come on, Goro, the sooner we cover this area, the sooner we can get some sleep!"

"What are you girls doin' standing around?" someone shouted from a distance. "This ain't no social club!"

They rotated in that direction. Another *Nisei* soldier trotted across the two lanes, passing by children who were pulling a tin wagon, collecting junk off the streets. A dusty black vehicle puttered from behind, one of the few cars driven by someone bold enough to venture on the streets. Russell recognized the other soldier.

"Ikki!" he exclaimed. "What in the hell are you doing here?"

"*Konichi-wa!*" he greeted, beaming. "I thought you losers looked familiar! Halfway around the world and this is where we meet."

The three took turns shaking each other's hands. Russell was surprised how little Ikki had changed, other than thinning around his face and dark bags under his eyes which were common for most battle-wearied soldiers.

Russell alluded, "Out of all the shit-holes in Europe, you had to walk into mine!"

Ikki chuckled.

"What division's yours?" Shig asked.

"232nd Engineer. What about you?"

"522nd Artillery," Russell answered. "We were hoping to go deaf soon so we can start ignoring orders!"

"Well," Ikki laughed, "some guys have all the luck!"

"But you guys get to build bridges and things, right?" Shig interjected. "And not destroy them?"

Ikki's humor unexpectedly dropped. "If we're not too busy sweeping out mines."

Russell asked, "So, when did you get here?"

Ikki shifted his stance as if bothered by the sun. "Well, Russ, I'm not sure. It felt like yesterday, but it could of been last year. We keep on marching, or keep on wondering if this will be the last time we'll live today. The only reason I know what season it is is by watching leaves falling off, or it's always raining or snowing." He suddenly sneezed several times. "Goddamnit! I must be the only one allergic to war!"

Russell and Shig were a little stunned by his animosity.

Shig asked, "I suppose you don't have an extra smoke on ya?"

He blinked. "Yeah, sure." Opening his chest pocket, he removed a slightly bent cigarette. "Here."

"Thanks, man," Shig said, taking it. He reached inside his pocket to remove a lighter. Puffing, he resumed, "So, Ikki, it's been a couple of years. What's new with you?"

"I got married."

"I'll be damned!" Shig exclaimed. "So did I!"

"Congratulations!" Russell boasted, slapping Ikki's shoulder. "Who's the lucky gal?"

Ikki readjusted his rifle on his back to reach for his wallet in his rear pocket. He slipped out a photograph. "It's Susan Kuroda."

"Yeah, I know Susie," Russell commented, looking at the photo. "I always thought she was cute. Use to sit behind her in Social Studies back home."

Shig flexed a grin and nodded his approval.

"That's Susie," Ikki briefly smiled. "We got hitched the week before I had to report for duty. She's expecting sometime this month, you know."

"Well, well," Rusell grinned, "again, congratulations, man!"

"Wait a minute," Shig flinched. "You reported for duty only *nine* months ago?"

"Yeah. Why?"

"How long did you train before you were sent here?"

Ikki hesitated. "The usual six weeks."

Annoyed, he stared at Russell. "I'll be a monkey's ass. We only trained for thirteen goddamn months!"

Ikki replaced his wallet. "I'm glad this whole mess is finally over! I'm looking forward going back home and salvage what's left. If they don't send us to Japan, that is."

"The first thing I'm going to do is take a long, long, loooong hot shower!" Russell said. "Use up all the water and soap! After that, sleep for a month before I start working!"

Shig smirked. "Forget sleeping. Although I like the idea of laying in bed for a month," he winked, "with my wife!"

Ikki narrowed his eyes and stepped back. He tried to imagine the city at one time swarming with people and cars before the bombing. Before the occupation. He knew this city could be rebuilt; but that wasn't the real question. Yes, it was possible to rebuild cities and his life after being reduced to a grunt in a hypercritical system. The real question was based on how. How could he forgive the United States for taking away their homes, their rights, their lives, and even taking away his cousin? How could he rebuild his life after learning the values of suspicion, anger, and humiliation?

He glared at his ignorant friends, and said, "The first thing I'll do is burn this damn uniform. Then the second thing I'll do is denounce my American citizenship and live in Japan."

Shig and Russell gawked at him.

Russell asked, "Are you joking?"

"Why would I joke? I didn't choose to be here. I was drafted like any other dope! I didn't choose to leave my home. We were forced by the military. The very military we're serving in. How's that for a joke? Am I laughing? Are you laughing?"

Russell and Shig looked away, embarrassed. Irony had haunted them every since boot camp.

Ikki shook his head, and stated, "Listen, I'll see you guys around." He trudged off, hiking up the street until he turned a corner and vanished.

Shig puffed the borrowed cigarette. "I wouldn't want to carry that kind of burden around."

Russell began walking and remarked, "We all have our own to carry, Shig."

Following his friend, Shig walked in silence; their muddied boots clumping on the abandoned road full of rubble. Russell ventured off a side street, substantially narrower than the main one that circulated through the old city. Fractured buildings had dumped mounds of bricks on the path. Last week's series of bombings had finally crippled this city, leaving half of it utterly devastated. A hint of decaying bodies hovered in the air. Russell saw two dead German soldiers covered in heavy debris, and another lying in the middle of the street, his head facing down; his arms stretched out as if in the process of surrendering. Pools of dried blood deposited beside the crushed bodies. The Germans' uniforms hadn't been pillaged yet, revealing their enshrined medals on their chests. Russell and Shig excitedly approached the honorary find, knowing that someday these trophies would merit a great deal of money. Rummaging among the first two trapped by bricks, they removed the medals and the cufflinks. Russell ignored their faces and their youth, reminding himself what they did to the prisoners in Dachau, making them less human. They got what they deserved. He had to believe it to stop feeling sorry for them.

"These bastards didn't have a chance!" Shig boosted. "Looks like they were running away instead of fighting for their lives!"

Russell slid his small trophies inside his front pocket, then buttoned and patted it for security. "It's been awhile since we've seen them up so close."

"Thank God this will be the last time. Unless we have to go to Japan," he stepped back, holding the medals in his hand, "And if one of those soldiers may be a relative." He winced and tossed his cigarette. "I can't do the same thing to one of them. Just in case, you know?"

Russell hesitated, wondering if Kunio had been doing the same thing, wondering if he could pass up the opportunity out of respect for their parents. Shuddering, he decided to leave the third body alone as if to balance his repentance and guilt even though the body belonged to a Kraut. He turned around to backtrack to the main street to complete his duty. When he realized Shig wasn't following him, he halted six feet apart and exclaimed, "Hey bonehead! Aren't you coming?"

"In a minute!" he replied, stuffing his pockets. "The other one is an officer. His will be worth a hell of alot more!"

"Forget it! We got what we need."

Disregarding him, Shig stepped on top of the fallen bricks, toward the last dead German.

Russell sighed out of annoyance and rested his knuckles over his hips. The sun's shadow cornered them in the alley, in between the two skeleton structures. The rich blue sky lured a false impression of confidence. Russell watched his stubborn friend carefully brace his weight over the bulky fragments.

Shig leaned down, flipped the body over with a grunt, and froze. "Oh, Jesus!" he hissed. "Grenade!"

Russell felt as though he had been electrocuted. He wasn't sure if he yelled out "run" or just thought it, but within seconds he bolted inside a door's threshold. His ears loudly popped. Crumbling to the ground, he felt his chest explode and instantly blacked out.

CHAPTER THREE

Early September

MINIDOKA was left to decay. Mr. Hamaguchi knew it. The few people who straggled behind the barbed wire fence continued to live in doubt, fear, and silence. The second bomb, this new kind of bomb that freed such tremendous energy as to obliterate Nagasaki as well Hiroshima, repeated a familiar remorse that was felt after Pearl Harbor. News of Japan's unconditional surrender may have resolved peace but it couldn't resolve their confidence. Caught between two worlds, between two different senses of morality and justice, their relief was counterbalanced by sorrow: For their families still living in Japan. For their children who were scattered across the United States like fallen leaves. For their ambivalent future.

Mr. Hamaguchi closed his suitcase. Grit and dust buried the wooden floor, the chairs and table, and the shelves. Since his wife's death, since his children's departures, his motivation to perform housework rarely occurred. Sometimes a couple of his wife's friends would feel sorry for him and do his laundry. Sometimes he paid children five cents to clean the barrack. Like Bethany Yoshimura who had nothing else left to do; poor girl. Now that the war ended, so did the purpose of these camps.

Reaching for his hat that laid on the bed, he angled it as he had seen done by the younger generation. He padded his coat to make sure he hadn't forgotten anything: his wallet, his dismissal papers, his photo identification. This morning he had his hair trimmed, his face professional shaved; a treat he seldom indulged.

He bowed to his wife's bed with a Morning Glory resting on top of her pillow. "*Setsumi*," he began. "*Thank you for the children you gave me, and thank you for taking care of me when I had been unwell.*"

Clutching his suitcase and half-empty Pepsi bottle that held his homemade *saki*, he left the door gaping wide, letting any and all elements prey on the structure's bones. He secretly wished his grandsons could burn down this barrack, too. Perhaps the entire camp. Browsing the dull harsh environment one last time, he realized he could only remember a few incidents during his internment. The drinking had blotted, if not purged, his mind through the years. He had been sleeping, more or less, and he also realized how much time he wasted not protecting his family. His closed his eyes, ashamed. No wonder his wife resented him. No wonder his ancestors had been scolding him in his dreams. And he wasn't certain if he deserved their forgiveness. Opening his eyes, he began walking away from the makeshift dwelling, abandoning his makeshift memories. The eastern sun traced his path to the camp's entrance. Although Meito had made plans to pick him up at the barrack, he was tired of waiting inside the fence. Meito never spoke about the family riddle as to why he appeared different compared to the rest. Although distraught from knowing, like the first-born son that he was, Meito continued to shelter family honor.

Passing the vacant barracks, these rows and rows of military-green skeletons, and hearing the desert's gusts whistle and squeak through silence, he bore witness to the extinction of the camp. Lacking thousands upon thousands of people to generate life, noises, activities, even sleepy Winslow now seemed to have more breath in its rural existence. He intended to reestablish his barber/ laundry business. Without his wife, without his youth, it would be better not to resume farming.

He yielded at the tail end of his destination. Standing apart from the guard shack, which secured a bored, inexperienced guard who hunched over his stool and listened to the radio, Mr. Hamacughi also listened, straining to understand. Music escaped through the yawning windows. The popular swing-beat united a country-western flavor, recruiting Bing Crosby and The Andrew Sisters to portray American idealism. He had heard this song multiple times from other people's radio for a year, but he had never listened to "Don't Fence Me In." He only caught half of the words, yet they were enough to adequately recognize the irony. Despite his own cycles of disappointments, these regrets weren't unfamiliar. He remembered his father repeatedly telling him, "*Things cannot be helped in this world. What is done, is done. It is best to live by these words, shikata ga nai. You cannot alter history, but you can influence the future.*"

Setting his suitcase down, he raised the bottle in front of him and stared at the transparent liquid. He slowly moved the bottle to his left side and poured out the alcohol. When the bottle began to drip, he walked to a trash barrel, released it, allowing the glass to break inside. He vowed to his wife, as well as himself, that he would never swallow another poisonous drop. Returning to his suitcase, he sat on it and patiently waited for Meito to arrive. By tomorrow he would travel on the ferry, returning to his home of thirty-eight years. And by tomorrow he wouldn't have the need to remember these camps. Or reasons for his drinking.

Mid September

"I'VE missed you like crazy!" Tomiko exclaimed, embracing Jim.

He stroked her cheek and kissed her. The men's barrack retained the last two bachelors who sat on their cots, pretending to read the newspapers as they peeked over the article's edges. With nothing else to do, they waited and watched. Jim's blood rushed throughout his body, induced by his electrified heart. Even in her jeans and plaid shirt she radiated beauty. Every day, every hour, he thought about her. One of the few positive aspects in his life. Feeling the warmth of her lips reminded him how much he loved her, and how ready he was to marry her.

Releasing Tomiko, he affirmed, "I'm glad you're here!"

She beamed, squeezing his hands. "I plan to stay a couple of nights at the hospice before I head back to Seattle."

"Listen," he began, glancing at his intrusive roommates, "I know a place where we can have some privacy."

The bright sunset resided across the watchtowers' shells, glaring through their windows, revealing emptiness. Guards no longer occupied the tall wooden structures. Even the double-wire barricade which bisected the camp had now been opened. Most of the residential barracks were deserted, although people from the other camps began to arrive at Tule Lake. The WRA allowed this once turbulent camp to become a refuge for those who were unsure and scared. People anguished over another breakout of violence, just like the first onslaught following Pearl Harbor, once they reemerged into society. Stories of beatings and destruction of property scattered through the streets, initiating fear to those who began believing that the camps were indeed created for their own protection. Jim didn't worry about any of it as he held Tomiko's hand, guiding her, not wanting to let go again. He had missed her to the point that while lying awake for hours, he prayed his loneliness would just kill him. During those excruciating nights he began writing by the candle's torch, struggling to exhaust himself. It broke something inside. A drained liberation of some sort, ironically enough. He realized how much of an idiot, and a child at times, he had behaved: toward Tomiko and toward his friends.

"I saved all your letters," she said. "You can be very sweet when you want to."

He smiled. She seemed to have the power to suspend the world, to dissolve his anxieties, to induce calm. "That almost sounded like a compliment."

"That's because it almost was!"

They walked quietly together, arm in arm, glancing down the hollow street. Loose papers and bottles rolled alongside the tumbleweeds. Even a single shoe had been discarded, perhaps by accident during somebody's exodus.

"So, Jim. Where are we going?"

"It's not much further. This place's been empty for a while."

She blushed. "Really? What do you plan to do there? Redecorate?"

Smiling broadly, he replied, "If that's what it takes to inspire you."

Tomiko reclined her head on his shoulder. "Your letters were already inspiring. And I'm still carrying the ring you gave me around my neck." Walking in peacefulness for a time, she suddenly announced, "I had my college transcripts transferred to Seattle from Minneapolis. Two more years and I'll officially have my degree in journalism."

Jim began to panic. "What about starting a family?"

"I'd like to finish school before we have kids."

He thought for a moment. “It would be a waste if you invested all that time into something you can’t use.”

She pinched him, a little annoyed. “Who said I can’t? I can write articles at home, you know. If my mama could raise kids while pushing a plow, then I think I can do the same, except I would be pushing a pen instead!”

He nodded. “True. Which ones do you plan to write for? We don’t have a lot of options for ourselves.”

“Ye have little faith,” she grinned. “What do you think I’ve been doing for the last three years? I’ve already been putting together a portfolio.”

“Really? I didn’t know that.”

“Because you hadn’t *asked*.”

A cool wind prickled their bare necks, reminding them that summer was at an end.

Jim announced, “My papers haven’t been cleared yet, but soon. Very soon.”

“Why is it taking so long?”

“There are a couple of complications.” He hesitated, knowing Tomiko wouldn’t relish the explanation. “First of all, because of that stupid loyalty questionnaire, my citizenship has been revoked. Right now I don’t think Congress has any intentions to reinstate it for people like me.”

“People like you?”

“The undesirables. They still believe my refusal to answer is just cause for taking away my rights. My *rights*! I was born here for crying out loud! I committed no treason!” He strained to grip his temper, knowing if he didn’t restrict his emotions, he would say or do something he would regret. Curtly sighing, he maintained, “Which brings me to the other thing.” Again he hesitated. “I’ve asked for repatriation to Japan.”

“To Japan?” she gasped, lifting up her head. “Why?”

“It’s obvious we’re not wanted here.”

“But Japan? What makes you think it’ll be any better there?”

“How is it better here?”

She halted and removed her arm away from him. “I’ll give you three examples,” she insisted. “One: women have absolutely no rights there. I’m not giving up what rights I do have. Two: I don’t think we’ll be as welcomed as you believe. They just surrendered to the Americans. I’m pretty confident they’ll resent us. And three,” she began shaking her head and looking up at the flaming sky, “our home is here! Our family and friends! What do we really know about surviving in Japan? I don’t mind visiting, but to live there? Why do you think our parents there left to come here?”

He slid his hands inside his pockets, staring at the ground. “In other words, you won’t come with me.”

“Jim, you’re doing it again! You’re expecting me to follow without thinking how I would feel.”

He refuted, “You can still earn your degree in Japan.”

“I can barely read or write Japanese little alone speak it!”

"Within the last year I've been taking classes to improve mine. I can help you."

Tomiko flinched. "But I write in *English*, Jim."

"You'll have more possibilities of getting published in Japan than here."

"How do you figure? I'm a woman who's also American."

Stepping closer to her, Jim examined her frustrated face. He wanted so much for Tomiko to understand, for once, the importance of this opportunity to start fresh. "MacArthur is setting up the Japanese government to become more democratic," he defended. "Women will be allowed to vote."

She stared at him, and crossed her arms. "Why reinvent democracy *there* when we can work on it *here*?"

"What democracy?" he snapped. "Here in the States both you and I are far from the majority! We didn't put ourselves in these camps! Or strip our dignity. At least in Japan we won't be singled out as spies or outcasts. We won't have to worry if a group of racists will attack us or vandalize our homes."

Tomiko peered at him, wondering how he became so angry, so resentful. He wasn't like that when they were children, just quiet, shy. Even in high school. Before the camps. "I don't see how by running off will make things perfect," she stated. "If we do, then how can we support our brothers and friends, like Russell, who are risking their lives to better ours? How can we tell them 'thanks, but no thanks?'"

He brooded for a moment. "That was their choice. I didn't ask them to."

Startled by his answer, she stepped back. "That's it, then? You won't even consider how they may be improving our lives?"

Jim grunted and scratched the side of his neck. "Just because I don't agree with them doesn't mean I disrespect their commitment. They chose to defend the integrity of our race. I'm choosing to preserve ours. And right now the only way I see it is to apply for repatriation. I'm proud of my Japanese heritage. Aren't you?"

She looked away, hurt by his insensitivity. "That's not the point, Jim. I am proud of my heritage." Struggling not to cry, she proceeded, "The question I have for you is, which do you love more? Me or your pride?"

He flinched. He knew this day would come when she would find an excuse to leave him. Stepping back, he asked in turn, "Maybe the real question is which do you love more? Me or a country that hates us?"

She slowly shook her head and began to walk backward. "Just remember this, Jim: I'm not the one who's demanding this unconditional need." Turning around, folding her arms tightly across her chest, she announced, "I'll be at the hospice in case you change your mind!"

Late September

KUNIO had removed his cap, hiding it in between his belt. He also loosened his collar to adopt not only for comfort around his sweaty neck, but to appear more casual in his foreign outfit, blending with the locals as if he were a Japanese citizen. It amazed him how by simply separating his cap from his head that people didn't notice that he was wearing an American uniform, assuming he was one of their own. The tan color intermingled as easily as soy sauce and noodles.

Not to mention that many villagers were unfamiliar with the differences; and Kunio doubted whether they cared. Most farmers were concerned with survival; the next harvest; their families. He doubted if they even had seen a motion picture let alone outsiders. But as soon as he replaced his cap to its proper position, people bowed their respect toward their occupier. He could imagine what they were *truly* thinking. One of his unit pals had visited Japan in the late thirties as an exchange student for a semester. He told Kunio he probably would have felt more welcome at a Ku Klux Klan's rally. Although his friend wasn't beaten, the fierce belligerence in their eyes and violent insults made it extremely clear that, despite his Japanese face, it was his American attachment they despised. And yet in America, it was Kunio's face that people mistrusted.

"You're crazy looking for your relatives now," he heard one of his buddies repeat in his mind. "You should at least wait until one of us gets a pass also before going off by yourself."

"I'm not worried," Kunio replied.

"Just make sure your gun's loaded and doesn't get stuck in this goddamn humidity."

"The war's over. These people have nothing left to fight with. And they have no food. They don't even have the energy to retaliate." He paused, grinning. "Believe me, I'm more worried about *you* catching syphilis than *me* catching a bullet!"

Kunio had been walking, alone, for over a mile to the other side of Misumi Island after he rode in a boat with an elderly man and a five year old girl, giving them a melted Hershey bar as payment. Japan seemed empty of young men. Many of the streets and roads were cluttered with elders and girls. Traveling from what he guessed was about forty miles from Nagasaki, riding in Uncle Sam's jeeps, natives' carts, and two boats, he saw boys no older than thirteen wearing military uniforms; some with crutches or arm slings and bloodied bandages around their heads. Sometimes he saw Goro's youth mixed inside their lost childhood. Although Goro was hardly a boy anymore. Hardly worth comparing him to those childish faces.

Tripping on the unpaved trail, Kunio muttered a curse. Although relieved to escape Nagasaki for a time, he was exhausted. And overburdened by guilt. He understood the regulations of war and the need to quickly end it, nevertheless he still couldn't help think which dead body might be a relative. Witnessing fractured buildings did not equal to the charred victims stumbling along. And the burnt shadows on the walls. It was then he knew how lucky he and his family were by living in the United States. If his parents hadn't immigrated, this could be them. And he felt guilty for thinking it, as if he were the favorable one who cheated destiny.

Sighting the village in front of him, Kunio slowed his pace. He saw thin ripples of smoke glide up from the huts for dinner preparations. The smell of fish and seaweed made him yearn for a plate, realizing his own hunger. A few villagers were walking to their homes, some carrying buckets of water, some carrying babies, some wearing straw hats. The women wore similar clothes as the men with flabby knickers and v-neck shirts, unlike the city folk who either wore *kimonos* or, ironically, Western attire. As much as the extremists protested against Western culture, he would have thought they would also refuse to buy Western slacks, skirts, and suits.

Nervously rubbing his hands, he proceeded, feeling out of place while he stood on the trail surrounded by the foreign trees. Kunio had never met his mother's relatives, nor did his mother acquire recent photos of them from the last three decades. He remembered his mother lamenting countless times: "*If my mother were to die today, I would not know about it. This is the fate I accepted for believing in a better life. Sometimes I do not know which is better.*" For years he had measured how his mother had sacrificed one family for another. Her sadness often caused him to feel inadequate; as if being the second son was second best compared to her original family in Japan. Today he hoped to make amends. Something that would bring peace for his mother in her afterlife. Except that he didn't know whether her relatives would be sympathetic; after all, they might perceive him as a barbarian instead of family.

Fireflies wandered through the early stuffy evening. Aimless. Indifferent. The loud insects inflated his headache, the moisture sticking his clothes to his skin. To some extent, he learned to tolerate the discomfort. After a year serving in the Pacific, squatting in thick brushes, listening for Japanese transmissions to crack, hating the environment taught him how to like it anyway. At least Japan was further up the equator and had been spared from the jungle's thorny harness. And its diseases. And its large snakes. In many ways southern Japan reminded him of home. Low mountain ranges slumped in the horizon like a serpent's skeleton, away from the sea, away from the sharp rocks. Dense greenery, sharpened by pines or fat trees, all unifying the peacefulness. Segmented-rectangular fields were untouched by war, perhaps too far south and remote from factories and politics. The two bombs left Japan's countryside undisturbed by their poisonous ashes. His mother spoke of nirvana, and it seemed, from a distance and without knowing death, that a paradise could exist here.

The villagers began staring at him when he emerged onto their turf. Perplexity and fear were easily exposed; like their island without a military, without any other means of self defense.

Kunio bowed to a middle-aged man. "*Excuse me. I am looking for the Sugimoto family. I am their grandson from America.*"

The man at first stared. He peered at Kunio, examining a novelty who stood in his ancestral village. Kunio waited, continuing to hold his cap, glancing at the man's stubby fingers that clutched a line of fish.

"*I will take you to their home*," the man replied.

The villager limped as his dinner swung by his waist side. His calves were wrapped up to his small knees like an Egyptian mummy, his slipper-like shoes stained in mud. Kunio tried to imagine his mother as a child in this old community who probably knew no other life. Until he had left Bainbridge Island, neither did he. It amazed him how people lived in huts, without electricity, without indoor plumbing, without a radio to attach them to the modern world. A hurricane or earthquake could easily destroy the feeble structures. He thought about the detention camps that were primitive, crude, most definitely a demeaning reminder that despite being a citizen, he was still considered a foreigner in his own country. So belonging somewhere certainly invited security. Wasn't that what every living soul wanted?

The man stopped. Pointing to a hut that shouldered a sleeping dog, he said, "*Here it is*."

"*Domo arigato*," Kunio again bowed.

The man grunted with a nod, then limped away.

Time seemed to have roped around Kunio's ankles and he couldn't budge. Since four a.m. that morning, he had been on the move. Halting at the brink of his journey, he felt lost. He didn't know what to say first or how to begin. He didn't know if they would accept or reject him. He didn't know if they had forgiven his mother for deserting them by running away to become a picture bride. Gently knocking on the bamboo door, he waited for it to open. A moment elapsed before a woman in her sixties stood before him. Puzzled, apprehensive, she stared past her wrinkly draped eyelids.

He cleared his throat and said, "*Good evening. I am the son of Setsumi Sugimoto. I have traveled many miles to deliver a message*."

KUNIO had perched on the floor, his knees folded underneath his legs, his hands properly resting over his thighs. He watched his grandmother sob while holding the photograph he gave her. In that photo it displayed all members of the Hamaguchi family on a Fourth of July picnic. Children and grandchildren. Three generations squatting or standing in two rows under a fully blossomed tree. It was the last family photo taken just before Pearl Harbor.

His aunt, the one who had greeted him at the door, settled in between them, around the square mat where full teacups remained. She was fifteen years older than his mother, and the second oldest out of twelve children. Directly across from her sat his thirty-year-old cousin; born with Down syndrome. Kunio would glance at him and flicker a smile. His cousin would then snigger and embellish a grin, flaunting his crooked teeth.

Having their heads bent, they respectfully waited for the elder in the room to speak first. Kunio tired not to twitch out of his nervousness. He glanced around the tightly sculpted hut which smelt of fish, wet earth, and bitter incense. Although small in size, it still managed to divide three rooms, partitioned by sliding paper doors that hid the sleeping areas. A few ancestral scrolls hung on the bamboo walls. His grandmother began wiping her weathered-beaten cheeks. Her petite hands trembled as she laid the photograph on her lap. Already covering eighty some years, her aging body had succumbed to pains and shrinkage.

"*I cannot believe I have outlived four children*," she quivered. "*But I am glad I have many grandchildren. And so healthy, too*." She stared at Kunio. "*Are you the first born of my Setsumi?*"

"*Nai, obasan*," he replied. "*His name is Meito*."

She moaned, blinking. "*Then you are the first born of Setsumi's second husband?*"

He stared at her. What was she talking about? Instead of challenging her, knowing she must be too old and a bit confused, he stuttered, "*Ah- hai, obasan.*"

Raising the photo directly in front of her, she sighed. "*It was not my doing, you understand. I did not want to lose Setsumi. Her father, my husband. . . it was my duty to be faithful to his wishes even though I hated him for a long time.*" She closed her eyes and tears reemerged. "*I wanted to see her one more time before I died.*" Kunio's aunt squeezed her arm for support, tears also inflating. "*But you are here,*" his grandmother managed to utter. "*And for that I am grateful.*"

Kunio was relieved. Greatly relieved. Sitting next to relatives he had never met before felt like walking barefoot on sand, the soft cool grains clinging between his toes. Yet a sadness stumbled into his path. All those decades his mother suffered, wondering; all those years stained from not getting to know his extended family, and then he understood it was time to fill the hole.

* * *

THE tranquil wind, pushed by the ferry and ocean air, delivered a neglected childhood memory. Its calming manner sifted the blood in Goro's brain like warm sand through his fingers. The rounded mountains, sheathed in green and the hazy sunrise remained identical to his recollections. A comforting thing. A distant thing. The smell of salted raw fish instead of salted fresh blood brought relief and satisfaction.

He was coming home. He finally was coming home.

Most of his family had already returned, expecting his arrival. He scratched under his black eye patch. He thought about his great, great-grandfather, Minoru, the seaman with a dead eye, too. Irony was not lost on him. People glanced at his deformities: his missing leg, his missing eye, and his cast arm opposite of his crutch. Were they uncomfortable because he was a broken soldier? Or were they uncomfortable because he was a broken *Jap*? He really didn't give a damn. He felt too old and tired to care anymore. Instead he smiled and nodded at the few familiar faces. They awkwardly stretched a grin, but turned away. Who truly had the nerve to insult an enlisted man; a hero with colorful decorations attached to his uniform, attached to his flesh? Even if he was Japanese! Goro readjusted his stable leg, rocking his crutch, rocking his plastered arm, yet stood firmly on the floor. No more would he sit and let life hoist him around.

Raising his chin, he saw a small boy, dark hair with radiant blue eyes, walk to him; his small hand tucked in pocket, his bony legs bouncing. The boy's tanned cap and corduroy suspenders kept his youth; about the age of four. Astonishment relished in his blinking; an innocent puzzlement flooding his curiosity.

The boy bluntly said, "You wook wike a pirate!"

He looked down at the kid. "Arg, I suppose I do, matey."

"Wha' happen?"

The plumpness of the boy's finger tip arched under his pink lip. Goro lifted a brow, equally curious. He found it amusing that only a child was allowed to ask a stranger such a personal question and assumed a direct answer.

"A grenade got me."

"Wow!"

"Yeah, wow," he lamented. Although counselors at the hospital told him repeatedly he was faultless, that nobody was at fault, he could still hear the explosion at night. If the dumb bastard hadn't gotten greedy, or if Goro had been more persistent, then Shig would be returning to San Pedro. The military couldn't even send his corpse back to his family. The grenade ripped him completely apart.

The boy blinked. "You a Jap?"

He became irritated. "I'm an American. Just like you. But I'm *Japanese-American.*"

The boy squinted. "Daddy says Japs is he'dens."

"Have you met a heathen?" Goro questioned.

"I dunno."

"Has your dad actually met a heathen?"

"He figh's wif Japs. He almos' got kilt!"

Feeling some sympathy, because a child should never have to experience an unfortunate death of a parent, he persisted, "But how does your dad know what a heathen is?"

The boy again squinted and squeezed the corner of his mouth. "He's smart!"

"Unless he's a god, I doubt he knows everything!"

"You don't!" the boy exhaled, offended.

Goro pricked a grin. The boy seemed more awake than most American boys of his age who were safely isolated from the war. The boy was lucky. He escaped the blistering gun shells and shrapnel. Goro remembered Italian children digging into the army's trash cans, covered in soot, mud, and specks of blood. They smelled worse than a mangy dog reeking of spoilt sewage. The children stunk so badly that Goro could hardly finish his K-rations when they were around. And yet staring at this boy's clean face and washed clothes only perpetuated his guilt. The same guilt and horror he felt in Dachau. Nothing was right.

He scratched under his eye patch and asked, "What's your name, kid?"

The boy stretched his arms from behind. "Weo Juner."

Goro squinted at the boy, scratching his forehead, not understanding what he had said.

"Leo Jr!" a man's voice bellowed, vibrating past people's hats and skirts.

Turning his head, Goro saw a bulky man, almost shaped like bull with blond hair flinging wildly. A woman stepped out of his path, clutching the rail, glaring at the brute. Stunned, Goro hadn't seen Leo Riley in four years. His football shoulders remained the same, but his belly jiggled and rounded out like a water balloon. For an instant, his face almost favored Callis.

Grabbing his son's small arm, he scolded, "What did I tell you about wandering off?"

He glared at Goro, unable to recognize a forgotten classmate. A genuine hatred penetrated his light eyes, slaying childhood memories. They once wore varsity jackets that projected an elitist club in Winslow High. They were jocks. They were gods. Now they were somehow undeclared enemies based on misconstrued ideals. As Leo yanked his son away, the boy began to whine and cry.

"Leo Riley!" Goro blurted. "How are you?"

Leo stopped. The muscles in his neck strained like rope, silently creaking. He continued to blaze at Goro, dumbfounded. People became quiet, watching, speculating.

"Who in the hell are you?" Leo snapped.

"Russell! Russell Hamaguchi! Class of '44. Or at least it would have been."

Leo harshly blinked a few times. "My God! I didn't recognize you!"

He stepped back, pulling his crying son, telling him to shut up. Goro privately sneered, not altogether astonished how Leo hadn't changed a bit. Still insensitive. Still the bully. His brown slacks and crisp white shirt indicated that he refused to farm his father's land, and thus renting it to others. His hands were too polished to argue otherwise. The little boy rubbed his nose, sniffling, afraid to anger his father more so.

"My God," Leo repeated, barely splitting a smile. "I heard they was gonna let you people fight in Europe. How about that? I get sent to Guam. You go to Europe." He chortled. "You think it would be the other way! Send the Japs to fight the Japs! Now that would be something!"

Goro shifted his jaw. He had always wanted to tell Leo off. Jokes about being Asian echoed in his head. "How do you make Chop Suey? You flog a Chink with a noodle! Get it? Noodles and a Chink?"

"Of course," Leo babbled on, "it makes sense not putting you people in the Pacific. Not only couldn't we tell you guys apart, but how do we know you won't switch over to the other side?"

Goro stood upright, trying to submerge the desire to beat him with his crutch. "You've always been an idiot, Leo. Did you know that? If it weren't for my people breaking an' interpreting Japanese codes, in the Pacific, your body would be decaying on the beach."

Leo punched out his chest and spouted, "My buddies were murdered because of your people!"

"It wasn't my people! We were too busy fighting Nazis on the other side of the world!"

"Your people beheaded my friends! Sticking their heads on bayonets! Torturing them! Using their rotting bodies for barricades!"

"Don't you get it? It wasn't *my* people! We're all Americans! *Americans!*"

Leo's eyes soon saturated with tears, his face burning with red fervor. He continued to yell obscenities and threats while four men, two in sailor suits, two civilians, struggled to chain him, pushing him away from Goro. The little boy wailed and trembled. A few women gasped, covering their mouths and shaking their heads. Leo hammered his words, repeating, "The hell you say! The hell you say!" until he collapsed, sobbing, crippled.

A man asked Goro, "Are you alright, Russell?"

Goro strained his neck. It was Officer Dandridge. The Clark Gable look-alike. The one who let them keep his father's *samurai* sword. He didn't wear his police uniform or any other uniform that day, just camouflaged in casual clothes.

"Yeah!" he heaved, trying to control his anger. He fought and nearly died for his country, and still people like Leo couldn't make the distinction.

Dandridge softly asked, "Are you sure?"

Goro nodded. Breathing heavily, he couldn't believe Leo's outrageous burst. But then he wasn't in his right mind set, obviously. Shifting around to examine Leo, he felt sorry for him. Leo, still hunched like a wounded cub, grabbed his son, clenching, afraid to let go. His confused son coughed and sniffled, crying out for his mother. Leo's sobs spattered, his body left weakened. It was apparent Leo didn't see a former classmate: he saw the face of brutality. And Goro was perfectly aware that the Japanese military had scarred many people. Civilians as well as POWs. On some odd level he understood where Leo's frame of mind descended. Goro's nightmares didn't stop either. They assaulted him just before sleep and persisted the minute he awoke. Faces of men he killed. Faces from the German concentration camp.

"If there's anything I do for you," Dandridge began, "please, let me know. It's real good to see you again, Russell. Welcome back."

Goro shook his hand and smiled his appreciation. The ferry slowed, tarried, and docked. The twenty minute trip ended, and finally Goro's journey came to a complete halt. He delayed until Leo trotted out of sight with his quiet son at hand. Saying his farewell to Dandridge and unbinding his grip on the rail, Goro hobbled off the ferry, swinging his leg, swinging his crutch. A trail of sunlight contoured his tan uniform, following him down the dock, grazing the luscious cedar trees. How he had missed the perfectly tall greenery; safe and undamaged. Green and not yellow or scarlet. The tree's faint perfume sweetened his homecoming.

He noticed Meito standing in front of his car and surprisingly enough, in front of a newly paved road. Meito's checkered short-sleeve shirt slightly rippled in the breeze. With his hands hidden in his pockets, his forehead hidden under his hat, he leaned on one leg. Goro thought he appeared like a posing figure in a photograph. Meito stared passed him, searching for a war hero in one piece. Goro had decided not to inform his family about what he had lost. He refused to worry them at that time. It had been fifteen months since the two brothers had seen each other. Time quickly tossed age aside and Goro returned unrecognizable.

Meito finally stared at him. His broad face hadn't altered much with the exception of a couple of wrinkles. He had gained weight, too. Healthy, muscular, more fit than inside those camps. Goro's thinness hid under his uniform, although it could be seen sagging under his cheekbones and bony fingers.

Puzzlement wounded Meito's face. All he could do was stare. "Goro?" he asked. "My God, is that you?"

The expression behind his brother's eyes nearly frightened him. He peeled a smile and said, "What's left of me anyway." He slipped his trembling fingers inside his pocket and pulled out a fat cross from the Third Reich. "The Jerrys might of got some of me, but I got something of them!"

Meito released his hands from his pockets, dangling uselessly at his waist. He pinched his thick brows and peered at the grey cross. "It's big," he numbly stated.

"Yeah, I know! It was around his neck. Like some sort of badge of honor."

Meito looked at him again. It wasn't as if he lacked pride for his little brother's heroism, he just wondered if it was worth it. He did understand the need to perverse freedom from mad men, cleaning up the mess they had made, but why did it have to be Goro? Or Kunio? Meito's flat feet disclaimed his eligibility of the draft. He certainly didn't feel ashamed. Best to his abilities, he kept his family from completely slipping apart. And he was damned proud of it! Kunio would be the last one to return home.

Meito gently expressed, slinging his arm around his brother's shoulder, "Come on, *ototo*, Gerdie and the rest are waiting for you. Welcome home, little brother. It's been a long, long time!"

CHAPTER FOUR

Early October

JIM'S barrack converted into emptiness after his last roommate departed yesterday. Everyone was in the process of either returning home or journeying toward the Midwest, East Coast, or Japan. Today he had to make a decision where to go. He had been postponing it for the last two weeks. "It's time to start over, Jim," his roommate had mentioned with a suitcase in his hand. "You can't stay in limbo forever." Limbo. Now that constituted a chilling warning with no place to stay; no place to go.

He frowned at the form. The stapled sheets appeared pompous on his tiny square table. His used typewriter sat behind the government form as if overshadowing his final decision. He had typed out the paperwork last week with the exception of signing and dating it. Half the men on his block had turned in their requests for repatriation to Japan. Some were already on the ship voyaging that way. Jim hadn't made the commitment as of yet, not absolutely convinced he should, although not absolutely convinced he should stay in the United States, either. Undergoing the camps. Sam's death. The weekly harassments late at night. It should be natural leaving. Unfortunately it also it would mean leaving Tomiko. That weekend she stayed they argued. She left upset, angered, and also in limbo. Not knowing what to do, he continued to sit and stare with a fan blowing directly on body.

He heard footsteps squeaking up the outside staircase. Turning to face the door across the room, he waited for the knocking. He wondered who wanted to see him. Standing up, he walked to the front, passing by the empty bunks and naked walls with pin holes where the photos used to hang. He quickly opened the door. Holding his breath, he couldn't move. His father stood on the top step. His hat shaded his glasses, protecting his eyes from the sun's glare. His long-sleeved shirt and slacks were wrinkled; his face revealing a day's worth of prickling growth. He gripped a suitcase with both hands in front of his stomach.

"Jimmu," he began, looking away, blinking rapidly. "I hoped to find you here still. May I come in?"

Speechless, he nodded and stepped back to allow his father to enter. Shutting the door, Jim watched him remove his hat as he set his luggage down. His father's hair had been thinning and graying.

Mr. Yoshimura wiped his forehead with a handkerchief. He examined his son who stood erect with his hands firmly folded together like a man holding importance. He had hoped someday Jim would finally mature into his fated role.

"Do you hafe a glass of wata?" he asked, slapping his dried tongue.

Jim wet his lips, lulling in a moment of stupefaction. Questions accelerated his thoughts: When did the government decided to release him and why after all those years? What was he doing here anyway? Did he know that his once honorable son no longer carried the American citizenship he was so proud of and believed it could protect Jim? Would he be just as ashamed of him as of John?

Instead he answered, "*Hai*, but the water will be warm, Papa."

"Is fine," he said.

Mr. Yoshimura sighed and sluggishly paced in a circle while Jim retrieved a glass next to a pitcher from another table close by.

"There you are," Jim said.

Reaching for the glass, a part of Mr. Yoshimura wanted to reach for his son's hand, to embrace him. Since they were in privacy, he could show affection without bringing embarrassment, however he knew his son continued to bear too much anger. Quietly sipping, he scanned around to see what kind of conditions Jim had been living in for the last year. The hollowness reminded him of where he had been.

Jim stated, "You should have written about your release. I could have been better prepared."

As he drank, the warm water didn't flow down his throat as nicely as he would have liked. It certainty didn't ease his thirst. "I did not hafe time," he replied, raising his brows. "By da time I write eferyone and send off da letters, I'm on da train, heading home."

"Speaking of which, why didn't you just go home first?"

"Yur motha writes me an' informs me you want to go to Japan." He paused, and switched languages. "*This would not be a wise decision. Especially now. Hiroshima, as I understand, is completely destroyed. Completely.*" He stopped to close his eyes. Imagining how his former home appeared in burnt ruins and then not knowing how many family members survived, the unthinkable strangled his heart. He knew he couldn't return there for a long period, if he ever chose to return. He had nothing. He would go back to nothing.

"I won't be going to Hiroshima," Jim affirmed. "Not all parts of Japan are destroyed. Although I am sorry that your home . . ." his speech stumbled, trying to find the proper words for something so terrible, "that your childhood home is being in the process of reconstruction."

Mr. Yoshimura opened his eyes. "Dare is no future in Japan at dis time. Not for at leas' ten years."

"Unless you can guarantee a better future here, I don't see how Japan could be much worse."

Glancing up at Jim, he steadily explained, "I came to dis country with only hope. Dare was a time when I could say proudly, 'I hafe great success in America. I hafe healthy children. I own my businesses an' because of my education, people come to me for help.'" He circled his fingers around the glass, gently rocking it. Despite the doubts that rattled through his fingers, he needed to display strength. "I still hafe my dignity, an' so do you. We can start ova."

"With what, Papa? With a hundred dollars in the account to find another house? Or to even start another business? You've lost all your land, and we have no property to our names! And do you even know that my citizenship has been revoked? I no longer exist! I no longer can purchase properties or can no longer take out loans. I'm sorry, Papa, but I don't see your vision. And to be truthful, I never have."

Mr. Yoshimura walked to one of the few scatters chairs to sit down. As he watched Jim's frustration manifest into stone, he felt like the perfect failure. One son who chose to kill himself because of his own quick anger. Another so enraged, so resentful, he would rather leave his family to find his despairing peace. Rose and her husband had decided to stay in Chicago. They weren't interested in returning to Bainbridge Island. His family was collapsing. Then, during the three years of war, his savings had been depleted from paying storage, paying taxes he still owed from his business and vehicle, and the move back to Bainbridge. He was at a point where he could do nothing to prevent further decay. The decades he had pushed himself to achieve strength, success, and opportunities for his family now seemed superficial.

"*I know I have not been the ideal father*," he began. "*Each day I am more aware of the mistakes I have made. Maybe if I listened more, then perhaps you would have decided to stay for a while longer.*"

Jim wasn't certain what to think. Always absolute, uncompromising, his father had patterned the Japanese discipline. But something had snapped in him, exposing this ordinary fragility.

"Well, I haven't finalized anything, yet," Jim admitted. "The paperwork is still lying on my table."

He looked up. "*If you are having doubts, then it is an omen that you should not go.*"

"I don't believe in omens. The only reason I'm hesitating is because of Tomiko."

"Tomiko? Ah yes, yur motha wrote to me about her. You two hafe been . . . dating, I belief, for some time." He hesitated and sighed. "Do you wish to marry Tomiko?"

Jim began fidgeting. "Marriage isn't the problem. She won't go with me to Japan."

Mr. Yoshimura nodded and half-smiled. "She is ah smart girl."

"Papa," he asserted. "I don't mean to sound ungrateful, but this isn't your problem. I'm aware of the past between Tomiko's family and ours. I've already spoke to Tomiko and her father about the situation, and they're fine with it. So, there's really no need to keep bringing it up."

He extended his gaze towards his son. "*I need to know which reason you choose to leave America. Is it because of the war*," he paused, realizing if he said the forbidden name out loud, it would feel like slashing a vein. "*Or is it because of . . . John?*"

Jim's body temperature surged and he started to pace aimlessly like paper trapped in floods of wind. "And how will knowing make you feel better?"

Mr. Yoshimura sharply blinked. Jim had never spoken to him in a spiteful tone before. "*For the last three years, as I could do very little at the prison, I had much time to meditate*." He closed his eyes, not confident on how much vulnerability he should surrender, especially to his only living son. "*When I would watch the sun's glare behind the mountains, it was as if my life was glaring directly in my face. Since I could go nowhere to hide, my regrets rose at night . . . swelling my mind and heart*." His hands trembled. He began breathing heavily, his voice weakening. "*I know I have aged twenty more years. My sins have taken those years out of my life. I have already lost one son. I do not want to loose another*."

"Papa," Jim began, tensing his muscles, struggling to withhold his pain. "*The war has changed many people.*"

Mr. Yoshimura shook his head, angered that he was not able to control his emotions. Angered and blinded.

Jim continued, "*You will not lose me, Papa, even if I decide to go to Japan. The war is over, so you have little to worry about*."

"*I am amazed how much you resemble John. Sometimes I see two sons in one face*." He exhaled a few times to regain his strength and reopened his eyes. "*I know this is not fair to you, Jimmu. You have your own talents and resilience. I am proud of you. I have always been proud of you*."

Jim didn't know how to respond. Hearing those words, particularly from his father, left him impaired; crippled. His father's criticisms had mounted in his head for years, hovering, echoing, pushing him to be the ideal son, this ideal Japanese son in American society. No question John had felt the same demands.

Jim placed his hand on his father's knee and began what he had planned to tell his father for over two years. "There's something you need to know about John, Papa." Mr. Yoshimura remained quiet, anxious. "Tomiko told me it wasn't his baby. Kiyoko . . ." he stopped, not sure what word to use to describe this untouchable subject. "Kiyoko had been . . . she was . . . taken advantage of by another boy. She had been *forced*, you understand."

Startled, Mr. Yoshimura peered at his son. He sat upright, blinking furiously. Panic and guilt exploded in his chest. He couldn't believe it. It would be impossible to conceive. Did he accuse John of disgracing the family for the wrong reason? A careless reason?

He shot up and wheezed, "What hafe I done? What hafe I done!"

Jim also rose. "What do you mean?"

"My God! Oh, God!" he sputtered, stumbling backward, collapsing on an empty cot. He squeezed his eyes so tightly it bled tears. "If I had not broken John . . . if I had been humble and patient, not so prideful, then perhaps John would have found reason to live. I killed my son! I killed my son!"

His voice decayed and unexpectedly he wept. Placing his hand over his forehead, the glass slipped out of his other hand and cracked on the floor. The remaining water soaked through the wood and dust. He felt his body withering, his bones splintering, every minor movement heightened his pain.

Jim was shocked. He stood with his hands loose at his waist, numbed. His father had never wept for John, yet now, in the middle of a desert, he finally did. Jim couldn't bear watching him cry. And it stung him like a thousand wasps. Not knowing what to do or say, he walked to his father, slipping out Tomiko's handkerchief and knelt beside him. His father jerked to the side to avoid facing him and removed his glasses to cover his eyes with his hand. Jim held out the handkerchief. He wanted to embrace him, to console him, but while his father had turned away from him, Jim could only return his duty with a formal gesture.

"*I am so ashamed!*" Mr. Yoshimura gasped.

"Papa, don't," he whispered.

Mr. Yoshimura slouched, allowing his elbows to support himself from completely falling down. Jim instinctively positioned his hands as if to catch him. Now reduced to a mediocre man, his father no longer seemed immortal or callous. That last year had taught Jim how difficult it was to appear sturdy in body and mind. To use wisdom based on one's ability and experiences. Fear of making mistakes. It proved more difficult than he realized. Tears began to blister, yet Jim refused to cry. "Take this," he urged, his own voice weakening.

His father seemed trapped, unable to leave his grief, surprisingly like himself. His sobs grew louder, more exhausting, tormenting Jim. He closed his eyes to bury his father's disturbing image, wishing he were someplace else. Suddenly, he felt clutches and a forceful pull. His father continued sobbing on his shoulder, his arms around Jim's back. Jim opened his eyes. His hands shook. For an instant, he couldn't breathe. As tears burned down his cheeks, he held his father in turn.

It was then he knew that his father had always loved him.

* * *

JOE and George's laughter soared through the opened window, rising above the trees. Their laughter seemed to ease Goro's tightened muscles and trailed a memory of normalcy. He lay awake but felt as if he were dreaming. This balanced serenity entered his nightmares and his nightmares entered his consciousness. Although Goro knew the warmth of a real bed was real, his body still elevated above everything, in the stillness, in the chill and sweat. For a moment, he didn't know where he laid, though he recognized Joe and George's laughter. Bainbridge Island. An unsung asylum. Despite that he now remembered he was home, he continued feeling as though he slept in a unfamiliar place, like the other places: a gypsy, a refugee, a soldier.

Music faintly chanted in his room. Jesus, how he missed it! The soft sounds of the clarinets. The skipping trumpets. Ballads of voices harmonizing. Then a faint odor of battered fish and fried rice pursued up the staircases and through the gaps of the door. The scent aroused his nose. It had to be lunch time. He slept during the morning, during breakfast, and dreamt of chaos. Dead friends lived in his dreams, and yet died repeatedly as he watched them choke on their own blood, lying in reddened mud, soaked in their own piss. But he was home.

He jerked upward. A piercing pain raised him. Panting like a dog, he stared at the narrow room. The yellowed wallpaper peeled from the ceiling, displaying weeping willows on all the walls. It was quiet. He was alone. Footsteps crept up the stairs, popping and creaking. He saw a shadow under the bottom of the door. Two knocks rattled.

"Yeah," he responded.

Gertrude announced, "There's someone here to see you, Goro."

Clenching his brows, he groggily asked, "Who is it?"

She hesitated. "I think you should come out and see."

"Well, who is it?" he demanded, aggravated.

"I'll meet you downstairs."

The stairs began to creak as she walked down the steps. Grunting, he swung his leg over the side and reached for his crutch. Who in the hell could it be? Dave, as far as he knew, remained somewhere in France, guarding the people from themselves as the U.S. attempted to smooth out the peace process. If another friend stopped by, why didn't Gertrude just say who it was? Was it Leo? He snickered. A day in hell would freeze over the day Leo would apologize. Wearing only his boxers, he snatched his brother's striped shirt and fastened three buttons. To dress fully resolved in taking too long. He wobbled down the narrow hallway, but stopped at in front of a hanging mirror. He looked at himself. His youth had lost its roundness and became detailed. His cheeks were more defined, his face discovering wrinkles and hair. Rubbing his prickly chin, he flexed his mouth to study his teeth. His Adam's apple bulged. Goro almost didn't recognize himself. Sometime between leaving boot camp and lying at a hospital in England, he changed. He wished his mother could see the difference. He wished she could see that she no longer needed to worry for him. He no longer was a boy. And for the first time, he liked his face, even with his imperfections.

Descending down the steps required perfect balance. He leaned his shoulder into the wall to preserve stability as he hopped each step delicately between his one leg and one crutch. Meito had insisted that he sleep downstairs with his two cousins where connivance laid at hand. Goro wanted privacy. Not only that, despite his handicaps, he refused to be treated like an invalid. He looked down the steps. Maria. She sat on the tan couch beside Gertrude, wearing a black dress. He stopped. Feeling embarrassed for not dressing properly, he quietly grunted. His white boxers loosely hinged around his bony waist. The short-sleeved shirt barely covered his front, exposing his half naked chest.

Maria glanced away. He looked too different. He looked inhuman with his missing leg and patched-eye.

No one said anything for a moment.

"I've made some tea!" Gertrude declared. "Would you like some, Maria?"

Maria turned to look at her and nervously smiled. "Yes. Tank you."

Goro proceeded down the staircase while Gertrude entered the kitchen. Maria appeared different. She had cut her long hair, allowing it to sweep across her cheeks. She had bangs, too, slicing off her childhood locks. Her face thinned, losing the gentle roundness, making her short nose appear as if it were longer, slimmer. But her large oval eyes remained the same. God, they were still beautiful, expressive. He finally reached the bottom, breathing unevenly, and plopped into an easy chair. He waited for her to speak first. She slumped forward, curling her fingers together, nibbling on her bottom red lip. Goro studied her. He wanted to touch her again, kiss her, but her wedding ring squelched that fantasy. She had married someone else. He should have proposed a long time ago, before the evacuation, before boot camp, before she lost her virginity.

"I hear," she started, searching to end the painful silence, "dat you ah fight in Italy. An' Germany."

"Yeah," he replied in a hollow tone.

"What Italy like? It be pretty?"

He sighed. Frivolous chit-chat only prolonged her visit. What did she want? Friendship? To apologize? To resolve things? "It's very pretty," he began. "The countryside anyway. Maybe someday I'll go back when it's put back together again. Visit Rome when it's not in ruins." He chortled. "That may be awhile!"

Maria sat quietly. He located her regrets as well as dwelling on his own. A popular song, "Sentimental Journey," danced between them as if they had danced with each other through the years. The soothing voice of Doris Day almost solaced the ache.

Exasperated, Goro blurted, "So, why are you here, Maria? I haven't seen you in over four years. You're married. I'm tired!" He lowered his voice, his tone suddenly drained. "What do you want from me?"

She seemed astonished, blinking feverishly and leaning back. She then closed her eyes, trying to spare her tears. For a moment he felt sorry for her. What did he expect? Neither really knew when or if he would return. He made a promise neither of them could keep. It was only luck that rescued him from death, no other reason.

Maria managed to say, "Na'ting. I wan' na'ting from you. I only," she paused, glancing at him, brushing her wet cheek, "I only wish to ah see you again. I be glad you alife. Dat's all."

He looked at her again. "Listen, I'm sorry for coming off so gruff. I'm not myself these days. Mario's a good man. I'm happy for the both of you," he lied, attempting to cast off his animosity. His bitterness, he understood, would not make his situation any better. "Do you have any kids?"

She unlatched her breath in a series of short huffs. She was trying not to cry. "Yes. A daughta. Her name be Alice. She be ah two years old."

Prying open a smile, Goro asked, "Where is she?"

"At home wit my ah fahda."

Gertrude, with an apron bandaged around her chubby hips, carried a tin tray with a tea set, passing by the Cathedral radio. The very same radio Meito had given to him while in Manzanar. She politely poured the hot tea as the trickling of the dark water would disguise the awkward silence.

"I like this song," Gertrude said, handing a cup to Goro, glancing at him with a promising grin. "I think it's romantic." She revolved to give Maria a full cup. "Makes you almost forget about the hard times."

Goro glared at his sister-in-law and blandly stated, "Thank you, Gerdie. I got it from here."

She coyly beamed. Amelia's cries echoed from the kitchen where she sat in a highchair. "I better tend to her needs," Gertrude announced. "Nice to see you again, Maria. You look very nice."

"Tank you," she whispered, blushing.

He watched Gertrude shuffle out of the room, a pleasing grin still stuck on her face. The song persisted to bathe the room in a soothing, warm sensation. Returning to Maria, he wondered why she was wearing black.

"Where is Mario?" he asked.

Maria instantly cuffed her hand over her eyes. She began sobbing. He then understood.

"I'm so sorry," he said, realizing how insensitive he just sounded by asking her so bluntly, especially when men were dying all over the world. He reclined back, feeling pricks up his back as his guilt punctured further through his stomach. For every three men who survived, at least two were dead.

Maria set the saucer on the coffee table and removed a perfectly ironed handkerchief. She covered her nose while she sobbed. Goro hobbled to her and sat down, letting her cry into his chest. The warmth of her body made him realize how much he had loved Maria. And he knew there was a stronger reason for her visit. He knew she had missed him after all those years. She had missed him because she still loved him.

* * *

TOMIKO walked down the ferry's plank while guiding her bicycle beside other passengers. Her books dangled at the rear, tightly wrapped with a leather strap. During the days when the sun made even a partial appearance, she rode her bike to college. Other times, she walked to the ferry and would then take the bus to class. Although it might have been more convenient living in the city, she felt more secure living on her island. The only hostile group which tried to assemble in Winslow was immediately disbanded by Officer Dandridge. He threatened to put them in jail if they undertook an antagonistic coalition again. Yet, throughout the State of Washington, as well as Oregon and California, boycotts against produce grown by the *Nikkei* farmers recurred and multiplied. Anti-Japanese signs on certain businesses' windows lingered like gun powder after numerous discharges. Pearl Harbor's legacy still branded them as traitors. Many continued to believe it. Why else would those camps have existed if they didn't do something wrong?

Tomiko straddled her bicycle and began pedaling up the hill, cherishing the luscious cedar trees she had missed considerably. Her absence felt longer. Much longer than twelve hundred days. Turning off the main street, she cruised through the peaceful town and coasted by her high school on the outskirts. It appeared tiny, her old school. Nothing more than two rectangles shaped in an upside-down T. She remembered how gigantic it once seemed. Not any more.

Oddly she could still feel sand in her shoes. And still tasted the dirt in her mouth during the violent storms. Someday she hoped she would stop feeling those memories. As she compressed the weeks with her studies, she now filled much of her time with little consideration of wanting to remember.

And then she would think about Jim. Two weeks and counting since she left him behind in Tule Lake. He hadn't written to her, no doubt continuing to brood over his self-importance. Sometimes she would miss him to the point of opening another book to replace the emptiness. Other times she would become so angry at his arrogance she would throw things across the room. She was tired of waiting and not knowing what to wait for. If she hadn't received a letter by this weekend, she would have to start considering other options.

She veered off another road, unpaved and bumpy. She was returning home. A stable home. One with walls and doors and sturdy wood. One without snakes and scorpions and wide cavities. Her parents had found it on a patch of farmland, renting it from a Swedish couple. The land was smaller than the first one, but it was at least another beginning. Reeling up the dirt driveway, she saw someone sleeping on the swing porch, his head perched on his hand, his elbow securing his weight. She then recognized him and her heart choked upward into her throat.

"Jim?" she gasped, bracing the bicycle while anchoring her feet on the ground. He jerked and turned to look at her. She excitedly asked, "What are you doing here?"

Standing up and clearing his throat, he replied, "I've thought about what you said to me last time." He traveled down the steps and nervously walked to her, not knowing how she would react or knowing if she would ultimately reject him. Stopping at the bike's handles, he rested his hands over hers, admiring the perfection of her scarred fingers, feeling the warmth of her skin. "As much as I've been thinking about the advantages of going to Japan . . . it won't amount to much if you're not beside me. Every time I think about leaving this damn place," he hesitated, biting his lip, shaking his head, "I can't leave you. You're more important to me."

She smiled as tears awakened. She had never loved him as much as now. "It's about time you admitted it! I was ready to give up on you!"

Startled, he blinked at her. "So soon?"

"Soon?" she laughed. "I've only been waiting since Roosevelt's second term, you ninny!"

"IS SOMEBODY going to get that?" Goro hollered.

Closing the kitchen cabinet, he set a can of tuna on the counter, next to a loaf of bread and lettuce. The doorbell rang again. He pivoted his body to peek out the door's portal. Not knowing where Gertrude vanished, perhaps outside hanging-up wet laundry, and with Meito helping their father reopen the business, Goro was left alone. Grunting, he hopped to the portal where his crutches reclined, grabbed them, and swung toward the front door. The bell rang for the third time. He bumped into the telephone that perched on top of a thin end table. Although he had adapted using one eye, the other now replaced by glass, his vision sometimes misled his balance. That and the damn pair of crutches. Next week he would get his prosthetic leg, thank God! Readjusting his stance, he opened the door.

Stunned, he dropped a smile. "For crying out loud! I didn't think they would let your kind out!"

Jim glanced at his missing leg while shaking his hand, trying not to appear so shocked. Tomiko had informed him about his condition, therefore not to stare. He then studied Goro's face, surprised by how much weight he had lost, and by the quality of the fake eye. He honestly couldn't tell which one was which, until one eye moved and the other didn't of course.

Returning a half-smile, he replied, "What do you mean- *my* kind?"

"You know, the incorrigibles."

Sliding both hands inside his pockets, he said, "The same could apply to you."

Goro chuckled and hopped backward. "Well, since you're here, you might as well come in."

Jim stepped inside where he could smell faint ointment hovering with fried okra.

Goro briefly studied him. He didn't seem as constipated-looking as the last few times. No, he seemed relaxed with his hands casually stored in his pockets instead of rigidly suspended at his waistline. And his posture was gently slumped, not stiff like an ancient pillar. But above all, he was actually beaming.

"I'm making a sandwich," Goro announced, shutting the door. "Want one?"

"Why not?"

Jim followed Goro into the kitchen, but leaned against the portal. He watched his friend set the crutches beside an open cabinet and retrieved two plates. As he began to juggle the can opener, the preserved tuna, the jar of Mayo, Jim was relieved that Goro had survived Europe. If he had to visit his grave instead, he didn't know whether Goro's sacrifice would had been justified or wasted. Even now Jim still wasn't convinced. Goro could no longer be who he was: an athlete, the wrestling champion, the robust fighter.

He asked, "So, Goro, when did you decide to restore your original name?"

Tearing off the lettuce leaves, he said, "This year. I figured it was best."

"How so?"

Goro placed the leaves on one plate. "If I'm going to be proud of my unit, what we did and how we did it," he paused to lean over and slide a knife out of its wooden holder, "and believe me when I say I haven't known a better group of men. It's that kind of pressure that brings out a man's true nature. And boy, we really had our share cut out for us!" He began slicing the loaf of bread, straining to seclude his burdened memories. "If I'm going to be proud of them, then I need to be proud of my name. The name my parents gave me. If I'm going to have pride in this country, then I need to have pride in myself first. Otherwise, why bother defending our rights? Our freedom?"

Jim rubbed his neck and slowly exhaled, staring at his own feet. Goro had a point. Whereas he had found pride in his dual heritage at Tule Lake, Goro found it on the other side of the fence. Whereas Jim scribbled into the political field, like his father, aiding people with their problems, Goro enlisted into the battlefield, hoping to clear a path for their future.

"You've always had determination," Jim proclaimed, "that's for certain. And I've always admired it, believe it or not." He returned his gaze at his friend, affirming his sincerity. "I can only imagine what you've gone through over there. I am thankful you're still here."

"Me, too!" he snorted, twisting the jar of Mayo open.

"But," he said, "it still bothers me why you chose to do it. Why would you fight for a country that *refuses* to fight for you?"

Goro stopped. He hunched over the counter and squinted. "That's a damn good question. Ikki thinks the same way. We bumped into each other in Austria, in a city I really don't care remembering. Shig was blown to pieces trying to get a stupid souvenir off of a dead German." He swallowed what felt like a burning stone, causing his skin to prickle. He could still hear the explosion ringing in his ears every time he thought about it.

Jim was startled. Although there was much about Shig he disliked, he knew Shig and passed time with him because of Goro. Not only that, he was also Goro's friend. "I'm sorry," he expressed. "I didn't know."

Inhaling a couple of times to regain his senses, he turned to look at Jim. "How's your folks these days? I've heard they're renting a place on Adams' property."

Looking down, he gnawed on his bottom lip before answering. "Well, they're getting by. My mother's working at a flower shop in Seattle, but um . . . my father isn't . . . doing as well." He closed his eyes when he sighed. "He barely leaves the house. He keeps the curtains shut in fear that someone might be watching him. He can't sleep at night." Jim sighed again, shaking his head. "I . . . I would have . . . never thought . . ." then his voice weakened.

"I know," Goro said. "My dad shuts himself in a room listening to old Japanese records alot of the time." Clearing his voice, he quickly asked, "Why haven't you already gone to Japan? I've heard you wanted to go there."

He straightened his stance. "Because . . . because my father asked me not to. And because I can't leave Tomiko behind."

Goro slowly nodded, revealing a partial grin. "Exactly. There's something worth fighting for. We all want a better life. And I really do believe that someday things will get better. It has to. It can't get any worse!"

Jim frowned. "How can you be that optimistic? Our father's bank accounts are dwindled to nearly nothing. They lost their businesses. Their homes. Their dignity. And you," he pointed, "you're now left as a . . . " he suddenly stumbled over his tongue, realizing what he was about to blurt out. "Left amputated."

Awed, Goro stared at him momentarily, then ruptured into laughter. Jim immediately blushed. "You can say it, Jim!" he urged. "Handicapped! I'm handicapped!" He continued to laugh, shaking his head. "Left *amputated!* What kind of wording is that?"

Removing his hands from his pockets, Jim tightly folded his arms across his chest.

"Really," Goro snickered. "It's okay. You're the last person I can take offence to! In the past you called me ignorant, stupid, selfish, and childish. You even managed to insult my other friends." He pointed in turn. "If I can forgive you for everything, then I've run out of things to forgive!"

Jim lowered his chin, leaking a grin. He had been working to improve his social graces since then. "Seriously though," Jim maintained, his grin withering. "How do you do it? How do you *not* let things get to you?"

"Oh, they get to me," Goro replied, reaching for the can opener to cut into the tuna. "They get to me alright, but I try not to dwell on it. I could easily let people like Leo, Callis, or even the war break me into pieces. I could, except it wouldn't accomplish anything."

"I can't do that."

"Sure you can," he quipped, spreading the mayonnaise first, then the tuna. After placing the complete sandwich on a plate, he extended it to Jim. "Just click your heels three times *omono*, because there really is no place like home! And you know what else? Kunio found my mother's family in Japan. Got a couple of letters from him."

Jim walked forward to take the treat. "That's a nice start."

Squinting, Goro paused and crossed his arms. "Also found out a family secret." He again paused, tilting his head. "My mother had a *first* husband. Back in Japan. After he was killed in a fishing accident she remarried as a picture bride to my father."

"I guess it goes to show you that everyone must have something to hide."

"Oh, it gets better!" he exclaimed. "Come to find out, Meito is the son of her first husband. So he's really my *half*-brother!"

Jim was speechlessness.

"We've always joked about Meito being the milkman's baby," Goro chortle, "and now we've learned that he's really the *fisherman's* baby!"

"How can you joke about something as serious as that?" he remarked, not amused. "It's certainly something you don't mention to others."

Slowly sighing, Goro looked at the floor for a moment. "Well, Jim, it's a done deal. Can't change it. And it's not as though I'm telling *everyone,* for crying out loud!" He looked up. "I'm only telling you. I know I can trust you."

Awestruck, Jim glanced at the sandwich his friend made for him. He flickered a grin and without the need to verbally thank him. The then asked, "Now that you're back home, what do you plan to do?"

"I passed the high school exams the army gave me. Next spring I plan to enroll into a business college. Thank God this new G.I. bill will pay for it all!"

Jim reclined on the counter, a bit envious. He had wanted to attend college as well, unfortunately without the finances and without his citizenship to inquire for grants or scholarships, pursuing a higher education would be impossible. He was now in the same status as his father.

Goro finished making his lunch and eagerly bit into it. Chewing, he asked, "What about you? What grand plans are you conspiring?"

His smile widened. "We're planning a March wedding."

"No kidding! It's about time!"

"I'd like for you to be my best man."

Stunned, Goro blinked a few times. He had never thought Jim would ever take him seriously. Ever. Recovering his breath, he said, "I'm honored, Jim."

He nodded. "Don't disappoint me. I'm expecting one helluva bachelor's party."

"You got it," he winked.

Jim's smile dwindled as he set the plate on the counter and began to peel the crust off the white bread. "I also want to open my own business, but," he hesitated, glancing at Goro, "until my citizenship is reinstated, if it's ever reinstated, I won't be eligible for any kind of a loan."

Baffled, he peered at him. "They haven't given your citizenship back?"

He bitterly chortled. "As if they *had* the right to take it in the first place!"

None of it made sense. Goro never understood the process of revoking their citizenship, then out of the blue, fabricating exceptions through the draft. Meito later told him the WRA urged the *Nisei* who weren't in the military to take another loyalty test to renew their citizenship like a valid driver's license. Most refused. Why take the unnecessary test when they were *already* American-born in America? Eventually the government dismissed the second test.

"Well," Goro nibbled, thinking. "What kind of business are you wanting?"

"I want to upscale my father's grocery store. Make it accessible for everyone and not just for the Japanese community."

He stopped chewing. "That would mean you would have to be nice to people."

Jim frowned. "It's not an impossible task."

"For you it is."

"You're not helping, Russell," he flinched, "I mean, *Goro*!"

Smiling, Goro took one more mouthful before hopping to the cooler to retrieve a bottle of milk.

Jim brooded for a moment. "I want to ask you something."

After gulping from the bottle, he put it back inside. "Sure, okay."

He paused. "I was wondering if you would like to go into business with me."

Goro froze. He had seen and heard bizarre things so far in his life. Especially during battle when men started hallucinating from lack of sleep and ceaseless anxieties. But what Jim requested had beat them all. Clearing his throat, he managed to ask, "What about your father?"

"To be honest, he doesn't have the faith to start from scratch again. And since he lost everything during the war, he has no collateral to apply for a loan. Plus, neither of us have our citizenships, so no bank will give us business loans."

Leaning on the other counter across from him, Goro cautiously inquired, "But why me? Are you that desperate?"

"Because I trust you. I can think of nobody else, aside from Tomiko, of course, who I'd rather do this with." He examined his friend's reluctance. "And I'm glad you're considering wanting to go business school. So, with my experience and brains, combined with your personality and education, I figure we have a chance to succeed."

He crossed his arms, staring at the door's portal. "It would be at least a couple of years before this could happen."

"That's fine," Jim replied. "I'll wait. I'll just work some odd jobs until then."

"What's your father going to do with the rest of his life? I mean, I've always thought your dad would always be in business."

Jim glanced away and released a grim sigh. "He can't anymore. I think he mentioned working for the Johnsons as an accountant, though."

Goro looked at him, not entirely convinced. "What does Tomiko think about it?"

"She has no objections. In fact, she thinks we'll work well together."

"Yeah, but," he shrugged, "we argue a lot. How's *that* gonna work?"

Jim chuckled, remembering how he himself usually started the bickering, often not knowing why, other than it just felt good. However, within the last year, as he accepted more responsibilities as part of the Block Committee, he learned to disagree more tastefully by not blurting out every negative thought that transgressed through his mind.

"Well, *omono-san*," he explained, "it's not why we argue, but how we argue. We seem to keep a balance. That's how it's going to work."

Goro tipped a brow, surprised by Jim's encouragement. He sensed much of it came from Tomiko, which he held no complaints.

Jim pursued, "I can understand why you're hesitant. And I just want to say . . ." he hesitated, lowering his head, straining. "I just want to say you're the best friend I ever had. I do appreciate everything you've done for me. I'm just sorry I haven't done the same for you."

Goro still sat in silence, trying to comprehend it all. "You're the most peculiar man I know."

Grinning, he replied, "I know."

Chuckling, he extending his right hand. "Okay, *omono-san.* I'm game if you're game. "

Jim leaned forward to shake his hand. Smiling proudly, he returned to his sandwich and starting eating. If anything honorable were to come from their ordeal, it was this friendship. One that might not have existed otherwise.

CHAPTER FIVE

Mid Spring, 1992

CARS surged over the paved highway like fallen leaves driven up creek by an overwhelming force. Its fumes drowned the cedar trees' faint sweetness as well as the salty air. Winslow's downtown interior had been decorated for the Strawberry Festival, inviting tourists and outsiders. Shops and restaurants expanded past its original blocks. Newer buildings, mixed with the restored ones, preserved the bygone days of the American West, preserving American idealism. However, the island outgrew its rural image. Franchises. Hotels. An opulent Japanese Garden enticing outside business and acquiring a popular reputation. Bicycle rentals. Pizza deliveries. Bainbridge was becoming a retreat from city life without denying modern conveniences. The locals, nevertheless, tolerated and perhaps even profited from its transformation.

GORO parked his '87 Buick LeSabre in front of his business, inside the handicap parking space. Getting out of his car, swinging his plastic leg as if it were real, he left his vehicle unlocked, not worried about theft or vandal. Wearing his golf cap and checkered trousers, he starting walking toward the automatic sliding doors. His sixty-eighth birthday was only three months away. Graying hair, somewhat receding above his forehead, agreed with his wrinkles. Twenty pounds heavier, wrestling with his high cholesterol and minor arthritis, he aimed to uphold optimism. Most of the time he could. And that was good enough, enjoying his full retirement, especially after discovering golf. It had kindled a forgotten feeling of sport and glory. Even with his artificial leg and eye, golf allowed him to master his imperfections as if he didn't have any. He had hung his six awards in the spare bedroom, alongside other five children's accomplishments, whether in sports or academics. That room was devoted to success. Even second or third place trophies hung on the wall. They still mattered. And he made sure his children understood it.

"Hey, Goro! Thought that was you!"

Turning around, he saw his childhood friend, Dave Lundberg, who was rolling a shopping cart back into the row. His curly hair had forfeited its thickness, now reduced to a thinning whiteness. A rounded belly overlapped his belt. And when he walked, he walked with a limp. But his rich blue eyes had retained their loyal brilliance.

"Well if it isn't my twin!" Goro exclaimed. Dave had also lost his left leg while fighting in Europe. The irony led into a private joke about appearing like twins. Extending his hand, Goro continued, "How've you been, Dave? Haven't seen you on the course this week!"

Shaking his hand, he replied, "That's because my grandkids were visiting!"

"Good, always good."

"How's the wife?"

"Maria's fine. When she's not complaining how little housework I don't contribute to!"

Dave chuckled. "Welcome to the club, my friend."

Sighing, he remarked, "But, unfortunately, my dog's not doing so well. She's getting so old it's coming to the point I may have to put her down."

"Oh," he said sympathetically, "sorry to hear it."

"Since I don't have the heart," Goro began, playfully shaking his head, "I figure I'd let you take care of her instead. You did a good job last time I recall!"

Dave frowned. All those years he had felt terrible about Zasshu dying in his backyard during the war, despite understanding it was only a matter of time for that poor mutt.

"That's not funny," he replied. "You know under the circumstances I couldn't tell you Zasshu lived only a month after you left."

"I know," he smiled. "You were so nervous trying to tell me. The way you were acting I thought you had cancer!" He readjusted his stance, his smile fading. "When you stopped writing about my dog, I knew. I knew." Dave awkwardly glanced away. The day was too beautiful to remember the ugliness. Goro tugged on his cap. "Good seeing you, Dave. Call me and we'll see if we can swing a few. Okay?"

He nodded. "Sure, okay. Take care, Goro."

Again shaking his hand, he replied, "You, too, Dave. Gotta grab some stuff for the wife!"

"Boy, our lives keep crossing the same path!" he chortled.

"That's what makes us twins!"

Laughing, Dave waved and returned to his car, also parked in another handicapped spot. As Goro entered his store, he greeted some of the people he knew and headed to the rear. The lunch hour rush clogged the open register lines. And would repeat just before dinner. The business developed into more than a simple grocery. Transforming Yoshi's Groceries into The Village Market, he and Jim generated it into a chain which extended throughout Washington and parts of Oregon. An endeavor they wouldn't had expected fifty years ago. It never ceased to amaze him how they first started with a dinky store, offering no more than three aisles of produce, and now their store exceeded twenty. At least both their fathers witnessed the growth before their passings. They couldn't have been more proud of their sons.

Photographs of the island, as well as Seattle and the rest of the Puget Sound area, were also for sale in the store, all taken by Jim. After they returned from the war, Jim resumed his photography, never dismissing Ansel Adams' encouragement and never took it for granted.

"Hello, Alice!" Goro approached, smiling widely.

"Hey, Dad!" she returned, stepping down from a stepladder, holding a clipboard. Her thickly permed hair bordered her face. She favored Maria at when she was in her late forties, but also inherited traits from her biological father. After one year of marrying her mother, Goro adopted her as one of his own and never treated her any differently. "Mom has you running her errands, eh?"

"I made a deal with her. For every time I golf," he paused to raise his index finger, "without her griping, I have to bring back something from her list."

She grinned. "Sounds like a deal made in heaven."

"Heaven is a state of mind," he winked. "And as long as your mother's idea of heaven means bargaining, then there's *my* peace of mind!"

Laughing, she said, "Be good, Dad! Don't be so ornery!"

"You sound just like your mother," he grinned. "She's been telling me that for decades!"

"Yes- I *know*," she said.

"Where's Jim? Is that workaholic floating around here?"

The Strawberry Festival always encouraged more business, for it seemed as popular as Christmas. Jim made sure there was enough in stock: paper plates, plastic silverware, napkins, sodas, and even kept Bainbridge Island T-shirts on hand for the tourists. In addition to the store's responsibilities, Jim volunteered to be part of the festival's committee, arranging the coordination for tomorrow's parade. Jim's seventeen year-old granddaughter would be crowned as the town's beauty queen.

"He's in the back with John," Alice replied.

"Ahh," he whisked. "Like father, like son. And you had to marry one of them."

"Not my fault, Dad," she winked, "you're the one who went into business with him!"

Nodding, thinking, he said, "You're right. It is my fault."

As Goro walked off, waving, Alice climbed back up the step ladder to continue her inventory. Strolling past the meat and cheese sections, he slipped through the swinging doors and steered to a hidden room off to the side, separate from stacks of nonperishable foods and a large cooler.

Knocking on the partially opened door, he announced, "Delivery."

Jim, who sat behind a desk, turned around and smiled. His hair had lightened, mixed with thick streaks of silver. Within the last thirty years he maintained a mustache which he thought appeared more distinguished. His glasses were thicker. And following Tomiko's death, who once struggled with

Parkinson's disease, he had been losing weight, reverting to the weight of his thirties.

"Well," Jim began, "I thought I felt the earth shake. I should have known it was you."

Goro flickered a grin. "The presence of greatness always shakes the earth. Haven't you learned?

"I think the real question is haven't you learned that riding in those golf carts doesn't take off the pounds?"

He rubbed his gut. "I'm proud of this paunch. It took me forty years to earn it!"

"You tell him," John interjected. Leaning against a tall metal filing cabinet, he favored more of his grandfather than his parents. His short nose, broad lips, and thin glasses eerily reflected the photos of his grandfather from sixty years ago. And yet, being nine years younger than Alice, the jokes about marrying an older woman never completely faded. Especially from Goro.

"Afternoon, John," Goro responded. "Are you keeping this old fool in line?"

Walking to the door, he patted his father-in-law's shoulder. "You can train domesticated pets, but once they've been in the wild you can never *retrain* them!" Looking at his father, he nodded, "See you later, Dad. I'll go ahead and put in those requests."

"Good," Jim replied. "And make sure Bob doesn't talk you into buying more than we need!"

"You keep forgetting I'm not Alice!" he pointed while he exited. "I know when to say no!"

Returning to Goro, folding his hands over his chest, he asked, "So, what brings you by?"

The small windowless office lingered in a musty odor. Tomiko's photo hung above a six year old computer, next to Jim's family reunion photo with seven children, twenty-three grandchildren, and his two sisters with their immediate families. Beside those photos rested a framed newspaper clipping about Jim winning second term as mayor.

Resting his other hand over his hip, Goro opened more somberly, "Got the newsletter about tomorrow's meeting."

Jim brooded. "I thought it necessary to discuss Bush's apology check. Primarily for the *Nikkon* community."

Blinking, he gnawed his lip. "So, you think the recognition is too late?"

"Late? I think the whole situation should have never happened at all!" he snapped. "But since it did happen, and since the damage has already been done," he hesitated, "yes, I think the effort is beyond mending. Where was the compensation for our folks? They lost everything . . . *everything* during the war! And you know it wasn't until in '53 that my citizenship was finally reinstated!" He readjusted in his seat and tried to clear his throat as it tightened with each memory. "And that year I spent in Tule Lake," he shook his head, "every now and again I wake up thinking another damn raid is about to take place. I can't help but hide my valuables around the house. Just in case!"

Goro remained calm. "I wake up in the middle of the night, too, with bad dreams. But I know they're only dreams and I have the rest of the day to look forward to."

"And Tomiko," he continued, glancing at her photo as though she was still sitting right beside him, "could never get over the dirt. The house was never clean enough. You remember when she almost had a breakdown after the kids were born? She worried any amount of dirt would make the kids sick, always taking them to the doctor to make sure."

Sighing, Goro stepped forward. "And yet we rarely talk to our kids about our experiences. Why is that?"

Jim flinched. "Well, who wants to relive all that nonsense?"

"Which brings us back to the check. Don't you think the gesture at least acknowledges responsibility?" He paused. "Twenty thousand isn't a bad size, Jim."

He removed his glasses to rub his eyes. The whole idea of distributing checks fifty years later seemed not only insulting, but worthless. Replacing his glasses, he said, "I don't need it. I don't want it! As far as I'm concerned, the government can shove it up its ass! We've made a living without their help then and I'll be goddamned if I need it now!"

"Is this how you'll conduct the meeting?"

"Everyone will have their say and then decide what to do with their checks. That's how it'll be conducted."

He again sighed. "We could use our checks to pass it on to our children. Or grandchildren. Use them to give them a better start than what we had."

"And we *still* did that on our own without the government's help," he grumbled.

Goro frowned, weighing the odds. "We are fortunate enough to live in a country that allows the growth of our success. We were able to rebuild. Look how long it took Japan and Europe to rebuild itself."

Jim wheeled his chair around to look Tomiko's picture, searching for some comfort to ease his aggravation. Every day he missed her. And for three years he found difficulty trying to get out of bed, but miraculously the business and community functions gave him enough reason to. Wheeling around again, he stated, "Don't misunderstand me, Goro. There are aspects in my life I'm grateful for. It's just that . . ." he glanced away, "there are aspects in this life I can't forget."

"You mean forgive," he affirmed.

Jim squinted, trying to preserve his composure. "I'm not accepting the check like some sort of bribe."

"It's an apology."

"It's an excuse, that's what it is! Trying to buy us off because they feel real damn bad!"

Goro scoffed, "And by not cashing in the check, tax deductible I might add, that'll really show 'em!"

"It's the principle. I couldn't live with myself if I reinforced their stupid mistakes."

Shaking his head, Goro shuffled to the door. "Just remember, Jim, nothing will change unless we rise above it. And I like to believe we have."

SHUTTING the car door, Goro shifted the paper bag full of groceries in his arms and started walking to his front porch. Hedges and a white-picket fence decorated his ranch house, complementing the ripened lawn. Rounded cement blocks guided the short path to the porch. Before he could reach for the door knob, Maria opened it.

Startled, he said. "Did you miss me that much?"

Standing in her pastel slacks and flowered shirt, she revealed an eager grin. "Something come for you in da mail. It's in da living room."

He grinned. "It's not even my birthday yet. I like the odds."

As he entered, she took the bag and followed him. He could still smell bacon from the early morning loafing in the rooms. A long box laid on the coffee table, over a couple of *Good Housekeeping* magazines. Their brown furniture pieces hadn't been replaced since the late 60's. Curious, Goro sat down and studied the box. An envelope was taped to the front.

Not recognizing the sender, he asked his wife, "Who's Charles Armstrong?"

She playfully shrugged. "Read da letta first. Find out who it is."

"Well, I'm gonna need . . ." he stopped when he discovered the letter opener placed on top of the box. Looking up, he suspiciously squinted. "I suppose you weren't expecting this by any chance?"

Smiling, she walked to the kitchen to put the grocery bag away. He began to poke the tape and pulled the envelope off. Tearing through, he removed a single sheet of paper and read the handwritten message:

Dear Mr. Hamaguchi,
You don't know me but I've spent the last few years trying to find you. You see, my father was an FBI agent. When he retired and when no claimed some of the confiscated items, he took a few things home with him, which was common at that time. After my father's passing, I never have felt comfortable keeping some of the items knowing they belonged to someone else. So I began to research and came across your name. I spoke to your wife on a couple of occasions to verify the information and now I'm giving back what was your family's in the first place. I hope this will bring some peace of mind for you and your family.
Sincerely, Charles Armstrong

Goro's heart quickly pulsated. Was it possible? Was it actually possible after five decades? Taking the letter opener, he slit through the crease to open the box. Then dipping through the white Styrofoam peanuts, he removed a long narrow object rolled in bubble-wrap. Carefully unrolling it, he found his father's *samurai* sword, polished and in the same condition as he once remembered it. Overwhelmed, dazed, he stared at the sword, breathing heavily while tears formed. After all that time, he had forgotten, perhaps more so wanting to forget about the family sword, because of what it exemplified: Loss. Humiliation.

Bigotry. But now it exemplified something else: Acknowledgment. Respect. Forgiveness.

Maria reentered the room and knelt beside her husband. Placing her hand over his knee, she eased a smile, knowing how important this meant to him.

JIM sat in his thirteen year old vehicle, a Ford with tan interior, staring at the steering wheel. Goro's words wouldn't leave his head. They had wearied his mind for the last few hours of the day. The upcoming meeting also wearied him, not certain what to make of this long overdue acknowledgment. After dwelling over the government's gesture regarding the check, he came close to ripping it up. Very close, yet Goro's voice rattled inside his brain, reciting a strong point: *use the money for someone else's future*. Then, perhaps it didn't matter as much that restitutions arrived half a century later. Jim had already rebuilt his life without it. So the money wasn't about him. Or what happened decades ago. Nonetheless, it should signify that hysterical discrimination should never repeat itself.

Realizing he couldn't sit in limbo forever, he finally decided to open the door and walked inside Bainbridge Island Bank. As he entered, a few other people stood in line, listening to the faint elevator music in the background. When his turn came, he removed his wallet to slip out the check.

The cashier, a young woman in her early twenties with thick eyebrows and having her bangs hair sprayed high in a salute, unfolded the check. She stared at it. "My goodness!" she gasped. "I've never seen a tax refund this big before!"

"It's not a tax refund, Maggie," he replied, reluctantly. "It's compensation from the war."

"Oh," she nodded, curious to inquire, but reserved her questions. "Where would you like this deposited?"

"Personal checkings." He watched her fill out a slip and handed it to him. Reaching for a pen, he supplied his consent. "There you are, Maggie. Thanks for your help."

"Always a pleasure, Mr. Yoshimura. I'll see you at the parade."

"With bells and whistles," he winked.

As Jim left the bank, he remembered his mother reminding him to laugh three times: once in praise, once in promise, and once with purpose. He planned to donate the money, praising the memory of Tomiko. And for others who were suffering the identical disease, defining his purpose. But most of all, he would forgive a world that perhaps deserved another promise.

About the Author:

K.P. Kollenborn is her pen name which she chose for two reasons: One- it is her mother's maiden name. They are grandchildren of German immigrants who migrated from Texas to Kansas prior to the American Civil War. Two- it's not a very common surname and no doubt she is somehow related to all the remaining Kollenborns in the United States one way or another.

K.P. Kollenborn has been writing since childhood however she does have a B.A. in History. Instead of applying a degree in creative writing, she wanted to focus on learning and understanding what motivates people of certain time periods. Also, she was fortunate to have been trained by one the top ten writing teachers in the US, the late Leonard Bishop, and author of *Dare to be a Great Writer*. When she had graduated Kansas State University, she wrote historical book reviews for *The Sunflower Press* about the Japanese-Americans. In addition to writing, she draws, paints, creates graphic design, composes music, and is an amateur photographer.

Even though she is from Kansas, she enjoys venturing into other worlds from around the globe which is why her writing focuses on diversity. With fluid accessibility to modern media and traveling opportunities, her Midwestern world can expand and explore beyond her own backyard. She writes, "Submitting to a moment in time allows us to remember, or to muse even, over our society's past. Although writing can educate as well as entertain, yet what makes art incredibly amazing, to that of paintings, photographs, and music, it transposes emotion into another form of humanity, and therefore, it is our humanity which keeps all of us striving for an improved future."

Currently she resides outside of Kansas City, KS with her husband and two daughters.

SIDENOTE

***Eyes Behind Belligerence* was written, designed, produced and published by its author. Because independent publishers and writers should be held to the same high standards as the mainstream publishing industry, I encourage you to post an honest and objective review of this book in the online bookstore of your choice. Such dialogue only serves the cause of good writers and good readers.**

Questions for Book Clubs

1.) Why do you think the beginning of the novel starts with a suicide? And how does it bring out the cultural prejudices?
2.) Compare Russell's friendships between Dave and Leo and why do you think he is friends with both?
3.) How does Mr. Yoshimura demonstrates his leadership in the community? And how is it taken away after Pearl Harbor?
4.) Why does Maria's father distrust Russell and how does his distrust impact their relationship?
5.) The introduction of Katsuji at Jim's house begins with agitation and arrogance. What role does Katsuji play in the development of pro-Japan movement? And what points are understandable to Katsuji's plight of being a Kibei?
6.) There is some dispute about the Hamaguchi's Samurai sword. How is the respect of the sword handled between the local police and the FBI and why do you think there is a contrast?
7.) The Yoshimuras and Hamaguchi's have different family cores. In what ways make these two families contradictory in values even though they are from the same community?
8.) Why do you think Russell tries to help out Jim when Jim is beaten by the school's bully even though they are not friends at this point?
9.) How do you think the death of Jim's brother has impacted him to the point that when Jim is sent to the principal's office he doesn't defend himself? And how does it continue to resonate throughout the novel?
10.) How do you see the symbolism of the photo that hangs in Jim's room of his ancestor and the implications of clashing cultures?
11.) How do you see the irony of arriving at Manzanar on April 1st?
12.) Mr. Woodard is a historical figure, as well as General DeWitt, Dorthea Lange, Fred Korematsu, and Ansel Adams. How are these real figures relevant to the storyline?
13.) The color yellow is frequently intertwined throughout the novel. What do you think it represents?
14.) How do the camp's conditions affect the characters physically and morally?
15.) *Little Women* and *Of Mice and Men* are mentioned in book. What do you think the signification of these references to gender and friendship mean between the characters?
16.) At what point in the novel do Jim and Russell finally become friends? And how does their shared experiences solidify their friendship?
17.) Why do you think Russell befriends someone like Shig? And why does Russell choose to make Shikami his enemy?
18.) Why do you think Russell wants to shed off his Japanese traditions so badly? And at what point does he decide to embrace them?

19.) How would you describe Jim's relationship with his father and how it changes after years of separation?
20.) Describe the conflicts between the Japanese-American community in regards to gender, generational gaps, where a person was born, and other races. Discuss the cultural differences between Japanese traditions and American ideals.
21.) How are Russell's love interests different and why is he attracted to both? What makes each girl unusual in the Japanese traditional sense of courtship?
22.) Why is Jim leery about wanting to date Tomiko? And what is it about their past which unites them?
23.) Sadaye has a love interest via letter writing. Why would it be forbidden for her to engage in such a romance?
24.) What do you think the canary in Jim's dream symbolizes?
25.) Why is the Terminal Island Gang so feared?
26.) Why are the Zoot Suits greeted with great apprehension within the community?
27.) When Tom joins Ted Tanka's group, how do you see the prejudices within their own community?
28.) There is a common theme about changing identities, therefore what do you think the growth of Tom's mustache represents? And what does it mean when he finally shaves it off?
29.) While Mr. Yoshimura is awaiting trial in Montana, why do you think his own people grow resentful towards him?
30.) When do you start seeing political problems inside Manzanar? And what are the events that lead up to the riot?
31.) What roles do Director Bridges, Assistant Director Petty, Katsuji, Sadaye, Ted, Saburo, and Choichi play in the development of the riot?
32.) How does the aftermath of the riot transform Russell, Jim, Ikki, Tom and Rose?
33.) Compare the bitterness Mr. and Mrs. Hamaguchi harbor for each other and how it contrasts based on their gender.
34.) Morning Glories are mentioned in Jim's dream and are giving as a gift by Tomiko. What do you think these flowers represent?
35.) Describe the mixed reactions when an army recruiter tries to enlist men into the military.
36.) What significance do you see when Russell makes the references to Andy Rooney being short and still was able to establish a career? How does Russell wish to make that connection? Particularly in American culture where men who have strength and power are often tall and white?
37.) What are the reasons the Bainbridge Islanders want to leave Manzanar and relocate to Minidoka? Why do you think they never quite felt comfortable living in the same space as those from California? And why was Russell reluctant to tell his Californian friends about the move?
38.) What is the signification of Russell standing up to Callis?

39.) When Rose is asked if she is Korean, why doesn't she correct the passenger?
40.) How does Russell feel when reuniting with the rest of him family in Minidoka?
41.) Describe the mixed reactions to the questionnaire that is required of everyone to answer and what is the purpose of this questionnaire?
42.) Even though Jim has been separated from his father for quite some time, in what ways does he start emulating his father but is oblivious to it? In what ways is he still different from his father?
43.) What is the fight about between Jim and Russell and how do their decisions about their future formulate a rift in their friendship?
44.) Parts four and five greatly tie up the family connection. How does this unify identity and community relations?
45.) At what point does Jim finally stand up for himself?
46.) Even in boot camp, why do you think there still is prejudice within their unit? Especially Shig who is distrustful of Roku?
47.) With the understanding of the Quaker's past as peacemakers in American history, how does their influence continue to help the Japanese-American camps? How does that make them different than the rest of American society?
48.) Aside from the racism that Russell encounters, other forms of racism are apparent. How are these experiences similar and different for Russell and Shig while in Mississippi?
49.) How do you see the irony of Mr. North's name who lives in the South?
50.) At what point does Russell finally stand up for what he believes in? How does he handle the situation with Earl Ray, Shig, and the young woman whom he meets at the USO?
51.) What is the importance of Kunio joining the MIS (Military Intelligence Service)? And how would this experience help him accept his dual heritage?
52.) How do you sense Mr. Hamaguchi's disappointment with his life at the funeral?
53.) What is the significance of Jim replacing his brother's memory with Russell's friendship?
54.) How does Bethany feel isolated while sitting in her classroom? And how does she feel with all the changes going on around her while she is still stuck in camp?
55.) How does Jim take on responsibilities at Tule Lake which emulate following his father's path in the Japanese-American community?
56.) Describe the encounter between Jim and Shikami and how they regard each other differs from their experiences in Manzanar.
57.) Compare Russell's and Shig's reactions of Dachau in correlation to their familiarity of American concentration camps.
58.) Ikki has a very different perspective of the war. How does it contrast with Russell's view?
59.) How has Russell's war experience lead him to choose to use his birth name again?

60.) Why would the circumstances be different for Shig and Russell to take war trophies from dead Germans than if they were to take them from Japanese soldiers?
61.) How does Mr. Hamaguchi finally let go of his experiences in camp?
62.) Why does Jim feel compelled to leave the U.S. for Japan? And how does his view differ from that of Tomiko?
63.) What is the significance of Kunio reuniting with his mother's side of the family?
64.) There are two references about using sand as metaphors for both Kunio and Goro. How are these relevant to paying homage to returning to one's birthplace?
65.) When Goro encounters Leo again on the ferry, how have the dynamics of their childhood relationship changed?
66.) While Jim is in limbo as to where he should go after leaving Tule Lake, his father makes a visit. How has their relationship changed?
67.) There is a constant referral to making of promises. What does each of these promises mean and how do they reflect the development of the characters?
68.) There's a list of cultural references throughout the novel such as "Sold American,"The Shadow, Little Orphan Annie, *The Letter, My Favorite Spy, The Human Comedy,* "You're a Sap Mr. Jap," "All God's Chuldrun's Got Rhythm," "Let's Get Away from it All," Lon Cheney, *The Odyssey, The Great Dictator, Born Free and Equal*, "Don't Fence Me In" and "Sentimental Journey." These were chosen to represent other themes. What do you think each reference represents in regards to the development of the story?
69.) What is the significance of Goro's family Samurai word being returned?
70.) What is the significance of Jim cashing in Bush's apology check?

BIBLIGRAPHY

Armor, John. *Manzanar*. New York: Times Book, 1988.

Gesensway, Deborah and Roseman, Mindy. *Beyond Words: Images from America's Concentration Camps. Ithaca*, New York: Cornell University Press, 1987.

Hosokawa, Bill. *Nisei: The Quiet Americans*. New York: William Morrow and Company. 1969.

Houston, Jeanne Wakatsuki and Houston, James. *Farewell to Manzanar: A True Story of Japanese American Experience During and After the World War II Interment*. Boston, Massachusetts: Houghton Mifflin Harcourt, 1973.

Inouye, Daniel K. and Elliott, Lawrence. *Journey to Washington*. New Jersey: Prentice-Hall. 1968.

Kessler, Lauren. *Stubborn Twig: Three Generations in the Life of a Japanese American Family*. New York, New York: Plume, 1994.

Kunitomi-Embrey, Sue. *Manzanar Martyr: An interview with Harry Y. Ueno*. Fullerton, California: Oral History Program, California State University, 1986.

Manzanar National Historic Resource Study, Volume One and Volume Two.

Tateishi, John. *And Justice for All: An Oral History of the Japanese American Detention Centers*. New York, New York: Random House, 1984.

Uchida, Yoshiko. *Desert Exile: The Uprooting of a Japanese-American Family*. Seattle, Washington: University of Washington Press, 1982.

Weglyn, Michi. *Years of Infamy: The Untold Story of America's Concentration Camps*. New York: William Morrow and Company. 1976.

Yoo, David. *Growing Up Nisei: Race, Generation and Culture Among Japanese Americans of California, 1924-1949*. Chicago, Illinois: University of Illinois Press, 2000.

CPSIA information can be obtained at www.ICGtesting.com
Printed in the USA
LVOW101813020413

327242LV00023B/870/P